THE UN-DEAD

THE UN-DEAD

The DRACULA novel [1], rewritten
to include Stoker's deleted characters
and events [2]

[Revised Edition]

Joel H. Emerson,
in a posthumous collaboration with
Bram Stoker

Library of Congress Control Number:		2007900276
ISBN:	Hardcover	978-1-4257-5040-4
	Softcover	978-1-4257-5031-2

This book was printed in the United States of America.

To order additional copies of this book, contact:
Xlibris Corporation
1-888-795-4274
www.Xlibris.com
Orders@Xlibris.com
38628

DEDICATION

This work is dedicated to Bram Stoker.

SPECIAL THANKS

I would like to thank several people who helped me throughout this project: my loving wife Rebekah for putting up with my late hours of typing; Elizabeth Miller and Robert Eighteen-Bisang, for their invaluable assistance with Bram Stoker's notes and manuscript; Elizabeth Fuller, of the Rosenbach Museum and Library, for her help with my research; my mother Phyllis Emerson, for her help in editing; and especially Cecelia L. Gruss, without whose assistance this work would never have been completed in the first place.

Introduction

Should you one day find yourself in the great city of Philadelphia, be sure to take time away from the hustle and bustle to stroll down the old herringbone sidewalk of a remarkably quiet side street by the name of Delancey Place. There, nestled amidst the historic buildings, and cooled by the shade of towering sycamores, is situated a building of rust-red masonry and grey mortar. The short flight of white marble stairs will bring you to a matching stone archway, framing a beautiful set of oaken doors. To one side hangs a simple black sign with white letters that form the word "Rosenbach."

Within the walls of this unassuming building, you will meet a most unique and remarkable person. You should know her when you see her: a woman of dark hair and trim build, dressed in functional attire, with thin spectacles and a scholastic ring. Of all the treasures and curiosities stored within the recesses of these halls, she can bring to you an item of particular interest, one that came to rest here from across oceans of water and time. Within a box made of stiff buckram is held this treasure: a collection of four grey folders, each containing page after page of yellowed paper sealed in transparent mylar.

These are the personal writing notes of Abraham Stoker, detailing nearly a decade of contemplation and research from which he would ultimately form his literary masterpiece. Should you carefully turn through these brittle pages, you will find that Mr. Stoker omitted a number of characters and events from the final work that he presented to the public over a century ago.

Hours later, when you have studied this treasure to your heart's content, you will cross over the marble threshold and walk down to the street below, back into the day-lit world of the living, one far removed from the dark night of Victorian London which you were, for a brief moment in time, a part of. As you make your way along the old street, you might find yourself wondering what might Stoker's novel have been like, had he chosen not to abbreviate it as he did . . .

What would it have been like for Jonathan Harker to journey through Munich and foreshadowing museums and opera houses, stroll through macabre funeral homes, and ultimately encounter a vampiress in the graveyard of an abandoned village? Or for the Count to attended a dinner at the house of one of his own victims? Or for the small band of heroes to attempt to carry out their illicit plans for revenge while under the scrutiny of a police inspector? Or for the adventurous Quincey Morris to journey alone to Transylvania in search of clues?

These "what ifs" are exactly what this work is about. What you hold in your hands is my humble attempt to flesh out, as it were, the original story of **Dracula**. Using the notes from the Rosenbach, as well as other writings of Stoker, I have modified the original text and woven into it whole new sentences, paragraphs and even entire chapters.

It is my hope that this book will encourage those who have never read Stoker's novel to do so now, for his masterpiece goes so much deeper than any Hollywood adaptation, delving into the troubled issues of society and nationality, gender and sex, science and religion, and so many more concerns that plagued his—and still our own—era. And for those who have already read the original text, this book should prove all the more interesting, adding a variety of new twists and turns to the traditional storyline.

My additions to Stoker's masterpiece have been written to be as close to the author's own style as possible, and indeed, several modified excerpts from Stoker's other works have been used for the sake of authenticity. Furthermore, you will find nearly two hundred endnotes marked throughout the text, to impart insights into Stoker's working notes and how they pertain to the modifications made to his original novel.

So close the curtains, pull up a chair by the fire, and delve into a version of **Dracula** that is closer to what Bram Stoker originally envisioned than anything you've ever read before . . .

Acknowledgements

In addition to my own writing, the body of this work contains a modified text of Bram Stoker's *Dracula* and *Dracula's Guest*, as well as modified excerpts from Stoker's ***The Man, The Coming of Abel Behenna, The Lady of the Shroud, The Judge's House, The Jewel of Seven Stars, Under the Sunset, The Lair of the White Worm, Personal Reminiscences of Henry Irving,*** and the Icelandic edition of *Dracula*. I have double-checked my own knowledge of Stoker's writing Notes with ***Bram Stoker's Notes for Dracula: A Facsimile Edition*** by Robert Eighteen-Bisang and Elizabeth Miller. I have also incorporated what is currently known of Stoker's Manuscript—information recently made available to the public in Leslie Klinger's ***The New Annotated Dracula***. Furthermore, adaptations of letters between Stoker and Walt Whitman have been used, as well as newspaper articles pertaining to the 1888 Jack the Ripper Murders printed in **"The Daily News," "The London Times," "The Evening News,"** and **"The East London Adviser."** Finally, some inspiration for a few plot points has been derived from the films **NOSFERATU** (1922), **DRACULA** (1931), and **DRACULA** (1979). It is with great respect and much thanksgiving that I have incorporated all of these sources of knowledge into this single work. Many changes inspired by the listed sources have been minor—the change of a word or the addition of a phrase—and merely serve to add flavor to the text. So as not to disrupt the natural flow of the novel, I have only cited with endnotes those changes that I felt were the most critical (which, even so, produced well over two hundred endnotes).

To My Dear Friend Hommy-Beg[3]

How these papers have been placed in sequence will be made manifest in the reading of them. All needless matters have been eliminated, so that a history almost at variance with the possibilities of later-day belief may stand forth as simple fact. There is throughout no statement of past things wherein memory may err, for all the records chosen are exactly contemporary, given from the stand-points and within the range of knowledge of those who made them.[4]

The reader of this story will very soon understand how the events outlined in these pages have been gradually drawn together to make a logical whole. Apart from excising minor details which I considered unnecessary, I have let the people involved relate their experiences in their own way; but, for obvious reasons, I have changed the names of the people[5] and places concerned. In all other respects I leave the manuscript unaltered, in deference to the wishes of those who have considered it their duty to present it before the eyes of the public.

I am quite convinced that there is no doubt whatever that the events here described really took place, however unbelievable and incomprehensible they might appear at first sight. And I am further convinced that they must always remain to some extent incomprehensible, although continuing research in psychology and natural sciences may, in years to come, give logical explanations of such strange happenings which, at present, neither scientists nor the secret police can understand. I state again that this mysterious tragedy which is here described is completely true in all its external respects, though naturally I have reached a different conclusion on certain points than those involved in the story. But the events are incontrovertible, and so many people know of them that they cannot be denied.

This series of crimes has not yet passed from the memory—a series of crimes which appear to have originated from the same source, and which at the same time created as much repugnance in people everywhere as the murders of Jack the Ripper, which came into the story a little later.[6] Various people's minds will go back to the remarkable group of foreigners who for many seasons together played a dazzling part in the life of the aristocracy here in London; and some will remember that one of them disappeared suddenly without apparent reason, leaving no trace.[7]

All the people who have willingly—or unwillingly—played a part in this remarkable story are known generally and well respected. Both Jonathan Harker and his wife (who is a woman of character) and the Sewards are my friends and have been so for many years, and I have never doubted that they were telling the truth; and the highly respected scientist, who appears here under a pseudonym, will also be too famous all over the educated world for his real name, which I have not desired to specify, to be hidden from people—least of all those who have from experience learnt to value and respect his genius and accomplishments, though they adhere to his views on life no more than I. But in our times it ought to be clear to all serious-thinking men that "there are more things in heaven and earth than are dreamt of in your philosophy."

—Bram Stoker

BOOK I

TRANSYLVANIA[8]

CHAPTER ONE[9]

IN THE YEAR OF OUR LORD 1888[10]

Letter[11] from Sir John Paxton[12] to Peter Hawkins[13]

March 21

Sir,

I have the honour to forward to you the enclosed, which was sent to the Society in care of myself. I regret that I am unacquainted with the sender, and that I can impart no further information upon the matter.

Respectfully,
Sir John Paxton
President, Incorporated Law Society

Letter[14] from Dracula to Peter Hawkins,
in the care of Sir John Paxton

4 March (Old Style)[15]

My dear Mr. Hawkins,

Your good name has more than once come to my ear by a dear friend of mine and of yours, who is one who also makes use of your services, even as I wish to now. So it is with great pleasure that I write to you, so that I may enlist your aid.

The dream of my old age is to live in your illustrious country. Thus it is that I wish to buy an English estate. I trust that you are willing to conduct this business on behalf of an aging gentleman of honorable family. Mr. James Malcolm of

Courts & Co will assure you of my intent. Answer at your earliest opportunity; I anxiously await your reply.

Very truly yours,
Dracula[16]

P.S. My copy of the Law List is somewhat antiquated, and, as you may have changed your residence since it was published, I have sent this letter in care of Sir John Paxton, to insure it reaches you in a timely manner.

Letter[17] from Peter Hawkins to Count Dracula, Transylvania

(manifold duplicate kept for records)

March 23

My Lord,

Your Lordship shows great kindness in entrusting me with the purchase of your new English estate. I undertake this happy commission most willingly, and shall accommodate your Lordship's needs in any way which is in my power.

It would be most helpful if your Lordship would convey an idea of the kind of estate being sought. Would a town or a country property be more desirable? If country, does your Lordship take pleasure in hunting and fishing? The acreage, the manner and number of buildings, a disposition to easy entertainment or to peaceful solitude,—all are matters of import to the purchase.

Once your Lordship has communicated his wishes, I shall have my clerk Harker to immediately begin a search for suitable properties. I would attend to the matter personally, but am presently suffering from a case of gout, and cannot travel with ease or efficiency.

I am, my Lord,
Your Lordship's humble servant,
Peter Hawkins

Letter[18] from Dracula to Peter Hawkins

18 March (Old Style)[19]

My Friend,

For many centuries my family has made our home in this ancient castle. To live in a modern house would surely kill me. Look then, if you will, for a house of venerable age. I desire that it shall be near London.

Do not concern yourself with the condition of the house. I shall make my own improvements. A consecrated chapel or church on the property is essential[20], and it must be from no later than the fifteenth century.[21]

The size of the estate is not important; I do not require much ground. Let there be a stream or small river on the land.[22] As to fields or woods for hunting, one may hunt elsewhere. I shall not entertain, but shall enter the city for amusement and companionship.

You write of a "Harker" who will search for my new home. Do you enlist an assistant to aid you? It interests me to learn how my friend Peter Hawkins goes about his business. I am certain that, if you have selected him, he will be most trustworthy[23], and a man of good taste. I shall however make a small request: that if your assistant speaks German, you shall discharge him of this task.[24]

I know that the excellent judgment of Peter Hawkins will procure for me a fine English home. May you have good fortune in the conduct of your search.

Your friend,
Dracula

Letter[25] from Jonathan Harker to Peter Hawkins

12 April

Dear Sir,

I have gathered the addresses of several properties from our colleagues at the Inns of Chancery. I shall begin pursuing them at once.

Affectionately,
Jonathan Harker

Letter[26], Jonathan Harker to Peter Hawkins

13 April

Dear Sir,

I fear I have had no success with the aforementioned addresses; there is nothing in Cornwall that meets any of the Count's requirements, though there are three more properties to visit closer to London. I shall make my way back there straight away in the hopes that, despite their proximity to the city, they will still meet with your client's wishes. I will write to you with my findings.

Affectionately,
Jonathan Harker

Letter[27], Jonathan Harker to Peter Hawkins

15 April

Dear Sir,

As tomorrow is Sunday, there will be little I can do for our client until the following day. As such, I believe I shall pay Mina a visit at the school, for now that I have passed my examinations, I believe the time has come for me to fulfill the duty for which she has patiently waited.

Affectionately,
Jonathan Harker

Letter[28] from Miss Katherine Reed[29] to Miss Lucy Westenra

17 April

Dearest Lucy,

It was so good to see you again at the last Pop. Was I mistaken, or did I see you accompanied by not one or two, but *three* handsome men over the course of that evening? I seem to recall an American who often spoke in their slang, and of course our old friend Dr. Seward, and that very handsome one with the curly hair. It seemed the latter—Lord Godalming's son, was he not?—was the only one you had eyes for. It should not be long now, I would wager, before any one of them proposes. Unless, of course, you beat them to it and propose first. I know you find such talk the stuff of silliness, but did not Miss Norman[30] do the proposing when her day came?

Oh, how lucky you are, now that you have finished your terms at the Chatham school. I have but a month to go before the term is over and I am free at last from this gilded cage . . . but it seems such an age away. The only bright spot in our lives here is Mina. You will, I know, remember how pleasant and kind she is, and how well she exemplifies the etiquette and decorum she teaches us, and yet how she is very much the New Woman (though I dare say she would be rather appalled to hear herself described in such a way). I am pleased that her life may soon be brightened as well, which is the very reason why I am writing:

A gentleman paid us a visit yesterday. It was such an odd thing for a man to come calling on our school, much less on a Sunday, and so when I saw him I could not help but take note. He was young and lean, with a handsome and dignified face. There was a resolute look in his blue eyes which betrayed the seriousness of this visit.

You will think it highly improper of me, I know, but I must confess I could not help but follow behind to see where he was going. When he turned into the lounge, where I know Miss Mina was wont to read on Sundays, I crept forward, silent as a mouse, and paused by the open archway to listen.

"Wilhelmina," the man's voice said, his tone grave and strong, and yet there was the faintest hint of trembling. "I have here a letter from Lincoln's Inn, which informs me that I passed my examination. Now I may properly provide for a future, for myself and for . . . for a wife. Your safety, your life, your happiness are all-in-all to me. When will you let them be my care?"[31]

I did not hear the answer, for it must have been very soft and low, nor did I hear another sound for a very long time. Then I heard his footsteps approaching, I retreated down the hall, and then started forward again at a leisurely pace, so that, when he passed through the arch, it would appear that I was simply walking by. Perhaps by seeing his expression, I would know what Miss Mina's answer was. And my dear, I believe I could have simply remained standing there, caught in the act of eavesdropping, and the good suitor would have paid me no mind, so joyful and far off was the look upon his face as he came out.

After we passed each other, I glanced through the door, and found Mina sitting in her favorite chair, her book in her lap, and tears rolling down her flushed cheeks. I knew, of course, that they were tears of joy (or at least was fairly sure they were such, for one can never truly know on such an occasion), but a passerby, unaware of what had transpired, and seeing a girl in tears while a man is walking away, might not have come to such a benign conclusion. So, playing the part of that passerby, I hurried in to her.

I don't know if she would have confided in me otherwise, but she was indeed in a joyful state, just as her good suitor was, and told me the whole story. She toyed with the new ring on her finger, a simple band of gold. As best as I can remember, these were some of her words, put down in a fair semblance of order:

"I never knew my mother or father, but only knew of them, that they came here from Scotland . . ." What a surprise that was to hear! Not that her family was Scottish, of course—with a name like Murray and that wonderful red hair, it was not difficult to guess—but rather that she was an orphan[32], for truly I have seen noble ladies who do not carry themselves as well as she. But here, let me continue on. "I dare say we were taken with each other right from the start, for we had much in common; he lost his parents at an early age, and has struggled to make a life for himself, just as I have. Though I would have said 'yes,' and he knew it, he did not think it proper to ask for my hand just then, as he was still only a solicitor's clerk. But just last week he received word from Lincoln's Inn that he passed his examination, and is now a full-fledged solicitor!"

I asked if she would continue to be a schoolmistress here, she smiled a bright smile, that was in no way regretful, and said "No, I have decided to work with Jonathan and help him with his career. I am endeavoring to learn shorthand and the typewriter, so that I can stenograph for him after we are married." I could not help feel a bit disappointed, for she was giving up her own independence, which is a hard thing for a woman to come by. She saw something of my concern, and of course knew my disposition regarding such matters, and offered a comment:

"Oh Kate, is there such a great difference in being an assistant to the schoolmistress—for that is all I still am, though I am very pleased and thankful for it—and being an assistant to a solicitor? Either way, I am under another's authority. Only now, at this school, I am in a position of duty and necessity, but soon I will be doing my duty out of love." I had no argument prepared for that, and even if I did, I had no desire to dampen her happiness. "I must be off now," she continued. "As I leave my teaching in school for good and all at the end of term, I must be very exact in all my ways up to the end."[33] So I wished her the best and gave her a hug and a kiss, and left her in peace.

I just could not wait to share this wonderful news with someone. But there is the bell, and I must go now.

Your loving,
Kate

P.S. It occurs to me that perhaps I should have asked Mina's permission before sharing her story with you. But the letter is written, the deed is done, and I can't help but send it. Good-bye again!

Letter[34], Lucy Westenra to Kate Reed

19 April

My dearest Kate,

Well, I suppose I did spend at least a small measure of my time at the concert with those three gentlemen . . . at least long enough to learn their names. The American is Quincey P. Morris[35] (isn't it peculiar how they always insist on including the initial?), who is an inventor[36] from Texas who holds patents on a number of devices—locks and bolts, rifles and pistols, and such similar mechanical things. He's a smart fellow, to be sure, but he looks and talks more like a rugged adventurer than an inventor; and his family is quite wealthy from oil and gold. His friend is the good doctor John Seward, though everyone calls him Jack, and who has under his control an immense lunatic asylum in Purfleet. They are both fine men, both well off, and about as true as they come. They were invited by the Hon. Arthur Holmwood, who is indeed, as you surmised, the Lord Godalming's son. My father—God rest his soul—was good friends with Lord Godalming; the two were introduced years ago at the Windham by a rather eccentric gentleman whose name escapes me. Arthur and Mother have become reacquainted just recently, and I find them often talking together at Hillingham.

As for passing Mina's story on to me, do not fret over disclosing her confidence; Mina and I have been friends since children. I have long known of her love for Jonathan, and I received her letter just before yours, telling of her engagement. At the suggestion of Mr. Holmwood, we will be taking our summer holiday together at Whitby; as I recall, you often find yourself there as well, do you not, to visit your relatives? Perhaps we will see you and your friend Mr. Aytown[37] there, once the term has passed . . .

Your loving,
Lucy

Letter[38], Jonathan Harker to Peter Hawkins

April 18

Dear Sir,

I have taken photographs of a possible home for our client, and thought it best to stay in town to develop the films. This account should precede me only by half a day, but I am anxious to communicate to you without delay the unexpected results of my labours.

The return journey to London was uneventful. Mina will be gratified to know that the trains ran promptly, according to the schedules she is so fond of memorizing. Having arrived at Waterloo Station, I took a cab once again to the Inns.

After an abbreviated luncheon, I immediately went round to the estate agents. Unfortunately, the choice property after which we had inquired was sold, as of Tuesday. I then went out to see the second property, which proved to be unsuitable, as there is no water on the estate itself. Although the River Medway runs a scant quarter mile from the edge of the property, there is no question of the Count's actually owning an access. The Earl of Essex would of course allow him sporting privileges, but he is disinclined to sell a section of the riverbank itself. A third mansion, visited the following morning, likewise failed to fulfill one of the Count's requirements, as the chapel (though splendid) is clearly of more recent date than was represented to us in the agent's letter. My mission seemed, if not doomed to failure, at least doomed to frustration.

Fortunately, the evening of my arrival, my path crossed with that of Sir Charles Bagley, who insisted that I lunch with him the following day at his club. Though I hardly know him, I did not wish to offend so good a friend of yours, so accepted his offer with pleasure (and, I must admit, with the hope of gleaning some pearls of wisdom from so learned a jurist!). Sir Charles inquired most feelingly after your health, and sends his and Lady Constance's love and best regards.

Naturally, at lunch, the conversation turned to the reason for which I had come into town. Mindful of your instructions (but without, I hope, breaching the Count's confidentiality), I apprised Sir Charles of the situation, including some of its more eccentric qualities—which are not, Sir Charles assures me, so unusual, given a wealthy, foreign, aristocratic client! Curiously, not long afterward, a gentleman approached our table, who introduced himself as Mr. Renfield, a solicitor himself[39]. He was perhaps the age of sixty, yet carried himself with a strength disproportionate to his age. There was an odd gleam in his eyes, a shiftiness of gaze that did not sit well with me, but he seemed genial enough.

"Pardon my intrusion, but are you, good sir, Mr. Harker?" he inquired.

"I am," I replied.

"The same Mr. Harker who is in the employ of the good solicitor Mr. Hawkins?"

"I am," I replied again.

"And who is searching for an old estate with a stream, on the instructions of a foreign client?"

"I am," I replied a third time with growing astonishment.

"Ah, how wonderful! If I may be so bold as to mention it, good sir," he said, "there is an estate called Carfax available in the neighborhood of Purfleet, which possesses such features as you desire. I myself will have a home near to there shortly, or so say my friends and family, and I would be more than pleased to have your foreign nobleman as a neighbor." Perplexed, I reached immediately for pen and paper, to make note of the address, but found—to my great surprise—on looking up, that he was no longer there.

I did not know whether to be grateful for the tip, or vexed at its incompleteness, or baffled as to its mysterious origin. Nevertheless, as my other leads had come to a dead end, I had nothing to lose by making my way to Purfleet that afternoon and hiring a local man to drive me about the neighborhood. On a by-road I found the property, which indeed is called Carfax. Were it not for the Count's very specific directives, I would hesitate to recommend it, as it is, to my mind, a very dismal, cheerless sort of place. My local guide says that it has not been inhabited for decades, though it has only been for sale a short time, as the owner—one Mr. Archibald Winter-Suffield, a wealthy man who no doubt had kept the estate purely for investment—has just died.

I was able to find the agent listed on the battered sign, and made an inspection of the premises. The house itself is quite old, possibly dating, in parts, from Norman times. We could not go into the chapel, as the agent had no key, but even to my untrained eye it is evidently of similar antiquity. A deep pool and a wide stream on the grounds empty into the Thames nearby. As the Count wishes to make his own improvements, the dilapidated condition of the estate would seem to be no object; the asking price reflects the need for extensive repairs, as it is astonishingly low.

As mentioned, I have taken numerous photographs, so that the Count may see for himself the property he may be purchasing. While the photographs are being developed, I shall visit the British Museum (which is not far from my lodgings), in the hope of learning something about Transylvania. As one of us must likely go there in the near future, this seems to me the wisest use of the additional time at my disposal.

I am inexpressibly grateful for your generosity, and for the confidence you have shown in entrusting me, so new a solicitor, with such important business. May this letter, dear Sir, find your health much improved. I hope to see both you and Mina by this time tomorrow.

Affectionately,
Jonathan Harker

Letter[40], Peter Hawkins to Dracula

(manifold duplicate kept for records)

19 April

My Lord,

May we humbly present to you the enclosed, in regard to an estate for your Lordship's consideration. The property, known as Carfax, consists in all of twenty acres and is an easy drive from London. My assistant, Mr. Harker, has taken numerous photographs of the mansion and the grounds for your Lordship's perusal, and has also appended a sketch of the interior plan of the house.

The estate meets fully your Lordship's requirements as to age and terrain. The chapel dates from the time of King Richard the First—that is, from the time of the Third Crusade. There are both a standing pool and a running stream in the park. Your Lordship will note that extensive renovations to the house are indeed necessary; we can, if your Lordship so desires, engage a builder to complete the work before the date of your Lordship's intended residency.

If Carfax meets with your Lordship's approval, there are documents which must be signed, transferring ownership of the estate. Unfortunately, I cannot travel myself, owing to recent illness. Mr. Harker is competent and capable in every way, and I have complete confidence in his treatment of your Lordship's business.

Your obedient servant,
Peter Hawkins

Telegram[41], Dracula to Hawkins

24 April

My Friend,

Excellently done. Let Mr. Harker travel at his earliest convenience to the Quatre Saisons Hotel, Munich, to await further instructions. A room shall be kept for him there.

—Dracula

Peter Hawkin's Journal

25 April—The young bird has at last flown the nest, and Harker is by now well on his way to Transylvania. I would not have wished for his first real assignment to be such a heavy undertaking, but the gout would have rendered me a poor servant to the Count, and I must think of the needs of our client. Jonathan is young and strong, and such a journey is made for the likes of him, not for an old fool like me.

I have no doubt Jonathan will make a fine solicitor; I fear I have not told him as much, but I have come to look upon him as a son (especially since the day his own parents died, and given that my own family has long since passed on), and fully intend to make him my partner upon his return. I have already commissioned work on the new sign for our office—"The Law Firm of Hawkins and Harker." The young lad has a keen intellect and an even temper, and will certainly need both in good measure when dealing with some of our more demanding clients and colleagues.

While my thoughts still linger on demanding people, I must record here that it appears Jonathan was aided in locating the estate by Mr. Renfield, who is perhaps the most eccentric of all my colleagues. How he came to know of Carfax, and of our desire to locate such a property, is beyond me. Ah, no matter. Time will tell, as it always does. Case in point, I certainly had my doubts about associating with Renfield in the first place, and he has been a source of disquiet ever since, but the *Aeneid* assured me he would play a pivotal role in our lives, if indeed I interpreted the prophetic line correctly. Until now I had not been able to appreciate any positive effect he has had, but I see that Virgil was ultimately correct yet again.

Ah! I am reminded of my remissness; I was so much in pain with this last attack that I never fulfilled my usual practice of *sortes virgilianae*[42] with regard to the Count. I will take down my copy of *Aeneid* at once.

Later—I am sorely troubled indeed, and my head and heart ache now as badly as my poor joints. When I, as always without so much as a glance at what I was doing, lest it influence the outcome, opened the *Aeneid* and allowed the point of my finger to fall where it wont, I looked and found Virgil's oracle opened to the sixth book, with my finger upon line 530, which read:

"My boat conveys no living bodies o'er"[43]

What could such grim tidings mean? I have read the line over and over again, but am no closer to having an answer than when my eye first beheld the words. What first came to mind was the Stoics' tale of how a certain Simonides buried a body, which later spoke to him in a dream and advised him not to start out the next day on a certain ship. He took the corpse's advice and tarried, and later found that all those who had sailed out on the ship were lost at sea[44].

With such thoughts in mind, I considered the possibility that I may have placed Jonathan in peril by sending him in my place, for he, by necessity, must cross the Straits by a ferry boat. By the time this realization came to me, it was too late to stop him, for he was no doubt already making the crossing, but I did inquire as to the conditions of the Straits; the reply to my wire was that the weather at

Dover is fine indeed, and there has been no report of any trouble in the waters. Perhaps the danger—if there is indeed any danger at all—lies further ahead for Jonathan; yet the rest of his journey is to be by train and coach, so I am at a loss as to what "My boat conveys no living bodies o'er" could mean for him.

There is naught else to do now, but to watch and wait . . .

CHAPTER

TWO[45]

Jonathan Harker's Journal

(Kept in shorthand)

25 April—Left Charing Cross promptly at 8:50 P.M., on a London Chatham train, and arrived in Dover as scheduled to undertake my first crossing of the Straits. As this will be my first journey abroad, I will endeavor to keep an accurate and detailed account, to serve as an aid when describing my adventure to Mina upon my return.

Until only a few decades ago, as I hear Mr. Hawkins tell it, such a crossing of the Straits was a dreaded event, for the waters of Dover Bay were shallow, with dangerous offshore banks and rocky shoals that sent many a larger ship to a watery grave. In order to make the journey to Calais in relative safety, one was required to make use of small ferry boats, and even then it was necessary to wait until the highest tide, so as to keep from becoming shipwrecked on submerged rocks. And, being as light as they were, the ferries were tossed about so by wind and waves that seasickness was all too common among such unfortunate travelers. But much has changed since then. With the construction of the Admiralty Pier, which extends well beyond the shallows, one is now able to make the crossing on larger, more comfortable ships.

Through a bit of practical innovation, my train was able to run out along tracks set into the top of the pier itself to where a steamer (owned and operated by the same London Chatham company) patiently waited. Though the pier was certainly convenient, relative to the difficulties that had come before, in truth I think it would have been far better if the English Tunnel Company had completed its work on digging their way to France beneath the Straits. Should this have been the case, I could have simply continued onward in my current seat, straight through to France. But after those infamous quarrels over the Suez Canal, such plans to connect the two countries were put to an abrupt halt. (The project was not a total loss, though, as coal and iron ore were found in the tunnel's depths.)

Watching out the window as my train made its way along the pier, I had the brief and unsettling impression that we were traveling across a bridge that had yet to be completed on the other end, for I could see ahead where the track simply ended, with nothing but dark waters beyond. But the sensation passed quickly, and in due time I reached the end of the pier, where the great turret stood at its tireless watch. Eden's guardian Cherubim might have flaming swords to defend Paradise, but Dover's turret housed two guns of such power as to be able to hurl explosive shells nearly seven miles. Woe be to any foreign invader who would dare cross the threshold into England!

My traps were lifted aboard the waiting steamer, and I settled in for the crossing. If there is any benefit to not being able to travel straight through a tunnel, it was this: that the view of Dover at night is truly breathtaking, with the angelic radiance of the lighthouses and the eerie luminescence of the chalk white cliffs. The greatest of these cliffs was, without doubt, Shakespeare Cliff, whose high and bending head looked fearfully down into the confined depths below. Perhaps Matthew Arnold put it best into words when he wrote:

"The sea is calm tonight, the tide is full, the moon lies fair upon the straits. On the French coast, the light gleams, and is gone: the cliffs of England stand, glimmering and vast, out in the tranquil bay."

And the poet's words certainly held true this night, for while Dover was bright, even ethereal, in the silver glow of the moon, Calais was dark, with swollen clouds hanging above its shores. Cruel lightning flashed much farther to the west and south, where the storm seemed to stretch back without end. As I sit here aboard the steamer, writing in my journal, I wonder if I will have to pass through that storm before my journey is done . . .

26 April—Arrived in Paris from Calais at 5:50 A.M. While here, I took the advice of Baedeker's "Austria" and had my English currency exchanged for French gold, which I am assured will be readily accepted on all the legs of my journey.

The Gare de l'Est, which faces the Boulevard du Strasbourg and is built on the site of the Saint Laurent Fair, was a grand affair decorated with a statue of Strasbourg himself. While preparing to board the train that would carry me on a direct service to Munich, I saw on a neighboring track the famous Orient Express.

As I am quite fond of trains—an interest that I happily share with Mina—I could not help but take pause and admire Nagelmackers' marvel.

The engine was a powerful 2-4-0 Class 500, with a freshly washed and polished black boiler, and sturdy double frames. Coupled behind its coal car were two fourgons, followed by two sleepers (which looked to be quite heavy, with six wheels to a car), and finally a luxurious dining coach.

Since the sleepers were being boarded on the opposite side, I felt secure in drawing closer to the Express. There were a number of wooden crates piled here and there upon the platform, and I took note that one of the larger ones sat conveniently near to an as yet deserted window of the coach. Though highly unbecoming of a proper Englishman, I could not resist the temptation, and so, setting aside my traps, and glancing around me like a sheepish schoolboy, I pulled myself up upon the crate for a quick look inside.

The sleeper compartment was decked out with all the trappings of an elegant hotel, with cabinets and lamps and mirrors and the like. There were wide and comfortable looking bench seats for sitting during the day, and four spacious berths for sleeping at night. From the size of the car, I estimated that there might be as many as six such compartments contained within the saloon; or rather five, for I had heard that a portion of each car had been set aside for washbasins and toilet compartments! As no one had called attention to my impropriety, I repeated the same maneuver at the dining car, and found a baroque interior lit by gas chandeliers. The seats were upholstered in embossed leather, and the paneling was in teak and mahogany inlaid with elaborate marquetry and gilt. If the rumors were true, a five-course meal of French delicacies was served each day in this car.

But now my own train was being boarded in earnest, and, fearing some sort of reprisal for my harmless curiosity, I quickly collected my traps and made my way back. As I stepped aboard, the conductor gave me a look that was part reprimand and part bemused sympathy, but said nothing about my actions one way or the other. Once I was aboard and nestled in for my long journey, I wasted no time in recording these recollections of the Wagons-Lit Express.

What I would not give to be able to make a journey on the Express with Mina! But even with my income of a solicitor's clerk and Mina's salary as an assistant schoolmistress, I doubt that anything short of supernatural intervention would ever allow us to be to partake in such luxury.

Later—Left Paris at 8:25 A.M., and arrived in Munich at 8:35 P.M. on a direct service[46]. It was quite late, and I was eager to get settled in to the Quatre Saisons for the night, where the Count had apparently arranged with the maître d'hôtel to hold a room for me[47]. I had expected to be given a room at the Marienbad or perhaps the Auracher Hof[48], but to stay at the Quatre Saisons would be a treat indeed!

Upon stepping down from the cab, I found my temporary residence to be an impressive five-story affair, set along the Maximilianstrasse thoroughfare. The façade of the Quatre Saisons—or the Vier Jahreszeiten, as they call it here—was unique to say the least, being a queer blending of Gothic architecture, harsh lines and sharp angles, and countless faux oval windows out of which peered the stone busts of people from all classes and walks of life; I was able to make out what appeared to be a waiter and a Chinaman, just to name two.

I understand that the design of the thoroughfare, and the Quatre Saisons in particular, had been the result of a famous architectural competition held by the Bavarian king Maximilian II, who wished Munich to have something akin to the renowned Champs Elysées of Paris. The hotel had taken six years to build, and was finally opened in 1858. Its owners, the Schimon family, made certain that their hotel would be renovated with each new luxury and advancement. To wit, the hotel has just recently had its own accumulators installed, which now provide electrical power to some one thousand bulbs; by way of comparison, the city of Munich has only some four thousand bulbs in its entirety. Though a costly affair to maintain, such innovation has paid off, for on any given day, over one hundred members of royalty can be found staying here.

As I entered the hotel, I found a beautiful stained glass cupola fixed into the ceiling of the luxurious lobby, depicting, appropriately, the four seasons. The room that the maître d'hôtel showed me to was quite large, with its own fireplace. What's more, it had an odd sort of bathtub that looked something akin to a rocking chair. The maître d' explained that the rocking motion of the tub, when filled with hot water (courtesy of the hotel's own steam engine!), would provide great rejuvenation with regard to the blood. He said that my benefactor had insisted on my staying as healthy as possible on my long journey. It was thoughtful of the Count to be so considerate of my health and well-being, and I must not fail to thank him for this when we at last meet.

My room is very pleasing to me, not because it is decked out with more accommodations than a solicitor's clerk could hope for, but because it affords me ample amounts of quiet and solitude. With the thick walls of the hotel, the only sounds that intrude upon my thoughts are the echoes of my own footfalls, the clinking of my teacup, and the crackling of the fire. It all reminded me of the quarters to which I had exiled myself while studying for the exams only a few months back.

I find it somehow queer that I, who would never otherwise be able to enjoy such as the Quatre Saisons, find its greatest boon the peace and quiet, while the Count, who must enjoy luxuries as those found here, wishes to leave the peace and quiet (for he must dwell in near isolation, judging by the maps I studied at the British Museum) for the bustle of London. Such are the ironies of life, I suppose.

It is late now, and as I supped on the train, I will finish my cup of tea, and settle in for the night.

27 April[49]—I dined today in the hotel. Having followed the stairway down, I found the dining room to be a unique combination of a vinothèque, lounge, restaurant and pub, being comprised of a series of interconnected open rooms with high arched ceilings. The meal was a called "schweinebraten mit knödel," which was roast pork with a sort of dumpling, with a large helping of spiced potatoes, and accompanied by a most excellent wine. The dessert was something the waiter called "kaiserschmarrn." It was an egg pudding of sorts, with raisins and almonds mixed in. It was brought to the table, then set ablaze. When the flames died away, the waiter dusted it with some sugar.

In the Count's last telegram to me in London, which signaled my departure, he mentioned that I should abide at the Quatre Saisons to await further instructions, but that, as I would undoubtedly have a few days to myself, I might well enjoy a tour of the more noteworthy attractions of Munich. Specifically, he mentioned the Pinakothek museum[50], the Royal Court and National Theatre's performance of "The Flying Dutchman," and the famous Munich "Dead House."

After spending so many hours of sitting yesterday, I thought it best to stretch my legs a bit today. So after I had dined and freshened up, I took a leisurely stroll to the museum, a refreshing walk which took just over an hour. I had greatly enjoyed my visit to the British Museum while in London, and so was eager to see what Munich had to offer. As it turned out, the Pinakothek was impressive indeed. The structure itself, though of a relatively simple and functional façade of the post Renaissance type, was incredibly long; I paused in the spacious courtyard and counted the large arched windows, finding that there were twenty-four of them, twelve on either side of the main doorway. The interior of the museum seemed to be overfilled with paintings from the last five centuries. The ground floor housed mainly the works of the old German masters, while the upper level contained a more interesting variety: Dutch, Flemish, Italian, French, and Spanish, to name a few. I had the rare privilege of viewing works by Peter Paul Rubens, Albrecht Dürer, Titian, Poussin, even daVinci. On prominent display was "Canigani Holy Family," the first work of Raphael to be brought to Germany. And, if the legend is true, the building's foundation stone was laid on the anniversary of Raphael's death as a tribute to him.

Oddly enough, it was an obscure oil painting, of artist unknown, which most fascinated me. Indeed, I returned to it several times, leaving behind the renowned masters, to study it more closely. I was enough of a student of church history to recognize it as depicting the martyrdom of Saint Andrew, which, as tradition dictates, consists of a bearded man being fastened to an "X" shaped cross (as opposed to the typical "T" variety). What was most unusual about this painting was that Saint Andrew's gaze was not facing up expectantly toward heaven, nor with forgiveness toward those binding his hands and legs; rather, he was looking with a curious sidelong glance toward a figure in the background, whose appearance and dress were remarkably different from that of those around him. The figure wore a robe or cloak of sorts, and atop his head was a cap adorned with a jeweled star, which might have served as a primitive crown in whatever barbaric age and land in which this man had lived. The face of the nobleman was hard, with high cheekbones and a thin hooked nose, below which was a thick dark moustache. The eyes were especially large and piercing, and, though obviously meant to be gazing upon the crucifixion, yet managed to follow one around the room.[51]

28 April—After I had supped, I took a cab to the Court Theatre, for I understood from the hotel staff that there would be a performance of "The Flying Dutchman" today, a favorite there since Wagner's patronage by King Ludwig II. Perhaps it was the strangeness of the city, but I could not help but feel that someone was watching me the whole time, though I did not manage to catch anyone looking my way. The journey did not take long at all, for the theatre was located along the same thoroughfare as my hotel. I spotted it a ways off. The theatre was of a Greek design (complete with portico and triangular pediment), but was of relatively new construct, having been rebuilt after a fire had destroyed its predecessor.

I was shown to my seat, and in due course, the curtains opened, revealing a most exquisite set.[52] The stage was truly immense, and looked remarkably like the little Cornish port of Pencastle I had holidayed at in early April of last year, when the sun had seemingly come to stay after a long and bitter winter. Boldly and blackly the rocks—and I had no doubt they were hewn of real stone, given the wealth and resources such a theatre must have at its disposal—stood out against a background of shaded blue, where the counterfeit sky faded into a misty hue at the far horizon. The sea was painted as if of sapphire, save where it became the deep emerald green of what I imagined to be fathomless depths under the cliffs. On the slopes the grass was parched and brown. The spikes of furze bushes were ashy grey, but the golden yellow of their flowers streamed along the hillside, dipping out in lines as the rock cropped up, and lessening into patches and dots till finally it died away all together at the jutting cliffs.

The little harbour opened from the sea between towering cliffs, and behind a lonely rock, pierced with many caves and blow-holes through which—were this grand display truly along the shores and not within these theatre walls—the sea in storm time might well send its thunderous voice, together with a fountain of drifting spume. From hence, the stream wound inland in a serpentine course, guarded at its entrance by two little curving piers to left and right. These had the look of being roughly built of dark slates placed endways and held together with great beams bound with iron bands.

This stream had been made to look deep at the mouth, with here and there, where it widened, patches of broken rock exposed and full of holes where I would fully expect crabs and lobsters might be found at the ebb of the tide. From amongst the rocks rose sturdy posts, akin to those used for warping in the little coasting vessels which might frequent such a port.

At either side of the river was a row of cottages down almost on the level of high tide. They were pretty cottages, strongly and snugly built, with trim narrow gardens in front, full of old-fashioned plants, flowering currants, coloured primroses, wallflower, and stonecrop. Over the fronts of many of them climbed clematis and wisteria. The window sides and door posts of all were as white as snow, and the little pathway to each was paved with light coloured stones. At some of the doors were tiny porches, whilst at others were rustic seats cut from tree trunks or from old barrels; in nearly every case the window ledges were filled with boxes or pots of flowers or foliage plants.

The sea was calm and the sun bright, but across the sea were strange lines of darkness and light, and close in to shore the rocks were fringed with foam. The wind, which unseen stagehands had somehow produced, had backed, as they say, and came in sharp, cold puffs. The blow-holes, which ran from the rocky bay without to the harbour within, were booming at intervals, and the seagulls were screaming ceaselessly as they wheeled about on their thin wires at the entrance of the port.

The lights slowly dimmed and the colours changed to those of dusk. Then it was that a wild storm came on. The sea rose and lashed the coast, and the room darkened so that it was only by the flash of lightning that anything could be seen. And presently, by one such flash, a 'ketch' was seen drifting under only a jib outside the port. All eyes and all glasses were concentrated on her, waiting for the next flash. The ship was small at first, rocking to and fro upon the waves upstage. But with each new flash, the ship was closer and larger, until at last it was at its full size downstage, where Daland and his crew sought shelter in the cove from the raging storm.

It was then that the Flying Dutchman appeared on the horizon. Unlike Daland's vessel, the Dutchman seemed untouched by the storm, sailing with great speed and grace. All was dark for a few moments, and then, at the next lightning flash (after which the lights remained up, though dim) the ghost ship had appeared downstage. Its three black masts flew blood red sails, which slowly and silently furled themselves as its undying Captain stepped ashore. In his face was the ghastly pallor of a phantom and in his eyes shown the wild glamour of the lost; in his every tone and action there was the stamp of death[53]. Later in the performance, when the drunken crew of Daland's ship call their taunts over, the

Dutchman's rigging, by some secret trick, suddenly bursts into crackling blue flame as the waves rise and rock beneath its black hull. A truly magnificent design.

If only the Captain and Senta had been played by ones such as Henry Irving and Ellen Terry. Ten years ago I was afforded the opportunity to see Irving perform in Wills's "Vanderdecken," a piece quite similar to this "Flying Dutchman," and had been quite overawed by his performance. Irving gave the wonderful impression of a dead man fictitiously alive[54]. Nevertheless, the performances today were satisfactory, and the story compelling indeed, telling of young Eric's struggle to keep his love, Senta, from falling victim to the phantom Captain's quest for a bride. I could not help but notice that the actors who played Senta and Eric bore a striking resemblance to Mina and myself. This proved to be unaccountably distressing (considering Eric fails and Senta does indeed become wooed, even unto death, by the Captain), a condition made worse by the sensation of that unseen touch of another's gaze upon my back through the performance. It was all a silly bit of rubbish, of course, but I could not shake the feeling, and more than once I felt the hairs on the back of my neck rise. When the performance had ended and the curtain closed, I turned around to, if nothing else, either confirm or discount my suspicions. Just above me was a private viewing box; it was oddly empty, though all the others remained occupied with people, which led me to wonder if this one had been suddenly vacated in the moment before I turned.

The whole experience was a bit overwhelming, and so I elected to sup in the quiet comfort of my quarters tonight, rather than return to the dining room. I have no desire for any more mysterious gazes falling upon me today.

29 April—As I had yet to receive word from the Count, I decided that today would be an excellent day to stroll through the Dead House. Along the way, I stopped in at an imbiss and ate something called "weisswurst," which was a sort of white veal sausage, delicately seasoned, and served with a grainy sweet mustard. By and by, I came to the Sendling Gate, or "Victory Gate," that had been built some five hundred years ago; only the two main towers remained intact from that era, the rest being of more recent construction. From there I walked down Thalkirchner until I reached the gate of Gottesacker—the Southern Cemetery. As I understand it, this was once a place of burial for paupers, but nearly a hundred years ago the churchyards of Munich were closed and this became the city's main cemetery. Strolling through the rows of stones, I came upon many an important name: the scientist Ohm, the artists Schwanthaler and Stieler, the architects Fischer and Klenze, and too many more to list here.

Nearer the Gate, I found situated the famous Leichenhaus, or "Dead House," a semi-circular building with an open colonnade at the front. In the rear of the building there have been constructed three large rooms for the reception of the dead. It is here that the friends and family of the deceased are afforded two boons.

First, the body is laid in a peaceful rest upon a bier, thus being removed from the confined dwelling of the survivors and placed in a respectful location, so that all those who care to can come and mourn. Second, it grants the survivors peace of mind that there should be no premature burial of their loved one. Regarding the latter, this assurance is accomplished in two ways; not only is there no interment until the first clear signs of decomposition have appeared, but additionally there is a string which connects one finger of the deceased to a bell. Should he only have been suffering a profound sleep, and find himself awake amidst the biers of the dead, he need only make the smallest movement of his finger, and the bell would ring, alerting the nearby warder of this joyous revival. Just as the Baroness Tautphoeus described it, the Dead House is "where all dead go, high and lowly, and with bells on hands and feet to wait to see if any spark of life is there—staying two days."

Upon one of the slabs I noticed a corpse of particular interest. I could not get overly close, for the body was set far back on a bier, nestled in among large arrangements of flowers. From where I stood I could see that the deceased had been a tall man, with a strong face, and a thin, beaky nose. It reminded me somewhat of the portrait I had spent much time studying at the museum, save that the corpse had a long dark beard, not the moustache in the painting. But what so caught my eye was that, despite the pallor of death, the cheeks and lips were flushed as if in life, and the lips were bright red. The eyes too were open, dead and dark[55], yet still clear as if alive. From there I moved on to view the other bodies on display, and lingered among the biers of the children and babies for quite some time . . . perhaps longer than I should, for such morbid curiosity can not be healthy. Though, in my defense, that room seemed to be where most of the onlookers congregated.

Just after sundown, as I was preparing to summon a cab to make my way back to the hotel, I overheard snatches of a conversation between the watchmen, from which I could make out a few words. It would seem that they were excited about a body being missing from one of the rooms. Apparently one of the watchmen had noticed a body of a rather lively appearance, but when pulse and heart and breath had been searched for, there was none to be found. Unconvinced, the man had gone to find another who might check again for signs of life, but upon their return to the bier, the body was gone! Just which one it was he could not say, for all corpses that remained were accounted for in their ledgers, with none missing. The watchmen were wondering between themselves how a body could have appeared in the rooms without being recorded in the ledgers, and then vanish without a trace.

I felt certain I knew which corpse it was they were searching for, so I returned to the room to see for myself, and was not at all surprised to find that the body of the tall man was no longer among the flowers. I considered telling the watchmen about it, but as I was unnerved enough as it was, and as I was a foreigner to them, and one who barely spoke their language, I thought it best for them to figure out this mystery—if it could be solved—in their own good time. So, without further delay, I returned to the hotel[56].

Upon my arrival at the Quatre Saisons, I found waiting for me a telegram from the Count, informing me that arrangements had been made for my journey to Bistritz in two days. I must confess that, while my stay in Munich has thus far been a wondrous experience, each day has become progressively more disconcerting than the last, and I will be eager to be on my way.

CHAPTER THREE[57]

Jonathan Harker's Journal, Continued

30 April, Munich—When we started for our drive the sun was shining brightly on Munich, and the air was full of the joyousness of early summer. Just as we were about to depart, Herr Delbrück (the maître d'hôtel of the Quatre Saisons, where I was staying) came down, bareheaded, to the carriage and, after wishing me a pleasant drive, said to the coachman, still holding his hand on the handle of the carriage door:

"Remember you are back by nightfall. The sky looks bright but there is a shiver in the north wind that says there may be a sudden storm. But I am sure you will not be late." Here he smiled, and added, "for you know what night it is."

Johann answered with an emphatic, "Ja, mein Herr," and, touching his hat, drove off quickly. When we had cleared the town, I said, after signaling to him to stop:

'Tell me, Johann, what is tonight?'

He crossed himself, as he answered laconically: 'Walpurgis nacht.' Then he took out his watch, a great, old-fashioned German silver thing as big as a turnip, and looked at it, with his eyebrows gathered together and a little impatient shrug of his shoulders. I realised that this was his way of respectfully protesting against the unnecessary delay, and sank back in the carriage, merely motioning him to proceed. He started off rapidly, as if to make up for lost time. Every now and then the horses seemed to throw up their heads and sniff the air suspiciously. On such occasions I often looked round in alarm. The road was pretty bleak, for we were traversing a sort of high, wind-swept plateau. As we drove, I saw another road that looked but little used, and which seemed to dip through a little, winding valley. It looked so inviting that, even at the risk of offending him, I called Johann to stop—and when he had pulled up, I told him I would like to drive down that road. He made all sorts of excuses, and frequently crossed himself as he spoke. This somewhat piqued my curiosity, so I asked him various questions. He answered fencingly, and repeatedly looked at his watch in protest. Finally I said:

'Well, Johann, I want to go down this road. I shall not ask you to come unless you like; but tell me why you do not like to go, that is all I ask.' For answer he seemed to throw himself off the box, so quickly did he reach the ground. Then he stretched out his hands appealingly to me, and implored me not to go. There was just enough of English mixed with the German for me to understand the drift of his talk. He seemed always just about to tell me something—the very idea of which evidently frightened him; but each time he pulled himself up, saying, as he crossed himself: 'Walpurgis nacht!'

I tried to argue with him, but it was difficult to argue with a man when I did not know the subtleties of his language. The advantage certainly rested with him, for although he began to speak in English, of a very crude and broken kind, he always got excited and broke into his native tongue—and every time he did so, he looked at his watch. Then the horses became restless and sniffed the air. At this he grew very pale, and, looking around in a frightened way, he suddenly jumped forward, took them by the bridles and led them on some twenty feet. I followed, and asked why he had done this. For answer he crossed himself, pointed to the spot we had left and drew his carriage in the direction of the other road, indicating a cross, and said, first in German, then in English: 'Buried him—him what killed themselves.'

I remembered the old custom of burying suicides at cross-roads: 'Ah! I see, a suicide. How interesting!' But for the life of me I could not make out why the horses were frightened.

Whilst we were talking, we heard a sort of sound between a yelp and a bark. It was far away; but the horses got very restless, and it took Johann all his time to quiet them. He was pale, and said, 'It sounds like a wolf—but yet there are no wolves here now.'

'No?' I said, questioning him; 'isn't it long since the wolves were so near the city?'

'Long, long,' he answered, 'in the spring and summer; but with the snow the wolves have been here not so long.'

Whilst he was petting the horses and trying to quiet them, dark clouds drifted rapidly across the sky. The sunshine passed away, and a breath of cold wind seemed to drift past us. It was only a breath, however, and more in the nature of a warning than a fact, for the sun came out brightly again. Johann looked under his lifted hand at the horizon and said:

'The storm of snow, he comes before long time.' Then he looked at his watch again, and, straightway holding his reins firmly—for the horses were still pawing the ground restlessly and shaking their heads—he climbed to his box as though the time had come for proceeding on our journey.

I felt a little obstinate and did not at once get into the carriage.

'Tell me,' I said, 'about this place where the road leads,' and I pointed down.

Again he crossed himself and mumbled a prayer, before he answered, 'It is unholy.'

'What is unholy?' I enquired.

'The village.'

'Then there is a village?'

'No, no. No one lives there hundreds of years.' My curiosity was piqued, 'But you said there was a village.'

'There was.'

'Where is it now?'

Whereupon he burst out into a long story in German and English, so mixed up that I could not quite understand exactly what he said, but roughly I gathered that long ago, hundreds of years, men had died there and been buried in their graves; and sounds were heard under the clay, and when the graves were opened, men and women were found rosy with life, and their mouths red with blood. And so, in haste to save their lives (aye, and their souls!—and here he crossed himself) those who were left fled away to other places, where the living lived, and the dead were dead and not—not something. He was evidently afraid to speak the last words. As he proceeded with his narration, he grew more and more excited. He told me how, some three decades past, a man had come to the town to rid the land of its evil. The stranger had proclaimed he was successful, and yet something of the evil remained; to this day no one would go near the ruins.

As he concluded his tale, it seemed as if his imagination had finally got hold of him, and he ended in a perfect paroxysm of fear—white-faced, perspiring, trembling and looking round him, as if expecting that some dreadful presence would manifest itself there in the bright sunshine on the open plain. Finally, in an agony of desperation, he cried:

'Walpurgis nacht!' and pointed to the carriage for me to get in. All my English blood rose at this, and, standing back, I said:

'You are afraid, Johann—you are afraid. Go home; I shall return alone; the walk will do me good.' The carriage door was open. I took from the seat my oak walking-stick—which I always carry on my holiday excursions—and closed the door, pointing back to Munich, and said, 'Go home, Johann—Walpurgis nacht doesn't concern Englishmen.'

The horses were now more restive than ever, and Johann was trying to hold them in, while excitedly imploring me not to do anything so foolish. I pitied the poor fellow, he was deeply in earnest; but all the same I could not help laughing. His English was quite gone now. In his anxiety he had forgotten that his only means of making me understand was to talk my language, so he jabbered away in his native German. It began to be a little tedious. After giving the direction, 'Home!' I turned to go down the cross-road into the valley.

With a despairing gesture, Johann turned his horses towards Munich. I leaned on my stick and looked after him. He went slowly along the road for a while: then there came over the crest of the hill a man tall and thin. I could see so much in the distance. When he drew near the horses, they began to jump and kick about, then to scream with terror. Johann could not hold them in; they bolted down the road, running away madly. I watched them out of sight, then looked for the stranger, but I found that he, too, was gone.

With a light heart I turned down the side road through the deepening valley to which Johann had objected. There was not the slightest reason, that I could see, for his objection; and I daresay I tramped for a couple of hours without thinking of time or distance, and certainly without seeing a person or a house. So far as the place was concerned, it was desolation, itself. But I did not notice this particularly till, on turning a bend in the road, I came upon a scattered fringe of wood; then I recognized that I had been impressed unconsciously by the desolation of the region through which I had passed.

I sat down to rest myself, and began to look around. It struck me that it was considerably colder than it had been at the commencement of my walk—a sort of sighing sound seemed to be around me, with, now and then, high overhead, a sort of muffled roar. Looking upwards I noticed that great thick clouds were drifting rapidly across the sky from North to South at a great height. There were signs of coming storm in some lofty stratum of the air. I was a little chilly, and, thinking that it was the sitting still after the exercise of walking, I resumed my journey.

The ground I passed over was now much more picturesque. There were no striking objects that the eye might single out; but in all there was a charm of beauty. I took little heed of time and it was only when the deepening twilight forced itself upon me that I began to think of how I should find my way home. The brightness of the day had gone. The air was cold, and the drifting of clouds high overhead was more marked. They were accompanied by a sort of far-away rushing sound, through which seemed to come at intervals that mysterious cry which the driver had said came from a wolf. For a while I hesitated. I had said I would see the deserted village, so on I went, and presently came on a wide stretch of open country, shut in by hills all around. Their sides were covered with trees which spread down to the plain, dotting, in clumps, the gentler slopes and hollows which showed here and there. I followed with my eye the winding of the road, and saw that it curved close to one of the densest of these clumps and was lost behind it.

As I looked there came a cold shiver in the air, and the snow began to fall. I thought of the miles and miles of bleak country I had passed, and then hurried on to seek the shelter of the wood in front. Darker and darker grew the sky, and faster and heavier fell the snow, till the earth before and around me was a glistening white carpet the further edge of which was lost in misty vagueness. The road was here but crude, and when on the level its boundaries were not so marked, as when it passed through the cuttings; and in a little while I found that I must have strayed from it, for I missed underfoot the hard surface, and my feet sank deeper in the grass and moss. Then the wind grew stronger and blew with ever increasing force, till I was fain to run before it. The air became icy-cold, and in spite of my exercise I began to suffer. The snow was now falling so thickly and whirling around me in such rapid eddies that I could hardly keep my eyes open. Every now and then the heavens were torn asunder by vivid lightning, and in the flashes I could see ahead of me a great mass of trees, chiefly yew and cypress all heavily coated with snow.

I was soon amongst the shelter of the trees, and there, in comparative silence, I could hear the rush of the wind high overhead. Presently the blackness of the storm had become merged in the darkness of the night. By-and-by the storm seemed to be passing away: it now only came in fierce puffs or blasts. At such moments the weird sound of the wolf appeared to be echoed by many similar sounds around me.

Now and again, through the black mass of drifting cloud, came a straggling ray of moonlight, which lit up the expanse, and showed me that I was at the edge of a dense mass of cypress and yew trees. As the snow had ceased to fall, I walked out from the shelter and began to investigate more closely. It appeared to me that, amongst so many old foundations as I had passed, there might be still standing a house in which, though in ruins, I could find some sort of shelter for a while. As I skirted the edge of the copse, I found that a low wall encircled it, and following this. I presently found an opening. Here the cypresses formed an alley leading up to a square mass of some kind of building. Just as I caught sight of this, however, the drifting clouds obscured the moon, and I passed up the path in darkness. The wind must have grown colder, for I felt myself shiver as I walked; but there was hope of shelter, and I groped my way blindly on.

I stopped, for there was a sudden stillness. The storm had passed; and, perhaps in sympathy with nature's silence, my heart seemed to cease to beat. But this was only momentarily; for suddenly the moonlight broke through the clouds, showing me that I was in a graveyard, and that the square object before me was a great massive tomb of marble, as white as the snow that lay on and all around it. With the moonlight there came a fierce sigh of the storm, which appeared to resume its course with a long, low howl, as of many dogs or wolves. I was awed and shocked, and felt the cold perceptibly grow upon me till it seemed to grip me by the heart. Then while the flood of moonlight still fell on the marble tomb, the storm gave further evidence of renewing, as though it was returning on its track. Impelled by some sort of fascination, I approached the sepulchre to see what it was, and why such a thing stood alone in such a place. I walked around it, and read, over the Doric door, in German:

COUNTESS DOLINGEN OF GRATZ
IN STYRIA
SOUGHT AND FOUND DEATH
1801[58]

On the top of the tomb, seemingly driven through the solid marble—for the structure was composed of a few vast blocks of stone—was a great iron spike or stake. On going to the back I saw, graven in great Russian letters:

'The dead travel fast.'

There was something so weird and uncanny about the whole thing that it gave me a turn and made me feel quite faint. I began to wish, for the first time, that I had taken Johann's advice. Here a thought struck me, which came under almost mysterious circumstances and with a terrible shock. This was Walpurgis Night!

Walpurgis Night, when, according to the belief of millions of people, the devil was abroad—when the graves were opened and the dead came forth and walked. When all evil things of earth and air and water held revel. This very place the driver had specially shunned. This was the depopulated village of centuries ago. This was where the suicide lay; and this was the place where I was alone—unmanned, shivering with cold in a shroud of snow with a wild storm gathering again upon me! It took all my philosophy, all the religion I had been taught, all my courage, not to collapse in a paroxysm of fright.

And now a perfect tornado burst upon me. The ground shook as though thousands of horses thundered across it; and this time the storm bore on its icy wings, not snow, but great hailstones which drove with such violence that they might have come from the thongs of Balearic slingers—hailstones that beat down leaf and branch and made the shelter of the cypresses of no more avail than though their stems were standing-corn. At the first I had rushed to the nearest tree; but I was soon fain to leave it and seek the only spot that seemed to afford refuge, the deep Doric doorway of the marble tomb. There, crouching against the massive bronze door, I gained a certain amount of protection from the beating of the hailstones, for now they only drove against me as they ricocheted from the ground and the side of the marble. I saw that some sort of mortar or putty had long ago been pressed into the spaces around the door, thus sealing it shut.

As I leaned against the door, it moved slightly and opened inwards, and in doing so broke apart the dried seal around the door. The shelter of even a tomb was welcome in that pitiless tempest, and I was about to enter it when there came a flash of forked-lightning that lit up the whole expanse of the heavens. In the instant, as I am a living man, I saw, as my eyes were turned into the darkness of the tomb, a beautiful woman, with rounded cheeks and red lips, seemingly sleeping on a bier, though pierced through with the iron stake from above. As the thunder broke overhead, I was grasped as by the hand of a giant and hurled out into the storm. The whole thing was so sudden that, before I could realize the shock, moral as well as physical, I found the hailstones beating me down. At the same time I had a strange, dominating feeling that I was not alone. I looked towards the tomb. Just then there came another blinding flash, which seemed to strike the iron stake that surmounted the tomb and to pour through to the earth, blasting and crumbling the marble, as in a burst of flame. The dead woman rose for a moment of agony, while she was lapped in the flame, and her bitter scream of pain was drowned in the thundercrash. The last thing I heard was this mingling of dreadful sound, as again I was seized in the giant-grasp and dragged away, while the hailstones beat on me, and the air around seemed reverberant with the howling of wolves. The last sight that I remembered was a vague, white, moving mass, as if all the graves around me had sent out the phantoms of their sheeted-dead, and that they were closing in on me through the white cloudiness of the driving hail.

Gradually there came a sort of vague beginning of consciousness; then a sense of weariness that was dreadful. For a time I remembered nothing; but slowly my senses returned. My feet seemed positively racked with pain, yet I could not move them. They seemed to be numbed. There was an icy feeling at the back of my neck and all down my spine, and my ears, like my feet, were dead, yet in torment; but there was in my breast a sense of warmth which was, by comparison, delicious. It was as a nightmare—a physical nightmare, if one may use such an expression; for some heavy weight on my chest made it difficult for me to breathe.

This period of semi-lethargy seemed to remain a long time, and as it faded away I must have slept or swooned. Then came a sort of loathing, like the first stage of sea-sickness, and a wild desire to be free from something—I knew not what. A vast stillness enveloped me, as though all the world were asleep or dead—only broken by the low panting as of some animal close to me. I felt a warm rasping at my throat, then came a consciousness of the awful truth, which chilled me to the heart and sent the blood surging up through my brain. Some great animal was lying on me and now licking my throat. I feared to stir, for some instinct of prudence bade me lie still; but the brute seemed to realise that there was now some change in me, for it raised its head. Through my eyelashes I saw above me the two great flaming eyes of a gigantic wolf. Its sharp white teeth gleamed in the gaping red mouth, and I could feel its hot breath fierce and acrid upon me.

For another spell of time I remembered no more. Then I became conscious of a low growl, followed by a yelp, renewed again and again. Then, seemingly very far away, I heard a 'Holloa! holloa!' as of many voices calling in unison. Cautiously I raised my head and looked in the direction whence the sound came; but the cemetery blocked my view. The wolf still continued to yelp in a strange way, and a red glare began to move round the grove of cypresses, as though following the sound. As the voices drew closer, the wolf yelped faster and louder. I feared to make either sound or motion. Nearer came the red glow, over the white pall which stretched into the darkness around me. Then all at once from beyond the trees there came at a trot a troop of horsemen bearing torches. The wolf rose from my breast and made for the cemetery. I saw one of the horsemen (soldiers by their caps and their long military cloaks) raise his carbine and take aim. A companion knocked up his arm, and I heard the ball whizz over my head. He had evidently taken my body for that of the wolf. Another sighted the animal as it slunk away, and a shot followed. Then, at a gallop, the troop rode forward—some towards me, others following the wolf as it disappeared amongst the snow-clad cypresses.

As they drew nearer I tried to move, but was powerless, although I could see and hear all that went on around me. Two or three of the soldiers jumped from their horses and knelt beside me. One of them raised my head, and placed his hand over my heart.

'Good news, comrades!' he cried. 'His heart still beats!'

Then some brandy was poured down my throat; it put vigour into me, and I was able to open my eyes fully and look around. Lights and shadows were moving among the trees, and I heard men call to one another. They drew together, uttering frightened exclamations; and the lights flashed as the others came pouring out of the cemetery pell-mell, like men possessed. When the further ones came close to us, those who were around me asked them eagerly:

'Well, have you found him?'

The reply rang out hurriedly:

'No! no! Come away quick—quick! This is no place to stay, and on this of all nights!'

'What was it?' was the question, asked in all manner of keys. The answer came variously and all indefinitely as though the men were moved by some common impulse to speak, yet were restrained by some common fear from giving their thoughts.

'It—it—indeed!' gibbered one, whose wits had plainly given out for the moment.

'A wolf—and yet not a wolf!' another put in shudderingly.

'No use trying for him without the sacred bullet,' a third remarked in a more ordinary manner.

'Serve us right for coming out on this night! Truly we have earned our thousand marks!' were the ejaculations of a fourth.

'There was blood on the broken marble,' another said after a pause—'the lightning never brought that there. And for him—is he safe? Look at his throat! See, comrades, the wolf has been lying on him and keeping his blood warm.'

The officer looked at my throat and replied:

'He is all right; the skin is not pierced. What does it all mean? We should never have found him but for the yelping of the wolf.'

'What became of it?' asked the man who was holding up my head, and who seemed the least panic-stricken of the party, for his hands were steady and without tremor. On his sleeve was the chevron of a petty officer.

'It went to its home,' answered the man, whose long face was pallid, and who actually shook with terror as he glanced around him fearfully. 'There are graves enough there in which it may lie. Come, comrades—come quickly! Let us leave this cursed spot.'

The officer raised me to a sitting posture, as he uttered a word of command; then several men placed me upon a horse. He sprang to the saddle behind me, took me in his arms, gave the word to advance; and, turning our faces away from the cypresses, we rode away in swift, military order.

As yet my tongue refused its office, and I was perforce silent. I must have fallen asleep; for the next thing I remembered was finding myself standing up, supported by a soldier on each side of me. It was almost broad daylight, and to the north a red streak of sunlight was reflected, like a path of blood, over the waste of snow. The officer was telling the men to say nothing of what they had seen, except that they found an English stranger, guarded by a large dog.

'Dog! that was no dog,' cut in the man who had exhibited such fear. 'I think I know a wolf when I see one.'

The young officer answered calmly: 'I said a dog.'

'Dog!' reiterated the other ironically. It was evident that his courage was rising with the sun; and, pointing to me, he said, 'Look at his throat. Is that the work of a dog, master?'

Instinctively I raised my hand to my throat, and as I touched it I cried out in pain. The men crowded round to look, some stooping down from their saddles; and again there came the calm voice of the young officer:

'A dog, as I said. If aught else were said we should only be laughed at.'

I was then mounted behind a trooper, and we rode on into the suburbs of Munich. Here we came across a stray carriage, into which I was lifted, and it was driven off to the Quatre Saisons—the young officer accompanying me, whilst a trooper followed with his horse, and the others rode off to their barracks.

When we arrived, Herr Delbrück rushed so quickly down the steps to meet me, that it was apparent he had been watching within. Taking me by both hands he solicitously led me in. The officer saluted me and was turning to withdraw, when I recognized his purpose, and insisted that he should come to my rooms. Over a glass of wine I warmly thanked him and his brave comrades for saving me. He replied simply that he was more than glad, and that Herr Delbrück had at the first taken steps to make all the searching party pleased; at which ambiguous utterance the maître d'hôtel smiled, while the officer pleaded duty and withdrew.

'But Herr Delbrück,' I enquired, 'how and why was it that the soldiers searched for me?'

He shrugged his shoulders, as if in depreciation of his own deed, as he replied:

'I was so fortunate as to obtain leave from the commander of the regiment in which I served, to ask for volunteers.'

'But how did you know I was lost?' I asked.

'The driver came hither with the remains of his carriage, which had been upset when the horses ran away.'

'But surely you would not send a search-party of soldiers merely on this account?'

'Oh, no!' he answered; 'but even before the coachman arrived, I had this telegram from the Boyar whose guest you are,' and he took from his pocket a telegram which he handed to me, and I read:

> Bistritz.
>
> Be careful of my guest—his safety is most precious to me. Should aught happen to him, or if he be missed, spare nothing to find him and ensure his safety. He is English and therefore adventurous. There are often dangers from snow and wolves and night. Lose not a moment if you suspect harm to him. I answer your zeal with my fortune.
>
> —Dracula.

As I held the telegram in my hand, the room seemed to whirl around me; and, if the attentive maître d'hôtel had not caught me, I think I should have fallen. There was something so strange in all this, something so weird and impossible to imagine, that there grew on me a sense of my being in some way the sport of opposite forces—the mere vague idea of which seemed in a way to paralyze me. I was certainly under some form of mysterious protection. From a distant country had come, in the very nick of time, a message that took me out of the danger of the snow-sleep and the jaws of the wolf.

CHAPTER FOUR[59]

Jonathan Harker's Journal, Continued

3 May. Bistritz—Left Munich at 8:35 P.M., on 1st May, arriving at Vienna early next morning; should have arrived at 6:46, but train was an hour late. God be praised that my stay in Munich has come to an end! Buda-Pesth, by comparison, seems a wonderful place, from the glimpse which I got of it from the train and the little I could walk through the streets. I feared to go very far from the station, as we had arrived late and would start as near the correct time as possible.

The impression I had was that we were leaving the West and entering the East; the most western of splendid bridges over the Danube, which is here of noble width and depth, took us among the traditions of Turkish rule.

We left in pretty good time, and came after nightfall to Klausenburgh. Here I stopped for the night at the Hotel Royale. I had for dinner, or rather supper, a chicken done up some way with red pepper, which was very good but thirsty. (*mem.*, get recipe for Mina.) I asked the waiter, and he said it was called "paprika hendl," and that, as it was a national dish, I should be able to get it anywhere along the Carpathians.

I found my smattering of German very useful here, indeed, I don't know how I should be able to get on without it.

Having had some time at my disposal when in London, I had visited the British Museum, and made search among the books and maps in the library regarding Transylvania; it had struck me that some foreknowledge of the country could hardly fail to have some importance in dealing with a nobleman of that country.

I find that the district he named is in the extreme east of the country, just on the borders of three states, Transylvania, Moldavia, and Bukovina, in the midst of the Carpathian mountains; one of the wildest and least known portions of Europe.

I was not able to light on any map or work giving the exact locality of the Castle Dracula, as there are no maps of this country as yet to compare with our own Ordnance Survey Maps; but I found that Bistritz, the post town named by Count Dracula, is a fairly well-known place. I shall enter here some of my notes, as they may refresh my memory when I talk over my travels with Mina.

In the population of Transylvania there are four distinct nationalities: Saxons in the South, and mixed with them the Wallachs, who are the descendants of the Dacians; Magyars in the West, and Szekelys in the East and North. I am going among the latter, who claim to be descended from Attila and the Huns. This may be so, for when the Magyars conquered the country in the eleventh century they found the Huns settled in it.

I read that every known superstition in the world is gathered into the horseshoe of the Carpathians, as if it were the centre of some sort of imaginative whirlpool; if so my stay may be very interesting. (*mem.*, I must ask the Count all about them.)

I did not sleep well, though my bed was comfortable enough, for I had all sorts of queer dreams of the Dead House at Munich which gets more strange and terrible whenever I think of it. It all seems so strange and mysterious.[60] There was a dog howling all night under my window, which may have had something to do with it; or it may have been the paprika, for I had to drink up all the water in my carafe, and was still thirsty. And I am certain that my recent hallucinations during the strain and cold of being caught in the snowstorm, and my subsequently having been saved by that great dog or wolf or whatever it may have been, played no small role in my insomnia. Towards morning I slept and was wakened by the continuous knocking at my door, so I guess I must have been sleeping soundly then.

I had for breakfast more paprika, and a sort of porridge of maize flour which they said was "mamaliga," and egg-plant stuffed with forcemeat, a very excellent dish, which they call "impletata." (*mem.*, get recipe for this also.)

I had to hurry breakfast, for the train started a little before eight, or rather it ought to have done so, for after rushing to the station at 7:30 I had to sit in the carriage for more than an hour before we began to move.

It seems to me that the further east you go the more unpunctual are the trains. What ought they to be in China?

All day long we seemed to dawdle through a country which was full of beauty of every kind. Sometimes we saw little towns or castles on the top of steep hills such as we see in old missals; sometimes we ran by rivers and streams which seemed from the wide stony margin on each side of them to be subject to great floods. It takes a lot of water, and running strong, to sweep the outside edge of a river clear.

At every station there were groups of people, sometimes crowds, and in all sorts of attire. Some of them were just like the peasants at home or those I saw coming through France and Germany, with short jackets, and round hats, and home-made trousers; but others were very picturesque.

The women looked pretty, except when you got near them, but they were very clumsy about the waist. They had all full white sleeves of some kind or other, and most of them had big belts with a lot of strips of something fluttering from them like the dresses in a ballet, but of course there were petticoats under them.

The strangest figures we saw were the Slovaks, who were more barbarian than the rest, with their big cow-boy hats, great baggy dirty-white trousers, white linen shirts, and enormous heavy leather belts, nearly a foot wide, all studded over with brass nails. They wore high boots, with their trousers tucked into them, and had long black hair and heavy black moustaches. They are very picturesque, but do not look prepossessing. On the stage they would be set down at once as some old Oriental band of brigands. They are, however, I am told, very harmless and rather wanting in natural self-assertion.

It was on the dark side of twilight when we got to Bistritz, which is a very interesting old place. Being practically on the frontier—for the Borgo Pass leads from it into Bukovina—it has had a very stormy existence, and it certainly shows marks of it. Fifty years ago a series of great fires took place, which made terrible havoc on five separate occasions. At the very beginning of the seventeenth century it underwent a siege of three weeks and lost 13,000 people, the casualties of war proper being assisted by famine and disease.

Count Dracula had directed me to go to the Golden Krone Hotel, which I found, to my great delight, to be thoroughly old-fashioned, for of course I wanted to see all I could of the ways of the country.

I was evidently expected, for when I got near the door I faced a cheery-looking elderly woman in the usual peasant dress—white undergarment with a long double apron, front, and back, of coloured stuff fitting almost too tight for modesty. When I came close she bowed and said, "The Herr Englishman?"

"Yes," I said, "Jonathan Harker."

She smiled, and gave some message to an elderly man in white shirtsleeves, who had followed her to the door.

He went, but immediately returned with a letter:

> "My friend—Welcome to the Carpathians. I am anxiously expecting you. Sleep well tonight, and in the morning see something of the beautiful bastioned town, Bistritz. At three tomorrow the diligence will start for Bukovina; a place on it is kept for you. At the Borgo Pass my carriage will await you and will bring you to me. I trust that your journey from London has been a happy one, and that you will enjoy your stay in my beautiful land.
>   —Your friend, Dracula."

4 May—Wrote a few lines to Mina this morning. Naturally I did not make mention of my adventures in Munich, but instead noted all of the places I had

been thus far, so that at some future time we may together investigate the many interesting places still remaining. Later I found that my landlord had got a letter from the Count, directing him to secure the best place on the coach for me; but on making inquiries as to details he seemed somewhat reticent, and pretended that he could not understand my German.

This could not be true, because up to then he had understood it perfectly; at least, he answered my questions exactly as if he did.

He and his wife, the old lady who had received me, looked at each other in a frightened sort of way. He mumbled out that the money had been sent in a letter, and that was all he knew. When I asked him if he knew Count Dracula, and could tell me anything of his castle, both he and his wife crossed themselves, and, saying that they knew nothing at all, simply refused to speak further. It was so near the time of starting that I had no time to ask anyone else, for it was all very mysterious and not by any means comforting.

Just before I was leaving, the old lady came up to my room and said in a hysterical way: "Must you go? Oh! Young Herr, must you go?" She was in such an excited state that she seemed to have lost her grip of what German she knew, and mixed it all up with some other language which I did not know at all. I was just able to follow her by asking many questions. When I told her that I must go at once, and that I was engaged on important business, she asked again:

"Do you know what day it is?" I answered that it was the fourth of May. She shook her head as she said again:

"Oh, yes! I know that! I know that, but do you know what day it is?"

On my saying that I did not understand, she went on:

"It is the eve of St. George's Day. Do you not know that tonight, when the clock strikes midnight, all the evil things in the world will have full sway? Do you know where you are going, and what you are going to?" She was in such evident distress that I tried to comfort her, but without effect. Finally, she went down on her knees and implored me not to go; at least to wait a day or two before starting.

It was all very ridiculous but I did not feel comfortable. However, there was business to be done, and I could allow nothing to interfere with it.

I tried to raise her up, and said, as gravely as I could, that I thanked her, but my duty was imperative, and that I must go.

She then rose and dried her eyes, and taking a crucifix from her neck offered it to me.

I did not know what to do, for, as an English Churchman, I have been taught to regard such things as in some measure idolatrous, and yet it seemed so ungracious to refuse an old lady meaning so well and in such a state of mind.

She saw, I suppose, the doubt in my face, for she put the rosary round my neck and said, "For your mother's sake," and went out of the room.

I am writing up this part of the diary whilst I am waiting for the coach, which is, of course, late; and the crucifix is still round my neck.

Whether it is the old lady's fear, or the many ghostly traditions of this place, or the crucifix itself, I do not know, but I am not feeling nearly as easy in my mind as usual.

If this book should ever reach Mina before I do, let it bring my goodbye. Here comes the coach!

5 May. The Castle—The gray of the morning has passed, and the sun is high over the distant horizon, which seems jagged, whether with trees or hills I know not, for it is so far off that big things and little are mixed.

I am not sleepy, and, as I am not to be called till I awake, naturally I write till sleep comes.

There are many odd things to put down, and, lest who reads them may fancy that I dined too well before I left Bistritz, let me put down my dinner exactly.

I dined on what they called "robber steak"—bits of bacon, onion, and beef, seasoned with red pepper, and strung on sticks, and roasted over the fire, in simple style of the London cat's meat!

The wine was Golden Mediasch, which produces a queer sting on the tongue, which is, however, not disagreeable.

I had only a couple of glasses of this, and nothing else until supper, with which I had two glasses of old Tokay—the nicest wine I ever tasted; but I did not take as much as I should have liked for I feared it might be too strong and the Count might want to talk business at once. A roast chicken was my supper.

When I got on the coach, the driver had not taken his seat, and I saw him talking to the landlady.

They were evidently talking of me, for every now and then they looked at me, and some of the people who were sitting on the bench outside the door—came and listened, and then looked at me, most of them pityingly. I could hear a lot of words often repeated, queer words, for there were many nationalities in the crowd, so I quietly got my polyglot dictionary from my bag and looked them out.

I must say they were not cheering to me, for amongst them were "Ordog"—Satan, "Pokol"—hell, "stregoica"—witch, "vrolok" and "vlkoslak"—both mean the same thing, one being Slovak and the other Servian for something that is either werewolf or vampire. (*mem.*, I must ask the Count about these superstitions.)

When we started, the crowd round the inn door, which had by this time swelled to a considerable size, all made the sign of the cross and pointed two fingers towards me.

With some difficulty, I got a fellow passenger to tell me what they meant. He would not answer at first, but on learning that I was English, he explained that it was a charm or guard against the evil eye.

This was not very pleasant for me, just starting for an unknown place to meet an unknown man. But everyone seemed so kind-hearted, and so sorrowful, and so sympathetic that I could not but be touched.

I shall never forget the last glimpse which I had of the inn yard and its crowd of picturesque figures, all crossing themselves, as they stood round the wide archway, with its background of rich foliage of oleander and orange trees in green tubs clustered in the centre of the yard.

Then our driver, whose wide linen drawers covered the whole front of the boxseat,—"gotza" they call them—cracked his big whip over his four small horses, which ran abreast, and we set off on our journey.

I soon lost sight and recollection of ghostly fears in the beauty of the scene as we drove along, although had I known the language, or rather languages, which my fellow-passengers were speaking, I might not have been able to throw them off so easily. Before us lay a green sloping land full of forests and woods, with here and there steep hills, crowned with clumps of trees or with farmhouses, the blank gable end to the road. There was everywhere a bewildering mass of fruit blossom—apple, plum, pear, cherry. And as we drove by I could see the green grass under the trees spangled with the fallen petals. In and out amongst these green hills of what they call here the "Mittel Land" ran the road, losing itself as it swept round the grassy curve, or was shut out by the straggling ends of pine woods, which here and there ran down the hillsides like tongues of flame. The road was rugged, but still we seemed to fly over it with a feverish haste. I could not understand then what the haste meant, but the driver was evidently bent on losing no time in reaching Borgo Prund. I was told that this road is in summertime excellent, but that it had not yet been put in order after the winter snows. In this respect it is different from the general run of roads in the Carpathians, for it is an old tradition that they are not to be kept in too good order. Of old the Hospadars would not repair them, lest the Turk should think that they were preparing to bring in foreign troops, and so hasten the war which was always really at loading point.

Beyond the green swelling hills of the Mittel Land rose mighty slopes of forest up to the lofty steeps of the Carpathians themselves. Right and left of us they towered, with the afternoon sun falling full upon them and bringing out all the glorious colours of this beautiful range, deep blue and purple in the shadows of the peaks, green and brown where grass and rock mingled, and an endless perspective of jagged rock and pointed crags, till these were themselves lost in the distance, where the snowy peaks rose grandly. Here and there seemed mighty rifts in the mountains, through which, as the sun began to sink, we saw now and again the white gleam of falling water. One of my companions touched my arm as we swept round the base of a hill and opened up the lofty, snow-covered peak of a mountain, which seemed, as we wound on our serpentine way, to be right before us.

"Look! Isten szek!"—"God's seat!"—and he crossed himself reverently.

As we wound on our endless way, and the sun sank lower and lower behind us, the shadows of the evening began to creep round us. This was emphasized by the fact that the snowy mountain-top still held the sunset, and seemed to glow out with a delicate cool pink. Here and there we passed Cszeks and slovaks, all in picturesque attire, but I noticed that goitre was painfully prevalent. By the roadside were many crosses, and as we swept by, my companions all crossed themselves. Here and there was a peasant man or woman kneeling before a shrine, who did not even turn round as we approached, but seemed in the self-surrender of devotion to have neither eyes nor ears for the outer world. There were many things new to me. For instance, hay-ricks in the trees, and here and there very beautiful masses of weeping birch, their white stems shining like silver through the delicate green of the leaves.

Now and again we passed a leiter-wagon—the ordinary peasants's cart—with its long, snakelike vertebra, calculated to suit the inequalities of the road. On this were sure to be seated quite a group of homecoming peasants, the Cszeks with their white, and the Slovaks with their coloured sheepskins, the latter carrying lance-fashion their long staves, with axe at end. As the evening fell it began to get very cold, and the growing twilight seemed to merge into one dark mistiness the gloom of the trees, oak, beech, and pine, though in the valleys which ran deep between the spurs of the hills, as we ascended through the Pass, the dark firs stood out here and there against the background of late-lying snow. Sometimes, as the road was cut through the pine woods that seemed in the darkness to be closing down upon us, great masses of greyness which here and there bestrewed the trees, produced a peculiarly weird and solemn effect, which carried on the thoughts and grim fancies engendered earlier in the evening, when the falling sunset threw into strange relief the ghost-like clouds which amongst the Carpathians seem to wind ceaselessly through the valleys. Sometimes the hills were so steep that, despite our driver's haste, the horses could only go slowly. I wished to get down and walk up them, as we do at home, but the driver would not hear of it. "No, no," he said. "You must not walk here. The dogs are too fierce." And then he added, with what he evidently meant for grim pleasantry—for he looked round to catch the approving smile of the rest—"And you may have enough of such matters before you go to sleep." The only stop he would make was a moment's pause to light his lamps.

When it grew dark there seemed to be some excitement amongst the passengers, and they kept speaking to him, one after the other, as though urging him to further speed. He lashed the horses unmercifully with his long whip, and with wild cries of encouragement urged them on to further exertions. Then through the darkness I could see a sort of patch of grey light ahead of us, as though there were a cleft in the hills. The excitement of the passengers grew greater. The crazy coach rocked on its great leather springs, and swayed like a boat tossed on a stormy sea. I had to hold on. The road grew more level, and we appeared to fly along. Then the mountains seemed to come nearer to us on each side and to frown down upon us. We were entering on the Borgo Pass. One by one several of the passengers offered me gifts, which they pressed upon me with an earnestness which would take no denial. These were certainly of an odd and varied kind, but each was given in simple good faith, with a kindly word, and a blessing, and that same strange mixture of fear-meaning movements which I had seen outside the hotel at Bistritz—the sign of the cross and the guard against the evil eye. Then, as we flew along, the driver leaned forward, and on each side the passengers, craning over the edge of the coach, peered eagerly into the darkness. It was evident that something very exciting was either happening or expected, but though I asked each passenger, no one would give me the slightest explanation. This state of excitement kept on for some little time. And at last we saw before us the Pass opening out on the eastern side. There were dark, rolling clouds overhead, and in the air the heavy, oppressive sense of thunder. It seemed as though the mountain range had separated two atmospheres, and that now we had got into the thunderous one. I was now myself looking out for the conveyance which was to take me to the Count. Each moment I expected to see the glare of lamps through the blackness, but all was dark. The only light was the flickering rays of our own lamps, in which the steam from our hard-driven horses rose in a white cloud. We could see now the sandy road lying white before us, but there was on it no sign of a vehicle. The passengers drew back with a sigh of gladness, which seemed to mock my own disappointment. I was already thinking what I had best do, when the driver, looking at his watch, said to the others something which I could hardly hear, it was spoken so quietly and in so low a tone, I thought it was "An hour less than the time." Then turning to me, he spoke in German worse than my own.

"There is no carriage here. The Herr is not expected after all. He will now come on to Bukovina, and return tomorrow or the next day, better the next day." Whilst he was speaking the horses began to neigh and snort and plunge wildly, so that the driver had to hold them up. Then, amongst a chorus of screams from the peasants and a universal crossing of themselves, a caleche, with four horses, drove up behind us, overtook us, and drew up beside the coach. I could see from the flash of our lamps as the rays fell on them, that the horses were coal-black and splendid animals. They were driven by a tall man, with a long brown beard and a great black hat, which seemed to hide his face from us. I could only see the gleam of a pair of very bright eyes, which seemed red in the lamplight, as he turned to us. Looking at him, even in this dim light, I could not help but think of the man on the bier, who had vanished from the Dead House.

He said to the driver, "You are early tonight, my friend."

The man stammered in reply, "The English Herr was in a hurry."

To which the stranger replied, "That is why, I suppose, you wished him to go on to Bukovina. You cannot deceive me, my friend. I know too much, and my horses are swift."

As he spoke he smiled, and the lamplight fell on a hard-looking mouth, with very red lips and sharp-looking teeth, as white as ivory. One of my companions whispered to another the line from Burger's "Lenore":

"Denn die Todten reiten Schnell." ("For the dead travel fast.")

I could not help but shudder, in recollection of those very same words carved into the Munich tomb. The strange driver evidently heard the words, for he looked up with a gleaming smile. The passenger turned his face away, at the same time putting out his two fingers and crossing himself. "Give me the Herr's luggage," said the driver, and with exceeding alacrity my bags were handed out and put in the caleche. Then I descended from the side of the coach, as the caleche was close alongside, the driver helping me with a hand which caught my arm in a grip of steel. His strength must have been prodigious.

Without a word he shook his reins, the horses turned, and we swept into the darkness of the pass. As I looked back I saw the steam from the horses of the coach by the light of the lamps, and projected against it the figures of my late companions crossing themselves. Then the driver cracked his whip and called to his horses, and off they swept on their way to Bukovina. As they sank into the darkness I felt a strange chill, and a lonely feeling come over me. But a cloak was thrown over my shoulders, and a rug across my knees, and the driver said in excellent German—"The night is chill, mein Herr, and my master the Count bade me take all care of you. There is a flask of slivovitz (the plum brandy of the country) underneath the seat, if you should require it."

I did not take any, but it was a comfort to know it was there all the same. I felt a little strangely, and not a little frightened. I think had there been any alternative I should have taken it, instead of prosecuting that unknown night journey. The carriage went at a hard pace straight along, then we made a complete turn and went along another straight road. It seemed to me that we were simply going over and over the same ground again, and so I took note of some salient point, and found that this was so. I would have liked to have asked the driver what this all meant, but I really feared to do so, for I thought that, placed as I was, any protest would have had no effect in case there had been an intention to delay.

By-and-by, however, as I was curious to know how time was passing, I struck a match, and by its flame looked at my watch. It was within a few minutes of midnight. This gave me a sort of shock, for I suppose the general superstition about midnight was increased by my recent experiences. I waited with a sick feeling of suspense.

Then a dog began to howl somewhere in a farmhouse far down the road, a long, agonized wailing, as if from fear. The sound was taken up by another dog, and then another and another, till, borne on the wind which now sighed softly through the Pass, a wild howling began, which seemed to come from all over the country, as far as the imagination could grasp it through the gloom of the night.

At the first howl the horses began to strain and rear, but the driver spoke to them soothingly, and they quieted down, but shivered and sweated as though after a runaway from sudden fright. Then, far off in the distance, from the mountains on each side of us began a louder and a sharper howling, that of wolves, which affected both the horses and myself in the same way. For I was minded to jump from the caleche and run, whilst they reared again and plunged madly, so that the driver had to use all his great strength to keep them from bolting. In a few minutes, however, my own ears got accustomed to the sound, and the horses so far became quiet that the driver was able to descend and to stand before them.

He petted and soothed them, and whispered something in their ears, as I have heard of horse-tamers doing, and with extraordinary effect, for under his caresses they became quite manageable again, though they still trembled. The driver again took his seat, and shaking his reins, started off at a great pace. This time, after going to the far side of the Pass, he suddenly turned down a narrow roadway which ran sharply to the right.

Soon we were hemmed in with trees, which in places arched right over the roadway till we passed as through a tunnel. And again great frowning rocks guarded us boldly on either side. Though we were in shelter, we could hear the rising wind, for it moaned and whistled through the rocks, and the branches of the trees crashed together as we swept along. It grew colder and colder still, and fine, powdery snow began to fall, so that soon we and all around us were covered with a white blanket. The keen wind still carried the howling of the dogs, though this grew fainter as we went on our way. The baying of the wolves sounded nearer and nearer, as though they were closing round on us from every side. I grew dreadfully afraid, and the horses shared my fear. The driver, however, was not in the least disturbed. He kept turning his head to left and right, but I could not see anything through the darkness.

Suddenly, away on our left I saw a faint flickering blue flame. The driver saw it at the same moment. He at once checked the horses, and, jumping to the ground, disappeared into the darkness. I did not know what to do, the less as the howling of the wolves grew closer. But while I wondered, the driver suddenly appeared again, and without a word took his seat, and we resumed our journey. I think I must have fallen asleep and kept dreaming of the incident, for it seemed to be repeated endlessly, and now looking back, it is like a sort of awful nightmare. Once the flame appeared so near the road, that even in the darkness around us I could watch the driver's motions. He went rapidly to where the blue flame arose, it must have been very faint, for it did not seem to illumine the place around it at all, and gathering a few stones, formed them into some device.

Once there appeared a strange optical effect. When he stood between me and the flame he did not obstruct it, for I could see its ghostly flicker all the same. This startled me, but as the effect was only momentary, I took it that my eyes deceived me straining through the darkness. Then for a time there were no blue flames, and we sped onwards through the gloom, with the howling of the wolves around us, as though they were following in a moving circle.

At last there came a time when the driver went further afield than he had yet gone, and during his absence, the horses began to tremble worse than ever and to snort and scream with fright. I could not see any cause for it, for the howling of the wolves had ceased altogether. But just then the moon, sailing through the black clouds, appeared behind the jagged crest of a beetling, pine-clad rock, and by its light I saw around us a ring of wolves, with white teeth and lolling red tongues, with long, sinewy limbs and shaggy hair. They were a hundred times more terrible in the grim silence which held them than even when they howled. For myself, I felt a sort of paralysis of fear. It is only when a man feels himself face to face with such horrors that he can understand their true import, and my experience in the storm near Munich was not calculated to ease my mind. As I looked at them I unconsciously put my hand to my throat which was still sore from the licking of the grey wolf's file-like tongue.[61]

All at once the wolves began to howl as though the moonlight had had some peculiar effect on them. The horses jumped about and reared, and looked helplessly round with eyes that rolled in a way painful to see. But the living ring of terror encompassed them on every side, and they had perforce to remain within it. I called to the coachman to come, for it seemed to me that our only chance was to try to break out through the ring and to aid his approach, I shouted and beat the side of the caleche, hoping by the noise to scare the wolves from the side, so as to give him a chance of reaching the trap. How he came there, I know not, but I heard his voice raised in a tone of imperious command, and looking towards the sound, saw him stand in the roadway. As he swept his long arms, as though brushing aside some impalpable obstacle, the wolves fell back and back further still. Just then a heavy cloud passed across the face of the moon, so that we were again in darkness.

When I could see again the driver was climbing into the caleche, and the wolves disappeared. This was all so strange and uncanny that a dreadful fear came upon me, and I was afraid to speak or move. The time seemed interminable as we swept on our way, now in almost complete darkness, for the rolling clouds obscured the moon.

We kept on ascending, with occasional periods of quick descent, but in the main always ascending, till waking up from a sort of reverie or sleep into which I must have fallen I found the driver in the act of pulling up the horses in the courtyard of a vast ruined castle, from whose tall black windows came no ray of light, and whose broken battlements showed a jagged line against the sky.

CHAPTER FIVE[62]

Jonathan Harker's Journal, Continued

5 May—I must have been asleep, for certainly if I had been fully awake I must have noticed the approach of such a remarkable place. In the gloom the courtyard looked of considerable size, and as several dark ways led from it under great round arches, it perhaps seemed bigger than it really is. I have not yet been able to see it by daylight.

When the caleche stopped, the driver jumped down and held out his hand to assist me to alight. Again I could not but notice his prodigious strength. His hand actually seemed like a steel vice that could have crushed mine if he had chosen. Then he took my traps, and placed them on the ground beside me as I stood close to a great door, old and studded with large iron nails, and set in a projecting doorway of massive stone. I could see even in the dim light that the stone was massively carved, but that the carving had been much worn by time and weather. As I stood, the driver jumped again into his seat and shook the reins. The horses started forward, and trap and all disappeared down one of the dark openings.

I stood in silence where I was, for I did not know what to do. Of bell or knocker there was no sign. Through these frowning walls and dark window openings it was not likely that my voice could penetrate. The time I waited seemed endless, and I felt doubts and fears crowding upon me. What sort of place had I come to, and among what kind of people? What sort of grim adventure was it on which I had embarked? Was this a customary incident in the life of a solicitor's clerk sent out to explain the purchase of a London estate to a foreigner? Solicitor's clerk! Mina would not like that. Solicitor, for just before leaving London I got word that my examination was successful, and I am now a full-blown solicitor! I began to rub my eyes and pinch myself to see if I were awake. It all seemed like a horrible nightmare to me, and I expected that I should suddenly awake, and find myself at home, with the dawn struggling in through the windows, as I had now and again felt in the morning after a day of overwork. But my flesh answered the pinching test, and my eyes were not to be deceived. I was indeed awake and among the Carpathians, and as far as I knew miles and miles away from any human being except the man who brought me here. All I could do now was to be patient, and to wait the coming of morning.

Just as I had come to this conclusion I heard a heavy step approaching behind the great door, and saw through the chinks the gleam of a coming light. I do not think I was ever so glad to see anything in my life, for the sense of loneliness and fear was becoming intolerable. Then there was the sound of rattling chains and the clanking of massive bolts drawn back. A key was turned with the loud grating noise of long disuse, and the great door swung back.

Within, stood a tall old man, clean shaven save for a long white moustache, and clad in black from head to foot, without a single speck of colour about him anywhere. He held in his hand an antique silver lamp, in which the flame burned without a chimney or globe of any kind, throwing long quivering shadows as it flickered in the draught of the open door. The old man motioned me in with his right hand with a courtly gesture, saying in excellent English, but with a strange intonation.

"Welcome to my house! Enter freely and of your own free will!" He made no motion of stepping to meet me, but stood like a statue, as though his gesture of welcome had fixed him into stone. The instant, however, that I had stepped over the threshold, he moved impulsively forward, and holding out his hand grasped mine with a strength which made me wince, an effect which was not lessened by the fact that it seemed cold as ice, more like the hand of a dead than a living man. Again he said.

"Welcome to my house! Enter freely. Go safely, and leave something of the happiness you bring!" The strength of the handshake was so much akin to that which I had noticed in the driver, whose face I had not seen, that for a moment I doubted if it were not the same person to whom I was speaking. So to make sure, I said interrogatively, "Count Dracula?"

He bowed in a courtly way as he replied, "I am Dracula, and I bid you welcome, Mr. Harker, to my house. Come in, the night air is chill, and you must need to eat and rest." As he was speaking, he put the lamp on a bracket on the wall, and stepping out, took my luggage. He had carried it in before I could forestall him. I protested, but he insisted.

"Nay, sir, you are my guest. It is late, and my people are not available. Let me see to your comfort myself." He insisted on carrying my traps along the passage, and then up a great winding stair, and along another great passage, on whose stone floor our steps rang heavily. At the end of this he threw open a heavy door, and I rejoiced to see within a well-lit room in which a table was spread for supper, and on whose mighty hearth a great fire of logs, freshly replenished, flamed and flared.

The Count halted, putting down my bags, closed the door, and crossing the room, opened another door, which led into a small octagonal room lit by a single lamp, and seemingly without a window of any sort. Passing through this, he opened another door, and motioned me to enter. It was a welcome sight. For here was a great bedroom well lighted and warmed with another log fire, also added to but lately, for the top logs were fresh, which sent a hollow roar up the wide chimney. The Count himself left my luggage inside and withdrew, saying, before he closed the door.

"You will need, after your journey, to refresh yourself by making your toilet. I trust you will find all you wish. When you are ready, come into the other room, where you will find your supper prepared."

The light and warmth and the Count's courteous welcome seemed to have dissipated all my doubts and fears. Having then reached my normal state, I discovered that I was half famished with hunger. So making a hasty toilet, I went into the other room.

I found supper already laid out. My host, who stood on one side of the great fireplace, leaning against the stonework, made a graceful wave of his hand to the table, and said,

"I pray you, be seated and sup how you please. You will I trust, excuse me that I do not join you, but I have dined already, and I do not sup."

I handed to him the sealed letter which Mr. Hawkins had entrusted to me. He opened it and read it gravely. Then, with a charming smile, he handed it to me to read. One passage of it, at least, gave me a thrill of pleasure.

> "I must regret that an attack of gout, from which malady I am a constant sufferer, forbids absolutely any traveling on my part for some time to come. But I am happy to say I can send a sufficient substitute, one in whom I have every possible confidence. He is a young man, full of energy and talent in his own way, and of a very faithful disposition. He is discreet and silent, and has grown into manhood in my service. He shall be ready to attend on you when you will during his stay, and shall take your instructions in all matters."

The Count himself came forward and took off the cover of a dish, and I fell to at once on an excellent roast chicken. This, with some cheese and a salad and a bottle of old Tokay, of which I had two glasses, was my supper. During the time

I was eating it the Count asked me many questions as to my journey, and I told him by degrees all I had experienced. He seemed very interested, especially at my adventures in Munich. When I told him of the wolf which lay on my chest saving my life in the cold, and whose howling seemed to direct the soldiers to where I was, he appeared quite excited.[63]

By this time I had finished my supper, and by my host's desire had drawn up a chair by the fire and begun to smoke a cigar which he offered me, at the same time excusing himself that he did not smoke. I had now an opportunity of observing him, and found him of a very marked physiognomy.

His face was a strong, a very strong, aquiline, with high bridge of the thin nose and peculiarly arched nostrils, with lofty domed forehead, and hair growing scantily round the temples but profusely elsewhere. His eyebrows were very massive, almost meeting over the nose, and with bushy hair that seemed to curl in its own profusion. The mouth, so far as I could see it under the heavy moustache, was fixed and rather cruel-looking, with peculiarly sharp white teeth. These protruded over the lips, whose remarkable ruddiness showed astonishing vitality in a man of his years. For the rest, his ears were pale, and at the tops extremely pointed. The chin was broad and strong, and the cheeks firm though thin. The general effect was one of extraordinary pallor.

Hitherto I had noticed the backs of his hands as they lay on his knees in the firelight, and they had seemed rather white and fine. But seeing them now close to me, I could not but notice that they were rather coarse, broad, with squat fingers. Strange to say, there were hairs in the centre of the palm. The nails were long and fine, and cut to a sharp point. As the Count leaned over me and his hands touched the wound at my throat, I could not repress a shudder. Perhaps there is a morbid susceptibility about a wound and that we fear any approach to touching it[64]—or it may have been that as the Count leaned over me that his breath was rank, but a horrible feeling of nausea came over me, which, do what I would, I could not conceal.

The Count, evidently noticing it, drew back. And with a grim sort of smile, which showed more than he had yet done his protuberant teeth, sat himself down again on his own side of the fireplace. We were both silent for a while, and as I looked towards the window I saw the first dim streak of the coming dawn. There seemed a strange stillness over everything. But as I listened, I heard as if from down below in the valley the howling of many wolves. The Count's eyes gleamed, and he said.

"Listen to them, the children of the night. What music they make!" Seeing, I suppose, some expression in my face strange to him, he added, "Ah, sir, you dwellers in the city cannot enter into the feelings of the hunter." Then he rose and said.

"But you must be tired. Your bedroom is all ready, and tomorrow you shall sleep as late as you will. I have to be away till the afternoon, so sleep well and dream well!" With a courteous bow, he opened for me himself the door to the octagonal room, and I entered my bedroom.

I am all in a sea of wonders. I doubt. I fear. I think strange things, which I dare not confess to my own soul. God keep me, if only for the sake of those dear to me!

7 May—It is again early morning, but I have rested and enjoyed the last twenty-four hours. I slept till late in the day, and awoke of my own accord. When I had dressed myself I went into the room where we had supped, and found a cold breakfast laid out, with coffee kept hot by the pot being placed on the hearth. There was a card on the table, on which was written—"I have to be absent for a while. Do not wait for me. D." I set to and enjoyed a hearty meal. When I had done, I looked for a bell, so that I might let the servants know I had finished, but I could not find one. There are certainly odd deficiencies in the house, considering the extraordinary evidences of wealth which are round me. The table service is of gold, and so beautifully wrought that it must be of immense value. The candles are fine green tapers that burn with a peculiar blue flame (which, I must say, had an unnerving resemblance to the fires I witnessed on my initial journey to the castle)[65]. The curtains and upholstery of the chairs and sofas and the hangings of my bed are of the costliest and most beautiful fabrics, and must have been of fabulous value when they were made, for they are centuries old, though in excellent order. I saw something like them in Hampton Court, but they were worn and frayed and moth-eaten. But still in none of the rooms is there a mirror. There is not even a toilet glass on my table, and I had to get the little shaving glass from my bag before I could either shave or brush my hair. I have not yet seen a servant anywhere, or heard a sound near the castle except the howling of wolves. Some time after I had finished my meal, I do not know whether to call it breakfast or dinner, for it was between five and six o'clock when I had it, I looked about for something to read, for I did not like to go about the castle until I had asked the Count's permission. There was absolutely nothing in the room, book, newspaper, or even writing materials, so I opened another door in the room and found a sort of library. The door opposite mine I tried, but found locked.

In the library I found, to my great delight, a vast number of English books, whole shelves full of them, and bound volumes of magazines and newspapers. A table in the centre was littered with English magazines and newspapers, though none of them were of very recent date. The books were of the most varied kind, history, geography, politics, political economy, botany, geology, law, all relating to England and English life and customs and manners. There were even such books of reference as the London Directory, the "Red" and "Blue" books, Whitaker's Almanac, the Army and Navy Lists, a copy of *Aeneid*[66] and it somehow gladdened my heart to see it, the Law List.

Whilst I was looking at the books, the door opened, and the Count entered. He saluted me in a hearty way, and hoped that I had had a good night's rest. Then he went on.

"I am glad you found your way in here, for I am sure there is much that will interest you. These companions," and he laid his hand on some of the books, "have been good friends to me, and for some years past, ever since I had the idea of going to London, have given me many, many hours of pleasure. Through them I have come to know your great England, and to know her is to love her. I long to go through the crowded streets of your mighty London, to be in the midst of the whirl and rush of humanity, to share its life, its change, its death, and all that makes it what it is. But alas! As yet I only know your tongue through books. To you, my friend, I look that I know it to speak."

"But, Count," I said, "You know and speak English thoroughly!" He bowed gravely.

"I thank you, my friend, for your all too-flattering estimate, but yet I fear that I am but a little way on the road I would travel. True, I know the grammar and the words, but yet I know not how to speak them."

"Indeed," I said, "You speak excellently."

"Not so," he answered. "Well, I know that, did I move and speak in your London, none there are who would not know me for a stranger. That is not enough for me. Here I am noble. I am a Boyar. The common people know me, and I am master. But a stranger in a strange land, he is no one. Men know him not, and to know not is to care not for. I am content if I am like the rest, so that no man stops if he sees me, or pauses in his speaking if he hears my words, 'Ha, ha! A stranger!' I have been so long master that I would be master still, or at least that none other should be master of me. You come to me not alone as agent of my friend Peter Hawkins, of Exeter, to tell me all about my new estate in London. You shall, I trust, rest here with me a while, so that by our talking I may learn the English intonation. And I would that you tell me when I make error, even of the smallest, in my speaking. I am sorry that I had to be away so long today, but you will, I know forgive one who has so many important affairs in hand."

Of course I said all I could about being willing, and asked if I might come into that room when I chose. He answered, "Yes, certainly," and added.

"You may go anywhere you wish in the castle, except where the doors are locked, where of course you will not wish to go. There is reason that all things are as they are, and did you see with my eyes and know with my knowledge, you would perhaps better understand." I said I was sure of this, and then he went on.

"We are in Transylvania, and Transylvania is not England. Our ways are not your ways, and there shall be to you many strange things. Nay, from what you have told me of your experiences already, you know something of what strange things there may be."

This led to much conversation, and as it was evident that he wanted to talk, if only for talking's sake, I asked him many questions regarding things that had already happened to me or come within my notice. Sometimes he sheered off the subject, or turned the conversation by pretending not to understand, but generally he answered all I asked most frankly. Then as time went on, and I had got somewhat bolder, I asked him of some of the strange things of the preceding night, as for instance, why the coachman went to the places where he had seen the blue flames.[67] He then explained to me that it was commonly believed that on a certain night of the year, last night, in fact, when all evil spirits are supposed to have unchecked sway, a blue flame is seen over any place where treasure has been concealed.

"That treasure has been hidden," he went on, "in the region through which you came last night, there can be but little doubt. For it was the ground fought over for centuries by the Wallachian, the Saxon, and the Turk. Why, there is hardly a foot of soil in all this region that has not been enriched by the blood of men, patriots or invaders. In the old days there were stirring times, when the Austrian and the Hungarian came up in hordes, and the patriots went out to meet them, men and women, the aged and the children too, and waited their coming on the rocks above the passes, that they might sweep destruction on them with their artificial avalanches. When the invader was triumphant he found but little, for whatever there was had been sheltered in the friendly soil."

"But how," said I, "can it have remained so long undiscovered, when there is a sure index to it if men will but take the trouble to look?" The Count smiled, and as his lips ran back over his gums, the long, sharp, canine teeth showed out strangely. He answered.

"Because your peasant is at heart a coward and a fool! Those flames only appear on one night, and on that night no man of this land will, if he can help it, stir without his doors. And, dear sir, even if he did he would not know what to do. Why, even the peasant that you tell me of who marked the place of the flame would not know where to look in daylight even for his own work. Even you would not, I dare be sworn, be able to find these places again?"

"There you are right," I said. "I know no more than the dead where even to look for them." Then we drifted into other matters.

"Come," he said at last, "tell me of London and of the house which you have procured for me." With an apology for my remissness, I went into my own room to get the papers from my bag. Whilst I was placing them in order I heard a rattling of china and silver in the next room, and as I passed through, noticed that the table had been cleared and the lamp lit, for it was by this time deep into the dark. The lamps were also lit in the study or library, and I found the Count lying on the sofa, reading, of all things in the world, an English Bradshaw's Guide. When I came in he cleared the books and papers from the table, and with him I went into plans and deeds and figures of all sorts. He was interested in everything, and asked me a myriad questions about the place and its surroundings. He clearly had studied beforehand all he could get on the subject of the neighbourhood, for he evidently at the end knew very much more than I did. When I remarked this, he answered.

"Well, but, my friend, is it not needful that I should? When I go there I shall be all alone, and my friend Harker Jonathan, nay, pardon me. I fall into my country's habit of putting your patronymic first, my friend Jonathan Harker will not be by my side to correct and aid me. He will be in Exeter, miles away, probably working at papers of the law with my other friend, Peter Hawkins. So!"

We went thoroughly into the business of the purchase of the estate at Purfleet. When I had told him the facts and got his signature to the necessary papers, and had written a letter with them ready to post to Mr. Hawkins, he began to ask me how I had come across so suitable a place. I read to him the notes which I had made at the time, and which I inscribe here.

"At Purfleet, on a byroad, I came across just such a place as seemed to be required, and where was displayed a dilapidated notice that the place was for sale. It was surrounded by a high wall, of ancient structure, built of heavy stones, and has not been repaired for a large number of years. The closed gates are of heavy old oak and iron, all eaten with rust.

"The estate is called Carfax, no doubt a corruption of the old Quatre Face, as the house is four sided, agreeing with the cardinal points of the compass." Here the Count smiled, just barely, as if to himself, and I could not help but wonder if I had gotten the etymology of the name incorrect. But as he did not correct me, I continued on with my description.[68] "It contains in all some twenty acres, quite surrounded by the solid stone wall above mentioned. There are many trees on it, which make it in places gloomy, and there is a deep, dark-looking pond or small lake, evidently fed by some springs, as the water is clear and flows away in a fair-sized stream. The house is very large and of all periods back, I should say, to mediaeval times, for one part is of stone immensely thick, with only a few windows high up and heavily barred with iron. It looks like part of a keep, and is close to an old chapel or church. I could not enter it, as I had not the key of the door leading to it from the house, but I have taken with my Kodak views of it from various points. The house had been added to, but in a very straggling way, and I can only guess at the amount of ground it covers, which must be very great. There are but few houses close at hand, one being a very large house only recently added to and formed into a private lunatic asylum. It is not, however, visible from the grounds."

When I had finished, he said, "I am glad that it is old and big. I myself am of an old family, and to live in a new house would kill me. A house cannot be made habitable in a day, and after all, how few days go to make up a century. I rejoice also that there is a chapel of old times. We Transylvanian nobles love not to think that our bones may lie amongst the common dead. I seek neither gaiety nor mirth, not the bright voluptuousness of much sunshine and sparkling waters which please the young and gay. I am no longer young, and my heart, through weary years of mourning over the dead, is not attuned to mirth. Moreover, the walls of my castle are broken. The shadows are many, and the wind breathes cold through the broken battlements and casements. I love the shade and the shadow, and would be alone with my thoughts when I may." Somehow his words and his look did not seem to accord, or else it was that his cast of face made his smile look malignant and saturnine.

Presently, w

ith an excuse, he left me, asking me to pull my papers together. He was some little time away, and I began to look at some of the books around me. One was an atlas, which I found opened naturally to England, as if that map had been much used. On looking at it I found in certain places little rings marked, and on examining these I noticed that one was near London on the east side, manifestly where his new estate was situated. The other two were Exeter, and Whitby on the Yorkshire coast. There seemed some little ground for surmise here—of London and Exeter I knew but why Whitby? As for London itself, it looked as though the city had a cut through it, as if it had been marked with the point of a knife.[69]

It was the better part of an hour when the Count returned. "Aha!" he said. "Still at your books? Good! But you must not work always. Come! I am informed that your supper is ready." He took my arm, and we went into the next room, where I found an excellent supper ready on the table. The Count again excused himself, as he had dined out on his being away from home. But he sat as on the previous night, and chatted whilst I ate. After supper I smoked, as on the last evening, and the Count stayed with me, chatting and asking questions on every conceivable subject, hour after hour. I felt that it was getting very late indeed, but I did not say anything, for I felt under obligation to meet my host's wishes in every way. I was not sleepy, as the long sleep yesterday had fortified me, but I could not help experiencing that chill which comes over one at the coming of the dawn, which is like, in its way, the turn of the tide. They say that people who are near death die generally at the change to dawn or at the turn of the tide. Anyone who has when tired, and tied as it were to his post, experienced this change in the atmosphere can well believe it. All at once we heard the crow of the cock coming up with preternatural shrillness through the clear morning air.

Count Dracula, jumping to his feet, said, "Why there is the morning again! How remiss I am to let you stay up so long. You must make your conversation regarding my dear new country of England less interesting, so that I may not forget how time flies by us," and with a courtly bow, he quickly left me.

I went into my room and drew the curtains, but there was little to notice. My window opened into the courtyard, all I could see was the warm grey of quickening sky. So I pulled the curtains again, and have written of this day.

8 May—I began to fear as I wrote in this book that I was getting too diffuse. But now I am glad that I went into detail from the first, for some day it may be of interest to me or to others; there is something so strange about this place and all in it that I cannot but feel uneasy. I wish I were safe out of it, or that I had never come. It may be that this strange night existence is telling on me, but would that that were all! If there were any one to talk to I could bear it, but there is no one. I have only the Count to speak with, and he—I fear I am myself the only living soul within the place. Let me be prosaic so far as facts can be. It will help me to bear up, and imagination must not run riot with me. If it does I am lost. Let me say at once how I stand, or seem to.

I only slept a few hours when I went to bed, and feeling that I could not sleep any more, got up. I had hung my shaving glass by the window, and was just beginning to shave. Suddenly I felt a hand on my shoulder, and heard the Count's voice saying to me, "Good morning." I started, for it amazed me that I had not seen him, since the reflection of the glass covered the whole room behind me. In starting I had cut myself slightly, but did not notice it at the moment. Having answered the Count's salutation, I turned to the glass again to see how I had been mistaken. This time there could be no error, for the man was close to me, and I could see him over my shoulder. But there was no reflection of him in the mirror! The whole room behind me was displayed, but there was no sign of a man in it, except myself.

This was startling, and coming on the top of so many strange things, was beginning to increase that vague feeling of uneasiness which I always have when the Count is near. But at the instant I saw that the cut had bled a little, and the blood was trickling over my chin. I laid down the razor, turning as I did so half round to look for some sticking plaster. When the Count saw my face, his eyes blazed with a sort of demoniac fury, and he suddenly made a grab at my throat. I drew away and his hand touched the string of beads which held the crucifix. It made an instant change in him, for the fury passed so quickly that I could hardly believe that it was ever there.

"Take care," he said, "take care how you cut yourself. It is more dangerous that you think in this country." Then seizing the shaving glass, he went on, "And this is the wretched thing that has done the mischief. It is a foul bauble of man's vanity. Away with it!" And opening the window with one wrench of his terrible hand, he flung out the glass, which was shattered into a thousand pieces on the stones of the courtyard far below. Then he withdrew without a word. It is very annoying, for I do not see how I am to shave, unless in my watch-case or the bottom of the shaving pot, which is fortunately of metal.

When I went into the dining room, breakfast was prepared, but I could not find the Count anywhere. So I breakfasted alone. It is strange that as yet I have not seen the Count eat or drink. He must be a very peculiar man! After breakfast I did a little exploring in the castle. I went out on the stairs, and found a room looking towards the South.

The view was magnificent, and from where I stood there was every opportunity of seeing it. The castle is on the very edge of a terrific precipice. A stone falling from the window would fall a thousand feet without touching anything! As far as the eye can reach is a sea of green tree tops, with occasionally a deep rift where there is a chasm. Here and there are silver threads where the rivers wind in deep gorges through the forests.

But I am not in heart to describe beauty, for when I had seen the view I explored further. Doors, doors, doors everywhere, and all locked and bolted. In no place save from the windows in the castle walls is there an available exit. The castle is a veritable prison, and I am a prisoner!

CHAPTER

SIX[70]

Jonathan Harker's Journal, Continued

When I found that I was a prisoner a sort of wild feeling came over me. I rushed up and down the stairs, trying every door and peering out of every window I could find, but after a little the conviction of my helplessness overpowered all other feelings. When I look back after a few hours I think I must have been mad for the time, for I behaved much as a rat does in a trap. When, however, the conviction had come to me that I was helpless I sat down quietly, as quietly as I have ever done anything in my life, and began to think over what was best to be done. I am thinking still, and as yet have come to no definite conclusion. Of one thing only am I certain. That it is no use making my ideas known to the Count. He knows well that I am imprisoned, and as he has done it himself, and has doubtless his own motives for it, he would only deceive me if I trusted him fully with the facts. So far as I can see, my only plan will be to keep my knowledge and my fears to myself, and my eyes open. I am, I know, either being deceived, like a baby, by my own fears, or else I am in desperate straits, and if the latter be so, I need, and shall need, all my brains to get through.

I had hardly come to this conclusion when I heard the great door below shut, and knew that the Count had returned. He did not come at once into the library, so I went cautiously to my own room and found him making the bed. This was odd, but only confirmed what I had all along thought, that there are no servants in the house. When later I saw him through the chink of the hinges of the door laying the table in the dining room, I was assured of it. For if he does himself all these menial offices, surely it is proof that there is no one else in the castle, it must have been the Count himself who was the driver of the coach that brought me here. This is a terrible thought, for if so, what does it mean that he could control the wolves, as he did, by only holding up his hand for silence? How was it that all the people at Bistritz and on the coach had some terrible fear for me? What meant the giving of the crucifix, of the garlic, of the wild rose, of the mountain ash, of the rye?[71]

Bless that good, good woman who hung the crucifix round my neck! For it is a comfort and a strength to me whenever I touch it. It is odd that a thing which I have been taught to regard with disfavour and as idolatrous should in a time of loneliness and trouble be of help. Is it that there is something in the essence of the thing itself, or that it is a medium, a tangible help, in conveying memories of sympathy and comfort? Some time, if it may be, I must examine this matter and try to make up my mind about it. In the meantime I must find out all I can about Count Dracula, as it may help me to understand. Tonight he may talk of himself, if I turn the conversation that way. I must be very careful, however, not to awake his suspicion.

Midnight—I have had a long talk with the Count. I asked him a few questions on Transylvania history, and he warmed up to the subject wonderfully. In his speaking of things and people, and especially of battles, he spoke as if he had been present at them all. This he afterwards explained by saying that to a Boyar the pride of his house and name is his own pride, that their glory is his glory, that their fate is his fate. Whenever he spoke of his house he always said "we," and spoke almost in the plural, like a king speaking. I wish I could put down all he said exactly as he said it, for to me it was most fascinating. It seemed to have in it a whole history of the country. He grew excited as he spoke, and walked about the room pulling his great white moustache and grasping anything on which he laid his hands as though he would crush it by main strength. One thing he said which I shall put down as nearly as I can, for it tells in its way the story of his race.

"We Szekelys have a right to be proud, for in our veins flows the blood of many brave races who fought as the lion fights, for lordship. Here, in the whirlpool of European races, the Ugric tribe bore down from Iceland the fighting spirit which Thor and Wodin gave them, which their Berserkers displayed to such fell intent on the seaboards of Europe, aye, and of Asia and Africa too, till the peoples thought that the werewolves themselves had come. Here, too, when they came, they found the Huns, whose warlike fury had swept the earth like a living flame, till the dying peoples held that in their veins ran the blood of those old witches, who, expelled from Scythia had mated with the devils in the desert. Fools, fools! What devil or what witch was ever so great as Attila, whose blood is in these veins?" He held up his arms. "Is it a wonder that we were a conquering race, that we were proud, that when the Magyar, the Lombard, the Avar, the Bulgar, or the Turk poured his thousands on our frontiers, we drove them back? Is it strange that when Arpad and his legions swept through the Hungarian fatherland he found us here when he reached the frontier, that the Honfoglalas was completed there? And when the Hungarian flood swept eastward, the Szekelys were claimed as kindred by the victorious Magyars, and to us for centuries was trusted the guarding of the frontier of Turkeyland. Aye, and more than that, endless duty of the frontier guard, for as the Turks say, 'water sleeps, and the enemy is sleepless.' Who more gladly than we throughout the Four Nations received the 'bloody sword,' or at its warlike call flocked quicker to the standard of the King? When was redeemed that great shame of my nation, the shame of Cassova, when the flags of the Wallach and the Magyar went down beneath the Crescent? Who was it but one of my own race who as Voivode crossed the Danube and beat the Turk on his own ground? This was a Dracula indeed! Woe was it that his own unworthy brother, when he had fallen, sold his people to the Turk and brought the shame of slavery on them! Was it not this Dracula, indeed, who inspired that other of his race who in a later age again and again brought his forces over the great river into Turkeyland, who, when he was beaten back, came again, and again, though he had to come alone from the bloody field where his troops were being slaughtered, since he knew that he alone could ultimately triumph! They said that he thought only of himself. Bah! What good are peasants without a leader? Where ends the war without a brain and heart to conduct it? Again, when, after the battle of Mohacs, we threw off the Hungarian yoke, we of the Dracula blood were amongst their leaders, for our spirit would not brook that we were not free. Ah, young sir, the Szekelys, and the Dracula as their heart's blood, their brains, and their swords, can boast a record that mushroom growths like the Hapsburgs and the Romanoffs can never reach. The warlike days are over. Blood is too precious a thing in these days of dishonourable peace, and the glories of the great races are as a tale that is told."

It was by this time close on morning, and we went to bed. (mem., this diary seems horribly like the beginning of the "Arabian Nights," for everything has to break off at cockcrow, or like the ghost of Hamlet's father.)

12 May—Let me begin with facts, bare, meager facts, verified by books and figures, and of which there can be no doubt. I must not confuse them with experiences which will have to rest on my own observation, or my memory of them. Last evening when the Count came from his room he began by asking me questions on legal matters and on the doing of certain kinds of business. I had spent the day wearily over books, and, simply to keep my mind occupied, went over some of the matters I had been examined in at Lincoln's Inn. There was a certain method in the Count's inquiries, so I shall try to put them down in sequence. The knowledge may somehow or some time be useful to me hereafter—or to others.

First, he asked if a man in England might have two solicitors or more. I told him he might have a dozen if he wished, but that it would not be wise to have more than one solicitor engaged in one transaction, as only one could act at a time, and that to change would be certain to militate against his interest. He seemed thoroughly to understand, and went on to ask if there would be any practical difficulty in having one man to attend, say, to banking, and another to look after shipping, in case local help were needed in a place far from the home of the banking solicitor. I asked to explain more fully, so that I might not by any chance mislead him, so he said,

"I shall illustrate. Your friend and mine, Mr. Peter Hawkins, from under the shadow of your beautiful cathedral at Exeter, which is far from London, buys for me through your good self my place at London. Good! Now here let me say frankly, lest you should think it strange that I have sought the services of one so far off from London instead of some one resident there, that my motive was that no local interest might be served save my wish only, and as one of London residence might, perhaps, have some purpose of himself or friend to serve, I went thus afield to seek my agent, whose labours should be only to my interest. Now, suppose I, who have much of affairs, wish to ship goods, say, to Newcastle, or Durham, or Harwich, or Dover, might it not be that it could with more ease be done by consigning to one in these ports?"

I answered that certainly it would be most easy, but that we solicitors had a system of agency one for the other, so that local work could be done locally on instruction from any solicitor, so that the client, simply placing himself in the hands of one man, could have his wishes carried out by him without further trouble.

"But," said he, "I could be at liberty to direct myself. Is it not so?"

"Of course," I replied, and "Such is often done by men of business, who do not like the whole of their affairs to be known by any one person."

"Good!" he said, and then went on to ask about the means of making consignments and the forms to be gone through, and of all sorts of difficulties which might arise, but by forethought could be guarded against. I explained all these things to him to the best of my ability, and he certainly left me under the impression that he would have made a wonderful solicitor, for there was nothing that he did not think of or foresee. For a man who was never in the country, and who did not evidently do much in the way of business, his knowledge and acumen were wonderful. When he had satisfied himself on these points of which he had spoken, and I had verified all as well as I could by the books available, he suddenly stood up and said, "Have you written since your first letter to our friend Mr. Peter Hawkins, or to any other?"

It was with some bitterness in my heart that I answered that I had not, that as yet I had not seen any opportunity of sending letters to anybody.

"Then write now, my young friend," he said, laying a heavy hand on my shoulder, "write to our friend and to any other, and say, if it will please you, that you shall stay with me until a month from now."

"Do you wish me to stay so long?" I asked, for my heart grew cold at the thought.

"I desire it much, nay I will take no refusal. When your master, employer, what you will, engaged that someone should come on his behalf, it was understood that my needs only were to be consulted. I have not stinted. Is it not so?"

What could I do but bow acceptance? It was Mr. Hawkins' interest, not mine, and I had to think of him, not myself, and besides, while Count Dracula was speaking, there was that in his eyes and in his bearing which made me remember that I was a prisoner, and that if I wished it I could have no choice. The Count saw his victory in my bow, and his mastery in the trouble of my face, for he began at once to use them, but in his own smooth, resistless way.

"I pray you, my good young friend, that you will not discourse of things other than business in your letters. It will doubtless please your friends to know that you are well, and that you look forward to getting home to them. Is it not so?" As he spoke he handed me three sheets of note paper and three envelopes. They were all of the thinnest foreign post, and looking at them, then at him, and noticing his quiet smile, with the sharp, canine teeth lying over the red underlip, I understood as well as if he had spoken that I should be more careful what I wrote, for he would be able to read it. So I determined to write only formal notes now, but to write fully to Mr. Hawkins in secret, and also to Mina, for to her I could write shorthand, which would puzzle the Count, if he did see it. When I had written my two letters I sat quiet, reading a book whilst the Count wrote several notes, referring as he wrote them to some books on his table. Then he took up my two and placed them with his own, and put by his writing materials, after which, the instant the door had closed behind him, I leaned over and looked at the letters, which were face down on the table. I felt no compunction in doing so for under the circumstances I felt that I should protect myself in every way I could.

One of the letters was directed to Samuel F. Billington, No. 7, The Crescent, Whitby, another to Herr Leutner, Varna. The third was to Coutts & Co., London, and the fourth to Herren Klopstock & Billreuth, bankers, Buda Pesth. The second and fourth were unsealed. I was just about to look at them when I saw the door handle move. I sank back in my seat, having just had time to resume my book before the Count, holding still another letter in his hand, entered the room. He took up the letters on the table and stamped them carefully, and then turning to me, said,

"I trust you will forgive me, but I have much work to do in private this evening. You will, I hope, find all things as you wish." At the door he turned, and after a moment's pause said, "Let me advise you, my dear young friend. Nay, let me warn you with all seriousness, that should you leave these rooms you will not by any chance go to sleep in any other part of the castle. It is old, and has many memories, and there are bad dreams for those who sleep unwisely. Be warned! Should sleep now or ever overcome you, or be like to do, then haste to your own chamber or to these rooms, for your rest will then be safe. But if you be not careful in this respect, then," He finished his speech in a gruesome way, for he motioned with his hands as if he were washing them. I quite understood. My only doubt was as to whether any dream could be more terrible than the unnatural, horrible net of gloom and mystery which seemed closing around me.

Later—I endorse the last words written, but this time there is no doubt in question. I shall not fear to sleep in any place where he is not. I have placed the crucifix over the head of my bed, I imagine that my rest is thus freer from dreams, and there it shall remain.

When he left me I went to my room. After a little while, not hearing any sound, I came out and went up the stone stair to where I could look out towards the South. There was some sense of freedom in the vast expanse, inaccessible though it was to me, as compared with the narrow darkness of the courtyard. Looking out on this, I felt that I was indeed in prison, and I seemed to want a breath of fresh air, though it were of the night. I am beginning to feel this nocturnal existence tell on me. It is destroying my nerve. I start at my own shadow, and am full of all sorts of horrible imaginings. God knows that there is ground for my terrible fear in this accursed place! I looked out over the beautiful expanse, bathed in soft yellow moonlight till it was almost as light as day. In the soft light the distant hills became melted, and the shadows in the valleys and gorges of velvety blackness. The mere beauty seemed to cheer me. There was peace and comfort in every breath I drew. As I leaned from the window my eye was caught by something moving a storey below me, and somewhat to my left, where I imagined, from the order of the rooms, that the windows of the Count's own room would look out. The window at which I stood was tall and deep, stone-mullioned, and though weatherworn, was still complete. But it was evidently many a day since the case had been there. I drew back behind the stonework, and looked carefully out.

What I saw was the Count's head coming out from the window. I did not see the face, but I knew the man by the neck and the movement of his back and arms. In any case I could not mistake the hands which I had had some many opportunities of studying. I was at first interested and somewhat amused, for it is wonderful how small a matter will interest and amuse a man when he is a prisoner. But my very feelings changed to repulsion and terror when I saw the whole man slowly emerge from the window and begin to crawl down the castle wall over the dreadful abyss, face down with his cloak spreading out around him like great wings. At first I could not believe my eyes. I thought it was some trick of the moonlight, some weird effect of shadow, but I kept looking, and it could be no delusion. I saw the fingers and toes grasp the corners of the stones, worn clear of the mortar by the stress of years, and by thus using every projection and inequality move downwards with considerable speed, just as a lizard moves along a wall.

What manner of man is this, or what manner of creature, is it in the semblance of man? I feel the dread of this horrible place overpowering me. I am in fear, in awful fear, and there is no escape for me. I am encompassed about with terrors that I dare not think of.

15 May—Once more I have seen the count go out in his lizard fashion. He moved downwards in a sidelong way, some hundred feet down, and a good deal to the left. He vanished into some hole or window. When his head had disappeared, I leaned out to try and see more, but without avail. The distance was too great to allow a proper angle of sight. I knew he had left the castle now, and thought to use the opportunity to explore more than I had dared to do as yet. I went back to the room, and taking a lamp, tried all the doors. They were all locked, as I had expected, and the locks were comparatively new. But I went down the stone stairs to the hall where I had entered originally. I found I could pull back the bolts easily enough and unhook the great chains. But the door was locked, and the key was gone! That key must be in the Count's room. I must watch should his door be unlocked, so that I may get it and escape. I went on to make a thorough examination of the various stairs and passages, and to try the doors that opened from them. One or two small rooms near the hall were open, but there was nothing to see in them except old furniture, dusty with age and moth-eaten. At last, however, I found one door at the top of the stairway which, though it seemed locked, gave a little under pressure. I tried it harder, and found that it was not really locked, but that the resistance came from the fact that the hinges had fallen somewhat, and the heavy door rested on the floor. Here was an opportunity which I might not have again, so I exerted myself, and with many efforts forced it back so that I could enter. I was now in a wing of the castle further to the right than the rooms I knew and a storey lower down. From the windows I could see that the suite of rooms lay along to the south of the castle, the windows of the end room looking out both west and south. On the latter side, as well as to the former, there was a great precipice. The castle was built on the corner of a great rock, so that on three sides it was quite impregnable, and great windows were placed here where sling, or bow, or culverin could not reach, and consequently light and comfort, impossible to a position which had to be guarded, were secured. To the west was a great valley, and then, rising far away, great jagged mountain fastnesses, rising peak on peak, the sheer rock studded with mountain ash and thorn, whose roots clung in cracks and crevices and crannies of the stone. This was evidently the

portion of the castle occupied by the ladies in bygone days, for the furniture had more an air of comfort than any I had seen.

The windows were curtainless, and the yellow moonlight, flooding in through the diamond panes, enabled one to see even colours, whilst it softened the wealth of dust which lay over all and disguised in some measure the ravages of time and moth. My lamp seemed to be of little effect in the brilliant moonlight, but I was glad to have it with me, for there was a dread loneliness in the place which chilled my heart and made my nerves tremble. Still, it was better than living alone in the rooms which I had come to hate from the presence of the Count, and after trying a little to school my nerves, I found a soft quietude come over me. Here I am, sitting at a little oak table where in old times possibly some fair lady sat to pen, with much thought and many blushes, her ill-spelt love letter, and writing in my diary in shorthand all that has happened since I closed it last. It is the nineteenth century up-to-date with a vengeance. And yet, unless my senses deceive me, the old centuries had, and have, powers of their own which mere "modernity" cannot kill.

Later: The morning of 16 May—God preserve my sanity, for to this I am reduced. Safety and the assurance of safety are things of the past. Whilst I live on here there is but one thing to hope for, that I may not go mad, if, indeed, I be not mad already. If I be sane, then surely it is maddening to think that of all the foul things that lurk in this hateful place the Count is the least dreadful to me, that to him alone I can look for safety, even though this be only whilst I can serve his purpose. Great God! Merciful God, let me be calm, for out of that way lies madness indeed. I begin to get new lights on certain things which have puzzled me. Up to now I never quite knew what Shakespeare meant when he made Hamlet say, "My tablets! Quick, my tablets! 'tis meet that I put it down," etc., For now, feeling as though my own brain were unhinged or as if the shock had come which must end in its undoing, I turn to my diary for repose. The habit of entering accurately must help to soothe me.

The Count's mysterious warning frightened me at the time. It frightens me more now when I think of it, for in the future he has a fearful hold upon me. I shall fear to doubt what he may say!

When I had written in my diary and had fortunately replaced the book and pen in my pocket I felt sleepy. The Count's warning came into my mind, but I took pleasure in disobeying it. The sense of sleep was upon me, and with it the obstinacy which sleep brings as outrider. The soft moonlight soothed, and the wide expanse without gave a sense of freedom which refreshed me. I determined not to return tonight to the gloom-haunted rooms, but to sleep here, where, of old, ladies had sat and sung and lived sweet lives whilst their gentle breasts were sad for their menfolk away in the midst of remorseless wars. I drew a great couch out of its place near the corner, so that as I lay, I could look at the lovely view to east and south, and unthinking of and uncaring for the dust, composed myself for sleep. I suppose I must have fallen asleep. I hope so, but I fear, for all that followed was startlingly real, so real that now sitting here in the broad, full sunlight of the morning, I cannot in the least believe that it was all sleep.

I was not alone. The room was the same, unchanged in any way since I came into it. I could see along the floor, in the brilliant moonlight, my own footsteps marked where I had disturbed the long accumulation of dust. In the moonlight opposite me were three young women, ladies by their dress and manner. I thought at the time that I must be dreaming when I saw them, they threw no shadow on the floor. They came close to me, and looked at me for some time, and then whispered together. Two were dark, and had high aquiline noses, like the Count, and great dark, piercing eyes, that seemed to be almost red when contrasted with the pale yellow moon. The other was fair, as fair as can be, with great masses of golden hair and eyes like pale sapphires. I seemed somehow to know her face, and to know it in connection with some dreamy fear, but I could not recollect at the moment how or where.

All three had brilliant white teeth that shone like pearls against the ruby of their voluptuous lips. There was something about them that made me uneasy, some longing and at the same time some deadly fear. I felt in my heart a wicked, burning desire that they would kiss me with those red lips. It is not good to note this down, lest some day it should meet Mina's eyes and cause her pain, but it is the truth. They whispered together, and then they all three laughed, such a silvery, musical laugh, but as hard as though the sound never could have come through the softness of human lips. It was like the intolerable, tingling sweetness of waterglasses when played on by a cunning hand. The fair girl shook her head coquettishly, and the other two urged her on.

One said, "Go on! You are first, and we shall follow. Yours is the right to begin."

The other added, "He is young and strong. There are kisses for us all."

I lay quiet, looking out from under my eyelashes in an agony of delightful anticipation. The fair girl advanced and bent over me till I could feel the movement of her breath upon me. Sweet it was in one sense, honey-sweet, and sent the same tingling through the nerves as her voice, but with a bitter underlying the sweet, a bitter offensiveness, as one smells in blood. She started back and pointed to my throat where the rubbing of the wolf's tongue. Her eyes flashed angrily with bitter disgust,[72] before the cruel smile returned to her red lips and she drew close once more.

I was afraid to raise my eyelids, but looked out and saw perfectly under the lashes. The girl went on her knees, and bent over me, simply gloating. There was a deliberate voluptuousness which was both thrilling and repulsive, and as she arched her neck she actually licked her lips like an animal, till I could see in the moonlight the moisture shining on the scarlet lips and on the red tongue as it lapped the white sharp teeth. Lower and lower went her head as the lips went below the range of my mouth and chin and seemed to fasten on my throat. Then she paused, and I could hear the churning sound of her tongue as it licked her teeth and lips, and I could feel the hot breath on my neck. Then the skin of my throat began to tingle as one's flesh does when the hand that is to tickle it approaches nearer, nearer. I could feel the soft, shivering touch of the lips on the super sensitive skin of my throat, and the hard dents of two sharp teeth, just touching and pausing there. I closed my eyes in languorous ecstasy and waited, waited with beating heart.

But at that instant, another sensation swept through me as quick as lightning. I was conscious of the presence of the Count, and of his being as if lapped in a storm of fury. As my eyes opened involuntarily I saw his strong hand grasp the slender neck of the fair woman and with giant's power draw it back, the blue eyes transformed with fury, the white teeth champing with rage, and the fair cheeks blazing red with passion. But the Count! Never did I imagine such wrath and fury, even to the demons of the pit. His eyes were positively blazing. The red light in them was lurid, as if the flames of hell fire blazed behind them. His face was deathly pale, and the lines of it were hard like drawn wires. The thick eyebrows that met over the nose now seemed like a heaving bar of white-hot metal. With a fierce sweep of his arm, he hurled the woman from him, and then motioned to the others, as though he were beating them back. It was the same imperious gesture that I had seen used to the wolves. In a voice which, though low and almost in a whisper seemed to cut through the air and then ring in the room he said,

"How dare you touch him, any of you? How dare you cast eyes on him when I had forbidden it? Back, I tell you all! This man belongs to me! Beware how you meddle with him, or you'll have to deal with me."

The fair girl, with a laugh of ribald coquetry, turned to answer him. "You yourself never loved. You never love!" On this the other women joined, and such a mirthless, hard, soulless laughter rang through the room that it almost made me faint to hear. It seemed like the pleasure of fiends.

Then the Count turned, after looking at my face attentively, and said in a soft whisper, "Yes, I too can love. You yourselves can tell it from the past. Is it not so? Well, now I promise you that when I am done with him you shall kiss him at your will. Now go! Go! I must awaken him, for there is work to be done." As he spoke I was looking at the fair woman and it suddenly dawned on me that she was the woman—or her image—that I had seen on Walpurgis night.[73] So then it had been no dream, nor was she destroyed in her tomb, but rather freed from it!

"Are we to have nothing tonight?" said one of them, with a low laugh, as she pointed to the bag which he had thrown upon the floor, and which moved as though there were some living thing within it. For answer he nodded his head. One of the women jumped forward and opened it. If my ears did not deceive me there was a gasp and a low wail, as of a half smothered child. The women closed round, whilst I was aghast with horror. But as I looked, they disappeared, and with them the dreadful bag. There was no door near them, and they could not have passed me without my noticing. They simply seemed to fade into the rays of the moonlight and pass out through the window, for I could see outside the dim, shadowy forms for a moment before they entirely faded away.

Then the horror overcame me, and I sank down unconscious.

CHAPTER SEVEN[74]

Jonathan Harker's Journal, Continued

I awoke in my own bed. If it be that I had not dreamt, the Count must have carried me here. I tried to satisfy myself on the subject, but could not arrive at any unquestionable result. To be sure, there were certain small evidences, such as that my clothes were folded and laid by in a manner which was not my habit. My watch was still unwound, and I am rigorously accustomed to wind it the last thing before going to bed, and many such details. But these things are no proof, for they may have been evidences that my mind was not as usual, and, for some cause or another, I had certainly been much upset. I must watch for proof. Of one thing I am glad. If it was that the Count carried me here and undressed me, he must have been hurried in his task, for my pockets are intact. I am sure this diary would have been a mystery to him which he would not have brooked. He would have taken or destroyed it. As I look round this room, although it has been to me so full of fear, it is now a sort of sanctuary, for nothing can be more dreadful than those awful women, who were, who are, waiting to suck my blood.

18 May—I have been down to look at that room again in daylight, for I must know the truth. When I got to the doorway at the top of the stairs I found it closed. It had been so forcibly driven against the jamb that part of the woodwork was splintered. I could see that the bolt of the lock had not been shot, but the door is fastened from the inside. I fear it was no dream, and must act on this surmise.

19 May—I am surely in the toils. Last night the Count asked me in the suavest tones to write three letters, one saying that my work here was nearly done, and

that I should start for home within a few days, another that I was starting on the next morning from the time of the letter, and the third that I had left the castle and arrived at Bistritz. I would fain have rebelled, but felt that in the present state of things it would be madness to quarrel openly with the Count whilst I am so absolutely in his power. And to refuse would be to excite his suspicion and to arouse his anger. He knows that I know too much, and that I must not live, lest I be dangerous to him. My only chance is to prolong my opportunities. Something may occur which will give me a chance to escape. I saw in his eyes something of that gathering wrath which was manifest when he hurled that fair woman from him. He explained to me that posts were few and uncertain, and that my writing now would ensure ease of mind to my friends. And he assured me with so much impressiveness that he would countermand the later letters, which would be held over at Bistritz until due time in case chance would admit of my prolonging my stay, that to oppose him would have been to create new suspicion. I therefore pretended to fall in with his views, and asked him what dates I should put on the letters.

He calculated a minute, and then said, "The first should be June 12, the second June 19, and the third June 29."

I know now the span of my life. God help me!

28 May—There is a chance of escape, or at any rate of being able to send word home. A band of Szgany have come to the castle, and are encamped in the courtyard. These are gipsies. I have notes of them in my book. They are peculiar to this part of the world, though allied to the ordinary gipsies all the world over. There are thousands of them in Hungary and Transylvania, who are almost outside all law. They attach themselves as a rule to some great noble or boyar, and call themselves by his name. They are fearless and without religion, save superstition, and they talk only their own varieties of the Romany tongue.

I shall write some letters home, and shall try to get them to have them posted. I have already spoken to them through my window to begin acquaintanceship. They took their hats off and made obeisance and many signs, which however, I could not understand any more than I could their spoken language . . .

I have written the letters. Mina's is in shorthand, and I simply ask Mr. Hawkins to communicate with her. To her I have explained my situation, but without the horrors which I may only surmise. It would shock and frighten her to death were I to expose my heart to her. Should the letters not carry, then the Count shall not yet know my secret or the extent of my knowledge . . . .

I have given the letters. I threw them through the bars of my window with a gold piece, and made what signs I could to have them posted. The man who took them pressed them to his heart and bowed, and then put them in his cap.

I could do no more. I stole back to the study, and began to read. As the Count did not come in, I have written here . . .

The Count has come. He sat down beside me, and said in his smoothest voice as he opened two letters, "The Szgany has given me these, of which, though I know not whence they come, I shall, of course, take care. See!"—He must have looked at it.—"One is from you, and to my friend Peter Hawkins. The other,"—here he caught sight of the strange symbols as he opened the envelope, and the dark look came into his face, and his eyes blazed wickedly,—"The other is a vile thing, an outrage upon friendship and hospitality! It is not signed. Well! So it cannot matter to us." And he calmly held letter and envelope in the flame of the lamp till they were consumed.

Then he went on, "The letter to Hawkins, that I shall, of course send on, since it is yours. Your letters are sacred to me. Your pardon, my friend, that unknowingly I did break the seal. Will you not cover it again?" He held out the letter to me, and with a courteous bow handed me a clean envelope.

I could only redirect it and hand it to him in silence. When he went out of the room I could hear the key turn softly. A minute later I went over and tried it, and the door was locked.

When, an hour or two after, the Count came quietly into the room, his coming awakened me, for I had gone to sleep on the sofa. He was very courteous and very cheery in his manner, and seeing that I had been sleeping, he said, "So, my friend, you are tired? Get to bed. There is the surest rest. I may not have the pleasure of talk tonight, since there are many labours to me, but you will sleep, I pray."

I passed to my room and went to bed, and, strange to say, slept without dreaming. Despair has its own calms.

31 May—This morning when I woke I thought I would provide myself with some papers and envelopes from my bag and keep them in my pocket, so that I might write in case I should get an opportunity, but again a surprise, again a shock!

Every scrap of paper was gone, and with it all my notes, my memoranda, relating to railways and travel, my letter of credit, in fact all that might be useful to me were I once outside the castle. I sat and pondered awhile, and then some thought occurred to me, and I made search of my portmanteau and in the wardrobe where I had placed my clothes.

The suit in which I had travelled was gone, and also my overcoat and rug. I could find no trace of them anywhere. This looked like some new scheme of villainy . . .

17 June—This morning, as I was sitting on the edge of my bed cudgelling my brains, I heard without a crackling of whips and pounding and scraping of horses' feet up the rocky path beyond the courtyard. With joy I hurried to the window,

and saw drive into the yard two great leiter-wagons, each drawn by eight sturdy horses, and at the head of each pair a Slovak, with his wide hat, great nail-studded belt, dirty sheepskin, and high boots. They had also their long staves in hand. I ran to the door, intending to descend and try and join them through the main hall, as I thought that way might be opened for them. Again a shock, my door was fastened on the outside.

Then I ran to the window and cried to them. They looked up at me stupidly and pointed, but just then the "hetman" of the Szgany came out, and seeing them pointing to my window, said something, at which they laughed.

Henceforth no effort of mine, no piteous cry or agonized entreaty, would make them even look at me. They resolutely turned away. The leiter-wagons contained great, square boxes, with handles of thick rope. These were evidently empty by the ease with which the Slovaks handled them, and by their resonance as they were roughly moved.

When they were all unloaded and packed in a great heap in one corner of the yard, the Slovaks were given some money by the Szgany, and spitting on it for luck, lazily went each to his horse's head. Shortly afterwards, I heard the crackling of their whips die away in the distance.

24 June—Last night the Count left me early, and locked himself into his own room. As soon as I dared I ran up the winding stair, and looked out of the window, which opened South. I thought I would watch for the Count, for there is something going on. The Szgany are quartered somewhere in the castle and are doing work of some kind. I know it, for now and then, I hear a far-away muffled sound as of mattock and spade, and, whatever it is, it must be the end of some ruthless villainy.

I had been at the window somewhat less than half an hour, when I saw something coming out of the Count's window. I drew back and watched carefully, and saw the whole man emerge. It was a new shock to me to find that he had on the suit of clothes which I had worn whilst travelling here, and slung over his shoulder the terrible bag which I had seen the women take away. There could be no doubt as to his quest, and in my garb, too! This, then, is his new scheme of evil, that he will allow others to see me, as they think, so that he may both leave evidence that I have been seen in the towns or villages posting my own letters, and that any wickedness which he may do shall by the local people be attributed to me.

It makes me rage to think that this can go on, and whilst I am shut up here, a veritable prisoner, but without that protection of the law which is even a criminal's right and consolation.

I thought I would watch for the Count's return, and for a long time sat doggedly at the window. Then I began to notice that there were some quaint little specks floating in the rays of the moonlight. They were like the tiniest grains of dust, and they whirled round and gathered in clusters in a nebulous sort of way. I watched them with a sense of soothing, and a sort of calm stole over me. I leaned back in the embrasure in a more comfortable position, so that I could enjoy more fully the aerial gambolling.

Something made me start up, a low, piteous howling of dogs somewhere far below in the valley, which was hidden from my sight. Louder it seemed to ring in my ears, and the floating moats of dust to take new shapes to the sound as they danced in the moonlight. I felt myself struggling to awake to some call of my instincts. Nay, my very soul was struggling, and my half-remembered sensibilities were striving to answer the call. I was becoming hypnotized!

Quicker and quicker danced the dust. The moonbeams seemed to quiver as they went by me into the mass of gloom beyond. More and more they gathered till they seemed to take dim phantom shapes. And then I started, broad awake and in full possession of my senses, and ran screaming from the place.

The phantom shapes, which were becoming gradually materialised from the moonbeams, were those three ghostly women to whom I was doomed.

I fled, holding the crucifix before me, and felt somewhat safer in my own room, where there was no moonlight, and where the lamp was burning brightly.

When a couple of hours had passed I heard something stirring in the Count's room, something like a sharp wail quickly suppressed. And then there was silence, deep, awful silence, which chilled me. With a beating heart, I tried the door, but I was locked in my prison, and could do nothing. I sat down and simply cried.

As I sat I heard a sound in the courtyard without, the agonized cry of a woman. I rushed to the window, and throwing it up, peered between the bars.

There, indeed, was a woman with dishevelled hair, holding her hands over her heart as one distressed with running. She was leaning against the corner of the gateway. When she saw my face at the window she threw herself forward, and shouted in a voice laden with menace, "Monster, give me my child!"

She threw herself on her knees, and raising up her hands, cried the same words in tones which wrung my heart. Then she tore her hair and beat her breast, and abandoned herself to all the violences of extravagant emotion. Finally, she threw herself forward, and though I could not see her, I could hear the beating of her naked hands against the door.

Somewhere high overhead, probably on the tower, I heard the voice of the Count calling in his harsh, metallic whisper. His call seemed to be answered from far and wide by the howling of wolves. Before many minutes had passed a pack of them poured, like a pent-up dam when liberated, through the wide entrance into the courtyard.

There was no cry from the woman, and the howling of the wolves was but short. Before long they streamed away singly, licking their lips.

I could not pity her, for I knew now what had become of her child, and she was better dead.

What shall I do? What can I do? How can I escape from this dreadful thing of night, gloom, and fear?

25 June—No man knows till he has suffered from the night how sweet and dear to his heart and eye the morning can be. When the sun grew so high this morning that it struck the top of the great gateway opposite my window, the high spot which it touched seemed to me as if the dove from the ark had lighted there. My fear fell from me as if it had been a vaporous garment which dissolved in the warmth.

I must take action of some sort whilst the courage of the day is upon me. Last night one of my post-dated letters went to post, the first of that fatal series which is to blot out the very traces of my existence from the earth.

Let me not think of it. Action!

It has always been at night-time that I have been molested or threatened, or in some way in danger or in fear. I have not yet seen the Count in the daylight. Can it be that he sleeps when others wake, that he may be awake whilst they sleep? If I could only get into his room! But there is no possible way. The door is always locked, no way for me.

Yes, there is a way, if one dares to take it. Where his body has gone why may not another body go? I have seen him myself crawl from his window. Why should not I imitate him, and go in by his window? The chances are desperate, but my need is more desperate still. I shall risk it. At the worst it can only be death, and a man's death is not a calf's, and the dreaded Hereafter may still be open to me. God help me in my task! Goodbye, Mina, if I fail. Goodbye, my faithful friend and second father. Goodbye, all, and last of all Mina!

Same day, later—I have made the effort, and God helping me, have come safely back to this room. I must put down every detail in order. I went whilst my courage was fresh straight to the window on the south side, and at once got outside on this side. The stones are big and roughly cut, and the mortar has by process of time been washed away between them. I took off my boots, and ventured out on the desperate way. I looked down once, so as to make sure that a sudden glimpse of the awful depth would not overcome me, but after that kept my eyes away from it. I know pretty well the direction and distance of the Count's window, and made for it as well as I could, having regard to the opportunities available. I did not feel dizzy, I suppose I was too excited, and the time seemed ridiculously short till I found myself standing on the window sill and trying to raise up the sash. I was filled with agitation, however, when I bent down and slid feet foremost in through the window. Then I looked around for the Count, but with surprise and gladness, made a discovery. The room was empty! It was barely furnished with odd things, which seemed to have never been used.

The furniture was something the same style as that in the south rooms, and was covered with dust. I looked for the key, but it was not in the lock, and I could not find it anywhere. The only thing I found was a great heap of gold in one corner, gold of all kinds, Roman, and British, and Austrian, and Hungarian, and Greek and Turkish money, covered with a film of dust, as though it had lain long in the ground. None of it that I noticed was less than three hundred years old. There were also chains and ornaments, some jewelled, but all of them old and stained.

At one corner of the room was a heavy door. I tried it, for, since I could not find the key of the room or the key of the outer door, which was the main object of my search, I must make further examination, or all my efforts would be in vain. It was open, and led through a stone passage to a circular stairway, which went steeply down.

I descended, minding carefully where I went for the stairs were dark, being only lit by loopholes in the heavy masonry. At the bottom there was a dark, tunnel-like passage, through which came a deathly, sickly odour, the odour of old earth newly turned. As I went through the passage the smell grew closer and heavier. At last I pulled open a heavy door which stood ajar, and found myself in an old ruined chapel, which had evidently been used as a graveyard. The roof was broken, and in two places were steps leading to vaults, but the ground had recently been dug over, and the earth placed in great wooden boxes, manifestly those which had been brought by the Slovaks.

There was nobody about, and I made a search over every inch of the ground, so as not to lose a chance. I went down even into the vaults, where the dim light struggled, although to do so was a dread to my very soul. Into two of these I went, but saw nothing except fragments of old coffins and piles of dust. In the third, however, I made a discovery.

There, in one of the great boxes, of which there were fifty in all, on a pile of newly dug earth, lay the Count! He was either dead or asleep. I could not say which, for eyes were open and stony, but without the glassiness of death, and the cheeks had the warmth of life through all their pallor. The lips were as red as ever. But there was no sign of movement, no pulse, no breath, no beating of the heart.

I bent over him, and tried to find any sign of life, but in vain. He could not have lain there long, for the earthy smell would have passed away in a few hours. By the side of the box was its cover, pierced with holes here and there. I thought he might have the keys on him, but when I went to search I saw the dead eyes, and in them dead though they were, such a look of hate, though unconscious of me or my presence, that I fled from the place, and leaving the Count's room by the window, crawled again up the castle wall. Regaining my room, I threw myself panting upon the bed and tried to think.

29 June—Today is the date of my last letter, and the Count has taken steps to prove that it was genuine, for again I saw him leave the castle by the same window, and in my clothes. As he went down the wall, lizard fashion, I wished I had a gun or some lethal weapon, that I might destroy him. But I fear that no weapon wrought alone by man's hand would have any effect on him. I dared not wait to see him return, for I feared to see those weird sisters—how right was Shakespeare, no one would believe that after three hundred years one should see in this fastness of Europe the counterpart of the witches of Macbeth.[75] I came back to the library, and read there till I fell asleep.

I was awakened by the Count, who looked at me as grimly as a man could look as he said, "Tomorrow, my friend, we must part. You return to your beautiful England, I to some work which may have such an end that we may never meet. Your letter home has been dispatched. Tomorrow I shall not be here, but all shall be ready for your journey. In the morning come the Szgany, who have some labours of their own here, and also come some Slovaks. When they have gone, my carriage shall come for you, and shall bear you to the Borgo Pass to meet the diligence from Bukovina to Bistritz. But I am in hopes that I shall see more of you at Castle Dracula."

I suspected him, and determined to test his sincerity. Sincerity! It seems like a profanation of the word to write it in connection with such a monster, so I asked him point-blank, "Why may I not go tonight?"

"Because, dear sir, my coachman and horses are away on a mission."

"But I would walk with pleasure. I want to get away at once."

He smiled, such a soft, smooth, diabolical smile that I knew there was some trick behind his smoothness. He said, "And your baggage?"

"I do not care about it. I can send for it some other time."

The Count stood up, and said, with a sweet courtesy which made me rub my eyes, it seemed so real, "You English have a saying which is close to my heart, for its spirit is that which rules our boyars, 'Welcome the coming, speed the parting guest.' Come with me, my dear young friend. Not an hour shall you wait in my house against your will, though sad am I at your going, and that you so suddenly desire it. Come!" With a stately gravity, he, with the lamp, preceded me down the stairs and along the hall. Suddenly he stopped. "Hark!"

Close at hand came the howling of many wolves. It was almost as if the sound sprang up at the rising of his hand, just as the music of a great orchestra seems to leap under the baton of the conductor. After a pause of a moment, he proceeded, in his stately way, to the door, drew back the ponderous bolts, unhooked the heavy chains, and began to draw it open.

To my intense astonishment I saw that it was unlocked. Suspiciously, I looked all round, but could see no key of any kind.

As the door began to open, the howling of the wolves without grew louder and angrier. Their red jaws, with champing teeth, and their blunt-clawed feet as they leaped, came in through the opening door. I knew then that to struggle at the moment against the Count was useless. With such allies as these at his command, I could do nothing.

But still the door continued slowly to open, and only the Count's body stood in the gap. Suddenly it struck me that this might be the moment and means of my doom. I was to be given to the wolves, and at my own instigation. There was a diabolical wickedness in the idea great enough for the Count, and as the last chance I cried out, "Shut the door! I shall wait till morning." And I covered my face with my hands to hide my tears of bitter disappointment.

With one sweep of his powerful arm, the Count threw the door shut, and the great bolts clanged and echoed through the hall as they shot back into their places.

In silence we returned to the library, and after a minute or two I went to my own room. The last I saw of Count Dracula was his kissing his hand to me, with a red light of triumph in his eyes, and with a smile that Judas in hell might be proud of.

When I was in my room and about to lie down, I thought I heard a whispering at my door. I went to it softly and listened. Unless my ears deceived me, I heard the voice of the Count.

"Back! Back to your own place! Your time is not yet come. Wait! Have patience! Tonight is mine. Tomorrow, tomorrow night[76] is yours!"

There was a low, sweet ripple of laughter, and in a rage I threw open the door, and saw without the three terrible women licking their lips. As I appeared, they all joined in a horrible laugh, and ran away.

I came back to my room and threw myself on my knees. It is then so near the end? Tomorrow! Tomorrow! Lord, help me, and those to whom I am dear!

30 June—These may be the last words I ever write in this diary. I slept till just before the dawn, and when I woke threw myself on my knees, for I determined that if Death came he should find me ready.

At last I felt that subtle change in the air, and knew that the morning had come. Then came the welcome cockcrow, and I felt that I was safe. With a glad heart, I opened the door and ran down the hall. I had seen that the door was unlocked, and now escape was before me. With hands that trembled with eagerness, I unhooked the chains and threw back the massive bolts.

But the door would not move. Despair seized me. I pulled and pulled at the door, and shook it till, massive as it was, it rattled in its casement. I could see the bolt shot. It had been locked after I left the Count.

Then a wild desire took me to obtain the key at any risk, and I determined then and there to scale the wall again, and gain the Count's room. He might kill me, but death now seemed the happier choice of evils. Without a pause I rushed up to the east window, and scrambled down the wall, as before, into the Count's room. It was empty, but that was as I expected. I could not see a key anywhere, but the heap of gold remained. I went through the door in the corner and down the winding stair and along the dark passage to the old chapel. I knew now well enough where to find the monster I sought.

The great box was in the same place, close against the wall, but the lid was laid on it, not fastened down, but with the nails ready in their places to be hammered home.

I knew I must reach the body for the key, so I raised the lid, and laid it back against the wall. And then I saw something which filled my very soul with horror. There lay the Count, but looking as if his youth had been half restored. The cheeks were fuller, and the white skin seemed ruby-red underneath. The mouth was redder than ever, for on the lips were gouts of fresh blood, which trickled from the corners of the mouth and ran down over the chin and neck. Even the deep, burning eyes seemed set amongst swollen flesh, for the lids and pouches underneath were bloated. It seemed as if the whole awful creature were simply gorged with blood. He lay like a filthy leech, exhausted with his repletion.

I shuddered as I bent over to touch him, and every sense in me revolted at the contact, but I had to search, or I was lost. The coming night might see my own body a banquet in a similar way to those horrid three. I felt all over the body, but no sign could I find of the key. Then I stopped and looked at the Count. There was a mocking smile on the bloated face which seemed to drive me mad. This was the being I was helping to transfer to London, where, perhaps, for centuries to come he might, amongst its teeming millions, satiate his lust for blood, and create a new and ever-widening circle of semi-demons to batten on the helpless.

The very thought drove me mad. A terrible desire came upon me to rid the world of such a monster. There was no lethal weapon at hand, but I seized a shovel which the workmen had been using to fill the cases, and lifting it high, struck, with the edge downward, at the hateful face. But as I did so the head turned, and the eyes fell upon me, with all their blaze of basilisk horror. The sight seemed to paralyze me, and the shovel turned in my hand and glanced from the face, merely making a deep gash above the forehead. The shovel fell from my hand across the box, and as I pulled it away the flange of the blade caught the edge of the lid which fell over again, and hid the horrid thing from my sight. The last glimpse I had was of the bloated face, blood-stained and fixed with a grin of malice which would have held its own in the nethermost hell.

I thought and thought what should be my next move, but my brain seemed on fire, and I waited with a despairing feeling growing over me. As I waited I heard in the distance a gipsy song sung by merry voices coming closer, and through their song the rolling of heavy wheels and the cracking of whips. The Szgany and the Slovaks of whom the Count had spoken were coming. With a last look around and at the box which contained the vile body, I ran from the place and gained the Count's room, determined to rush out at the moment the door should be opened. With strained ears, I listened, and heard downstairs the grinding of the key in the great lock and the falling back of the heavy door. There must have been some other means of entry, or some one had a key for one of the locked doors.

Then there came the sound of many feet tramping and dying away in some passage which sent up a clanging echo. I turned to run down again towards the vault, where I might find the new entrance, but at the moment there seemed to come a violent puff of wind, and the door to the winding stair blew to with a shock that set the dust from the lintels flying. When I ran to push it open, I found that it was hopelessly fast. I was again a prisoner, and the net of doom was closing round me more closely.

As I write there is in the passage below a sound of many tramping feet and the crash of weights being set down heavily, doubtless the boxes, with their freight of earth. There was a sound of hammering. It is the box being nailed down. Now I can hear the heavy feet tramping again along the hall, with many other idle feet coming behind them.

The door is shut, the chains rattle. There is a grinding of the key in the lock. I can hear the key withdrawn, then another door opens and shuts. I hear the creaking of lock and bolt.

Hark! In the courtyard and down the rocky way the roll of heavy wheels, the crack of whips, and the chorus of the Szgany as they pass into the distance.

I am alone in the castle with those horrible women. Faugh! Mina is a woman, and there is naught in common. They are devils of the Pit!

I shall not remain alone with them. I shall try to scale the castle wall farther than I have yet attempted. I shall take some of the gold with me, lest I want it later. I may find a way from this dreadful place.

And then away for home! Away to the quickest and nearest train! Away from the cursed spot, from this cursed land, where the devil and his children still walk with earthly feet!

At least God's mercy is better than that of those monsters, and the precipice is steep and high. At its foot a man may sleep, as a man. Goodbye, all. Mina!

BOOK II

TRAGEDY[77]

CHAPTER EIGHT[78]

Letter from Miss Mina Murray to Miss Lucy Westenra

9 May.

My dearest Lucy,

Forgive my long delay in writing, but I have been simply overwhelmed with work. The life of an assistant schoolmistress is sometimes trying. I am longing to be with you, and by the sea, where we can talk together freely and build our castles in the air. I have been working very hard lately, because I want to keep up with Jonathan's studies, and I have been practicing shorthand very assiduously. When we are married I shall be able to be useful to Jonathan, and if I can stenograph well enough I can take down what he wants to say in this way and write it out for him on the typewriter, at which also I am practicing very hard.

He and I sometimes write letters in shorthand, and he is keeping a stenographic journal of his travels abroad. When I am with you I shall keep a diary in the same way. I don't mean one of those two-pages-to-the-week-with-Sunday-squeezed-in-a-corner diaries, but a sort of journal which I can write in whenever I feel inclined.

I do not suppose there will be much of interest to other people, but it is not intended for them. I may show it to Jonathan some day if there is in it anything worth sharing, but it is really an exercise book. I shall try to do what I see lady journalists do, interviewing and writing descriptions and trying to remember conversations. I am told that, with a little practice, one can remember all that goes on or that one hears said during a day.

However, we shall see. I will tell you of my little plans when we meet. I have just had a few hurried lines from Jonathan from Transylvania. He is well, and will be returning in about a week. I am longing to hear all his news. It must be nice to see strange countries. I wonder if we, I mean Jonathan and I, shall ever see them together. There is the ten o'clock bell ringing. Goodbye.

Your loving
Mina

Tell me all the news when you write. You have not told me anything for a long time. I hear rumours, and especially of a tall, handsome, curly-haired man??? If they are true, I do not know how to say how glad I am that you are so happy. Every blessing, my dear, on you both. I shall try to tell you when we meet how I feel.

Letter, Lucy Westenra to Mina Murray

17, Chatham Street
Wednesday

My dearest Mina,

I must say you tax me very unfairly with being a bad correspondent. I wrote you twice since we parted, and your last letter was only your second. Besides, I have nothing to tell you. There is really nothing to interest you.

Town is very pleasant just now, and we go a great deal to picture-galleries and for walks and rides in the park. As to the tall, curly-haired man, I suppose it was the one who was with me at the last Pop. Someone has evidently been telling tales, and I believe I can guess who it was too.

That was Mr. Holmwood. He often comes to see us, and he and Mamma get on very well together, they have so many things to talk about in common. I almost envy mother sometimes for her knowledge when she can talk to people whilst I have to sit by like a dumb animal and smile a stereotyped smile till I find myself blushing at being an incarnate lie. And it is so silly and childish to blush and without reason too.[79] At each visit, he brings her a special tea that his own father uses to calm his nerves. His family has it imported from the wilds of Central Europe.

We met some time ago a man that would just do for you, if you were not already engaged to Jonathan. He is an excellent parti, being handsome, well off, and of good birth. He is a doctor and really clever. Just fancy! He is only nine-and-twenty, and he has an immense lunatic asylum all under his own care. Mr. Holmwood introduced him to me, and he called here to see us, and often comes now. I think he is one of the most resolute men I ever saw, and yet the most calm. He seems absolutely imperturbable. I can fancy what a wonderful power he must have over his patients. He has a curious habit of looking one straight in the face, as if trying to read one's thoughts. He tries this on very much with me, but I flatter myself he has got a tough nut to crack. I know that from my glass.

Do you ever try to read your own face? I do, and I can tell you it is not a bad study, and gives you more trouble than you can well fancy if you have never tried it.

He says that I afford him a curious psychological study, and I humbly think I do. I do not, as you know, take sufficient interest in dress to be able to describe the new fashions. Dress is a bore. That is slang again, but never mind. Arthur says that every day.

There, it is all out, Mina, we have told all our secrets to each other since we were children. We have slept together and eaten together, and laughed and cried together, and now, though I have spoken, I would like to speak more. Oh, Mina, couldn't you guess? I love him. I am blushing as I write, for although I think he loves me, he has not told me so in words. That is not love at all—no, nor the least like it. Love is a holy thing. We used to be ashamed of those things then—as we well might be. I glory in my love now. But, oh, Mina, I love him. I love him! There, that does me good.

I wish I were with you, dear, sitting by the fire undressing, as we used to sit, and I would try to tell you what I feel. I do not know how I am writing this even to you. I am afraid to stop, or I should tear up the letter, and I don't want to stop, for I do so want to tell you all. I wish you knew the man—he is so noble and brave and tender and true. How the girls would laugh in school if they saw this letter. I must stop. I feel so happy that I could go on writing for ever—telling you my secret is just like telling Arthur that I love him, only of course not quite the same. Mina, if a time should come when,—after he had told me that he loved me, of course—I should be able to whisper to him, "Arthur, I love you!" Let me hear from you at once, and tell me all that you think about it. Mina, pray for my happiness.

Lucy

P.S.—I need not tell you this is a secret. Goodnight again. L.

Letter, Lucy Westenra to Mina Murray

24 May

My dearest Mina,

Thanks, and thanks, and thanks again for your sweet letter. It was so nice to be able to tell you and to have your sympathy.

My dear, it never rains but it pours. How true the old proverbs are. Here am I, who shall be twenty in September, and yet I never had a proposal till today, not a real proposal, and today I had three. Just fancy! Three proposals in one day! Isn't it awful! I feel sorry, really and truly sorry, for two of the poor fellows. Oh, Mina, I am so happy that I don't know what to do with myself. And three proposals! But, for goodness' sake, don't tell any of the girls, or they would be getting all sorts of extravagant ideas, and imagining themselves injured and slighted if in their very first day at home they did not get six at least. Some girls are so vain! You and I, Mina dear, who are engaged and are going to settle down soon soberly into old married women, can despise vanity. Well, I must tell you about the three, but you must keep it a secret, dear, from every one except, of course, Jonathan. You will tell him, because I would, if I were in your place, certainly tell Arthur. A woman ought to tell her husband everything. Don't you think so, dear? And I must be fair. Men like women, certainly their wives, to be quite as fair as they are. And women, I am afraid, are not always quite as fair as they should be.

Well, my dear, number One came to me just before lunch; or rather, I came to him, as Mother and I were visiting Purfleet at his invitation. I told you of him, Dr. John Seward, the lunatic asylum man, with the strong jaw and the good forehead. He showed us all through his large house, which also served as his place of work, and introduced us to a few of the more hospitable patients. One in particular struck me as a rather gentlemanly fellow—Mr. Renfield, I believe the doctor said his name was. Indeed, at the time I was introduced to him he appeared quite sane, so far as my limited experience could tell, and even he ventured with me into a brief discussion on theology, in which I remember distinctly him saying "My dear Miss Westenra, you must always be vigilant, for the day of the Lord shall come upon you like a thief in the night. Whosoever eats of His flesh and drinks of His blood shall not perish, but have everlasting life." Then, even as we were talking, a small fly passed between us, and he, not even breaking off from our discussion, grabbed it out of the air and popped it in his mouth and swallowed it between sentences. Before that moment, I would have questioned why he was even locked up here in such a place, so you can see what a poor judge of sanity I am!

Afterward, Dr. Seward took us on a tour of the grounds, which was surrounded by a high wall. At one spot along the way I was able to take a peek over the wall, and beheld a marvelous old mansion. He said that, until just recently, it had been vacant, with a sign posted at its door, but now the sign has been taken down as if the property has been sold, though he has seen no one yet come to take possession of it. He found it all to be something of a mystery, but seeing my interest, he promised to do his best to get permission from its new owner—should he ever encounter him—to allow me to see the inside of the house for myself[80].

There was a moment, just before lunch was served, when we had a few moments away from Mother (I found out later that he had beforehand asked her permission to propose, and she knew all along why Dr. Seward had asked us to the asylum today, and so had purposefully given us a moment alone). He was very cool outwardly, but was nervous all the same. He had evidently been schooling himself as to all sorts of little things, and remembered them, and when he wanted to appear at ease he kept playing with a lancet in a way that made me nearly scream. He spoke to me, Mina, very straightforwardly. He told me how dear I was to him, though he had known me so little, and what his life would be with me to help and cheer him. He was going to tell me how unhappy he would be if I did not care for him, but when he saw me cry he said he was a brute and would not add to my present trouble. Then he broke off and asked if I could love him in time, and when I shook my head his hands trembled, and then with some hesitation he asked me if I cared already for any one else. He put it very nicely, saying that he did not want to wring my confidence from me, but only to know, because if a woman's heart was free a man might have hope. And then, Mina, I felt a sort of duty to tell him that there was some one. I found myself almost wishing that there was not some one else, for there is something in my heart which is pulled in his direction; if there had not been another, I would have accepted his proposal on the spot.[81] But I only told him that there was indeed another, and then he stood up, and he looked very strong and very grave as he took both my hands in his and said he hoped I would be happy, and that If I ever wanted a friend I must count him one of my best and truest who would do for me anything that a man might do. How either of us managed to make it through lunch I cannot say . . .

Oh, Mina dear, I can't help crying, and you must excuse this letter being all blotted. Being proposed to is all very nice and all that sort of thing, but it isn't at all a happy thing when you have to see a poor fellow, whom you know loves you honestly, going away and looking all broken hearted, and to know that, no matter what he may say at the moment, you are passing out of his life. My dear, I must stop here at present, I feel so miserable, though I am so happy.

Evening.

Arthur has just gone, and I feel in better spirits than when I left off, so I can go on telling you about the day.

Well, my dear, number Two came after I returned home from lunch. He is such a nice fellow, an American from Texas, and he looks so young and so fresh that it seems almost impossible that he has been to so many places and has such adventures. I sympathize with poor Desdemona when she had such a stream poured in her ear, even by a black man. I suppose that we women are such cowards that we think a man will save us from fears, and we marry him. I know now what I would do if I were a man and wanted to make a girl love me. No, I don't, for there was Mr. Morris telling us his stories, and Arthur never told any, and yet . . .

My dear, I am somewhat previous. Mr. Quincy P. Morris found me alone. It seems that a man always does find a girl alone. No, he doesn't, for Arthur tried twice to make a chance, and I helping him all I could, I am not ashamed to say it now. I must tell you beforehand that Mr. Morris doesn't always speak slang, that is to say, he never does so to strangers or before them, for he is really well educated and has exquisite manners, but he found out that it amused me to hear him talk American slang, and whenever I was present, and there was no one to be shocked, he said such funny things. I am afraid, my dear, he has to invent it all, for it fits exactly into whatever else he has to say. But this is a way slang has. I do not know myself if I shall ever speak slang. I do not know if Arthur likes it, as I have never heard him use any as yet.

Well, Mr. Morris sat down beside me and looked as happy and jolly as he could, but I could see all the same that he was very nervous. He took my hand in his, and said ever so sweetly . . .

"Miss Lucy, I know I ain't good enough to regulate the fixin's of your little shoes, but I guess if you wait till you find a man that is you will go join them seven young women with the lamps when you quit. Won't you just hitch up alongside of me and let us go down the long road together, driving in double harness?"

Well, he did look so good humoured and so jolly that it didn't seem half so hard to refuse him as it did poor Dr. Seward. So I said, as lightly as I could, that I did not know anything of hitching, and that I wasn't broken to harness at all yet. Then he said that he had spoken in a light manner, and he hoped that if he had made a mistake in doing so on so grave, so momentous, an occasion for him, I would forgive him. He really did look serious when he was saying it, and I couldn't help feeling a sort of exultation that he was number Two in one day. And then, my dear, before I could say a word he began pouring out a perfect torrent of love-making, laying his very heart and soul at my feet. He looked so earnest over it that I shall never again think that a man must be playful always, and never earnest, because he is merry at times. I suppose he saw something in my face which checked him, for he suddenly stopped, and said with a sort of manly fervour that I could have loved him for if I had been free . . .

"Lucy, you are an honest hearted girl, I know. I should not be here speaking to you as I am now if I did not believe you clean grit, right through to the very depths of your soul. Tell me, like one good fellow to another, is there any one else that you care for? And if there is I'll never trouble you a hair's breadth again, but will be, if you will let me, a very faithful friend."

My dear Mina, why are men so noble when we women are so little worthy of them? Here was I almost making fun of this great hearted, true gentleman. I burst into tears, I am afraid, my dear, you will think this a very sloppy letter in more ways than one, and I really felt very badly.

Why can't they let a girl marry three men, or as many as want her, and save all this trouble? But this is heresy, and I must not say it. I am glad to say that, though I was crying, I was able to look into Mr. Morris' brave eyes, and I told him out straight . . .

"Yes, there is some one I love, though he has not told me yet that he even loves me." I was right to speak to him so frankly, for quite a light came into his face, and he put out both his hands and took mine, I think I put them into his, and said in a hearty way . . .

"That's my brave girl. It's better worth being late for a chance of winning you than being in time for any other girl in the world. Don't cry, my dear. If it's for me, I'm a hard nut to crack, and I take it standing up. If that other fellow doesn't know his happiness, well, he'd better look for it soon, or he'll have to deal with me. Little girl, your honesty and pluck have made me a friend, and that's rarer than a lover, it's more selfish anyhow. My dear, I'm going to have a pretty lonely walk between this and Kingdom Come. Won't you give me one kiss? It'll be something to keep off the darkness now and then. You can, you know, if you like, for that other good fellow, or you could not love him, hasn't spoken yet."

That quite won me, Mina, for it was brave and sweet of him, and noble too, to a rival, wasn't it? And he so sad, so I leant over and kissed him.

He stood up with my two hands in his, and as he looked down into my face, I am afraid I was blushing very much, he said, "In my part of the world, when one man takes another's hand and calls him friend, he'll die for him if need be. Little girl, I hold your hand, and you've kissed me on the mouth. I call you pard and by the Almighty if ever need be I'll die for you and yours. Thank you for your sweet honesty to me, and goodbye."

He wrung my hand, and taking up his hat, went straight out of the room without looking back, without a tear or a quiver or a pause, and I am crying like a baby.

Oh, why must a man like that be made unhappy when there are lots of girls about who would worship the very ground he trod on? I know I would if I were free, only I don't want to be free. My dear, this quite upset me, and I feel I cannot write of happiness just at once, after telling you of it, and I don't wish to tell of the number Three until it can be all happy. Ever your loving . . .

Lucy

P.S.—Oh, about number Three, I needn't tell you of number Three, need I? Besides, it was all so confused. It seemed only a moment from his coming into the room till both his arms were round me, and he was kissing me. I am very, very happy, and I don't know what I have done to deserve it. I must only try in the future to show that I am not ungrateful to God for all His goodness to me in sending to me such a lover, such a husband, and such a friend.

Goodbye.

Dr. Seward's Case-Book

(Kept in phonograph)

25 May—Ebb tide in appetite today. Cannot eat, cannot rest, so diary instead. Since my rebuff of yesterday I have a sort of empty feeling. Nothing in the world seems of sufficient importance to be worth the doing. As I knew that the only cure for this sort of thing was work, I went amongst the patients. I picked out one who has since afforded me a study of much interest. He was the one that Lucy had found to be so fascinating, and is so quaint that I am determined to understand him as well as I can. Today I seemed to get nearer than ever before to the heart of his mystery.

I questioned him more fully than I had ever done, with a view to making myself master of the facts of his hallucination. In my manner of doing it there was, I now see, something of cruelty. I seemed to wish to keep him to the point of his madness, a thing which I avoid with the patients as I would the mouth of hell.

(Mem., Under what circumstances would I not avoid the pit of hell?) *Omnia Romae venalia sunt.* Hell has its price! If there be anything behind this instinct it will be valuable to trace it afterwards accurately, so I had better commence to do so, therefore . . .

R.M. Renfield[82], age 59. Former solicitor, brought to us on 30 June. Sanguine temperament, great physical strength, morbidly excitable, periods of gloom, ending in some fixed idea which I cannot make out. I presume that the sanguine temperament itself and the disturbing influence end in a mentally-accomplished finish, a possibly dangerous man, probably dangerous if unselfish. In selfish men caution is as secure an armour for their foes as for themselves. What I think of on this point is, when self is the fixed point the centripetal force is balanced with the centrifugal. When duty, a cause, etc., is the fixed point, the latter force is paramount, and only accident or a series of accidents can balance it.

Letter, Quincey P. Morris to Hon. Arthur Holmwood

25 May.

My dear Art,

We've told yarns by the campfire in the prairies, and dressed one another's wounds after trying a landing at the Marquesas, and drunk healths on the shore of Titicaca. There are more yarns to be told, and other wounds to be healed, and another health to be drunk. Won't you let this be at my campfire tomorrow night? I have no hesitation in asking you, as I know a certain lady is engaged to a certain dinner party, and that you are free. There will only be one other, our old pal at the Korea, Jack Seward. He's coming, too, and we both want to mingle our weeps over the wine cup, and to drink a health with all our hearts to the happiest man in all the wide world, who has won the noblest heart that God has made and best worth winning. We promise you a hearty welcome, and a loving greeting, and a health as true as your own right hand. We shall both swear to leave you at home if you drink too deep to a certain pair of eyes. Come!

Yours, as ever and always,
Quincey P. Morris

Telegram from Arthur Holmwood to Quincey P. Morris

26 May

Count me in every time. I bear messages which will make both your ears tingle.

—Art

CHAPTER NINE[83]

Mina Murray's Journal

24 July. Whitby—Lucy met me at the station, looking sweeter and lovelier than ever, and we drove up to the house at the Crescent in which they have rooms. This is a lovely place, and I am so very happy that Mr. Holmwood suggested it to Lucy.

The little river, the Esk, runs through a deep valley, which broadens out as it comes near the harbour. A great viaduct runs across, with high piers, through which the view seems somehow further away than it really is. The valley is beautifully green, and it is so steep that when you are on the high land on either side you look right across it, unless you are near enough to see down. The houses of the old town—the side away from us, are all red-roofed, and seem piled up one over the other anyhow, like the pictures we see of Nuremberg. Right over the town is the ruin of Whitby Abbey, which was sacked by the Danes, and which is the scene of part of "Marmion," where the girl was built up in the wall. It is a most noble ruin, of immense size, and full of beautiful and romantic bits. There is a legend that a white lady is seen in one of the windows. Between it and the town there is another church, the parish one, round which is a big graveyard, all full of tombstones. This is to my mind the nicest spot in Whitby, for it lies right over the town, and has a full view of the harbour and all up the bay to where the headland called Kettleness stretches out into the sea. It descends so steeply over the harbour that part of the bank has fallen away, and some of the graves have been destroyed.

In one place part of the stonework of the graves stretches out over the sandy pathway far below. There are walks, with seats beside them, through the churchyard, and people go and sit there all day long looking at the beautiful view and enjoying the breeze.

I shall come and sit here often myself and work. Indeed, I am writing now, with my book on my knee, and listening to the talk of three old men who are sitting beside me. They seem to do nothing all day but sit here and talk.

The harbour lies below me, with, on the far side, one long granite wall stretching out into the sea, with a curve outwards at the end of it, in the middle of which is a lighthouse. A heavy seawall runs along outside of it. On the near side, the seawall makes an elbow crooked inversely, and its end too has a lighthouse. Between the two piers there is a narrow opening into the harbour, which then suddenly widens.

It is nice at high water, but when the tide is out it shoals away to nothing, and there is merely the stream of the Esk, running between banks of sand, with rocks here and there. Outside the harbour on this side there rises for about half a mile a great reef, the sharp edge of which runs straight out from behind the south lighthouse. At the end of it is a buoy with a bell, which swings in bad weather, and sends in a mournful sound on the wind.

They have a legend here that when a ship is lost bells are heard out at sea. I must ask the old man about this. He is coming this way . . .

He is a funny old man[84]. He must be awfully old, for his face is gnarled and twisted like the bark of a tree. He tells me that he is nearly a hundred, and that he was a sailor in the Greenland fishing fleet when Waterloo was fought. He is, I am afraid, a very sceptical person, for when I asked him about the bells at sea and the White Lady at the abbey he said very brusquely,

"I wouldn't fash masel' about them, miss. Them things be all wore out. Mind, I don't say that they never was, but I do say that they wasn't in my time. They be all very well for comers and trippers, an' the like, but not for a nice young lady like you. Them feet-folks from York and Leeds that be always eatin' cured herrin's and drinkin' tea an' lookin' out to buy cheap jet would creed aught. I wonder masel' who'd be bothered tellin' lies to them, even the newspapers, which is full of fool-talk."[85]

I thought he would be a good person to learn interesting things from, so I asked him if he would mind telling me something about the whale fishing in the old days. He was just settling himself to begin when the clock struck six, whereupon he laboured to get up, and said,

"I must gang ageeanwards home now, miss. My grand-daughter don't like to be kept waitin' when the tea is ready, for it takes me time to crammle aboon the grees, for there be a many of 'em, and miss, I lack belly-timber sairly by the clock."[86]

He hobbled away, and I could see him hurrying, as well as he could, down the steps. The steps are a great feature on the place. They lead from the town to the church, there are hundreds of them, I do not know how many, and they wind up in a delicate curve. The slope is so gentle that a horse could easily walk up and down them.

I think they must originally have had something to do with the abbey. I shall go home too. Lucy went out, visiting with her mother, and as they were only duty calls, I did not go.

Letter, from Katherine Reed to Mr. and Mrs. Reed

21 July

Dearest Mamma and Papa—

We arrived safely in Whitby after several delays, which were most exasperating! We nearly missed the train, owing to Francis having forgot some necessary colour or brush or something, which he believed he would never be able to get in such a small town. So we had to go back for it. Then the train, which did leave on time, was delayed *en route* because of cows on the line or some such nonsense. Why a cow would want to get out of a nice green field to stand on railway tracks is beyond me! But then they are just poor dumb creatures.

Grampapa Joseph—who Francis, amusingly, still insists on calling "Mr. Swales"—met us at the station[87]. Though he grumped about our tardiness, he was clearly pleased to see us. He wore, for the occasion, an amazing, ancient vest which he had dug up from who knows where. Walrus hide, I guess, or something equally Arctic, from one of the whalers he's been on. I shall ask him to tell me about it—no doubt he will eagerly oblige!

He had cleared a corner of the shed for Francis, as a makeshift studio. Francis was visibly moved—after all, he hadn't even met him!—and declares that he does not mind sharing his working space with spars and ropes and all Grampapa's other flotsam. Francis hopes, anyway, to work mostly out of doors. But it was very sweet of Grampapa, and the shed will be so useful to Francis if it should rain.

Your affectionate daughter
Kate

Francis Aytown's Sketch Diary

21 July—We have arrived in Whitby. Kate is quite right: it is a veritable Paradise. The clear light, the foaming waves, the dramatic sweep of the cliffs—all conspire to captivate the senses. The pure fresh air, carrying the wild scent of the sea, invigorates both mind and spirit. And the light—the light! I cannot say enough about it. One would have to be a poor artist indeed to paint badly in so lovely a place.

Though I would gladly succumb wholly to the beauty of Nature, She does not buy paintings. Buyers are often more interested in depictions of human pursuits, so I turned reluctantly to the town itself—and was pleasantly surprised. That other great Power, Man—who so often desecrates what Nature has wrought—has here succeeded, over the centuries, in building a charming seaside town. Many of the buildings are quite old and interesting. Of particular note are the imposing church—its ancient graveyard—and the ruined abbey, mysterious and dark, with its empty windows. Together with the quays, the fishing fleet, and the quaint Whitby natives (of whom our host is one!), there is every source of inspiration here for the willing artist.

Thanks to the proceeds from my last portrait, the French easel is loaded with an assortment of Winsor & Newton's finest paints and brushes, and I have for myself a new leather painter's apron. The large canvases which I had sent ahead have arrived in excellent condition. It pleases me to be able to afford such good materials; nothing should impede the *rapport* between the painter and his subject.

All that remains is to prepare myself. Tomorrow I shall spend the day in opening myself, as it were, to the spirit of the place, its *ambiance*—in roaming it from sunrise to sunset, and allowing it to infuse my sensibilities. My Muse has been quite absent of late, and I must find a way to reconnect with it. To that end, I must now to bed . . .

22 July—As planned, by dawn I was high up on the East Cliff, looking eastward out over the sea. Sunrise was a symphony of delicate colour. In the clear air, a few gulls wheeled and called: a sublime vista, if ever one there were. I spent over an hour there, observing the changing play of light and colour, till all that remained was a brilliant blue mirrored softly and greyly in the waves. Then, recalling my happy mission, I moved on to other, more southerly prospects. Some walkers were now about, enjoying the early morning air and the beautiful view; we nodded to each other in passing.

A number of painters had set up in various places between the Abbey and Robin Hood's Bay. I chose not to reveal myself as one of them, but studied their work briefly, with an air of careless affectation, as any casual onlooker might. Though a few appear to be truly gifted artists, many were lacking: their technique was unsubtle, sometimes even crude. "Impressionistic" brushwork is more often messy than impressive.

The lunch Kate had packed allowed me to spend the day rambling the coast. I made quick sketches of some particularly favorable sites, in the hope of recognizing and revisiting them at a later time. But mostly I immersed myself in the beauty of the sky and the sea. It was not till late afternoon that I returned to town.

Descending the steps from the church and the Abbey, I noted the view of the quays along the upper harbour, the colourful hues of fishing vessels with their nets outspread. It will make a fine midday painting, requiring strong light. Though tempted to detour, I left the investigation of the quays for another day; there can be no better guide to them than Mr. Swales.

Letter, Kate to Mr. and Mrs. Reed

28 July

Dearest Mamma and Papa—

You will never guess who we have run into! Mina Murray and Lucy Westenra are here on holiday, and they have already met Grampapa! He was somewhat chagrined to learn that the "pretty young lasses," who have listened so avidly to his lurid tales, are actually our friends. They are coming to tea the day after tomorrow. Mrs. Westenra is here too, and may join us.

The postman is coming, so I will close for now. A hundred kisses to you both, from—

Your affectionate daughter,
Kate

Mina Murray's Journal

28 July—Lucy and I had an afternoon tea with Kate, who is here on holiday visiting her grandfather. Mrs. Westenra had intended to join us, but was simply not feeling up to the task.

Kate was, of course, very eager to hear more about our fiancés Jonathan and Arthur, and I have no doubt that everyone at the school shall soon hear everything we've said of them (and, I daresay, some things we never said at all!).

She, in turn, introduced us to Francis Aytown, a young man whom she has often spoken of but that we until now never had the opportunity to meet. He is an artist—and a rather talented one at that, by the looks of his sketches—who has been a playmate to Kate since they were children, much as Lucy and I have been. He is rather an eccentric fellow, if one can judge by his length of hair and choice of clothing. They are quite happy and friendly with one another, and at first I took them to be at the very least engaged, but was shocked to discover he had yet to propose. I must say that the affection they demonstrate toward one another, especially in public, was less than proper. But such forward behavior is, no doubt, yet another aspect of the "New Woman" philosophy that Kate has embraced. Having spent a good deal of time teaching etiquette and decorum to Kate, I could not help but feel a twinge of disappointment in her behavior. Still, we were not in school, and Lucy seemed relatively unconcerned, so I held my tongue until the topic of conversation had moved past their relationship.

It was then we learned some surprising and pleasant news, for as it turns out, the old man we met just a few days earlier—Mr. Swales, is his name—is Kate's grandfather! Her face reddened somewhat to hear of our encounters with him (odd, that this should cause her to blush, whereas her relationship to Francis does not!).

After tea, we took a stroll through the tombstones. Kate pointed out two epitaphs of interest. The first was that of a James Reed, who was "Drowned in Liverpool, 7/1/1859, aet. 23." The second read "Ann Swales, 6th February 1795, aet. 100."[88] James was her grandfather, while Ann—from her mother's side—was Mr. Swales' own grandmother. She says that many of those buried here Mr. Swales knew personally. Perhaps he will tell us of them next time we meet.

1 August—I came up here an hour ago with Lucy, and we had a most interesting talk with my old friend and the two others who always come and join him. He is evidently the Sir Oracle of them, and I should think must have been in his time a most dictatorial person.

He will not admit anything, and down faces everybody. If he can't out-argue them he bullies them, and then takes their silence for agreement with his views.

Lucy was looking sweetly pretty in her white lawn frock. She has got a beautiful colour since she has been here.

I noticed that the old men did not lose any time in coming and sitting near her when we sat down. She is so sweet with old people, I think they all fell in love with her on the spot. Even my old man succumbed and did not contradict her, but gave me double share instead. I got him on the subject of the legends, and he went off at once into a sort of sermon. I must try to remember it and put it down.

"It be all fool-talk, lock, stock, and barrel, that's what it be and nowt else. These bans an' wafts an' boh-ghosts an' bar-guests an' bogles an' all anent them is only fit to set bairns an' dizzy women a'belderin.' They be nowt but air-blebs. They, an' all grims an' signs an' warnin's, be all invented by parsons an' illsome berk-bodies an' railway touters to skeer an' scunner hafflin's, an' to get folks to do somethin' that they don't other incline to. It makes me ireful to think o' them. Why, it's them that, not content with printin' lies on paper an' preachin' them out of pulpits, does want to be cuttin' them on the tombstones. Look here all around you in what airt ye will. All them steans, holdin' up their heads as well as they can out of their pride, is acant, simply tumblin' down with the weight o' the lies wrote on them, 'Here lies the body' or 'Sacred to the memory' wrote on all of them, an' yet in nigh half of them there bean't no bodies at all, an' the memories of them bean't cared a pinch of snuff about, much less sacred. Lies all of them, nothin' but lies of one kind or another! My gog, but it'll be a quare scowderment at the Day of Judgment when they come tumblin' up in their death-sarks, all jouped together an' trying' to drag their tombsteans with them to prove how good they was, some of them trimmlin' an' dithering, with their hands that dozzened an' slippery from lyin' in the sea that they can't even keep their gurp o' them."[89]

I could see from the old fellow's self-satisfied air and the way in which he looked round for the approval of his cronies that he was "showing off," so I put in a word to keep him going.

"Oh, Mr. Swales, you can't be serious. Surely these tombstones are not all wrong?"

"Yabblins! There may be a poorish few not wrong, savin' where they make out the people too good, for there be folk that do think a balm-bowl be like the sea, if only it be their own. The whole thing be only lies. Now look you here. You come here a stranger, an' you see this kirkgarth."

I nodded, for I thought it better to assent, though I did not quite understand his dialect. I knew it had something to do with the church.

He went on, "And you consate that all these steans be aboon folk that be haped here, snod an' snog?" I assented again. "Then that be just where the lie comes in. Why, there be scores of these laybeds that be toom as old Dun's 'baccabox on Friday night."

He nudged one of his companions, and they all laughed. "And, my gog! How could they be otherwise? Look at that one, the aftest abaft the bier-bank, read it!"[90]

I went over and read, "Edward Spencelagh, master mariner, murdered by pirates off the coast of Andres, April, 1854, age 30." When I came back Mr. Swales went on,

"Who brought him home, I wonder, to hap him here? Murdered off the coast of Andres! An' you consated his body lay under! Why, I could name ye a dozen whose bones lie in the Greenland seas above," he pointed northwards, "or where the currants may have drifted them. There be the steans around ye. Ye can, with your young eyes, read the small print of the lies from here. This Braithwaite Lowery, I knew his father, lost in the Lively off Greenland in '20, or Andrew Woodhouse, drowned in the same seas in 1777, or John Paxton, drowned off Cape Farewell a year later, or old John Rawlings, whose grandfather sailed with me, drowned in the Gulf of Finland in '50. Do ye think that all these men will have to make a rush to Whitby when the trumpet sounds? I have me antherums aboot it! I tell ye that when they got here they'd be jommlin' and jostlin' one another that way that it 'ud be like a fight up on the ice in the old days, when we'd be at one another from daylight to dark, an' tryin' to tie up our cuts by the aurora borealis."[91] This was evidently local pleasantry, for the old man cackled over it, and his cronies joined in with gusto.

"But," I said, "surely you are not quite correct, for you start on the assumption that all the poor people, or their spirits, will have to take their tombstones with them on the Day of Judgment. Do you think that will be really necessary?"

"Well, what else be they tombstones for? Answer me that, miss!"

"To please their relatives, I suppose."

"To please their relatives, you suppose!" This he said with intense scorn. "How will it pleasure their relatives to know that lies is wrote over them, and that everybody in the place knows that they be lies?"

He pointed to a stone at our feet which had been laid down as a slab, on which the seat was rested, close to the edge of the cliff. "Read the lies on that stone," he said.

The letters were upside down to me from where I sat, but Lucy was more opposite to them, so she leant over and read, "Sacred to the memory of George Canon, who died, in the hope of a glorious resurrection, on July 29, 1873, falling from the rocks at Kettleness. This tomb was erected by his sorrowing mother to her dearly beloved son. 'He was the only son of his mother, and she was a widow.' Really, Mr. Swales, I don't see anything very funny in that!" She spoke her comment very gravely and somewhat severely.

"Ye don't see aught funny! Ha-ha! But that's because ye don't gawm the sorrowin' mother was a hell-cat that hated him because he was acrewk'd, a regular lamiter he was, an' he hated her so that he committed suicide in order that she mightn't get an insurance she put on his life. He blew nigh the top of his head off with an old musket that they had for scarin' crows with. 'twarn't for crows then, for it brought the clegs and the dowps to him. That's the way he fell off the rocks. And, as to hopes of a glorious resurrection, I've often heard him say masel' that he hoped he'd go to hell, for his mother was so pious that she'd be sure to go to heaven, an' he didn't want to addle where she was. Now isn't that stean at any rate," he hammered it with his stick as he spoke, "a pack of lies? And won't it make Gabriel keckle when Geordie comes pantin' ut the grees with the tompstean balanced on his hump, and asks to be took as evidence!"[92]

I did not know what to say, but Lucy turned the conversation as she said, rising up, "Oh, why did you tell us of this? It is my favourite seat, and I cannot leave it, and now I find I must go on sitting over the grave of a suicide."

"That won't harm ye, my pretty, an' it may make poor Geordie gladsome to have so trim a lass sittin' on his lap. That won't hurt ye. Why, I've sat here off an' on for nigh twenty years past, an' it hasn't done me no harm. Don't ye fash about them as lies under ye, or that doesn' lie there either! It'll be time for ye to be getting scart when ye see the tombsteans all run away with, and the place as bare as a stubble-field. There's the clock, and 'I must gang. My service to ye, ladies!"[93] And off he hobbled.

Lucy and I sat awhile, and it was all so beautiful before us that we took hands as we sat, and she told me all over again about Arthur and their coming marriage. That made me just a little heart-sick, for I haven't heard from Jonathan for a whole month.

The same day. I came up here alone, for I am very sad. There was no letter for me. I hope there cannot be anything the matter with Jonathan. The clock has just struck nine. I see the lights scattered all over the town, sometimes in rows where the streets are, and sometimes singly. They run right up the Esk and die away in the curve of the valley. To my left the view is cut off by a black line of roof of the old house next to the abbey. The sheep and lambs are bleating in the fields away behind me, and there is a clatter of donkeys' hoofs up the paved road below. The band on the pier is playing a harsh waltz in good time, and further along the quay there is a Salvation Army meeting in a back street. Neither of the bands hears the other, but up here I hear and see them both. I wonder where Jonathan is and if he is thinking of me! I wish he were here.

Francis Aytown's Sketch Journal

28 July—At teatime, met some friends of Kate's, who happen also to be staying in Whitby. The one, Lucy, is hardly a person at all—too flighty and dainty for my taste! The glories of life—freedom, romance, adventure—are impossible to share with such a woman, if not with most women. The other new arrival, Mina, might prove an exception. Though conservative, she has a good deal more character than most, and she'd make a good painting because of it. (*mem.*, must keep a hand in at portraits! I am in danger of being seduced altogether by the beauty and mystery of the natural world, and so must make it a point to sketch whichever passers-by strike my fancy, to keep up my skill.)

Dr. Seward's Case-Book

5 June—The case of Renfield grows more interesting the more I get to understand the man. He has certain qualities very largely developed, selfishness, secrecy, and purpose.

I wish I could get at what is the object of the latter. He seems to have some settled scheme of his own, but what it is I do not know. His redeeming quality is a love of animals, though, indeed, he has such curious turns in it that I sometimes imagine he is only abnormally cruel. His pets are of odd sorts.

Just now his hobby is catching flies. He has at present such a quantity that I have had myself to expostulate. To my astonishment, he did not break out into a fury, as I expected, but took the matter in simple seriousness. He thought for a moment, and then said, "May I have three days? I shall clear them away." Of course, I said that would do. I must watch him.

18 June—He has turned his mind now to spiders, and has got several very big fellows in a box. He keeps feeding them his flies, and the number of the latter is becoming sensibly diminished, although he has used half his food in attracting more flies from outside to his room.

1 July—His spiders are now becoming as great a nuisance as his flies, and today I told him that he must get rid of them.

He looked very sad at this, so I said that he must clear out some of them, at all events. He cheerfully acquiesced in this, and I gave him the same time as before for reduction.

He disgusted me much while with him, for when a horrid blowfly, bloated with some carrion food, buzzed into the room, he caught it, held it exultantly for a few moments between the finger and thumb of his left hand (using his left thumb nail, which he had grown exceptionally long[94], to pin the insect in place), and before I knew what he was going to do, put it in his mouth and ate it.

I scolded him for it, but he argued quietly that it was very good and very wholesome, that it was life, strong life, and gave life to him. This gave me an idea, or the rudiment of one. I must watch how he gets rid of his spiders.

He has evidently some deep problem in his mind, for he keeps a little notebook in which he is always jotting down something. whole pages of it are filled with masses of figures, generally single numbers added up in batches, and then the totals added in batches again, as though he were focussing some account, as the auditors put it.

8 July—There is a method in his madness, and the rudimentary idea in my mind is growing. It will be a whole idea soon, and then, oh, unconscious cerebration, you will have to give the wall to your conscious brother.

I kept away from my friend for a few days, so that I might notice if there were any change. Things remain as they were except that he has parted with some of his pets and got a new one.

He has managed to get a sparrow, and has already partially tamed it. His means of taming is simple, for already the spiders have diminished. Those that do remain, however, are well fed, for he still brings in the flies by tempting them with his food.

19 July—We are progressing. My friend has now a whole colony of sparrows, and his flies and spiders are almost obliterated. When I came in he ran to me and said he wanted to ask me a great favour, a very, very great favour. And as he spoke, he fawned on me like a dog.

I asked him what it was, and he said, with a sort of rapture in his voice and bearing, "A kitten, a nice, little, sleek playful kitten, that I can play with, and teach, and feed, and feed, and feed!"

I was not unprepared for this request, for I had noticed how his pets went on increasing in size and vivacity, but I did not care that his pretty family of tame sparrows should be wiped out in the same manner as the flies and spiders. So I said I would see about it, and asked him if he would not rather have a cat than a kitten.

His eagerness betrayed him as he answered, "Oh, yes, I would like a cat! I only asked for a kitten lest you should refuse me a cat. No one would refuse me a kitten, would they?"

I shook my head, and said that at present I feared it would not be possible, but that I would see about it. His face fell, and I could see a warning of danger in it, for there was a sudden fierce, sidelong look which meant killing. The man is an undeveloped homicidal maniac. I shall test him with his present craving and see how it will work out, then I shall know more.

10 pm—I have visited him again and found him sitting in a corner brooding. When I came in he threw himself on his knees before me and implored me to let him have a cat, that his salvation depended upon it.

I was firm, however, and told him that he could not have it, whereupon he went without a word, and sat down, gnawing his fingers, in the corner where I had found him. I shall see him in the morning early.

20 July—Visited Renfield very early, before attendant went his rounds. Found him up and humming a tune. He was spreading out his sugar, which he had saved, in the window, and was manifestly beginning his fly catching again, and beginning it cheerfully and with a good grace.

I looked around for his birds, and not seeing them, asked him where they were. He replied, without turning round, that they had all flown away. There were a few feathers about the room and on his pillow a drop of blood. I said nothing, but went and told the keeper to report to me if there were anything odd about him during the day.

11 am—The attendant has just been to see me to say that Renfield has been very sick and has disgorged a whole lot of feathers. "My belief is, doctor," he said, "that he has eaten his birds, and that he just took and ate them raw!"

11 pm—I gave Renfield a strong opiate tonight, enough to make even him sleep, and took away his pocketbook to look at it. The thought that has been buzzing about my brain lately is complete, and the theory proved.

My homicidal maniac is of a peculiar kind. I shall have to invent a new classification for him, and call him a zoophagous (life-eating) maniac. What he desires is to absorb as many lives as he can, and he has laid himself out to achieve it in a cumulative way. He gave many flies to one spider and many spiders to one bird, and then wanted a cat to eat the many birds. What would have been his later steps?

It would almost be worth while to complete the experiment. It might be done if there were only a sufficient cause. Men sneered at vivisection, and yet look at its results today! Why not advance science in its most difficult and vital aspect, the knowledge of the brain?

Had I even the secret of one such mind, did I hold the key to the fancy of even one lunatic, I might advance my own branch of science to a pitch compared with which Burdon-Sanderson's physiology or Ferrier's brain knowledge would be as nothing. If only there were a sufficient cause! I must not think too much of this, or I may be tempted. A good cause might turn the scale with me, for may not I too be of an exceptional brain, congenitally?

How well the man reasoned. Lunatics always do within their own scope, but with the simplicity of lunacy he valued all lives the same. His note book proves it. One fly is a life and the total of its lives goes into one spider's, but he only adds one for the spider when the total passes into the bird and the bird in turn counted only one when it passed into him. I wonder at how many lives he values a man, or if at only one. He has closed the account most accurately, and today begun a new record. How many of us begin a new record with each day of our lives?

To me it seems only yesterday that my whole life ended with my new hope, and that truly I began a new record. So it shall be until the Great Recorder sums me up and closes my ledger account with a balance to profit or loss.

Oh, Lucy, Lucy, I cannot be angry with you, nor can I be angry with my friend whose happiness is yours, but I must only wait on hopeless and work. Work! Work!

If I could have as strong a cause as my poor mad friend there, a good, unselfish cause to make me work, that would be indeed happiness.

Mina Murray's Journal

26 July—I am anxious, and it soothes me to express myself here. It is like whispering to one's self and listening at the same time. And there is also something about the shorthand symbols that makes it different from writing. I am unhappy about Lucy and about Jonathan. I had not heard from Jonathan for some time, and was very concerned, but yesterday dear Mr. Hawkins, who is always so kind, sent me a letter from him. I had written asking him if he had heard, and he said the enclosed had just been received. It is only a line dated from Castle Dracula, and says that he is just starting for home. That is not like Jonathan. I do not understand it, and it makes me uneasy.

Lucy is to be married in the autumn, and she is already planning out her dresses and how her house is to be arranged. I sympathise with her, for I do the same, only Jonathan and I will start in life in a very simple way, and shall have to try to make both ends meet.

Mr. Holmwood, he is the Hon. Arthur Holmwood, only son of Lord Godalming, is coming up here very shortly, as soon as he can leave town, for his father is not very well, and I think dear Lucy is counting the moments till he comes.

She wants to take him up in the seat on the churchyard cliff and show him the beauty of Whitby. I daresay it is the waiting which disturbs her. She will be all right when he arrives.

27 July—No news from Jonathan. I am getting quite uneasy about him, though why I should I do not know, but I do wish that he would write, if it were only a single line.

Thank God, Lucy's health keeps up. Mr. Holmwood has been suddenly called to Ring to see his father, who has been taken seriously ill. Lucy frets at the postponement of seeing him, but it does not touch her looks. She is a trifle stouter, and her cheeks are a lovely rose-pink. She has lost the anemic look which she had. I pray it will all last.

3 August—Another week gone by, and no news from Jonathan, not even to Mr. Hawkins, whom I have heard. Oh, I do hope he is not ill. He surely would have written. I look at that last letter of his, but somehow it does not satisfy me. It does not read like him, and yet it is his writing. There is no mistake of that.

Francis Aytown's Sketch Journal

5 August—Rain this morning. As I had already done everything needful in my *ersatz* studio, Kate & I made our way to the famous Whitby Museum, to see its curiosities. Of course we have seen natural curiosities in London, but not in such profusion—and this is the very place of their excavation. Giant snails, the skeletons of strange fishes—and most imposing of all, great toothed, winged beasts, the remains of which were found below the town. It is thrilling to think of this place as it once was—bare of human life, with the great soaring creatures as the lords of the coast.

The local people, in their backward way, have colourful explanations for it all; so that curved, claw-like ancient mussels can be nothing other than the Devil's toenails, and the great winged beasts are the remains of ancient dragons. Strange, though, that these same rustic folk can produce such accomplished artisans. There are here masterful carvers of jet—the black funerary stone. Kate has bought an exquisitely detailed, flowered comb, worked from such smooth black stone.

All my pieces thus far are good, but not great. I must find something or someone to inspire better work. But the arrival of one's Muse cannot be rushed, I know, and so I must be patient.

Mina Murray's Journal

6 August—Another three days, and no news. This suspense is getting dreadful. If I only knew where to write to or where to go to, I should feel easier. But no one has heard a word of Jonathan since that last letter. I must only pray to God for patience.

Lucy is more excitable than ever, but is otherwise well. Last night was very threatening, and the fishermen say that we are in for a storm. I must try to watch it and learn the weather signs.

Today is a gray day, and the sun as I write is hidden in thick clouds, high over Kettleness. Everything is gray except the green grass, which seems like emerald amongst it, gray earthy rock, gray clouds, tinged with the sunburst at the far edge, hang over the gray sea, into which the sandpoints stretch like gray figures. The sea is tumbling in over the shallows and the sandy flats with a roar, muffled in the sea-mists drifting inland. The horizon is lost in a gray mist. All vastness, the clouds are piled up like giant rocks, and there is a 'brool' over the sea that sounds like some passage of doom.

I wonder that Kate's companion is painting on such a day, but he seemed quite cheerful, in his usual spot. "Extraordinary atmosphere," he said, and I could not but agree, though for different reasons. I suppose there *is* much to be seen, though I find it oppressive, not beautiful.

Dark figures are on the beach here and there, sometimes half shrouded in the mist, and seem 'men like trees walking.' The fishing boats are racing for home, and rise and dip in the ground swell as they sweep into the harbour, bending to the scuppers. Here comes old Mr. Swales. He is making straight for me, and I can see, by the way he lifts his hat, that he wants to talk.

I have been quite touched by the change in the poor old man. When he sat down beside me, he said in a very gentle way, "I want to say something to you, miss."

I could see he was not at ease, so I took his poor old wrinkled hand in mine and asked him to speak fully.

So he said, leaving his hand in mine, "I'm afraid, my deary, that I must have shocked you by all the wicked things I've been sayin' about the dead, and such like, for weeks past, but I didn't mean them, and I want ye to remember that when I'm gone. We aud folks that be daffled, and with one foot abaft the krok-hooal, don't altogether like to think of it, and we don't want to feel scart of it, and that's why I've took to makin' light of it, so that I'd cheer up my own heart a bit. But, Lord love ye, miss, I ain't afraid of dyin', not a bit, only I don't want to die if I can help it. My time must be nigh at hand now, for I be aud, and a hundred years is too much for any man to expect. And I'm so nigh it that the Aud Man is already whettin' his scythe. Ye see, I can't get out o' the habit of caffin' about it all at once. The chafts will wag as they be used to. Some day soon the Angel of Death will sound his trumpet for me. But don't ye dooal an' greet, my deary!"—for he saw that I was crying—"if he should come this very night I'd not refuse to answer his call. For life be, after all, only a waitin' for somethin' else than what we're doin,' and death be all that we can rightly depend on. But I'm content, for it's comin' to me, my deary, and comin' quick. It may be comin' while we be lookin' and wonderin.' Maybe it's in that wind out over the sea that's bringin' with it loss and wreck, and sore distress, and sad hearts. Look! Look!" he cried suddenly. "There's something in that wind and in the hoast beyont that sounds, and looks, and tastes, and smells like death. It's in the air. I feel it comin.' Lord, make me answer cheerful, when my call comes!"[95] He held up his arms devoutly, and raised his hat. His mouth moved as though he were praying. After a few minutes' silence, he got up, shook hands with me, and blessed me, and said goodbye, and hobbled off. It all touched me, and upset me very much.

I was glad when the coastguard came along, with his spyglass under his arm. He stopped to talk with me, as he always does, but all the time kept looking at a strange ship.

"I can't make her out," he said. "She's a Russian, by the look of her. But she's knocking about in the queerest way. She doesn't know her mind a bit. She seems to see the storm coming, but can't decide whether to run up north in the open, or to put in here. Look there again! She is steered mighty strangely, for she doesn't mind the hand on the wheel, changes about with every puff of wind. We'll hear more of her before this time tomorrow."

CHAPTER TEN[96]

Cutting from *The Dailygraph*, 8 August

(Pasted in Mina Murray's Journal)
From a correspondent.

Whitby[97]

One of the greatest and suddenest storms on record has just been experienced here, with results both strange and unique. The weather had been somewhat sultry, but not to any degree uncommon in the month of August. Saturday evening was as fine as was ever known, and the great body of holiday-makers laid out yesterday for visits to Mulgrave Woods, Robin Hood's Bay, Rig Mill, Runswick, Staithes, and the various trips in the neighborhood of Whitby. The steamers Emma and Scarborough made trips up and down the coast, and there was an unusual amount of 'tripping' both to and from Whitby. The day was unusually fine till the afternoon, when some of the gossips who frequent the East Cliff churchyard, and from the commanding eminence watch the wide sweep of sea visible to the north and east, called attention to a sudden show of 'mares tails' high in the sky to the northwest. The wind was then blowing from the south-west in the mild degree which in barometrical language is ranked 'No. 2, light breeze.'

The coastguard on duty at once made report, and one old fisherman, who for more than half a century has kept watch on weather signs from the East Cliff, foretold in an emphatic manner the coming of a sudden storm. The approach of sunset was so very beautiful, so grand in its masses of splendidly coloured clouds, that there was quite an assemblage on the walk along the cliff in the old churchyard to enjoy the beauty. Before the sun dipped below the black mass of Kettleness, standing boldly athwart the western sky, its downward way was marked by myriad clouds of every sunset colour, flame, purple, pink, green, violet, and all the tints of gold, with here and there masses not large, but of seemingly absolute blackness, in all sorts of shapes, as well outlined as colossal silhouettes. The experience was not lost on the painters, and doubtless some of the sketches of the 'Prelude to the Great Storm' will grace the R. A and R. I. walls in May next.

More than one captain made up his mind then and there that his 'cobble' or his 'mule,' as they term the different classes of boats, would remain in the harbour till the storm had passed. The wind fell away entirely during the evening, and at midnight there was a dead calm, a sultry heat, and that prevailing intensity which, on the approach of thunder, affects persons of a sensitive nature.

There were but few lights in sight at sea, for even the coasting steamers, which usually hug the shore so closely, kept well to seaward, and but few fishing boats were in sight. The only sail noticeable was a foreign schooner with all sails set, which was seemingly going westwards. The foolhardiness or ignorance of her officers was a prolific theme for comment whilst she remained in sight, and efforts were made to signal her to reduce sail in the face of her danger. Before the night shut down she was seen with sails idly flapping as she gently rolled on the undulating swell of the sea.

"As idle as a painted ship upon a painted ocean."

Shortly before ten o'clock the stillness of the air grew quite oppressive, and the silence was so marked that the bleating of a sheep inland or the barking of a dog in the town was distinctly heard, and the band on the pier, with its lively French air, was like a dischord in the great harmony of nature's silence. A little after midnight came a strange sound from over the sea, and high overhead the air began to carry a strange, faint, hollow booming.

Then without warning the tempest broke. With a rapidity which, at the time, seemed incredible, and even afterwards is impossible to realize, the whole aspect of nature at once became convulsed. The waves rose in growing fury, each over-topping its fellow, till in a very few minutes the lately glassy sea was like a roaring and devouring monster. White-crested waves beat madly on the level sands and rushed up the shelving cliffs. Others broke over the piers, and with their spume swept the lanthorns of the lighthouses which rise from the end of either pier of Whitby Harbour.

The wind roared like thunder, and blew with such force that it was with difficulty that even strong men kept their feet, or clung with grim clasp to the iron stanchions. It was found necessary to clear the entire pier from the mass of onlookers, or else the fatalities of the night would have increased manifold. To add to the difficulties and dangers of the time, masses of sea-fog came drifting inland. White, wet clouds, which swept by in ghostly fashion, so dank and damp and cold that it needed but little effort of imagination to think that the spirits of those lost at sea were touching their living brethren with the clammy hands of death, and many a one shuddered as the wreaths of sea-mist swept by.

At times the mist cleared, and the sea for some distance could be seen in the glare of the lightning, which came thick and fast, followed by such peals of thunder that the whole sky overhead seemed trembling under the shock of the footsteps of the storm.

Some of the scenes thus revealed were of immeasurable grandeur and of absorbing interest. The sea, running mountains high, threw skywards with each wave mighty masses of white foam, which the tempest seemed to snatch at and whirl away into space. Here and there a fishing boat, with a rag of sail, running madly for shelter before the blast, now and again the white wings of a storm-tossed seabird. On the summit of the East Cliff the new searchlight was ready for experiment, but had not yet been tried. The officers in charge of it got it into working order, and in the pauses of onrushing mist swept with it the surface of the sea. Once or twice its service was most effective, as when a fishing boat, with gunwale under water, rushed into the harbour, able, by the guidance of the sheltering light, to avoid the danger of dashing against the piers. As each boat achieved the safety of the port there was a shout of joy from the mass of people on the shore, a shout which for a moment seemed to cleave the gale and was then swept away in its rush.

Before long the searchlight discovered some distance away a schooner with all sails set, apparently the same vessel which had been noticed earlier in the evening. The wind had by this time backed to the east, and there was a shudder amongst the watchers on the cliff as they realised the terrible danger in which she now was.

Between her and the port lay the great flat reef on which so many good ships have from time to time suffered, and, with the wind blowing from its present quarter, it would be quite impossible that she should fetch the entrance of the harbour.

It was now nearly the hour of high tide, but the waves were so great that in their troughs the shallows of the shore were almost visible, and the schooner, with all sails set, was rushing with such speed that, in the words of one old salt, "she must fetch up somewhere, if it was only in hell." Then came another rush of sea-fog, greater than any hitherto, a mass of dank mist, which seemed to close on all things like a gray pall, and left available to men only the organ of hearing, for the roar of the tempest, and the crash of the thunder, and the booming of the mighty billows came through the damp oblivion even louder than before. The rays of the searchlight were kept fixed on the harbour mouth across the East Pier, where the shock was expected, and men waited breathless.

The wind suddenly shifted to the northeast, and the remnant of the sea fog melted in the blast. And then, *mirabile dictu*, between the piers, leaping from wave to wave as it rushed at headlong speed, swept the strange schooner before the blast, with all sail set, and gained the safety of the harbour. The searchlight followed her, and a shudder ran through all who saw her, for lashed to the helm was a corpse, with drooping head, which swung horribly to and fro at each motion of the ship. No other form could be seen on the deck at all.

A great awe came on all as they realised that the ship, as if by a miracle, had found the harbour, unsteered save by the hand of a dead man! However, all took place more quickly than it takes to write these words. The schooner paused not, but rushing across the harbour, pitched herself on that accumulation of sand and gravel washed by many tides and many storms into the southeast corner of the pier jutting under the East Cliff, known locally as Tate Hill Pier. The method of her arrival is thus graphically given in the words of one bystander—merely reduced into conventional phrase for the benefit of those to whom the Yorkshire dialect is not familiar: "She ran in as soft as a seal flappin' under an ice floe!"

There was of course a considerable concussion as the vessel drove up on the sand heap. Every spar, rope, and stay was strained, and some of the 'top-hammer' came crashing down. But, strangest of all, the very instant the shore was touched, an immense dog sprang up on deck from below, as if shot up by the concussion, and running forward, jumped from the bow on the sand.

Making straight for the steep cliff, where the churchyard hangs over the laneway to the East Pier so steeply that some of the flat tombstones, thruffsteans or through-stones, as they call them in Whitby vernacular, actually project over where the sustaining cliff has fallen away, it disappeared in the darkness, which seemed intensified just beyond the focus of the searchlight.

It so happened that there was no one at the moment on Tate Hill Pier, as all those whose houses are in close proximity were either in bed or were out on the heights above. Thus the coastguard on duty on the eastern side of the harbour, who at once ran down to the little pier, was the first to climb aboard. The men working the searchlight, after scouring the entrance of the harbour without seeing anything, then turned the light on the derelict and kept it there. The coastguard ran aft, and when he came beside the wheel, bent over to examine it, and recoiled at once as though under some sudden emotion. This seemed to pique general curiosity, and quite a number of people began to run.

It is a good way round from the West Cliff by the Draw-bridge to Tate Hill Pier, but your correspondent is a fairly good runner, and came well ahead of the crowd. When I arrived, however, I found already assembled on the pier a crowd, whom the coastguard and police refused to allow to come on board. By the courtesy of the chief boatman, I was, as your correspondent, permitted to climb on deck, and was one of a small group who saw the dead seaman whilst actually lashed to the wheel.

It was no wonder that the coastguard was surprised, or even awed, for not often can such a sight have been seen. The man was simply fastened by his hands, tied one over the other, to a spoke of the wheel. Between the inner hand and the wood was a crucifix, the set of beads on which it was fastened being around both wrists and wheel, and all kept fast by the binding cords. The poor fellow may have been seated at one time, but the flapping and buffeting of the sails had worked through the rudder of the wheel and had dragged him to and fro, so that the cords with which he was tied had cut the flesh to the bone.

Accurate note was made of the state of things, and a doctor, Surgeon J. M. Caffyn, of 33, East Elliot Place, who came immediately after me, declared, after making examination, that the man must have been dead for quite two days.

In his pocket was a bottle, carefully corked, empty save for a little roll of paper, which proved to be the addendum to the log.

The coastguard said the man must have tied up his own hands, fastening the knots with his teeth. The fact that a coastguard was the first on board may save some complications later on, in the Admiralty Court, for coastguards cannot claim the salvage which is the right of the first civilian entering on a derelict. Already, however, the legal tongues are wagging, and one young law student is loudly asserting that the rights of the owner are already completely sacrificed, his property being held in contravention of the statues of mortmain, since the tiller, as emblemship, if not proof, of delegated possession, is held in a dead hand.

Indeed, the young man was so confident of his position in the matter that he immediately arranged for an auctioneer[98] to handle the matter of selling what salvage may be uncovered within. The two men set about at once inspecting the cargo, only to find that the ship contained only fifty great wooden boxes filled with mould. However, one of those boxes held within it an unexpected surprise indeed—yet another corpse, its arms folded over his chest as if it were a body in a coffin![99]

Unlike that of the captain, which had taken the brunt of the storm, this corpse was quite well preserved, being, as it was, safely below deck. It was of an older man, tall and thin, and dressed all in black. Indeed, it seemed so very incorrupt that Dr. Caffyn was called back aboard the ship (in lieu of the divisional surgeon, who is presently recovering from an illness) to confirm that the body was in fact dead, and not merely in a deep sleep.[100]

It is needless to say that the dead steersman has been reverently removed from the place where he held his honourable watch and ward till death, a steadfastness as noble as that of the young Casabianca, and placed in the mortuary, along with that of the body found within the crate, to await inquest.

Already the sudden storm is passing, and its fierceness is abating. Crowds are scattering backward, and the sky is beginning to redden over the Yorkshire wolds. A few have remained behind in curiosity, to see if any of the crew shall wash up on shore, though such a thing is unlikely at this late date.[101]

I shall send, in time for your next issue, further details of the derelict ship which found her way so miraculously into harbour in the storm.

Cutting from *The Dailygraph*, 9 August

The sequel to the strange arrival of the derelict in the storm last night is almost more startling than the thing itself. It turns out that the schooner is Russian from Varna, and is called the *Demeter*[102]. She is almost entirely in ballast of silver sand, in addition to the small amount of cargo. The ship's manifest said nothing about a body being shipped for burial, so it was suspected at the time that either the man had stowed himself away in the box in order to sneak aboard the ship only to become trapped within it and die, or that the box containing the corpse was brought aboard in Varna by mistake, having been thought to be one of the other boxes, so similar the boxes may have been in appearance[103].

The rights of the young law student were successfully contested, and his auctioneer was dismissed. The cargo was consigned to a Whitby solicitor, Mr. S.F. Billington, of 7, The Crescent, who this morning went aboard and took formal possession of the goods. The Russian consul, too, acting for the charter-party, took formal possession of the ship, and paid all harbour dues, etc.

Nothing is talked about here today except the strange coincidence. The officials of the Board of Trade have been most exacting in seeing that every compliance has been made with existing regulations. As the matter is to be a 'nine days wonder,' they are evidently determined that there shall be no cause of other complaint.

A good deal of interest was abroad concerning the dog which landed when the ship struck, and more than a few of the members of the S.P.C.A., which is very strong in Whitby, have tried to befriend the animal. To the general disappointment, however, it was not to be found. It seems to have disappeared entirely from the town. It may be that it was frightened and made its way on to the moors, where it is still hiding in terror.

There are some who look with dread on such a possibility, lest later on it should in itself become a danger, for it is evidently a fierce brute. Early this morning a large dog, a half-bred mastiff belonging to a coal merchant close to Tate Hill Pier, was found dead in the roadway opposite its master's yard. It had been fighting, and manifestly had had a savage opponent, for its throat was torn away, and its belly was slit open as if with a savage claw such as a tiger wields. One of our local scientists has photographed its eyes in the hopes that he may be able to reproduce the image of the last thing it saw whilst alive.[104] This dog's death is generally attributed to the newcomer, and a close watch is being kept for the latter lest it should cause further harm to either brute or human. What's more, the newcomer appears to have tried digging up one of the graves, for the soil was found freshly turned[105].

Later—By the kindness of the Board of Trade inspector, I have been permitted to look over the log book of the Demeter, which was in order up to within three days, but contained nothing of special interest except as to facts of missing men. The greatest interest, however, is with regard to the paper found in the bottle, which was today produced at the inquest. And a more strange narrative than the two between them unfold it has not been my lot to come across.

As there is no motive for concealment, I am permitted to use them, and accordingly send you a transcript, simply omitting technical details of seamanship and supercargo. It almost seems as though the captain had been seized with some kind of mania before he had got well into blue water, and that this had developed persistently throughout the voyage. Of course my statement must be taken *cum grano*, since I am writing from the dictation of a clerk of the Russian consul, who kindly translated for me, time being short.

Log of the *Demeter*

Varna to Whitby

Written 18 July, things so strange happening, that I shall keep accurate note henceforth till we land.

On 6 July we finished taking in cargo, silver sand and boxes of earth. At noon set sail. East wind, fresh. Crew, five hands . . . two mates, cook, and myself, (captain).

On 11 July at dawn entered Bosphorus. Boarded by Turkish Customs officers. Backsheesh. All correct. Under way at 4 P.M.

On 12 July through Dardanelles. More Customs officers and flagboat of guarding squadron. Backsheesh again. Work of officers thorough, but quick. Want us off soon. At dark passed into Archipelago.

On 13 July passed Cape Matapan. Crew dissatisfied about something. Seemed scared, but would not speak out.

On 14 July was somewhat anxious about crew. Men all steady fellows, who sailed with me before. Mate could not make out what was wrong. They only told him there was SOMETHING, and crossed themselves. Mate lost temper with one of them that day and struck him. Expected fierce quarrel, but all was quiet.

On 16 July mate reported in the morning that one of the crew, Petrofsky, was missing. Could not account for it. Took larboard watch eight bells last night, was relieved by Amramoff, but did not go to bunk. Men more downcast than ever. All said they expected something of the kind, but would not say more than there was SOMETHING aboard. Mate getting very impatient with them. Feared some trouble ahead.

On 17 July, yesterday, one of the men, Olgaren, came to my cabin, and in an awestruck way confided to me that he thought there was a strange man aboard the ship. He said that in his watch he had been sheltering behind the deckhouse, as there was a rain storm, when he saw a tall, thin man, who was not like any of the crew, come up the companionway, and go along the deck forward and disappear. He followed cautiously, but when he got to bows found no one, and the hatchways were all closed. He was in a panic of superstitious fear, and I am afraid the panic may spread. To allay it, I shall today search the entire ship carefully from stem to stern.

Later in the day I got together the whole crew, and told them, as they evidently thought there was some one in the ship, we would search from stem to stern. First mate angry, said it was folly, and to yield to such foolish ideas would demoralise the men, said he would engage to keep them out of trouble with the handspike. I let him take the helm, while the rest began a thorough search, all keeping abreast, with lanterns. We left no corner unsearched. As there were only the big wooden boxes, there were no odd corners where a man could hide. Men much relieved when search over, and went back to work cheerfully. First mate scowled, but said nothing.

22 July—Rough weather last three days, and all hands busy with sails, no time to be frightened. Men seem to have forgotten their dread. Mate cheerful again, and all on good terms. Praised men for work in bad weather. Passed Gibraltar and out through Straits. All well.

24 July—There seems some doom over this ship. Already a hand short, and entering the Bay of Biscay with wild weather ahead, and yet last night another man lost, disappeared. Like the first, he came off his watch and was not seen again. Men all in a panic of fear, sent a round robin, asking to have double watch, as they fear to be alone. Mate angry. Fear there will be some trouble, as either he or the men will do some violence.

28 July—Four days in hell, knocking about in a sort of maelstrom, and the wind a tempest. No sleep for any one. Men all worn out. Hardly know how to set a watch, since no one fit to go on. Second mate volunteered to steer and watch, and let men snatch a few hours sleep. Wind abating, seas still terrific, but feel them less, as ship is steadier.

29 July—Another tragedy. Had single watch tonight, as crew too tired to double. When morning watch came on deck could find no one except steersman. Raised outcry, and all came on deck. Thorough search, but no one found. Are now without second mate, and crew in a panic. Mate and I agreed to go armed henceforth and wait for any sign of cause.

30 July—Last night. Rejoiced we are nearing England. Weather fine, all sails set. Retired worn out, slept soundly, awakened by mate telling me that both man of watch and steersman missing. Only self and mate and two hands left to work ship.

1 August—Two days of fog, and not a sail sighted. Had hoped when in the English Channel to be able to signal for help or get in somewhere. Not having

power to work sails, have to run before wind. Dare not lower, as could not raise them again. We seem to be drifting to some terrible doom. Mate now more demoralised than either of men. His stronger nature seems to have worked inwardly against himself. Men are beyond fear, working stolidly and patiently, with minds made up to worst. They are Russian, he Roumanian.

2 August, midnight—Woke up from few minutes sleep by hearing a cry, seemingly outside my port. Could see nothing in fog. Rushed on deck, and ran against mate. Tells me he heard cry and ran, but no sign of man on watch. One more gone. Lord, help us! Mate says we must be past Straits of Dover, as in a moment of fog lifting he saw North Foreland, just as he heard the man cry out. If so we are now off in the North Sea, and only God can guide us in the fog, which seems to move with us, and God seems to have deserted us.

3 August—At midnight I went to relieve the man at the wheel and when I got to it found no one there. The wind was steady, and as we ran before it there was no yawing. I dared not leave it, so shouted for the mate. After a few seconds, he rushed up on deck in his flannels. He looked wild-eyed and haggard, and I greatly fear his reason has given way. He came close to me and whispered hoarsely, with his mouth to my ear, as though fearing the very air might hear. "It is here. I know it now. On the watch last night I saw It, like a man, tall and thin, and ghastly pale. It was in the bows, and looking out. I crept behind It, and gave it my knife, but the knife went through It, empty as the air." And as he spoke he took the knife and drove it savagely into space. Then he went on, "But It is here, and I'll find It. It is in the hold, perhaps in one of those boxes. I'll unscrew them one by one and see. You work the helm." And with a warning look and his finger on his lip, he went below. There was springing up a choppy wind, and I could not leave the helm. I saw him come out on deck again with a tool chest and lantern, and go down the forward hatchway. He is mad, stark, raving mad, and it's no use my trying to stop him. He can't hurt those big boxes, they are invoiced as clay, and to pull them about is as harmless a thing as he can do. So here I stay and mind the helm, and write these notes. I can only trust in God and wait till the fog clears. Then, if I can't steer to any harbour with the wind that is, I shall cut down sails, and lie by, and signal for help . . .

It is nearly all over now. Just as I was beginning to hope that the mate would come out calmer, for I heard him knocking away at something in the hold, and work is good for him, there came up the hatchway a sudden, startled scream, which made my blood run cold, and up on the deck he came as if shot from a gun, a raging madman, with his eyes rolling and his face convulsed with fear. "Save me! Save me!" he cried, and then looked round on the blanket of fog. His horror turned to despair, and in a steady voice he said, "You had better come too, captain, before it is too late. He is there! I know the secret now. The sea will save me from Him, and it is all that is left!" Before I could say a word, or move forward to seize him, he sprang on the bulwark and deliberately threw himself into the sea. I suppose I know the secret too, now. It was this madman who had got rid of the men one by one, and now he has followed them himself. God help me! How am I to account for all these horrors when I get to port? When I get to port! Will that ever be?

4 August—Still fog, which the sunrise cannot pierce, I know there is sunrise because I am a sailor, why else I know not. I dared not go below, I dared not leave the helm, so here all night I stayed, and in the dimness of the night I saw it, Him! God, forgive me, but the mate was right to jump overboard. It was better to die like a man. To die like a sailor in blue water, no man can object. But I am captain, and I must not leave my ship. But I shall baffle this fiend or monster, this SOMETHING which my crew called "nosferatu," for I shall tie my hands to the wheel when my strength begins to fail, and along with them I shall tie that which He, It, dare not touch. And then, come good wind or foul, I shall save my soul, and my honour as a captain. I am growing weaker, and the night is coming on. If He can look me in the face again, I may not have time to act . . . If we are wrecked, mayhap this bottle may be found, and those who find it may understand. If not . . . well, then all men shall know that I have been true to my trust. God and the Blessed Virgin and the Saints help a poor ignorant soul trying to do his duty . . .

Of course the verdict was an open one. There is no evidence to adduce, and whether or not the man himself committed the murders there is now none to say. The folk here hold almost universally that the captain is simply a hero, and he is to be given a public funeral. Already it is arranged that his body is to be taken with a train of boats up the Esk for a piece and then brought back to Tate Hill Pier and up the abbey steps, for he is to be buried in the churchyard on the cliff. The owners of more than a hundred boats have already given in their names as wishing to follow him to the grave.

No trace has ever been found of the great dog, at which there is much mourning, for, with public opinion in its present state, he would, I believe, be adopted by the town. As for the body found within the crate—though how or why he came aboard we may never know, we do know now how he died, for the log tells of how the mate stabbed such the very man with his knife. Of course, he claimed that his blade passed harmlessly through the stowaway, thus denying to his captain the heinous outcome of the murderous act. The mate must have been the one to have hidden the body within one of the boxes. That Dr. Caffyn reports a deep cut present on the forehead lends credence to the suspicion of foul play. But as the mate is now dead by his own hand, there is little more to do in this matter.

Tomorrow will see the funeral of the captain, and so will end this one more 'mystery of the sea.'

CHAPTER ELEVEN[106]

Mina Murray's Journal

8 August—Lucy was very restless all night, and I too, could not sleep. The storm was fearful, and as it boomed loudly among the chimney pots, it made me shudder. When a sharp puff came it seemed to be like a distant gun.

Early in the morning we both got up and went down to the harbour to see if anything had happened in the night. There were very few people about, and though the sun was bright, and the air clear and fresh, the big, grim-looking waves, that seemed dark themselves because the foam that topped them was like snow, forced themselves in through the mouth of the harbour, like a bullying man going through a crowd. Somehow I felt glad that Jonathan was not on the sea last night, but on land. But, oh, is he on land or sea? Where is he, and how? I am getting fearfully anxious about him. If I only knew what to do, and could do anything!

9 August—Arthur came by to see Lucy today. They took a long walk along the beach; when they returned, Lucy had a curious brooch fastening her shawl. She says Arthur found it in the shore, near where the *Demeter* had been lodged, and guessed that it had come in with the ship.[107] Later, Lucy commented that she never actually saw Arthur pick anything up out of the sand, and made a guess that he had simply invented a "tall tale"—that's more of Lucy's new slang—as an excuse for giving her a gift. I might have agreed, except for the peculiar design of the brooch. It was expertly wrought, and very old by the look of it. It had the appearance of an eight-pointed star, with a large square ruby set in its centre.[108]

The jewel gives me an odd feeling to look upon it, for when the light hits it a certain way, it seems that the ruby is no ruby at all, but rather clear glass, and hollow, with something red contained therein. When Arthur left I tried to persuade her to remove it, reasoning with her that the edges were old and worn and sharp, and she might injure herself. But she would have none of it.

Francis Aytown's Sketch Journal

9 August—A fine day for painting; up before sunrise. Did a few sketches of shipwreck onlookers in the half-light of dawn.

Glorious sunrise after storm, nicely lit view of shipwreck; I dare say I did the scene fair justice.

Painters are neither so populous as to crowd each other nor so rare as to attract onlookers. Not like before the storm.

Quick ink sketches, studies for paintings: Waves, ships, gulls, Kate perched on a rock scowling into the sun. Careless girl—she'll be burnt as I.

Good likenesses all, Kate agreed, save for the pale gentleman; they said his face wasn't quite right. Such untrained eyes, they have.

We all retire early.

Same day, 9pm—Have I lost my eye for judgment? Reviewing the day's work, shocked by the poor quality of one sketch in particular: the gent, which I had remembered as quite good. Kate was right in her critique of that piece, after all. And he should have been easy fellow to draw, too; I can see his face in my mind's eye, with his strong sharp features and fascinating eyes. I really cannot allow distracting visits from Kate if she has this effect on my work.

Letter, Kate to Mr. and Mrs. Reed

10 August

Papa, Mamma,

The most horrible thing has happened. Grampapa Joseph has been the victim of a terrible accident—he is dead! He must have climbed up to the graveyard—a favorite vantage point, we had a tremendous storm last night and he often views—viewed, the harbour from there, and he slipped and broke his neck on one of the stones. The coastguard found him early this morning; he must have gone up as soon as it got light, to see the damage.

We will stay till after the funeral Thursday. What we shall do then, I cannot say. Francis has his heart set on staying. He seems to have become fixated on something here, some inspiration that seems just beyond his reach . . .

I am so sorry for you, Mamma, as I know Grampapa Joseph meant very much to you, and I know it will be difficult for you not to be able to attend the services. I will write again as quickly as I may, to tell you our plans.

Your loving daughter
Kate

Francis Aytown's Sketch Journal

10 August—Up early again; was rewarded by seeing the object of my frustration, sitting on a bench looking out to sea, where the first light of dawn was beginning to break. I took the opportunity to study him. Not quite such a fop as I thought. There is something strangely commanding about him. A military man, perhaps; not of the Indias, not with that pale skin. The Crimea? He could even be Russian. But then what is he doing here? I sense a romantic history . . . Captured a near-exact likeness this time.

Same day, late morning—Kate's grandfather found dead this morning. Oddly, he died at the same bench upon which I saw my gentleman sitting at sunrise. Surely the old man's body was not there when I was doing the sketch? No, impossible; I would have seen it. Wouldn't I?

It's that pale gent's sketch from yesterday, confound it!—I can't stop thinking about that fellow's face; how I thought my rendition was so superb at the time, then found it to be so very wrong later. The incident has addled my brain, frustrated my confidence. But at least my sketch of him this morning was satisfactory. I shall study it now, to prove to myself I have not lost my eye for faces . . .

This is insanity! My morning's sketch of the pale stranger, which I thought was so superb, I see now is worse than my first attempt. It bears no resemblance to what I remember of him, and yet his image in my mind seems clearer than ever. Worse yet—and I dare not ever make mention of this to Kate—I see in my sketch that there is a body lying by the bench, no doubt that of Mr. Swales, which I must have included unconsciously in my rendition. How could I have been so absorbed with studying the gentleman that I simply drew what surrounded him—even a corpse!—without noticing anything but the man himself?

Ah, the sea captain's funeral is about to get underway, and I must attend to my painting. Perhaps it will distract me.

Same day, evening—The funeral is really superb piece; it should fetch a handsome price in London, if Barrett's will take it. A few more like these, and the trip will have been well worth it! Still, I find myself unable to resist the absurd desire to keep looking at the funeral painting, as if it would no longer be as good as remembered. Of course it remains perfect, just like before; it is only that man's image that changes.

And how his face, even as a vision in my mind's eye, speaks volumes to me—it is sensual, soulful—Is this why he is so difficult to draw? Is there some subtlety of his character that eludes my pen? I must discover more about him. I know, I shall look for him tonight, and endeavor to follow him.

Why is painting this one portrait so difficult? It's like chasing a ghost . . .

Mina Murray's Journal[109]

10 August—It would seem that Lucy, although she is so well, has suddenly taken to her old habit of walking in her sleep. Again, Lucy was restless during the night; but strangely enough, she did not wake this time, but got up twice and dressed herself. There was an odd concentration about her which I do not understand, even in her sleep she seems to be watching me. She tried the door, and finding it locked, went about the room searching for the key. Fortunately, each time I awoke in time and managed to undress her without waking her, and got her back to bed.

It is a very strange thing, this sleep-walking, for as soon as her will is thwarted in any physical way, her intention, if there be any, disappears, and she yields herself almost exactly to the routine of her life.

I have spoken to her mother about it, and we have decided that I am to lock the door of our room every night. Mrs. Westenra has got an idea that sleep-walkers always go out on roofs of houses and along the edges of cliffs and then get suddenly wakened and fall over with a despairing cry that echoes all over the place.

Poor dear, she is naturally anxious about Lucy, and she tells me that her husband, Lucy's father, had the same habit, that he would get up in the night and dress himself and go out, if he were not stopped.

Later—The funeral of the poor sea captain today was most touching. Every boat in the harbour seemed to be there, and the coffin was carried by captains all the way from Tate Hill Pier up to the churchyard. Lucy came with me, and we went early to our old seat, whilst the cortege of boats went up the river to the Viaduct and came down again. We had a lovely view, and saw the procession nearly all the way. The poor fellow was laid to rest near our seat so that we stood on it, when the time came and saw everything.

Poor Lucy seemed much upset. She was restless and uneasy all the time, and I cannot but think that her dreaming at night is telling on her. She is quite odd in one thing. She will not admit to me that there is any cause for restlessness, or if there be, she does not understand it herself.

There is an additional cause in that poor Mr. Swales was found dead this morning on our seat, his neck being broken. He had evidently, as the doctor said, fallen back in the seat in some sort of fright, for there was a look of fear and horror on his face that the men said made them shudder. Poor dear old man! We must call upon our dear Kate to see how she is holding up.

Lucy is so sweet and sensitive that she feels influences more acutely than other people do. Just now she was quite upset by a little thing which I did not much heed, though I am myself very fond of animals.

One of the men who came up here often to look for the boats was followed by his dog. The dog is always with him. They are both quiet persons, and I never saw the man angry, nor heard the dog bark. During the service the dog would not come to its master, who was on the seat with us, but kept a few yards off, barking and howling. Its master spoke to it gently, and then harshly, and then angrily. But it would neither come nor cease to make a noise. It was in a fury, with its eyes savage, and all its hair bristling out like a cat's tail when puss is on the war path.

Finally the man too got angry, and jumped down and kicked the dog, and then took it by the scruff of the neck and half dragged and half threw it on the tombstone on which the seat is fixed. The moment it touched the stone the poor thing began to tremble. It did not try to get away, but crouched down, quivering and cowering, and was in such a pitiable state of terror that I tried, though without effect, to comfort it. No doubt it smelled something of the great beast which, after escaping the shipwreck, appears to have been digging at the very grave over which our seat rested.

Lucy was full of pity, too, but she did not attempt to touch the dog, but looked at it in an agonized sort of way. I greatly fear that she is of too super sensitive a nature to go through the world without trouble. She will be dreaming of this tonight, I am sure. The whole agglomeration of things, the ship steered into port by a dead man, his attitude, tied to the wheel with a crucifix and beads, the touching funeral, the dog, now furious and now in terror, will all afford material for her dreams.

I think it will be best for her to go to bed tired out physically, so I shall take her for a long walk by the cliffs to Robin Hood's Bay and back. She ought not to have much inclination for sleep-walking then.

Cutting from *The Dailygraph*, 10 August

Some mysteries, it would seem, do not wish to remain buried. The body of the man which had been found within one of the cargo crates of the wrecked *Demeter*, has since vanished from the mortuary, where it was being held to await a proper burial. The police have been investigating the matter, but thus far they have no signs of burglary or vandalism to account for its disappearance. The general belief is that some of the more superstitions peoples of Whitby, perhaps thinking that the dead man was a "Jonah"—the cause of the incidents aboard the *Demeter*—stole the body during the night in order to deal with it in some manner intended to break whatever "curse" it may have brought here with it. Thus far, there have been no leads to solving this case, so we can only watch and wait to see if the body resurfaces.

CHAPTER

TWELVE[110]

Mina Murray's Journal

Same day, 11 o'clock P.M.—Oh, but I am tired! If it were not that I had made my diary a duty I should not open it tonight. We had a lovely walk. Lucy, after a while, was in gay spirits, owing, I think, to some dear cows who came nosing towards us in a field close to the lighthouse, and frightened the wits out of us. I believe we forgot everything, except of course, personal fear, and it seemed to wipe the slate clean and give us a fresh start. We had a capital "severe tea" at Robin Hood's Bay in a sweet little old-fashioned inn, with a bow window right over the seaweed-covered rocks of the strand. I believe we should have shocked even our very own "New Woman" Kate with our appetites. Men are more tolerant, bless them! Then we walked home with some, or rather many, stoppages to rest, and with our hearts full of a constant dread of wild bulls.

Lucy was really tired, and we intended to creep off to bed as soon as we could. The young curate came in, however, and Mrs. Westenra asked him to stay for supper. Lucy and I had both a fight for it with the dusty miller. I know it was a hard fight on my part, and I am quite heroic. I think that some day the bishops must get together and see about breeding up a new class of curates, who don't take supper, no matter how hard they may be pressed to, and who will know when girls are tired.

Lucy is asleep and breathing softly. She has more colour in her cheeks than usual, and looks, oh so sweet. If Mr. Holmwood fell in love with her seeing her only in the drawing room, I wonder what he would say if he saw her now. Some of the 'New Women' writers will some day start an idea that men and women should be allowed to see each other asleep before proposing or accepting. But I suppose the 'New Woman' won't condescend in future to accept. She will do the proposing herself. And a nice job she will make of it too! There's some consolation in that. I am so happy tonight, because dear Lucy seems better. I really believe she has turned the corner, and that we are over her troubles with dreaming. I should be quite happy if I only knew if Jonathan . . . God bless and keep him.

11 August—Diary again. No sleep now, so I may as well write. I am too agitated to sleep. We have had such an adventure, such an agonizing experience. I fell asleep as soon as I had closed my diary . . . . Suddenly I became broad awake, and sat up, with a horrible sense of fear upon me, and of some feeling of emptiness around me. The room was dark, so I could not see Lucy's bed. I stole across and felt for her. The bed was empty. I lit a match and found that she was not in the room. The door was shut, but not locked, as I had left it. I feared to wake her mother, who has been more than usually ill lately, even with her use of Arthur's special tea, so threw on some clothes and got ready to look for her. As I was leaving the room it struck me that the clothes she wore might give me some clue to her dreaming intention. Dressing-gown would mean house, dress outside. Dressing-gown and dress were both in their places. "Thank God," I said to myself, "she cannot be far, as she is only in her nightdress."

I ran downstairs and looked in the sitting room. Not there! Then I looked in all the other rooms of the house, with an ever-growing fear chilling my heart. Finally, I came to the hall door and found it open. It was not wide open, but the catch of the lock had not caught. The people of the house are careful to lock the door every night, so I feared that Lucy must have gone out as she was. There was no time to think of what might happen. A vague over-mastering fear obscured all details.

I took a big, heavy shawl—Lucy's, the one with that dreadful new brooch, which I would not have taken, except that I was in a hurry and it was the first one I saw—and ran out. The clock was striking one as I was in the Crescent, and there was not a soul in sight. I ran along the North Terrace, but could see no sign of the white figure which I expected. At the edge of the West Cliff above the pier I looked across the harbour to the East Cliff, in the hope or fear, I don't know which, of seeing Lucy in our favourite seat.

There was a bright full moon, with heavy black, driving clouds, which threw the whole scene into a fleeting diorama of light and shade as they sailed across. For a moment or two I could see nothing, as the shadow of a cloud obscured St. Mary's Church and all around it. Then as the cloud passed I could see the ruins of the abbey coming into view, and as the edge of a narrow band of light as sharp as a sword-cut moved along, the church and churchyard became gradually visible. Whatever my expectation was, it was not disappointed, for there, on our favourite seat, the silver light of the moon struck a half-reclining figure, snowy white. The coming of the cloud was too quick for me to see much, for shadow shut down on light almost immediately, but it seemed to me as though something dark stood behind the seat where the white figure shone, and bent over it. What it was, whether man or beast, I could not tell.

I did not wait to catch another glance, but flew down the steep steps to the pier and along by the fish-market to the bridge, which was the only way to reach the East Cliff. The town seemed as dead, for not a soul did I see. I rejoiced that it was so, for I wanted no witness of poor Lucy's condition. The time and distance seemed endless, and my knees trembled and my breath came laboured as I toiled up the endless steps to the abbey. I must have gone fast, and yet it seemed to me as if my feet were weighted with lead, and as though every joint in my body were rusty.

When I got almost to the top I could see the seat and the white figure, for I was now close enough to distinguish it even through the spells of shadow. There was undoubtedly something, long and black, bending over the half-reclining white figure. I called in fright, "Lucy! Lucy!" and something raised a head, and from where I was I could see a white face and red, gleaming eyes.

Lucy did not answer, and I ran on to the entrance of the churchyard. As I entered, the church was between me and the seat, and for a minute or so I lost sight of her. When I came in view again the cloud had passed, and the moonlight struck so brilliantly that I could see Lucy half reclining with her head lying over the back of the seat. She was quite alone, and there was not a sign of any living thing about.

When I bent over her I could see that she was still asleep. Her lips were parted, and she was breathing, not softly as usual with her, but in long, heavy gasps, as though striving to get her lungs full at every breath. As I came close, she put up her hand in her sleep and pulled the collar of her nightdress close around her, as though she felt the cold. I flung the warm shawl over her, and drew the edges tight around her neck, for I dreaded lest she should get some deadly chill from the night air, unclad as she was. I feared to wake her all at once, so, in order to have my hands free to help her, I fastened the shawl at her throat with the brooch. But I must have been clumsy in my anxiety and pinched or pricked her with it, for by-and-by, when her breathing became quieter, she put her hand to her throat again and moaned, and I saw the brooch had blood on it.[111] When I had her carefully wrapped up I put my shoes on her feet, and then began very gently to wake her.

At first she did not respond, but gradually she became more and more uneasy in her sleep, moaning and sighing occasionally. At last, as time was passing fast, and for many other reasons, I wished to get her home at once, I shook her forcibly, till finally she opened her eyes and awoke. She did not seem surprised to see me, as, of course, she did not realize all at once where she was.

Lucy always wakes prettily, and even at such a time, when her body must have been chilled with cold, and her mind somewhat appalled at waking unclad in a churchyard at night, she did not lose her grace. She trembled a little, and clung to me. When I told her to come at once with me home, she rose without a word, with the obedience of a child. As we passed along, the gravel hurt my feet, and Lucy noticed me wince. She stopped and wanted to insist upon my taking my shoes, but I would not. However, when we got to the pathway outside the churchyard, where there was a puddle of water, remaining from the storm, I daubed my feet with mud, using each foot in turn on the other, so that as we went home, no one, in case we should meet any one, should notice my bare feet.

Fortune favoured us, and we got home without meeting a soul. Once we saw a man, who seemed not quite sober, passing along a street in front of us. But we hid in a door till he had disappeared up an opening such as there are here, steep little closes, or 'wynds,' as they call them in Scotland. My heart beat so loud all the time sometimes I thought I should faint. I was filled with anxiety about Lucy, not only for her health, lest she should suffer from the exposure, but for her reputation in case the story should get wind. When we got in, and had washed our feet, and had said a prayer of thankfulness together, I tucked her into bed. Before falling asleep she asked, even implored, me not to say a word to any one, even her mother, about her sleep-walking adventure.

I hesitated at first, to promise, but on thinking of the state of her mother's health, and how the knowledge of such a thing would fret her, and think too, of how such a story might become distorted, nay, infallibly would, in case it should leak out, I thought it wiser to do so. I hope I did right. I have locked the door, and the key is tied to my wrist, so perhaps I shall not be again disturbed. Lucy is sleeping soundly. The reflex of the dawn is high and far over the sea . . .

Same day, noon—All goes well. Lucy slept till I woke her and seemed not to have even changed her side. The adventure of the night does not seem to have harmed her, on the contrary, it has benefited her, for she looks better this morning than she has done for weeks. I was sorry to notice that my clumsiness with the pin hurt her. Indeed, it might have been serious, for the skin of her throat was pierced. I must have pinched up a piece of loose skin and have transfixed it, for there are two little red points like pin-pricks, and on the band of her nightdress was a drop of blood. When I apologized and was concerned about it, she laughed and petted me, and said she did not even feel it. Fortunately it cannot leave a scar, as it is so tiny.

Same day, night—We passed a happy day. The air was clear, and the sun bright, and there was a cool breeze. We took our lunch to Mulgrave Woods, Mrs. Westenra driving by the road and Lucy and I walking by the cliff-path and joining her at the gate. I felt a little sad myself, for I could not but feel how absolutely happy it would have been had Jonathan been with me. But there! I must only be patient. In the evening we strolled in the Casino Terrace, and heard some good music by Spohr and Mackenzie, and went to bed early. Lucy seems more restful than she has been for some time, and fell asleep at once. I shall lock the door and secure the key the same as before, though I do not expect any trouble tonight.

Francis Aytown's Sketch Journal

11 August—I am beside myself with fear and indecision, for surely I cannot trust my own sanity. And yet I know I am sane, so surely I can trust myself and my own eyes. I have made the effort, and stayed awake during the night to observe the gentleman—though now I must wonder if he is either gentle or even a man.

I had searched and searched through the night, but without success, and was about to give up my quest, when a saw something white move in the distance. With as much haste and silence as I could manage, I approached, and saw the figure to be Miss Lucy, clad in nothing but her dressing-gown. She walked slowly, but with purpose, toward the bench she and Miss Mina favored. Then He appeared, clad all in black, rising slowly from behind the bench as might a specter from the grave. Had he been there the whole time, and I merely did not see him for his dark attire? Even now I cannot be sure, though if I were forced to say, I believe I would that he had not been there before, but indeed had risen from the grave beneath the bench.

As I watched, he lay her down upon the bench and bent over her, the black folds of his cloak spreading about them like the wings of some great bat, hiding them from my view. I found myself frozen in place, unable to move, for I could not bear to take my eyes off the scene. Was Miss Lucy not engaged to be married? And yet she had come here of her own free will, to this man, this creature.

Then I heard another voice, Miss Mina's, cry out "Lucy, Lucy," and at the sound the creature, the pale King, lifted his head, and I saw his bared white teeth and gleaming red eyes quite clearly. A cloud passed before the moon, and all was in shadow for a long minute. And yet, from my vantage, I could still see with relative ease. To my amazement, before my very eyes, I saw the figure sink into the ground below the bench, as if he were nothing more than vapour.[112] When the light returned, the King was gone, and Miss Mina rushed to attend Miss Lucy. The girl, now clearly visible in the moonlight, was now as pale as the man she had been with. For a moment I thought her to be dead, but Miss Mina was able to rouse her sufficiently to walk.

Before they could see me, I withdrew and made my way back to the Crescent. I fear I was so stunned from my encounter with Death—for who else could he have been but the scytheman, whose love-making could leave a girl so pale?—that I would have seemed drunk to anyone who saw me. But no one did see me, at least not that I could tell. Once I thought I heard faint footsteps, but when I looked, there was no one there.

What am I to do? I cannot get the vision of Him—the pale face, the red eyes—out of my head. Nor, I dare say, would I want to even if I could; it is as if He is, at long last, the very incarnation of the Muse I have been searching for . . .

Same day, later—I have kept myself away from Kate all day, painting. I am loath to paint from memory, but this time I gave it my all. In the end, I created a rendition of last night's scene at the bench. It looked good to me when I had finished it . . . better than good, masterful! I dare say even that it is the best work I have ever done, but then, all of my attempts to paint Him appeared successful at the time. So I left it alone for a long time. And when I returned . . . it was still as perfect as I remembered it!

For once, His face remained true to my memory, perhaps because this time I had endeavored to paint Him as He truly was, with his pale flesh and red eyes, rather than the illusory mask He hid behind when He thought others to be watching.

I was right—he is my Muse made flesh. This indeed must be "the Love that dare not speak its name." I know now what I must do . . .

Mina Murray's Journal

12 August—My expectations were wrong, for twice during the night I was wakened by Lucy trying to get out. She seemed, even in her sleep, to be a little impatient at finding the door shut, and went back to bed under a sort of protest. I woke with the dawn, and heard the birds chirping outside of the window. Lucy woke, too, and I was glad to see, was even better than on the previous morning. All her old gaiety of manner seemed to have come back, and she came and snuggled in beside me and told me all about Arthur. I told her how anxious I was about Jonathan, and then she tried to comfort me. Well, she succeeded somewhat, for, though sympathy can't alter facts, it can make them more bearable.

13 August—Another quiet day, and to bed with the key on my wrist as before. Again I awoke in the night, and found Lucy sitting up in bed, still asleep, pointing to the window. I got up quietly, and pulling aside the blind, looked out. It was brilliant moonlight, and the soft effect of the light over the sea and sky, merged together in one great silent mystery, was beautiful beyond words. Between me and the moonlight flitted a great bat, coming and going in great whirling circles. Once or twice it came quite close, but was, I suppose, frightened at seeing me, and flitted away across the harbour towards the abbey. When I came back from the window Lucy had lain down again, and was sleeping peacefully. She did not stir again all night.

Letter, from Francis Aytown to "King Death"
left on the bench above George Canon's tomb at sundown,
accompanied by a painting[113]

14 August

King Death—for I know not what else to call you,

If you are the man I take you to be, you will like this letter. If you are not I don't care whether you like it or not and only ask you to put it into the fire without reading any farther. I don't think there is a man living, even you, who are above the prejudice of the class of small-minded men, who wouldn't like to get a letter from a younger man, a stranger—a man living in an atmosphere prejudiced to the truths you sing and your manner of singing them. And I have seen you sing your truths, to the young lady upon this very bench three nights past. You are a true man, and I would like to be one myself, and so I would be towards you as a brother and as a pupil to his master.

Shelley wrote to William Godwin and they became friends. I am not Shelley and you are not Godwin and so I will only hope that sometime I may meet you face to faced and perhaps shake hands with you. If I ever do, it will be one of the greatest pleasures of my life. If you care to know who it is that writes this, my name is Francis Aytown. I live at 346 Piccadilly, London. I am an artist—a painter—who lives upon a small income and upon the generosity of my friend Katherine Reed. I am twenty-four years old. I am six feet two inches high and twelve stones weight naked and used to be forty-one or forty-two inches round the chest. I am ugly but strong and determined and have a large bump over my eyebrows. I have a heavy jaw and a big mouth and thick lips, sensitive nostrils, a snub nose, and straight hair. I am equal in temper and cool in disposition and have a large amount of self control and am naturally secretive to the world. I take a delight in letting people I don't like see the worst side of me. Now I have told you all I know about myself.

Be assured of this, King Death, that I have been more candid with you, have said more about myself to you than I have ever said to anyone else, even to Kate. How sweet a thing it is for a strong healthy man with woman's eyes and a child's wishes to feel that he can speak so to a man who can be if he wishes, father and brother and wife to his soul. I don't think you will laugh, King Death, nor despise me, but at all events I thank you. I must return to London today, and so I leave you with this painting, of when I first saw you as you truly are, for it is the only thanks I know how to give.

Your Servant,
Francis Aytown

Mina Murray's Journal

14 August—On the East Cliff, reading and writing all day. Lucy seems to have become as much in love with the spot as I am, and it is hard to get her away from it when it is time to come home for lunch or tea or dinner. This afternoon she made a funny remark. We were coming home for dinner, and had come to the top of the steps up from the West Pier and stopped to look at the view, as we generally do. The setting sun, low down in the sky, was just dropping behind Kettleness. The red light was thrown over on the East Cliff and the old abbey, and seemed to bathe everything in a beautiful rosy glow. We were silent for a while, and suddenly Lucy murmured as if to herself . . .

"His red eyes again! They are just the same." It was such an odd expression, coming apropos of nothing, that it quite startled me. I slewed round a little, so as to see Lucy well without seeming to stare at her, and saw that she was in a half dreamy state, with an odd look on her face that I could not quite make out, so I said nothing, but followed her eyes. She appeared to be looking over at our own seat, whereon was a dark figure seated alone. I was quite a little startled myself, for it seemed for an instant as if the stranger had great eyes like burning flames, but a second look dispelled the illusion. The red sunlight was shining on the windows of St. Mary's Church behind our seat, and as the sun dipped there was just sufficient change in the refraction and reflection to make it appear as if the light moved. I called Lucy's attention to the peculiar effect, and she became herself with a start, but she looked sad all the same. It may have been that she was thinking of that terrible night up there. We never refer to it, so I said nothing, and we went home to dinner. Lucy had a headache and went early to bed. I saw her asleep, and went out for a little stroll myself.

I walked along the cliffs to the westward, and was full of sweet sadness, for I was thinking of Jonathan. When coming home, it was then bright moonlight, so bright that, though the front of our part of the Crescent was in shadow, everything could be well seen, I threw a glance up at our window, and saw Lucy's head leaning out. I opened my handkerchief and waved it. She did not notice or make any movement whatever. Just then, the moonlight crept round an angle of the building, and the light fell on the window. There distinctly was Lucy with her head lying up against the side of the window sill and her eyes shut. She was fast asleep, and by her, seated on the window sill, was something that looked like a good-sized bird. I was afraid she might get a chill, so I ran upstairs, but as I came into the room she was moving back to her bed, fast asleep, and breathing heavily. She was holding her hand to her throat, as though to protect it from the cold.

I did not wake her, but tucked her up warmly. I have taken care that the door is locked and the window securely fastened.

She looks so sweet as she sleeps, but she is paler than is her wont, and there is a drawn, haggard look under her eyes which I do not like. I fear she is fretting about something. I wish I could find out what it is.

15 August—Rose later than usual. Lucy was languid and tired, and slept on after we had been called. We had a happy surprise at breakfast. Arthur's father is better, and wants the marriage to come off soon. Lucy is full of quiet joy, and her mother is glad and sorry at once. Later on in the day she told me the cause. She is grieved to lose Lucy as her very own, but she is rejoiced that she is soon to have some one to protect her. Poor dear, sweet lady! She confided to me that she has got her death warrant. She has not told Lucy, and made me promise secrecy. Her doctor told her that within a few months, at most, she must die, for her heart is weakening. At any time, even now, a sudden shock would be almost sure to kill her. Ah, we were wise to keep from her the affair of the dreadful night of Lucy's sleep-walking.

17 August—No diary for two whole days. I have not had the heart to write. Some sort of shadowy pall seems to be coming over our happiness. No news from Jonathan, and Lucy seems to be growing weaker, whilst her mother's hours are numbering to a close. I do not understand Lucy's fading away as she is doing. She eats well and sleeps well, and enjoys the fresh air, but all the time the roses in her cheeks are fading, and she gets weaker and more languid day by day. At night I hear her gasping as if for air.

I keep the key of our door always fastened to my wrist at night, but she gets up and walks about the room, and sits at the open window. Last night I found her leaning out when I woke up, and when I tried to wake her I could not.

She was in a faint. When I managed to restore her, she was weak as water, and cried silently between long, painful struggles for breath. When I asked her how she came to be at the window she shook her head and turned away.

I trust her feeling ill may not be from that unlucky prick of the safety-pin. I looked at her throat just now as she lay asleep, and the tiny wounds seem not to have healed. They are still open, and, if anything, larger than before, and the edges of them are faintly white. They are like little white dots with red centres. Unless they heal within a day or two, I shall insist on the doctor seeing about them.

Letter, Samuel F. Billington & Son, Solicitors, Whitby to Messrs. Carter, Paterson & Co., London

17 August.

Dear Sirs,

Herewith please receive invoice of goods sent by Great Northern Railway. Same are to be delivered at Carfax, near Purfleet, immediately on receipt at goods station King's Cross. The house is at present empty, but enclosed please find keys, all of which are labeled.

You will please deposit the boxes, fifty in number, which form the consignment, in the partially ruined building forming part of the house and marked 'A' on rough diagrams enclosed. Your agent will easily recognize the locality, as it is the ancient chapel of the mansion. The goods leave by the train at 9:30 tonight, and will be due at King's Cross at 4:30 tomorrow afternoon. As our client wishes the delivery made as soon as possible, we shall be obliged by your having teams ready at King's Cross at the time named and forthwith conveying the goods to destination. In order to obviate any delays possible through any routine requirements as to payment in your departments, we enclose cheque herewith for ten pounds, receipt of which please acknowledge. Should the charge be less than this amount, you can return balance, if greater, we shall at once send cheque for difference on hearing from you. You are to leave the keys on coming away in the main hall of the house, where the proprietor may get them on his entering the house by means of his duplicate key.

Pray do not take us as exceeding the bounds of business courtesy in pressing you in all ways to use the utmost expedition.

We are, dear Sirs,
Faithfully yours,
Samuel F. Billington & Son

Letter, Messrs. Carter, Paterson & Co., London
To Messrs. Billington & Son, Whitby

21 August.

Dear Sirs,

We beg to acknowledge 10 pounds received and to return cheque of 1 pound, 17s, 9d, amount of overplus, as shown in receipted account herewith. Goods are delivered in exact accordance with instructions, and keys left in parcel in main hall, as directed.

We are, dear Sirs,
Yours respectfully,
Pro Carter, Paterson & Co.

Mina Murray's Journal

18 August—I am happy today, and write sitting on the seat in the churchyard. Lucy is ever so much better. Last night she slept well all night, and did not disturb me once.

The roses seem coming back already to her cheeks, though she is still sadly pale and wan-looking. If she were in any way anemic I could understand it, but she is not. She is in gay spirits and full of life and cheerfulness. All the morbid reticence seems to have passed from her, and she has just reminded me, as if I needed any reminding, of that night, and that it was here, on this very seat, I found her asleep.

As she told me she tapped playfully with the heel of her boot on the stone slab and said,

"My poor little feet didn't make much noise then! I daresay poor old Mr. Swales would have told me that it was because I didn't want to wake up Geordie."

As she was in such a communicative humour, I asked her if she had dreamed at all that night.

Before she answered, that sweet, puckered look came into her forehead, which Arthur, I call him Arthur from her habit, says he loves, and indeed, I don't wonder that he does. Then she went on in a half-dreaming kind of way, as if trying to recall it to herself.

"I didn't quite dream, but it all seemed to be real. I only wanted to be here in this spot. I don't know why, for I was afraid of something, I don't know what. I remember, though I suppose I was asleep, passing through the streets and over the bridge. A fish leaped as I went by, and I leaned over to look at it, and I heard a lot of dogs howling. The whole town seemed as if it must be full of dogs all howling at once, as I went up the steps. Then I had a vague memory of something long and dark with red eyes, just as we saw in the sunset, and something very sweet and very bitter all around me at once. And then I seemed sinking into deep green water, and there was a singing in my ears, as I have heard there is to drowning men, and then everything seemed passing away from me. My soul seemed to go out from my body and float about the air. I seem to remember that once the West Lighthouse was right under me, and then there was a sort of agonizing feeling, as if I were in an earthquake, and I came back and found you shaking my body. I saw you do it before I felt you."

Then she began to laugh. It seemed a little uncanny to me, and I listened to her breathlessly. I did not quite like it, and thought it better not to keep her mind on the subject, so we drifted on to another subject, and Lucy was like her old self again. When we got home the fresh breeze had braced her up, and her pale cheeks were really more rosy. Her mother rejoiced when she saw her, and we all spent a very happy evening together.

19 August—Joy, joy, joy! Although not all joy. At last, news of Jonathan. The dear fellow has been ill, that is why he did not write. I am not afraid to think it or to say it, now that I know. Mr. Hawkins sent me on the letter, and wrote himself, oh so kindly. I am to leave in the morning and go over to Jonathan, and to help to nurse him if necessary, and to bring him home. Mr. Hawkins says it would not be a bad thing if we were to be married out there. I have cried over the good

Sister's letter till I can feel it wet against my bosom, where it lies. It is of Jonathan, and must be near my heart, for he is in my heart. My journey is all mapped out, and my luggage ready. I am only taking one change of dress. Lucy will bring my trunk to London and keep it till I send for it, for it may be that . . . I must write no more. I must keep it to say to Jonathan, my husband. The letter that he has seen and touched must comfort me till we meet.

Letter, Sister Agatha, Hospital of St. Joseph and Ste. Mary, Buda-Pesth, to Miss Willhelmina Murray

12 August,

Dear Madam.

I write by desire of Mr. Jonathan Harker, who is himself not strong enough to write, though progressing well, thanks to God and St. Joseph and Ste. Mary. He has been under our care for nearly six weeks, suffering from a violent brain fever. He wishes me to convey his love, and to say that by this post I write for him to Mr. Peter Hawkins, Exeter, to say, with his dutiful respects, that he is sorry for his delay, and that all of his work is completed. He will require some few weeks' rest in our sanatorium in the hills, but will then return. He wishes me to say that he has not sufficient money with him, and that he would like to pay for his staying here, so that others who need shall not be wanting for help.

Believe me,
Yours, with sympathy and all blessings.
Sister Agatha

P.S.—My patient being asleep, I open this to let you know something more. He has told me all about you, and that you are shortly to be his wife. All blessings to you both! He has had some fearful shock, so says our doctor, and in his delirium his ravings have been dreadful, of wolves and poison and blood, of ghosts and demons, and I fear to say of what. Be careful of him always that there may be nothing to excite him of this kind for a long time to come. The traces of such an illness as his do not lightly die away. We should have written long ago, but we knew nothing of his friends, and there was nothing on him, nothing that anyone could understand. He came in the train from Klausenburg, and the guard was told by the station master there that he rushed into the station shouting for a ticket for home. Seeing from his violent demeanour that he was English, they gave him a ticket for the furthest station on the way thither that the train reached.

Be assured that he is well cared for. He has won all hearts by his sweetness and gentleness. He is truly getting on well, and I have no doubt will in a few weeks be all himself. But be careful of him for safety's sake. There are, I pray God and St. Joseph and Ste. Mary, many, many, happy years for you both.

Dr. Seward's Case-Book

19 August—Strange and sudden change in Renfield last night. About eight o'clock he began to get excited and sniff about as a dog does when setting. The attendant was struck by his manner, and knowing my interest in him, encouraged him to talk. He is usually respectful to the attendant and at times servile, but tonight, the man tells me, he was quite haughty. Would not condescend to talk with him at all.

All he would say was, "I don't want to talk to you. You don't count now. The master is at hand."

The attendant thinks it is some sudden form of religious mania which has seized him. If so, we must look out for squalls, for a strong man with homicidal and religious mania at once might be dangerous. The combination is a dreadful one.

At nine o'clock I visited him myself. His attitude to me was the same as that to the attendant. In his sublime self-feeling the difference between myself and the attendant seemed to him as nothing. It looks like religious mania, and he will soon think that he himself is God.

These infinitesimal distinctions between man and man are too paltry for an Omnipotent Being. How these madmen give themselves away! The real God taketh heed lest a sparrow fall. But the God created from human vanity sees no difference between an eagle and a sparrow. Oh, if men only knew!

For half an hour or more Renfield kept getting excited in greater and greater degree. I did not pretend to be watching him, but I kept strict observation all the same. All at once that shifty look came into his eyes which we always see when a madman has seized an idea, and with it the shifty movement of the head and back which asylum attendants come to know so well. He became quite quiet, and went and sat on the edge of his bed resignedly, and looked into space with lack-luster eyes.

I thought I would find out if his apathy were real or only assumed, and tried to lead him to talk of his pets, a theme which had never failed to excite his attention.

At first he made no reply, but at length said testily, "Bother them all! I don't care a pin about them."

"What" I said. "You don't mean to tell me you don't care about spiders?" (Spiders at present are his hobby and the notebook is filling up with columns of small figures.)

To this he answered enigmatically, "The Bride maidens rejoice the eyes that wait the coming of the bride. But when the bride draweth nigh, then the maidens shine not to the eyes that are filled."

He would not explain himself, but remained obstinately seated on his bed all the time I remained with him.

I am weary tonight and low in spirits. I cannot but think of Lucy, and how different things might have been. If I don't sleep at once, chloral, the modern Morpheus! I must be careful not to let it grow into a habit. No, I shall take none tonight! I have thought of Lucy, and I shall not dishonour her by mixing the two. If need be, tonight shall be sleepless.

Later—Glad I made the resolution, gladder that I kept to it. I had lain tossing about, and had heard the clock strike only twice, when the night watchman came to me, sent up from the ward, to say that Renfield had escaped. I threw on my clothes and ran down at once. My "fly-man" patient, as I always think of him, is too dangerous a person to be roaming about. Those ideas of his might work out dangerously with strangers.

The attendant was waiting for me. He said he had seen him not ten minutes before, seemingly asleep in his bed, when he had looked through the observation trap in the door. His attention was called by the sound of the window being wrenched out. He ran back and saw his feet disappear through the window, and had at once sent up for me. He was only in his night gear, and cannot be far off.

The attendant thought it would be more useful to watch where he should go than to follow him, as he might lose sight of him whilst getting out of the building by the door. He is a bulky man, and couldn't get through the window.

I am thin, so, with his aid, I got out, but feet foremost, and as we were only a few feet above ground landed unhurt.

The attendant told me the patient had gone to the left, and had taken a straight line, so I ran as quickly as I could. As I got through the belt of trees I saw a white figure scale the high wall which separates our grounds from those of the deserted house.

I ran back at once, told the watchman to get three or four men immediately and follow me into the grounds of Carfax, in case our friend might be dangerous. I got a ladder myself, and crossing the wall, dropped down on the other side. I could see Renfield's figure just disappearing behind the angle of the house, so I ran after him. On the far side of the house I found him pressed close against the old iron-bound oak door of the chapel.

He was talking, apparently to some one, but I was afraid to go near enough to hear what he was saying, lest I might frighten him, and he should run off.

Chasing an errant swarm of bees is nothing to following a naked lunatic, when the fit of escaping is upon him! After a few minutes, however, I could see that he did not take note of anything around him, and so ventured to draw nearer to him, the more so as my men had now crossed the wall and were closing him in. I heard him say . . .

"I am here to do your bidding, Master. I am your slave, and you will reward me, for I shall be faithful. I have worshipped you long and afar off. Now that you are near, I await your commands, and you will not pass me by, will you, dear Master, in your distribution of good things?"

He is a selfish old beggar anyhow. He thinks of the loaves and fishes even when he believes his is in a real Presence. His manias make a startling combination. When we closed in on him he fought like a tiger. He is immensely strong, for he was more like a wild beast than a man.

I never saw a lunatic in such a paroxysm of rage before, and I hope I shall not again. It is a mercy that we have found out his strength and his danger in good time. With strength and determination like his, he might have done wild work before he was caged.

He is safe now, at any rate. Jack Sheppard himself couldn't get free from the strait waistcoat that keeps him restrained, and he's chained to the wall in the padded room.

His cries are at times awful, but the silences that follow are more deadly still, for he means murder in every turn and movement.

Just now he spoke coherent words for the first time. "I shall be patient, Master. It is coming, coming, coming!"

So I took the hint, and came to the room where the "fly-man" was being held. He was gazing with hopeful wonder toward the window, so I went over to look as well. I thought I saw something, or someone, moving about the grounds, and so hurried outside. I circled the entire property, but found no one, save for a tall man passing on the street. It was a strange trick of the moon light, to be sure, but it appeared that he cast no shadow what so ever.[114] I was too excited to sleep, but this diary has quieted me, and I feel I shall get some sleep tonight.

Letter from "King Death" to Francis Aytown[115]

19 August
346 Piccadilly

My dear young man,

Your letter has been most welcome to me. You did well to write to me so unconventionally, so fresh, so manly, and so affectionately, too. I, too, desire it that we shall one day personally meet each other. I dare say that time may be soon. Meantime I send you my friendship and thanks.

—D.

CHAPTER
THIRTEEN[116]

Research Notes of Alfred Singleton

19 August—While I am pleased that my article on the Whitby shipwreck was published in the local *Dailygraph*, I am still hopeful that I will succeed in writing a fuller account—one that includes a far deeper study of the supernatural elements this story is simply rife with—that can be published by the *Journal of the Occult*. As they have published several of my writings in the past, I am confident that this one will be a success as well. Indeed, they have already contacted me about my preliminary submission on the Whitby incident, and it has met with the approval of the *Journal's* editor. But as the record is as yet unfinished, I must do some follow-up investigation, so that a more complete article might be published.

After reviewing my previous research notes, I came to the conclusion that contacting Miss Katherine Reed—whose name and address I acquired, among others, during the course of my interviews—would be the most prudent action. My reason for this choice was two-fold:

First, generally speaking, when an event has no direct impact on a person's life, the details of it oft become altered or indistinct with the passage of time, or are forgotten altogether. But with the case of Miss Reed, her grandfather, one Mr. Swales, was found dead of fright and a broken neck within a day after the storm. So far as I can tell, he was the only casualty native to Whitby (save for a coal merchant's mastiff) at the time of and immediately following the shipwreck. While such a death had neither bearing on nor a solid connection to the shipwreck itself—and as such I did not include his passing in the article for the *Dailygraph*—it may yet have significance to the *Journal's* readers. And in any event, it undoubtedly had great significance to Miss Reed; if anyone will have the clearest memory of that unfortunate day, it will be she.

Second, I distinctly recall that Miss Reed had an acquaintance of sorts, one Francis Aytown, who had produced some excellent paintings of the stormy seas and of the *Demeter* herself, both while she was still afar off and after she had come ashore, as well as some sketches of the sea captain's funeral. With his permission, I will use my Kodak to make a photographic essay of his works to include in my next report.

Letter from Alfred Singleton to Katherine Reed

19 August
346 Piccadilly

Dear Miss Reed,

I pray you will pardon my writing, as it may serve only to dredge up unwanted memories. I am most grateful for your description of the events surrounding the storm and shipwreck of two weeks past. As I'm sure you read in the *Dailygraph* article, I did not make mention of the unfortunate accident involving your grandfather Mr. Swales, just as you requested, so as to not add the subject matter to the local gossip.

The reason for my writing you is this: I have the desire to conduct further interviews regarding the storm of 8 August at Whitby, and all that transpired after. If you are willing, may I call upon you in Piccadilly at your earliest convenience? I would like to speak with you more about that fateful week, and also, if I may, discover from you how I might make contact with Mr. Aytown, so that I might seek his permission to photograph those of his paintings and sketches which concern that same period of time. Again, my pardon, and with many thanks as well.

Sincerely,
Alfred Singleton
Independent Correspondent

Telegram, Miss Reed to Mr. Singleton

22 August

Come for supper on 24 August. Mr. Aytown will be there, as will others of our friends from Whitby, some of whom may be of assistance to you.

—Katherine Reed

Alfred Singleton's Notes

24 August, night. Piccadilly—I write this on the train, having just recently departed from the residence of Miss Reed. Though I am quite tired, I must record the details of the evening before tonight's dreaming can diminish facts into half-truths and outright fiction.

I arrived for supper at the Piccadilly home. I took my time before making my presence known, however, so that I might have the opportunity to study the vacant house across the street. It was in outward appearance quite similar to that of Miss Reed's, for it too was set high on its foundations, with a steep set of steps leading up to the great door. That it had been unoccupied for some time was clearly evident; the paint was blackened and pealing, the windows were dark with dust. A notice-board stood in front of the balcony, stating the residence was for sale through Mitchell, Sons, & Candy.

There was about that house an air of unwholesomeness, a sort of foreboding that went beyond what it's shadowed and derelict appearance might in and of itself inspire. I have, over the years, come to trust such intuitions, having made good use of them on my various investigations. Therefore, I would wager that if there is not already something malign afoot within those walls, there will be in short order, for evil calls to evil. (*mem.*, The address of the house—347—seems somehow familiar to me. I must consult my old notes on the matter, for there was or is, I seem to recall, something peculiar about the history of the residence which came to light in a prior bit of research I had done on another article for the *Journal of the Occult*).

But the hour was growing late, and I turned my attention to the matter at hand. I knocked at the door, and was shown in by the maid. The décor of Miss Reed's home was rather Bohemian; I was none too surprised at this, given the untraditional manner in which she carries herself, especially with regard to the dubious nature of her relationship with Mr. Aytown.

The maid took me to the salon, and announced my arrival. As supper was still nearly one half hour from being served, I had ample opportunity to meet the other guests who were already conversing there. Aside from myself, there were eleven others. Five of these, being Mr. Aytown, Miss Reed, Mr. Billington, Mr. Young, and Dr. Caffyn, were found to be of direct importance to my research. The remaining six, though they were certainly cordial enough, had no apparent connection to my project whatsoever, so I have not bothered to record my conversations with them in this ledger. In addition to myself and these eleven, there was also apparently a mysterious thirteenth guest who was due to arrive later, but I shall deal with that encounter in its proper time. So, to the five:

Mr. Francis Aytown—an acquaintance, shall we say, of Miss Reed, who makes his living as a painter. Mr. Aytown appears to be in his mid twenties, is rather tall, and dresses in an unorthodox manner—black velvet trimmed with fur, with a fairly open shirt front. He seems to be of a melancholic temperament, as artists are often wont to have, and has a quiet and intellectual, even poetic, manner of speech.

Evidentially Miss Reed had informed him of my intentions, for no sooner than I had introduced myself than he eagerly showed me to the second floor of the house, and into a large room which it would seem our hostess has been allowing him to use as a studio. Seeing his presence so firmly established in Miss Reed's home, I found myself having the rather improper thought that they might actually be living under the same roof, despite their not being wed. But as such matters concerned neither me nor my report, I did not bother to inquire on that particular matter.

In any event, in that studio he had arranged on easels a number of canvases for me to photograph. He agreed to allow the *Journal* print copies of his work, if only I would make mention of his name in the article, as well as include the address of his new gallery (the opening of which, incidentally, is the cause of this celebratory supper we were to enjoy this evening). The paintings themselves were quite remarkable. Three in particular caught my eye:

The first was of the evening before the storm, titled "Prelude to the Great Storm" (the very one I mentioned in passing in the *Dailygraph* article). The work depicted a view of the sunset over the bay, with black masses of clouds standing out boldly against the myriad of sunset-colours. Directly in front of the golden orb of the sun was the silhouette of the ill-fated schooner, all sails set. This was, he explained, the night of 8 August, just before the storm began to roll in.

The second was entitled "Mystery of the Sea." It was a beautiful—if macabre—rendering of the shipwreck itself. Mr. Aytown had captured the moment in eerie detail; the derelict resting upon the great sand mound of Tate Hill Pier, the poor dead sea-captain still dutifully at the helm, the great waves still churning in the background as if the water itself was a living thing in rage over its lost prize, and the whole scene illuminated by the great searchlight atop the East Cliff.

The third was of the sea-captain's somber funeral, which immortalized the particular details of the ceremony: the cortège of boats upon the river, the gathering of mourners in the cemetery, and the like. I noticed that the vantage point of the viewer was quite near the seat where Miss Reed's grandfather was found dead. In Mr. Aytown's depiction, there were two women standing upon the seat itself, apparently in an effort to get a better view of the proceedings. They were both quite lovely, one with red curls and the other with dark, shiny hair.[117] Oddly, there was a dog near to the foot of the bench, quite obviously in the act of barking. At first I thought it was barking at the funeral procession, but then, as I looked more closely, I saw that it was barking at the bench seat the two ladies were upon. The expression the dog's face held—for indeed animals have faces as expressive as any human's, if not more so—was a particular mixture of savage rage and pure terror that I have seen only a time or two in the past. If I was not mistaken, the animal had the "angel eyes" markings upon its brow, the same as those upon the great mastiff that was found dead after the storm. I asked him about the spots above the dog's eyes, inquiring if they were intentional representations of actual spots he had seen upon the original subject. He confirmed that indeed they were. Very curious . . .

Mr. Aytown excused himself for a moment, leaving me to record copies of his paintings with my Kodak. When I had completed my task, I caught sight of some other paintings and sketches nestled in a corner of the room. Curious to see if there was anything else that might be useful to my research, I went over to study them. While they all were obviously scenes of Whitby, there was nothing to indicate they would be of any use to me (or so I thought at the time). Indeed, the shipwreck appeared in none of them, as the focus of each work seemed to be upon a particular figure.

The man in the various works was tall, dressed all in black, with a long dark beard, a crooked nose, and piercing eyes. Clearly the painter had been having difficulty capturing the man's face correctly, for in each attempt he looked somewhat different, and some of the half-finished paintings had the face scraped off entirely, perhaps in preparation to try again, or perhaps in simple frustration. In all of the renditions, though, the man's face was unnaturally pale and seemed to be frozen in a rictus of death; if this were indeed the subject's true complexion, perhaps this pallor was the cause of Mr. Aytown's uncharacteristic difficulties?[118] I could not help but notice how similar the man was to the description of the supposed stowaway described in the *Demeter's* logbook, and made a mental memorandum of it.

Miss Katherine Reed—a woman of Yorkshire descent, though she clearly has been absent long enough to have lost her accent. She is young, near twenty, and of fair complexion and hair.

She is also the granddaughter of the late Mr. Swales, who was himself native of Yorkshire. Mr. Swales was found dead the morning of 10 August. The cause of his death was a broken neck, which the local doctor (one Doctor J.M. Caffyn, who I shall write of in due time) stated had been the result from falling backward over the seat overlooking the Whitby graveyard. The countenance of Mr. Swales' face was said (again by the good Dr Caffyn) to have been frozen in a rictus of fear, as if he had seen something horrific enough to cause him to stumble in the first place.

The thought occurred to me that might not the great wolf that had been seen leaping from the wreckage of the *Demeter* have come upon him suddenly, given him a great fright and causing him to stumble and break his neck? When asked about it, Miss Reed said the wayward animal was never found or seen again, though it had been blamed for the death of a coal merchant's mastiff, which had been found slain (presumably having been bested by the newcomer) on 9 August. Of course, I already knew of this from other sources. But she did provide a new tidbit of information for me: there was a second dog, a somewhat smaller one, found dead of similar causes as the mastiff. Curiously, the second dog had been discovered under the same seat upon which Mr. Swales had died. When I inquired as to the appearance of the second dog, she described it in a way that sounded very much like the one pictured in Mr. Aytown's paintings.

How very troubling, that two dogs with the "angel eyes" markings—which, according to folklore, made them both keenly sensitive to the presence of supernatural evil—would have both been found slain after the storm. And then, to have one of those unfortunate dogs found in a painting, pictured barking at the very seat that both it and Mr. Swales had died upon was quite disconcerting—and intriguing—indeed.

When I asked Miss Reed about the seat itself, she replied that it was very old, and had just beneath it the resting place of one George Canon, whom Mr. Swales told her was a suicide. Quite disconcerting, indeed.

Mr. Billington—the younger half of "S. F. Billington, of Samuel F. Billington & Son, Solicitors," located at 7 The Crescent, Whitby.

The young gentleman, a sincere and honourable man, was understandably reluctant to divulge anything beyond what he would consider common knowledge, for the sake of his client's privacy. He did add some measure of detail to what information I already had, however—that there were a total of fifty boxes that arrived aboard the *Demeter*, each filled with what the invoice labeled as "common earth, to be used for experimental purposes." The boxes—and presumably the earth therein—originated in Transylvania and were loaded into the ship at Varna. They have since been delivered to their destination.

Naturally, he would divulge neither this destination nor the owners of the boxes. But shortly thereafter I was approached by one William Young (who is here with his sister, who seemed never far behind him)[119], who had apparently overheard our conversation and offered to be of assistance in this matter.

William Young—the law student who was present at the initial boarding of the wrecked *Demeter*, the one whom I wrote of in the *Dailygraph*, who had insisted that the statues of mortmain should have forfeited the cargo's owner of any rights to the salvage[120].

He was a shrewd and skeptical character[121], to be sure, and had made sure that he was the first civilian to board the shipwreck, though he did not make it aboard before the coastguard discovered the body of the captain. But as coastguards cannot claim salvage rights, undoubtedly Mr. Young was still certain that he, as the first civilian present, would be granted such rights by the Admiralty Court, and had even brought in an auctioneer to handle the whole affair.

Of course, his claim was refuted, and there was ultimately nothing worth salvaging on the ship anyway, but nevertheless the young lawyer seemed to hold a grudge against the Billington solicitors over their having his declaration overruled. So now he was hoping that by offering me the information that Mr. Billington would not, that he might have a small amount of revenge against him. While I can hardly condone such a prideful and selfish motive, I was far too interested in what he had to offer to criticize him or turn down his aid.

According to Mr. Young, who had apparently pursued the matter further than he should have been allowed to legally, the owner of the boxes is one Count DeVille, who owns an estate called Carfax, located in Purfleet. All fifty boxes were delivered to Carter, Paterson & Co by way of the Great Northern Railway and the King's Cross station. Mr. Young admits he gave up the pursuit of his salvage rights at this point, and can only assume that from this point Carter *etc. etc.* had fulfilled their obligations and delivered the goods to Carfax.

I of course thanked the embittered young man for his information, but in the most noncommittal way possible under the circumstances.

Doctor J.M. Caffyn—a surgeon of 33 East Elliot Place, Whitby, who had provided the initial estimate of the sea-captain's time of death, as well as took charge of the stowaway's body found within one of the cargo boxes.

With regard to the body found within one of the cargo boxes, which was later found to be missing, he seemed reluctant to speak. Finally, he related to me a peculiar story, which I've seen fit to record here verbatim:

"When the corpse was found in the cargo hold, I was called back aboard to examine it, seeing as how the regional surgeon was unavailable for the task, and found myself struck by how fresh and life-like the body was. And yet, with no discernable heartbeat or breath, I had to officially conclude that he was in fact deceased. Still, even when the body was brought to the mortuary, I could not help but feel there may be some sort of life left within the poor man. As you may know, there have been many cases reported, even in our own day, of people who have been thought by friends and family and surgeons alike to be dead, only to recover from whatever it was that had ailed them, and awoke once more, much to the surprise of all concerned. Well, before too much time had passed, I wanted to see for myself if there was any chance the man could be restored to life. I tried everything I could think of, from smelling salts to brandy, and even a large injection of fresh blood into his veins, but there seemed to be no effect. I had given up all hope for him, and had to believe he had been dead all along, or at least so deeply and irreversibly comatose that he may as well be dead. But when I returned to the room again that night for one more look, I found the body to be gone! In a burst of pride, I thought to myself 'Ah! My efforts were a success! The man is restored to life!' . . . but then I thought better of it. I'm sure you can see why I did not mention my attempt at restoration to anyone at the time, for it would be apparent that I had been the one to take and hide away the body, in an effort to make a name for myself as one who was skilled enough in medicine as to be able to revive even the dead."[122]

About this time, we were all called to supper, and we gathered in the dining room. There were thirteen seats positioned around a large table, which left one vacant after we had all been seated, as our "mystery guest" had yet to arrive. Soft music played from a nearby phonograph. Our meal was that of dressed crab, and though it had been prepared wonderfully, I did not partake of an overly large helping, as such a dish has been known to produce queer dreams in some.[123]

As the evening wore on, Miss Reed suggested that we all play a story-telling game. She produced a bowl filled with little scraps of paper, each folded and with a number written on it. We all would draw out our paper, and open it to see what number we had. Whoever had "1" would go first and would begin to tell a story, and after a few minutes they would stop, leaving it up to the "2" person to continue, and so on until we had made our way around the entire table and the story was completed.[124] We all found this to be a splendid idea, and so agreed to proceed.

Miss Reed, who appropriately ended up with the "1" began the story thus:[125]

"Far, far away, there is a beautiful Country which no human eye has ever seen in waking hours. Under the Sunset it lies, where the distant horizon bounds the day, and where the clouds, splendid with light and colour, give a promise of the glory and beauty which encompass it. Sometimes it is given to us to see it in dreams. Now and again come, softly, Angels who fan with their great white wings the aching brows, and place cool hands upon the sleeping eyes. Then soars away the spirit of the sleeper. Up from the dimness and murkiness of the night season it springs. Away through the purple clouds it sails. It flies through the vast expanse of light and air. Through the deep blue of heaven's vault it flies; and sweeping over the far-off horizon, rests in the fair Land Under the Sunset."

How excellent! Miss Reed had provided us a promising beginning; it was short enough to retain the interest of her listeners, yet provided many avenues through which the story could be expounded by those who would speak after her. So there she left off, and it was the turn of the good doctor Caffyn:

"This Country is like our own Country in many ways. It has men and women, kings and queens, rich and poor; it has houses, and trees, and fields, and birds, and flowers. There is day there and night also; and heat and cold, and sickness and health. The hearts of men and women, and boys and girls, beat as they do here. There are the same sorrows and the same joys; and the same hopes and the same fears. If a child from that Country was beside a child here you could not tell the difference between them, save that the clothes alone are different. They talk the same language as we do ourselves. They do not know that they are different from us; and we do not know that we are different from them. When they come to us in their dreams we do not know they are strangers; and when we go to their Country in our dreams we seem to be at home. Perhaps this is because good people's homes are in their hearts; and wheresoever they may be they have peace."

The good doctor was predictably mundane in his description of the inhabitants, but he did at least manage to include the aspect of dream-time visitations that Miss Reed had invented. And so we moved on to Mr. Billington:

"The Country Under the Sunset was for long ages a wondrous and pleasant Land. Nothing there was which was not beautiful and sweet and pleasant. It was only when sin came that things there began to lose their perfect beauty. Even now it is a wondrous and pleasant land. As the sun is strong there, by the sides of every road are planted great trees which spread out their thick branches. So the travelers have shelter as they pass. The milestones are fountains of sweet cold water, so clear and bright that when the wayfarer comes to one he sits down on the carved stone seat beside it and gives a sigh of relief, for he knows that there is rest. When it is sunset here, it is the middle of the day there. The clouds gather and shade the Land from the great heat. Then for a little while everything goes to sleep. This sweet, peaceful hour is called the Rest Time. When it comes the birds stop their singing, and lie close under the wide eaves of the houses, or in the branches of the trees where they join the stems. The fishes stop darting about in the water, and lie close under the stones, with their fins and tails as still as if they were dead. The sheep and the cattle lie under the trees. The men and women get into hammocks slung between trees or under the verandahs of their houses. Then, when the sun has ceased to glare so fiercely and the clouds have melted away, the living things all wake up."

The scene he described was vivid enough to make me wonder if he had seem something like it on one of his travels, so that, in truth, he was relating to us an actual memory. But now it was my turn to speak. As the matter of those slain dogs was still weighing heavily upon my mind, I made use of them in my addition:

"The only living things that are not asleep in the Rest Time are the dogs. They lie quite quiet, only half asleep, with one eye open and one ear cocked; keeping watch all the time. Then if any stranger comes during the hour of Rest, the dogs rise up and look at him, softly, without barking, lest they should disturb anyone. They know if the new comer is harmless; and if it be so they lie down again, and the stranger lies down too till the Rest Time is over. But if the dogs think that the stranger is come to do any harm, they bark loudly and growl. The cows begin to low and the sheep to bleat, and the birds to chirp and sing their loudest notes, but without any music in them; and even the fishes begin to dart about and splash the water. The men awake and jump out of their hammocks, and seize their weapons. Then it is an evil time for the intruder. Straightway he is brought into the Court and tried, and if found guilty sentenced, and either put into prison or banished. Then the men go back to their hammocks, and all living things retire again till the Rest Time is over. It is the same in the night as in the Rest Time, if an intruder comes to do harm. In the night only the dogs are awake, and the sick people and their nurses."

Now it was Mr. Young's turn. His lack of interest in this game was well-concealed, a credit to his shrewd nature, but it still visible to a trained observer such as myself. He made his addition—which involved the notion of being trapped (as perhaps he felt at this particular gathering, or in his career in general?)—thankfully brief:

"No one can leave the Country Under the Sunset except in one direction. Those who go there in dreams, or who come in dreams to our world, come and go they know not how; but if an inhabitant tries to leave it, he cannot except by one way. If he tries any other way he goes on and on, turning without knowing it, till he comes to the one place where only he can depart." After a moment's pause, perhaps feeling he had not measured up to those who had come before him (which, of course, he had not), he added quickly: "This place is called the Portal, and there the Angels keep guard."

Mr. Aytown spoke next. His words were slow and thoughtful, and were tinged with a kind of wistful longing:

"Farther off, away towards the Portal, the country gets wilder and wilder. Beyond this there are dense forests and great mountains full of deep caverns, as dark as night. Here wild animals and all cruel things have their home. Then come bogs and fens and deep shaky morasses, and thick jungles. Then all becomes so wild that the road gets lost altogether. In the wild places beyond this no man knows what dwells. Some say that the Giants who still exist, live there, and that all poisonous plants there grow. They say that there is a wicked wind there that brings out the seeds of all evil things and scatters them over the earth. Some there are who say that the same wicked wind brings out also the Diseases and Plagues that there exist. Others say that Famine lives there in the marshes, and that he stalks out when men are wicked—so wicked that the Spirits who guard the land are weeping so bitterly that they do not see him pass. It is whispered that Death has his kingdom in the Solitudes beyond the marshes, and lives in a castle so awful to look at that no one has ever seen it and lived to tell what it is like. Also it is told that all the evil things that live in the marshes are the disobedient Children of Death who have left their home and cannot find their way back again. But no man knows where the Castle of King Death is. All men and women, boys and girls, and even little wee children should so live that when they have to enter the Castle and see the grim King, they may not fear to behold his face . . ."

No sooner had he uttered this last line than the maid broke in with the announcement of a late arrival to dinner: "Count DeVille."[126]

CHAPTER
FOURTEEN[127]

Alfred Singleton's Notes, Continued

At the point the maid had announced the arrival of the Count, we had all become so thoroughly engrossed in our game that we had lost nearly all connection with reality, and the abrupt intrusion of her words into our fanciful tale came as quite a shock; indeed, more than one of us "jumped in our seats" as the saying goes. With a start, all eyes turned toward the door, and as the maid stepped aside, King Death himself entered the room right out of our storytelling game—or so it seemed, to look upon his visage.

He was tall, and dressed all in black. His face was feral and sensual, with a thin, beak-like nose. His hair was quite dark, and pulled back behind unusually pointed ears. His eyebrows were thick, and served to shadow a pair of eyes that seemed to gleam red from their dark orbits. His thin red lips, over which hung a pair of particularly long eyeteeth, were framed by a black moustache and long beard and which came to a point.

For a moment it seemed the hands of the clock ceased to move, and we all gazed in silence and wonder upon this man, each of us perhaps wondering if, by some spell woven in through our story telling, we had ourselves called this apparition into being from the mists of our own imaginings. But then the Count moved, breaking the spell, and bowed in a courtly manner similar to that seen given by delegates from the East. When he spoke, his pronunciation was nearly flawless, save for a few inflections I could not quite place, but which nevertheless placed his origins beyond our borders. While I typically concern myself with recording facts rather than recounting conversation, I found the dialogue of this evening of particular interest, and so will endeavor to catalogue it here:

"Good evening," the late arrival was the first to speak, "I am Count DeVille. Miss Reed, I thank you for your most kind invitation into your home."

"Count," Miss Reed returned his bow, as did we all, now that we found ourselves able to move of our own accord. All of us, that is, save for Mr. Aytown. He still seemed quite stunned by the Count's presence, and remained fixed in place. Our hostess spoke quickly to cover for her acquaintance's lapse: "Please forgive dear Francis."

"But of course. Are you well, good sir?" the Count turned to ask Mr. Aytown in the suavest of tones. "You seem a trifle . . . pale."

Kate answered for him when he made no reply of his own, "Oh yes, he's quite well; he's just so surprised to see you again."

"Again?" The Count replied with an arched brow and a look toward Mr. Aytown. "Have we met?" I could have been mistaken, but there seemed to be something in his voice, or in his hard, dark eyes, that made me think that he knew exactly who Mr. Aytown was.

"N—n—no. Well, yes, in a way," the artist stammered out. "You see, I saw you at—at Whitby, not very long ago, and . . ."

"And poor Francis has been trying to paint your portrait ever since," Miss Reed added. "He has been having a time with it. I've never known him to have so much difficulty capturing someone's face before. So when I saw you inspecting the property across the way, I simply had to invite you over to meet him."

"I have not had a portrait painted of me in some time. I am honoured," the Count said, bowing again to Mr. Aytown, who blushed like a schoolboy might, though at last he too remembered to bow in turn.

"Ah, Count DeVille," said the young Mr. Billington, "we haven't actually met."

"Count, this is . . ." Kate began, but our guest finished the introduction for her.

"Yes, Mr. Billington, my new English solicitor, who so carefully handled my goods aboard the ill-fated *Demeter*." Here I could not help but notice Mr. Young grimace at the memory of his loss of salvage rights. "I must say I have greatly enjoyed our correspondence."

"As have I."

"What a terrible shame about the *Demeter* and it's crew," Dr. Caffyn lamented. "It's too bad they did not survive the journey as well as your cargo."

"Yes, a pity," the Count seemed to agree, but then said "Had they lived, the ship would have undoubtedly arrived in a more timely manner."

"But, what of that poor fellow found in the crate?" the doctor continued, visibly stunned by the Count's insensitivity to death and the dead.[128] "Surely he was one of your own countrymen, Count. His features were somewhat like your own, though his were much older."

"It could very well be, considering from whence the ship sailed." Seeing, perhaps, his remiss in showing such absolute despisal for death, added "You must not think I care nothing for the dead, good doctor, it is only that, where I am from, death is so very common as to be a way of life. In a way, though, I do feel somewhat responsible for the loss of the ship's crew; after all, I had chartered the very ship they were doomed to sail upon. I especially grieve for that poor lad who threw himself to the sea; blood is far too precious a thing to be spilt in times such as these."

"Ah, did you happen to read that article in the local paper about it, Count?" I ventured, noting that he knew of the mate's suicide. Surprisingly, he indicated he had not, so I added "It seems that the poor captain had kept an addendum to the ship's logbook."

"Oh?" the Count replied in obvious surprise. "Such a thing was not lost at sea?"

"No indeed. He kept it on his person, you see, sealed in a bottle, to be found after the death he knew was upon him. It told a strange tale of ghosts and plague and death. But there was one word in the last entry that was quite strange, something that seemed to mean 'un-dead.' The word was 'nosferatu,' I do believe."

"Ah, yes. Nosferatu. The meaning of such a word does prove difficult when translating into English. Perhaps something more along the lines of 'unclean' or 'plague carrier' might suffice. I trust such discussion is not frightening to anyone?"

"Oh, but I do love to be frightened!" Mr. Aytown said impulsively.

"Do you?" our guest replied with an amused smile.

Soon we were all reseated, with the Count having been placed in a position of honour that had been held for him. Hot food and wine were brought and placed before him, though at the moment he seemed more interested in conversation than dining.

"Forgive me, Count, but do you . . . do you mean to say that you are planning to move here? That is, across the street?" Mr. Aytown asked hesitantly.

"Yes, indeed," the newcomer replied. "It is quite an extraordinary house. I dare say that before long we will be neighbors."

"Your presence will be most welcome," Kate said, "though I must say that I can't imagine how anyone could spend even a day in that old place."

"A house, Miss Reed, cannot be made habitable in a day. I am from an old family, and am somewhat fixed in my ways. To live in a new house would be quite impossible for me."

Here there came a pause in the conversation, during which Mr. Aytown offered the count something to drink.

"No, thank you, Mr. Aytown," was his response. "I never drink wine."

After a time, the staff came around to remove the plates. I noticed the Count had neither eaten nor drank of anything that was before him, when he relinquished his dinner without objection. We all retired to the parlour, where Miss Reed and Mr. Aytown and a few of the other guests danced. As the Count seemed disinclined to dance at the moment, I sat near him.

"So, you have come to England to settle down?"

"Settle down? No, quite the opposite. I have found your England, and the great London, to be a most fascinating place, so full of life, and of unexpected . . . curiosities." It seemed to me his gaze traveled to our hosts as he spoke. "I wish to walk its streets, to share in its humanity, its life, even its death."

"You seem to have a great lust for life, Count."

"Ah, how very well you phrase it," he replied to me, though he kept his gaze fixed upon Miss Reed and Mr. Aytown. Suddenly, Mr. Aytown collapsed on the floor in front of Miss Reed, with whom he had been dancing.

"Francis!" Miss Reed quickly knelt down beside him, as the other guests rushed over to help.

"I'm all right," the young man insisted after he had been helped to his feet. "Just a little dizzy, is all."

"Dr. Caffyn," Miss Reed beckoned to her guest. "Do you have any laudanum with you?"

"With your permission and with all due respect, Miss Reed," the Count interjected before the doctor could answer, "there is no need to taint this good man's blood with such medications." He then directed himself to Mr. Aytown. "Good sir, I fear you have been under much strain this evening, and my unexpected presence is no doubt the cause."

"Oh, no, Count. It's not you at all. It's just this pain in my head; it runs all the way down into my neck . . ."

"I can remove this pain," the Count said in tone that was not boastful, but simply matter of fact. Mr. Aytown seemed at once intrigued and fearful.

"How would you do such a thing?" he inquired.

"Such pain yields readily to suggestion."

"Ah, if you mean hypnotism, he's probably better off with the pain," Dr Caffyn said.

"Why is that?" Miss Reed asked her dubious guest. The Count answered for him.

"I suspect your friend is envisioning an ugly waving of the arms with many passes before the eyes. My ways are rather more direct. Please, sir, sit here." At his prompting, Mr. Aytown took a seat across from the Count, facing him, and Miss Reed dimmed the lights for them. "Look at me, Mr. Aytown." The Count's eyes, which had previously been quite dark, now seemed to more than reflect the flickering light that remained, burning like red embers. As Mr. Aytown stared into those strange eyes, his own seemed to cloud over and lose their focus, though the Count had said or done nothing to induce such a state (I have seen other hypnotists that have required several minutes and soothing words to bring about such relaxation). When he spoke, his voice was deep and resonant. "When I will you to do a thing, it shall be done, now and for always. Do you understand?"

"Yes," the young man mummured.

"Then listen, and obey my command. From now on, you have no pain. Do you hear me?"

"Yes," he again replied dully, like one only half awake.

"Good. When you awaken, you shall remember nothing of this. Now, awake!" All at once the man's eyes were open and clear, and the lines of pain that had creased his face only minutes before were gone. "How do you feel, Mr. Aytown?"

"I feel . . . wonderful. Free. The pain is gone!" (Yes, I thought to my self, gone . . . along with his free will!)

"Excellent. I am most gratified to have been of service." And with that, the festivities resumed. The Count danced with Miss Reed (though I noticed how Mr. Aytown watched the proceedings with obvious jealousy), and conversation was reduced to the idle and pointless chatter so common to such affairs. As for myself, I had but one final question to ask, and that was to inquire of the Count in a straightforward way if he himself had made the journey here on the *Demeter*. He would of course deny it, but I am by nature an excellent judge of honesty, and am certain that I would be able to tell if he was telling the truth.

Yet, I could not bring myself to ask him. It was as if something within me had risen up to choke back my words, to weaken my very nerve. Such feelings were uncommon, but not unheard of in my particular line of work. More than once I had been hindered in such a manner during investigations for the *Journal*, and each time I was glad for my silence later, for in hindsight there was great danger in the asking.

But, as I could not let the matter go completely, I asked by what means he made his journey to England, if not through Whitby. He replied that he had first arrived through Dover prior to his making the journey to Whitby. Here I must confess that my previous boasting was in vain, because, for the life of me, I could not discern whether or not he had lied (*mem.*, check with Customs House to validate or refute the Count's story).

So from here on I contented myself with merely observing the Count. His mannerisms were refined and elegant, yet somehow restrained, as if his actions and thoughts were not of one accord. Of particular note was his reaction—or rather, lack there of—to the various changes in music of the phonograph. While his manner of dance was elegant and sophisticated, it was performed with such a rehearsed precision and an absolute lack of emotion, as if he were thoroughly unmoved by what the phonograph was playing, that for a moment I wondered if he might be tone deaf.[129]

By then the hour had grown late, and my time at Miss Reed's was at an end. I excused myself at the first convenient opportunity, and made my way to the station. And here I sit on the train, completing my notes. I am pleased with my notes on the *Demeter* incident, and yet, I believe I shall hold off sending in the article for a time. There is something else afoot here, and I must look into it further before considering the matter closed.

25 August—Spoke with contact in Dover. Apparently, there has been no record of a Count DeVille listed in the Custom's House ledger[130]. It is an odd thought, yet I am certain that the Count was somehow aboard the *Demeter*, though surely he could not have been the corpse found below deck . . .

26 August—Have tracked down the mention of 347 Piccadilly in my research notes. It was the residence of the late Archibald Winter-Suffield. He was a wealthy man, who owned several properties throughout the land—Piccadilly, Purfleet, Mile End, and Bermondsey, among others. Yet, despite his financial security, he was apparently quite dissatisfied with life, and committed suicide. From what I inferred from my discussions with Mr. Billington and Mr. Young, it would seem that Count DeVille has already purchased the Purfleet estate called Carfax (though the purchase was carried out in a peculiar way, which did not directly entail the use of Winter-Suffield's regular solicitor, one Mr. Renfield), and by his own admission he is now moving into the Piccadilly home.

When last the Count was in Whitby, there were deaths at the grave of a suicide. Now he is to dwell in one or more homes of a suicide. I must study this matter with closer scrutiny, and keep watch for unusual happenings . . .

CHAPTER FIFTEEN[131]

Letter, Mina Harker to Lucy Westenra

Buda-Pesth,
24 August.

My dearest Lucy,

I know you will be anxious to hear all that has happened since we parted at the railway station at Whitby.

Well, my dear, I got to Hull all right, and caught the boat to Hamburg, and then the train on here. I feel that I can hardly recall anything of the journey, except that I knew I was coming to Jonathan, and that as I should have to do some nursing, I had better get all the sleep I could. I found my dear one, oh, so thin and pale and weak-looking. All the resolution has gone out of his dear eyes, and that quiet dignity which I told you was in his face has vanished. He is only a wreck of himself, and he does not remember anything that has happened to him for a long time past. At least, he wants me to believe so, and I shall never ask.

He has had some terrible shock, and I fear it might tax his poor brain if he were to try to recall it. Sister Agatha, who is a good creature and a born nurse, tells me that he wanted her to tell me what they were, but she would only cross herself, and say she would never tell. That the ravings of the sick were the secrets of God, and that if a nurse through her vocation should hear them, she should respect her trust.

She is a sweet, good soul, and the next day, when she saw I was troubled, she opened up the subject my poor dear raved about, added, 'I can tell you this much, my dear. That it was not about anything which he has done wrong himself, and you, as his wife to be, have no cause to be concerned. He has not forgotten you or what he owes to you. His fear was of great and terrible things, which no mortal can treat of.'

I do believe the dear soul thought I might be jealous lest my poor dear should have fallen in love with any other girl. The idea of my being jealous about Jonathan! And yet, my dear, let me whisper, I felt a thrill of joy through me when I knew that no other woman was a cause for trouble. I am now sitting by his bedside, where I can see his face while he sleeps. He is waking!

When he woke he asked me for his coat, as he wanted to get something from the pocket. I asked Sister Agatha, and she brought all his things. I saw amongst them was his notebook, and was going to ask him to let me look at it, for I knew that I might find some clue to his trouble, but I suppose he must have seen my wish in my eyes, for he sent me over to the window, saying he wanted to be quite alone for a moment.

Then he called me back, and he said to me very solemnly, 'Wilhelmina,' I knew then that he was in deadly earnest, for he has never called me by that name since he asked me to marry him, 'You know, dear, my ideas of the trust between husband and wife. There should be no secret, no concealment. I have had a great shock, and when I try to think of what it is I feel my head spin round, and I do not know if it was real of the dreaming of a madman. You know I had brain fever, and that is to be mad. The secret is here, and I do not want to know it. I want to take up my life here, with our marriage.' For, my dear, we had decided to be married as soon as the formalities are complete. 'Are you willing, Wilhelmina, to share my ignorance? Here is the book. Take it and keep it, read it if you will, but never let me know unless, indeed, some solemn duty should come upon me to go back to the bitter hours, asleep or awake, sane or mad, recorded here.' He fell back exhausted, and I put the book under his pillow, and kissed him. I have asked Sister Agatha to beg the Superior to let our wedding be this afternoon, and am waiting her reply . . .

She has come and told me that the Chaplain of the English mission church has been sent for. We are to be married in an hour, or as soon after as Jonathan awakes[132].

Lucy, the time has come and gone. I feel very solemn, but very, very happy. Jonathan woke a little after the hour, and all was ready, and he sat up in bed, propped up with pillows. He answered his 'I will' firmly and strong. I could hardly speak. My heart was so full that even those words seemed to choke me.

The dear sisters were so kind. Please, God, I shall never, never forget them, nor the grave and sweet responsibilities I have taken upon me. I must tell you of my wedding present. When the chaplain and the sisters had left me alone with my husband—oh, Lucy, it is the first time I have written the words 'my husband'—left me alone with my husband, I took the book from under his pillow, and wrapped it up in white paper, and tied it with a little bit of pale blue ribbon which was round my neck, and sealed it over the knot with sealing wax, and for my seal I used my wedding ring. Then I kissed it and showed it to my husband, and told him that I would keep it so, and then it would be an outward and visible sign for us all our lives that we trusted each other, that I would never open it unless it were for his own dear sake or for the sake of some stern duty. Then he took my hand in his, and oh, Lucy, it was the first time he took his wife's hand, and said that it was the dearest thing in all the wide world, and that he would go through all the past again to win it, if need be. The poor dear meant to have said a part of the past, but he cannot think of time yet, and I shall not wonder if at first he mixes up not only the month, but the year.

Well, my dear, what could I say? I could only tell him that I was the happiest woman in all the wide world, and that I had nothing to give him except myself, my life, and my trust, and that with these went my love and duty for all the days of my life. And, my dear, when he kissed me, and drew me to him with his poor weak hands, it was like a solemn pledge between us.

Lucy dear, do you know why I tell you all this? It is not only because it is all sweet to me, but because you have been, and are, very dear to me. It was my privilege to be your friend and guide when you came from the schoolroom to prepare for the world of life. I want you to see now, and with the eyes of a very happy wife, whither duty has led me, so that in your own married life you too may be all happy, as I am. My dear, please Almighty God, your life may be all it promises, a long day of sunshine, with no harsh wind, no forgetting duty, no distrust. I must not wish you no pain, for that can never be, but I do hope you will be always as happy as I am now. Goodbye, my dear. I shall post this at once, and perhaps, write you very soon again. I must stop, for Jonathan is waking. I must attend my husband!

Your ever-loving,
Mina Harker.

Letter, Lucy Westenra to Mina Harker

Whitby,
30 August.

My dearest Mina,

Oceans of love and millions of kisses, and may you soon be in your own home with your husband. I wish you were coming home soon enough to stay with us here. The strong air would soon restore Jonathan. It has quite restored me. I have an appetite like a cormorant, am full of life, and sleep well. You will be glad to know that I have quite given up walking in my sleep. I think I have not stirred out of my bed for a week, that is when I once got into it at night. Arthur says I am getting fat. By the way, I forgot to tell you that Arthur is here. We have such walks and drives, and rides, and rowing, and tennis, and fishing together, and I love him more than ever. He tells me that he loves me more, but I doubt that, for at first he told me that he couldn't love me more than he did then. But this is nonsense. There he is, calling to me. So no more just at present from your loving,

Lucy.

P.S.—Mother sends her love. She seems no better, poor dear.
P.P.S.—We are to be married on 28 September.

Letter, Kate to Mr. and Mrs. Reed

31 August

Dearest Mamma and Papa,

We have a new neighbor, and of foreign royalty no less!

His name is Count DeVille. Francis had spotted him in Whitby during our holiday, and had the worst of times trying to capture his image on canvas. And then, just last week, I found him inspecting the property across the way—the old Winter-Suffield place. How odd, that of all the places he could have purchased, he hit upon the same street as Francis. It was as if he somehow knew Francis' need to see his face again.

The opportunity was too much to pass by, and so introduced myself (not the proper thing to do, I know, but I did it anyway), and invited him to dinner without telling Francis. Oh Mamma, Papa, you should have seen the look on his face when he saw the Count walk in! The moment was truly priceless. I believe the surprise of it all was too much for Francis though, and he nearly fainted while we were dancing. But the Count used some sort of Eastern hypnosis, and cured him on the spot. The two of them have been firm friends ever since.

Our new friend seems to me to be quite lonely—a stranger in a strange land—and greatly enjoys our company. Curiously, though he enjoys recounting tales of ancient battles and blood feuds and odd legends, he has never mentioned specifically from where he hailed, but would only say that it was a "land beyond a great forest."

Well, you know how much I love a good mystery, so I took it upon myself to trace his origins. My one real clue was a name he mentioned in one of his tales, a place called the Scholomance, which he seemed to indicate was not that far from his own home. So the following day I had my and Mina's good friend from the Lyceum pay a visit to the reading room of the British Museum on my behalf, for he already has a letter of introduction, and visits there quite often.

My friend tells me there is a book there by Emily Gerard[133], in which is described the Scholomance. It was, or still may be, a legendary school of sorts situated near a lake in the Carpathian mountains, just above the city of Hermannstadt. This would then place the Count's home as being in Transylvania, or at least a nearby province. I believe I shall bring up Transylvania at our next dinner, and see if he takes note of my discovery. In the meantime, dear Francis is out with our neighbor even as I write this, showing him through his new home of London.

I shall write you soon, and as always, I am—

Your loving daughter,

Kate

Cutting from *The Daily News*, 1 September[134]

A shocking murder was discovered in Whitechapel yesterday morning. Shortly before four o'clock Police constable Neil found a woman lying in Buck's row, Thomas street, with her throat cut from ear to ear. The body, which was immediately removed to a mortuary, was also fearfully mutilated. The deceased has been identified as Mary Ann Nicholls, thirty six years of age, who was recently an inmate of Lambeth Workhouse. No clue to the murderer has, however, yet been obtained.

Dr. Seward's Case-Book

20 August—The case of Renfield grows even more interesting. He has now so far quieted that there are spells of cessation from his passion. For the first week after his attack he was perpetually violent. Then one night, just as the moon rose, he grew quiet, and kept murmuring to himself. "Now I can wait. Now I can wait."

The attendant came to tell me, so I ran down at once to have a look at him. He was still in the strait waistcoat and in the padded room, but the suffused look had gone from his face, and his eyes had something of their old pleading. I might almost say, cringing, softness. I was satisfied with his present condition, and directed him to be relieved. The attendants hesitated, but finally carried out my wishes without protest.

It was a strange thing that the patient had humour enough to see their distrust, for, coming close to me, he said in a whisper, all the while looking furtively at them, "They think I could hurt you! Fancy me hurting you! The fools!"

It was soothing, somehow, to the feelings to find myself disassociated even in the mind of this poor madman from the others, but all the same I do not follow his thought. Am I to take it that I have anything in common with him, so that we are, as it were, to stand together. Or has he to gain from me some good so stupendous that my well being is needful to Him? I must find out later on. Tonight he will not speak. Even the offer of a kitten or even a full-grown cat will not tempt him.

He will only say, "I don't take any stock in cats. I have more to think of now, and I can wait. I can wait."

After a while I left him. The attendant tells me that he was quiet until just before dawn, and that then he began to get uneasy, and at length violent, until at last he fell into a paroxysm which exhausted him so that he swooned into a sort of coma.

. . . Three nights has the same thing happened, violent all day then quiet from moonrise to sunrise. I wish I could get some clue to the cause. It would almost seem as if there was some influence which came and went. Happy thought! We shall tonight play sane wits against mad ones. He escaped before without our help. Tonight he shall escape with it. We shall give him a chance, and have the men ready to follow in case they are required.

23 August—"The expected always happens." How well Disraeli knew life. Our bird when he found the cage open would not fly, so all our subtle arrangements were for naught. At any rate, we have proved one thing, that the spells of quietness last a reasonable time. We shall in future be able to ease his bonds for a few hours each day. I have given orders to the night attendant merely to shut him in the padded room, when once he is quiet, until the hour before sunrise. The poor soul's body will enjoy the relief even if his mind cannot appreciate it. Hark! The unexpected again! I am called. The patient has once more escaped.

Later—Another night adventure. Renfield artfully waited until the attendant was entering the room to inspect. Then he dashed out past him and flew down the passage. I took my pistol and sent word for the attendants to take their nets and follow. Again he went into the grounds of the deserted house, and we found him in the same place, pressed against the old chapel door. When he saw me he became furious, and had not the attendants seized him in time, he would have killed me or I should have had to shoot him in self-defense. As we were holding him a strange thing happened. He suddenly redoubled his efforts, and then as suddenly grew calm. I looked round instinctively, but could see nothing. Then I caught the patient's eye and followed it, but could trace nothing as it looked into the moonlight sky, except a big bat, which was flapping its silent and ghostly way to the west. Bats usually wheel about, but this one seemed to go straight on, as if it knew where it was bound for or had some intention of its own.

The patient grew calmer every instant, and presently said, "You needn't tie me. I shall go quietly!" Without trouble, we came back to the house. I feel there is something ominous in his calm, and shall not forget this night.

Lucy Westenra's Diary

Hillingham, 24 August—I must imitate Mina, and keep writing things down. Then we can have long talks when we do meet. I wonder when it will be. I wish she were with me again, for I feel so unhappy. Last night I seemed to be dreaming again just as I was at Whitby. Perhaps it is the change of air, or getting home again. It is all dark and horrid to me, for I can remember nothing. But I am full of vague fear, and I feel so weak and worn out. When Arthur came to lunch with a fresh batch of purple tea leaves for Mother, he looked quite grieved when he saw me, and I hadn't the spirit to try to be cheerful. I wonder if I could sleep in mother's room tonight. Her room is higher up and as mine looks out on the verandah I seem to hear every sound that goes on round the house! I shall make an excuse to try.

25 August—Another bad night. Mother did not seem to take to my proposal. She seems not too well herself again, and doubtless she fears to worry me. I tried to keep awake, and succeeded for a while, but when the clock struck twelve it waked me from a doze, so I must have been falling asleep. There was a sort of scratching or flapping at the window, but I did not mind it, and as I remember no more, I suppose I must have fallen asleep. More bad dreams. I wish I could remember them. This morning I am horribly weak. My face is ghastly pale, and my throat pains me. It must be something wrong with my lungs, for I don't seem to be getting air enough. I shall try to cheer up when Arthur comes, or else I know he will be miserable to see me so.

Letter, Arthur to Dr. Seward

Albemarle Hotel,
31 August

My dear Jack,

I want you to do me a favour. Lucy is ill, that is she has no special disease, but she looks awful, and is getting worse every day. I have asked her if there is any cause, I not dare to ask her mother, for to disturb the poor lady's mind about her daughter in her present state of health would be fatal. Mrs. Westenra has confided to me that her doom is spoken, disease of the heart, though poor Lucy does not know it yet. I am sure that there is something preying on my dear girl's mind. I am almost distracted when I think of her. To look at her gives me a pang. I told her I should ask you to see her, and though she demurred at first, I know why, old fellow, she finally consented. It will be a painful task for you, I know, old friend, but it is for her sake, and I must not hesitate to ask, or you to act. You are to come to lunch at Hillingham tomorrow, two o'clock, so as not to arouse any suspicion in Mrs. Westenra, and after lunch Lucy will take an opportunity of being alone with you. I am filled with anxiety, and want to consult with you alone as soon as I can after you have seen her. Do not fail!

Arthur[135]

Telegram, Arthur Holmwood to Seward

1 September

Am summoned to see my father, who is worse. Am writing. Write me fully by tonight's post to Ring. Wire me if necessary.

Letter from Dr. Seward to Arthur Holmwood

2 September

My dear old fellow,

With regard to Miss Westenra's health I hasten to let you know at once that in my opinion there is not any functional disturbance or any malady that I know of. At the same time, I am not by any means satisfied with her appearance. She is woefully different from what she was when I saw her last. Of course you must bear in mind that I did not have full opportunity of examination such as I should wish. Our very friendship makes a little difficulty which not even medical science or custom can bridge over. I had better tell you exactly what happened, leaving you to draw, in a measure, your own conclusions. I shall then say what I have done and propose doing.

I found Miss Westenra in seemingly gay spirits. Her mother was present, and in a few seconds I made up my mind that she was trying all she knew to mislead her mother and prevent her from being anxious. I have no doubt she guesses, if she does not know, what need of caution there is.

We lunched alone, and as we all exerted ourselves to be cheerful, we got, as some kind of reward for our labours, some real cheerfulness amongst us. Then Mrs. Westenra went to lie down, and Lucy was left with me. We went into her boudoir, and till we got there her gaiety remained, for the servants were coming and going.

As soon as the door was closed, however, the mask fell from her face, and she sank down into a chair with a great sigh, and hid her eyes with her hand. When I saw that her high spirits had failed, I at once took advantage of her reaction to make a diagnosis.

She said to me very sweetly, 'I cannot tell you how I loathe talking about myself.' I reminded her that a doctor's confidence was sacred, but that you were grievously anxious about her. She caught on to my meaning at once, and settled that matter in a word. 'Tell Arthur everything you choose. I do not care for myself, but for him!' So I am quite free.

I could easily see that she was somewhat bloodless, but I could not see the usual anemic signs, and by the chance, I was able to test the actual quality of her blood, for in opening a window which was stiff a cord gave way, and she cut her hand slightly with broken glass. It was a slight matter in itself, but it gave me an evident chance, and I secured a few drops of the blood and have analysed them.

The qualitative analysis give a quite normal condition, and shows, I should infer, in itself a vigorous state of health. In other physical matters I was quite satisfied that there is no need for anxiety, but as there must be a cause somewhere, I have come to the conclusion that it must be something mental.

She complains of difficulty breathing satisfactorily at times, and of heavy, lethargic sleep, with dreams that frighten her, but regarding which she can remember nothing. She says that as a child, she used to walk in her sleep, and that when in Whitby the habit came back, and that once she walked out in the night and went to East Cliff, where Miss Murray found her. But she assures me that of late the habit has not returned.

I am in doubt, and so have done the best thing I know of. I have written to my old friend and master, Professor Van Helsing[136], of Amsterdam, who knows as much about obscure diseases as any one in the world. I have asked him to come over, and as you told me that all things were to be at your charge, I have mentioned to him who you are and your relations to Miss Westenra. This, my dear fellow, is in obedience to your wishes, for I am only too proud and happy to do anything I can for her.

Van Helsing would, I know, do anything for me for a personal reason, so no matter on what ground he comes, we must accept his wishes. He is a seemingly arbitrary man, this is because he knows what he is talking about better than any one else. He is a philosopher and a metaphysician, and one of the most advanced scientists of his day, and he has, I believe, an absolutely open mind. This, with an iron nerve, a temper of the ice-brook, and indomitable resolution, self-command, and toleration exalted from virtues to blessings, and the kindliest and truest heart that beats, these form his equipment for the noble work that he is doing for mankind, work both in theory and practice, for his views are as wide as his all-embracing sympathy. I tell you these facts that you may know why I have such confidence in him. I have asked him to come at once. I shall see Miss Westenra tomorrow again. She is to meet me at the Stores, so that I may not alarm her mother by too early a repetition of my call.

Yours always.
John Seward

Letter, Abraham Van Helsing, M.D., D.Ph., D.Lit., etc., etc., to Dr. Seward

2 September.

My good Friend,

When I received your letter I am already coming to you. By good fortune I can leave just at once, without wrong to any of those who have trusted me. Were fortune other, then it were bad for those who have trusted, for I come to my friend when he call me to aid those he holds dear. Tell your friend that when that time you suck from my wound so swiftly the poison of the gangrene from that knife that our other friend, too nervous, let slip, you did more for him when he wants my aids and you call for them than all his great fortune could do. But it is pleasure added to do for him, your friend, it is to you that I come. Have then rooms for me at the Great Eastern Hotel, so that I may be near at hand, and please it so arrange that we may see the young lady not too late on tomorrow, for it is likely that I may have to return here that night. But if need be I shall come again in three days, and stay longer if it must. Till then goodbye, my friend John.

Van Helsing

Letter, Dr. Seward to Hon. Arthur Holmwood

3 September

My dear Art,

Van Helsing has come and gone. He came on with me to Hillingham, and found that, by Lucy's discretion, her mother was lunching out, so that we were alone with her.

Van Helsing made a very careful examination of the patient. He is to report to me, and I shall advise you, for of course I was not present all the time. He is, I fear, much concerned, but says he must think. When I told him of our friendship and how you trust to me in the matter, he said, 'You must tell him all you think. Tell him him what I think, if you can guess it, if you will. Nay, I am not jesting. This is no jest, but life and death, perhaps more.' I asked what he meant by that, for he was very serious. This was when we had come back to town, and he was having a cup of tea before starting on his return to Amsterdam. He would not give me any further clue. You must not be angry with me, Art, because his very reticence means that all his brains are working for her good. He will speak plainly enough when the time comes, be sure. So I told him I would simply write an account of our visit, just as if I were doing a descriptive special article for *The Daily Telegraph*. He seemed not to notice, but remarked that the smuts of London were not quite so bad as they used to be when he was a student here. I am to get his report tomorrow if he can possibly make it. In any case I am to have a letter.

Well, as to the visit, Lucy was more cheerful than on the day I first saw her, and certainly looked better. She had lost something of the ghastly look that so upset you, and her breathing was normal. She was very sweet to the Professor (as she always is), and tried to make him feel at ease, though I could see the poor girl was making a hard struggle for it.

I believe Van Helsing saw it, too, for I saw the quick look under his bushy brows that I knew of old. Then he began to chat of all things except ourselves and diseases and with such an infinite geniality that I could see poor Lucy's pretense of animation merge into reality. Then, without any seeming change, he brought the conversation gently round to his visit, and suavely said,

"My dear young miss, I have the so great pleasure because you are so much beloved. That is much, my dear, even were there that which I do not see. They told me you were down in the spirit, and that you were of a ghastly pale. To them I say 'Pouf!'" And he snapped his fingers at me and went on. "But you and I shall show them how wrong they are. How can he,' and he pointed at me with the same look and gesture as that with which he pointed me out in his class, on, or rather after, a particular occasion which he never fails to remind me of, 'know anything of a young ladies? He has his madmen to play with, and to bring them back to happiness, and to those that love them. It is much to do, and, oh, but there are rewards in that we can bestow such happiness. But the young ladies! He has no wife nor daughter, and the young do not tell themselves to the young, but to the old, like me, who have known so many sorrows and the causes of them. So, my dear, we will send him away to smoke the cigarette in the garden, whiles you and I have little talk all to ourselves." I took the hint, and strolled about, and presently the professor came to the window and called me in. He looked grave, but said, "I have made careful examination, but there is no functional cause. With you I agree that there has been much blood lost, it has been but is not. But the conditions of her are in no way anemic. I have asked her to send me her maid, that I may ask just one or two questions, that so I may not chance to miss nothing. I know well what she will say. And yet there is cause. There is always cause for everything. I must go back home and think. You must send me the telegram every day, and if there be cause I shall come again. The disease, for not to be well is a disease, interest me, and the sweet, young dear, she interest me too. She charm me, and for her, if not for you or disease, I come."

As I tell you, he would not say a word more, even when we were alone. And so now, Art, you know all I know. I shall keep stern watch. I trust your poor father is rallying. It must be a terrible thing to you, my dear old fellow, to be placed in such a position between two people who are both so dear to you. I know your idea of duty to your father, and you are right to stick to it. But if need be, I shall send you word to come at once to Lucy, so do not be over-anxious unless you hear from me.

Letter, Kate to Mr. and Mrs. Reed

4 September

Mamma, Papa,

Something is wrong with Francis. He eats far too little, and he sleep far too much . . . at least while the sun is up. During the night he locks himself away in his studio, but he won't show me what he has been doing. He has become quiet and thoughtful, and when I try and talk with him he assures me that everything is fine, but gets angry if I press the issue.

As I had begun to worry about his health, of both his mind and body, I asked my old friend Jack Seward—you remember him, right? the one who had courted me for a time, before he finally gave up and moved on to my friend Lucy—if he would be so kind as to come by and have a look at Francis. (Honestly, I would have preferred having Dr. Caffyn make the trip in from Whitby instead, but he was unavailable). Old Jack agreed, and came to our house earlier today.

Thinking Francis to be still asleep, I invited Jack to sit with me in the parlour. I had tea brought in for us, and we caught ourselves up to the date on each other's lives. It appears his proposal to Lucy was not accepted after all, poor fellow, though as it turns out she did accept that of his good friend Arthur Holmwood (that is, the son of Lord Godalming). To make matters worse for Jack, it sounds like Lucy has taken ill, and Mr. Holmwood has asked him to be her physician. How very awkward that must be! Then it was my turn, and I told him all about school and our holiday in Whitby, but when I was just about to tell Jack all about our new neighbor, Francis came in, dressed for the day and wearing his leather painting apron.

"I though I heard voices down here," he said, obviously in a sour mood, and all but glowering at Jack.

"Ah, Francis, you're awake!" I greeted him, quite surprised to see him up and about after these past few days of lethargy. "This is Jack Seward. He's a doctor, you see, and I've asked him to—"

"Oh yes, I remember the name of Jack Seward," Francis interrupted, now even more irritated than before.

"Have we met, sir?" Jack inquired as he stood to greet him.

"No, but I do remember quite well Kate talking about you. You had courted her for a time, had you not?"

"Well yes, that is true," Jack replied, blushing slightly with the awkwardness of the meeting. "But that time has passed. Kate—ah, Miss Reed—has asked me here to see you. She is concerned about your health these last few days."

"My health is quite fine, thank you. In fact, I've never felt better. Now if you'll excuse me, *Jack*" he said his name with a degree of sarcasm that surprised me, "I have some work to do. Good day." And with that he was gone. I can't help but feel that Francis took my meeting with Jack to be something more than it really was; I believe the good doctor must have thought the same thing, and, still flustered, excused himself to return to his work in Purfleet.

Oh Mamma and Papa, poor Francis has been so preoccupied of late as it is, and now I believe I've only made matters worse. Yet I simply can't let things continue as they have been. Any advice you could offer would be very much appreciated.

Your loving daughter,
Kate

Dr. Seward's Case-Book

4 September—Zoophagous patient still keeps up our interest in him. He had only one outburst and that was yesterday at an unusual time. Just before the stroke of noon he began to grow restless. The attendant knew the symptoms, and at once summoned aid. Fortunately the men came at a run, and were just in time, for at the stroke of noon he became so violent that it took all their strength to hold him. In about five minutes, however, he began to get more quiet, and finally sank into a sort of melancholy, in which state he has remained up to now. The attendant tells me that his screams whilst in the paroxysm were really appalling. I found my hands full when I got in, attending to some of the other patients who were frightened by him. Indeed, I can quite understand the effect, for the sounds disturbed even me, though I was some distance away. It is now after the dinner hour of the asylum, and as yet my patient sits in a corner brooding, with a dull, sullen, woe-begone look in his face, which seems rather to indicate than to show something directly. I cannot quite understand it.

Later—Another change in my patient. At five o'clock I looked in on him after my return from seeing Kate, and found him seemingly as happy and contented as he used to be. He was catching flies and eating them, and was keeping note of his capture by making nailmarks on the edge of the door between the ridges of padding. When he saw me, he came over and apologized for his bad conduct, and asked me in a very humble, cringing way to be led back to his own room, and to have his notebook again. I thought it well to humour him, so he is back in his room with the window open. He has the sugar of his tea spread out on the window sill, and is reaping quite a harvest of flies. He is not now eating them, but putting them into a box, as of old, and is already examining the corners of his room to find a spider. I tried to get him to talk about the past few days, for any clue to his thoughts would be of immense help to me, but he would not rise. For a moment or two he looked very sad, and said in a sort of far away voice, as though saying it rather to himself than to me.

"All over! All over! He has deserted me. No hope for me now unless I do it myself!" Then suddenly turning to me in a resolute way, he said, "Doctor, won't you be very good to me and let me have a little more sugar? I think it would be very good for me."

"And the flies?" I said.

"Yes! The flies like it, too, and I like the flies, therefore I like it." And there are people who know so little as to think that madmen do not argue. I procured him a double supply, and left him as happy a man as, I suppose, any in the world. I wish I could fathom his mind.

Midnight—Another change in him. I had been to see Miss Westenra, whom I found much better, and had just returned, and was standing at our own gate looking at the sunset, when once more I heard him yelling. As his room is on this side of the house, I could hear it better than in the morning. It was a shock to me to turn from the wonderful smoky beauty of a sunset over London, with its lurid lights and inky shadows and all the marvelous tints that come on foul clouds even as on foul water, and to realize all the grim sternness of my own cold stone building, with its wealth of breathing misery, and my own desolate heart to endure it all. I reached him just as the sun was going down, and from his window saw the red disc sink. As it sank he became less and less frenzied, and just as it dipped he slid from the hands that held him, an inert mass, on the floor. It is wonderful, however, what intellectual recuperative power lunatics have, for within a few minutes he stood up quite calmly and looked around him. I signalled to the attendants not to hold him, for I was anxious to see what he would do. He went straight over to the window and brushed out the crumbs of sugar. Then he took his fly box, and emptied it outside, and threw away the box. Then he shut the window, and crossing over, sat down on his bed. All this surprised me, so I asked him, "Are you going to keep flies any more?"

"No," said he. "I am sick of all that rubbish!" He certainly is a wonderfully interesting study. I wish I could get some glimpse of his mind or of the cause of his sudden passion. Stop. There may be a clue after all, if we can find why today his paroxysms came on at high noon and at sunset. Can it be that there is a malign influence of the sun at periods which affects certain natures, as at times the moon does others? We shall see.

Letter, Kate to Mr. and Mrs. Reed

8 September

Mamma, Papa,

Thank you for your letter. Your advice is sound, and though it pains me to even think on it, I fear you could be right in that Francis may be seeing another woman. In hindsight, he has seemed awfully "love sick," as they call it. And the "sickness" must be growing worse, for he no longer seems willing or able to hide his melancholy from me. Though he does make a solid effort to hide his mood from the Count DeVille. At first I came to welcome his visits, for the time he is here is the only time that Francis seems like his old self again. But there is a peculiarity about that man I can not quite place. I have seen him more than once standing at one of the upper windows of his mansion, staring without blinking, like a dead man—sometimes at passers by on the street below, but most often at our own house. A strange man, indeed.

Oh, but I cannot for the life of me fathom what girl Francis has been seeing! Or even how he has gone about such liaisons, for that matter, for he sleeps his days away and paints all night. He hasn't even been out of the house for over a week, though the Count has asked Francis to show him more of London tonight. Perhaps such a task as assisting our neighbor in his acclamation to England will do him some good.

I have not the heart to write further now, but I will let you know if I should discover anything new, or if he himself admits to such a relationship on his own.

Your loving daughter,
Kate

Cutting from *The London Times*, 11 September[137]

The Whitechapel Murders

Two arrests were made yesterday, but it is very doubtful whether the murderer is in the hands of the police. The members of the Criminal Investigation Department are assisting the divisional police at the East-end in their endeavours to elucidate the mystery in which these crimes are involved. Yesterday morning Detective Sergeant Thicke, of the H Division, who has been indefatigable in his inquiries respecting the murder of Annie Chapman at 29, Hanbury Street, Spitalfields, on Saturday morning, succeeded in capturing a man whom he believed to be "Leather Apron." It will be recollected that this person obtained an evil notoriety during the inquiries respecting this and the recent murders committed in Whitechapel, owing to the startling reports that had been freely circulated by many of the women living in the district as to outrages alleged to have been committed by him. Sergeant Thicke, who has had much experience of the thieves and their haunts in this portion of the metropolis, has, since he has been engaged in the present inquiry, been repeatedly assured by some of the most well-known characters of their abhorrence of the fiendishness of the crime, and they have further stated that if they could only lay hands on the murderer they would hand him over to justice. These and other circumstances convinced the officer and those associated with him that the deed was in no way traceable to any of the regular thieves or desperadoes at the East-end.

At the same time a sharp look-out was kept on the common lodginghouses, not only in this district, but in other portions of the metropolis. Several persons bearing a resemblance to the description of the person in question have been arrested, but, being able to render a satisfactory account of themselves, were allowed to go away. Shortly after 8 o'clock yesterday morning Sergeant Thicke, accompanied by two or three other officers, proceeded to 22, Mulberry Street and knocked at the door. It was opened by a Polish Jew named Pizer, supposed to be "Leather Apron." Thicke at once took hold of the man, saying, "You are just the man I want." He then charged Pizer with being concerned in the murder of the woman Chapman, and to this he made no reply. The accused man, who is a boot finisher by trade, was then handed over to other officers and the house was searched. Thicke took possession of five sharp long-bladed knives—which, however, are used by men in Pizer's trade—and also several old hats. With reference to the latter, several women who stated they were acquainted with the prisoner, alleged he has been in the habit of wearing different hats. Pizer, who is about 33, was then quietly removed to the Leman Street Police station, his friends protesting that he knew nothing of the affair, that he had not been out of the house since Thursday night, and is of a very delicate constitution. The friends of the man were subjected to a close questioning by the police. It was still uncertain, late last night, whether this man remained in custody or had been liberated. He strongly denies that he is known by the name of "Leather Apron."

The following official notice has been circulated throughout the metropolitan police district and all police stations throughout the country: "Description of a man who entered a passage of the house at which the murder was committed of a prostitute at 2 A.M. on the 8th.—Age 37; height, 5ft. 7in.; rather dark beard and moustache. Dress-shirt, dark vest and trousers, black scarf, and black felt hat. Spoke with a foreign accent."

Telegram, Seward, London, to Van Helsing, Amsterdam

4 September—Patient still better today.

Telegram, Seward, London, to Van Helsing, Amsterdam

5 September—Patient greatly improved. Good appetite, sleeps naturally, good spirits, colour coming back.

Telegram, Seward, London, to Van Helsing, Amsterdam

6 September—Terrible change for the worse. Come at once. Do not lose an hour. I hold over telegram to Holmwood till have seen you.

CHAPTER SIXTEEN[138]

Letter, Dr. Seward to Hon. Arthur Holmwood

6 September

My dear Art,

My news today is not so good. Lucy this morning had gone back a bit. There is, however, one good thing which has arisen from it. Mrs. Westenra was naturally anxious concerning Lucy, and has consulted me professionally about her. I took advantage of the opportunity, and told her that my old master, Van Helsing, the great specialist, was coming to stay with me, and that I would put her in his charge conjointly with myself. So now we can come and go without alarming her unduly, for a shock to her would mean sudden death, and this, in Lucy's weak condition, might be disastrous to her. We are hedged in with difficulties, all of us, my poor fellow, but, please God, we shall come through them all right. If any need I shall write, so that, if you do not hear from me, take it for granted that I am simply waiting for news, In haste,

Yours ever,
John Seward

Dr. Seward's Case-Book

7 September—The first thing Van Helsing said to me when we met at Liverpool Street was, "Have you said anything to our young friend, the lover of her?"

"No," I said. "I waited till I had seen you, as I said in my telegram. I wrote him a letter simply telling him that you were coming, as Miss Westenra was not so well, and that I should let him know if need be."

"Right, my friend," he said. "Quite right! Better he not know as yet. Perhaps he will never know. I pray so, but if it be needed, then he shall know all. And, my good friend John, let me caution you. You deal with the madmen. All men are mad in some way or the other, and inasmuch as you deal discreetly with your madmen, so deal with God's madmen too, the rest of the world. You tell not your madmen what you do nor why you do it. You tell them not what you think. So you shall keep knowledge in its place, where it may rest, where it may gather its kind around it and breed. You and I shall keep as yet what we know here, and here." He touched me on the heart and on the forehead, and then touched himself the same way. "I have for myself thoughts at the present. Later I shall unfold to you."

"Why not now?" I asked. "It may do some good. We may arrive at some decision." He looked at me and said, "My friend John, when the corn is grown, even before it has ripened, while the milk of its mother earth is in him, and the sunshine has not yet begun to paint him with his gold, the husbandman he pull the ear and rub him between his rough hands, and blow away the green chaff, and say to you, 'Look! He's good corn, he will make a good crop when the time comes.'"

I did not see the application and told him so. For reply he reached over and took my ear in his hand and pulled it playfully, as he used long ago to do at lectures, and said, "The good husbandman tell you so then because he knows, but not till then. But you do not find the good husbandman dig up his planted corn to see if he grow. That is for the children who play at husbandry, and not for those who take it as of the work of their life. See you now, friend John? I have sown my corn, and Nature has her work to do in making it sprout, if he sprout at all, there's some promise, and I wait till the ear begins to swell." He broke off, for he evidently saw that I understood. Then he went on gravely, "You were always a careful student, and your case book was ever more full than the rest. And I trust that good habit have not fail. Remember, my friend, that knowledge is stronger than memory, and we should not trust the weaker. Even if you have not kept the good practice, let me tell you that this case of our dear miss is one that may be, mind, I say may be, of such interest to us and others that all the rest may not make him kick the beam, as your people say. Take then good note of it. Nothing is too small. I counsel you, put down in record even your doubts and surmises. Hereafter it may be of interest to you to see how true you guess. We learn from failure, not from success!"

When I described Lucy's symptoms, the same as before, but infinitely more marked, he looked very grave, but said nothing. He took with him a bag in which were many instruments and drugs, "the ghastly paraphernalia of our beneficial trade," as he once called, in one of his lectures, the equipment of a professor of the healing craft.

When we were shown in, Mrs. Westenra met us. She was alarmed, but not nearly so much as I expected to find her. Nature in one of her beneficent moods has ordained that even death has some antidote to its own terrors. Here, in a case where any shock may prove fatal, matters are so ordered that, from some cause or other, the things not personal, even the terrible change in her daughter to whom she is so attached, do not seem to reach her. It is something like the way dame Nature gathers round a foreign body an envelope of some insensitive tissue which can protect from evil that which it would otherwise harm by contact. If this be an ordered selfishness, then we should pause before we condemn any one for the vice of egoism, for there may be deeper root for its causes than we have knowledge of.

I used my knowledge of this phase of spiritual pathology, and set down a rule that she should not be present with Lucy, or think of her illness more than was absolutely required. She assented readily, so readily that I saw again the hand of Nature fighting for life. Van Helsing and I were shown up to Lucy's room. If I was shocked when I saw her yesterday, I was horrified when I saw her today.

She was ghastly, chalkily pale. The red seemed to have gone even from her lips and gums, and the bones of her face stood out prominently. Her breathing was painful to see or hear. Van Helsing's face grew set as marble, and his eyebrows converged till they almost touched over his nose. Lucy lay motionless, and did not seem to have strength to speak, so for a while we were all silent. Then Van Helsing beckoned to me, and we went gently out of the room. The instant we had closed the door he stepped quickly along the passage to the next door, which was open. Then he pulled me quickly in with him and closed the door. "My god!" he said. "This is dreadful. There is not time to be lost. She will die for sheer want of blood to keep the heart's action as it should be. There must be a transfusion of blood at once. Is it you or me?"

"I am younger and stronger, Professor. It must be me."

"Then get ready at once. I will bring up my bag. I am prepared."

I went downstairs with him, and as we were going there was a knock at the hall door. When we reached the hall, the maid had just opened the door, and Arthur was stepping quickly in. He rushed up to me, saying in an eager whisper,

"Jack, I was so anxious. I read between the lines of your letter, and have been in an agony. The dad was better, so I ran down here to see for myself. Is not that gentleman Dr. Van Helsing? I am so thankful to you, sir, for coming."

When first the Professor's eye had lit upon him, he had been angry at his interruption at such a time, but now, as he took in his stalwart proportions and recognized the strong young manhood which seemed to emanate from him, his eyes gleamed. Without a pause he said to him as he held out his hand,

"Sir, you have come in time. You are the lover of our dear miss. She is bad, very, very bad. Nay, my child, do not go like that." For he suddenly grew pale and sat down in a chair almost fainting. "You are to help her. You can do more than any that live, and your courage is your best help."

"What can I do?" asked Arthur hoarsely. "Tell me, and I shall do it. My life is hers, and I would give the last drop of blood in my body for her."

The Professor has a strongly humorous side, and I could from old knowledge detect a trace of its origin in his answer.

"My young sir, I do not ask so much as that, not the last!"

"What shall I do?" There was fire in his eyes, and his open nostrils quivered with intent. Van Helsing slapped him on the shoulder.

"Come!" he said. "You are a man, and it is a man we want. You are better than me, better than my friend John." Arthur looked bewildered, and the Professor went on by explaining in a kindly way.

"Young miss is bad, very bad. She wants blood, and blood she must have or die. My friend John and I have consulted, and we are about to perform what we call transfusion of blood, to transfer from full veins of one to the empty veins which pine for him. John was to give his blood, as he is the more young and strong than me."—Here Arthur took my hand and wrung it hard in silence.—"But now you are here, you are more good than us, old or young, who toil much in the world of thought. Our nerves are not so calm and our blood so bright than yours!"

Arthur turned to him and said, "If you only knew how gladly I would die for her you would understand . . ." He stopped with a sort of choke in his voice.

"Good boy!" said Van Helsing. "In the not-so-far-off you will be happy that you have done all for her you love. Come now and be silent. You shall kiss her once before it is done, but then you must go, and you must leave at my sign. Say no word to Madame. You know how it is with her. There must be no shock, any knowledge of this would be one. Come!"

We all went up to Lucy's room. Arthur by direction remained outside. Lucy turned her head and looked at us, but said nothing. She was not asleep, but she was simply too weak to make the effort. Her eyes spoke to us, that was all.

Van Helsing took some things from his bag and laid them on a little table out of sight. Then he mixed a narcotic, and coming over to the bed, said cheerily, "Now, little miss, here is your medicine. Drink it off, like a good child. See, I lift you so that to swallow is easy. Yes." She had made the effort with success.

It astonished me how long the drug took to act. This, in fact, marked the extent of her weakness. The time seemed endless until sleep began to flicker in her eyelids. At last, however, the narcotic began to manifest its potency, and she fell into a deep sleep. When the Professor was satisfied, he called Arthur into the room, and bade him strip off his coat. Then he added, "You may take that one little kiss whiles I bring over the table. Friend John, help to me!" So neither of us looked whilst he bent over her.

Van Helsing, turning to me, said, "He is so young and strong, and of blood so pure that we need not defibrinate it."

Then with swiftness, but with absolute method, Van Helsing performed the operation. As the transfusion went on, something like life seemed to come back to poor Lucy's cheeks, and through Arthur's growing pallor the joy of his face seemed absolutely to shine. After a bit I began to grow anxious, for the loss of blood was telling on Arthur, strong man as he was. It gave me an idea of what a terrible strain Lucy's system must have undergone that what weakened Arthur only partially restored her.

But the Professor's face was set, and he stood watch in hand, and with his eyes fixed now on the patient and now on Arthur. I could hear my own heart beat. Presently, he said in a soft voice, "Do not stir an instant. It is enough. You attend him. I will look to her."

When all was over, I could see how much Arthur was weakened. I dressed the wound and took his arm to bring him away, when Van Helsing spoke without turning round, the man seems to have eyes in the back of his head, "The brave lover, I think, deserve another kiss, which he shall have presently." And as he had now finished his operation, he adjusted the pillow to the patient's head. As he did so the narrow black velvet band which she seems always to wear round her throat, buckled with an old diamond buckle which her lover had given her, was dragged a little up, and showed a red mark on her throat.

Arthur did not notice it, but I could hear the deep hiss of indrawn breath which is one of Van Helsing's ways of betraying emotion. He said nothing at the moment, but turned to me, saying, "Now take down our brave young lover, give him of the port wine, and let him lie down a while. He must then go home and rest, sleep much and eat much, that he may be recruited of what he has so given to his love. He must not stay here. Hold a moment! I may take it, sir, that you are anxious of result. Then bring it with you, that in all ways the operation is successful. You have saved her life this time, and you can go home and rest easy in mind that all that can be is. I shall tell her all when she is well. She shall love you none the less for what you have done. Goodbye."

When Arthur had gone I went back to the room. Lucy was sleeping gently, but her breathing was stronger. I could see the counterpane move as her breast heaved. By the bedside sat Van Helsing, looking at her intently. The velvet band again covered the red mark. I asked the Professor in a whisper, "What do you make of that mark on her throat?"

"What do you make of it?"

"I have not examined it yet," I answered, and then and there proceeded to loose the band. Just over the external jugular vein there were two punctures, not large, but not wholesome looking. There was no sign of disease, but the edges were white and worn looking, as if by some trituration. It at once occurred to me that this wound, or whatever it was, might be the means of that manifest loss of blood. But I abandoned the idea as soon as it formed, for such a thing could not be. The whole bed would have been drenched to a scarlet with the blood which the girl must have lost to leave such a pallor as she had before the transfusion.

"Well?" said Van Helsing.

"Well," said I. "I can make nothing of it."

The Professor stood up. "I must go back to Amsterdam tonight," he said "There are books and things there which I want. You must remain here all night, and you must not let your sight pass from her."

"Shall I have a nurse?" I asked.

"We are the best nurses, you and I. You keep watch all night. See that she is well fed, and that nothing disturbs her. You must not sleep all the night. Later on we can sleep, you and I. I shall be back as soon as possible. And then we may begin."

"May begin?" I said. "What on earth do you mean?"

"We shall see!" he answered, as he hurried out. He came back a moment later and put his head inside the door and said with a warning finger held up, "Remember, she is your charge. If you leave her, and harm befall, you shall not sleep easy hereafter!"

8 September—I sat up all night with Lucy. The opiate worked itself off towards dusk, and she waked naturally. She looked a different being from what she had been before the operation. Her spirits even were good, and she was full of a happy vivacity, but I could see evidences of the absolute prostration which she had undergone. When I told Mrs. Westenra that Dr. Van Helsing had directed that I should sit up with her, she almost pooh-poohed the idea, pointing out her daughter's renewed strength and excellent spirits. I was firm, however, and made preparations for my long vigil. When her maid had prepared her for the night I came in, having in the meantime had supper, and took a seat by the bedside.

She did not in any way make objection, but looked at me gratefully whenever I caught her eye. After a long spell she seemed sinking off to sleep, but with an effort seemed to pull herself together and shook it off. It was apparent that she did not want to sleep, so I tackled the subject at once.

"You do not want to sleep?"

"No. I am afraid."

"Afraid to go to sleep! Why so? It is the boon we all crave for."

"Ah, not if you were like me, if sleep was to you a presage of horror!"

"A presage of horror! What on earth do you mean?"

"I don't know. Oh, I don't know. And that is what is so terrible. All this weakness comes to me in sleep, until I dread the very thought."

"But, my dear girl, you may sleep tonight. I am here watching you, and I can promise that nothing will happen."

"Ah, I can trust you!" she said.

I seized the opportunity, and said, "I promise that if I see any evidence of bad dreams I will wake you at once."

"You will? Oh, will you really? How good you are to me. Then I will sleep!" And almost at the word she gave a deep sigh of relief, and sank back, asleep.

All night long I watched by her. She never stirred, but slept on and on in a deep, tranquil, life-giving, health-giving sleep. Her lips were slightly parted, and her breast rose and fell with the regularity of a pendulum. There was a smile on her face, and it was evident that no bad dreams had come to disturb her peace of mind.

In the early morning her maid came, and I left her in her care and took myself back home, for I was anxious about many things. I sent a short wire to Van Helsing and to Arthur, telling them of the excellent result of the operation. My own work, with its manifold arrears, took me all day to clear off. It was dark when I was able to inquire about my zoophagous patient. The report was good. He had been quite quiet for the past day and night. A telegram came from Van Helsing at Amsterdam whilst I was at dinner, suggesting that I should be at Hillingham tonight, as it might be well to be at hand, and stating that he was leaving by the night mail and would join me early in the morning.

9 September—I was pretty tired and worn out when I got to Hillingham. For two nights I had hardly had a wink of sleep, and my brain was beginning to feel that numbness which marks cerebral exhaustion. Lucy was up and in cheerful spirits. When she shook hands with me she looked sharply in my face and said,

"No sitting up tonight for you. You are worn out. I am quite well again. Indeed, I am, and if there is to be any sitting up, it is I who will sit up with you."

I would not argue the point, but went and had my supper. Lucy came with me, and, enlivened by her charming presence, I made an excellent meal, and had a couple of glasses of the more than excellent port. Then Lucy took me upstairs, and showed me a room next her own, where a cozy fire was burning.

"Now," she said. "You must stay here. I shall leave this door open and my door too. You can lie on the sofa for I know that nothing would induce any of you doctors to go to bed whilst there is a patient above the horizon. If I want anything I shall call out, and you can come to me at once."

I could not but acquiesce, for I was dog tired, and could not have sat up had I tried. So, on her renewing her promise to call me if she should want anything, I lay on the sofa, and forgot all about everything.

Lucy Westenra's Diary

9 September—I feel so happy tonight. I have been so miserably weak, that to be able to think and move about is like feeling sunshine after a long spell of east wind out of a steel sky. Somehow Arthur feels very, very close to me. I seem to

feel his presence warm about me. I suppose it is that sickness and weakness are selfish things and turn our inner eyes and sympathy on ourselves, whilst health and strength give love rein, and in thought and feeling he can wander where he wills. I know where my thoughts are. If only Arthur knew! My dear, my dear, your ears must tingle as you sleep, as mine do waking. Oh, the blissful rest of last night! How I slept, with that dear, good Dr. Seward watching me. And tonight I shall not fear to sleep, since he is close at hand and within call. Thank everybody for being so good to me. Thank God! Goodnight Arthur.

Dr. Seward's Case-Book

10 September—I was conscious of the Professor's hand on my head, and started awake all in a second. That is one of the things that we learn in an asylum, at any rate.

"And how is our patient?"

"Well, when I left her, or rather when she left me," I answered.

"Come, let us see," he said. And together we went into the room.

The blind was down, and I went over to raise it gently, whilst Van Helsing stepped, with his soft, cat-like tread, over to the bed.

As I raised the blind, and the morning sunlight flooded the room, I heard the Professor's low hiss of inspiration, and knowing its rarity, a deadly fear shot through my heart. As I passed over he moved back, and his exclamation of horror, "Gott in Himmel!" needed no enforcement from his agonized face. He raised his hand and pointed to the bed, and his iron face was drawn and ashen white. I felt my knees begin to tremble.

There on the bed, seemingly in a swoon, lay poor Lucy, more horribly white and wan-looking than ever. Even the lips were white, and the gums seemed to have shrunken back from the teeth, as we sometimes see in a corpse after a prolonged illness.

Van Helsing raised his foot to stamp in anger, but the instinct of his life and all the long years of habit stood to him, and he put it down again softly.

"Quick!" he said. "Bring the brandy."

I flew to the dining room, and returned with the decanter. He wetted the poor white lips with it, and together we rubbed palm and wrist and heart. He felt her heart, and after a few moments of agonizing suspense said,

"It is not too late. It beats, though but feebly. All our work is undone. We must begin again. There is no young Arthur here now. I have to call on you yourself this time, friend John." As he spoke, he was dipping into his bag, and producing the instruments of transfusion. I had taken off my coat and rolled up my shirt sleeve. There was no possibility of an opiate just at present, and no need of one. and so, without a moment's delay, we began the operation.

After a time, it did not seem a short time either, for the draining away of one's blood, no matter how willingly it be given, is a terrible feeling, Van Helsing held up a warning finger. "Do not stir," he said. "But I fear that with growing strength she may wake, and that would make danger, oh, so much danger. But I shall precaution take. I shall give hypodermic injection of morphia." He proceeded then, swiftly and deftly, to carry out his intent.

The effect on Lucy was not bad, for the faint seemed to merge subtly into the narcotic sleep. It was with a feeling of personal pride that I could see a faint tinge of colour steal back into the pallid cheeks and lips. No man knows, till he experiences it, what it is to feel his own lifeblood drawn away into the veins of the woman he loves.

The Professor watched me critically. "That will do," he said. "Already?" I remonstrated. "You took a great deal more from Art." To which he smiled a sad sort of smile as he replied,

"He is her lover, her fiance. You have work, much work to do for her and for others, and the present will suffice."

When we stopped the operation, he attended to Lucy, whilst I applied digital pressure to my own incision. I laid down, while I waited his leisure to attend to me, for I felt faint and a little sick. By and by he bound up my wound, and sent me downstairs to get a glass of wine for myself. As I was leaving the room, he came after me, and half whispered.

"Mind, nothing must be said of this. If our young lover should turn up unexpected, as before, no word to him. It would at once frighten him and enjealous him, too. There must be none. So!"

When I came back he looked at me carefully, and then said, "You are not much the worse. Go into the room, and lie on your sofa, and rest awhile, then have much breakfast and come here to me."

I followed out his orders, for I knew how right and wise they were. I had done my part, and now my next duty was to keep up my strength. I felt very weak, and in the weakness lost something of the amazement at what had occurred. I fell asleep on the sofa, however, wondering over and over again how Lucy had made such a retrograde movement, and how she could have been drained of so much blood with no sign any where to show for it. I think I must have continued my wonder in my dreams, for, sleeping and waking my thoughts always came back to the little punctures in her throat and the ragged, exhausted appearance of their edges, tiny though they were.

Lucy slept well into the day, and when she woke she was fairly well and strong, though not nearly so much so as the day before. When Van Helsing had seen her, he went out for a walk, leaving me in charge, with strict injunctions that I was not to leave her for a moment. I could hear his voice in the hall, asking the way to the nearest telegraph office.

Lucy chatted with me freely, and seemed quite unconscious that anything had happened. I tried to keep her amused and interested. When her mother came up to see her, she did not seem to notice any change whatever, but said to me gratefully,

"We owe you so much, Dr. Seward, for all you have done, but you really must now take care not to overwork yourself. You are looking pale yourself. You want a wife to nurse and look after you a bit, that you do!" As she spoke, Lucy turned crimson, though it was only momentarily, for her poor wasted veins could not stand for long an unwonted drain to the head. The reaction came in excessive pallor as she turned imploring eyes on me. I smiled and nodded, and laid my finger on my lips. With a sigh, she sank back amid her pillows.

Van Helsing returned in a couple of hours, and presently said to me. "Now you go home, and eat much and drink enough. Make yourself strong. I stay here tonight, and I shall sit up with little miss myself. You and I must watch the case, and we must have none other to know. I have grave reasons. No, do not ask me. Think what you will. Do not fear to think even the most not-improbable. Goodnight."

In the hall two of the maids came to me, and asked if they or either of them might not sit up with Miss Lucy. They implored me to let them, and when I said it was Dr. Van Helsing's wish that either he or I should sit up, they asked me quite piteously to intercede with the 'foreign gentleman.' I was much touched by their kindness. Perhaps it is because I am weak at present, and perhaps because it was on Lucy's account, that their devotion was manifested. For over and over again have I seen similar instances of woman's kindness. I got back here in time for a late dinner, went my rounds, all well, and set this down whilst waiting for sleep. It is coming.

11 September—This afternoon I went over to Hillingham. Found Van Helsing in excellent spirits, and Lucy much better. Shortly after I had arrived, a big parcel from abroad came for the Professor. He opened it with much impressment, assumed, of course, and showed a great bundle of white flowers.

"These are for you, Miss Lucy," he said.

"For me? Oh, Dr. Van Helsing!"

"Yes, my dear, but not for you to play with. These are medicines." Here Lucy made a wry face. "Nay, but they are not to take in a decoction or in nauseous form, so you need not snub that so charming nose, or I shall point out to my friend Arthur what woes he may have to endure in seeing so much beauty that he so loves so much distort. Aha, my pretty miss, that bring the so nice nose all straight again. This is medicinal, but you do not know how. I put him in your window, I make pretty wreath, and hang him round your neck, so you sleep well. Oh, yes! They, like the lotus flower, make your trouble forgotten. It smell so like the waters of Lethe, and of that fountain of youth that the Conquistadores sought for in the Floridas, and find him all too late."

Whilst he was speaking, Lucy had been examining the flowers and smelling them. Now she threw them down saying, with half laughter, and half disgust,

"Oh, Professor, I believe you are only putting up a joke on me. Why, these flowers are only common garlic. 'No sugar in mine thank you,' as Mr. Morris would say."[139]

To my surprise, Van Helsing rose up and said with all his sternness, his iron jaw set and his bushy eyebrows meeting,

"No trifling with me! I never jest! There is grim purpose in what I do, and I warn you that you do not thwart me. Take care, for the sake of others if not for your own." Then seeing poor Lucy scared, as she might well be, he went on more gently, "Oh, little miss, my dear, do not fear me. I only do for your good, but there is much virtue to you in those so common flowers. See, I place them myself in your room. I make myself the wreath that you are to wear. But hush! No telling to others that make so inquisitive questions. We must obey, and silence is a part of obedience, and obedience is to bring you strong and well into loving arms that wait for you. Now sit still a while. Come with me, friend John, and you shall help me deck the room with my garlic, which is all the way from Haarlem, where my friend Vanderpool raise herb in his glass houses all the year. I had to telegraph yesterday, or they would not have been here."

We went into the room, taking the flowers with us. The Professor's actions were certainly odd and not to be found in any pharmacopeia that I ever heard of. First he fastened up the windows and latched them securely. Next, taking a handful of the flowers, he rubbed them all over the sashes, as though to ensure that every whiff of air that might get in would be laden with the garlic smell. Then with the wisp he rubbed all over the jamb of the door, above, below, and at each side, and round the fireplace in the same way. It all seemed grotesque to me, and presently I said, "Well, Professor, I know you always have a reason for what you do, but this certainly puzzles me. It is well we have no sceptic here, or he would say that you were working some spell to keep out an evil spirit."

"Perhaps I am!" He answered quietly as he began to make the wreath which Lucy was to wear round her neck.

We then waited whilst Lucy made her toilet for the night, and when she was in bed he came and himself fixed the wreath of garlic round her neck. The last words he said to her were,

"Take care you do not disturb it, and even if the room feel close, do not tonight open the window or the door."

"I promise," said Lucy. "And thank you both a thousand times for all your kindness to me! Oh, what have I done to be blessed with such friends?"

As we left the house in my fly, which was waiting, Van Helsing said, "Tonight I can sleep in peace, and sleep I want, two nights of travel, much reading in the day between, and much anxiety on the day to follow, and a night to sit up, without to wink. Tomorrow in the morning early you call for me, and we come together to see our pretty miss, so much more strong for my 'spell' which I have work. Ho, ho!"

He seemed so confident that I, remembering my own confidence two nights before and with the baneful result, felt awe and vague terror. It must have been my weakness that made me hesitate to tell it to my friend, but I felt it all the more, like unshed tears.

CHAPTER SEVENTEEN[140]

Lucy Westenra's Diary

12 September—How good they all are to me. I quite love that dear Dr. Van Helsing. I wonder why he was so anxious about these flowers. He positively frightened me, he was so fierce. And yet he must have been right, for I feel comfort from them already. Somehow, I do not dread being alone tonight, and I can go to sleep without fear. I shall not mind any flapping outside the window. Oh, the terrible struggle that I have had against sleep so often of late, the pain of sleeplessness, or the pain of the fear of sleep, and with such unknown horrors as it has for me! How blessed are some people, whose lives have no fears, no dreads, to whom sleep is a blessing that comes nightly, and brings nothing but sweet dreams. Well, here I am tonight, hoping for sleep, and lying like Ophelia in the play, with 'virgin crants and maiden strewments.' I never liked garlic before, but tonight it is delightful! There is peace in its smell. I feel sleep coming already. Goodnight, everybody.

13 September—I had the most terrible dream last night, one quite different, I believe, than any other dreams that I've had of late, and one so perfectly vivid that even now I am not quite certain that it was only a dream.

It was well into the darkness of night when I heard a noise at the window, a rattling much like the wind makes from time to time. I awoke, or dreamed I awoke, at least to a small degree, just enough to take the noise to be the wind. Thus thinking little of it, my half-conscious mind began to slide back toward the blissful oblivion of sleep. It was then that there came a new sound to my ears, one like a faint scratching or scraping that, while soft, was still sufficient to set every nerve on edge and send chills through me. I was so frightened that

I was hardly able to move, and seemed quite paralyzed where I lay, but with a supreme effort of will I forced my eyes to open and my head to turn, though rather sluggishly, toward the sound. I saw through the glass a tall man, with a pale face and burning red eyes, who seemed very familiar to me, but was all the more terrifying for that familiarity.

While I watched, he, as yet unaware of my waking gaze, busied himself by trying to scratch away the seal around one of the small panes of glass, using his own nails which certainly seemed long and sharp enough for the task. But, for whatever reason, he was unable to succeed with that particular seal, and so he moved his attention to another pane, and then another, with as little success as before. In time—I know not whether moments or hours—he became aware of my state of wakefulness, such as it was, and at last ceased his incessant scratching.

As his red eyes turned to meet mine, I became keenly aware that he was somehow speaking to me; or rather that he was communicating with me, for no actual words were exchanged, through the connection of our gazes. His eyes conveyed to mine his clear desire that I should turn the latch and open the window for him. But we both found, perhaps to our mutual surprise, that I would not, or could not, rise from my bed to comply with his wishes. His burning red orbs held the promise of certain retribution if I continued to refuse him, but still I held back, though whether it was through my own fear, or stubborn will, or the very hand of Providence I cannot say.

I thought the man would surely be filled with rage, but his face remained impassive. With the patience of a demon he studied the window for a moment more before stepping back from it. Presently, he lifted his arms outward and upward, as if praying, and stood there motionless. Within but moments, a small bat suddenly appeared and thudded against the window. This one was followed by another, and then another, and yet another after that. Rats, too, began to appear, dozens of them, gnawing and scratching at the window. Though the panes rattled and shook, they miraculously remained quite secure against the onslaught of vermin. Then, as quickly as they had appeared, the small creatures vanished back into the night, leaving me alone with the pale figure, with only glass and some of Van Helsing's flowers between us.

Again he retained that impassive, perhaps now even curious or thoughtful, look upon his ghostly face. And then, as I watched, he seemed to dissolve into a dark clouded mass of fog or mist that rolled up against the glass in waves, swirling about in a manner both cunning and intelligent, not like the simple mists of night that drift about upon the wind, as if it would slide between whatever miniscule gaps might exist about the window. But this too proved to be as unsuccessful as any of his other attempts.

When the fog coalesced once more into its solid, or mostly solid, form, gone at last was the thoughtful look upon the pale face, having now been replaced with a scowl of frustration. He seemed to snarl like an animal, and as I saw how white and long and sharp his teeth were, my hand, seemingly of its own accord, moved up to clutch protectively at my throat. I watched in growing horror, though unable to look away, as he clenched his hands into fists, digging his talon-like nails into his own palms in the process. When blood began to flow freely from his wounds, he flung his arms forward in a sudden movement, the motion of which served to shower the window with a spray of red ichor. This, more than anything else, seemed to have something of the effect he desired, for the blood seemed to move of its own accord to slip through the tiny chinks around the glass panes. But even as the pale man—oh so pale, as pale as death—smiled in triumph, the blood began to boil away, as if from a great heat, as it seeped through to my side of the window. And his diabolical grin at once contorted into a mask of rage, of frustrated desire, and of inexplicable confusion. He paced back and forth before the window like a caged animal, though of course it was I who was in the "cage," albeit a seemingly safe and impenetrable one so far as he was concerned, and glared at me with those terrible eyes.

Somewhere in the distance a dog began to howl, and soon it was accompanied by its fellows, until the night air was filled with the crescendo. All at once the tall figure paused, and his countenance of rage slipped away, replaced by one of cunning inspiration. For a moment longer I was held in his gaze, and then he was gone, melted back into the night from whence he came. As for myself, I must have fallen instantly into unconsciousness, for I remember nothing more until the light of day filled my room.

When at last I was fully awake, I went at once to the window. Gone were all traces of blood, if even there ever had been any; the only thing out of the ordinary was the scent of the garlic flowers that Van Helsing had rubbed about the window last night. I had heard Dr. Seward say to the Professor last night that their peculiar use of the garlic flowers was like "working some spell to keep out an evil spirit." I wonder if somehow, by accident, my doctors had indeed set into motion some ancient and forgotten spell with their medicines, which served to keep that man, the creature, at bay all through the night. Or, could it be that this "spell" was cast through no accident at all, but intentional on their part?[141]

Dr. Seward's Case-Book

13 September—Called at the Berkeley and found Van Helsing, as usual, up to time. The carriage ordered from the hotel was waiting. The Professor took his bag, which he always brings with him now.

Let all be put down exactly. Van Helsing and I arrived at Hillingham at eight o'clock. It was a lovely morning. The bright sunshine and all the fresh feeling of early autumn seemed like the completion of nature's annual work. The leaves were turning to all kinds of beautiful colours, but had not yet begun to drop from the trees. When we entered we met Mrs. Westenra coming out of the morning room. She is always an early riser. She greeted us warmly and said,

"You will be glad to know that Lucy is better. The dear child is still asleep. I looked into her room and saw her, but did not go in, lest I should disturb her." The Professor smiled, and looked quite jubilant. He rubbed his hands together, and said, "Aha! I thought I had diagnosed the case. My treatment is working."

To which she replied, "You must not take all the credit to yourself, doctor. Lucy's state this morning is due in part to me."

"How do you mean, ma'am?" asked the Professor.

"Well, I was anxious about the dear child in the night, and went into her room. She was sleeping soundly, so soundly that even my coming did not wake her. But the room was awfully stuffy. There were a lot of those horrible, strong-smelling flowers about everywhere, and she had actually a bunch of them round her neck. I feared that the heavy odour would be too much for the dear child in her weak state, so I took them all away and opened a bit of the window to let in a little fresh air. You will be pleased with her, I am sure."

She moved off into her boudoir, where she usually breakfasted early. As she had spoken, I watched the Professor's face, and saw it turn ashen gray. He had been able to retain his self-command whilst the poor lady was present, for he knew her state and how mischievous a shock would be. He actually smiled on her as he held open the door for her to pass into her room. But the instant she had disappeared he pulled me, suddenly and forcibly, into the dining room and closed the door.

Then, for the first time in my life, I saw Van Helsing break down. He raised his hands over his head in a sort of mute despair, and then beat his palms together in a helpless way. Finally he sat down on a chair, and putting his hands before his face, began to sob, with loud, dry sobs that seemed to come from the very racking of his heart.

Then he raised his arms again, as though appealing to the whole universe. "God! God! God!" he said. "What have we done, what has this poor thing done, that we are so sore beset? Is there fate amongst us still, send down from the pagan world of old, that such things must be, and in such way? This poor mother, all unknowing, and all for the best as she think, does such thing as lose her daughter body and soul, and we must not tell her, we must not even warn her, or she die, then both die. Oh, how we are beset! How are all the powers of the devils against us!"

Suddenly he jumped to his feet. "Come," he said, "come, we must see and act. Devils or no devils, or all the devils at once, it matters not. We must fight him all the same." He went to the hall door for his bag, and together we went up to Lucy's room.

Once again I drew up the blind, whilst Van Helsing went towards the bed. This time he did not start as he looked on the poor face with the same awful, waxen pallor as before. He wore a look of stern sadness and infinite pity.

"As I expected," he murmured, with that hissing inspiration of his which meant so much. Without a word he went and locked the door, and then began to set out on the little table the instruments for yet another operation of transfusion of blood. I had long ago recognized the necessity, and begun to take off my coat, but he stopped me with a warning hand. "No!" he said. "Today you must operate. I shall provide. You are weakened already." As he spoke he took off his coat and rolled up his shirtsleeve.

Again the operation. Again the narcotic. Again some return of colour to the ashy cheeks, and the regular breathing of healthy sleep. This time I watched whilst Van Helsing recruited himself and rested.

Presently he took an opportunity of telling Mrs. Westenra that she must not remove anything from Lucy's room without consulting him. That the flowers were of medicinal value, and that the breathing of their odour was a part of the system of cure. Then he took over the care of the case himself, saying that he would watch this night and the next, and would send me word when to come.

After another hour Lucy waked from her sleep, fresh and bright and seemingly not much the worse for her terrible ordeal.

What does it all mean? I am beginning to wonder if my long habit of life amongst the insane is beginning to tell upon my own brain.

Lucy Westenra's Diary

17 September—Four days and nights of peace. I am getting so strong again that I hardly know myself. It is as if I had passed through some long nightmare, and had just awakened to see the beautiful sunshine and feel the fresh air of the morning around me. I have a dim half remembrance of long, anxious times of waiting and fearing, darkness in which there was not even the pain of hope to make present distress more poignant. And then long spells of oblivion, and the rising back to life as a diver coming up through a great press of water. Since, however, Dr. Van Helsing has been with me, all this bad dreaming seems to have passed away. The noises that used to frighten me out of my wits, the flapping against the windows, the distant voices which seemed so close to me, the harsh sounds that came from I know not where and commanded me to do I know not what, have all ceased. I go to bed now without any fear of sleep. I do not even try to keep awake. I have grown quite fond of the garlic, and a boxful arrives for me every day from Haarlem. Tonight Dr. Van Helsing is going away, as he has to be for a day in Amsterdam. But I need not be watched. I am well enough to be left alone.

Thank God for Mother's sake, and dear Arthur's, and for all our friends who have been so kind! I shall not even feel the change, for last night Dr. Van Helsing slept in his chair a lot of the time. I found him asleep twice when I awoke. But I did not fear to go to sleep again, although the boughs or bats or something flapped almost angrily against the window panes.

Cutting from *The Pall Mall Gazette*, 18 September.
The Escaped Wolf Perilous Adventure of our Interviewer

Interview with the Keeper in the Zoological Gardens

After many inquiries and almost as many refusals, and perpetually using the words 'PALL MALL GAZETTE' as a sort of talisman, I managed to find the keeper of the section of the Zoological Gardens in which the wolf department is included. Thomas Bilder lives in one of the cottages in the enclosure behind the elephant house, and was just sitting down to his tea when I found him. Thomas and his wife are hospitable folk, elderly, and without children, and if the specimen I enjoyed of their hospitality be of the average kind, their lives must be pretty comfortable. The keeper would not enter on what he called business until the supper was over, and we were all satisfied. Then when the table was cleared, and he had lit his pipe, he said,

"Now, Sir, you can go on and arsk me what you want. You'll excoose me refoosin' to talk of perfeshunal subjucts afore meals. I gives the wolves and the jackals and the hyenas in all our section their tea afore I begins to arsk them questions."

"How do you mean, ask them questions?" I queried, wishful to get him into a talkative humor.

"'Ittin' of them over the 'ead with a pole is one way. Scratchin' of their ears in another, when gents as is flush wants a bit of a show-orf to their gals. I don't so much mind the fust, the 'ittin of the pole part afore I chucks in their dinner, but I waits till they've 'ad their sherry and kawffee, so to speak, afore I tries on with the ear scratchin.' Mind you," he added philosophically, "there's a deal of the same nature in us as in them theer animiles. Here's you a-comin' and arskin' of me questions about my business, and I that grump-like that only for your bloomin' 'arf-quid I'd 'a' seen you blowed fust 'fore I'd answer. Not even when you arsked me sarcastic like if I'd like you to arsk the Superintendent if you might arsk me questions. Without offence did I tell yer to go to 'ell?"

"You did."

"An' when you said you'd report me for usin' obscene language that was 'ittin' me over the 'ead. But the 'arf-quid made that all right. I weren't a-goin' to fight, so I waited for the food, and did with my 'owl as the wolves and lions and tigers does. But, lor' love yer 'art, now that the old 'ooman has stuck a chunk of her tea-cake in me, an' rinsed me out with her bloomin' old teapot, and I've lit hup, you may scratch my ears for all you're worth, and won't even get a growl out of me. Drive along with your questions. I know what yer a-comin' at, that 'ere escaped wolf."

"Exactly. I want you to give me your view of it. Just tell me how it happened, and when I know the facts I'll get you to say what you consider was the cause of it, and how you think the whole affair will end."

"All right, guv'nor. This 'ere is about the 'ole story. That'ere wolf what we called Bersicker was one that was brought to us just last month. He was a nice well-behaved wolf, that never gave no trouble to talk of. I'm more surprised at 'im for wantin' to get out nor any other animile in the place. But, there, you can't trust wolves no more nor women."

"Don't you mind him, Sir!" broke in Mrs. Tom, with a cheery laugh. "'E's got mindin' the animiles so long that blest if he ain't like a old wolf 'isself! But there ain't no 'arm in 'im."

"Well, Sir, it was about two hours after feedin' yesterday when I first hear my disturbance. I was makin' up a litter in the monkey house for a young puma which is ill. But when I heard the yelpin' and 'owlin' I kem away straight. There was Bersicker a-tearin' like a mad thing at the bars as if he wanted to get out. There wasn't much people about that day, and close at hand was only one man, a tall, thin chap, with a 'ook nose and a pointed beard, with a few white hairs runnin' through it. He had a 'ard, cold look and red eyes, and I took a sort of mislike to him, for it seemed as if it was 'im as they was hirritated at. He 'ad white kid gloves on 'is 'ands, and he pointed out the animiles to me and says, 'Keeper, these wolves seem upset at something.'

"'Maybe it's you,' says I, for I did not like the airs as he give 'isself. He didn't get angry, as I 'oped he would, but he smiled a kind of insolent smile, with a mouth full of white, sharp teeth. 'Oh no, they wouldn't like me,' 'e says.

"'Ow yes, they would,' says I, a-imitatin' of him. 'They always like a bone or two to clean their teeth on about tea time, which you 'as a bagful.'

"Well, it was a odd thing, but when the animiles see us a-talkin' they lay down, and when I went over to Bersicker he let me stroke his ears same as ever. That there man kem over, and blessed but if he didn't put in his hand and stroke the old wolf's ears too!

"'Tyke care,' says I. 'Bersicker is quick.'

"'Never mind,' he says. 'I'm used to 'em!'

"'Are you in the business yourself?' I says, tyking off my 'at, for a man what trades in wolves, anceterer, is a good friend to keepers.

"'Nom' says he, 'not exactly in the business, but I 'ave made pets of several.' and with that he lifts his 'at as perlite as a lord, and walks away. As he did, I heard the other animiles—the eagle and the lion—get all angry like at the man as he went by[142]. Old Bersicker kep' a-lookin' arter 'im till 'e was out of sight, and then went and lay down in a corner and wouldn't come hout the 'ole hevening. Well, larst night, so soon as the moon was hup, the wolves here all began a-'owling. There warn't nothing for them to 'owl at. There warn't no one near, except some one that was evidently a-callin' a dog somewheres out back of the gardings in the Park road. Once or twice I went out to see that all was right, and it was, and then the 'owling stopped. Just before twelve o'clock I just took a look round afore turnin' in, an,' bust me, but when I kem opposite to old Bersicker's cage I see the rails broken and twisted about and the cage empty. And that's all I know for certing."

"Did any one else see anything?"

"One of our gard'ners was a-comin' 'ome about that time from a 'armony, when he sees a big gray dog comin' out through the garding 'edges. At least, so he says, but I don't give much for it myself, for if he did 'e never said a word about it to his missis when 'e got 'ome, and it was only after the escape of the wolf was made known, and we had been up all night a-huntin' of the Park for Bersicker, that he remembered seein' anything. My own belief was that the 'armony 'ad got into his 'ead."

"Now, Mr. Bilder, can you account in any way for the escape of the wolf?"

"Well, Sir," he said, with a suspicious sort of modesty, "I think I can, but I don't know as 'ow you'd be satisfied with the theory."

"Certainly I shall. If a man like you, who knows the animals from experience, can't hazard a good guess at any rate, who is even to try?"

"Well then, Sir, I accounts for it this way. It seems to me that 'ere wolf escaped—simply because he wanted to get out."

From the hearty way that both Thomas and his wife laughed at the joke I could see that it had done service before, and that the whole explanation was simply an elaborate sell. I couldn't cope in badinage with the worthy Thomas, but I thought I knew a surer way to his heart, so I said, "Now, Mr. Bilder, we'll consider that first half-sovereign worked off, and this brother of his is waiting to be claimed when you've told me what you think will happen."

"Right y'are, Sir," he said briskly. "Ye'll excoose me, I know, for a-chaffin' of ye, but the old woman her winked at me, which was as much as telling me to go on."

"Well, I never!" said the old lady.

"My opinion is this. That 'ere wolf is a'idin' of, somewheres. The gard'ner wot didn't remember said he was a-gallopin' northward faster than a horse could go, but I don't believe him, for, yer see, Sir, wolves don't gallop no more nor dogs does, they not bein' built that way. Wolves is fine things in a storybook, and I dessay when they gets in packs and does be chivyin' somethin' that's more afeared than they is they can make a devil of a noise and chop it up, whatever it is. But, Lor' bless you, in real life a wolf is only a low creature, not half so clever or bold as a good dog, and not half a quarter so much fight in 'im. This one ain't been used to fightin' or even to providin' for hisself, and more like he's somewhere round the Park a'hidin' an' a'shiverin' of, and if he thinks at all, wonderin' where he is to get his breakfast from. Or maybe he's got down some area and is in a coal cellar. My eye, won't some cook get a rum start when she sees his green eyes a-shinin' at her out of the dark! If he can't get food he's bound to look for it, and mayhap he may chance to light on a butcher's shop in time. If he doesn't, and some nursemaid goes out walkin' or orf with a soldier, leavin' of the hinfant in the perambulator—well, then I shouldn't be surprised if the census is one babby the less. That's all."

I was handing him the half-sovereign, when something came bobbing up against the window, and Mr. Bilder's face doubled its natural length with surprise.

"God bless me!" he said. "If there ain't old Bersicker come back by 'isself!"

He went to the door and opened it, a most unnecessary proceeding it seemed to me. I have always thought that a wild animal never looks so well as when some obstacle of pronounced durability is between us. A personal experience has intensified rather than diminished that idea.

After all, however, there is nothing like custom, for neither Bilder nor his wife thought any more of the wolf than I should of a dog. The animal itself was a peaceful and well-behaved as that father of all picture-wolves, Red Riding Hood's quondam friend, whilst moving her confidence in masquerade.

The whole scene was a unutterable mixture of comedy and pathos. The wicked wolf that for a half a day had paralyzed London and set all the children in town shivering in their shoes, was there in a sort of penitent mood, and was received and petted like a sort of vulpine prodigal son. Old Bilder examined him all over with most tender solicitude, and when he had finished with his penitent said,

"There, I knew the poor old chap would get into some kind of trouble. Didn't I say it all along? Here's his head all cut and full of broken glass. 'E's been a-gettin' over some bloomin' wall or other. It's a shyme that people are allowed to top their walls with broken bottles. This 'ere's what comes of it. Come along, Bersicker."

He took the wolf and locked him up in a cage, with a piece of meat that satisfied, in quantity at any rate, the elementary conditions of the fatted calf, and went off to report.

I came off too, to report the only exclusive information that is given today regarding the strange escapade at the Zoo.

Dr. Seward's Case-Book

17 September—I was engaged after dinner in my study posting up my books, which, through press of other work and the many visits to Lucy, had fallen sadly into arrear. Suddenly the door was burst open, and in rushed my patient, with

his face distorted with passion. I was thunderstruck, for such a thing as a patient getting of his own accord into the Superintendent's study is almost unknown.

Without an instant's notice he made straight at me. He had a dinner knife in his hand, and as I saw he was dangerous, I tried to keep the table between us. He was too quick and too strong for me, however, for before I could get my balance he had struck at me and cut my left wrist rather severely.

Before he could strike again, however, I got in my right hand and he was sprawling on his back on the floor. My wrist bled freely, and quite a little pool trickled on to the carpet. I saw that my friend was not intent on further effort, and occupied myself binding up my wrist, keeping a wary eye on the prostrate figure all the time. When the attendants rushed in, and we turned our attention to him, his employment positively sickened me. He was lying on his belly on the floor licking up, like a dog, the blood which had fallen from my wounded wrist. He was easily secured, and to my surprise, went with the attendants quite placidly, simply repeating over and over again, "The blood is the life! The blood is the life! It is the cup of the new covenant which the Lord has poured out for his bride, of which she now drinks! For any who eat of His flesh and drink of His blood shall not perish, but have everlasting life!"

I cannot afford to lose blood just at present. I have lost too much of late for my physical good, and then the prolonged strain of Lucy's illness and its horrible phases is telling on me. I am over excited and weary, and I need rest, rest, rest. Happily Van Helsing has not summoned me, so I need not forego my sleep. Tonight I could not well do without it.

Telegram, Van Helsing, Antwerp, to Seward, Carfax

(Sent to Carfax, Sussex, as no county given,
delivered late by twenty-two hours.)

17 September—Do not fail to be at Hillingham tonight. If not watching all the time, frequently visit and see that flowers are as placed, very important, do not fail. Shall be with you as soon as possible after arrival.

Dr. Seward's Case-Book

18 September—Just off train to London. The arrival of Van Helsing's telegram filled me with dismay. A whole night lost, and I know by bitter experience what may happen in a night. Of course it is possible that all may be well, but what may have happened? Surely there is some horrible doom hanging over us that every possible accident should thwart us in all we try to do. I shall take this cylinder with me, and then I can complete my entry on Lucy's phonograph.

Memorandum left by Lucy Westenra

17. September, Night—I write this and leave it to be seen, so that no one may by any chance get into trouble through me. This is an exact record of what took place tonight. I feel I am dying of weakness, and have barely strength to write, but it must be done if I die in the doing.

I went to bed as usual, taking care that the flowers were placed as Dr. Van Helsing directed, and soon fell asleep.

I was waked by the flapping at the window, which had begun after that sleep-walking on the cliff at Whitby when Mina saved me, and which now I know so well. I was not afraid, but I did wish that Dr. Seward was in the next room, as Dr. Van Helsing said he would be, so that I might have called him. I tried to sleep, but I could not. Then there came to me the old fear of sleep, and I determined to keep awake. Perversely sleep would try to come then when I did not want it. So, as I feared to be alone, I opened my door and called out. "Is there anybody there?" There was no answer. I was afraid to wake mother, and so closed my door again. Then outside in the shrubbery I heard a sort of howl like a dog's, but more fierce and deeper. I went to the window and looked out, but could see nothing, except a big bat, which had evidently been buffeting its wings against the window. So I went back to bed again, but determined not to go to sleep. Presently the door opened, and mother looked in. Seeing by my moving that I was not asleep, she came in and sat by me. She said to me even more sweetly and softly than her wont,

"I was uneasy about you, darling, and came in to see that you were all right."

I feared she might catch cold sitting there, and asked her to come in and sleep with me, so she came into bed, and lay down beside me. She did not take off her dressing gown, for she said she would only stay a while and then go back to her own bed. As she lay there in my arms, and I in hers the flapping and buffeting came to the window again. She was startled and a little frightened, and cried out, "What is that?"

I tried to pacify her, and at last succeeded, and she lay quiet. But I could hear her poor dear heart still beating terribly. After a while there was the howl again out in the shrubbery, and then a pattering of quick paws on the verandah, and shortly after there was a crash at the window, and a lot of broken glass was hurled on the floor. The window blind blew back with the wind that rushed in, and in the aperture of the broken panes there was the head of a great, gaunt gray wolf.

Mother cried out in a fright, and struggled up into a sitting posture, and clutched wildly at anything that would help her. Amongst other things, she clutched the wreath of flowers that Dr. Van Helsing insisted on my wearing round my neck, and tore it away from me. For a second or two she sat up, pointing at the wolf, and there was a strange and horrible gurgling in her throat. Then she fell over, as if struck with lightning, and her head hit my forehead and made me dizzy for a moment or two.

The room and all round seemed to spin round. I kept my eyes fixed on the window, but the wolf drew his head back, and a whole myriad of little specks seemed to come blowing in through the broken window, and wheeling and circling round like the pillar of dust that travelers describe when there is a simoon in the desert. I tried to stir, but there was some spell upon me, and dear Mother's poor body, which seemed to grow cold already, for her dear heart had ceased to beat, weighed me down, and I remembered no more for a while.

The time did not seem long, but very, very awful, till I recovered consciousness again. Somewhere near, a passing bell was tolling. The dogs all round the neighbourhood were howling, and in our shrubbery, seemingly just outside, a nightingale was singing. I was dazed and stupid with pain and terror and weakness, but the sound of the nightingale seemed like the voice of my dead mother come back to comfort me. The sounds seemed to have awakened the maids, too, for I could hear their bare feet pattering outside my door. I called to them, and they came in, and when they saw what had happened, and what it was that lay over me on the bed, they screamed out. The wind rushed in through the broken window, and the door slammed to. They lifted off the body of my dear mother, and laid her, covered up with a sheet, on the bed after I had got up. They were all so frightened and nervous that I directed them to go to the dining room and each have a glass of wine. The door flew open for an instant and closed again. The maids shrieked, and then went in a body to the dining room, and I laid what flowers I had on my dear mother's breast. When they were there I remembered what Dr. Van Helsing had told me, but I didn't like to remove them, and besides, I would have some of the servants to sit up with me now. I was surprised that the maids did not come back. I called them, but got no answer, so I went to the dining room to look for them.

My heart sank when I saw what had happened. They all four lay helpless on the floor, breathing heavily. The decanter of sherry was on the table half full, but there was a queer, acrid smell about. I was suspicious, and examined the decanter. It smelt of laudanum, and looking on the sideboard, I found that the bottle which Mother's doctor uses for her—oh! did use—was empty. What am I to do? What am I to do? I am back in the room with Mother. I cannot leave her, and I am alone, save for the sleeping servants, whom some one has drugged. Alone with the dead! I dare not go out, for I can hear the low howl of the wolf through the broken window.

The air seems full of specks, floating and circling in the draught from the window, and the lights burn blue and dim. What am I to do? God shield me from harm this night! I shall hide this paper in my breast, where they shall find it when they come to lay me out. My dear mother gone! It is time that I go too. Goodbye, dear Arthur, if I should not survive this night. God keep you, dear, and God help me!

CHAPTER EIGHTEEN[143]

---

18 September

Mamma and Papa,

Today is, without any sense of exaggeration, the very worst day of my life. Though I do not have a memory for fine details as does my friend Mina, and I abhor writing lengthy letters, I will try my best to make this as specific and factual as I can, so that you can better understand what is happening in my life. So, to begin:

I suppose I should have been more satisfied with myself for being the first at the tryst. The conventional idea, in the minds of most women and of all men, is that a woman should never be the first. But real women, those in whom the heart beats strong, and whose blood can leap, know better. These are the commanders of men. In them sex calls to sex, all unconsciously at first; and men answer to their call, as they to men's.

Two opposite feelings strove for dominance as I found myself on the hilltop of our country estate, alone. One a feeling natural enough to any one, and especially to a girl, of relief that a dreaded hour had been postponed; the other of chagrin that I was the first.

After a few moments, however, one of the two militant thoughts became dominant: the feeling of chagrin. With a pang I thought if I had been a man and summoned for such a purpose, how I would have hurried to the trysting-place; how the flying of my feet would have vied with the quick rapturous beating of my heart! With a little sigh and perhaps even a blush, I remembered that Francis did not know the purpose of the meeting; that he was a friend almost brought up with me since boy and girl times; that he had often been summoned in similar terms and for the most trivial of social purposes.

206

For nearly half an hour I sat on the rustic seat under the shadow of the great oak, looking, half unconscious of its beauty and yet influenced by it, over the wide landscape stretched at my feet.

In spite of my disregard of conventions, I was no fool; the instinct of wisdom was strong within me, so strong that in many ways it ruled my conscious efforts. Had any one told me at the time that my preparations for this interview were made deliberately with some of the astuteness that dominated the Devil when he took Jesus to the top of a high mountain and showed Him all the kingdoms of the earth at His feet, I would have, and with truth, denied it with indignation. Nevertheless it was a fact that I had, in all unconsciousness, chosen for the meeting a spot which would evidence to a man, consciously or unconsciously, the desirability for his own sake of acquiescence in my views and wishes. For all this spreading landscape was my possession—that is, the land which I would in time inherit from you both—which my husband would share.

The half-hour passed in waiting had in one way its advantages to me: though I'm sure I was still as high strung as ever, I acquired a larger measure of control over myself. The nervous tension, however, was so complete physically that all my faculties were acutely awake; very early I became conscious of a distant footstep.

To my straining ears the footsteps seemed wondrous slow, and more wondrous regular; I felt instinctively that I would have liked to have listened to a more hurried succession of less evenly-marked sounds. But notwithstanding these thoughts, and the qualms which came in their turn, the sound of the coming feet brought me great joy. For, after all, they were coming; and coming just in time to prevent the sense of disappointment at their delay gaining firm foothold. It was only when the coming was assured that I felt how strong had been the undercurrent of my apprehension lest they should not come at all.

As Francis drew near, I sank softly into a seat, doing so with a guilty feeling of acting a part. When he actually came into the grove he found me, I'm sure, seemingly lost in a reverie as I gazed out over the wide expanse in front of me. He was hot after his walk, and with something very like petulance threw himself into a cane armchair, exclaiming as he did so with the easy insolence of old familiarity:

'What a girl you are, Kate! dragging a fellow all the way up here. Couldn't you have fixed it down below somewhere if you wanted to see me?'

Strangely enough, as it seemed to me, I did not dislike his tone of mastery. There was something in it which satisfied me. Perhaps it was the unconscious recognition of his manhood, as opposed to my womanhood, which soothed in a peaceful way. It was easy to yield to a dominant man. I was never more womanly than when I answered him softly:

'It was rather unfair; but I thought you would not mind coming so far. It is so cool and delightful here; and we can talk without being disturbed.' Francis was lying back in his chair fanning himself with his wide-brimmed straw hat, with outstretched legs wide apart and resting on the back of his heels. He replied with grudging condescension:

'Yes, it's cool enough after the hot tramp over the fields and through the wood. It's not so good as the house, though, in one way: a man can't get a drink here. I say, Kate, it wouldn't be half bad if there were a shanty put up here like those at the Grands Mulets or on the Matterhorn. There could be a tap laid on where a fellow could quench his thirst on a day like this!'

Before my eyes floated a momentary vision of a romantic chalet with wide verandah and big windows looking over the landscape; a great wide stone hearth; quaint furniture made from the gnarled branches of trees; skins on the floor; and the walls adorned with antlers, great horns, and various trophies of the chase. And amongst them Francis, in a picturesque suit, lolling back just as at present and smiling with a loving look in his eyes as I handed him a great blue-and-white Munich beer mug topped with cool foam. I found there to be a soft mystery in my voice as I answered:

'Perhaps, Francis, there will some day be such a place here!' He seemed to grumble as he replied:

'I wish it was here now. Some day seems a long way off!'

This seemed a good opening for me; for the fear of the situation was again beginning to assail me, and I felt that if I did not enter on my task at once, its difficulty might overwhelm me. I felt angry with myself that there was a change in my voice as I said:

'Some day may mean—can mean everything. Things needn't be a longer way off than we choose ourselves, sometimes!'

'I say, that's a good one! Do you mean to say that because I am some day to own that London gallery I can do as I like with it at once, whilst my uncle the banker still holds the deed? Unless you want me to shoot the old man by accident when we go out on the First and take the scroll from him.' He laughed a short, unmeaning masculine laugh which jarred somewhat on me. I did not, however, mean to be diverted from my main purpose, so I went on quickly:

'You know quite well, Francis, that I don't mean anything of the kind. But there was something I wanted to say to you, and I wished that we should be alone. Can you not guess what it is?'

'No, I'll be hanged if I can!' was his response, lazily given.

Despite my resolution I turned my head; I could not meet his eyes. It cut me with a sharp pain to notice when I turned again that he was not looking at me. He continued fanning himself with his hat as he gazed out at the view. I felt that the critical moment of my life had come, that it was now or never as to my fulfilling my settled intention. So with a rush I went on my way:

'Francis, you and I have been friends a long time. You know my views on some points, and that I think a woman should be as free to act as a man!' I paused; words and ideas did not seem to flow with the readiness I expected. Francis's arrogant assurance completed the dragging me back to earth which my own self-consciousness began:

'Drive on, old girl! I know you're a crank from Crankville on some subjects. Let us have it for all you're worth. I'm on the grass and listening.'

I paused. 'A crank from Crankville!'—this after my nights of sleepless anxiety; after the making of the resolution which had cost me so much, and which was now actually in process of realisation. Was it all worth so much? Why not abandon it now? . . . Abandon it! Abandon a resolution! All the obstinacy of my nature—which I often classed it myself as firmness—rose in revolt. I shook my head angrily, pulled myself together, and went on:

'That may be! though it's not what I call myself, or what I am usually called, so far as I know. At any rate my convictions are honest, and I am sure you will respect them as such, even if you do not share them.' I did not see the ready response in his face which I expected, and so hurried on: 'It has always seemed to me that a—when a woman has to speak to a man she should do so as frankly as she would like him to speak to her, and as freely. Francis, I-I,' as I halted, a sudden idea, winged with possibilities of rescuing procrastination came to me. I went on more easily:

'I know you are in trouble about money matters. Why not let me help you?' He sat up and looked at me and said genially:

'Well, Kate, you are a good old sort! No mistake about it. Do you mean to say you would help me to pay my debts, when my own uncle has refused to do so any more?'

'It would be a great pleasure to me, Francis, to do anything for your good or your pleasure.'

There was a long pause; we both sat looking down at the ground. My heart beat loud; I feared that he must hear it. I was consumed with anxiety, and with a desolating wish to be relieved from the strain of saying more. Surely, surely Francis could not be so blind as not to see the state of things! . . . He would surely seize the occasion; throw aside his diffidence and relieve me! . . . His words made a momentary music in my ears as he spoke:

'And is this what you asked me to come here for?'

But then the words filled me with a great shame. I felt myself in a dilemma. It had been no part of my purpose to allude to his debts. Viewed in the light of what was to follow, it would seem to him that I was trying to foreclose his affection. That could not be allowed to pass; the error must be rectified. And yet! . . . And yet this very error must be cleared up before I could make my full wish apparent. I seemed to find myself compelled by inexorable circumstances into an unlooked-for bluntness. In any case I was forced to face the situation. I must say that my pluck did not fail me; it was with a very noble and graceful simplicity that I turned to my companion and said:

'Francis, I did not quite mean that. It would be a pleasure to me to be of that or any other service to you, if I might be so happy! But I never meant to allude to your debts. Oh! Francis, can't you understand! If you were my husband—or—or going to be, all such little troubles would fall away from you. But I would not for the world have you think . . . '

Here my very voice failed me. I could not speak what was in my mind; I turned away, hiding in my hands my face which fairly seemed to burn. This, I thought, was the time for a true lover's opportunity! Oh, if I had been a man, and a woman had so appealed, how I would have sprung to her side and taken her in my arms, and in a wild rapture of declared affection have swept away all the pain of her shame!

But I remained alone. There was no springing to my side; no rapture of declared affection; no obliteration of my shame. I had to bear it all alone. There, in the open; under the eyes that I would fain have seen any other phase of my distress. My heart beat loud and fast; I waited to gain my self-control.

Francis Aytown has his faults, plenty of them, and I see now that he was in truth composed of an amalgam of far baser metals than I had ever thought; but he had been born of gentle blood and reared amongst gentlefolk. While he did not quite understand the cause or the amount of my concern, he could not but recognise my distress. He must have realised that it had followed hard upon my most generous intention towards himself. He could not, therefore, do less than try to comfort me, and he began his task in a conventional way, but with a blundering awkwardness which was all manlike. He took my hand and held it in his; this much at any rate he had learned in sitting on stairs or in conservatories after extra dances. He said as tenderly as he could, but with an impatient gesture:

'Forgive me, Kate! I suppose I have said or done something which I shouldn't. But I don't know what it is; upon my honour I don't. Anyhow, I am truly sorry for it. Cheer up, old girl! I'm not your husband, you know; so you needn't be distressed.'

Here I took my courage *a deux mains*. If Francis would not speak then I must. It was manifestly impossible that the matter could be left in its present state.

'Francis,' I said softly and solemnly, 'might not that some day be?'

Francis, in addition to being an egotist and the very incarnation of selfishness (for such has he become of late), was a prig of the first water. He had been reared altogether in convention. Home life had taught him many things, wise as well as foolish; but had tended to fix his conviction that affairs of the heart should proceed on adamantine lines of conventional decorum. It never even occurred to him that a lady could so far step from the confines of convention as to take the initiative in a matter of affection. In his blind ignorance he blundered brutally. He struck better than he knew, as, meaning only to pass safely by an awkward conversational corner, he replied:

'No jolly fear of that! You're too much of a boss for me!' The words and the levity with which they were spoken struck me as with a whip. I must have turned for an instant as pale as ashes; then the red blood rushed from my heart, and I felt my face and neck dyed crimson. It was not a blush, it was a suffusion. In his ignorance Francis must have thought it was the former, and went on with what he considered his teasing.

'Oh yes! You know you always want to engineer a chap your own way and make him do just as you wish. The man who has the happiness of marrying you, Kate, will have a hard row to hoe!' His 'chaff' with its utter want of refinement seemed to me, in my high-strung earnest condition, nothing short of brutal, and for a few seconds produced a feeling of repellence. But it is in the nature of things that opposition of any kind arouses the fighting instinct of a naturally dominant nature.

I can see now that I lost sight of my femininity in the pursuit of my purpose; and as this was to win the man to my way of thinking, I took the logical course of answering his argument. If Francis Aytown had purposely set himself to stimulate my efforts in this direction he could hardly have chosen a better way. It came somewhat as a surprise to me, when I heard my own words:

'I would make a good wife, Francis! A husband whom I loved and honoured would, I think, not be unhappy!' The sound of my own voice speaking these words, though the tone was low and tender and more self-suppressing by far than was my wont, seemed to peal like thunder in my own ears. My last bolt seemed to have sped. The blood rushed to my head, and I had to hold on to the arms of the rustic chair or I would have fallen forward.

The time seemed long before Francis spoke again; every second seemed an age. I seemed to have grown tired of waiting for the sound of his voice, for it was with a kind of surprise that I heard him say:

'You limit yourself wisely, Kate!'

'How do you mean?' I asked, making a great effort to speak.

'You would promise to love and honour; but there isn't anything about obeying. Perhaps your old friend Jack might be one to put up with your stubbornness, but most husbands would not tolerate it.'

As he spoke Francis stretched himself again luxuriously, and laughed with the intellectual arrogance of a man who is satisfied with a joke, however inferior, of his own manufacture. I looked at him with a long look which began in anger—that anger which comes from an unwonted sense of impotence, and ends in tolerance, the intermediate step being admiration. It is the primeval curse that a woman's choice is to her husband; and it is an important part of the teaching of a British gentlewoman, knit in the very fibres of her being by the remorseless etiquette of a thousand years, that she be true to him. The man who has in his person the necessary powers or graces to evoke admiration in his wife, even for a passing moment, has a stronghold unconquerable as a rule by all the deadliest arts of mankind.

Francis Aytown was certainly good to look upon as he lolled at his ease on that summer morning. Tall, straight, supple. Though he had for some time distained propriety and preferred his hair longer and his attire more effeminate than was the norm, it was still quite clear that he had been raised a typical British gentleman of the educated class, with all parts of the body properly developed and held in some kind of suitable poise.

As I looked, the anxiety and chagrin which tormented me seemed to pass. I realised that here was a nature different from my own, and which should be dealt with in a way unsuitable to myself; and the conviction seemed to make the action which it necessitated more easy as well as more natural to me. Perhaps for the first time in my life I understood that it may be necessary to apply to individuals a standard of criticism unsuitable to self-judgment. My recognition might have been summed up in the thought which ran through my mind:

'One must be a little lenient with a man one loves!'

I, when once I had allowed the spirit of toleration to work within me, felt immediately its calming influence. It was with brighter thoughts and better humour that I went on with her task. But a task only, it seemed to me now; a means to an end which I desired.

'Francis, tell me seriously, why do you think I gave you the trouble of coming out here?'

'Upon my soul, Kate, I don't know.'

'You don't seem to care either, lolling like that when I am serious!' The words were acid, but the tone was soft and friendly, familiar and genuine, putting quite a meaning of its own on them. Francis looked at me indolently:

'I like to loll.'

'But can't you even guess, or try to guess, what I ask you?'

'I can't guess,' Francis replied. 'The day's too hot, and that shanty with the drinks is not built yet.'

'Or may never be!' Again he looked at me sleepily.

'Never be! Why not?'

'Because, Francis, it may depend on you.'

'All right then. Drive on! Hurry up the architect and the jerry-builder!'

I felt another quick blush leap to my cheeks. Did he at last realize what I was asking? Was he consenting to be my husband? His words were full of meaning, though the tone lacked something; but the news was too good. I could not accept it at once; I decided to myself to wait a short time. Ere many seconds had passed I rejoiced that I had done so as he went on:

'I hope you'll give me a say before that husband of yours comes along. He might be a blue-ribbonite; and it wouldn't do to start such a shanty for rot-gut!'

Again a cold wave swept over me. The absolute difference of feeling between the man and myself; his levity against my earnestness, his callous blindness to my purpose, even the commonness of his words chilled me. For a few seconds I wavered again in my intention; but once again his comeliness and my own obstinacy joined hands and took me back to my path. With chagrin I felt that my words almost stuck in my throat, as summoning up all my resolution I went on:

'It would be for you I would have it built, Francis!' The man sat up quickly.

'For me?' he asked in a sort of wonderment.

'Yes, Francis, for you and me!' I turned away; my blushes so overcame me that I could not look at him. When I faced round again he was standing up, his back towards me.

I stood up also. He was silent for a while; so long that the silence became intolerable, and I spoke:

'Francis, I am waiting!' He turned round and said slowly, the absence of all emotion from his face chilling me till I felt my face blanch:

'I don't think I would worry about it!'

Now, you know I have always been plucky, and whenever I was face to face with any difficulty I was all myself. Francis did not look pleasant; his face was hard and there was just a suspicion of anger. Strangely enough, this last made the next step easier to me; I said slowly:

'All right! I think I understand!'

He turned from me and stood looking out on the distant prospect. Then I felt that the blow which I had all along secretly feared had fallen on me. But my pride as well as my obstinacy now rebelled. I would not accept a silent answer. There must be no doubt left to torture me afterwards. I would take care that there was no mistake. Schooling myself to the task, and pressing one hand for a moment to my side as though to repress the beating of my heart, I came behind him and touched him tenderly on the arm.

'Francis,' I said softly, 'are you sure there is no mistake? Do you not see that I am asking you,' I intended to say 'to be my husband,' but I could not utter the words, they seemed to stick in my mouth, so I finished the sentence: 'that I be your wife?'

The moment the words were spoken—the bare, hard, naked, shameless words—the revulsion came. As a lightning flash shows up the blackness of the night the appalling truth of what I had done was forced upon me. The blood rushed to my head till cheeks and shoulders and neck seemed to burn. Covering my face with my hands I sank back on the seat crying silently bitter tears that seemed to scald my eyes and my cheeks as they ran.

Francis was angry. When it dawned upon him what was the purpose of my speech, he had been shocked. Young men are so easily shocked by breaches of convention made by women they respect! And his pride was hurt. I could almost hear the thoughts running through this mind: 'Why should I have been placed in such a ridiculous position! I did not love Kate in that way; and she should have known it. I liked her and all that sort of thing; but what right had she to assume that I loved her?'

All the weakness of his moral nature came out in his petulance. It was boyish that his eyes filled with tears. He knew it, and that made him more angry than ever, and, with manifest intention to wound, he answered me:

'What a girl you are, Kate. You are always doing something or other to put a chap in the wrong and make him ridiculous. I thought you were joking—not a good joke either! Upon my soul, I don't know what I've done that you should fix on me! I wish to goodness—'

If I had suffered the red terror before, I suffered the white terror now. It was not injured pride, it was not humiliation, it was not fear; it was something vague and terrible that lay far deeper than any of these. Under ordinary circumstances I would have liked to have spoken out my mind and given back as good as I got; and even as the thoughts whirled through my brain they came in a torrent of vague vituperative eloquence. But now my tongue was tied. Instinctively I knew that I had put it out of my power to revenge, or even to defend myself. I was tied to the stake, and must suffer without effort and in silence.

Most humiliating of all was the thought that I must propitiate the man who had so wounded me. All love for him had in the instant passed from me; or rather I realised fully the blank, bare truth that I had never really loved him at all. Had I really loved him, even a blow at his hands would have been acceptable; but now . . .

I shook the feelings and thoughts from me as a bird does the water from its wings; and, with the courage and strength and adaptability of my nature, addressed myself to the hard task which faced me in the immediate present. With what I hoped was an eloquent, womanly gesture I arrested the torrent of Francis' indignation; and, as he paused in surprised obedience, I said:

'That will do, Francis! It is not necessary to say any more; and I am sure you will see, later on, that at least there was no cause for your indignation! I have done an unconventional thing, I know; and I dare say I shall have to pay for it in humiliating bitterness of thought later on! But please remember we are all alone! This is a secret between us; no one else need ever know or suspect it!'

I rose as I concluded. The quiet dignity of my speech and bearing brought back Francis in some way to his sense of duty as a gentleman. He began, in a sheepish way, to make an apology:

'I'm sure I beg your pardon, Katherine.' But again I held the warning hand:

'There is no need for pardon; the fault, if there were any, was mine alone. It was I, remember, who asked you to come here and who introduced and conducted this melancholy business. I have asked you several things, Francis, and one more I will add—'tis only one: that you will forget!'

"Forget?" he said at first in surprise, then again in anger. "Forget! How can I forget such a thing? It's that doctor friend of yours, isn't it. The two of you must have cooked up this scheme to humiliate me. Well, I won't forget this . . . this insult! And I won't forgive you, you or 'doctor Jack.' That's a name I won't forget. I'll see you both pay for this."

And so he left me, there on the hill of our family's estate, at an utter loss for words, or the strength with which to speak them, should I have had any. I doubted I should ever see him again, except that he would, of course, wish to collect his canvasses and belongings from my home.

I was going to pay you a visit, for I was so near your home, but it was then that the idea came to me, like a bolt out of the blue. I would endeavor to return to my own home before him, and should I succeed, I would look through his studio—my studio! for the room belongs to me, not him!—and see just what it is he has been up to these past few weeks. If indeed this tremendous change in personality has come over him because of another woman, he has undoubtedly been making paintings of her. He always paints that which occupies his thoughts; I know this, for once upon a time all he would paint was me. So now I would look upon her face, if only upon a canvas, and see who it is that has stolen Francis from me, so that if ever we were to meet . . .

Forgive me, Mamma and Papa. I know such thoughts are not lady-like, but then I have never been much of a lady, have I? In any event, such thoughts were, by and large, misplaced. I did return home before Francis, and I did enter the studio—for though he had been keeping it locked, I of course had a spare—and when I walked in, I found he had indeed been painting portraits of his new obsession.

Oh, and here is the horror of it, for the canvasses were not of a woman at all, but were of a man! Indeed, they were of our neighbor, Count DeVille. You'll remember the tall somber man I've told you about, the one Francis has been trying to paint ever since our holiday at Whitby. I now fear that his frustration has grown into a morbid obsession, for there were literally dozens of paintings and sketches of the Count strewn about the room, and in each one the face looked like that of a corpse or skull. Whereas before Francis had endeavored to paint DeVille as a man, but had been thwarted by a cadaverous look that had continually crept into the attempts, now it seemed he had given up entirely trying to make the man look even remotely human, but instead was now purposefully painting him as if dead!

This is, I know, the longest letter I have ever written you, and I doubt I shall ever bring myself to write one such as this again, but I wanted to let you know all every detail that has happened. Though you have patiently indulged me and my novel ideas, you have long warned me about my lack of respect for tradition. I wanted to say that I see now that I should have listened to you. I have failed to win Francis' heart, and my own heart has grown cold toward him in the process. But though we shall never be man and wife, I would still be his friend. And now that friendship may too be lost forever, and to a man! And not even to a man, but to the mere a painting of a man.

I can write no more today . . .

Your daughter,
Kate

CHAPTER NINETEEN[144]

Dr. Seward's Case-Book

18 September—I drove at once to Hillingham and arrived early. Keeping my cab at the gate, I went up the avenue alone. I knocked gently and rang as quietly as possible, for I feared to disturb Lucy or her mother, and hoped to only bring a servant to the door. After a while, finding no response, I knocked and rang again, still no answer. I cursed the laziness of the servants that they should lie abed at such an hour, for it was now ten o'clock, and so rang and knocked again, but more impatiently, but still without response. Hitherto I had blamed only the servants, but now a terrible fear began to assail me. Was this desolation but another link in the chain of doom which seemed drawing tight round us? Was it indeed a house of death to which I had come, too late? I know that minutes, even seconds of delay, might mean hours of danger to Lucy, if she had had again one of those frightful relapses, and I went round the house to try if I could find by chance an entry anywhere.

I could find no means of ingress. Every window and door was fastened and locked, and I returned baffled to the porch. As I did so, I heard the rapid pit-pat of a swiftly driven horse's feet. They stopped at the gate, and a few seconds later I met Van Helsing running up the avenue. When he saw me, he gasped out, "Then it was you, and just arrived. How is she? Are we too late? Did you not get my telegram?"

I answered as quickly and coherently as I could that I had only got his telegram early in the morning, and had not lost a minute in coming here, though I was still weak from the deep cut in my wrist. When he asked me of it, I told him of Renfield's attack on me, and how he lapped at my blood, and had carried on so about a bride and blood. He paused and raised his hat as he said solemnly, "How often are the mad gifted with senses beyond our own! So, already has he fed his blood to dear Lucy! Then I fear we are too late. God's will be done!"

With his usual recuperative energy, he went on, "Come. If there be no way open to get in, we must make one. Time is all in all to us now."

We went round to the back of the house, where there was a kitchen window. The Professor took a small surgical saw from his case, and handing it to me, saying, "You are a surgeon—this is your work," and pointed to the iron bars which guarded the window. I attacked them at once and had very soon cut through three of them. Then with a long, thin knife we pushed back the fastening of the sashes and opened the window. I helped the Professor in, and followed him. There was no one in the kitchen or in the servants' rooms, which were close at hand. We tried all the rooms as we went along, and in the dining room, dimly lit by rays of light through the shutters, found four servant women lying on the floor. There was no need to think them dead, for their stertorous breathing and the acrid smell of laudanum in the room left no doubt as to their condition.

Van Helsing and I looked at each other, and as we moved away he said, "We can attend to them later." Then we ascended to Lucy's room. For an instant or two we paused at the door to listen, but there was no sound that we could hear. With white faces and trembling hands, we opened the door gently, and entered the room.

How shall I describe what we saw? On the bed lay two women, Lucy and her mother. The latter lay farthest in, and she was covered with a white sheet, the edge of which had been blown back by the draught through the broken window, showing the drawn, white, face, with a look of terror fixed upon it. By her side lay Lucy, with face white and still more drawn. The flowers which had been round her neck we found upon her mother's bosom, and her throat was bare, showing the two little wounds which we had noticed before, but looking horribly white and mangled. Without a word the Professor knelt down beside the bed and groaned outwardly as he said an inward prayer as he bend forward, his head almost touching poor Lucy's breast. Then he gave a quick turn of his head, as of one who listens, and leaping to his feet, he cried out to me, "It is not yet too late! Quick! Quick! Bring the brandy!"

I flew downstairs and returned with it, taking care to smell and taste it, lest it, too, were drugged like the decanter of sherry which I found on the table. The maids were still breathing, but more restlessly, and I fancied that the narcotic was wearing off. I did not stay to make sure, but returned to Van Helsing. He rubbed the brandy, as on another occasion, on her lips and gums and on her wrists and the palms of her hands. He said to me, "I can do this, all that can be at the present. You go wake those maids. Flick them in the face with a wet towel, and flick them hard. Make them get heat and fire and a warm bath. This poor soul is nearly as cold as that beside her. She will need be heated before we can do anything more."

I went at once, and found little difficulty in waking three of the women. The fourth was only a young girl, and the drug had evidently affected her more strongly so I lifted her on the sofa and let her sleep.

The others were dazed at first, but as remembrance came back to them they cried and sobbed in a hysterical manner. I was stern with them, however, and would not let them talk. I told them that one life was bad enough to lose, and if they delayed they would sacrifice Miss Lucy. So, sobbing and crying they went about their way, half clad as they were, and prepared fire and water. Fortunately, the kitchen and boiler fires were still alive, and there was no lack of hot water. We got a bath and carried Lucy out as she was and placed her in it. Whilst we were busy chafing her limbs there was a knock at the hall door. One of the maids ran off, hurried on some more clothes, and opened it. Then she returned and whispered to us that there was a gentleman who had come with a message from Mr. Holmwood. I bade her simply tell him that he must wait, for we could see no one now. She went away with the message, and, engrossed with our work, I clean forgot all about him.

I never saw in all my experience the Professor work in such deadly earnest. I knew, as he knew, that it was a stand-up fight with death, and in a pause told him so. He answered me in a way that I did not understand, but with the sternest look that his face could wear.

"If that were all, I would stop here where we are now, and let her fade away into peace, for I see no light in life over her horizon." He went on with his work with, if possible, renewed and more frenzied vigour.

Presently we both began to be conscious that the heat was beginning to be of some effect. Lucy's heart beat a trifle more audibly to the stethoscope, and her lungs had a perceptible movement. Van Helsing's face almost beamed, and as we lifted her from the bath and rolled her in a hot sheet to dry her he said to me, "The first gain is ours! Check to the King!"

We took Lucy into another room, which had by now been prepared, and laid her in bed and forced a few drops of brandy down her throat. I noticed that Van Helsing tied a soft silk handkerchief round her throat. She was still unconscious, and was quite as bad as, if not worse than, we had ever seen her.

Van Helsing called in one of the women, and told her to stay with her and not to take her eyes off her till we returned, and then beckoned me out of the room.

"We must consult as to what is to be done," he said as we descended the stairs. In the hall he opened the dining room door, and we passed in, he closing the door carefully behind him. The shutters had been opened, but the blinds were already down, with that obedience to the etiquette of death which the British woman of the lower classes always rigidly observes. The room was, therefore, dimly dark. It was, however, light enough for our purposes. Van Helsing's sternness was somewhat relieved by a look of perplexity. He was evidently torturing his mind about something, so I waited for an instant, and he spoke.

"What are we to do now? Where are we to turn for help? We must have another transfusion of blood, and that soon, or that poor girl's life won't be worth an hour's purchase. You are exhausted already. I am exhausted too. I fear to trust those women, even if they would have courage to submit. What are we to do for some one who will open his veins for her?"

"What's the matter with me, anyhow?"

The voice came from the sofa across the room, and its tones brought relief and joy to my heart, for they were those of Quincey Morris.

Van Helsing started angrily at the first sound, but his face softened and a glad look came into his eyes as I cried out, "Quincey Morris!" and rushed towards him with outstretched hands.

"What brought you here?" I cried as our hands met.

"I guess Art is the cause."

He handed me a telegram.—'Have not heard from Seward for three days, and am terribly anxious. Cannot leave. Father still in same condition. Send me word how Lucy is. Do not delay.—Holmwood.'

"I think I came just in the nick of time. You know you have only to tell me what to do."

Van Helsing strode forward, and took his hand, looking him straight in the eyes as he said, "A brave man's blood is the best thing on this earth when a woman is in trouble. You're a man and no mistake. Well, the devil may work against us for all he's worth, but God sends us men when we want them."

Once again we went through that ghastly operation. I have not the heart to go through with the details. Lucy had got a terrible shock and it told on her more than before, for though plenty of blood went into her veins, her body did not respond to the treatment as well as on the other occasions. Her struggle back into life was something frightful to see and hear. However, the action of both heart and lungs improved, and Van Helsing made a sub-cutaneous injection of morphia, as before, and with good effect. Her faint became a profound slumber. The Professor watched whilst I went downstairs with Quincey Morris, and sent one of the maids to pay off one of the cabmen who were waiting.

I left Quincey lying down after having a glass of wine, and told the cook to get ready a good breakfast. Then a thought struck me, and I went back to the room where Lucy now was. When I came softly in, I found Van Helsing with a sheet or two of note paper in his hand. He had evidently read it, and was thinking it over as he sat with his hand to his brow. There was a look of grim satisfaction in his face, as of one who has had a doubt solved. He handed me the paper saying only, "It dropped from Lucy's breast when we carried her to the bath."

When I had read it, I stood looking at the Professor, and after a pause asked him, "In God's name, what does it all mean? Was she, or is she, mad, or what sort of horrible danger is it?" I was so bewildered that I did not know what to say more. Van Helsing put out his hand and took the paper, saying,

"Do not trouble about it now. Forget it for the present. You shall know and understand it all in good time, but it will be later. And now what is it that you came to me to say?" This brought me back to fact, and I was all myself again.

"I came to speak about the certificate of death. If we do not act properly and wisely, there may be an inquest, and that paper would have to be produced. I am in hopes that we need have no inquest, for if we had it would surely kill poor Lucy, if nothing else did. I know, and you know, and the other doctor who attended her knows, that Mrs. Westenra had disease of the heart, and we can certify that she died of it. Let us fill up the certificate at once, and I shall take it myself to the registrar and go on to the undertaker."

"Good, oh my friend John! Well thought of! Truly Miss Lucy, if she be sad in the foes that beset her, is at least happy in the friends that love her. One, two, three, all open their veins for her, besides one old man. Ah, yes, I know, friend John. I am not blind! I love you all the more for it! Now go."

In the hall I met Quincey Morris, with a telegram for Arthur telling him that Mrs. Westenra was dead, that Lucy also had been ill, but was now going on better, and that Van Helsing and I were with her. I told him where I was going, and he hurried me out, but as I was going said,

"When you come back, Jack, may I have two words with you all to ourselves?" I nodded in reply and went out. I found no difficulty about the registration, and arranged with the local undertaker to come up in the evening to measure for the coffin and to make arrangements.

When I got back Quincey was waiting for me. I told him I would see him as soon as I knew about Lucy, and went up to her room. She was still sleeping, and the Professor seemingly had not moved from his seat at her side. From his putting his finger to his lips, I gathered that he expected her to wake before long and was afraid of fore-stalling nature. So I went down to Quincey and took him into the breakfast room, where the blinds were not drawn down, and which was a little more cheerful, or rather less cheerless, than the other rooms.

When we were alone, he said to me, "Jack Seward, I don't want to shove myself in anywhere where I've no right to be, but this is no ordinary case. You know I loved that girl and wanted to marry her, but although that's all past and gone, I can't help feeling anxious about her all the same. What is it that's wrong with her? The Dutchman, and a fine old fellow he is, I can see that, said that time you two came into the room, that you must have another transfusion of blood, and that both you and he were exhausted. Now I know well that you medical men speak *in camera*, and that a man must not expect to know what they consult about in private. But this is no common matter, and whatever it is, I have done my part. Is not that so?"

"That's so," I said, and he went on.

"I take it that both you and Van Helsing had done already what I did today. Is not that so?"

"That's so."

"And I guess Art was in it too. When I saw him four days ago down at his own place he looked queer. I have not seen anything pulled down so quick since I was on the Pampas and had a mare that I was fond of go to grass all in a night. One of those big bats that they call vampires had got at her in the night, and what with his gorge and the vein left open, there wasn't enough blood in her to let her stand up, and I had to put a bullet through her as she lay. Jack, if you may tell me without betraying confidence, Arthur was the first, is not that so?"

As he spoke the poor fellow looked terribly anxious. He was in a torture of suspense regarding the woman he loved, and his utter ignorance of the terrible mystery which seemed to surround her intensified his pain. His very heart was bleeding, and it took all the manhood of him, and there was a royal lot of it, too, to keep him from breaking down. I paused before answering, for I felt that I must not betray anything which the Professor wished kept secret, but already he knew so much, and guessed so much, that there could be no reason for not answering, so I answered in the same phrase.

"That's so."

"And how long has this been going on?"

"About ten days."

"Ten days! Then I guess, Jack Seward, that that poor pretty creature that we all love has had put into her veins within that time the blood of four strong men. Man alive, her whole body wouldn't hold it." Then coming close to me, he spoke in a fierce half-whisper. "What took it out?"

I shook my head. "That," I said, "is the crux. Van Helsing is simply frantic about it, and I am at my wits' end. I can't even hazard a guess. There has been a series of little circumstances which have thrown out all our calculations as to Lucy being properly watched. But these shall not occur again. Here we stay until all be well, or ill."

Quincey held out his hand. "Count me in," he said. "You and the Dutchman will tell me what to do, and I'll do it."

When she woke late in the afternoon, Lucy's first movement was to feel in her breast, and to my surprise, produced the paper which Van Helsing had given me to read. The careful Professor had replaced it where it had come from, lest on waking she should be alarmed. Her eyes then lit on Van Helsing and on me too, and gladdened. Then she looked round the room, and seeing where she was, shuddered. She gave a loud cry, and put her poor thin hands before her pale face.

We both understood what was meant, that she had realised to the full her mother's death. So we tried what we could to comfort her. Doubtless sympathy eased her somewhat, but she was very low in thought and spirit, and wept silently and weakly for a long time. We told her that either or both of us would now remain with her all the time, and that seemed to comfort her. Towards dusk she fell into a doze. Here a very odd thing occurred. Whilst still asleep she took the paper from her breast and tore it in two. Van Helsing stepped over and took the pieces from her. All the same, however, she went on with the action of tearing, as though the material were still in her hands. Finally she lifted her hands and opened them as though scattering the fragments. Van Helsing seemed surprised, and his brows gathered as if in thought, but he said nothing.

19 September—All last night she slept fitfully, being always afraid to sleep, and something weaker when she woke from it. The Professor and I took in turns to watch, and we never left her for a moment unattended. Quincey Morris said nothing about his intention, but I knew that all night long he patrolled round and round the house.

When the day came, its searching light showed the ravages in poor Lucy's strength. She was hardly able to turn her head, and the little nourishment which she could take seemed to do her no good. At times she slept, and both Van Helsing and I noticed the difference in her, between sleeping and waking. Whilst asleep she looked stronger, although more haggard, and her breathing was softer. Her open mouth showed the pale gums drawn back from the teeth, which looked positively longer and sharper than usual. When she woke the softness of her eyes evidently changed the expression, for she looked her own self, although a dying one; she breathed heaving as though fighting for air. In the afternoon she asked for Arthur, and we telegraphed for him. Quincey went off to meet him at the station.

When he arrived it was nearly six o'clock, and the sun was setting full and warm, and the red light streamed in through the window and gave more colour to the pale cheeks. When he saw her, Arthur was simply choking with emotion, and none of us could speak. In the hours that had passed, the fits of sleep, or the comatose condition that passed for it, had grown more frequent, so that the pauses when conversation was possible were shortened. Arthur's presence, however, seemed to act as a stimulant. She rallied a little, and spoke to him more brightly than she had done since we arrived. He too pulled himself together, and spoke as cheerily as he could, so that the best was made of everything.

It is now nearly one o'clock, and he and Van Helsing are sitting with her. I am to relieve them in a quarter of an hour, and I am entering this on Lucy's phonograph. Until six o'clock they are to try to rest. I fear that tomorrow will end our watching, for the shock has been too great. The poor child cannot rally. God help us all.

Letter Mina Harker to Lucy Westenra

(Unopened by her)

17 September

My dearest Lucy,

It seems an age since I heard from you, or indeed since I wrote. You will pardon me, I know, for all my faults when you have read all my budget of news. Well, I got my husband back all right. When we arrived at Exeter there was a carriage waiting for us, and in it, though he had an attack of gout, Mr. Hawkins. He took us to his house, where there were rooms for us all nice and comfortable, and we dined together. He seemed happy to see us, almost unnaturally so, as if he had all along feared for our safety. After dinner Mr. Hawkins said,

"My dears, I want to drink your health and prosperity, and may every blessing attend you both. I am happy to see that for once Virgil was mistaken. I know you both from children, and have, with love and pride, seen you grow up. Now I want you to make your home here with me. I have left to me neither chick nor child. All are gone, and in my will I have left you everything." I cried, Lucy dear, as Jonathan and the old man clasped hands. Though I am still perplexed as to who or what Virgil might be, I was too filled with joy to ask, and have not had the opportunity to since. Oh, but our evening was a very, very happy one.

So here we are, installed in this beautiful old house, and from both my bedroom and the drawing room I can see the great elms of the cathedral close, with their great black stems standing out against the old yellow stone of the cathedral, and I can hear the rooks overhead cawing and cawing and chattering and chattering and gossiping all day, after the manner of rooks—and humans. I am busy, I need not tell you, arranging things and housekeeping. Jonathan and Mr. Hawkins are busy all day, for now that Jonathan is a partner, Mr. Hawkins wants to tell him all about the clients. Even now they are attending to the will of Arthur's father, the Lord Godalming. I am so sorry to hear of his untimely death; I know it must be a sad blow to your Arthur, and as such to you. Mr. Hawkins will conduct the proceedings himself later today, while Jonathan remains here to continue his recovery. Perhaps that is for the best anyway, for I would hate for my husband to have his first meeting with your own (or so soon to be your own) under such trying circumstances.

How is your dear mother getting on? I wish I could run up to town for a day or two to see you, dear, but I, dare not go yet, with so much on my shoulders, and Jonathan wants looking after still. He is beginning to put some flesh on his bones again, but he was terribly weakened by the long illness. Even now he sometimes starts out of his sleep in a sudden way and awakes all trembling until I can coax him back to his usual placidity. However, thank God, these occasions grow less frequent as the days go on, and they will in time pass away altogether, I trust. And now I have told you my news, let me ask yours. Where are you to be married, and who is to perform the ceremony, and what are you to wear, and is it to be a public or private wedding? Tell me all about it, dear, tell me all about everything, for there is nothing which interests you which will not be dear to me. Jonathan asks me to send his 'respectful duty,' but I do not think that is good enough from the junior partner of the important firm Hawkins & Harker. And so, as you love me, and he loves me, and I love you with all the moods and tenses of the verb, I send you simply his 'love' instead. Goodbye, my dearest Lucy, and blessings on you.

Yours,
Mina Harker

Report from Patrick Hennessey, M.D. M.R.C.S.L.K., Q.C.P.I., etc., etc., to John Seward, M.D.

20 September

My dear Sir,

   In accordance with your wishes, I enclose report of the conditions of everything left in my charge. With regard to patient, Renfield, there is more to say. He has had another outbreak, which might have had a dreadful ending, but which, as it fortunately happened, was unattended with any unhappy results. This afternoon a carrier's cart with two men made a call at the empty house whose grounds abut on ours, the house to which, you will remember, the patient twice ran away. The men stopped at our gate to ask the porter their way, as they were strangers.

   I was myself looking out of the study window, having a smoke after dinner, and saw one of them come up to the house. As he passed the window of Renfield's room, the patient began to rate him from within, and called him all the foul names he could lay his tongue to. The man, who seemed a decent fellow enough, contented himself by telling him to "shut up for a foul-mouthed beggar," whereon our man accused him of robbing him and wanting to murder him and said that he would hinder him if he were to swing for it. I opened the window and signed to the man not to notice, so he contented himself after looking the place over and making up his mind as to what kind of place he had got to by saying, "Lor' bless yer, sir, I wouldn't mind what was said to me in a bloomin' madhouse. I pity ye and the guv'nor for havin' to live in the house with a wild beast like that."

Then he asked his way civilly enough, and I told him where the gate of the empty house was. He went away followed by threats and curses and revilings from our man. I went down to see if I could make out any cause for his anger, since he is usually such a well-behaved man, and except his violent fits nothing of the kind had ever occurred. I found him, to my astonishment, quite composed and most genial in his manner. I tried to get him to talk of the incident, but he blandly asked me questions as to what I meant, and led me to believe that he was completely oblivious of the affair. It was, I am sorry to say, however, only another instance of his cunning, for within half an hour I heard of him again. This time he had broken out through the window of his room, and was running down the avenue. I called to the attendants to follow me, and ran after him, for I feared he was intent on some mischief. My fear was justified when I saw the same cart which had passed before coming down the road, having on it some great wooden boxes. The men were wiping their foreheads, and were flushed in the face, as if with violent exercise. Before I could get up to him, the patient rushed at them, and pulling one of them off the cart, began to knock his head against the ground. If I had not seized him just at the moment, I believe he would have killed the man there and then. The other fellow jumped down and struck him over the head with the butt end of his heavy whip. It was a horrible blow, but he did not seem to mind it, but seized him also, and struggled with the three of us, pulling us to and fro as if we were kittens. You know I am no lightweight, and the others were both burly men. At first he was silent in his fighting, but as we began to master him, and the attendants were putting a strait waistcoat on him, he began to shout, "I'll frustrate them! They shan't rob me! They shan't murder me by inches! I'll fight for my Lord and Master!" and all sorts of similar incoherent ravings. It was with very considerable difficulty that they got him back to the house and put him in the padded room. One of the attendants, Hardy, had a finger broken. However, I set it all right, and he is going on well.

The two carriers were at first loud in their threats of actions for damages, and promised to rain all the penalties of the law on us. Their threats were, however, mingled with some sort of indirect apology for the defeat of the two of them by a feeble madman. They said that if it had not been for the way their strength had been spent in carrying and raising the heavy boxes to the cart they would have made short work of him. They gave as another reason for their defeat the extraordinary state of drouth to which they had been reduced by the dusty nature of their occupation and the reprehensible distance from the scene of their labors of any place of public entertainment. I quite understood their drift, and after a stiff glass of strong grog, or rather more of the same, and with each a sovereign in hand, they made light of the attack, and swore that they would encounter a worse madman any day for the pleasure of meeting so "bloomin' good a bloke" as your correspondent. I took their names and addresses, in case they might be needed. They are as follows: Jack Smollet, of Dudding's Rents, King George's Road, Great Walworth, and Thomas Snelling, Peter Farley's Row, Guide Court, Bethnal Green. They are both in the employment of Harris & Sons, Moving and Shipment Company, Orange Master's Yard, Soho.

I shall report to you any matter of interest occurring here, and shall wire you at once if there is anything of importance.

Believe me, dear Sir,
Yours faithfully,
Patrick Hennessey.

Letter, Mina Harker to Lucy Westenra

(Unopened by her)

18 September

My dearest Lucy,

Such a sad blow has befallen us. Mr. Hawkins has died very suddenly. I fear the trip to the Ringwood estate was too much for him. Some may not think it so sad for us, but we had both come to so love him that it really seems as though we had lost a father. I never knew either father or mother, so that the dear old man's death is a real blow to me. Jonathan is greatly distressed. It is not only that he feels sorrow, deep sorrow, for the dear, good man who has befriended him all his life, and now at the end has treated him like his own son and left him a fortune which to people of our modest bringing up is wealth beyond the dream of avarice, but Jonathan feels it on another account. He says the amount of responsibility which it puts upon him makes him nervous. He begins to doubt himself.

I try to cheer him up, and my belief in him helps him to have a belief in himself. But it is here that the grave shock that he experienced tells upon him the most. Oh, it is too hard that a sweet, simple, noble, strong nature such as his, a nature which enabled him by our dear, good friend's aid to rise from clerk to master in a few years, should be so injured that the very essence of its strength is gone. Forgive me, dear, if I worry you with my troubles in the midst of your own happiness, but Lucy dear, I must tell someone, for the strain of keeping up a brave and cheerful appearance to Jonathan tries me, and I have no one here that I can confide in. I dread coming up to London, as we must do that day after tomorrow, for poor Mr. Hawkins left in his will that he was to be buried in the grave with his father. As there are no relations at all, Jonathan will have to be chief mourner. I shall try to run over to see you, dearest, if only for a few minutes. Forgive me for troubling you. With all blessings,

Your loving
Mina Harker

Letter, Kate to Mr. and Mrs. Reed

19 September

Mamma, Papa,

As Francis has yet to return to our house, I decided to look through his effects, in case I might find some clue as to his plans or whereabouts. In doing so, I came across his most recent sketch journal, which was filled mainly with his musings and drawings of Whitby. Near the end of journal, though, his writings and sketches become centered around the Count. It seems he even followed the man one night, and caught the Count at a romantic tryst with Lucy Westenra, of all people, though his thoughts on the matter were less romantic than they were morbid. He ends his last entry, of 11 August, with a decision to do something, though what he did not say.

It's all so bewildering, this change that has come over Francis since the arrival of the Count. I shall endeavor to speak with him on the matter when he returns. Until then, I believe the best course is to take a photograph of the Count for Francis to paint from. Perhaps then he can finish his work properly and put an end to this pointless obsession, and we can once again talk to one another in peace, if not in friendship.

To that end, I have been watching for the Count to enter or leave his new home, or to stand watching at his window, as I have seen him do before, but all I ever see is a bat flying to and fro. I shall continue to watch and wait with my camera, and will write soon . . .

Your daughter,
Kate

Dr. Seward's Case-Book

20 September—Only resolution and habit can let me make an entry tonight. I am too miserable, too low spirited, too sick of the world and all in it, including life itself, that I would not care if I heard this moment the flapping of the wings of the angel of death. And he has been flapping those grim wings to some purpose of late, Lucy's mother and Arthur's father, and now . . . Let me get on with my work.

I duly relieved Van Helsing in his watch over Lucy. We wanted Arthur to go to rest also, but he refused at first. It was only when I told him that we should want him to help us during the day, and that we must not all break down for want of rest, lest Lucy should suffer, that he agreed to go.

Van Helsing was very kind to him. "Come, my child," he said. "Come with me. You are sick and weak, and have had much sorrow and much mental pain, as well as that tax on your strength that we know of. You must not be alone, for to be alone is to be full of fears and alarms. Come to the drawing room, where there is a big fire, and there are two sofas. You shall lie on one, and I on the other, and our sympathy will be comfort to each other, even though we do not speak, and even if we sleep."

Arthur went off with him, casting back a longing look on Lucy's face, which lay in her pillow, almost whiter than the lawn. She lay quite still, and I looked around the room to see that all was as it should be. I could see that the Professor had carried out in this room, as in the other, his purpose of using the garlic. The whole of the window sashes reeked with it, and round Lucy's neck, over the silk handkerchief which Van Helsing made her keep on, was a rough chaplet of the same odorous flowers.

Lucy was breathing somewhat stertorously, and her face was at its worst, for the open mouth showed the pale gums. Her teeth, in the dim, uncertain light, seemed longer and sharper than they had been in the morning. In particular, by some trick of the light, the canine teeth looked longer and sharper than the rest.

I sat down beside her, and presently she moved uneasily. At the same moment there came a sort of dull flapping or buffeting at the window. I went over to it softly, and peeped out by the corner of the blind. There was a full moonlight, and I could see that the noise was made by a great bat, which wheeled around, doubtless attracted by the light, although so dim, and every now and again struck the window with its wings. When I came back to my seat, I found that Lucy had moved slightly, and had torn away the garlic flowers from her throat. I replaced them as well as I could, and sat watching her.

Presently she woke, and I gave her food, as Van Helsing had prescribed. She took but a little, and that languidly. There did not seem to be with her now the unconscious struggle for life and strength that had hitherto so marked her illness. It struck me as curious that the moment she became conscious she pressed the garlic flowers close to her. It was certainly odd that whenever she got into that lethargic state, with the stertorous breathing, she put the flowers from her, but that when she waked she clutched them close, There was no possibility of making any mistake about this, for in the long hours that followed, she had many spells of sleeping and waking and repeated both actions many times.

At six o'clock Van Helsing came to relieve me. Arthur had then fallen into a doze, and he mercifully let him sleep on. When he saw Lucy's face I could hear the hissing indraw of breath, and he said to me in a sharp whisper. "Draw up the blind. I want light!" Then he bent down, and, with his face almost touching Lucy's, examined her carefully. He removed the flowers and lifted the silk handkerchief from her throat. As he did so he started back and I could hear his ejaculation, "Mein Gott!" as it was smothered in his throat. I bent over and looked, too, and as I noticed some queer chill came over me. The wounds on the throat had absolutely disappeared.

For fully five minutes Van Helsing stood looking at her, with his face at its sternest. Then he turned to me and said calmly, "She is dying. It will not be long now. It will be much difference, mark me, whether she dies conscious or in her sleep. Wake that poor boy, and let him come and see the last. He trusts us, and we have promised him."

I went to the dining room and waked him. He was dazed for a moment, but when he saw the sunlight streaming in through the edges of the shutters he thought he was late, and expressed his fear. I assured him that Lucy was still asleep, but told him as gently as I could that both Van Helsing and I feared that the end was near. He covered his face with his hands, and slid down on his knees by the sofa, where he remained, perhaps a minute, with his head buried, praying, whilst his shoulders shook with grief. I took him by the hand and raised him up. "Come," I said, "my dear old fellow, summon all your fortitude. It will be best and easiest for her."

When we came into Lucy's room I could see that Van Helsing had, with his usual forethought, been putting matters straight and making everything look as pleasing as possible. He had even brushed Lucy's hair, so that it lay on the pillow in its usual shiny ripples. When we came into the room she opened her eyes, and seeing him, whispered softly, "Arthur! Oh, my love, I am so glad you have come!"

He was stooping to kiss her, when Van Helsing motioned him back. "No," he whispered, "not yet! Hold her hand, it will comfort her more."

So Arthur took her hand and knelt beside her, and she looked her best, with all the soft lines matching the angelic beauty of her eyes. Then gradually her eyes closed, and she sank to sleep. For a little bit her breast heaved softly, and her breath came and went like a tired child's.

And then insensibly there came the strange change which I had noticed in the night. Her breathing grew stertorous, the mouth opened, and the pale gums, drawn back, made the teeth look longer and sharper than ever. In a sort of sleep-waking, vague, unconscious way she opened her eyes, which were now dull and hard at once, and said in a soft, voluptuous voice, such as I had never heard from her lips, "Arthur! Oh, my love, I am so glad you have come! Kiss me!"

Arthur bent eagerly over to kiss her, but at that instant Van Helsing, who, like me, had been startled by her voice, swooped upon him, and catching him by the neck with both hands, dragged him back with a fury of strength which I never thought he could have possessed, and actually hurled him almost across the room.

"Not on your life!" he said, "not for your living soul and hers!" And he stood between them like a lion at bay.

Arthur was so taken aback that he did not for a moment know what to do or say, and before any impulse of violence could seize him he realised the place and the occasion, and stood silent, waiting.

I kept my eyes fixed on Lucy, as did Van Helsing, and we saw a spasm as of rage flit like a shadow over her face. The sharp teeth clamped together. Then her eyes closed, and she breathed heavily.

Very shortly after she opened her eyes in all their softness, and putting out her poor, pale, thin hand, took Van Helsing's great brown one, drawing it close to her, she kissed it. "My true friend," she said, in a faint voice, but with untellable pathos, "My true friend, and his! Oh, guard him, and give me peace!"

"I swear it!" he said solemnly, kneeling beside her and holding up his hand, as one who registers an oath. Then he turned to Arthur, and said to him, "Come, my child, take her hand in yours, and kiss her on the forehead, and only once."

Their eyes met instead of their lips, and so they parted. Lucy's eyes closed, and Van Helsing, who had been watching closely, took Arthur's arm, and drew him away.

And then Lucy's breathing became stertorous again, and all at once it ceased.

"It is all over," said Van Helsing. "She is dead!"

I took Arthur by the arm, and led him away to the drawing room, where he sat down, and covered his face with his hands, sobbing in a way that nearly broke me down to see.

I went back to the room, and found Van Helsing looking at poor Lucy, and his face was sterner than ever. Some change had come over her body. Death had given back part of her beauty, for her brow and cheeks had recovered some of their flowing lines. Even the lips had lost their deadly pallor. It was as if the blood, no longer needed for the working of the heart, had gone to make the harshness of death as little rude as might be.

"We thought her dying whilst she slept, And sleeping when she died."

I stood beside Van Helsing, and said, "Ah well, poor girl, there is peace for her at last. It is the end!"

He turned to me, and said with grave solemnity, "Not so, alas! Not so. It is only the beginning!"

When I asked him what he meant, he only shook his head and answered, "We can do nothing as yet. Wait and see."

Letter, Kate to Mr. and Mrs. Reed

20 September

Mamma, Papa,

I cannot recall a time that I have asked you for this, but would you pray for us, that is, for myself and Francis? I am no longer angry with him for spurning my advances, nor even with myself for failing to win his heart; I daresay that the luxury of such emotions has given way to utter dread.

Since my last letter to you, Francis has departed from our home. Or rather, he simply never returned. I was deceiving myself in thinking he would come back to me, but I was at least hoping to speak with him when he stopped by for his belongings.

The worst of it is, I don't know where he went. I thought that perhaps he had simply moved in across the way, and knocked at the door in vain more than a time or two. I have watched for him as well, for in what was once his studio there is a window which opens to a grand view of the DeVille mansion, but saw neither him nor even—until tonight—the Count.

You will recall from my last letter that I had hit upon the notion of photographing the Count to help ease Francis' fixation. To that end, I had set up my Kodak in the old studio, ready to capture the face of our neighbor on film. I wasted several evenings waiting in vain before I finally succeeded in taking his picture.

A horse and cart filled with long boxes had stopped in front of the house, and who did come to meet the driver but the Count himself! I cannot recall from where he appeared, though I don't believe it was from within the house. Though I thought it rather odd that he did not send servants out, I did not "look a gift horse in the mouth," as the say, and took the picture.

And here is the horror of it all, that the photograph turned out just like Francis' paintings. The Count's image is devoid of detail, the lines of his form blurred and indistinct. And his face! My God, but it looks for all the world like that of a man long dead![145] Francis had been painting him correctly all along, for it was our own eyes that were mistaken.

What horror has taken up residence so near to me? What hold does it have over poor Francis? I must find out these things, for both our sakes. Oh do pray for us, and keep us in your thoughts!

In all sincerity,
Your loving daughter,
Kate

CHAPTER TWENTY[146]

The Godalming Case Notes of Inspector Cotford[147]

19 September—It has come to my attention that renown philanthropist Edward Holmwood, the honourable Lord Godalming, has died suddenly. I say suddenly, for despite the newspaper accounts that state he had "finally succumbed to a prolonged illness of the heart," such news came as quite a surprise to many (including myself, who was counted among the friends of the deceased), for none knew him to be ill. Given his great standing, and given the contradictory accounts of his health, it seemed most proper that a visit be paid to his home, and so with due haste I made the trip to Surrey.

The trip from London to Surrey was quite a beautiful one, for that land is perhaps the most densely-wooded region left in all of England, being as it is, a portion of the ancient Andredswald. Within Surrey, surrounded by lush forests, is the Godalming Hundred, so having been named in ancient times, along with the other such Hundreds, because the land was fertile enough to support one hundred families.

I arrived at the station in Godalming, which has from long ago been a waypoint between London and Portsmouth. The town proper is quite ancient, having been mentioned by name in the will of King Alfred the Great, after Surrey's annexation by Wessex a thousand years ago. It was first colonized by the Godhelm Ingus—the clan of the Saxon chief Godehlm—and its history is evident in such buildings as the parish church I passed, which has a Saxon chancel and Norman tower. But, while ancient, it was also quite innovative. In ages past, its progressive wool industry allowed the town to grow quickly. The new town hall, on High Street and Church, was only built some seventy years ago, is very modern, rounded two-story "pepperpot" design, with open archways below and topped with a clock tower. What's more, thanks to the support of the Holmwoods, it was the first town in England to have a public supply of electricity, and the first in the world, so far as I know, to have electric street lamps.

As my carriage left the town far behind, and the streets became lanes, the forest grew thicker and thicker about us, until at last, upon turning down a long path, they opened up once more into a fast clearing in which rested the mansion of Ringwood (or simply "Ring," as the good Lord Godalming was fond of calling it). The estate was large and private, surrounded by a wide ring of Holm Oak (accounting, one would suppose, for both the name of the estate and the surname of the family).

I was promptly shown into the mansion. The interior was as beautiful as one would imagine, save that all the windows had been darkened by the staff in mourning. The fireplace was lit, however, and served to lessen the gloom. Above the mantle was the Godalming coat of arms: a red and black shield, adorned with smaller shields and a red rose, topped by a ram. The motto beneath read *libera deinde fidelis*—faithful because free.

As it happened, Arthur Holmwood, the only son of the late Lord Godalming, was not present. His staff was most cooperative, though, and explained he was presently attending to his fiancee, Lucy Westenra, at her Hillingham estate, as her mother has just died and she too is near death. How peculiar, that both the young man's father and his fiancee's mother would have died within a day of each other, and now to have his fiancee ill as well . . .

While disappointing, the absence of the Hon. Arthur Holmwood—now, one would suppose, the new Lord Godalming—did afford me the opportunity to freely question his staff. The maids confirmed that their late master had indeed been ill, and for approximately five months, and had been diagnosed with a progressively weakening heart. Having a knowledge of illnesses myself—a necessity my line of work—I inquired as to his symptoms. The description the maids gave certainly conformed to a malady of the heart, save for one detail, which was his being prone to nausea. Thinking perhaps it was due to his medications, I inquired about them, but was informed that the Lord Godalming had apparently not been one to follow a doctor's orders, and took nothing from the apothecary. He did, however, drink often an herbal tea made from rare flowers which only grew to the East, in the wilds of Central Europe. One of the girls sheepishly admitted to trying a sip of the tea once, and noted it had numbed her mouth to the point it made talking difficult for a time, and made her a bit queasy as well, which might indeed account for the peculiar symptoms exhibited by her late master.

I must note the staff seemed visibly worried about my visit, but as they did not demonstrate any nervous or guilty mannerisms, I suspect their only concern was for the health and happiness of Arthur Holmwood. I assured them I was merely here on a routine visit, given the late Lord Godalming's standing, and the great respect and admiration he had acquired throughout the land. This seemed to put them more at ease. I asked the staff not to concern the young Holmwood with my visit as of yet, for surely he had more than enough troubles resting upon him. They wholeheartedly agreed, for it was clear that each of them was deeply devoted to their young master, and were concerned for him enough as it was, and had no desire to worry him further.

Before I bade them farewell, I asked to see the body of the deceased. I was shown into the family chapel, which was quite old, where the body still rested while awaiting the funeral. The corpse had already been prepared by the undertaker, and was surrounded by a display of flowers. The flowers themselves were as attractive as they were unusual; the blooms were long, fairly cylindrical, though they squeezed in at the middle, and of a deep purple. Their general appearance seemed somehow familiar to me, but not their particular shape or colouring. I noticed there was a crude wooden crate off in a far corner, that seemed out of place amidst the otherwise elegant, if not somber, décor. I couldn't imagine they intended to use such a box for the Lord's coffin (though it would be the right size and shape for one), so I questioned one of the maids about it. She explained that it was a crate of earth the family recently had shipped in from Central Europe, which the purple flowers that filled the chapel grew naturally in.

With regard to the body of Lord Godalming, I only afforded myself a quick examination, for I did not wish to seem as if there were an official inquest (which, as of yet, it was not). I could see no sign of trauma, nor any white lines in the fingernails which would indicate arsenic poisoning. There was one noteworthy item: when I lifted his lids, though the eyes had already begun to cloud, I could still see through the milky tint enough to note his pupils, which should have been relaxed and dilated in death, were constricted down to a size no larger than the head of a pin.

I have a thought, a suspicion, one that needs either proving or refuting. I shall arrange a visit to Hillingham tomorrow under the pretense of paying my respects to the late Mrs. Westenra. In the mean time, I shall wire the law office of Mr. Peter Hawkins, whose name I was given by the staff of Ring as being the solicitor handling the Holmwood's affairs, to arrange to look through the will and papers concerning both the Holmwood and Westenra estates, to see if there are any legal ties between the two.

Later—Received word from the law office, stating Mr. Hawkins died suddenly of gout yesterday, with his firm now being managed by his partner, Jonathan Harker. How intriguing, that yet another person connected to the Holmwoods has perished. I shall call upon this Mr. Harker in due time, but first I must go to Hillingham at first light tomorrow, before too much time has passed.

20 September—I have been to Hillingham, and in time to examine the body of Mrs. Charlotte Westenra before her funeral. I was fearful I would not have the opportunity to see it before her burial, but as it happened, her service had been delayed for a day, in order that she might be buried with her daughter Lucy, who had died in the interim.

As I feared and suspected, the pupils of Mrs. Westenra were unnaturally constricted, just as the Lord Godalming's had been. Knowing for certain now that something was afoot, I inspected the eyes of her daughter as well. I had truthfully expected them to be likewise constricted, but to my surprise, the girl's pupils were not small at all. Indeed, they seemed quite large and clear and bright, as if she was merely sleeping and not dead at all. It was such an odd effect that I found myself caught in her dead gaze, and apparently stood motionless for some time before the undertaker's man startled me from my mental stupor. In any event, despite the lack of the peculiar pupil constriction, the significance of Lucy Westenra's untimely death, so close to that of her mother, *et al*, goes without saying.

I also had the opportunity to speak with Dr. John Seward, who had attended to Lucy Westenra near the end of her life. Rather than practicing in a hospital or a private facility, he is the head of an insane asylum in Purfleet. When questioned why Lucy was placed in his care, rather than that of a specialist, he explained that he undertook the task as a favor to Arthur Holmwood (once again, everything seems to come back to that man). He admitted his failure to diagnose her malady, and so had called upon the aid of the renowned Professor Van Helsing. That name was certainly familiar to me from my various studies into medicine, and so was quite impressed that his expertise would be needed in the first place, and that he would have consented to make the journey here at all . . . though it would seem even he was not able to save her life. With regard to Charlotte Westenra, though he was not involved in her care, Dr. Seward believed her diagnosis to be a malady of the heart—again, just as with Lord Godalming—and took great pains not to put any undo strain upon her.

Dr. Seward's Case-Book

21 September—The funeral was arranged for the next succeeding day, so that Lucy and her mother might be buried together. I attended to all the ghastly formalities, and the urbane undertaker proved that his staff was afflicted, or blessed, with something of his own obsequious suavity. Even the woman who performed the last offices for the dead remarked to me, in a confidential, brother-professional way, when she had come out from the death chamber,

"She makes a very beautiful corpse, sir. It's quite a privilege to attend on her. It's not too much to say that she will do credit to our establishment!"

I noticed that Van Helsing never kept far away. This was possible from the disordered state of things in the household. There were no relatives at hand, and as Arthur had to be back the next day to attend at his father's funeral, we were unable to notify any one who should have been bidden. Under the circumstances, Van Helsing and I took it upon ourselves to examine papers, etc. He insisted upon looking over Lucy's papers himself. I asked him why, for I feared that he, being a foreigner, might not be quite aware of English legal requirements, and so might in ignorance make some unnecessary trouble, especially since a police inspector had already been through once.

He answered me, "I know, I know. You forget that I am a lawyer as well as a doctor. But this is not altogether for the law. You knew that, when you avoided the coroner. I have more than him to avoid. There may be papers more, such as this."

As he spoke he took from his pocket book the memorandum which had been in Lucy's breast, and which she had torn in her sleep.

"When you find anything of the solicitor who is for the late Mrs. Westenra, seal all her papers, and write him tonight. For me, I watch here in the room and in Miss Lucy's old room all night, and I myself search for what may be. It is not well that her very thoughts go into the hands of strangers."

I went on with my part of the work, and in another half hour had found the name and address of Mrs. Westenra's solicitor and had written to him. All the poor lady's papers were in order. Explicit directions regarding the place of burial were given. I had hardly sealed the letter, when, to my surprise, Van Helsing walked into the room, saying,

"Can I help you friend John? I am free, and if I may, my service is to you."

"Have you got what you looked for?" I asked.

To which he replied, "I did not look for any specific thing. I only hoped to find, and find I have, all that there was, only some letters and a few memoranda, and a diary new begun. But I have them here, and we shall for the present say nothing of them. I shall see that poor lad tomorrow evening, and, with his sanction, I shall use some."

When we had finished the work in hand, he said to me, "And now, friend John, I think we may to bed. We want sleep, both you and I, and rest to recuperate. Tomorrow we shall have much to do, but for the tonight there is no need of us. Alas!"

Before turning in we went to look at poor Lucy. The undertaker had certainly done his work well, for the room was turned into a small chapelle ardente. There was a wilderness of beautiful white flowers, and death was made as little repulsive as might be. The end of the winding sheet was laid over the face. When the Professor bent over and turned it gently back, we both started at the beauty before us. The tall wax candles showing a sufficient light to note it well. All Lucy's loveliness had come back to her in death, and the hours that had passed, instead of leaving traces of 'decay's effacing fingers,' had but restored the beauty of life, till positively I could not believe my eyes that I was looking at a corpse.

The Professor looked sternly grave. He had not loved her as I had, and there was no need for tears in his eyes. He said to me, "Remain till I return," and left the room. He came back with a handful of wild garlic from the box waiting in the hall, but which had not been opened, and placed the flowers amongst the others on and around the bed. Then he took from his neck, inside his collar, a little gold crucifix, and placed it over the mouth. He restored the sheet to its place, and we came away.

I was undressing in my own room, when, with a premonitory tap at the door, he entered, and at once began to speak.

"Tomorrow I want you to bring me, before night, a set of post-mortem knives."

"Must we make an autopsy?" I asked.

"Yes and no. I want to operate, but not what you think. Let me tell you now, but not a word to another. I want to cut off her head and take out her heart. Ah! You a surgeon, and so shocked! You, whom I have seen with no tremble of hand or heart, do operations of life and death that make the rest shudder. Oh, but I must not forget, my dear friend John, that you loved her, and I have not forgotten it for is I that shall operate, and you must not help. I would like to do it tonight, but for Arthur I must not. He will be free after his father's funeral tomorrow, and he will want to see her, to see it. Then, when she is coffined ready for the next day, you and I shall come when all sleep. We shall unscrew the coffin lid, and shall do our operation, and then replace all, so that none know, save we alone."

"But why do it at all? The girl is dead. Why mutilate her poor body without need? And if there is no necessity for a post-mortem and nothing to gain by it, no good to her, to us, to science, to human knowledge, why do it? Without such it is monstrous."

For answer he put his hand on my shoulder, and said, with infinite tenderness, "Friend John, I pity your poor bleeding heart, and I love you the more because it does so bleed. If I could, I would take on myself the burden that you do bear. But there are things that you know not, but that you shall know, and bless me for knowing, though they are not pleasant things. John, my child, you have been my friend now many years, and yet did you ever know me to do any without good cause? I may err, I am but man, but I believe in all I do. Was it not for these causes that you send for me when the great trouble came? Yes! Were you not amazed, nay horrified, when I would not let Arthur kiss his love, though she was dying, and snatched him away by all my strength? Yes! And yet you saw how she thanked me, with her so beautiful dying eyes, her voice, too, so weak, and she kiss my rough old hand and bless me? Yes! And did you not hear me swear promise to her, that so she closed her eyes grateful? Yes!

"Well, I have good reason now for all I want to do. You have for many years trust me. You have believe me weeks past, when there be things so strange that you might have well doubt. Believe me yet a little, friend John. If you trust me not, then I must tell what I think, and that is not perhaps well. And if I work, as work I shall, no matter trust or no trust, without my friend trust in me, I work with heavy heart and feel, oh so lonely when I want all help and courage that may be!" He paused a moment and went on solemnly, "Friend John, there are strange and terrible days before us. Let us not be two, but one, that so we work to a good end. Will you not have faith in me?"

I took his hand, and promised him. I held my door open as he went away, and watched him go to his room and close the door. As I stood without moving, I saw one of the maids pass silently along the passage, she had her back to me, so did not see me, and go into the room where Lucy lay. The sight touched me. Devotion is so rare, and we are so grateful to those who show it unasked to those we love. Here was a poor girl putting aside the terrors which she naturally had of death to go watch alone by the bier of the mistress whom she loved, so that the poor clay might not be lonely till laid to eternal rest.

I must have slept long and soundly, for it was broad daylight when Van Helsing waked me by coming into my room. He came over to my bedside and said, "You need not trouble about the knives. We shall not do it."

"Why not?" I asked. For his solemnity of the night before had greatly impressed me.

"Because," he said sternly, "it is too late, or too early. See!" Here he held up the little golden crucifix.

"This was stolen in the night."

"How stolen," I asked in wonder, "since you have it now?"

"Because I get it back from the worthless wretch who stole it, from the woman who robbed the dead and the living. Her punishment will surely come, but not through me. She knew not altogether what she did, and thus unknowing, she only stole. Now we must wait." He went away on the word, leaving me with a new mystery to think of, a new puzzle to grapple with.

The forenoon was a dreary time, but at noon the solicitor came, Mr. Marquand, of Wholeman, Sons, Marquand & Lidderdale. He was very genial and very appreciative of what we had done, and took off our hands all cares as to details. During lunch he told us that Mrs. Westenra had for some time expected sudden death from her heart, and had put her affairs in absolute order. He informed us that, with the exception of a certain entailed property of Lucy's father which now, in default of direct issue, went back to a distant branch of the family, the whole estate, real and personal, was left absolutely to Arthur Holmwood. When he had told us so much he went on,

"Frankly we did our best to prevent such a testamentary disposition, and pointed out certain contingencies that might leave her daughter either penniless or not so free as she should be to act regarding a matrimonial alliance. Indeed, we pressed the matter so far that we almost came into collision, for she asked us if we were or were not prepared to carry out her wishes. Of course, we had then no alternative but to accept. We were right in principle, and ninety-nine times out of a hundred we should have proved, by the logic of events, the accuracy of our judgment.

"Frankly, however, I must admit that in this case any other form of disposition would have rendered impossible the carrying out of her wishes. For by her predeceasing her daughter the latter would have come into possession of the property, and, even had she only survived her mother by five minutes, her property would, in case there were no will, and a will was a practical impossibility in such a case, have been treated at her decease as under intestacy. In which case Lord Godalming, though so dear a friend, would have had no claim in the world. And the inheritors, being remote, would not be likely to abandon their just rights, for sentimental reasons regarding an entire stranger. I assure you, my dear sirs, I am rejoiced at the result, perfectly rejoiced."

He was a good fellow, but his rejoicing at the one little part, in which he was officially interested, of so great a tragedy, was an object-lesson in the limitations of sympathetic understanding.

He did not remain long, but said he would look in later in the day and see Lord Godalming. His coming, however, had been a certain comfort to us, since it assured us that we should not have to dread hostile criticism as to any of our acts. Arthur was expected at five o'clock, so a little before that time we visited the death chamber. It was so in very truth, for now both mother and daughter lay in it. The undertaker, true to his craft, had made the best display he could of his goods, and there was a mortuary air about the place that lowered our spirits at once.

Van Helsing ordered the former arrangement to be adhered to, explaining that, as Lord Godalming was coming very soon, it would be less harrowing to his feelings to see all that was left of his fiancee quite alone.

The undertaker seemed shocked at his own stupidity and exerted himself to restore things to the condition in which we left them the night before, so that when Arthur came such shocks to his feelings as we could avoid were saved.

Poor fellow! He looked desperately sad and broken. Even his stalwart manhood seemed to have shrunk somewhat under the strain of his much-tried emotions. He had, I knew, been very genuinely and devotedly attached to his father, and to lose him, and at such a time, was a bitter blow to him. With me he was warm as ever, and to Van Helsing he was sweetly courteous. But I could not help seeing that there was some constraint with him. The professor noticed it too, and motioned me to bring him upstairs. I did so, and left him at the door of the room, as I felt he would like to be quite alone with her, but he took my arm and led me in, saying huskily,

"You loved her too, old fellow. She told me all about it, and there was no friend had a closer place in her heart than you. I don't know how to thank you for all you have done for her. I can't think yet . . ."

Here he suddenly broke down, and threw his arms round my shoulders and laid his head on my breast, crying, "Oh, Jack! Jack! What shall I do? The whole of life seems gone from me all at once, and there is nothing in the wide world for me to live for."

I comforted him as well as I could. In such cases men do not need much expression. A grip of the hand, the tightening of an arm over the shoulder, a sob in unison, are expressions of sympathy dear to a man's heart. I stood still and silent till his sobs died away, and then I said softly to him, "Come and look at her."

Together we moved over to the bed, and I lifted the lawn from her face. God! How beautiful she was. Every hour seemed to be enhancing her loveliness. It frightened and amazed me somewhat. And as for Arthur, he fell to trembling, and finally was shaken with doubt as with an ague. At last, after a long pause, he said to me in a faint whisper, "Jack, is she really dead?"

I assured him sadly that it was so, and went on to suggest, for I felt that such a horrible doubt should not have life for a moment longer than I could help, that it often happened that after death faces become softened and even resolved into their youthful beauty, that this was especially so when death had been preceded by any acute or prolonged suffering. I seemed to quite do away with any doubt, and after kneeling beside the couch for a while and looking at her lovingly and long, he turned aside. I told him that that must be goodbye, as the coffin had to be prepared, so he went back and took her dead hand in his and kissed it, and bent over and kissed her forehead. He came away, fondly looking back over his shoulder at her as he came.

I left him in the drawing room, and told Van Helsing that he had said goodbye, so the latter went to the kitchen to tell the undertaker's men to proceed with the preparations and to screw up the coffin. When he came out of the room again I told him of Arthur's question, and he replied, "I am not surprised. Just now I doubted for a moment myself!"

We all dined together, and I could see that poor Art was trying to make the best of things. Van Helsing had been silent all dinner time, but when we had lit our cigars he said, "Lord . . ." but Arthur interrupted him.

"No, no, not that, for God's sake! Not yet at any rate. Forgive me, sir. I did not mean to speak offensively. It is only because my loss is so recent."

The Professor answered very sweetly, "I only used that name because I was in doubt. I must not call you 'Mr.' and I have grown to love you, yes, my dear boy, to love you, as Arthur."

Arthur held out his hand, and took the old man's warmly. "Call me what you will," he said. "I hope I may always have the title of a friend. And let me say that I am at a loss for words to thank you for your goodness to my poor dear." He paused a moment, and went on, "I know that she understood your goodness even better than I do. And if I was rude or in any way wanting at that time you acted so, you remember,"—the Professor nodded—"You must forgive me."

He answered with a grave kindness, "I know it was hard for you to quite trust me then, for to trust such violence needs to understand, and I take it that you do not, that you cannot, trust me now, for you do not yet understand. And there may be more times when I shall want you to trust when you cannot, and may not, and must not yet understand. But the time will come when your trust shall be whole and complete in me, and when you shall understand as though the sunlight himself shone through. Then you shall bless me from first to last for your own sake, and for the sake of others, and for her dear sake to whom I swore to protect."

"And indeed, indeed, sir," said Arthur warmly. "I shall in all ways trust you. I know and believe you have a very noble heart, and you are Jack's friend, and you were hers. You shall do what you like."

The Professor cleared his throat a couple of times, as though about to speak, and finally said, "May I ask you something now?"

"Certainly."

"You know that Mrs. Westenra left you all her property?"

"No, poor dear. I never thought of it."

"And as it is all yours, you have a right to deal with it as you will. I want you to give me permission to read all Miss Lucy's papers and letters. Believe me, it is no idle curiosity. I have a motive of which, be sure, she would have approved. I have them all here. I took them before we knew that all was yours, so that no strange hand might touch them, no strange eye look through words into her soul. I shall keep them, if I may. Even you may not see them yet, but I shall keep them safe. No word shall be lost, and in the good time I shall give them back to you. It is a hard thing that I ask, but you will do it, will you not, for Lucy's sake?"

Arthur spoke out heartily, like his old self, "Dr. Van Helsing, you may do what you will. I feel that in saying this I am doing what my dear one would have approved. I shall not trouble you with questions till the time comes."

The old Professor stood up as he said solemnly, "And you are right. There will be pain for us all, but it will not be all pain, nor will this pain be the last. We and you too, you most of all, dear boy, will have to pass through the bitter water before we reach the sweet. But we must be brave of heart and unselfish, and do our duty, and all will be well!"

I slept on a sofa in Arthur's room that night. Van Helsing did not go to bed at all. He went to and fro, as if patroling the house, and was never out of sight of the room where Lucy lay in her coffin, strewn with the wild garlic flowers, which sent through the odour of lily and rose, a heavy, overpowering smell into the night.

22 September—It is all over. Arthur has gone back to Ring, and has taken Quincey Morris with him. What a fine fellow is Quincey! I believe in my heart of hearts that he suffered as much about Lucy's death as any of us, but he bore himself through it like a moral Viking. If America can go on breeding men like that, she will be a power in the world indeed. Van Helsing is lying down, having a rest preparatory to his journey. He goes to Amsterdam tonight, but says he returns tomorrow night, that he only wants to make some arrangements which can only be made personally. He is to stop with me then, if he can. He says he has work to do in London which may take him some time. Poor old fellow! I fear that the strain of the past week has broken down even his iron strength. All the time of the burial he was, I could see, putting some terrible restraint on himself. When it was all over, we were standing beside Arthur, who, poor fellow, was speaking of his part in the operation where his blood had been transfused to his Lucy's veins. I could see Van Helsing's face grow white and purple by turns. Arthur was saying that he felt since then as if they two had been really married, and that she was his wife in the sight of God. None of us said a word of the other operations, and none of us ever shall. Arthur and Quincey went away together to the station, and Van Helsing and I came on here. The moment we were alone in the carriage he gave way to a regular fit of hysterics. He has denied to me since that it was hysterics, and insisted that it was only his sense of humor asserting itself under very terrible conditions. He laughed till he cried, and I had to draw down the blinds lest any one should see us and misjudge. And then he cried, till he laughed again, and laughed and cried together, just as a woman does. I tried to be stern with him, as one is to a woman under the circumstances, but it had no effect. Men and women are so different in manifestations of nervous strength or weakness! Then when his face grew grave and stern again I asked him why his mirth, and why at such a time. His reply was in a way characteristic of him, for it was logical and forceful and mysterious. He said,

"Ah, you don't comprehend, friend John. Do not think that I am not sad, though I laugh. See, I have cried even when the laugh did choke me. But no more think that I am all sorry when I cry, for the laugh he come just the same. Keep it always with you that laughter who knock at your door and say, 'May I come in?' is not true laughter. No! He is a king, and he come when and how he like. He ask no person, he choose no time of suitability. He say, 'I am here.' Behold, in example I grieve my heart out for that so sweet young girl. I give my blood for her, though I am old and worn. I give my time, my skill, my sleep. I let my other sufferers want that she may have all. And yet I can laugh at her very grave, laugh when the clay from the spade of the sexton drop upon her coffin and say 'Thud, thud!' to my heart, till it send back the blood from my cheek. My heart bleed for that poor boy, that dear boy, so of the age of mine own boy had I been so blessed that he live, and with his hair and eyes the same. He was lost to me in Munich, stoled from my wife in retribution, my payment for locking away an evil that was long a plague to those parts.

"There, you know now why I love him so. And yet when he say things that touch my husband-heart to the quick, and make my father-heart yearn to him as to no other man, not even you, friend John, for we are more level in experiences than father and son, yet even at such a moment King Laugh he come to me and shout and bellow in my ear, 'Here I am! Here I am!' till the blood come dance back and bring some of the sunshine that he carry with him to my cheek. Oh, friend John, it is a strange world, a sad world, a world full of miseries, and woes, and troubles. And yet when King Laugh come, he make them all dance to the tune he play. Bleeding hearts, and dry bones of the churchyard, and tears that burn as they fall, all dance together to the music that he make with that smileless mouth of him. And believe me, friend John, that he is good to come, and kind. Ah, we men and women are like ropes drawn tight with strain that pull us different ways. Then tears come, and like the rain on the ropes, they brace us up, until perhaps the strain become too great, and we break. But King Laugh he come like the sunshine, and he ease off the strain again, and we bear to go on with our labor, what it may be."

I did not like to wound him by pretending not to see his idea, but as I did not yet understand the cause of his laughter, I asked him. As he answered me his face grew stern, and he said in quite a different tone,

"Oh, it was the grim irony of it all, this so lovely lady garlanded with flowers, that looked so fair as life, till one by one we wondered if she were truly dead, she laid in that so fine marble house in that lonely churchyard, where rest so many of her kin, laid there with the mother who loved her, and whom she loved, and that sacred bell going "Toll! Toll! Toll!' so sad and slow, and those holy men, with the white garments of the angel, pretending to read books, and yet all the time their eyes never on the page, and all of us with the bowed head. And all for what? She is dead, so! Is it not?"

"Well, for the life of me, Professor," I said, "I can't see anything to laugh at in all that. Why, your expression makes it a harder puzzle than before. But even if the burial service was comic, what about poor Art and his trouble? Why his heart was simply breaking."

"Just so. Said he not that the transfusion of his blood to her veins had made her truly his bride?"

"Yes, and it was a sweet and comforting idea for him."

"Quite so. But there was a difficulty, friend John. If so that, then what about the others? Ho, ho! Then this so sweet maid is a polyandrist, and me, with my poor wife dead to me, but alive by Church's law, though no wits, all gone since the loss of our son, even I, who am faithful husband to this now-no-wife, am bigamist."

"I don't see where the joke comes in there either!" I said, and I did not feel particularly pleased with him for saying such things. He laid his hand on my arm, and said,

"Friend John, forgive me if I pain. I showed not my feeling to others when it would wound, but only to you, my old friend, whom I can trust. If you could have looked into my heart then when I want to laugh, if you could have done so when the laugh arrived, if you could do so now, when King Laugh have pack up his crown, and all that is to him, for he go far, far away from me, and for a long, long time, maybe you would perhaps pity me the most of all."

I was touched by the tenderness of his tone, and asked why.

"Because I know!"

And now we are all scattered, and for many a long day loneliness will sit over our roofs with brooding wings. Lucy lies in the tomb of her kin, a lordly death house in a lonely churchyard, away from teeming London, where the air is fresh, and the sun rises over Hampstead Hill, and where wild flowers grow of their own accord.

So I can finish this diary, and God only knows if I shall ever begin another. If I do, or if I even open this again, it will be to deal with different people and different themes, for here at the end, where the romance of my life is told, ere I go back to take up the thread of my life-work, I say sadly and without hope,

"Finis."

Inspector Cotford's Case Notes

22 September—Summary of findings to date:

Edward Holmwood, the Lord Godalming, died 17 September. Cause of death listed as "failure of heart," though symptoms suspicious. Survived by only son, Arthur Holmwood. Legal affairs handled through law firm of Hawkins & Harker.

Peter Hawkins, solicitor to the Holmwoods, died 18 September. Cause of death reportedly "gout" (*mem.* check to see if death directly resulted from gout or from the colchicine he surely would have used to treat it). Died shortly after handling the will of Lord Godalming. Law firm now in control of partner, Jonathan Harker.

Charlotte Westenra, died 18 September. Cause of death listed as "failure of heart," though she, as with Lord Godalming, had unusual symptoms. Also note that her certificate of death was filled out by Dr. Seward, rather than her own physician. Hillingham estate and inheritance left directly to Arthur Holmwood, the fiancé of her only daughter Lucy Westenra, through an unorthodox testamentary disposition arranged through law firm of Wholeman, Sons, Marquand & Lidderdale.

Lucy Westenra, died 20 September. Cause of death listed as "exhaustion" by Dr. Seward. Was fiancee of Arthur Holmwood. Hillingham estate and inheritance left to Arthur Holmwood, not through her own will, but through the will of her late mother, as described above.

There have been too many deaths—and peculiarities surrounding those deaths and subsequent legal matters—relating to Arthur Holmwood. There is little option now but to begin an official inquest into the matter immediately, before harm can befall anyone else.

The Westminster Gazette, 25 September

A Hampstead Mystery

The neighborhood of Hampstead is just at present exercised with a series of events which seem to run on lines parallel to those of what was known to the writers of headlines as "The Kensington Horror," or "The Stabbing Woman," or "The Woman in Black." During the past two or three days several cases have occurred of young children straying from home or neglecting to return from their playing on the Heath. In all these cases the children were too young to give any properly intelligible account of themselves, but the consensus of their excuses is that they had been with a "bloofer lady." It has always been late in the evening when they have been missed, and on two occasions the children have not been found until early in the following morning. It is generally supposed in the neighborhood that, as the first child missed gave as his reason for being away that a "bloofer lady" had asked him to come for a walk, the others had picked up the phrase and used it as occasion served. This is the more natural as the favourite game of the little ones at present is luring each other away by wiles. A correspondent writes us that to see some of the tiny tots pretending to be the "bloofer lady" is supremely funny. Some of our caricaturists might, he says, take a lesson in the irony of grotesque by comparing the reality and the picture. It is only in accordance with general principles of human nature that the "bloofer lady" should be the popular role at these al fresco performances. Our correspondent naively says that even Ellen Terry could not be so winningly attractive as some of these grubby-faced little children pretend, and even imagine themselves, to be.

There is, however, possibly a serious side to the question, for some of the children, indeed all who have been missed at night, have been slightly torn or wounded in the throat. The wounds seem such as might be made by a rat or a small dog, and although of not much importance individually, would tend to show that whatever animal inflicts them has a system or method of its own. The police of the division have been instructed to keep a sharp lookout for straying children, especially when very young, in and around Hampstead Heath, and for any stray dog which may be about.

The Westminster Gazette, 25 September Extra Special

The Hampstead Horror
Another Child Injured
The "Bloofer Lady"

We have just received intelligence that another child, missed last night, was only discovered late in the morning under a furze bush at the Shooter's Hill side of Hampstead Heath, which is perhaps, less frequented than the other parts. It has the same tiny wound in the throat as has been noticed in other cases. It was terribly weak, and looked quite emaciated. It too, when partially restored, had the common story to tell of being lured away by the "bloofer lady."

BOOK III

DISCOVERY[148]

CHAPTER TWENTY-ONE[149]

Mina Harker's Journal[150]

22 September—In the train to Exeter. Jonathan sleeping. It seems only yesterday that the last entry was made, and yet how much between then, in Whitby and all the world before me, Jonathan away and no news of him, and now, married to Jonathan, Jonathan a solicitor, a partner, rich, master of his business, Mr. Hawkins dead and buried, and Jonathan with another attack that may harm him. Some day he may ask me about it. Down it all goes. I am rusty in my shorthand, see what unexpected prosperity does for us, so it may be as well to freshen it up again with an exercise anyhow.

The service was very simple and very solemn. There were only ourselves and the servants there, one or two old friends of his from Exeter, his London agent, and a gentleman representing Sir John Paxton, the President of the Incorporated Law Society. Jonathan and I stood hand in hand, and we felt that our best and dearest friend was gone from us.

We came back to town quietly, taking a bus to Hyde Park Corner. Jonathan thought it would interest me to go into the Row for a while, so we sat down. But there were very few people there, and it was sad-looking and desolate to see so many empty chairs. It made us think of the empty chair at home. So we got up and walked down Piccadilly. Jonathan was holding me by the arm, the way he used to in the old days before I went to school. I felt it very improper, for you can't go on for some years teaching etiquette and decorum to other girls without the pedantry of it biting into yourself a bit. But it was Jonathan, and he was my husband, and we didn't know anybody who saw us, and we didn't care if they did, so on we walked.

As we made our way down the street, I caught sight of Kate. She was, as always, a very beautiful girl, today in a big cart-wheel hat and sitting in a victoria outside Guiliano's. I was about to call to her when I felt Jonathan clutch my arm so tight that he hurt me, and he said under his breath, "My God!"

I am always anxious about Jonathan, for I fear that some nervous fit may upset him again. So I turned to him quickly, and asked him what it was that disturbed him.

He was very pale, and his eyes seemed bulging out as, half in terror and half in amazement, he gazed at a tall, thin man, with a beaky nose and black moustache and pointed beard, who was also observing Kate. He was looking at her so hard that he did not see either of us, and so I had a good view of him. His face was not a good face. It was hard, and cruel, and sensual, and big white teeth, that looked all the whiter because his lips were so red, were pointed like an animal's. Jonathan kept staring at him, till I was afraid he would notice. I feared he might take it ill, he looked so fierce and nasty. I asked Jonathan why he was disturbed, and he answered, evidently thinking that I knew as much about it as he did, "Do you see who it is?"

"No, dear," I said. "I don't know him, who is it?" His answer seemed to shock and thrill me, for it was said as if he did not know that it was me, Mina, to whom he was speaking. "It is the man himself! It is the man from the Munich Dead House!"[151]

The poor dear was evidently terrified at something, very greatly terrified. I do believe that if he had not had me to lean on and to support him he would have sunk down. He kept staring. A man came out of the shop with a small parcel, and gave it to Kate, who then drove off together. I found it odd that the man with her was not Francis, but was too concerned about Jonathan to think on it long. The dark man kept his eyes fixed on Kate, and when the carriage moved up Piccadilly he followed in the same direction, and hailed a hansom. Jonathan kept looking after him, and said, as if to himself,

"I believe it is the Count, but he has grown young. He is just as I saw him at the Dead House![152] My God, if this be so! Oh, my God! My God! If only I knew! If only I knew!" He was distressing himself so much that I feared to keep his mind on the subject by asking him any questions, so I remained silent. I drew away quietly, and he, holding my arm, came easily. We walked a little further, and then went in and sat for a while in the Green Park. It was a hot day for autumn, and there was a comfortable seat in a shady place. After a few minutes' staring at nothing, Jonathan's eyes closed, and he went quickly into a sleep, with his head on my shoulder. I thought it was the best thing for him, so did not disturb him. In about twenty minutes he woke up, and said to me quite cheerfully,

"Why, Mina, have I been asleep! Oh, do forgive me for being so rude. Come, and we'll have a cup of tea somewhere."

He had evidently forgotten all about the dark stranger, as in his illness he had forgotten all that this episode had reminded him of. I don't like this lapsing into forgetfulness. It may make or continue some injury to the brain. I must not ask him, for fear I shall do more harm than good, but I must somehow learn the facts of his journey abroad. The time is come, I fear, when I must open the parcel, and know what is written. Oh, Jonathan, you will, I know, forgive me if I do wrong, but it is for your own dear sake.

Later—A sad homecoming in every way, the house empty of the dear soul who was so good to us. Jonathan still pale and dizzy under a slight relapse of his malady, and now a telegram from Van Helsing, whoever he may be. "You will be grieved to hear that Mrs. Westenra died five days ago, and that Lucy died the day before yesterday. They were both buried today."

Oh, what a wealth of sorrow in a few words! Poor Mrs. Westenra! Poor Lucy! Gone, gone, never to return to us! And poor, poor Arthur, to have lost such a sweetness out of his life! God help us all to bear our troubles.

23 September—Jonathan is better after a bad night. I am so glad that he has plenty of work to do, for that keeps his mind off the terrible things, and oh, I am rejoiced that he is not now weighed down with the responsibility of his new position. I knew he would be true to himself, and now how proud I am to see my Jonathan rising to the height of his advancement and keeping pace in all ways with the duties that come upon him. He will be away all day till late, for he said he could not lunch at home. He is meeting with an inspector from Scotland Yard, regarding the affairs Mr. Hawkins had been handling for the Lord Godalming.

My household work is done, so I shall take his foreign journal, and lock myself up in my room and read it.

24 September—I hadn't the heart to write last night, that terrible record of Jonathan's upset me so. Poor dear! How he must have suffered, whether it be true or only imagination. I wonder if there is any truth in it at all. Did he get his brain fever, and then write all those terrible things, or had he some cause for it all? I suppose I shall never know, for I dare not open the subject to him. And yet that man we saw yesterday! He seemed quite certain of him, poor fellow! I suppose it was the funeral upset him and sent his mind back on some train of thought.

He believes it all himself. I remember how on our wedding day he said "Unless some solemn duty come upon me to go back to the bitter hours, asleep or awake, mad or sane . . ." There seems to be through it all some thread of continuity. That fearful Count was coming to London . . . and truly he saw that other fearful man . . . and he thought now the Man of the Munich Dead House and Count Dracula were one.[153] If it should be, and he came to London, with its teeming millions . . . There may be a solemn duty, and if it come we must not shrink from it. I shall be prepared. I shall get my typewriter this very hour and begin transcribing. Then we shall be ready for other eyes if required. And if it be wanted, then, perhaps, if I am ready, poor Jonathan may not be upset, for I can speak for him and never let him be troubled or worried with it at all. If ever Jonathan quite gets over the nervousness he may want to tell me of it all, and I can ask him questions and find out things, and see how I may comfort him.

Inspector Cotford's Case Notes

23 September—Met today with Jonathan Harker, who is now the owner of the law firm of Hawkins & Harker (a name which he apparently intends to keep unchanged, in honour of the deceased). He came to my office promptly, bringing with him a number of documents pertaining to the matter in question. He was a young man, far younger than I would have expected, but his eyes shone with a strength and resolution that surpassed his age. His manner of speech revealed a keen and practical intelligence, but betrayed what I suspect were his humble beginnings, for his words were both friendly and direct, lacking completely the cold aloofness of such prigs as are typically found in legal firms.

All in all, I found Jonathan Harker to be an honest and intelligent man, who answered my questions in a forthright manner and helped me in every way he could. However, I noted at several intervals throughout our day together, he seemed to suffer from a transient form of weakness or exhaustion. When asked about it, he explained that, as Mr. Hawkins had become crippled with gout, he had made a long and difficult journey abroad to handle a legal matter in his place. There he came down with a malignant brain fever that caused him to remain in Buda Pesth for some time before his eventual return to England last week, and he is still weakened from the experience. (*mem.*, confirm departure and arrival dates with ship manifests, though I suspect all will be in order).

With regard to the legal matters that Mr. Hawkins had been conducting with Lord Godalming, the various papers Mr. Harker brought to me seemed all in order, spelling out clearly the transfer of inheritance. The Hon. Arthur Holmwood, being the only heir, received the title of Viscount[154], Lordship over the Godalming Hundred and Ringwood, as well as the whole estate, real and personal. There were, however, two items of possible interest that caught my eye:

First, the Holmwoods seemed to have had a regular influx of wealth from the bankers Herren Klopstock & Billreuth in Buda Pesth, which in turn received said wealth from a Salzburg bank house, without explanation as to the reason or ultimate source. These transactions had occurred at regular intervals, though the amount varied slightly from time to time, due to certain fees incurred for the changing of archaic gold denominations[155] into usable funds.

Second, there seemed to be a lengthy preparation regarding the statutes of peerage that had been made over the course of many years, which ultimately allowed for Arthur Holmwood to inherit the title of Viscount from Edward Holmwood without further question, as it seemed Arthur had, as a child, been adopted by the Holmwoods.

Letter, Van Helsing to Mrs. Harker

24 September
(Confidence)

Dear Madam,

I pray you to pardon my writing, in that I am so far friend as that I sent to you sad news of Miss Lucy Westenra's death. By the kindness of Lord Godalming, I am empowered to read her letters and papers, for I am deeply concerned about certain matters vitally important. In them I find some letters from you, which show how great friends you were and how you love her. Oh, Madam Mina, by that love, I implore you, help me. It is for others' good that I ask, to redress great wrong, and to lift much and terrible troubles, that may be more great than you can know. May it be that I see you? You can trust me. I am friend of Dr. John Seward and of Lord Godalming (that was Arthur of Miss Lucy). I must keep it private for the present from all. I should come to Exeter to see you at once if you tell me I am privilege to come, and where and when. I implore your pardon, Madam. I have read your letters to poor Lucy, and know how good you are and how your husband suffer. So I pray you, if it may be, enlighten him not, least it may harm.

Again your pardon, and forgive me.
Van Helsing

Telegram, Mrs. Harker to Van Helsing

25 September—Come today by quarter past ten train if you can catch it. Can see you any time you call.

—Wilhelmina Harker

Mina Harker's Journal

25 September—I cannot help feeling terribly excited as the time draws near for the visit of Dr. Van Helsing, for somehow I expect that it will throw some light upon Jonathan's sad experience, and as he attended poor dear Lucy in her last illness, he can tell me all about her. That is the reason of his coming. It is concerning Lucy and her sleep-walking, and not about Jonathan. Then I shall never know the real truth now! How silly I am. That awful journal gets hold of my

imagination and tinges everything with something of its own colour. Of course it is about Lucy. That habit came back to the poor dear, and that awful night on the cliff must have made her ill. I had almost forgotten in my own affairs how ill she was afterwards. She must have told him of her sleep-walking adventure on the cliff, and that I knew all about it, and now he wants me to tell him what I know, so that he may understand. I hope I did right in not saying anything of it to Mrs. Westenra. I should never forgive myself if any act of mine, were it even a negative one, brought harm on poor dear Lucy. I hope too, Dr. Van Helsing will not blame me. I have had so much trouble and anxiety of late that I feel I cannot bear more just at present.

I suppose a cry does us all good at times, clears the air as other rain does. Perhaps it was reading the journal yesterday that upset me, and then Jonathan went away this morning to stay away from me a whole day and night, the first time we have been parted since our marriage. I do hope the dear fellow will take care of himself, and that nothing will occur to upset him. It is two o'clock, and the doctor will be here soon now. I shall say nothing of Jonathan's journal unless he asks me. I am so glad I have typewritten out my own journal, so that, in case he asks about Lucy, I can hand it to him. It will save much questioning.

Later—He has come and gone. Oh, what a strange meeting, and how it all makes my head whirl round. I feel like one in a dream. Can it be all possible, or even a part of it? If I had not read Jonathan's journal first, I should never have accepted even a possibility. Poor, poor, dear Jonathan! How he must have suffered. Please the good God, all this may not upset him again. I shall try to save him from it. But it may be even a consolation and a help to him, terrible though it be and awful in its consequences, to know for certain that his eyes and ears and brain did not deceive him, and that it is all true. It may be that it is the doubt which haunts him, that when the doubt is removed, no matter which, waking or dreaming, may prove the truth, he will be more satisfied and better able to bear the shock. Dr. Van Helsing must be a good man as well as a clever one if he is Arthur's friend and Dr. Seward's, and if they brought him all the way from Holland to look after Lucy. I feel from having seen him that he is good and kind and of a noble nature. When he comes tomorrow I shall ask him about Jonathan. And then, please God, all this sorrow and anxiety may lead to a good end. I used to think I would like to practice interviewing. Jonathan's friend on "The Exeter News" told him that memory is everything in such work, that you must be able to put down exactly almost every word spoken, even if you had to refine some of it afterwards. Here was a rare interview. I shall try to record it verbatim.

It was half-past two o'clock when the knock came. I took my courage *a deux mains* and waited. In a few minutes Mary opened the door, and announced "Dr. Van Helsing."

I rose and bowed, and he came towards me, a man of medium weight, strongly built, with his shoulders set back over a broad, deep chest and a neck well balanced on the trunk as the head is on the neck. The poise of the head strikes me at once as indicative of thought and power. The head is noble, well-sized, broad, and large behind the ears. The face, clean-shaven, shows a hard, square chin, a large resolute, mobile mouth, a good-sized nose, rather straight, but with quick, sensitive nostrils, that seem to broaden as the big bushy brows come down and the mouth tightens. The forehead is broad and fine, rising at first almost straight and then sloping back above two bumps or ridges wide apart, such a forehead that the reddish hair cannot possibly tumble over it, but falls naturally back and to the sides. Big, dark blue eyes are set widely apart, and are quick and tender or stern with the man's moods. He said to me,

"Mrs. Harker, is it not?" I bowed assent.

"That was Miss Mina Murray?" Again I assented.

"It is Mina Murray that I came to see that was friend of that poor dear child Lucy Westenra. Madam Mina, it is on account of the dead that I come."

"Sir," I said, "you could have no better claim on me than that you were a friend and helper of Lucy Westenra." And I held out my hand. He took it and said tenderly,

"Oh, Madam Mina, I know that the friend of that poor little girl must be good, but I had yet to learn . . ." He finished his speech with a courtly bow. I asked him what it was that he wanted to see me about, so he at once began.

"I have read your letters to Miss Lucy. Forgive me, but I had to begin to inquire somewhere, and there was none to ask. I know that you were with her at Whitby. She sometimes kept a diary, you need not look surprised, Madam Mina. It was begun after you had left, and was an imitation of you, and in that diary she traces by inference certain things to a sleep-walking in which she puts down that you saved her. In great perplexity then I come to you, and ask you out of your so much kindness to tell me all of it that you can remember."

"I can tell you, I think, Dr. Van Helsing, all about it."

"Ah, then you have good memory for facts, for details? It is not always so with young ladies."

"No, doctor, but I wrote it all down at the time. I can show it to you if you like."

"Oh, Madam Mina, I will be grateful. You will do me much favour."

I could not resist the temptation of mystifying him a bit, I suppose it is some taste of the original apple that remains still in our mouths, so I handed him the shorthand diary. He took it with a grateful bow, and said, "May I read it?"

"If you wish," I answered as demurely as I could. He opened it, and for an instant his face fell. Then he stood up and bowed.

"Oh, you so clever woman!" he said. "I knew long that Mr. Jonathan was a man of much thankfulness, but see, his wife have all the good things. And will you not so much honour me and so help me as to read it for me? Alas! I know not the shorthand."

By this time my little joke was over, and I was almost ashamed. So I took the typewritten copy from my work basket and handed it to him.

"Forgive me," I said. "I could not help it, but I had been thinking that it was of dear Lucy that you wished to ask, and so that you might not have time to wait, not on my account, but because I know your time must be precious, I have written it out on the typewriter for you."

He took it and his eyes glistened. "You are so good," he said. "And may I read it now? I may want to ask you some things when I have read."

"By all means," I said, "read it over whilst I order lunch, and then you can ask me questions whilst we eat."

He bowed and settled himself in a chair with his back to the light, and became so absorbed in the papers, whilst I went to see after lunch chiefly in order that he might not be disturbed. When I came back, I found him walking hurriedly up and down the room, his face all ablaze with excitement. He rushed up to me and took me by both hands.

"Oh, Madam Mina," he said, "how can I say what I owe to you? This paper is as sunshine. It opens the gate to me. I am dazed, I am dazzled, with so much light, and yet clouds roll in behind the light every time. But that you do not, cannot comprehend. Oh, but I am grateful to you, you so clever woman. Madame," he said this very solemnly, "if ever Abraham Van Helsing can do anything for you or yours, I trust you will let me know. It will be pleasure and delight if I may serve you as a friend, as a friend, but all I have ever learned, all I can ever do, shall be for you and those you love. There are darknesses in life, and there are lights. You are one of the lights. You will have a happy life and a good life, and your husband will be blessed in you."

"But, doctor, you praise me too much, and you do not know me."

"Not know you, I, who am old, and who have studied all my life men and women, I who have made my specialty the brain and all that belongs to him and all that follow from him! And I have read your diary that you have so goodly written for me, and which breathes out truth in every line. I, who have read your so sweet letter to poor Lucy of your marriage and your trust, not know you! Oh, Madam Mina, good women tell all their lives, and by day and by hour and by minute, such things that angels can read. And we men who wish to know have in us something of angels' eyes. Your husband is noble nature, and you are noble too, for you trust, and trust cannot be where there is mean nature. And your husband, tell me of him. Is he quite well? Is all that fever gone, and is he strong and hearty?"

I saw here an opening to ask him about Jonathan, so I said, "He was almost recovered, but he has been greatly upset by Mr. Hawkins' death."

He interrupted, "Oh, yes. I know. I know. I have read your last two letters."

I went on, "I suppose this upset him, for when we were in town on Thursday last he had a sort of shock."

"A shock, and after brain fever so soon! That is not good. What kind of shock was it?"

"He thought he saw some one who recalled something terrible, something which led to his brain fever." And here the whole thing seemed to overwhelm me in a rush. The pity for Jonathan, the horror which he experienced, the whole fearful mystery of his diary, and the fear that has been brooding over me ever since, all came in a tumult. I suppose I was hysterical, for I threw myself on my knees and held up my hands to him, and implored him to make my husband well again. He took my hands and raised me up, and made me sit on the sofa, and sat by me. He held my hand in his, and said to me with, oh, such infinite sweetness,

"My life is a barren and lonely one, and so full of work that I have not had much time for friendships, but since I have been summoned to here by my friend John Seward I have known so many good people and seen such nobility that I feel more than ever, and it has grown with my advancing years, the loneliness of my life. Believe me, then, that I come here full of respect for you, and you have given me hope, hope, not in what I am seeking of, but that there are good women still left to make life happy, good women, whose lives and whose truths may make good lesson for the children that are to be. I am glad, glad, that I may here be of some use to you. For if your husband suffer, he suffer within the range of my study and experience. I promise you that I will gladly do all for him that I can, all to make his life strong and manly, and your life a happy one. Now you must eat. You are overwrought and perhaps over-anxious. Husband Jonathan would not like to see you so pale, and what he like not where he love, is not to his good. Therefore for his sake you must eat and smile. You have told me about Lucy, and so now we shall not speak of it, lest it distress. I shall stay in Exeter tonight, for I want to think much over what you have told me, and when I have thought I will ask you questions, if I may. And then too, you will tell me of husband Jonathan's trouble so far as you can, but not yet. You must eat now, afterwards you shall tell me all."

After lunch, when we went back to the drawing room, he said to me, "And now tell me all about him."

When it came to speaking to this great learned man, I began to fear that he would think me a weak fool, and Jonathan a madman, that journal is all so strange, and I hesitated to go on. But he was so sweet and kind, and he had promised to help, and I trusted him, so I said,

"Dr. Van Helsing, what I have to tell you is so queer that you must not laugh at me or at my husband. I have been since yesterday in a sort of fever of doubt. You must be kind to me, and not think me foolish that I have even half believed some very strange things."

He reassured me by his manner as well as his words when he said, "Oh, my dear, if you only know how strange is the matter regarding which I am here, it is you who would laugh. I have learned not to think little of any one's belief, no matter how strange it may be. I have tried to keep an open mind, and it is not the ordinary things of life that could close it, but the strange things, the extraordinary things, the things that make one doubt if they be mad or sane."

"Thank you, thank you a thousand times! You have taken a weight off my mind. If you will let me, I shall give you a paper to read. It is long, but I have typewritten it out. It will tell you my trouble and Jonathan's. It is the copy of his journal when abroad, and all that happened. I dare not say anything of it. You will read for yourself and judge. And then when I see you, perhaps, you will be very kind and tell me what you think."

"I promise," he said as I gave him the papers. "I shall in the morning, as soon as I can, come to see you and your husband, if I may."

"Jonathan will be here at half-past eleven, and you must come to lunch with us and see him then. You could catch the quick 3:34 train, which will leave you at Paddington before eight." He was surprised at my knowledge of the trains offhand, but he does not know that I have made up all the trains to and from Exeter, so that I may help Jonathan in case he is in a hurry.

So he took the papers with him and went away, and I sit here thinking, thinking I don't know what.

Letter (by hand), Van Helsing to Mrs. Harker

25 September, 6 o'clock

Dear Madam Mina,

I have read your husband's so wonderful diary. You may sleep without doubt. Strange and terrible as it is, it is true! I will pledge my life on it. I fear that he may have, through no fault of his own, helped to undo a good work I had once wrought near Munich many years ago, but that is of no matter now.

With regard to your husband's health, it may be worse for others, but for him and you there is no dread. He is a noble fellow, and let me tell you from experience of men, that one who would do as he did in going down that wall and to that room, aye, and going a second time, is not one to be injured in permanence by a shock. His brain and his heart are all right, this I swear, before I have even seen him, so be at rest. I shall have much to ask him of other things. I am blessed that today I come to see you, for I have learn all at once so much that again I am dazzled, dazzled more than ever, and I must think.

Yours the most faithful,
Abraham Van Helsing

Letter, Mrs. Harker to Van Helsing

25 September, 6:30 P.M.

My dear Dr. Van Helsing,

A thousand thanks for your kind letter, which has taken a great weight off my mind. And yet, if it be true, what terrible things there are in the world, and what an awful thing if that man, that monster, be really in London! I fear to think. I have this moment, whilst writing, had a wire from Jonathan, saying that he leaves by the 6:25 tonight from Launceston and will be here at 10:18, so that I shall have no fear tonight. Will you, therefore, instead of lunching with us, please come to breakfast at eight o'clock, if this be not too early for you? You can get away, if you are in a hurry, by the 10:30 train, which will bring you to Paddington by 2:35. Do not answer this, as I shall take it that, if I do not hear, you will come to breakfast.

Believe me,
Your faithful and grateful friend,
Mina Harker

Jonathan Harker's Journal

26 September—I thought never to write in this diary again, but the time has come. When I got home last night Mina had supper ready, and when we had supped she told me of Van Helsing's visit, and of her having given him the two diaries copied out, and of how anxious she has been about me. She showed me in the doctor's letter that all I wrote down was true. It seems to have made a new man of me. It was the doubt as to the reality of the whole thing that knocked me over. I felt impotent, and in the dark, and distrustful. But, now that I know, I am not afraid, even of the Count. He has succeeded after all, then, in his design in getting to London, and it was he I saw. He has got younger, and how? Van Helsing is the man to unmask him and hunt him out, if he is anything like what Mina says. We sat late, and talked it over. Mina is dressing, and I shall call at the hotel in a few minutes and bring him over.

He was, I think, surprised to see me. When I came into the room where he was, and introduced myself, he took me by the shoulder, and turned my face round to the light, and said, after a sharp scrutiny,

"But Madam Mina told me you were ill, that you had had a shock."

It was so funny to hear my wife called 'Madam Mina' by this kindly, strong-faced old man. I smiled, and said, "I was ill, I have had a shock, but you have cured me already."

"And how?"

"By your letter to Mina last night. I was in doubt, and then everything took a hue of unreality, and I did not know what to trust, even the evidence of my own senses. Not knowing what to trust, I did not know what to do, and so had only to keep on working in what had hitherto been the groove of my life. The groove ceased to avail me, and I mistrusted myself. Doctor, you don't know what it is to doubt everything, even yourself. No, you don't, you couldn't with eyebrows like yours."

He seemed pleased, and laughed as he said, "So! You are a physiognomist. I learn more here with each hour. I am with so much pleasure coming to you to breakfast, and, oh, sir, you will pardon praise from an old man, but you are blessed in your wife."

I would listen to him go on praising Mina for a day, so I simply nodded and stood silent.

"She is one of God's women, fashioned by His own hand to show us men and other women that there is a heaven where we can enter, and that its light can be here on earth. So true, so sweet, so noble, so little an egoist, and that, let me tell you, is much in this age, so sceptical and selfish. And you, sir . . . I have read all the letters to poor Miss Lucy, and some of them speak of you, so I know you since some days from the knowing of others, but I have seen your true self since last night. You will give me your hand, will you not? And let us be friends for all our lives."

We shook hands, and he was so earnest and so kind that it made me quite choky.

"And now," he said, "may I ask you for some more help? I have a great task to do, and at the beginning it is to know. You can help me here. Can you tell me what went before your going to Transylvania? Later on I may ask more help, and of a different kind, but at first this will do."

"Look here, Sir," I said, "does what you have to do concern the Count?"

"It does," he said solemnly.

"Then I am with you heart and soul. As you go by the 10:30 train, you will not have time to read them, but I shall get the bundle of papers. You can take them with you and read them in the train."

After breakfast I saw him to the station. When we were parting he said, "Perhaps you will come to town if I send for you, and take Madam Mina too."

"We shall both come when you will," I said.

I had got him the morning papers and the London papers of the previous night, and while we were talking at the carriage window, waiting for the train to start, he was turning them over. His eyes suddenly seemed to catch something in one of them, "The Westminster Gazette," I knew it by the colour, and he grew quite white. He read something intently, groaning to himself, "Mein Gott! Mein Gott! So soon! So soon!" I do not think he remembered me at the moment. Just then the whistle blew, and the train moved off. This recalled him to himself, and he leaned out of the window and waved his hand, calling out, "Love to Madam Mina. I shall write so soon as ever I can."

Dr. Seward's Case-Book

26 September—Truly there is no such thing as finality. Not a week since I said "Finis," and yet here I am starting fresh again, or rather going on with the record. Until this afternoon I had no cause to think of what is done. Renfield had become, to all intents, as sane as he ever was. He was already well ahead with his fly business, and he had just started in the spider line also, so he had not been of any trouble to me. I had a letter from Arthur, written on Sunday, and from it I gather that he is bearing up wonderfully well. Quincey Morris is with him, and that is much of a help, for he himself is a bubbling well of good spirits. Quincey wrote me a line too, and from him I hear that Arthur is beginning to recover something of his old buoyancy, so as to them all my mind is at rest. As for myself, I was settling down to my work with the enthusiasm which I used to have for it, so that I might fairly have said that the wound which poor Lucy left on me was becoming cicatrised.

Everything is, however, now reopened, and what is to be the end God only knows. I have an idea that Van Helsing thinks he knows, too, but he will only let out enough at a time to whet curiosity. He went to Exeter yesterday, and stayed there all night. Today he came back, and almost bounded into the room at about half-past five o'clock, and thrust last night's "Westminster Gazette" into my hand.

"What do you think of that?" he asked as he stood back and folded his arms.

I looked over the paper, for I really did not know what he meant, but he took it from me and pointed out a paragraph about children being decoyed away at Hampstead. It did not convey much to me, until I reached a passage where it described small puncture wounds on their throats. An idea struck me, and I looked up.

"Well?" he said.

"It is like poor Lucy's."

"And what do you make of it?"

"Simply that there is some cause in common. Whatever it was that injured her has injured them." I did not quite understand his answer.

"That is true indirectly, but not directly."

"How do you mean, Professor?" I asked. I was a little inclined to take his seriousness lightly, for, after all, four days of rest and freedom from burning, harrowing anxiety does help to restore one's spirits, but when I saw his face, it sobered me. Never, even in the midst of our despair about poor Lucy, had he looked more stern.

"Tell me!" I said. "I can hazard no opinion. I do not know what to think, and I have no data on which to found a conjecture."

"Do you mean to tell me, friend John, that you have no suspicion as to what poor Lucy died of, not after all the hints given, not only by events, but by me?"

"Of nervous prostration following a great loss or waste of blood."

"And how was the blood lost or wasted?" I shook my head.

He stepped over and sat down beside me, and went on, "You are a clever man, friend John. You reason well, and your wit is bold, but you are too prejudiced. You do not let your eyes see nor your ears hear, and that which is outside your daily life is not of account to you. Do you not think that there are things which you cannot understand, and yet which are, that some people see things that others cannot? But there are things old and new which must not be contemplated by men's eyes, because they know, or think they know, some things which other men have told them. Ah, it is the fault of our science that it wants to explain all, and if it explain not, then it says there is nothing to explain. But yet we see around us every day the growth of new beliefs, which think themselves new, and which are yet but the old, which pretend to be young, like the fine ladies at the opera. I suppose now you do not believe in corporeal transference. No? Nor in materialization. No? Nor in astral bodies. No? Nor in the reading of thought. No? Nor in hypnotism . . ."

"Yes," I said. "Charcot has proved that pretty well."

He smiled as he went on, "Then you are satisfied as to it. Yes? And of course then you understand how it act, and can follow the mind of the great Charcot, alas that he is no more, into the very soul of the patient that he influence. No? Then, friend John, am I to take it that you simply accept fact, and are satisfied to let from premise to conclusion be a blank? No? Then tell me, for I am a student of the brain, how you accept hypnotism and reject the thought reading. Let me tell you, my friend, that there are things done today in electrical science which would have been deemed unholy by the very man who discovered electricity, who would themselves not so long before been burned as wizards. There are always mysteries in life. Why was it that Methuselah lived nine hundred years, and 'Old Parr' one hundred and sixty-nine, and yet that poor Lucy, with four men's blood in her poor veins, could not live even one day? For, had she live one more day, we could save her. Do you know all the mystery of life and death? Do you know the altogether of comparative anatomy and can say wherefore the qualities of brutes are in some men, and not in others? Can you tell me why, when other spiders die small and soon, that one great spider lived for centuries in the tower of the old Spanish church and grew and grew, till, on descending, he could drink the oil of all the church lamps? Can you tell me why in the Pampas, ay and elsewhere, there are bats that come out at night and open the veins of cattle and horses and suck dry their veins, how in some islands of the Western seas there are bats which hang on the trees all day, and those who have seen describe as like giant nuts or pods, and that when the sailors sleep on the deck, because that it is hot, flit down on them and then, and then in the morning are found dead men, white as even Miss Lucy was?"

"Good God, Professor!" I said, starting up. "Do you mean to tell me that Lucy was bitten by such a bat, and that such a thing is here in London in the nineteenth century?"

He waved his hand for silence, and went on, "Can you tell me why the tortoise lives more long than generations of men, why the elephant goes on and on till he have sees dynasties, and why the parrot never die only of bite of cat or dog or other complaint? Can you tell me why men believe in all ages and places that there are men and women who cannot die? We all know, because science has vouched for the fact, that there have been toads shut up in rocks for thousands of years, shut in one so small hole that only hold him since the youth of the world. Can you tell me how the Indian fakir can make himself to die and have been buried, and his grave sealed and corn sowed on it, and the corn reaped and be cut and sown and reaped and cut again, and then men come and take away the unbroken seal and that there lie the Indian fakir, not dead, but that rise up and walk amongst them as before?"

Here I interrupted him. I was getting bewildered. He so crowded on my mind his list of nature's eccentricities and possible impossibilities that my imagination was getting fired. I had a dim idea that he was teaching me some lesson, as long ago he used to do in his study at Amsterdam. But he used them to tell me the thing, so that I could have the object of thought in mind all the time. But now I was without his help, yet I wanted to follow him, so I said,

"Professor, let me be your pet student again. Tell me the thesis, so that I may apply your knowledge as you go on. At present I am going in my mind from point to point as a madman, and not a sane one, follows an idea. I feel like a novice lumbering through a bog in a mist, jumping from one tussock to another in the mere blind effort to move on without knowing where I am going."

"That is a good image," he said. "Well, I shall tell you. My thesis is this, I want you to believe."

"To believe what?"

"To believe in things that you cannot. Let me illustrate. I heard once of an American who so defined faith, 'that faculty which enables us to believe things which we know to be untrue.' For one, I follow that man. He meant that we shall have an open mind, and not let a little bit of truth check the rush of the big truth, like a small rock does a railway truck. We get the small truth first. Good! We keep him, and we value him, but all the same we must not let him think himself all the truth in the universe."

"Then you want me not to let some previous conviction inure the receptivity of my mind with regard to some strange matter. Do I read your lesson aright?"

"Ah, you are my favourite pupil still. It is worth to teach you. Now that you are willing to understand, you have taken the first step to understand. You think then that those so small holes in the children's throats were made by the same that made the holes in Miss Lucy?"

"I suppose so."

He stood up and said solemnly, "Then you are wrong. Oh, would it were so! But alas! No. It is worse, far, far worse."

"In God's name, Professor Van Helsing, what do you mean?" I cried.

He threw himself with a despairing gesture into a chair, and placed his elbows on the table, covering his face with his hands as he spoke.

"They were made by Miss Lucy!"

CHAPTER

TWENTY-TWO[156]

Dr. Seward's Case-Book, Continued

For a while sheer anger mastered me. It was as if he had during her life struck Lucy on the face. I smote the table hard and rose up as I said to him, "Dr. Van Helsing, are you mad?"

He raised his head and looked at me, and somehow the tenderness of his face calmed me at once. "Would I were!" he said. "Madness were easy to bear compared with truth like this. Oh, my friend, why, think you, did I go so far round, why take so long to tell so simple a thing? Was it because I hate you and have hated you all my life? Was it because I wished to give you pain? Was it that I wanted, now so late, revenge for that time when you saved my life, and from a fearful death? Ah no!"

"Forgive me," said I.

He went on, "My friend, it was because I wished to be gentle in the breaking to you, for I know you have loved that so sweet lady. But even yet I do not expect you to believe. It is so hard to accept at once any abstract truth, that we may doubt such to be possible when we have always believed the 'no' of it. It is more hard still to accept so sad a concrete truth, and of such a one as Miss Lucy. Tonight I go to prove it. Dare you come with me?"

This staggered me. A man does not like to prove such a truth, Byron excepted from the category, jealousy.

"And prove the very truth he most abhorred."

He saw my hesitation, and spoke, "The logic is simple, no madman's logic this time, jumping from tussock to tussock in a misty bog. If it not be true, then proof will be relief. At worst it will not harm. If it be true! Ah, there is the dread.

Yet every dread should help my cause, for in it is some need of belief. Come, I tell you what I propose. First, that we go off now and see that child in the hospital. Dr. Vincent, of the North Hospital, where the papers say the child is, is a friend of mine, and I think of yours since you were in class at Amsterdam. He will let two scientists see his case, if he will not let two friends. We shall tell him nothing, but only that we wish to learn. And then . . ."

"And then?"

He took a key from his pocket and held it up. "And then we spend the night, you and I, in the churchyard where Lucy lies. This is the key that lock the tomb. I had it from the coffin man to give to Arthur."

My heart sank within me, for I felt that there was some fearful ordeal before us. I could do nothing, however, so I plucked up what heart I could and said that we had better hasten, as the afternoon was passing.

We found the child awake. It had had a sleep and taken some food, and altogether was going on well. Dr, Vincent took the bandage from its throat, and showed us the punctures. There was no mistaking the similarity to those which had been on Lucy's throat. They were smaller, and the edges looked fresher, that was all. We asked Vincent to what he attributed them, and he replied that it must have been a bite of some animal, perhaps a rat, but for his own part, he was inclined to think it was one of the bats which are so numerous on the northern heights of London. "Out of so many harmless ones," he said, "there may be some wild specimen from the South of a more malignant species. Some sailor may have brought one home, and it managed to escape, or even from the Zoological Gardens a young one may have got loose, or one be bred there from a vampire. These things do occur, you know. Only ten days ago a wolf got out, and was, I believe, traced up in this direction. For a week after, the children were playing nothing but Red Riding Hood on the Heath and in every alley in the place until this 'bloofer lady' scare came along, since then it has been quite a gala time with them. Even this poor little mite, when he woke up today, asked the nurse if he might go away. When she asked him why he wanted to go, he said he wanted to play with the 'bloofer lady.'"

"I hope," said Van Helsing, "that when you are sending the child home you will caution its parents to keep strict watch over it. These fancies to stray are most dangerous, and if the child were to remain out another night, it would probably be fatal. But in any case I suppose you will not let it away for some days?"

"Certainly not, not for a week at least, longer if the wound is not healed."

Our visit to the hospital took more time than we had reckoned on, and the sun had dipped before we came out. When Van Helsing saw how dark it was, he said,

"There is not hurry. It is more late than I thought. Come, let us seek somewhere that we may eat, and then we shall go on our way."

We dined at 'Jack Straw's Castle' along with a little crowd of bicyclists and others who were genially noisy. About ten o'clock we started from the inn. It was then very dark, and the scattered lamps made the darkness greater when we were once outside their individual radius. The Professor had evidently noted the road we were to go, for he went on unhesitatingly, but, as for me, I was in quite a mixup as to locality. As we went further, we met fewer and fewer people, till at last we were somewhat surprised when we met even the patrol of horse police going their usual suburban round. At last we reached the wall of the churchyard, which we climbed over. With some little difficulty, for it was very dark, and the whole place seemed so strange to us, we found the Westenra tomb. The Professor took the key, opened the creaky door, and standing back, politely, but quite unconsciously, motioned me to precede him. There was a delicious irony in the offer, in the courtliness of giving preference on such a ghastly occasion. My companion followed me quickly, and cautiously drew the door to, after carefully ascertaining that the lock was a falling, and not a spring one. In the latter case we should have been in a bad plight. Then he fumbled in his bag, and taking out a matchbox and a piece of candle, proceeded to make a light. The tomb in the daytime, and when wreathed with fresh flowers, had looked grim and gruesome enough, but now, some days afterwards, when the flowers hung lank and dead, their whites turning to rust and their greens to browns, when the spider and the beetle had resumed their accustomed dominance, when the time-discoloured stone, and dust-encrusted mortar, and rusty, dank iron, and tarnished brass, and clouded silver-plating gave back the feeble glimmer of a candle, the effect was more miserable and sordid than could have been imagined. It conveyed irresistibly the idea that life, animal life, was not the only thing which could pass away.

Van Helsing went about his work systematically. Holding his candle so that he could read the coffin plates, and so holding it that the sperm dropped in white patches which congealed as they touched the metal, he made assurance of Lucy's coffin. Another search in his bag, and he took out a turnscrew.

"What are you going to do?" I asked.

"To open the coffin. You shall yet be convinced."

Straightway he began taking out the screws, and finally lifted off the lid, showing the casing of lead beneath. The sight was almost too much for me. It seemed to be as much an affront to the dead as it would have been to have stripped off her clothing in her sleep whilst living. I actually took hold of his hand to stop him.

He only said, "You shall see," and again fumbling in his bag took out a tiny fret saw. Striking the turnscrew through the lead with a swift downward stab, which made me wince, he made a small hole, which was, however, big enough to admit the point of the saw. I had expected a rush of gas from the week-old corpse. We doctors, who have had to study our dangers, have to become accustomed to such things, and I drew back towards the door. But the Professor never stopped for a moment. He sawed down a couple of feet along one side of the lead coffin, and then across, and down the other side. Taking the edge of the loose flange, he bent it back towards the foot of the coffin, and holding up the candle into the aperture, motioned to me to look.

I drew near and looked. The coffin was empty. It was certainly a surprise to me, and gave me a considerable shock, but Van Helsing was unmoved. He was now more sure than ever of his ground, and so emboldened to proceed in his task. "Are you satisfied now, friend John?" he asked.

I felt all the dogged argumentativeness of my nature awake within me as I answered him, "I am satisfied that Lucy's body is not in that coffin, but that only proves one thing."

"And what is that, friend John?"

"That it is not there."

"That is good logic," he said, "so far as it goes. But how do you, how can you, account for it not being there?"

"Perhaps a body-snatcher," I suggested. "Some of the undertaker's people may have stolen it." I felt that I was speaking folly, and yet it was the only real cause which I could suggest.

The Professor sighed. "Ah well!" he said, "we must have more proof. Come with me."

He put on the coffin lid again, gathered up all his things and placed them in the bag, blew out the light, and placed the candle also in the bag. We opened the door, and went out. Behind us he closed the door and locked it. He handed me the key, saying, "Will you keep it? You had better be assured."

I laughed, it was not a very cheerful laugh, I am bound to say, as I motioned him to keep it. "A key is nothing," I said, "there are many duplicates, and anyhow it is not difficult to pick a lock of this kind."

He said nothing, but put the key in his pocket. Then he told me to watch at one side of the churchyard whilst he would watch at the other.

I took up my place behind a yew tree, and I saw his dark figure move until the intervening headstones and trees hid it from my sight.

It was a lonely vigil. Just after I had taken my place I heard a distant clock strike twelve, and in time came one and two. I was chilled and unnerved, and angry with the Professor for taking me on such an errand and with myself for coming. I was too cold and too sleepy to be keenly observant, and not sleepy enough to betray my trust, so altogether I had a dreary, miserable time.

Suddenly, as I turned round, I thought I saw something like a white streak, moving between two dark yew trees at the side of the churchyard farthest from the tomb. At the same time a dark mass moved from the Professor's side of the ground, and hurriedly went towards it. Then I too moved, but I had to go round headstones and railed-off tombs, and I stumbled over graves. The sky was overcast, and somewhere far off an early cock crew. A little ways off, beyond a line of scattered juniper trees, which marked the pathway to the church, a white dim figure flitted in the direction of the tomb. The tomb itself was hidden by trees, and I could not see where the figure had disappeared. I heard the rustle of actual movement where I had first seen the white figure, and coming over, found the Professor holding in his arms a tiny child. When he saw me he held it out to me, and said, "Are you satisfied now?"

"No," I said, in a way that I felt was aggressive.

"Do you not see the child?"

"Yes, it is a child, but who brought it here? And is it wounded?"

"We shall see," said the Professor, and with one impulse we took our way out of the churchyard, he carrying the sleeping child.

When we had got some little distance away, we went into a clump of trees, and struck a match, and looked at the child's throat. It was without a scratch or scar of any kind.

"Was I right?" I asked triumphantly.

"We were just in time," said the Professor thankfully.

We had now to decide what we were to do with the child, and so consulted about it. If we were to take it to a police station we should have to give some account of our movements during the night. At least, we should have had to make some statement as to how we had come to find the child. So finally we decided that we would take it to the Heath, and when we heard a policeman coming, would leave it where he could not fail to find it. We would then seek our way home as quickly as we could. All fell out well. At the edge of Hampstead Heath we heard a policeman's heavy tramp, and laying the child on the pathway, we waited and watched until he saw it as he flashed his lantern to and fro. We heard his exclamation of astonishment, and then we went away silently. By good chance we got a cab near the 'Spainiards,' and drove to town.

I cannot sleep, so I make this entry. But I must try to get a few hours' sleep, as Van Helsing is to call for me at noon. He insists that I go with him on another expedition.

27 September—It was two o'clock before we found a suitable opportunity for our attempt. The funeral held at noon was all completed, and the last stragglers of the mourners had taken themselves lazily away, when, looking carefully from behind a clump of alder trees, we saw the sexton lock the gate after him. We knew that we were safe till morning did we desire it, but the Professor told me that we should not want more than an hour at most. Again I felt that horrid sense of the reality of things, in which any effort of imagination seemed out of place, and I realised distinctly the perils of the law which we were incurring in our unhallowed

work. Besides, I felt it was all so useless. Outrageous as it was to open a leaden coffin, to see if a woman dead nearly a week were really dead, it now seemed the height of folly to open the tomb again, when we knew, from the evidence of our own eyesight, that the coffin was empty. I shrugged my shoulders, however, and rested silent, for Van Helsing had a way of going on his own road, no matter who remonstrated. He took the key, opened the vault, and again courteously motioned me to proceed. The place was not so gruesome as last night, but oh, how unutterably mean looking when the sunshine streamed in. Van Helsing walked over to Lucy's coffin, and I followed. He bent over and again forced back the leaden flange, and a shock of surprise and dismay shot through me.

There lay Lucy, seemingly just as we had seen her the night before her funeral. She was, if possible, more radiantly beautiful than ever, and I could not believe that she was dead. The lips were red, nay redder than before, and on the cheeks was a delicate bloom.

"Is this a juggle?" I said to him.

"Are you convinced now?" said the Professor, in response, and as he spoke he put over his hand, and in a way that made me shudder, pulled back the dead lips and showed the white teeth. "See," he went on, "they are even sharper than before. With this and this," and he touched one of the canine teeth and that below it, "the little children can be bitten. Are you of belief now, friend John?"

Once more argumentative hostility woke within me. I could not accept such an overwhelming idea as he suggested. So, with an attempt to argue of which I was even at the moment ashamed, I said, "She may have been placed here since last night."

"Indeed? That is so, and by whom?"

"I do not know. Someone has done it."

"And yet she has been dead one week. Most peoples in that time would not look so."

I had no answer for this, so was silent. Van Helsing did not seem to notice my silence. At any rate, he showed neither chagrin nor triumph. He was looking intently at the face of the dead woman, raising the eyelids and looking at the eyes, and once more opening the lips and examining the teeth. Then he turned to me and said,

"Here, there is one thing which is different from all recorded. Here is some dual life that is not as the common. She was bitten by the vampire when she was in a trance, sleep-walking, oh, you start. You do not know that, friend John, but you shall know it later, and in trance could he best come to take more blood. In trance she dies, and in trance she is UnDead, too. So it is that she differ from all other. Usually when the UnDead sleep at home," as he spoke he made a comprehensive sweep of his arm to designate what to a vampire was 'home,' "their face show what they are, but this so sweet that was when she not UnDead she go back to the nothings of the common dead. There is no malign there, see, and so it make hard that I must kill her in her sleep."

This turned my blood cold, and it began to dawn upon me that I was accepting Van Helsing's theories. But if she were really dead, what was there of terror in the idea of killing her?

He looked up at me, and evidently saw the change in my face, for he said almost joyously, "Ah, you believe now?"

I answered, "Do not press me too hard all at once. I am willing to accept. How will you do this bloody work?"

"I shall cut off her head and fill her mouth with garlic, and I shall drive a stake through her body."

It made me shudder to think of so mutilating the body of the woman whom I had loved. And yet the feeling was not so strong as I had expected. I was, in fact, beginning to shudder at the presence of this being, this UnDead, as Van Helsing called it, and to loathe it. Is it possible that love is all subjective, or all objective?

I waited a considerable time for Van Helsing to begin, but he stood as if wrapped in thought. Presently he closed the catch of his bag with a snap, and said,

"I have been thinking, and have made up my mind as to what is best. If I did simply follow my inclining I would do now, at this moment, what is to be done. But there are other things to follow, and things that are thousand times more difficult in that them we do not know. This is simple. She have yet no life taken, though that is of time, and to act now would be to take danger from her forever. But then we may have to want Arthur, and how shall we tell him of this? If you, who saw the wounds on Lucy's throat, and saw the wounds so similar on the child's at the hospital, if you, who saw the coffin empty last night and full today with a woman who have not change only to be more rose and more beautiful in a whole week, after she die, if you know of this and know of the white figure last night that brought the child to the churchyard, and yet of your own senses you did not believe, how then, can I expect Arthur, who know none of those things, to believe?

"He doubted me when I took him from her kiss when she was dying. I know he has forgiven me because in some mistaken idea I have done things that prevent him say goodbye as he ought, and he may think that in some more mistaken idea this woman was buried alive, and that in most mistake of all we have killed her. He will then argue back that it is we, mistaken ones, that have killed her by our ideas, and so he will be much unhappy always. Yet he never can be sure, and that is the worst of all. And he will sometimes think that she he loved was buried alive, and that will paint his dreams with horrors of what she must have suffered, and again, he will think that we may be right, and that his so beloved

was, after all, an UnDead. No! I told him once, and since then I learn much.
Now, since I know it is all true, a hundred thousand times more do I know that
he must pass through the bitter waters to reach the sweet. He, poor fellow, must
have one hour that will make the very face of heaven grow black to him, then
we can act for good all round and send him peace. My mind is made up. Let us
go. You return home for tonight to your asylum, and see that all be well. As for
me, I shall spend the night here in this churchyard in my own way. Tomorrow
night you will come to me to the Berkeley Hotel at ten of the clock. I shall send
for Arthur to come too, and also that so fine young man of America that gave
his blood. Later we shall all have work to do. I come with you so far as Piccadilly
and there dine, for I must be back here before the sun set."

So we locked the tomb and came away, and got over the wall of the churchyard,
which was not much of a task, and drove back to Piccadilly.

Note left by Van Helsing in his portmanteau, Berkley Hotel directed to John Seward, M.D. (not delivered)

27 September

Friend John,

I write this in case anything should happen. I go alone to watch in that
churchyard. It pleases me that the UnDead, Miss Lucy, shall not leave tonight,
that so on the morrow night she may be more eager. Therefore I shall fix some
things she like not, garlic and a crucifix, and so seal up the door of the tomb.
She is young as UnDead, and will heed. Moreover, these are only to prevent her
coming out. They may not prevail on her wanting to get in, for then the UnDead
is desperate, and must find the line of least resistance, whatsoever it may be. I
shall be at hand all the night from sunset till after sunrise, and if there be aught
that may be learned I shall learn it. For Miss Lucy or from her, I have no fear,
but that other to whom is there that she is UnDead, he have not the power to
seek her tomb and find shelter. He is cunning, as I know from Mr. Jonathan
and from the way that all along he have fooled us when he played with us for
Miss Lucy's life, and we lost, and in many ways the UnDead are strong. He
have always the strength in his hand of twenty men, even we four who gave our
strength to Miss Lucy it also is all to him. Besides, he can summon his wolf and
I know not what. So if it be that he came thither on this night he shall find me.
But none other shall, until it be too late. But it may be that he will not attempt
the place. There is no reason why he should. His hunting ground is more full
of game than the churchyard where the UnDead woman sleeps, and the one
old man watch.

Therefore I write this in case . . . Take the papers that are with this, the
diaries of Harker and the rest, and read them, and then find this great UnDead,

and cut off his head and burn his heart or drive a stake through it, so that the world may rest from him.

If it be so, farewell.
Van Helsing

Dr. Seward's Case-Book

28 September—It is wonderful what a good night's sleep will do for one. Yesterday I was almost willing to accept Van Helsing's monstrous ideas, but now they seem to start out lurid before me as outrages on common sense. I have no doubt that he believes it all. I wonder if his mind can have become in any way unhinged. Surely there must be some rational explanation of all these mysterious things. Is it possible that the Professor can have done it himself? He is so abnormally clever that if he went off his head he would carry out his intent with regard to some fixed idea in a wonderful way. I am loathe to think it, and indeed it would be almost as great a marvel as the other to find that Van Helsing was mad, but anyhow I shall watch him carefully. I may get some light on the mystery.

Letter, Kate to Mr. and Mrs. Reed

22 September

Mamma, Papa,

Many thanks, for your prayers must be working! I have acquired some aid in the form of a gentleman named Alfred Singleton. Mr. Singleton is the correspondent who wrote that most fascinating article about the Whitby shipwreck, the one I sent you a clipping of. We first met while he was conducting his interviews after that great storm. I saw him again when he came to supper not long ago, as he wanted to make further inquiries about that unfortunate incident.

You will remember, of course, how I described Francis' paintings and my own photograph of the Count. Without a doubt, these peculiarities place this foreign nobleman—whoever or whatever he may be—beyond the realm of conventional scientific thought. So I felt a bit of research into the matter was in order, and purchased a number of books and publications on the supernatural. Among these was a stack of magazines called the *Journal of the Occult*, and as I was reading through it, lo and behold I came across Mr. Singleton's name! Indeed, his name appeared in more than one of these publications.

As Mr. Singleton had called upon me for a favor for his research, I thought it only fair that I now call upon him, as he seemed especially suited to help me. I telegrammed him, and he came to Piccadilly to see me earlier today. After questioning about his occupation, he confessed that he was indeed an independent correspondent who wrote for various journals and papers—not just the *Dailygraph* of Whitby. Apparently, though, his main interest dealt with the supernatural, with most of his articles being published by the *Journal of the Occult*. He apologized for failing to mention this to me before, but explained that many people are put off by the idea of the *Journal* and become less than helpful during his interviews.

"Surely," I thought to myself, "he would believe me about the photograph I had taken of Count DeVille!" I could not help but wonder if it was Providence that had preordained my prior encounters with Mr. Singleton, so that he might now be in a position to be of assistance to me in this rather unorthodox matter. And yet, might he not simply be a writer of fiction, who published fanciful works merely for the coin? So I asked him straight away if he actually believed the things he wrote about in the *Journal of the Occult*. I fear I do not have my friend Mina's knack for remembering conversations *verbatim*, but his answer went something like this:

"Miss Reed. I write only about what I have seen and experienced, or, should I have had the misfortune of arriving late upon the scene, I always endeavor to record the statements only of direct eye witnesses—those who have themselves seen or experienced the event in question. Over the years, I have recorded a good many things that most men would rather turn their backs to or pretend aren't there, like children who hide from shadows under their bed sheets. I do put my confidence in neither legends born of ignorance, nor in the lofty writings of scholars and doctors, for the presumptions born of heeding such dross only serves to cloud reason and sensibility. If something is the truth, then it is the truth, regardless of what science and superstition may have to say about it."

Intrigued, and full of hope, I questioned him further. "Might you then believe in . . . in . . ." Here I paused, for I did not even have a name to put to the vague suspicions I had about the Count and what he might be.

"In what, my dear?" He prompted.

"In . . . well . . . *things*." I came out with at last. "In Creatures. In ghosts and evil spirits and worse, who may at times look like a man but in truth are anything but."

For the longest time he was silent, as if considering his next words carefully. Then he looked me directly in the eye and spoke with the utmost seriousness. "Is this to do with the Count DeVille?" A thrill of excitement, and a chill of fear, went through me at his words.

"Yes! Oh yes indeed it does! But, how did you know?"

"As you know, I have been investigating the 'ghost ship' incident. Along the way, I've encountered a number of details which—though they would not necessarily catch the attention of others—I have found to be rather disturbing. Are . . . are you certain you want to hear this?"

I suspect his last question was out of some sort of concern for my supposed frailty as a woman, perhaps thinking I would faint upon the mention of "ghosts," or the like. Normally I would have taken the opportunity to argue my views on the strengths of the modern woman, but given that I was in need of his immediate help, I chose to hold my tongue and simply replied "yes, please."

"Very well. Let's begin with the shipwreck. You read my article that described the log book?" I nodded that I had, and he continued. "The log repeatedly described an unknown man aboard the ship, and yet one was never found, save for that body that had been packed up with the dirt. The crew vanished one at a time, leaving the captain to fear for his very soul.

"Then, after the shipwreck, your grandfather was found dead at the grave of a suicide—the only known suicide's grave in that graveyard. And not long after, a small dog was also killed at the same spot. While that in itself could be merely a coincidence, I notice in Mr. Aytown's painting of the funeral scene that the dog had what are called 'angel eyes'—two spots on the brow above the real eyes. Such dogs have been known to have the ability to sense when there is supernatural evil afoot. And because the graves of suicides are unhallowed ground, evil spirits can easily find solace there. In addition to these two deaths, another dog—the mastiff—was also found killed, and it too had the same 'angel eyes' as the first."

Despite my resolve, I did find myself a bit shaken by all this, but forced myself to remain calm. I did not want to misunderstand anything he was saying, so I asked him straightaway "So then, do you think that some sort of evil was aboard the *Demeter*?"

"Yes," Mr. Singleton replied simply.

"And that this evil housed itself for a time in the suicide's grave, and was responsible for the death of Grampapa and those two dogs?"

"Yes," he replied again.

"And . . . do you believe that this evil has something to do with Count DeVille?"

"Yes. I believe this evil that arrived aboard that ill-fated ship, and the Count, are one and the same. Indeed, I am certain of it, for it is clear to me that the Count is none other than the body that was found to be within the box of earth."

"Please tell me, how did you hit upon that notion?" For my part, I certainly had no doubt that the Count was both evil and unnatural, but I couldn't help but wonder how Mr. Singleton had made the connection between those unusual occurrences at Whitby and my own problems here in Piccadilly.

"Through my various interviews, I discovered that the boxes of earth that were the cargo of *Demeter* were shipped to an ancient estate called Carfax in Purfleet. The purchaser of the estate is listed on the official documents as Count DeVille. In addition, both Carfax and the Piccadilly mansion across the way were both owned by a man named Winter-Suffield, who killed himself."

"Another suicide, like the Whitby grave!" I gasped, understanding the connection now between Whitby and London.

"Precisely." Mr. Singleton kindly waited for a moment for me to collect my thoughts, before he continued. "Miss Reed, I've told you all that I know, and how I have come to believe what I believe about Count DeVille. If I now may ask, how did you come to suspect the Count?"

"I . . . I'm afraid that Francis has somehow come under the influence of this creature. He first saw the Count in Whitby after the shipwreck, and decided to do a few sketches and paintings of him, as he is wont to do with people he finds interesting. Yet all of his attempts to paint the man turned out very wrong, and with each failed attempt, he became more and more obsessed with the Count. I have read as much in his journal.

"When the Count became our neighbor, this obsession worsened. I sensed this issue was dissolving the friendship Francis and I had, and I wanted to do something to bring us closer together. So I talked with Francis about . . . well, about our future. But our conversation did not end well. I know that artists can become fixated and depressed when things do not go well with their work, and thought this might be in part to blame for our argument. So I decided to help him with his painting by taking a photograph of our neighbor, so that Francis could simply work from the photograph and finally be done with his project. But the photo turned out . . . well, just like Francis' paintings, with the Count's face all ghostly and distorted."

"May I see the photo?" Mr. Singleton asked. I quickly retrieved it for him, and he studied it closely. After a time, he handed it back and inquired "Where is Mr. Aytown now?"

"I can't be certain. I haven't seen him in days, though I suspect he is with the Count. Mr. Singleton, will you help me discover exactly who the Count is, what he means to do with Francis, and how I might intervene?"

Mr. Singleton smiled the first genuine smile I believe I have seen on his face. "Miss Reed," he said, "It would be an honor."

He said he already had a good idea about what we were up against, but was reluctant to say more until he had done some further research. So instead we took a victoria down the street to one of the shops. I chose to remain outside while he went in, but soon wished I hadn't, for I felt a cold chill run up and down my spine, as if Death himself were watching me. But it was not long before Mr. Singleton returned with a package, and we made our way back to my home. I thought for a moment, as we were leaving, I saw Mina and Jonathan in Piccadilly, but Mr. Singleton was talking and I was too eager to listen to pay much attention to passersby. Mr. Singleton explained that the package contained a special sort of oil, and that I was to rub some of it onto each of the windowsills, and all around the door frames.

We parted ways once we reached my home. I went inside and eagerly opened the package . . . but all I found was a vial of pungent garlic oil! Though a bit perplexed, I did exactly as Mr. Singleton recommended. So now my home reeks of garlic, which makes my eyes water terribly. While I await word from Mr. Singleton, I believe I shall write to my dear friends Mina and Lucy. They were fond of that seat in Whitby where the suicide lay. Maybe one of them saw something unusual that could shed some light onto all of this. And if not, at least paying them a visit would be a good excuse for getting out of this house.

Your loving daughter,
Kate

CHAPTER
TWENTY-THREE[157]

Dr. Seward's Case-Book

28 September—Last night, at a little before ten o'clock, Arthur and Quincey came into Van Helsing's room. He told us all what he wanted us to do, but especially addressing himself to Arthur, as if all our wills were centred in his. He began by saying that he hoped we would all come with him too, "for," he said, "there is a grave duty to be done there. You were doubtless surprised at my letter?" This query was directly addressed to Lord Godalming.

"I was. It rather upset me for a bit. There has been so much trouble around my house of late that I could do without any more. I have been curious, too, as to what you mean.

"Quincey and I talked it over, but the more we talked, the more puzzled we got, till now I can say for myself that I'm about up a tree as to any meaning about anything."

"Me too," said Quincey Morris laconically.

"Oh," said the Professor, "then you are nearer the beginning, both of you, than friend John here, who has to go a long way back before he can even get so far as to begin."

It was evident that he recognized my return to my old doubting frame of mind without my saying a word. Then, turning to the other two, he said with intense gravity,

"I want your permission to do what I think good this night. It is, I know, much to ask, and when you know what it is I propose to do you will know, and only then how much. Therefore may I ask that you promise me in the dark, so that afterwards, though you may be angry with me for a time, I must not disguise from myself the possibility that such may be, you shall not blame yourselves for anything."

"That's frank anyhow," broke in Quincey. "I'll answer for the Professor. I don't quite see his drift, but I swear he's honest, and that's good enough for me."

"I thank you, Sir," said Van Helsing proudly. "I have done myself the honour of counting you one trusting friend, and such endorsement is dear to me." He held out a hand, which Quincey took.

Then Arthur spoke out, "Dr. Van Helsing, I don't quite like to 'buy a pig in a poke,' as they say in Scotland, and if it be anything in which my honour as a gentleman or my faith as a Christian is concerned, I cannot make such a promise. If you can assure me that what you intend does not violate either of these two, then I give my consent at once, though for the life of me, I cannot understand what you are driving at."

"I accept your limitation," said Van Helsing, "and all I ask of you is that if you feel it necessary to condemn any act of mine, you will first consider it well and be satisfied that it does not violate your reservations."

"Agreed!" said Arthur. "That is only fair. And now that the pourparlers are over, may I ask what it is we are to do?"

"I want you to come with me, and to come in secret, to the churchyard at Kingstead."

Arthur's face fell as he said in an amazed sort of way,

"Where poor Lucy is buried?"

The Professor bowed.

Arthur went on, "And when there?"

"To enter the tomb!"

Arthur stood up. "Professor, are you in earnest, or is it some monstrous joke? Pardon me, I see that you are in earnest." He sat down again, but I could see that he sat firmly and proudly, as one who is on his dignity. There was silence until he asked again, "And when in the tomb?"

"To open the coffin."

"This is too much!" he said, angrily rising again. "I am willing to be patient in all things that are reasonable, but in this, this desecration of the grave, of one who . . ." He fairly choked with indignation.

The Professor looked pityingly at him. "If I could spare you one pang, my poor friend," he said, "God knows I would. But this night our feet must tread in thorny paths, or later, and for ever, the feet you love must walk in paths of flame!"

Arthur looked up with set white face and said, "Take care, sir, take care!"

"Would it not be well to hear what I have to say?" said Van Helsing. "And then you will at least know the limit of my purpose. Shall I go on?"

"That's fair enough," broke in Morris.

After a pause Van Helsing went on, evidently with an effort, "Miss Lucy is dead, is it not so? Yes! Then there can be no wrong to her. But if she be not dead . . ."

Arthur jumped to his feet, "Good God!" he cried. "What do you mean? Has there been any mistake, has she been buried alive?" He groaned in anguish that not even hope could soften.

"I did not say she was alive, my child. I did not think it. I go no further than to say that she might be UnDead."

"UnDead! Not alive! What do you mean? Is this all a nightmare, or what is it?"

"There are mysteries which men can only guess at, which age by age they may solve only in part. Believe me, we are now on the verge of one. But I have not done. May I cut off the head of dead Miss Lucy?"

"Heavens and earth, no!" cried Arthur in a storm of passion. "Not for the wide world will I consent to any mutilation of her dead body. Dr. Van Helsing, you try me too far. What have I done to you that you should torture me so? What did that poor, sweet girl do that you should want to cast such dishonour on her grave? Are you mad, that you speak of such things, or am I mad to listen to them? Don't dare think more of such a desecration. I shall not give my consent to anything you do. I have a duty to do in protecting her grave from outrage, and by God, I shall do it!"

Van Helsing rose up from where he had all the time been seated, and said, gravely and sternly, "My Lord Godalming, I too, have a duty to do, a duty to others, a duty to you, a duty to the dead, and by God, I shall do it! All I ask you now is that you come with me, that you look and listen, and if when later I make the same request you do not be more eager for its fulfillment even than I am, then, I shall do my duty, whatever it may seem to me. And then, to follow your Lordship's wishes I shall hold myself at your disposal to render an account to you, when and where you will." His voice broke a little, and he went on with a voice full of pity.

"But I beseech you, do not go forth in anger with me. In a long life of acts which were often not pleasant to do, and which sometimes did wring my heart, I have never had so heavy a task as now. Believe me that if the time comes for you to change your mind towards me, one look from you will wipe away all this so sad hour, for I would do what a man can to save you from sorrow. Just think. For why should I give myself so much labor and so much of sorrow? I have come here from my own land to do what I can of good, at the first to please my friend John, and then to help a sweet young lady, whom too, I come to love. For her, I am ashamed to say so much, but I say it in kindness, I gave what you gave, the blood of my veins. I gave it, I who was not, like you, her lover, but only her physician and her friend. I gave her my nights and days, before death, after death, and if my death can do her good even now, when she is the dead UnDead, she shall have it freely." He said this with a very grave, sweet pride, and Arthur was much affected by it.

He took the old man's hand and said in a broken voice, "Oh, it is hard to think of it, and I cannot understand, but at least I shall go with you and wait."

It was just a quarter before twelve o'clock when we got into the churchyard over the low wall. The night was dark with occasional gleams of moonlight between the rents of the heavy clouds that scudded across the sky. We all kept somehow close together, with Van Helsing slightly in front as he led the way. When we had come close to the tomb I looked well at Arthur, for I feared the proximity to a place laden with so sorrowful a memory would upset him, but he bore himself well. I took it that the very mystery of the proceeding was in some way a counteractant to his grief. The Professor unlocked the door, and seeing a natural hesitation amongst us for various reasons, solved the difficulty by entering first himself. The rest of us followed, and he closed the door. He then lit a dark lantern and pointed to a coffin. Arthur stepped forward hesitatingly. Van Helsing said to me, "You were with me here yesterday. Was the body of Miss Lucy in that coffin?"

"It was."

The Professor turned to the rest saying, "You hear, and yet there is no one who does not believe with me.'

He took his screwdriver and again took off the lid of the coffin. Arthur looked on, very pale but silent. When the lid was removed he stepped forward. He evidently did not know that there was a leaden coffin, or at any rate, had not thought of it. When he saw the rent in the lead, the blood rushed to his face for an instant, but as quickly fell away again, so that he remained of a ghastly whiteness. He was still silent. Van Helsing forced back the leaden flange, and we all looked in and recoiled.

The coffin was empty!

For several minutes no one spoke a word. The silence was broken by Quincey Morris, "Professor, I answered for you. Your word is all I want. I wouldn't ask such a thing ordinarily, I wouldn't so dishonour you as to imply a doubt, but this racket goes a pile better than an honour or dishonour or fancy frills of any kind. Is this your doing? Honest Injun?"

"I swear to you by all that I hold sacred that I have not removed or touched her. What happened was this. Two nights ago my friend Seward and I came here, with good purpose, believe me. I opened that coffin, which was then sealed up, and we found it as now, empty. We then waited, and saw something white come through the trees. The next day we came here in daytime and she lay there. Did she not, friend John?"

"Yes."

"That night we were just in time. One more so small child was missing, and we find it, thank God, unharmed amongst the graves. Yesterday I came here before sundown, for at sundown the UnDead can move. I waited here all night till the sun rose, but I saw nothing. It was most probable that it was because I had laid over the clamps of those doors garlic, which the UnDead cannot bear, and other things which they shun. Last night there was no exodus, so tonight before the sundown I took away my garlic and other things. And so it is we find this coffin empty. But bear with me. So far there is much that is strange. Wait you with me outside, unseen and unheard, and things much stranger are yet to be. So," here he shut the dark slide of his lantern, "now to the outside." He opened the door, and we filed out, he coming last and locking the door behind him.

Oh! But it seemed fresh and pure in the night air after the terror of that vault. How sweet it was to see the clouds race by, and the passing gleams of the moonlight between the scudding clouds crossing and passing, like the gladness and sorrow of a man's life. How sweet it was to breathe the fresh air, that had no taint of death and decay. How humanizing to see the red lighting of the sky beyond the hill, and to hear far away the muffled roar that marks the life of a great city. Each in his own way was solemn and overcome. Arthur was silent, and was, I could see, striving to grasp the purpose and the inner meaning of the mystery. I was myself tolerably patient, and half inclined again to throw aside doubt and to accept Van Helsing's conclusions. Quincey Morris was phlegmatic in the way of a man who accepts all things, and accepts them in the spirit of cool bravery, with hazard of all he has at stake. Not being able to smoke, he cut himself a good-sized plug of tobacco and began to chew. As to Van Helsing, he was employed in a definite way. First he took from his bag a mass of what looked like thin, wafer-like biscuit, which was carefully rolled up in a white napkin. Next he took out a double handful of some whitish stuff, like dough or putty. He crumbled the wafer up fine, and opening the mouth of a wide necked phial, spread some red liquid over it;[158] he worked it into the mass between his hands. This he then took, and rolling it into thin strips, began to lay them into the crevices between the door and its setting in the tomb. I was somewhat puzzled at this, and being close, asked him what it was that he was doing. Arthur and Quincey drew near also, as they too were curious.

He answered, "I am closing the tomb so that the UnDead may not enter."

"And is that stuff you have there going to do it?"

"It is. It has worked before, once upon a time, to seal a tomb in Munich."

"What is that which you are using?" This time the question was by Arthur. Van Helsing reverently lifted his hat as he answered.

"The Host. I brought it from Amsterdam. I have an Indulgence."

It was an answer that appalled the most sceptical of us, and we felt individually that in the presence of such earnest purpose as the Professor's, a purpose which could thus use the to him most sacred of things, it was impossible to distrust. In respectful silence we took the places assigned to us close round the tomb, but hidden from the sight of any one approaching. I pitied the others, especially Arthur. I had myself been apprenticed by my former visits to this watching horror, and yet I, who had up to an hour ago repudiated the proofs, felt my heart sink within me. Never did tombs look so ghastly white. Never did cypress, or yew, or juniper so seem the embodiment of funeral gloom. Never did tree or grass wave or rustle so ominously. Never did bough creak so mysteriously, and never did the far-away howling of dogs send such a woeful presage through the night.

There was a long spell of silence, big, aching void, and then from the Professor a keen "S-s-s!" He pointed, and far down the avenue of yews we saw a white figure advance, a dim white figure, which held something dark at its breast. The figure stopped, and at the moment a ray of moonlight fell upon the masses of driving clouds, and showed in startling prominence a dark-haired woman, dressed in the cerements of the grave. We could not see the face, for it was bent down over what we saw to be a fair-haired child. There was a pause and a sharp little cry, such as a child gives in sleep, or a dog as it lies before the fire and dreams. We were starting forward, but the Professor's warning hand, seen by us as he stood behind a yew tree, kept us back. And then as we looked the white figure moved forwards again. It was now near enough for us to see clearly, and the moonlight still held. My own heart grew cold as ice, and I could hear the gasp of Arthur, as we recognized the features of Lucy Westenra. Lucy Westenra, but yet how changed. The sweetness was turned to adamantine, heartless cruelty, and the purity to voluptuous wantonness.

Van Helsing stepped out, and obedient to his gesture, we all advanced too. The four of us ranged in a line before the door of the tomb. Van Helsing raised his lantern and drew the slide. By the concentrated light that fell on Lucy's face we could see that the lips were crimson with fresh blood, and that the stream had trickled over her chin and stained the purity of her lawn death robe.

We shuddered with horror. I could see by the tremulous light that even Van Helsing's iron nerve had failed. Arthur was next to me, and if I had not seized his arm and held him up, he would have fallen.

When Lucy, I call the thing that was before us Lucy because it bore her shape, saw us she drew back with an angry snarl, such as a cat gives when taken unawares, then her eyes ranged over us. Lucy's eyes in form and colour, but Lucy's eyes unclean and full of hell fire, instead of the pure, gentle orbs we knew. At that moment the remnant of my love passed into hate and loathing. Had she then to be killed, I could have done it with savage delight. As she looked, her eyes blazed with unholy light, and the face became wreathed with a voluptuous smile. Oh, God, how it made me shudder to see it! With a careless motion, she flung to the ground, callous as a devil, the child that up to now she had clutched strenuously to her breast, growling over it as a dog growls over a bone. The child gave a sharp cry, and lay there moaning. There was a cold-bloodedness in the act which wrung a groan from Arthur. When she advanced to him with outstretched arms and a wanton smile he fell back and hid his face in his hands.

She still advanced, however, and with a languorous, voluptuous grace, said, "Come to me, Arthur. Leave these others and come to me. My arms are hungry for you. Come, and we can rest together. Come, my husband, come!"

There was something diabolically sweet in her tones, something of the tinkling of glass when struck, which rang through the brains even of us who heard the words addressed to another.

As for Arthur, he seemed under a spell, moving his hands from his face, he opened wide his arms. She was leaping for them, when Van Helsing sprang forward and held between them his little golden crucifix. She recoiled from it, and, with a suddenly distorted face, full of rage, dashed past him as if to enter the tomb.

When within a foot or two of the door, however, she stopped, as if arrested by some irresistible force. Then she turned, and her face was shown in the clear burst of moonlight and by the lamp, which had now no quiver from Van Helsing's nerves. Never did I see such baffled malice on a face, and never, I trust, shall such ever be seen again by mortal eyes. The beautiful colour became livid, the eyes seemed to throw out sparks of hell fire, the brows were wrinkled as though the folds of flesh were the coils of Medusa's snakes, and the lovely, blood-stained mouth grew to an open square, as in the passion masks of the Greeks and Japanese. If ever a face meant death, if looks could kill, we saw it at that moment.

And so for full half a minute, which seemed an eternity, she remained between the lifted crucifix and the sacred closing of her means of entry.

Van Helsing broke the silence by asking Arthur, "Answer me, oh my friend! Am I to proceed in my work?"

"Do as you will, friend. Do as you will. There can be no horror like this ever any more." And he groaned in spirit.

Quincey and I simultaneously moved towards him, and took his arms. We could hear the click of the closing lantern as Van Helsing held it down. Coming close to the tomb, he began to remove from the chinks some of the sacred emblem which he had placed there. We all looked on with horrified amazement as we saw, when he stood back, the woman, with a corporeal body as real at that moment as our own, pass through the interstice where scarce a knife blade could have gone. We all felt a glad sense of relief when we saw the Professor calmly restoring the strings of putty to the edges of the door.

When this was done, he lifted the child and said, "Come now, my friends. We can do no more till tomorrow. There is a funeral at noon, so here we shall all come before long after that. The friends of the dead will all be gone by two, and when the sexton locks the gate we shall remain. Then there is more to do, but not like this of tonight. As for this little one, he is not much harmed, and by tomorrow night he shall be well. We shall leave him where the police will find him, as on the other night, and then to home."

Coming close to Arthur, he said, "My friend Arthur, you have had a sore trial, but after, when you look back, you will see how it was necessary. You are now in the bitter waters, my child. By this time tomorrow you will, please God, have passed them, and have drunk of the sweet waters. So do not mourn over-much. Till then I shall not ask you to forgive me."

Arthur and Quincey came home with me, and we tried to cheer each other on the way. We had left behind the child in safety, and were tired. So we all slept with more or less reality of sleep.

Later—A little before twelve o'clock we three, Arthur, Quincey Morris, and myself, called for the Professor. It was odd to notice that by common consent we had all put on black clothes. Of course, Arthur wore black, for he was in deep mourning, but the rest of us wore it by instinct. We got to the graveyard by half-past one, and strolled about, keeping out of official observation, so that when the gravediggers had completed their task and the sexton under the belief that every one had gone, had locked the gate, we had the place all to ourselves. Van Helsing, instead of his little black bag, had with him a long leather one, something like a cricketing bag. It was manifestly of fair weight.

When we were alone and had heard the last of the footsteps die out up the road, we silently, and as if by ordered intention, followed the Professor to the tomb. He unlocked the door, and we entered, closing it behind us. Then he took from his bag the lantern, which he lit, and also two wax candles, which, when lighted, he stuck by melting their own ends, on other coffins, so that they might give light sufficient to work by. When he again lifted the lid off Lucy's coffin we all looked, Arthur trembling like an aspen, and saw that the corpse lay there in all its death beauty. But there was no love in my own heart, nothing but loathing for the foul Thing which had taken Lucy's shape without her soul. I could see even Arthur's face grow hard as he looked. Presently he said to Van Helsing, "Is this really Lucy's body, or only a demon in her shape?"

"It is her body, and yet not it. But wait a while, and you shall see her as she was, and is."

She seemed like a nightmare of Lucy as she lay there, the pointed teeth, the blood stained, voluptuous mouth, which made one shudder to see, the whole carnal and unspirited appearance, seeming like a devilish mockery of Lucy's sweet purity. Van Helsing, with his usual methodicalness, began taking the various contents from his bag and placing them ready for use. First he took out a soldering iron and some plumbing solder, and then a small oil lamp, which gave out, when lit in a corner of the tomb, gas which burned at a fierce heat with a blue flame, then his operating knives, which he placed to hand, and last a round wooden stake, some two and a half or three inches thick and about three feet long. One end of it was hardened by charring in the fire, and was sharpened to a fine point.

With this stake came a heavy hammer, such as in households is used in the coal cellar for breaking the lumps. To me, a doctor's preparations for work of any kind are stimulating and bracing, but the effect of these things on both Arthur and Quincey was to cause them a sort of consternation. They both, however, kept their courage, and remained silent and quiet.

When all was ready, Van Helsing said, "Before we do anything, let me tell you this. It is out of the lore and experience of the ancients and of all those who have studied the powers of the UnDead. When they become such, there comes with the change the curse of immortality. They cannot die, but must go on age after age adding new victims and multiplying the evils of the world. For all that die from the preying of the Undead become themselves Undead, and prey on their kind. And so the circle goes on ever widening, like as the ripples from a stone thrown in the water. Friend Arthur, if you had met that kiss which you know of before poor Lucy die, or again, last night when you open your arms to her, you would in time, when you had died, have become nosferatu, as they call it in Eastern Europe, and would for all time make more of those Un-Deads that so have filled us with horror. The career of this so unhappy dear lady is but just begun. Those children whose blood she sucked are not as yet so much the worse, but if she lives on, UnDead, more and more they lose their blood and by her power over them they come to her, and so she draw their blood with that so wicked mouth. But if she die in truth, then all cease. The tiny wounds of the throats disappear, and they go back to their play unknowing ever of what has been. But of the most blessed of all, when this now UnDead be made to rest as true dead, then the soul of the poor lady whom we love shall again be free. Instead of working wickedness by night and growing more debased in the assimilating of it by day, she shall take her place with the other Angels. So that, my friend, it will be a blessed hand for her that shall strike the blow that sets her free. To this I am willing, but is there none amongst us who has a better right? Will it be no joy to think of hereafter in the silence of the night when sleep is not, 'It was my hand that sent her to the stars. It was the hand of him that loved her best, the hand that of all she would herself have chosen, had it been to her to choose?' Tell me if there be such a one amongst us?"

We all looked at Arthur. He saw too, what we all did, the infinite kindness which suggested that his should be the hand which would restore Lucy to us as a holy, and not an unholy, memory. He stepped forward and said bravely, though his hand trembled, and his face was as pale as snow, "My true friend, from the bottom of my broken heart I thank you. Tell me what I am to do, and I shall not falter!"

Van Helsing laid a hand on his shoulder, and said, "Brave lad! A moment's courage, and it is done. This stake must be driven through her. It well be a fearful ordeal, be not deceived in that, but it will be only a short time, and you will then rejoice more than your pain was great. From this grim tomb you will emerge as though you tread on air. But you must not falter when once you have begun. Only think that we, your true friends, are round you, and that we pray for you all the time."

"Go on," said Arthur hoarsely. "Tell me what I am to do."

"Take this stake in your left hand, ready to place to the point over the heart, and the hammer in your right. Then when we begin our prayer for the dead, I shall read him, I have here the book, and the others shall follow, strike in God's name, that so all may be well with the dead that we love and that the UnDead pass away."

Arthur took the stake and the hammer, and when once his mind was set on action his hands never trembled nor even quivered. Van Helsing opened his missal and began to read, and Quincey and I followed as well as we could.

Arthur placed the point over the heart, and as I looked I could see its dint in the white flesh. Then he struck with all his might.

The thing in the coffin writhed, and a hideous, blood-curdling screech came from the opened red lips. The body shook and quivered and twisted in wild contortions. The sharp white teeth champed together till the lips were cut, and the mouth was smeared with a crimson foam. But Arthur never faltered. He looked like a figure of Thor as his untrembling arm rose and fell, driving deeper and deeper the mercy-bearing stake, whilst the blood from the pierced heart welled and spurted up around it. His face was set, and high duty seemed to shine through it. The sight of it gave us courage so that our voices seemed to ring through the little vault.

And then the writhing and quivering of the body became less, and the teeth ceased to champ, and the face to quiver. Finally it lay still. The terrible task was over.

The hammer fell from Arthur's hand. He reeled and would have fallen had we not caught him. The great drops of sweat sprang from his forehead, and his breath came in broken gasps. It had indeed been an awful strain on him—and on this of all nights, that which was to be their wedding night!—and had he not been forced to his task by more than human considerations he could never have gone through with it. For a few minutes we were so taken up with him that we did not look towards the coffin. When we did, however, a murmur of startled surprise ran from one to the other of us. We gazed so eagerly that Arthur rose, for he had been seated on the ground, and came and looked too, and then a glad strange light broke over his face and dispelled altogether the gloom of horror that lay upon it.

There, in the coffin lay no longer the foul Thing that we had so dreaded and grown to hate that the work of her destruction was yielded as a privilege to the one best entitled to it, but Lucy as we had seen her in life, with her face of unequalled sweetness and purity. True that there were there, as we had seen them in life, the traces of care and pain and waste. But these were all dear to us, for they marked her truth to what we knew. One and all we felt that the holy calm that lay like sunshine over the wasted face and form was only an earthly token and symbol of the calm that was to reign for ever.

Instinctively we all sank on our knees beside the coffin and sent forth our hearts in prayer. When we stood up, Van Helsing came and laid his hand on Arthur's shoulder, and said to him, "And now, Arthur my friend, dear lad, am I not forgiven?"

The reaction of the terrible strain came as he took the old man's hand in his, and raising it to his lips, pressed it, and said, "Forgiven! God bless you that you have given my dear one her soul again, and me peace." He put his hands on the Professor's shoulder, and laying his head on his breast, cried for a while silently, whilst we stood unmoving.

When he raised his head Van Helsing said to him, "And now, my child, you may kiss her. Kiss her dead lips if you will, as she would have you to, if for her to choose. For she is not a grinning devil now, not any more a foul Thing for all eternity. No longer she is the devil's UnDead. She is God's true dead, whose soul is with Him!"

Arthur bent and kissed her, and then we sent him and Quincey out of the tomb. The Professor and I sawed the top off the stake, leaving the point of it in the body. Then we cut off the head and filled the mouth with garlic. We soldered up the leaden coffin, screwed on the coffin lid, and gathering up our belongings, came away. When the Professor locked the door he gave the key to Arthur.

Outside the air was sweet, the sun shone, and the birds sang, and it seemed as if all nature were tuned to a different pitch. There was gladness and mirth and peace everywhere, for we were at rest ourselves on one account, and we were glad, though it was with a tempered joy.

Before we moved away Van Helsing said, "Now, my friends, one step of our work is done, one the most harrowing to ourselves. But there remains a greater task, to find out the author of all this our sorrow and to stamp him out. I have clues which we can follow, but it is a long task, and a difficult one, and there is danger in it, and pain. Shall you not all help me? We have learned to believe, all of us, is it not so? And since so, do we not see our duty? Yes! And do we not promise to go on to the bitter end?"

Each in turn, we took his hand, and the promise was made. Then said the Professor as we moved off, "Two nights hence you shall meet with me and dine together at seven of the clock with friend John. I shall entreat two others, two that you know not as yet, and I shall be ready to all our work show and our plans unfold. Friend John, you come with me home, for I have much to consult you about, and you can help me. Tonight I leave for Amsterdam, but shall return tomorrow night. And then begins our great quest. But first I shall have much to say, so that you may know what to do and to dread. Then our promise shall be made to each other anew. For there is a terrible task before us, and once our feet are on the ploughshare we must not draw back."

CHAPTER
TWENTY-FOUR[159]

Inspector Cotford's Case Notes

28 September—The maids of Hillingham, now under the employ of Arthur Holmwood (as the inheritor of the estate), proved even more enlightening than those of Ring. With regard to the topic of the Westenra ladies' illnesses and deaths, their four maids—who had clearly loved them both dearly—had much to say.

Their description of the symptoms present in Charlotte Westenra were nearly identical to those of the late Lord Godalming, down to the approximate five month duration and the nausea. Through a subtle line of questioning, one I am certain will not arouse their suspicions, I discovered that Mrs. Westenra's illness began shortly after Arthur Holmwood had begun courting Lucy Westenra.

Unlike her mother, Miss Lucy began her illness only within the last two months, upon her return from a holiday in Whitby. What's more, her symptoms were markedly different—weakness and lethargy during the day, and sleep-walking at night (a trait, they say, she inherited from her father, though she was thought to have outgrown it along with her childhood).

The maids confirmed that she was first treated by Dr. Seward (who, quite interestingly, they say proposed to her—and was turned down by her—on the very same day that Mr. Holmwood's own proposal was made and accepted). When his efforts to restore her failed, he called upon a "Dutchman" to handle her care. Of course I knew this to be Professor Van Helsing, from the brief encounter I had with Dr. Seward when here last.

Here the accounts of the Hillingham staff take a peculiar turn, yet each of the maids (who were questioned separately), though their stories varied here and there to a certain degree, all contain certain consistent pieces of disturbing information regarding the deaths of the Westenra ladies.

The maids attest that, sometime between the night of 17 September and the following morning, they were awoken by the sound of breaking glass and the howling of dogs outside (and later, upon cleaning up the mess, they found that some of the shards of broken glass were flecked with blood and bits of grey fur). When the maids arrived at the young lady's room, they heard her call out to them, so they opened the door, and found the dead body of the mother laying atop her. Once they had recovered somewhat from the shock of such a sight, the maids lifted the body off of Miss Lucy, placed it upon the bed, and covered it with a sheet, for its face was drawn and white and wide-eyed with terror. Miss Lucy then directed them to go downstairs and have a glass of wine to calm their nerves; they did so, and fell asleep from it at once. Three of four maids were awoken in the morning by Dr. Seward (who, along with Professor Van Helsing, had apparently broken into the house through a kitchen window); they made mention that Dr. Seward told them their wine had been doctored with a heavy amount of laudanum, though each of them insisted that none of them had been the one to add it to their drinks.

As for the fourth girl, she added that she has suffered from queer dreams. She told me of how, in her dreams, all was dark, save for two burning red eyes, and a deep voice which spoke from behind the eyes, though she could not recall precisely what the voice was instructing her to do, except that it had something to do with an invitation and the doctored wine[160]. As she is engaged to the man of the Westenras' undertaker[161], I can't help but think the morbid qualities which undoubtedly surrounded her fiancé played a role in this fanciful account.

The maids then, upon the direction of Dr. Seward, stoked up the fire and ran a hot bath, into which the doctors placed Miss Lucy, who looked to the girls as one already dead. While the doctors attended to Lucy, an American came to the house with a message from Arthur Holmwood; the American's name was Quincey P. Morris (or so his card said when presented at the door), who had been to Hillingham before, when had he proposed to Miss Lucy (yet another proposal, and one which was, like Dr. Seward's, given and rejected on the same day as that of Holmwood). But with regard to the doctors, one of the maids shyly confessed that she had ventured to look through a keyhole at what was afoot, for there were moans and groans and she feared that the men might have been taking advantage of their mistress. She described, in a shuddering way, how she saw the doctors pump blood out of the American though a tube and put it into Lucy's arm.

A transfusion of blood! Nearly all such attempts at restoring health ended in the death of the patient; either the doctors were mad, or far more advanced in their knowledge than all others. It would appear the latter, for apparently Miss

Lucy thence awoke and was able to cling to life for two more days. During that
span, Holmwood too came to the house, and the men each took their turn sitting
with her, as if to guard her from something. In the end, though, Miss Lucy joined
her mother in death.

When I asked each of them the frank question of whether or not they thought
foul play might be involved, none of them immediately said "no," though they
were reluctant to voice an affirmative opinion either. I asked if they thought any
of this mistress' three suitors might be to blame, they seemed horrified at the
thought, and assured me that all of their intentions seemed most honorable. "If
anyone is to blame," one said, "'tis that queer Dutchman." As for their new master,
the young Holmwood had doted over his fiancee and her mother (when he was
not away attending to his own father), and brought over imported tea from the
East now and again for Mrs. Westenra.

Again the tea. I asked if they had any of it left, and they went to search.
Before too long one of the maids returned with a small package. She explained
most of it had been thrown out, but this had apparently be set aside and forgotten
about until now. Upon opening the package, I found it to contain dried flowers.
Most of the petals and leaves were already crumbled to pieces, though some of
the flowers were still intact enough for me to see they were the same as were
growing at Ring. I resealed the package and slipped it into my pocket to take
back to the Yard. I noticed, as I did so, my fingertips seemed numb from where
I had touched the dried herbs.

Later—As I feared, the purple flowers are poisonous, or at least potentially so,
containing, as they do, *aconite*. Their familiarity to me when I first saw them was
due to their similarity to *aconitum napellus*, the common monkshood, though
with their variant shape and colouring, I did not recognize them at once. Having
consulted a variety of botanical journals, indexes of poisons, and pharmacopeias,
I have concluded that this particular variety of monkshood is called Carpathian
Wolfsbane. Little is known about this variety, save for an anecdotal gypsy poem
that had made its way into one of the articles:

> "Even those who are pure of heart,
> and say their prayers at night,
> can become a wolf, when the wolfsbane blooms
> and the moon is full and bright."

Certainly, the herb's use as a poison is not a foregone conclusion, for it is quite
possible that in small doses this wolfsbane may have medicinal qualities, just as
the common monkshood does (indeed, many things that are called poison are
still medicine in smaller doses). However, their involvement in the death of Lord

Godalming is at least possible, for the effects of ingesting this herb (even if the dose is not lethal) are constricted pupils and nausea. If too much of the herb is ingested at once, or for too long a time, death occurs from a weakening of the heart . . .

Two identical telegrams from Kate Reed, one to Lucy Westenra (unopened by her), one to Mina "Murray" (delivered late to Mina Harker's new Exeter address)

22 September

Good to see you in Whitby. Could you tell me if you noticed something unusual after the shipwreck? Reason for asking difficult to explain, but urgent.

—Katherine Reed

Telegram, Mina Harker to Kate Reed

28 September

Please come to my new home at 58 Cathedral Place, Exeter, at your earliest convenience. We may have much to discuss.

—Wilhelmina Harker

Mina Harker's Journal

29 September—I write this on the train to Paddington Station. Kate Reed, my old friend and pupil from school, is with me. She had apparently sent me a telegram nearly a week ago, but not knowing I had married and moved to Exeter, she had it sent to "Mina Murray" at my old address (needless to say, it did not arrive here until yesterday). She asked about unusual happenings after the *Demeter* came ashore in Whitby. She was not specific, which is rather unlike her, but only said that her "reason for asking is difficult to explain." As I read the note, the memory suddenly came to me about that day in Piccadilly on Thursday last, when Jonathan felt certain he had seen Count Dracula watching Kate. I had thought nothing of any danger to her at the time, for I had yet to read my dear husband's journal; nor did I think of any danger later, for the tall bearded man we saw did not match at all the description of the aged and clean-shaven Count in the journal. But with all Jonathan has been through, surely if anyone could recognize the Count it would be him! So could not that man have somehow been the Count in disguise? And had the dark man not been staring at Kate in that cruel and hungry manner?

Suddenly fearing for Kate, I replied to her by telegram and asked her to see me at once. Kate looked as beautiful as ever when Mary showed her in, but there was a wearied look in her eyes that I had become all too familiar with as of late.

"Will Francis not be joining us?" I asked conversationally as we sat down to tea.

"No, I'm afraid he no longer counts me as a friend. Which is part of the reason I wanted to talk with you and Lucy." Lucy! Poor Kate, she must still not know about our poor school friend. But it was clear she had much to say, so I held my tongue and waited for an opportune moment to break the news to her. "Mina," she continued, "you know I'm a headstrong woman. You've even said so yourself more than once. And I know we have different opinions about a woman's place in society, and we have, from time to time, argued with passion and intelligence on that topic. But, in our years together at the school, have you ever thought of me as . . . well, as irrational? Or superstitious? Or prone to flights of fancy?"

"Goodness no! Of all the girls, you were perhaps the farthest from such things." I kept my voice as lighthearted as I could, but a chill ran up my spine as she asked me this, for I was certain it would be the prelude to some new account of horror.

"Then please believe me, Mina, when I say that there was something terrible aboard that ship that wrecked at Whitby, and that this thing—this evil—is among us now!" There was a look of fear in her eyes—in eyes that I have only ever known to show intelligence and resolution—and I knew at that moment she spoke the truth, and that our troubles were somehow one and the same.

"I believe you, Kate. Oh, how I wish I didn't have cause to believe you, but I do have cause, so I know you tell the truth!"

"Oh, thank you Mina! But, by what cause do you believe me?" she asked in an eager tone that blended relief and dread. So I retrieved for her one of the manuscripts I had typed out and compiled of Jonathan's and my own journals. I sat quietly beside her as she read carefully through each page. I watched her face grow pale more than once, especially when reading the entry about our seeing that strange fellow watching Kate at Piccadilly, and again on the topic of our home coming to find Van Helsing's telegram about Lucy's death. I had Mary bring us some brandy, which Kate sipped from time to time. At last she finished, and sank back in mental and emotional exhaustion. After a bit more brandy, some of the colour returned to her face.

"So Lucy is dead . . ." she muttered the revelation to no one in particular. "And the Count is to blame."

"It would seem so," was all I could bring myself to say.

"But Mina, the man I've seen, whom I have since come to believe is the same evil which came first to Whitby and then to London, calls himself 'DeVille,' not 'Dracula.' And he looks different than the Count your fiancé—no, your husband!—encountered in Transylvania. Could he somehow be able to change his form, to grow older or younger at will? Or could . . . could there be two of them?" Kate whispered this last, as if unwilling to hear her own question.

"Kate, you said you had come in part because of Francis. What has he to do with all of this?"

"I fear his mind has become fixated on the Count. He saw him first at Whitby, and attempted to do some sketches and paintings of the man, as he often did with strangers he found interesting. But he was not able to recreate his likeness, and the more he tried, the worse his attempts became. I read in his journal that he even followed the Count one night and . . ." here she halted her speech abruptly, and grew quite pale.

"Kate? Kate, what is it? Tell me!" I implored her

"Mina . . . oh, Mina, I . . . I think he saw the Count with Lucy, the night you first found her on the seat. He wrote of such a scene in his journal."

"And he never said anything about it?" I breathed, stunned.

"No, not a word. I only found his journal after he left me."

"Left you? Why would he do such a thing?"

"Again, the Count is to blame. He moved into a vacant home across from us. It was as if he were following us, or rather, following Francis, as if he somehow knew of poor him and his frustrated desire to paint his portrait. I recognized him at once, and couldn't help but take the opportunity of inviting him over for dinner. I thought Francis would be pleased, which indeed he was, but as time passed he grew more and more obsessed with the Count. I felt him being pulled away from me, so I . . . I . . . Oh, Mina, I know how you will scold me for my impropriety, you who tried to impart on all of we girls a sense of decorum. But I felt it necessary at the time, so I . . . I asked him to be my husband."

"Kate! You didn't!"

"I did. Oh, I did. But he didn't want anything to do with it. So he left me and our home—only my home, now—and to where I know not. I have come to realize that I never loved him. Oh, I loved him as a friend, a companion from childhood who always let me say and do as I pleased without reprisal, but not the true love that a woman should have for a husband. Now I am glad, to a degree, that he turned my offer down, lest we both have been bound to one another by law but not by love. Still, even if he was not my true love, he was my true friend, and I would like him to be my true friend once more. For the sake of that friendship that once was, and may still one day be again, I decided I would be of some help to him in some way. In my naivety, I thought the best solution were for him to be over and done with painting the Count. So I secretly photographed our new neighbor, so I could give the picture to Francis to work from. But the picture turned out . . . well here, look for yourself."

Kate had brought with her the sketch book, from which she pulled out a photograph. When she handed it to me I almost dropped it in shock. The street and sidewalk and buildings were in clear focus, as was a wagon full of boxes and the driver, but the figure in the center of the picture was horribly distorted, as if being viewed through water. I could tell he was a tall man dressed in black, though the details were blurred at the edges. The skin of the hands and face appeared to be pale and rotten. And what's more, this blotched skin was transparent—not the kind of transparency that comes from too much movement during the photography, but rather the skin itself was able to be seen through right to the bone. And even the bones and clothes appeared not quite solid, for I was sure I could just barely make out a bit of the background through the figure.

"I've enlisted the aid of a gentleman well versed in the occult to help me deal with this man—the creature—and free Francis from whatever control it has over him."

"We have come upon like help as well, though he sought us out, rather than we him. Please, come with me to meet Professor Van Helsing, and tell him your story as you told it to me. If our troubles are indeed interwoven, I think we can be of great help to one another."

Kate agreed, and we made plans to set off at once. She was quite tired, and has slept most of the way beside me as I have written in my journal. I have thought long on her words, and upon one comment in particular . . . "could there be two of them?" The description of the bearded coachman who brought Jonathan to the castle matched a man we saw in Piccadilly, but neither was the same Count as the aged lord of Castle Dracula. Yet Jonathan sensed the Count, or at least something of him, in the younger man we saw in London. The thought of *two* such creatures now lurking among London's teeming millions was staggering. And if there were two that we were only now aware of, how many more might there be? Or how many yet to come? What plans might they have for us? If anyone can sort it out, it will be the Professor.

Poor Kate. Even if she never truly loved Francis, she at least held him to be a dear friend. And now, to have him in thrall to the Count, whether by his own choice or through coercion . . . I can hardly think of what it must be like to be the servant of such a creature. We can only hope and pray that it is not too late for him.

Cutting from *The Evening News*, 1 October[162]

THE WHITECHAPEL HORRORS

The East-end fiend is still abroad, and two other victims have become his prey. On Sunday morning a woman was found with her throat cut and her body partially mutilated in a court in Berner-street, Whitechapel, close by the International Club situated in that locality. The discovery seems to have been made at one in the morning by Mr. Lewis Diemschitz, the steward of the club. Another member of the club, Mr. Morris Eagle, had passed through the court at twenty minutes to one, and had not seen anything unusual near the premises. Even if it was too dark to see the body of this woman it is impossible to suppose that Morris Eagle would not have tripped over it had it been there when he went into the club. The inference is therefore this: if the woman was murdered and mutilated where she was found, the deed was done in the short period of twenty minutes—the deed was done in the time which the police surgeon said a medical expert would take to do it. The residents in the court knew nothing about the murder. Neither they nor the people in the club heard or had seen anything that led them to suspect that foul play was going on around them. About three-quarters of an hour after this corpse was found, another was discovered in Mitre-square, Aldgate. It was that of a woman with her throat cut, but in her case the inevitable abdominal mutilation had been accomplished. A watchman was on duty in a counting-house in the square at the time the assassin was operating. Firemen were also on duty at a station close by. Yet nobody heard or saw anything likely to rouse suspicion. The silence and secrecy in which the atrocities were perpetrated wrap them in an impenetrable veil of mystery for the moment. As in former cases the murderer seems to have been almost miraculously successful in securing his retreat. His success in this respect seems to indicate a wonderful power of combination and organisation—an amazing gift for calculating the chances against the success of his schemes or purposes. In fact, the similarity of the murders leads to the conclusion that they have been committed by the one man or the one gang. The worst of it is that we do not know what a "gang" may mean. It might mean an organisation of great extent, or only the partnership between a criminal and his "pal." Recent events seem to suggest that there is more than one individual in the horrid business.

Note left on the desk of Inspector Cotford

28 September

Inspector Cotford,

I dutifully followed Arthur Holmwood as you requested. Last night he left Ringwood and went straight away to the Berkely Hotel. Shortly thereafter he left with three men—an older gentleman who was carrying a little black doctor's bag, and two men of the suspect's approximate age (one seemed to me to be American, given his manner of dress). I followed them for a time, but lost them in the neighborhood of Hampstead. After a time, I caught sight of them again, they had with them a small fair-haired body that was seemingly asleep, being carried in the arms of the American. I followed them to the Heath, where they left the child in plain view before hurrying away.

Please pardon my actions, Inspector, but here I abandoned my assignment to see about the child, lest he die without any care. Thankfully, the boy seemed relatively unharmed, save for two small punctures in his neck that were already sealing closed. I quickly had him taken to North Hospital, where he is now under the care of Dr. Vincent, who has been put in charge of the other such children found near Hampstead Heath.

I returned to Berkely Hotel in time to see Arthur Holmwood leave with the two younger gentlemen (I would assume the older man remained at the hotel, but did not have the opportunity to confirm that assumption). The three men made the journey to Purfleet, to the lunatic asylum there.

The following morning the three men, dressed all in black, returned to the hotel, where they met with the older gentleman, also in black, and the four of them made their way toward Hampstead. I was able to stay with them this time, and watched as they made their way into the graveyard at Kingstead. It was around noon when they entered with other mourners, but stayed behind and well hidden until after the funeral was completed and everyone had gone. I watched them proceed from there to the Westenra tomb. Once there, the older gentleman removed some sort of white putty from the crack around the door, after which he unlocked the door and they all proceeded inside.

I crept closer, and could hear some sort of singing or chanting coming from within. Suddenly there came a loud knocking noise that repeated itself several times, and a hideous screech that chilled me to the bone. Before long it was all over. I heard one of the men—Holmwood, I believe—exclaim "God bless you that you have given my dear one her soul again, and me peace." I hid as two of the men—Holmwood and the American—came out of the tomb. Both were pale and strained, and Holmwood looked as if he had been crying. They waited as other sounds came from within: the sawing of wood, followed by a wet, cutting sound. Eventually the other two came out of the tomb, locked it, and all four left together.

Before they left the graveyard, the older gentleman said, as best as I can recall, "Now, my friends, one step of our work is done, one the most harrowing to ourselves. But there remains a greater task, to find out the author of all this our sorrow and to stamp him out. I have clues which we can follow, but it is a long task, and a difficult one, and there is danger in it, and pain. Shall you not all help me? We have learned to believe, all of us, is it not so? And since so, do we not see our duty? Yes! And do we not promise to go on to the bitter end?" Holmwood and the other two men agreed to this task, whatever it may be, and the elder continued "Two nights hence you shall meet with me and dine together at seven of the clock with friend John. I shall entreat two others, two that you know not as yet, and I shall be ready to all our work show and our plans unfold. Friend John, you come with me home, for I have much to consult you about, and you can help me. Tonight I leave for Amsterdam, but shall return tomorrow night. And then begins our great quest. But first I shall have much to say, so that you may know what to do and to dread. Then our promise shall be made to each other anew. For there is a terrible task before us, and once our feet are on the ploughshare we must not draw back."

I trust this has proven useful to you, Inspector. Feel free to call upon me again if needs be; as always, it is an honor and a pleasure to work under you.

Believe me,

Johnny Wright[163]

CHAPTER TWENTY-FIVE[164]

Dr. Seward's Case-Book

29 September—When we arrived at the Berkely Hotel, Van Helsing found a telegram waiting for him.

> "Am coming up by train with a friend. Jonathan at Whitby. Important news.
>
> —Mina Harker."

The Professor was delighted. "Ah, that wonderful Madam Mina," he said, "pearl among women! She arrive, but I cannot stay. She must go to your house, friend John. You must meet her at the station. Telegraph her en route so that she may be prepared. Watch what you say, until you know who this 'friend' of hers is and what he or she may already know of us."

When the wire was dispatched he had a cup of tea. Over it he told me of a diary kept by Jonathan Harker when abroad, and gave me a typewritten copy of it, as also of Mrs. Harker's diary at Whitby. "Take these," he said, "and study them well. When I have returned you will be master of all the facts, and we can then better enter on our inquisition. Keep them safe, for there is in them much of treasure. You will need all your faith, even you who have had such an experience as that of today. What is here told," he laid his hand heavily and gravely on the packet of papers as he spoke, "may be the beginning of the end to you and me and many another, or it may sound the knell of the UnDead who walk the earth. Read all, I pray you, with the open mind, and if you can add in any way to the story here told do so, for it is all important. You have kept a diary of all these so strange things, is it not so? Yes! Then we shall go through all these together when we meet." He then made ready for his departure and shortly drove off to Liverpool Street. I took my way to Paddington, where I arrived about fifteen minutes before the train came in.

The crowd melted away, after the bustling fashion common to arrival platforms, and I was beginning to feel uneasy, lest I might miss my guests, when to my surprise I caught sight of Kate, who was accompanied by a sweet-faced, dainty looking girl who stepped up to me. After a quick glance, she said, before Kate could introduce us, "Dr. Seward, is it not?"

"And you are Mrs. Harker!" I answered at once, whereupon she held out her hand.

"I knew you from the description of poor dear Lucy, but . . ." She stopped suddenly, and a quick blush overspread her face. The blush that rose to my own cheeks somehow set us both at ease, for it was a tacit answer to her own.

"Dr. Seward, this is Katherine Reed," Mrs. Harker said with a gesture toward Kate. It was clear she did not know of our prior relationship. Kate simply smiled at me and, with a good deal of amusement in her voice, said "Yes, I believe we've met before."

After the three of us exchanged a few words of pleasantries, I got their luggage, which included a typewriter, and we took the Underground to Fenchurch Street, after I had sent a wire to my housekeeper to have a sitting room and two bedrooms prepared at once for Mrs. Harker and Kate.

In due time we arrived. The women knew, of course, that the place was a lunatic asylum, but I could see that Mrs. Harker was unable to repress a shudder when we entered. Unaccountably, I was quite pleased to see that Kate showed far less concern over the surroundings as when she was here last autumn.

Mrs. Harker told me that, if they might, they would come presently to my study, as they had much to say. So here I am finishing my entry in my phonograph diary whilst I await them. As yet I have not had the chance of looking at the papers which Van Helsing left with me, though they lie open before me. I must get the two women interested in something, so that I may have an opportunity of reading them. They do not know how precious time is, or what a task we have in hand. I must be careful not to frighten them. Here they are!

Mina Harker's Journal

29 September—After I had tidied myself, I went down with Kate to Dr. Seward's study. At the door I paused a moment, for I thought I heard him talking with some one. As, however, he had pressed us to be quick, I knocked at the door, and on his calling out, "Come in," we entered.

To my intense surprise, there was no one with him. He was quite alone, and on the table opposite him was what I knew at once from the description to be a phonograph. I had never seen one, and was much interested.

"I hope we did not keep you waiting," I said, "but we stayed at the door as we heard you talking, and thought there was someone with you."

"Oh," he replied with a smile, "I was only entering my diary."

"Your diary?" Kate asked him in surprise.

"Yes," he answered. "I keep it in this." As he spoke he laid his hand on the phonograph.

I felt quite excited over it, and blurted out, "Why, this beats even shorthand! May I hear it say something?"

"Certainly," he replied with alacrity, and stood up to put it in train for speaking. Then he paused, and a troubled look overspread his face.

"The fact is," he began awkwardly, "I only keep my diary in it, and as it is entirely, almost entirely, about my cases it may be awkward, that is, I mean . . ." He stopped, and I tried to help him out of his embarrassment.

"You helped to attend dear Lucy at the end. Let Kate and I hear how she died, for all that we know of her, we shall be very grateful. She was very, very dear to us."

To my surprise, he answered, with a horrorstruck look in his face, "Tell you of her death? Not for the wide world!"

"Why not?" Kate asked boldly, in a tone that somehow blended both familiarity and annoyance with regard to the doctor, and perhaps even a bit of fright as well over what had truly befallen poor Lucy. I too felt as if some grave, terrible feeling was coming over me.

Again he paused, and I could see that he was trying to invent an excuse. At length, he stammered out, "You see, I do not know how to pick out any particular part of the diary."

Even while he was speaking an idea dawned upon him, and he said with unconscious simplicity, in a different voice, and with the naivete of a child, "that's quite true, upon my honour. Honest Indian!"

Kate and I could not but smile, at which he grimaced. "I gave myself away that time!" he said. "But do you know that, although I have kept the diary for months past, it never once struck me how I was going to find any particular part of it in case I wanted to look it up?"

By this time my mind was made up that the diary of a doctor who attended Lucy might have something to add to the sum of our knowledge of that terrible Being, and I said boldly, "Then, Dr. Seward, you had better let me copy it out for you on my typewriter."

He grew to a positively deathly pallor as he said, "No! No! No! For all the world. I wouldn't let you know that terrible story!"

Then it was terrible. My intuition was right! For a moment, I thought, and as my eyes ranged the room, unconsciously looking for something or some opportunity to aid me, they lit on a great batch of typewriting on the table. His eyes caught the look in mine, and without his thinking, followed their direction. As they saw the parcel he realised my meaning.

"You do not know me," I said. "When you have read those papers, my own diary and my husband's also, which I have typed, you will know me better. I have not faltered in giving every thought of my own heart in this cause. But, of course, you do not know me, yet, and I must not expect you to trust me so far."

He is certainly a man of noble nature. Poor dear Lucy was right about him. He stood up and opened a large drawer, in which were arranged in order a number of hollow cylinders of metal covered with dark wax, and said,

"You are quite right. I did not trust you because I did not know you. But I know you now, and let me say that I should have known you long ago. I know that Lucy told you of me. She told me of you too. May I make the only atonement in my power? Take the cylinders and hear them. The first half-dozen of them are personal to me, and they will not horrify you. Then you will know me better. Dinner will by then be ready. In the meantime I shall read over some of these documents, and shall be better able to understand certain things."

He carried the phonograph himself up to our sitting room and adjusted it for me. Now Kate and I shall learn something pleasant, I am sure. For it will tell us the other side of a true love episode of which I know one side already.

Dr. Seward's Case-Book

29 September—I was so absorbed in that wonderful diary of Jonathan Harker and that other of his wife that I let the time run on without thinking. Mrs. Harker and Kate were not down when the maid came to announce dinner, so I said, "They are possibly tired. Let dinner wait an hour," and I went on with my work. I had just finished Mrs. Harker's diary, when they came in. Though Kate seemed quite stalwart—perhaps overly so, as if to hide her true emotions—Mrs. Harker looked sweetly pretty, but very sad, and her eyes were flushed with crying. This somehow moved me much. Of late I have had cause for tears, God knows! But the relief of them was denied me, and now the sight of those sweet eyes, brightened by recent tears, went straight to my heart. So I said as gently as I could, "I greatly fear I have distressed you."

"Oh, no, not distressed me," she replied. "But I have been more touched than I can say by your grief. That is a wonderful machine, but it is cruelly true. It told us, in its very tones, the anguish of your heart. It was like a soul crying out to Almighty God. No one must hear them spoken ever again! See, I have tried to be useful. I have copied out the words on my typewriter, and none other need now hear your heart beat, as I did."

"No one need ever know, shall ever know," I said in a low voice. She laid her hand on mine and said very gravely, "Ah, but they must!"

"Must! but why?" I asked.

"Because it is a part of the terrible story, a part of poor Lucy's death and all that led to it. Because in the struggle which we have before us to rid the earth of this terrible monster we must have all the knowledge and all the help which we can get. I think that the cylinders which you gave me contained more than you intended me to know. But I can see that there are in your record many lights to this dark mystery. You will let me help, will you not?

"We know all up to a certain point, and I see already, though your diary only took us to 7 September, how poor Lucy was beset, and how her terrible doom was being wrought out. Jonathan and I have been working day and night since Professor Van Helsing saw us. He is gone to Whitby to get more information, and he will be here tomorrow to help us. And Kate is plagued with dangers and woes that are somehow a part of our own. We need have no secrets amongst us. Working together and with absolute trust, we can surely be stronger than if some of us were in the dark."

She looked at me so appealingly, and at the same time manifested such courage and resolution in her bearing, that I gave in at once to her wishes. "You shall," I said, "do as you like in the matter. God forgive me if I do wrong! There are terrible things yet to learn of. But if you have so far traveled on the road to poor Lucy's death, you will not be content, I know, to remain in the dark. Nay, the end, the very end, may give you a gleam of peace. Come, there is dinner. We must keep one another strong for what is before us. We have a cruel and dreadful task. When you have eaten you shall learn the rest, and I shall answer any questions you ask, if there be anything which you do not understand, though it was apparent to us who were present."

Mina Harker's Journal

29 September—After dinner, I came with Dr. Seward to his study, where I waited for him to bring back the phonograph from my room. Kate and I took a chair, and he arranged the phonograph so that we could touch it without getting up, and showed us how to stop it in case we should want to pause. Then he very thoughtfully took a chair and began to read with his back to us, so that we might be as free as possible to listen and understand. And so we began . . .

When the terrible story of Lucy's death, and all that followed, was done, Kate and I lay back in our chairs powerless. Fortunately neither of us is of a fainting disposition. When Dr. Seward saw us he jumped up with a horrified exclamation, and hurriedly taking a case bottle from the cupboard, gave us some brandy, which in a few minutes somewhat restored us.

My brain was all in a whirl, and only that there came through all the multitude of horrors, the holy ray of light that my dear Lucy was at last at peace, I do not think I could have borne it without making a scene. It is all so wild and mysterious, and strange that if I had not known Jonathan's experience in Transylvania, or had not seen Kate's photograph of the Count, I could not have believed. As it was, I didn't know what to believe, and so got out of my difficulty by attending to something else. I took the cover off my typewriter, and said to Dr. Seward,

"Let me write this all out now. We must be ready for Dr. Van Helsing when he comes. I have sent a telegram to Jonathan to come on here when he arrives in London from Whitby. In this matter dates are everything, and I think that if we get all of our material ready, and have every item put in chronological order, we shall have done much. You tell me that Lord Godalming and Mr. Morris are coming too. Let us be able to tell them when they come."

Dr. Seward agreed, and accordingly set the phonograph at a slow pace, and while Kate had a long talk with the doctor, I began to typewrite from the beginning of the seventeenth cylinder. I used manifold, and so took three copies of the diary, just as I had done with the rest. Dr. Seward finished his conversation with Kate; she excused herself to attend to an errand, while he went about his work of going his round of the patients. But when he had finished he came back and sat near me, reading, so that I did not feel too lonely whilst I worked. How good and thoughtful he is. The world seems full of good men, even if there are monsters in it.

It was late when I got through. By then Kate had returned, and when she saw that I had finished my work, she explained that she had asked our host if she might telegram her acquaintance, Mr. Singleton, whom she had enlisted in her own struggles with the Count. He consented, and she had wired for the gentleman to come tomorrow.

Before we left him for the night, I remembered what Jonathan put in his diary of the Professor's perturbation at reading something in an evening paper at the station at Exeter, so, seeing that Dr. Seward keeps his newspapers, I borrowed the files of 'The Westminster Gazette' and 'The Pall Mall Gazette' and took them to my room. I remember how much the 'Dailygraph' and 'The Whitby Gazette,' of which I had made cuttings, had helped us to understand the terrible events at Whitby when Count Dracula landed, so I shall look through the evening papers since then, and perhaps I shall get some new light. I am not sleepy, and the work will help to keep me quiet.

Dr. Seward's Case-Book

30 September—Mr. Harker arrived at nine o'clock. He got his wife's wire just before starting. He is uncommonly clever, if one can judge from his face, and full of energy. If this journal be true, and judging by one's own wonderful experiences, it must be, he is also a man of great nerve. That going down to the vault a second time was a remarkable piece of daring. After reading his account of it I was prepared to meet a good specimen of manhood, but hardly the quiet, businesslike gentleman who came here today.

Later—After lunch Harker and his wife went back to their own room with Kate, and as I passed a while ago I heard the click of the typewriter. They are hard at it. Mrs. Harker says that they are knitting together in chronological order every scrap of evidence they have. Harker has got the letters between the consignee of the boxes at Whitby and the carriers in London who took charge of them. He is now reading his wife's transcript of my diary. I wonder what they make out of it. Here he is . . .

Strange that it never struck me that the very next house might be the Count's hiding place! Goodness knows that we had enough clues from the conduct of the patient Renfield! The bundle of letters relating to the purchase of the house were with the transcript. Oh, if we had only had them earlier we might have saved poor Lucy! Stop! That way madness lies!

Harker has gone back, and is again collecting material. Kate too, has left to acquire some papers of her own. As always, I find Kate to be a fascinating woman, and quite unlike any other I have met. She is not one to play coy games or disguise her thoughts and feelings, as other women are wont, but is bold and forthright in a man-like sort of way. I would imagine she still holds firm to the "New Woman" mentality that is becoming popular throughout London. I fear they will have a hard time of it, these "New Women," for they fail to realize that the brains and humours of men and women function in different manners; a woman cannot think and feel and act as a man, at least not without driving herself—or her society—mad in the process. But still they try, and for her part Kate seems to have taken upon herself many of the finer masculine qualities of the heart and mind which she seems to covet, though I believe there is far more woman left in her than even she realizes.

But I digress. Both Kate and Mrs. Harker should return with their respective documents shortly, and Mrs. Harker says that by dinner time they will be able to show a whole connected narrative. She thinks that in the meantime I should see my "fly-man," as hitherto he has been a sort of index to the coming and going of the Count. I hardly see this yet, but when I get at the dates I suppose I shall. What a good thing that Mrs. Harker put my cylinders into type! We never could have found the dates otherwise.

I found Renfield sitting placidly in his room with his hands folded, smiling benignly. At the moment he seemed as sane as any one I ever saw. I sat down and talked with him on a lot of subjects, all of which he treated naturally. He then, of his own accord, spoke of going home, a subject he has never mentioned to my knowledge during his sojourn here. In fact, he spoke quite confidently of getting his discharge at once. I believe that, had I not had the chat with Harker and read the letters and the dates of his outbursts, I should have been prepared to sign for him after a brief time of observation. As it is, I am darkly suspicious. All those out-breaks were in some way linked with the proximity of the Count. What then does this absolute content mean? Can it be that his instinct is satisfied as to the vampire's ultimate triumph? Stay. He is himself zoophagous, and in his wild ravings outside the chapel door of the deserted house he always spoke of 'master.' This all seems confirmation of our idea. However, after a while I came away. My friend is just a little too sane at present to make it safe to probe him too deep with questions. He might begin to think, and then . . . So I came away. I mistrust these quiet moods of his, so I have given the attendant a hint to look closely after him, and to have a strait waistcoat ready in case of need.

Jonathan Harker's Journal

29 September, in train to London—When I received Mr. Billington's courteous message that he would give me any information in his power I thought it best to go down to Whitby and make, on the spot, such inquiries as I wanted. It was now my object to trace that horrid cargo of the Count's to its place in London. Later, we may be able to deal with it. Billington junior, a nice lad, met me at the station, and brought me to his father's house, where they had decided that I must spend the night. They are hospitable, with true Yorkshire hospitality, give a guest everything and leave him to do as he likes. They all knew that I was busy, and that my stay was short, and Mr. Billington had ready in his office all the papers concerning the consignment of boxes. It gave me almost a turn to see again one of the letters which I had seen on the Count's table before I knew of his diabolical plans. Everything had been carefully thought out, and done systematically and with precision. He seemed to have been prepared for every obstacle which might be placed by accident in the way of his intentions being carried out. To use an Americanism, he had 'taken no chances,' and the absolute accuracy with which his instructions were fulfilled was simply the logical result of his care. I saw the invoice, and took note of it.

"Fifty cases of common earth, to be used for the purpose of botanical experimentation."

Also the copy of the letter to Carter Paterson, and their reply. Of both these I got copies. This was all the information Mr. Billington could give me, so I went down to the port and saw the coastguards, the Customs Officers and the harbour master, who kindly put me in communication with the men who had actually received the boxes. Their tally was exact with the list, and they had nothing to add to the simple description 'fifty cases of common earth,' except that the boxes were 'main and mortal heavy,' and that shifting them was dry work. One of them added that it was hard lines that there wasn't any gentleman 'such like as like yourself, squire,' to show some sort of appreciation of their efforts in a liquid form. Another put in a rider that the thirst then generated was such that even the time which had elapsed had not completely allayed it. Needless to add, I took care before leaving to lift, forever and adequately, this source of reproach.

30 September—The station master was good enough to give me a line to his old companion the station master at King's Cross, so that when I arrived there in the morning I was able to ask him about the arrival of the boxes. He, too put me at once in communication with the proper officials, and I saw that their tally was correct with the original invoice. The opportunities of acquiring an abnormal thirst had been here limited. A noble use of them had, however, been made, and again I was compelled to deal with the result in ex post facto manner.

From thence I went to Carter Paterson's central office, where I met with the utmost courtesy. They looked up the transaction in their day book and letter book, and at once telephoned to their King's Cross office for more details. By good fortune, the men who did the teaming were waiting for work, and the official at once sent them over, sending also by one of them the way-bill and all the papers connected with the delivery of the boxes at Carfax. Here again I found the tally agreeing exactly. The carriers' men were able to supplement the paucity of the written words with a few more details. These were, I shortly found, connected almost solely with the dusty nature of the job, and the consequent thirst engendered in the operators. On my affording an opportunity, through the medium of the currency of the realm, of the allaying, at a later period, this beneficial evil, one of the men remarked,

"That 'ere 'ouse, guv'nor, is the rummiest I ever was in. Blyme! But it ain't been touched sence a hundred years. There was dust that thick in the place that you might have slep' on it without 'urtin' of yer bones. An' the place was that neglected that yer might 'ave smelled ole Jerusalem in it. But the old chapel, that took the cike, that did! Me and my mate, we thort we wouldn't never git out quick enough. Lor,' I wouldn't take less nor a quid a moment to stay there arter dark."

Having been in the house, I could well believe him, but if he knew what I know, he would, I think have raised his terms.

Of one thing I am now satisfied. That all those boxes which arrived at Whitby from Varna in the Demeter were safely deposited in the old chapel at Carfax. There should be fifty of them there, unless any have since been removed, as from Dr. Seward's diary I fear.

I shall try to see the carter who took away the boxes from Carfax when Renfield attacked them. By following up this clue we may learn a good deal.

Mina Harker's Journal

30 September—I am so glad that I hardly know how to contain myself. It is, I suppose, the reaction from the haunting fear which I have had, that this terrible affair and the reopening of his old wound might act detrimentally on Jonathan. I saw him leave for Whitby with as brave a face as could, but I was sick with apprehension. The effort has, however, done him good. He was never so resolute, never so strong, never so full of volcanic energy, as at present. It is just as that dear, good Professor Van Helsing said, he is true grit, and he improves under strain that would kill a weaker nature. He came back full of life and hope and determination. Kate, too, has returned with several of her own letters which she retrieved from her parents so they might be added to our document.

We have got everything in order for tonight. I feel myself quite wild with excitement. I suppose one ought to pity anything so hunted as the Count. That is just it. This thing is not human, not even a beast. To read Dr. Seward's account of poor Lucy's death, and what followed, is enough to dry up the springs of pity in one's heart.

Later—Lord Godalming and Mr. Morris arrived earlier than we expected. Dr. Seward was out on business, and had taken Jonathan with him, so Kate and I had to see them. Though Kate was far less unaffected, for she had not been as close to Lucy as I, it was to me a painful meeting, for it brought back all poor dear Lucy's hopes of only a few months ago.

Of course they had heard Lucy speak of me, and it seemed that Dr. Van Helsing, too, had been quite 'blowing my trumpet,' as Mr. Morris expressed it. Poor fellows, neither of them is aware that Kate and I know all about the proposals they made to Lucy. They did not quite know what to say or do, as they were ignorant of the amount of our knowledge. So they had to keep on neutral subjects.

Then Mr. Singleton arrived, which caused our topics of conversation to be further restricted, for we knew nothing of this man or what he knew of us. Kate, always one to be astute, could sense the change in conversation, and took Mr. Singleton aside, along with one of the manifold documents, so that she could bring his knowledge up to date. How clever Kate can be at times, for as soon as they separated themselves from us, Lord Godalming and Mr. Morris seemed more at ease, though they still seemed uncertain on how to proceed from here.

However, I thought the matter over, and came to the conclusion that the best thing I could do would be to post them on affairs right up to date, just as Kate was doing with Mr. Singleton. I knew from Dr. Seward's diary that they had been at Lucy's death, her real death, and that I need not fear to betray any secret before the time. So I told them, as well as I could, that I had read all the papers and diaries, and that I, along with my husband and Kate, having typewritten them, had just finished putting them in order. I gave them each a copy to read in the library. When Lord Godalming got his and turned it over, it does make a pretty good pile, he said, "Did you write all this, Mrs. Harker?"

I nodded, and he went on.

"I don't quite see the drift of it, but you people are all so good and kind, and have been working so earnestly and so energetically, that all I can do is to accept your ideas blindfold and try to help you. I have had one lesson already in accepting facts that should make a man humble to the last hour of his life. Besides, I know you loved my Lucy . . ."

Here he turned away and covered his face with his hands. I could hear the tears in his voice. Mr. Morris, with instinctive delicacy, just laid a hand for a moment on his shoulder, and then walked quietly out of the room. I suppose there is something in a woman's nature that makes a man free to break down before her and express his feelings on the tender or emotional side without feeling it derogatory to his manhood. For when Lord Godalming found himself alone with me he sat down on the sofa and gave way utterly and openly. I sat down beside him and took his hand. I hope he didn't think it forward of me, and that if he ever thinks of it afterwards he never will have such a thought. There I wrong him. I know he never will. He is too true a gentleman. I said to him, for I could see that his heart was breaking, "I loved dear Lucy, and I know what she was to you, and what you were to her. She and I were like sisters, and now she is gone, will you not let me be like a sister to you in your trouble? I know what sorrows you have had, though I cannot measure the depth of them. If sympathy and pity can help in your affliction, won't you let me be of some little service, for Lucy's sake?"

In an instant the poor dear fellow was overwhelmed with grief. It seemed to me that all that he had of late been suffering in silence found a vent at once. He grew quite hysterical, and raising his open hands, beat his palms together in a perfect agony of grief. He stood up and then sat down again, and the tears rained down his cheeks. I felt an infinite pity for him, and opened my arms unthinkingly. With a sob he laid his head on my shoulder and cried like a wearied child, whilst he shook with emotion.

We women have something of the mother in us that makes us rise above smaller matters when the mother spirit is invoked. I felt this big sorrowing man's head resting on me, as though it were that of a baby that some day may lie on my bosom, and I stroked his hair as though he were my own child. I never thought at the time how strange it all was.

After a little bit his sobs ceased, and he raised himself with an apology, though he made no disguise of his emotion. He told me that for days and nights past, weary days and sleepless nights, he had been unable to speak with any one, as a man must speak in his time of sorrow. There was no woman whose sympathy could be given to him, or with whom, owing to the terrible circumstance with which his sorrow was surrounded, he could speak freely.

"I know now how I suffered," he said, as he dried his eyes, "but I do not know even yet, and none other can ever know, how much your sweet sympathy has been to me today. I shall know better in time, and believe me that, though I am not ungrateful now, my gratitude will grow with my understanding. You will let me be like a brother, will you not, for all our lives, for dear Lucy's sake?"

"For dear Lucy's sake," I said as we clasped hands. "Ay, and for your own sake," he added, "for if a man's esteem and gratitude are ever worth the winning, you have won mine today. If ever the future should bring to you a time when you need a man's help, believe me, you will not call in vain. God grant that no such time may ever come to you to break the sunshine of your life, but if it should ever come, promise me that you will let me know."

He was so earnest, and his sorrow was so fresh, that I felt it would comfort him, so I said, "I promise."

So I came to my own room to copy out on the typewriter the papers that Lord Godalming gave me.[165] As I came along the corridor I saw Mr. Morris looking out of a window. He turned as he heard my footsteps. "How is Art?" he said. Then noticing my red eyes, he went on, "Ah, I see you have been comforting him. Poor old fellow! He needs it. No one but a woman can help a man when he is in trouble of the heart, and he had no one to comfort him."

He bore his own trouble so bravely that my heart bled for him. I saw the manuscript in his hand, and I knew that when he read it he would realize how much I knew, so I said to him, "I wish I could comfort all who suffer from the heart. Will you let me be your friend, and will you come to me for comfort if you need it? You will know later why I speak."

He saw that I was in earnest, and stooping, took my hand, and raising it to his lips, kissed it. It seemed but poor comfort to so brave and unselfish a soul, and impulsively I bent over and kissed him. The tears rose in his eyes, and there was a momentary choking in his throat. He said quite calmly, "Little girl, you will never forget that true hearted kindness, so long as ever you live!" Then he went into the study to his friend.

"Little girl!" The very words he had used to Lucy, and, oh, but he proved himself a friend.

Inspector Cotford's Case Notes

29 September—Wright showed me to the Westenra tomb. With the use of some skeleton keys, we forced the door and entered the tomb. The coffin of Lucy Westenra was soldered shut, and it took us some time to open it. When we did, what we found within was truly horrific. A shaft of wood had been driven through the poor girl's heart and her head cut free from her body. Wright was overcome, and had to leave for better air, but I remained within the tomb. There was much blood in the coffin, far too fresh for the length of time the girl had been dead, and far too much to have spilled from a heart that no longer beat. If I didn't know better, I would say the Westenra girl had still been alive when the stake was driven in, and indeed it seems there was a bit of a struggle within the coffin. Furthremore, there were grass stains at the hem of her grave clothes, and mud caked between her toes, as if indeed she had been walking amongst the tombs. Oddest of all was the look of absolute peace upon her face, a stark contrast to the violence seen elsewhere within the tomb. Could she have been buried alive last week, and then killed in truth only yesterday? I must consult with the undertaker forthwith.

Later—I have spoken to the undertaker, his man (who is, interestingly enough, engaged to the young maid of Hillingham), and the woman who performs the last offices of the dead. While all three assured me that Lucy Westenra was quite dead, there was a noticeable hesitation in their voices. When questioned further, they revealed that she had been, to their eyes, the most beautiful of all corpses they had ever seen, more beautiful even than living girls.

In addition, the woman, of her own accord, ventured to mention that someone had placed a golden crucifix upon the mouth of the corpse. At the first opportunity, she had removed the "idolatrous thing" (for clearly she was a devout English Churchwoman, who would, of course, shun all things Catholic), but was found out by "that crank of a Dutchman." He had accused her of stealing the crucifix for its gold, and took it from her. The good woman was, needless to say, quite offended by this Dutchman, but was also perplexed by his tone of voice, as if he were in truth more afraid as to the consequences of her action than angry as to the action itself.

This case grows more curious by the day. I believe I shall have to attend the gathering these men are planning tomorrow, to see what more may be uncovered before the arrests are made.

CHAPTER
TWENTY-SIX[166]

Dr. Seward's Case-Book

30 September—I got home at five o'clock, and found that Godalming, Morris, and Mr. Singleton had not only arrived, but had already studied the transcript of the various diaries and letters which Harker and his wonderful wife had made and arranged. Harker had not yet returned from his visit to the carriers' men, of whom Dr. Hennessey had written to me. Mrs. Harker gave us all a cup of tea, and I can honestly say that, for the first time since I have lived in it, this old house seemed like home. When we had finished, Mrs. Harker said,

"Dr. Seward, may I ask a favour? I want to see your patient Mr. Renfield, the one you call the fly-man. Do let me see him. What you have said of him in your diary interests me so much! And if I am not mistaken, he may well have been a colleague of Jonathan's old employer."

She looked so appealing and so pretty that I could not refuse her, and there was no possible reason why I should, so I took her with me. When I went into the room, I told the man that a lady would like to see him, to which he simply answered, "Why?"

"She is going through the house, and wants to see every one in it," I answered.

"Oh, very well," he said, "let her come in, by all means, but just wait a minute till I tidy up the place."

His method of tidying was peculiar, he simply swallowed all the flies and spiders in the boxes before I could stop him. It was quite evident that he feared, or was jealous of, some interference. When he had got through his disgusting task, he said cheerfully, "Let the lady come in," and sat down on the edge of his bed with his head down, but with his eyelids raised so that he could see her as she entered. For a moment I thought that he might have some homicidal intent. I remembered how quiet he had been just before he attacked me in my own study, and I took care to stand where I could seize him at once if he attempted to make a spring at her.

She came into the room with an easy gracefulness which would at once command the respect of any lunatic, for easiness is one of the qualities mad people most respect. She walked over to him, smiling pleasantly, and held out her hand.

"Good evening, Mr. Renfield," said she. "You see, I know you, for Dr. Seward has told me of you." He made no immediate reply, but eyed her all over intently with a set frown on his face. This look gave way to one of wonder, which merged in doubt, then to my intense astonishment he said, "You're not the girl the doctor wanted to marry, are you? You can't be, you know, for she's dead."

Mrs. Harker smiled sweetly as she replied, "Oh no! I have a husband of my own, to whom I was married before I ever saw Dr. Seward, or he me. I am Mrs. Harker."

"Then what are you doing here?"

"My husband and I are staying on a visit with Dr. Seward."

"Your husband? Is he the same Harker as who works for Peter Hawkins?"

"He is that man, though I fear Mr. Hawkins has since died."

"Yes, of course, he must be dead by now. The Master covers his own tracks well, does he not? Oh, madam, you must not stay!"

"But why not?"

"You too are in danger. Those whose paths cross too near the Master's do not live long, I'm afraid . . ."

I thought that this style of conversation might not be pleasant to Mrs. Harker, any more than it was to me, so I joined in, "How did you know I wanted to marry anyone?"

His reply was simply contemptuous, given in a pause in which he turned his eyes from Mrs. Harker to me, instantly turning them back again, "What an asinine question!"

"I don't see that at all, Mr. Renfield," said Mrs. Harker, at once championing me.

He replied to her with as much courtesy and respect as he had shown contempt to me, "You will, of course, understand, Mrs. Harker, that when a man is so loved and honoured as our host is, everything regarding him is of interest in our little community. Dr. Seward is loved not only by his household and his friends, but even by his patients, who, being some of them hardly in mental equilibrium, are apt to distort causes and effects. Since I myself have been an inmate of a lunatic asylum, I cannot but notice that the sophistic tendencies of some of its inmates lean towards the errors of *non causa* and *ignoratio elenche*."

I positively opened my eyes at this new development. Here was my own pet lunatic, the most pronounced of his type that I had ever met with, talking elemental philosophy, and with the manner of a polished gentleman. I wonder if it was Mrs. Harker's presence which had touched some chord in his memory. If this new phase was spontaneous, or in any way due to her unconscious influence, she must have some rare gift or power.

We continued to talk for some time, and seeing that he was seemingly quite reasonable, she ventured, looking at me questioningly as she began, to lead him to his favourite topic. I was again astonished, for he addressed himself to the question with the impartiality of the completest sanity. He even took himself as an example when he mentioned certain things.

"Why, I myself am an instance of a man who had a strange belief. Indeed, it was no wonder that my friends were alarmed, and insisted on my being put under control. I used to fancy that life was a positive and perpetual entity, and that by consuming a multitude of live things, no matter how low in the scale of creation, one might indefinitely prolong life. At times I held the belief so strongly that I actually tried to take human life. The doctor here will bear me out that on one occasion I tried to kill him for the purpose of strengthening my vital powers by the assimilation with my own body of his life through the medium of his blood, relying of course, upon the Scriptural phrase, 'For the blood is the life.' Though, indeed, the vendor of a certain nostrum has vulgarized the truism to the very point of contempt. Isn't that true, doctor?"

I nodded assent, for I was so amazed that I hardly knew what to either think or say, it was hard to imagine that I had seen him eat up his spiders and flies not five minutes before. Looking at my watch, I saw that I should go to the station to meet Van Helsing, so I told Mrs. Harker that it was time to leave.

She came at once, after saying pleasantly to Mr. Renfield, "Goodbye, and I hope I may see you often, under auspices pleasanter to yourself."

To which, to my astonishment, he replied, "Goodbye, my dear. I pray God I may never see your sweet face again. May He bless and keep you!"

When I went to the station to meet Van Helsing I left the boys behind me. Poor Art seemed more cheerful than he has been since Lucy first took ill, and Quincey is more like his own bright self than he has been for many a long day. They had by now become fast friends with Singleton, for it was clear that he was willing to believe, and what's more willing to help in any way he could, and in times such as these, that is more than cause enough for friendship.

Van Helsing stepped from the carriage with the eager nimbleness of a boy. He saw me at once, and rushed up to me, saying, "Ah, friend John, how goes all? Well? So! I have been busy, for I come here to stay if need be. All affairs are settled with me, and I have much to tell. Madam Mina is with you? Yes. And her so fine husband? And Arthur and my friend Quincey, they are with you, too? Good!"

As I drove to the house I told him of what had passed, of the addition of Kate and Mr. Singleton to our party, and of how my own diary had come to be of some use through Mrs. Harker's suggestion, at which the Professor interrupted me.

"Ah, that wonderful Madam Mina! She has man's brain, a brain that a man should have were he much gifted, and a woman's heart. The good God fashioned her for a purpose, believe me, when He made that so good combination. Friend John, up to now fortune has made that woman of help to us, after tonight neither she nor her friend Miss Kate must have anything to do with this so terrible affair. It is not good that they run a risk so great. We men are determined, nay, are we not pledged, to destroy this monster? But it is no part for women. Even if they be not harmed, their heart may fail them in so much and so many horrors and hereafter they may suffer, both in waking, from their nerves, and in sleep, from their dreams. And, besides, they are young women, Miss Kate not yet married and Madam Mina not so long married, and there may be other things to think of some time, if not now. You tell me they have wrote all, then they must consult with us, but tomorrow they say goodbye to this work, and we go alone."

I agreed heartily with him, and then I told him what we had found in his absence, that the house which Dracula had bought was the very next one to my own. He was amazed, and a great concern seemed to come on him.

"Oh that we had known it before!" he said, "for then we might have reached him in time to save poor Lucy. However, 'the milk that is spilt cries not out afterwards,' as you say. We shall not think of that, but go on our way to the end." Then he fell into a silence that lasted till we entered my own gateway. Before we went to prepare for dinner he said to Mrs. Harker, "I am told, Madam Mina, by my friend John that you and your husband have put up in exact order all things that have been, up to this moment."

"Not up to this moment, Professor," she said impulsively, "but up to this morning."

"But why not up to now? We have seen hitherto how good light all the little things have made. We have told our secrets, and yet no one who has told is the worse for it."

Mrs. Harker began to blush, and taking a paper from her pockets, she said, "Dr. Van Helsing, will you read this, and tell me if it must go in. It is my record of today. I too have seen the need of putting down at present everything, however trivial, but there is little in this except what is personal. Must it go in?"

The Professor read it over gravely, and handed it back, saying, "It need not go in if you do not wish it, but I pray that it may. It can but make your husband love you the more, and all us, your friends, more honour you, as well as more esteem and love." She took it back with another blush and a bright smile.

And so now, up to this very hour, all the records we have are complete and in order. The Professor took away one copy to study after dinner, and before our meeting, which is fixed for nine o'clock. The rest of us have already read everything, so when we meet in the study we shall all be informed as to facts, and can arrange our plan of battle with this terrible and mysterious enemy.

Campaign Diary, kept by Mina Harker

30 September—When we met in Dr. Seward's study two hours after dinner, which had been at six o'clock, we unconsciously formed a sort of board or committee. Professor Van Helsing took the head of the table, to which Dr. Seward motioned him as he came into the room. He made me sit next to him on his right, and asked me to act as secretary. Jonathan sat next to me. Kate and Mr. Singleton were beside Jonathan. Opposite us were Lord Godalming, Mr. Morris, and Dr. Seward, Lord Godalming being next the Professor.

The Professor said, "I may, I suppose, take it that we are all acquainted with the facts that are in these papers." We all expressed assent, and he went on, "Then it were, I think, good that I tell you something of the kind of enemy with which we have to deal. I shall then make known to you something of the history of this man, which has been ascertained for me. So we then can discuss how we shall act, and can take our measure according.

"There are such beings as vampires, some of us have evidence that they exist. Even had we not the proof of our own unhappy experience, the teachings and the records of the past give proof enough for sane peoples. I admit that at the first, I was sceptic. Were it not that through long years I have trained myself to keep an open mind, I could not have believed until such time as that fact thunder on my ear. 'See! See! I prove, I prove.' Alas! Had I known at first what now I know, nay, had I even guess at him, one so precious life had been spared to many of us who did love her. But that is gone, and we must so work, that other poor souls perish not, whilst we can save." This last he said with a look toward Kate, for he had read through her letters and knew it was her Francis who was quite probably in grave danger.

"The nosferatu do not die like the bee when he sting once. He is only stronger, and being stronger, have yet more power to work evil. This vampire which is amongst us is of himself so strong in person as twenty men, he is of cunning more than mortal, for his cunning be the growth of ages, he have still the aids of necromancy, which is, as his etymology imply, the divination by the dead, and all the dead that he can come nigh to are for him at command. He is brute, and more than brute, he is devil in callous, and the heart of him is not. He can, within his range, direct the elements, the storm, the fog, the thunder. He can command all the meaner things, the rat, and the owl, and the bat, the moth, and the fox, and the wolf, he can grow and become small, and he can at times vanish and come unknown. How then are we to begin our strike to destroy him? How shall we find his where, and having found it, how can we destroy?"

"My friends, this is much, it is a terrible task that we undertake, and there may be consequence to make the brave shudder. For if we fail in this our fight he must surely win, and then where end we? Life is nothing, I heed him not. But to fail here, is not mere life or death. It is that we become as him, that we henceforward become foul things of the night like him, without heart or conscience, preying on the bodies and the souls of those we love best. To us forever are the gates of heaven shut, for who shall open them to us again? We go on for all time abhorred by all, a blot on the face of God's sunshine, an arrow in the side of Him who died for man. But we are face to face with duty, and in such case must we shrink? For me, I say no, but then I am old, and life, with his sunshine, his fair places, his song of birds, his music and his love, lie far behind. You others are young. Some have seen sorrow, but there are fair days yet in store. What say you?"

Whilst he was speaking, Jonathan had taken my hand. I feared, oh so much, that the appalling nature of our danger was overcoming him when I saw his hand stretch out, but it was life to me to feel its touch, so strong, so self reliant, so resolute. A brave man's hand can speak for itself, it does not even need a woman's love to hear its music.

When the Professor had done speaking my husband looked in my eyes, and I in his, there was no need for speaking between us.

"I answer for Mina and myself," he said.

"Count me in, Professor," said Mr. Quincey Morris, laconically as usual.

"I am with you," said Lord Godalming, "for Lucy's sake, if for no other reason."

"To save my friend, I'm with you too," Kate added.

Mr. Singleton and Dr. Seward simply nodded in their turn.

The Professor stood up and, after laying his golden crucifix on the table, held out his hand on either side. I took his right hand, and Lord Godalming his left, I held Jonathan's hand, and he in turn held Mr. Singleton's, who held Kate's, who stretched across to Dr. Seward. So as we all took hands our solemn compact was made. I felt my heart icy cold, but it did not even occur to me to draw back. We resumed our places (though I took note that Kate left her hand in Dr. Seward's a moment after the rest of us had let go), and Dr. Van Helsing went on with a sort of cheerfulness which showed that the serious work had begun. It was to be taken as gravely, and in as businesslike a way, as any other transaction of life.

"Well, you know what we have to contend against, but we too, are not without strength. We have on our side power of combination, a power denied to the vampire kind, we have sources of science, we are free to act and think, and the hours of the day and the night are ours equally. In fact, so far as our powers extend, they are unfettered, and we are free to use them. We have self devotion in a cause and an end to achieve which is not a selfish one. These things are much.

"Now let us see how far the general powers arrayed against us are restrict, and how the individual cannot. In fine, let us consider the limitations of the vampire in general, and of this one in particular.

"All we have to go upon are traditions and superstitions. These do not at the first appear much, when the matter is one of life and death, nay of more than either life or death. Yet must we be satisfied, in the first place because we have to be, no other means is at our control, and secondly, because, after all these things, tradition and superstition, are everything. Does not the belief in vampires rest for others—though not, alas, for us—on them? A year ago which of us would have received such a possibility, in the midst of our scientific, sceptical, matter-of-fact nineteenth century? We even scouted a belief that we saw justified under our very eyes. Take it, then, that the vampire, and the belief in his limitations and his cure, rest for the moment on the same base. For, let me tell you, he is known everywhere that men have been. In old Greece, in old Rome, he flourish in Germany all over, in France, in India, even in the Chersonese, and in China, so far from us in all ways, there even is he, and the peoples for him at this day. He have follow the wake of the berserker Icelander, the devil-begotten Hun, the Slav, the Saxon, the Magyar. And before the Magyar, the Finn, from which the Magyar come.[167]

"So far, then, we have all we may act upon, and let me tell you that very much of the beliefs are justified by what we have seen in our own so unhappy experience. The vampire live on, and cannot die by mere passing of the time, he can flourish when that he can fatten on the blood of the living. Even more, we have seen amongst us that he can even grow younger, that his vital faculties grow strenuous, and seem as though they refresh themselves when his special pabulum is plenty. Jonathan saw him as old when in his afar off castle, where blood was scarce, and yet when he saw him again in London, with its teeming millions, the vampire was grown younger again, and Miss Kate has also encountered him in this form as well."

"Pardon me, Professor?" Kate interjected. "I have had a growing fear, since I first spoke with Mina, that there might actually be two such vampires in London. The younger man with the beard, who Mr. Harker saw as a coachman, and again in Piccadilly, and who I have encountered myself, seems altogether different than the old man of the castle. What's more, when the Demeter came ashore at Whitby, there was a wolf that leapt off the ship—no doubt a vampire, if he can indeed change forms—and yet the body of the old man was found in one of the boxes."

"Ah, Miss Kate!" Van Helsing replied with an approving smile. "Your logic is quite sound, so far as it goes. But I believe the wolf which was aboard the ship was indeed a wolf; I daresay even the same wolf which the Count later released from its cage, being as it was a kind of favored pet or servant. We have seen that the Count feeds only on women, for male prey he heeds not; see how Jonathan remained untouched at the castle, and your own good grandfather, God rest his soul, died not of a bite but only of a broken neck. It was to the wolf, I am quite certain, that the crew of the *Demeter* went to feed." From the look that was upon Kate's face, it was clear that she was not convinced of this explanation, but the Professor continued on:

"No, whatever others horrors we must face, we can be certain that there is only one vampire in England. His ability to grow old or young comes from his peculiar diet. But he cannot flourish without this diet, he eat not as others. Even friend Jonathan, who lived with him for weeks, did never see him eat, never! He throws no shadow. Your friend John saw that when he meet you on this road here. Alas! That you did not know of him then! He make in the mirror no reflect, as again Jonathan observe. He has the strength of many of his hand, witness again Jonathan when he shut the door against the wolves, and when he help him from the diligence too. He can transform himself to wolf, as we gather from the ship arrival in Whitby, when he tear open the dogs. He can be as bat, as Miss Kate saw him about his London house, as Madam Mina saw him on the window at Whitby, and as friend John saw him fly from this so near house, and as my friend Quincey saw him at the window of Miss Lucy.

"He can effect the thoughts of others, calling forth evil desires in some, and banishing good ones in others[168].

"He can come in mist which he create, that noble ship's captain proved him of this, but, from what we know, the distance he can make this mist is limited, and it can only be round himself.

"He come on moonlight rays as elemental dust, as again Jonathan saw those sisters in the castle of Dracula. He become so small, we ourselves saw Miss Lucy, ere she was at peace, slip through a hairbreadth space at the tomb door. He can, when once he find his way, come out from anything or into anything, no matter how close it be bound or even fused up with fire, solder you call it. He can see in the dark, no small power this, in a world which is one half shut from the light.

"He can make others like himself, should he feed his own blood to one of his choosing. The patient Renfield, raving in his madness, revealed as much to friend John the night poor Miss Lucy died, and in so doing, warned us of what she would become. Ah, but hear me through, for though he and certain ones of his choosing may seem immortal, it is an immortality limited to a degree that your own Gladstone would be pleased to hear of, for though he can do all these things, yet he is not free[169]. Nay, he is even more prisoner than the slave of the galley, than the madman in his cell.

"He cannot go where he lists, he who is not of nature has yet to obey some of nature's laws, why we know not. And indeed, nature abhors him. The dog is his enemy, and the horse lives in fear of him[170]. The leech, though drawn to his blood, will, once it has tasted, turn from him.[171] Even the rains are held back while he yet walks the land: Your London is known for its rain, is it not? And yet, since the vampire arrive, has the rain come even once of its own accord? I dare say not! Only when the vampire is fled or destroyed will the drought be gone[172].

"He may not enter anywhere at the first, unless there be some one of the household who bid him to come, though afterwards he can come as he please. His power ceases, as does that of all evil things, at the coming of the day. Only at certain times can he have limited freedom during the day-lit hours. If he be not at the place whither he is bound, he can only change himself at noon or at exact sunrise or sunset. These things we are told, and in this record of ours we have proof by inference. Thus, whereas he can do as he will within his limit, when he have his earth-home, his coffin-home, his hell-home, the place unhallowed, as we saw when he went to the grave of the suicide at Whitby, still at other time he can only change when the time come.

"It is said, too, that he can only pass running water at the slack or the flood of the tide. Then there are things which so afflict him that he has no power, as the garlic that we know of, and the rye which Jonathan experience; as for things sacred, as this symbol, my crucifix, that was amongst us even now when we resolve, to them he is nothing, but in their presence he take his place far off and silent with respect. There are others, too, which I shall tell you of, lest in our seeking we may need them. The branch of wild rose on his coffin keep him that he move not from it, a sacred bullet fired into the coffin kill him so that he be true dead, and as for the stake through him, we know already of its peace, or the cut off head that giveth rest. We have seen it with our eyes.

"Thus when we find the habitation of this man-that-was, we can confine him to his coffin and destroy him, if we obey what we know. But he is clever. I have asked my friend Arminius, of Buda-Pesth University, to make his record, and from all the means that are, he tell me of what he has been. He must, indeed, have been that Voivode Dracula who won his name against the Turk, over the great river on the very frontier of Turkeyland. If it be so, then was he no common man, for in that time, and for centuries after, he was spoken of as the cleverest and the most cunning, as well as the bravest of the sons of the 'land beyond the forest.' That mighty brain and that iron resolution went with him to his grave, and are even now arrayed against us.

"The Draculas were, says Arminius, a great and noble race, though now and again were scions who were held by their coevals to have had dealings with the Evil One. They learned his secrets in the Scholomance, amongst the mountains over Lake Hermanstadt, where the devil claims the tenth scholar as his due. In the records are such words as 'stregoica' witch, 'ordog' and 'pokol' Satan and hell, and in one manuscript this very Dracula is spoken of as 'wampyr,' which we all understand too well. There have been from the loins of this very one great men and good women, and their graves make sacred the earth where alone this foulness can dwell. For it is not the least of its terrors that this evil thing is rooted deep in all good, in soil barren of holy memories it cannot rest."

Whilst they were talking Mr. Morris was looking steadily at the window, and he now got up quietly, and went out of the room. There was a little pause, and then the Professor went on.

"And now we must settle what we do. We have here much data, and we must proceed to lay out our campaign. We know from the inquiry of Jonathan that from the castle to Whitby came fifty boxes of earth, all of which were delivered at Carfax, we also know that at least some of these boxes have been removed, perhaps to the Piccadilly house across from that of Miss Kate. For did she not see a cart arrive at that house the very same night that a cart left from Carfax? It seems to me, that our first step should be to ascertain whether all the rest remain in the house beyond that wall where we look today, or whether any more have been removed. If the latter, we must trace . . ."

Here we were interrupted in a very startling way. Outside the house came the sound of a pistol shot, the glass of the window was shattered with a bullet, which ricochetting from the top of the embrasure, struck the far wall of the room. I am afraid I am at heart a coward, for I shrieked out. The men all jumped to their feet, Lord Godalming flew over to the window and threw up the sash. As he did so we heard Mr. Morris' voice without, "Sorry! I fear I have alarmed you. I shall come in and tell you about it."

A minute later he came in and said, "It was an idiotic thing of me to do, and I ask your pardon, Mrs. Harker, most sincerely, I fear I must have frightened you terribly. But the fact is that whilst the Professor was talking there came a big bat and sat on the window sill. I have got such a horror of the damned brutes from recent events that I cannot stand them, and I went out to have a shot, as I have been doing of late of evenings, whenever I have seen one. You used to laugh at me for it then, Art."

"Did you hit it?" asked Dr. Van Helsing.

"I don't know, I fancy not, for it flew away into the wood." Without saying any more he took his seat, and the Professor began to resume his statement.

"We must trace each of these boxes, and when we are ready, we must either capture or kill this monster in his lair, or we must, so to speak, sterilize the earth, so that no more he can seek safety in it. Thus in the end we may find him in his form of man between the hours of noon and sunset, and so engage with him when he is at his most weak.

"And now for you, Madam Mina, and for you, Miss Kate, this night is the end until all be well. You are too precious to us to have such risk. When we part tonight, you no more must question. We shall tell you all in good time. We are men and are able to bear, but you must be our stars and our hope, and we shall act all the more free that you are not in the danger, such as we are."

324 JOEL H. EMERSON

All the men, even Jonathan, seemed relieved, but it did not seem to me good that they should brave danger and, perhaps lessen their safety, strength being the best safety, through care of me, but their minds were made up, and though it was a bitter pill for me to swallow, I could say nothing, save to accept their chivalrous care of me. I knew, though, that Kate would never swallow that same pill and accept such care from men, for chivalry to her is an anathema.

"Good sirs," Kate started out with an astounding degree of decorum, though I could hear the old spiteful tone rising in her voice, "I understand you are compelled to protect us, that is, Mina and I, but my good friend is still unaccounted for, and I must do all within my power to see to his safe return. I am, I should think, more capable than you may realize . . ."

"Miss Reed," Dr. Seward, who sat across from her, interjected with an honest and earnest voice, "Please do not think we are belittling either of you in asking you to stay behind, for with the powers this terrible menace appears to have at his disposal, any of us men could be laid low as easily as yourself, for what is the difference between the strength of a man and the strength of a woman, when weighted against the Count's own might? Nor is it your resolve we would question, but rather our own. If we five men confront the vampire together, and one or some or all might be killed in the process, then so be it. But if you were to come too, and were to find yourself at the mercy of our enemy, our resolve may fail, and we may be forced to give ground for your sake. Already we have lost one who was dear to us, and the thought of losing another . . ." Here the doctor had to pause, for his voice was about to break.

Kate, perhaps for the first time in her life, saw something into the heart of a man, and seemed moved by what she saw there. She reached out and took his hand, and said, "Then for your sake, and for the sake of these good men, I will stay here this night." The look of relief on Dr. Seward's face was immeasurable.

After a polite pause, Mr. Morris resumed the discussion, "As there is no time to lose, I vote we have a look at his house right now. Time is everything with him, and swift action on our part may save another victim."

From Mina Harker's Private Diary

I own that my heart began to fail me when the time for action came so close, but I did not say anything, for I had a greater fear that if I appeared as a drag or a hindrance to their work, they might even leave me out of their counsels altogether. They have now gone off to Carfax, with means to get into the house.

Manlike, they had told me to go to bed and sleep after I had typed out the notes of our meeting, as if a woman can sleep when those she loves are in danger! When the time of their return comes, I shall lie down, and pretend to sleep, lest Jonathan have added anxiety about me when he returns. Kate has stayed with me until now, and as my duty, such as it is, is complete, I shall retire to bed.

Dr. Seward's Case-Book

1 October, 4 A.M.—Just as we were about to leave the house, an urgent message was brought to me from Renfield to know if I would see him at once, as he had something of the utmost importance to say to me. I told the messenger to say that I would attend to his wishes in the morning, I was busy just at the moment.

The attendant added, "He seems very importunate, sir. I have never seen him so eager. I don't know but what, if you don't see him soon, he will have one of his violent fits." I knew the man would not have said this without some cause, so I said, "All right, I'll go now," and I asked the others to wait a few minutes for me, as I had to go and see my patient.

"Take me with you, friend John," said the Professor. "His case in your diary interest me much, and it had bearing, too, now and again on our case. I should much like to see him, and especial when his mind is disturbed."

"May I come also?" asked Lord Godalming.

"Me too?" said Quincey Morris.

"May I come?" said Harker.

"And I?" asked Singleton.

I nodded, and we all went down the passage together.

We found him in a state of considerable excitement, but far more rational in his speech and manner than I had ever seen him. There was an unusual understanding of himself, which was unlike anything I had ever met with in a lunatic, and he took it for granted that his reasons would prevail with others entirely sane. We all five went into the room, but none of the others at first said anything. His request was that I would at once release him from the asylum and send him home. This he backed up with arguments regarding his complete recovery, and adduced his own existing sanity.

"I appeal to your friends," he said, "they will, perhaps, not mind sitting in judgement on my case. By the way, you have not introduced me."

I was so much astonished, that the oddness of introducing a madman in an asylum did not strike me at the moment, and besides, there was a certain dignity in the man's manner, so much of the habit of equality, that I at once made the introduction, "Lord Godalming, Professor Van Helsing, Mr. Quincey Morris, of Texas, Mr. Jonathan Harker, Mr. Alfred Singleton . . . Mr. Renfield."

He shook hands with each of them, saying in turn, "Lord Godalming, I had the honour of seconding your father at the Windham. I grieve to know, by your holding the title, that he is no more. He was a man loved and honoured by all who knew him, and in his youth was, I have heard, the inventor of a burnt rum punch, much patronized on Derby night. Mr. Morris the inventor, you should be proud of your great state. Its reception into the Union was a precedent which may have far-reaching effects hereafter, when the Pole and the Tropics may hold

alliance to the Stars and Stripes. The power of Treaty may yet prove a vast engine
of enlargement, when the Monroe doctrine takes its true place as a political fable.
Mr. Singleton, your writings for the *Journal of the Occult* are most thorough and
enlightening to all who seek such esoteric knowledge. It is a rare thing to keep
such writing free of both baseless superstition and blind moderninity, and so
remain focused solely on the details. What shall any man say of his pleasure
at meeting Van Helsing? Sir, I make no apology for dropping all forms of
conventional prefix. When an individual has revolutionized therapeutics by his
discovery of the continuous evolution of brain matter, conventional forms are
unfitting, since they would seem to limit him to one of a class. You, gentlemen,
who by nationality, by heredity, or by the possession of natural gifts, are fitted to
hold your respective places in the moving world, I take to witness that I am as
sane as at least the majority of men who are in full possession of their liberties.
And I am sure that you, Dr. Seward, humanitarian and medico-jurist as well as
scientist, will deem it a moral duty to deal with me as one to be considered as
under exceptional circumstances." He made this last appeal with a courtly air of
conviction which was not without its own charm.

I think we were all staggered, save for Art, who studied my patient long and
hard, as if trying to discern something of his face. For my own part, I was under
the conviction, despite my knowledge of the man's character and history, that
his reason had been restored, and I felt under a strong impulse to tell him that
I was satisfied as to his sanity, and would see about the necessary formalities for
his release in the morning. I thought it better to wait, however, before making so
grave a statement, for of old I knew the sudden changes to which this particular
patient was liable. So I contented myself with making a general statement that
he appeared to be improving very rapidly, that I would have a longer chat with
him in the morning, and would then see what I could do in the direction of
meeting his wishes.

This did not at all satisfy him, for he said quickly, "But I fear, Dr. Seward,
that you hardly apprehend my wish. I desire to go at once, here, now, this very
hour, this very moment, if I may. Time presses, and in our implied agreement
with the old scytheman it is of the essence of the contract. I am sure it is only
necessary to put before so admirable a practitioner as Dr. Seward so simple, yet
so momentous a wish, to ensure its fulfillment."

He looked at me keenly, and seeing the negative in my face, turned to the
others, and scrutinized them closely. Not meeting any sufficient response, he
went on, "Is it possible that I have erred in my supposition?"

"You have," I said frankly, but at the same time, as I felt, brutally.

There was a considerable pause, and then he said slowly, "Then I suppose
I must only shift my ground of request. Let me ask for this concession, boon,
privilege, what you will. I am content to implore in such a case, not on personal

grounds, but for the sake of others. I am not at liberty to give you the whole of my reasons, but you may, I assure you, take it from me that they are good ones, sound and unselfish, and spring from the highest sense of duty.

"Could you look, sir, into my heart, you would approve to the full the sentiments which animate me. Nay, more, you would count me amongst the best and truest of your friends."

Again he looked at us all keenly. I had a growing conviction that this sudden change of his entire intellectual method was but yet another phase of his madness, and so determined to let him go on a little longer, knowing from experience that he would, like all lunatics, give himself away in the end. Van Helsing was gazing at him with a look of utmost intensity, his bushy eyebrows almost meeting with the fixed concentration of his look. He said to Renfield in a tone which did not surprise me at the time, but only when I thought of it afterwards, for it was as of one addressing an equal, "Can you not tell frankly your real reason for wishing to be free tonight? I will undertake that if you will satisfy even me, a stranger, without prejudice, and with the habit of keeping an open mind, Dr. Seward will give you, at his own risk and on his own responsibility, the privilege you seek."

He shook his head sadly, and with a look of poignant regret on his face. The Professor went on, "Come, sir, bethink yourself. You claim the privilege of reason in the highest degree, since you seek to impress us with your complete reasonableness. You do this, whose sanity we have reason to doubt, since you are not yet released from medical treatment for this very defect. If you will not help us in our effort to choose the wisest course, how can we perform the duty which you yourself put upon us? Be wise, and help us, and if we can we shall aid you to achieve your wish."

He still shook his head as he said, "Dr. Van Helsing, I have nothing to say. Your argument is complete, and if I were free to speak I should not hesitate a moment, but I am not my own master in the matter. I can only ask you to trust me. If I am refused, the responsibility does not rest with me."

I thought it was now time to end the scene, which was becoming too comically grave, so I went towards the door, simply saying, "Come, my friends, we have work to do. Goodnight."

As, however, I got near the door, a new change came over the patient. He moved towards me so quickly that for the moment I feared that he was about to make another homicidal attack. My fears, however, were groundless, for he held up his two hands imploringly, and made his petition in a moving manner. As he saw that the very excess of his emotion was militating against him, by restoring us more to our old relations, he became still more demonstrative. I glanced at Van Helsing, and saw my conviction reflected in his eyes, so I became a little more fixed in my manner, if not more stern, and motioned to him that his efforts were unavailing. I had previously seen something of the same constantly growing excitement in him when he had to make some request of which at the time he had thought much, such for instance, as when he wanted a cat, and I was prepared to see the collapse into the same sullen acquiescence on this occasion.

My expectation was not realised, for when he found that his appeal would not be successful, he got into quite a frantic condition. He threw himself on his knees, and held up his hands, wringing them in plaintive supplication, and poured forth a torrent of entreaty, with the tears rolling down his cheeks, and his whole face and form expressive of the deepest emotion.

"Let me entreat you, Dr. Seward, oh, let me implore you, to let me out of this house at once. Send me away how you will and where you will, send keepers with me with whips and chains, let them take me in a strait waistcoat, manacled and leg-ironed, even to gaol, but let me go out of this. You don't know what you do by keeping me here. I am speaking from the depths of my heart, of my very soul. You don't know whom you wrong, or how, and I may not tell. Woe is me! I may not tell. By all you hold sacred, by all you hold dear, by your love that is lost, by your hope that lives, for the sake of the Almighty, take me out of this and save my soul from guilt! Can't you hear me, man? Can't you understand? Will you never learn? Don't you know that I am sane and earnest now, that I am no lunatic in a mad fit, but a sane man fighting for his soul? Oh, hear me! Hear me! Let me go, let me go, let me go!"

I thought that the longer this went on the wilder he would get, and so would bring on a fit, so I took him by the hand and raised him up.

"Come," I said sternly, "no more of this, we have had quite enough already. Get to your bed and try to behave more discreetly."

He suddenly stopped and looked at me intently for several moments. Then, without a word, he rose and moving over, sat down on the side of the bed. The collapse had come, as on former occasions, just as I had expected.

When I was leaving the room, last of our party, he said to me in a quiet, well-bred voice, "You will, I trust, Dr. Seward, do me the justice to bear in mind, later on, that I did what I could to convince you tonight."

Inspector Cotford's Case Notes

1 October—I arrived at the Purfleet asylum well before seven last night, so that I could study how to best position myself to listen in on their conversation. It seemed most likely that any conversation would either be held in the dining room, or in the study, and most likely the latter, where the staff would be less likely to hear. As such, by making my way surreptitiously around the building, I located both rooms, and places outside of each where I might hid myself from

view. I settled in first behind a bush, near to the dining room window, and bided my time.

By seven o'clock, the dining room had filled with a number of people. From my view through the window, I could see that in attendance were Arthur Holmwood, Professor Van Helsing, Quincey Morris, Dr. Seward (to whom this house belonged), a gentleman I had never seen before, and, to my amazement, Jonathan Harker (the solicitor who beforehand had proven so helpful and, so I had thought, honest). There were also two women I did not recognize; one sat near to Harker, and by their words and actions I soon realised they must be married. Their discussion throughout dinner was reserved and wholly uninformative, save that I learned the one gentleman's name to be "Mr. Singleton," and the ladies to be "Madam Mina" (who I learned during the course of the conversation was indeed Mr. Harker's wife) and "Miss Kate."

As suspected, after dinner the party made their way out of the dining room. I hurried to secure my hiding spot by the window of the study, and had settled in just in time for their entry. Their discussion was as perplexing as it was enlightening (the subject matter of which I shall get to in due course), though I had few opportunities to peer in, as the American spent much of his time staring at the very window by which I was hiding, as if able to sense my presence there. At one point, he even left the room and came outside. When I saw him draw a revolver, I feared I had somehow "tipped my hand," as they say, and the game was up. But he had not seen me, crouched as I was behind the bush, but instead fired upon a large bat that had been circling about the window and which had eventually come to rest on the window sill. The shot went through the glass and startled one of the women inside. Holmwood threw open the window to see what was afoot, but when he closed it again I did not hear it latched.

The meeting concluded, the men left, and the women remained behind to type. It seemed, from their discussion, that they had been keeping a typewritten account of the entire affair which I was presently investigating! Oh how thankful I was now that the American had so foolishly fired upon that bat, and Holmwood, in his eagerness, failed to latch the window, for when the women had finished typing (which did not take long) and retired to bed, I opened the window from the outside and entered the study. At one end of the table was a phonograph with a number of wax cylinders, a typewriter, and three manifold documents of identical content. Again I found myself amazed, for the very first page involved Peter Hawkins, the Holmwood's solicitor. Flipping through the papers I found mentions of the Holmwoods, Westenras, *et al*, dating from April through today, containing even the dialogue of the meeting I had just witnessed. While I undoubtedly could have made the appropriate arrests before now, based on the evidence I had already accumulated, now I would surely have all I would need against these criminals, and so took one of the manifolds with me as I left the room through the window.

It was nearly dawn before I reached London. I shall sleep as well as I may, in order to have a fresh mind and renewed wits, before reading through this thick stack of papers with Wright tomorrow. I must trust that, given the late hour, nothing untoward shall happen until then.

CHAPTER
TWENTY-SEVEN[173]

Jonathan Harker's Journal

1 October, 5 A.M.—I went with the party to the search with an easy mind, for I think I never saw Mina so absolutely strong and well. I am so glad that she consented to hold back with her friend and let us men do the work. Somehow, it was a dread to me that she was in this fearful business at all, but now that her work is done, and that it is due to her energy and brains and foresight that the whole story is put together in such a way that every point tells, she may well feel that her part is finished, and that she can henceforth leave the rest to us. We were, I think, all a little upset by the scene with Mr. Renfield. When we came away from his room we were silent till we got back to the study. Mina had apparently finished the typing and had retired to bed. I noticed one of the documents was missing from the table, and concluded she had taken it with her to study before going to sleep.

Then Mr. Morris said to Dr. Seward, "Say, Jack, if that man wasn't attempting a bluff, he is about the sanest lunatic I ever saw, and if he isn't he's about fit to call Irving for the jack-pot.[174] I'm not sure, but I believe that he had some serious purpose, and if he had, it was pretty rough on him not to get a chance."

The rest of us were silent, but Dr. Van Helsing added, "Friend John, you know more lunatics than I do, and I'm glad of it, for I fear that if it had been to me to decide I would before that last hysterical outburst have given him free. But we live and learn, and in our present task we must take no chance, as my friend Quincey would say. All is best as they are."

Dr. Seward seemed to answer them both in a dreamy kind of way, "I don't know but that I agree with you. If that man had been an ordinary lunatic I

would have taken my chance of trusting him, but he seems so mixed up with
the Count in an indexy kind of way that I am afraid of doing anything wrong
by helping his fads. I can't forget how he prayed with almost equal fervor for
a cat, and then tried to tear my throat out with his teeth. Besides, he called
the Count 'lord and master,' and he may want to get out to help him in some
diabolical way. That horrid thing has the wolves and the rats and his own kind
to help him, so I suppose he isn't above trying to use a respectable lunatic. He
certainly did seem earnest, though. I only hope we have done what is best.
These things, in conjunction with the wild work we have in hand, help to
unnerve a man."

The Professor stepped over, and laying his hand on his shoulder, said in his
grave, kindly way, "Friend John, have no fear. We are trying to do our duty in a
very sad and terrible case, we can only do as we deem best. What else have we
to hope for, except the pity of the good God?"

Mr. Singleton had slipped away for a few minutes, but now he returned. He
held up a little silver whistle, as he remarked, "That old place may be full of rats,
and if so, I've got an antidote on call."

Having passed the wall, we took our way to the house, taking care to keep
in the shadows of the trees on the lawn when the moonlight shone out. When
we got to the porch the Professor opened his bag and took out a lot of things,
which he laid on the step, sorting them into five little groups, evidently one for
each. Then he spoke.

"My friends, we are going into a terrible danger, and we need arms of many
kinds. Our enemy is not merely spiritual. Remember that he has the strength of
twenty men, and that, though our necks or our windpipes are of the common
kind, and therefore breakable or crushable, his are not amenable to mere strength.
A stronger man, or a body of men more strong in all than him, can at certain
times hold him, but they cannot hurt him as we can be hurt by him. We must,
therefore, guard ourselves from his touch. Keep this near your heart." As he
spoke he lifted a little silver crucifix and held it out to me, I being nearest to him,
"put these flowers round your neck," here he handed to me a wreath of withered
garlic blossoms, "for other enemies more mundane—remember the wolf and the
rat—this revolver and this knife, and for aid in all, these so small electric lamps,
which you can fasten to your breast, and for all, and above all at the last, this,
which we must not desecrate needless."

This was a portion of Sacred Wafer, which he put in an envelope and handed
to me. Each of the others was similarly equipped. How odd it was, that even after
all we knew and all we had faced thus far, it seemed that each of us—save for Mr.
Singleton, who seemed to have an unwavering faith in such things—hesitated in
taking up the crucifix and garlic, as if still subconsciously incredulous as to their
effectiveness against one such as the Count.

"Now," he said, "friend Quincey, you are the expert here. Where are the skeleton keys? If so that we can open the door, we need not break house by the window, as before at Miss Lucy's."

Mr. Morris tried one or two skeleton keys, his knowledge and skill as an inventor and locksmith standing him in good stead[175]. Presently he got one to suit, after a little play back and forward the bolt yielded, and with a rusty clang, shot back. We pressed on the door, the rusty hinges creaked, and it slowly opened. It was startlingly like the image conveyed to me in Dr. Seward's diary of the opening of Miss Westenra's tomb, I fancy that the same idea seemed to strike the others, for with one accord they shrank back. The Professor was the first to move forward, and stepped into the open door.

"In manus tuas, Domine!" he said, crossing himself as he passed over the threshold. We closed the door behind us, lest when we should have lit our lamps we should possibly attract attention from the road. The Professor carefully tried the lock, lest we might not be able to open it from within should we be in a hurry making our exit. Then we all lit our lamps and proceeded on our search.

The light from the tiny lamps fell in all sorts of odd forms, as the rays crossed each other, or the opacity of our bodies threw great shadows. I could not for my life get away from the feeling that there was someone else amongst us. I suppose it was the recollection, so powerfully brought home to me by the grim surroundings, of that terrible experience in Transylvania. I think the feeling was common to us all, for I noticed that the others kept looking over their shoulders at every sound and every new shadow, just as I felt myself doing.

The whole place was thick with dust. The floor was seemingly inches deep, except where there were recent footsteps, in which on holding down my lamp I could see marks of hobnails where the dust was cracked. The walls were fluffy and heavy with dust, and in the corners were masses of spider's webs, whereon the dust had gathered till they looked like old tattered rags as the weight had torn them partly down. On a table in the hall was a great bunch of keys, with a time-yellowed label on each. They had been used several times, for on the table were several similar rents in the blanket of dust, similar to that exposed when the Professor lifted them.

He turned to me and said, "You know this place, Jonathan. You have copied maps of it, and you know it at least more than we do. Which is the way to the chapel?"

I had an idea of its direction, though on my former visit I had not been able to get admission to it, so I led the way, and after a few wrong turnings found myself opposite a low, arched oaken door, ribbed with iron bands.

"This is the spot," said the Professor as he turned his lamp on a small map of the house, copied from the file of my original correspondence regarding the purchase. With a little trouble we found the key on the bunch and opened the door. We were prepared for some unpleasantness, for as we were opening the door a faint, malodorous air seemed to exhale through the gaps, but none of us ever expected such an odour as we encountered. None of the others had met the Count at all at close quarters, and when I had seen him he was either in the fasting stage of his existence in his rooms or, when he was bloated with fresh blood, in a ruined building open to the air, but here the place was small and close, and the long disuse had made the air stagnant and foul. There was an earthy smell, as of some dry miasma, which came through the fouler air. But as to the odour itself, how shall I describe it? It was not alone that it was composed of all the ills of mortality and with the pungent, acrid smell of blood, but it seemed as though corruption had become itself corrupt. Faugh! It sickens me to think of it. Every breath exhaled by that monster seemed to have clung to the place and intensified its loathsomeness.

Under ordinary circumstances such a stench would have brought our enterprise to an end, but this was no ordinary case, and the high and terrible purpose in which we were involved gave us a strength which rose above merely physical considerations. After the involuntary shrinking consequent on the first nauseous whiff, we one and all set about our work as though that loathsome place were a garden of roses.

We made an accurate examination of the place, the Professor saying as we began, "The first thing is to see how many of the boxes are left, we must then examine every hole and corner and cranny and see if we cannot get some clue as to what has become of the rest."

A glance was sufficient to show how many remained, for the great earth chests were bulky, and there was no mistaking them.

There were only twenty-nine left out of the fifty! Once I got a fright, for, seeing Mr. Singleton suddenly turn and look out of the vaulted door into the dark passage beyond, I looked too, and for an instant my heart stood still. Somewhere, looking out from the shadow, I seemed to see the high lights of the Count's evil face, the ridge of the nose, the red eyes, the red lips, the awful pallor. It was only for a moment, for, as Mr. Singleton said, "I thought I saw a face, but it's gone now," I turned my lamp in the direction, and stepped into the passage. There was no sign of anyone, and as there were no corners, no doors, no aperture of any kind, but only the solid walls of the passage, there could be no hiding place even for him. I took it that fear had helped imagination, and said nothing.

A few minutes later I saw Morris step suddenly back from a corner, which he was examining. We all followed his movements with our eyes, for undoubtedly some nervousness was growing on us, and we saw a whole mass of phosphorescence, which twinkled like stars. We all instinctively drew back. The whole place was becoming alive with rats.

For a moment or two we stood appalled, all save Mr. Singleton, who was seemingly prepared for such an emergency. Rushing over to the great iron-bound oaken door, which Dr. Seward had described from the outside, and which I had seen myself, he turned the key in the lock, drew the huge bolts, and swung the door open. Then, taking his little silver whistle from his pocket, he blew a low, shrill call[176]. It was answered from behind Dr. Seward's house by the yelping of dogs, and after about a minute three terriers came dashing round the corner of the house. Unconsciously we had all moved towards the door, and as we moved I noticed that the dust had been much disturbed. The boxes which had been taken out had been brought this way. But even in the minute that had elapsed the number of the rats had vastly increased. They seemed to swarm over the place all at once, till the lamplight, shining on their moving dark bodies and glittering, baleful eyes, made the place look like a bank of earth set with fireflies. The dogs dashed on, but at the threshold suddenly stopped and snarled, and then, simultaneously lifting their noses, began to howl in most lugubrious fashion. The rats were multiplying in thousands, and we moved out.

Mr. Singleton lifted one of the dogs—which I noticed had two nearly luminous white spots on its brow, like a second pair of eyes—and carrying him in, placed him on the floor. The instant his feet touched the ground he seemed to recover his courage, and rushed at his natural enemies. They fled before him so fast that before he had shaken the life out of a score, the other dogs, which had by now been lifted in the same manner, had but small prey ere the whole mass had vanished.

With their going it seemed as if some evil presence had departed, for the dogs frisked about and barked merrily as they made sudden darts at their prostrate foes, and turned them over and over and tossed them in the air with vicious shakes. We all seemed to find our spirits rise. Whether it was the purifying of the deadly atmosphere by the opening of the chapel door, or the relief which we experienced by finding ourselves in the open I know not, but most certainly the shadow of dread seemed to slip from us like a robe, and the occasion of our coming lost something of its grim significance, though we did not slacken a whit in our resolution. We closed the outer door and barred and locked it, and bringing the dogs with us, began our search of the house. We found nothing throughout except dust in extraordinary proportions, and all untouched save for my own footsteps when I had made my first visit. Never once did the dogs exhibit any symptom of uneasiness, and even when we returned to the chapel they frisked about as though they had been rabbit hunting in a summer wood.

The morning was quickening in the east when we emerged from the front. Dr. Van Helsing had taken the key of the hall door from the bunch, and locked the door in orthodox fashion, putting the key into his pocket when he had done.

"So far," he said, "our night has been eminently successful. No harm has come to us such as I feared might be and yet we have ascertained how many boxes are missing, and we have for ever prevented his return to any of those that lie there. Henceforth he must find his unholy refuge in some other of the earth that he has brought or exist in one form by daylight save at noon or the turning of the tide. More than all do I rejoice that this, our first, and perhaps our most difficult and dangerous, step has been accomplished without the bringing thereinto our most sweet Madam Mina or Miss Kate, or troubling their waking or sleeping thoughts with sights and sounds and smells of horror which they might never forget. One lesson, too, we have learned, if it be allowable to argue a *particulari*, that the brute beasts which are to the Count's command are yet themselves not amenable to his spiritual power, for look, these rats that would come to his call, just as from his castle top he summon the wolves to your going and to that poor mother's cry, though they come to him, they run pell-mell from the so little dogs of our friend Alfred. We have other matters before us, other dangers, other fears, and that monster . . . He has not used his power over the brute world for the only or the last time tonight. So be it that he has gone elsewhere. Good! It has given us opportunity to cry 'check' in some ways in this chess game, which we play for the stake of human souls. And now let us go home. The dawn is close at hand, and we have reason to be content with our first night's work. It may be ordained that we have many nights and days to follow, if full of peril, but we must go on, and from no danger shall we shrink."

The house was silent when we got back, save for some poor creature who was screaming away in one of the distant wards, and a low, moaning sound from Renfield's room. The poor wretch was doubtless torturing himself, after the manner of the insane, with needless thoughts of pain.

I came tiptoe into our own room, and found Mina asleep, breathing so softly that I had to put my ear down to hear it. She looks paler than usual. I hope the meeting tonight has not upset her. I am truly thankful that she is to be left out of our future work, and even of our deliberations. It is too great a strain for a woman to bear. I did not think so at first, but I know better now. Therefore I am glad that it is settled. There may be things which would frighten her to hear, and yet to conceal them from her might be worse than to tell her if once she suspected that there was any concealment. Henceforth our work is to be a sealed book to her, till at least such time as we can tell her that all is finished, and the earth free from a monster of the nether world. I daresay it will be difficult to begin to keep silence after such confidence as ours, but I must be resolute, and tomorrow I shall keep dark over tonight's doings, and shall refuse to speak of anything that has happened. I rest on the sofa, so as not to disturb her.

1 October, later—I suppose it was natural that we should have all overslept ourselves, for the day was a busy one, and the night had no rest at all. Even Mina

must have felt its exhaustion, for though I slept till the sun was high, I was awake before her, and had to call two or three times before she awoke. Indeed, she was so sound asleep that for a few seconds she did not recognize me, but looked at me with a sort of blank terror, as one looks who has been waked out of a bad dream. She complained a little of being tired, and I let her rest till later in the day. We now know of twenty-one boxes having been removed, and if it be that several were taken in any of these removals we may be able to trace them all. Such will, of course, immensely simplify our labor, and the sooner the matter is attended to the better. I shall look up Thomas Snelling today.

Dr. Seward's Case-Book

1 October—It was towards noon when I was awakened by the Professor walking into my room. He was more jolly and cheerful than usual, and it is quite evident that last night's work has helped to take some of the brooding weight off his mind.

After going over the adventure of the night he suddenly said, "Your patient interests me much. May it be that with you I visit him this morning? Or if that you are too occupy, I can go alone if it may be. It is a new experience to me to find a lunatic who talk philosophy, and reason so sound."

I had some work to do which pressed, so I told him that if he would go alone I would be glad, as then I should not have to keep him waiting, so I called an attendant and gave him the necessary instructions. Before the Professor left the room I cautioned him against getting any false impression from my patient.

"But," he answered, "I want him to talk of himself and of his delusion as to consuming live things. He said to Madam Mina, as I see in your diary of yesterday, that he had once had such a belief. Why do you smile, friend John?"

"Excuse me," I said, "but the answer is here." I laid my hand on the typewritten matter. "When our sane and learned lunatic made that very statement of how he used to consume life, his mouth was actually nauseous with the flies and spiders which he had eaten just before Mrs. Harker entered the room."

Van Helsing smiled in turn. "Good!" he said. "Your memory is true, friend John. I should have remembered. And yet it is this very obliquity of thought and memory which makes mental disease such a fascinating study. Perhaps I may gain more knowledge out of the folly of this madman than I shall from the teaching of the most wise. After all, he already knew, in the way that madmen often come to know things beyond their ken, that the Vampire had given his blood to Lucy before even we ourselves saw her as Undead. Who knows what else may be learned?"

I went on with my work, and before long was through that in hand. It seemed that the time had been very short indeed, but there was Van Helsing back in the study.

"Do I interrupt?" he asked politely as he stood at the door.

"Not at all," I answered. "Come in. My work is finished, and I am free. I can go with you now, if you like."

"It is needless, I have seen him!"

"Well?"

"I fear that he does not appraise me at much. Our interview was short. When I entered his room he was sitting on a stool in the centre, with his elbows on his knees, and his face was the picture of sullen discontent. I spoke to him as cheerfully as I could, and with such a measure of respect as I could assume. He made no reply whatever. 'Don't you know me?' I asked. His answer was not reassuring. 'I know you well enough, you are the old fool Van Helsing. I wish you would take yourself and your idiotic brain theories somewhere else. Damn all thick-headed Dutchmen!' Not a word more would he say, but sat in his implacable sullenness as indifferent to me as though I had not been in the room at all. Thus departed for this time my chance of much learning from this so clever lunatic, so I shall go, if I may, and cheer myself with a few happy words with that sweet soul Madam Mina. Friend John, it does rejoice me unspeakable that she is no more to be pained, no more to be worried with our terrible things. Though we shall much miss her help, it is better so."

"I agree with you with all my heart," I answered earnestly, for I did not want him to weaken in this matter. "Mrs. Harker is better out of it. Things are quite bad enough for us, all men of the world, and who have been in many tight places in our time, but it is no place for a woman, and if she had remained in touch with the affair, it would in time infallibly have wrecked her."

So Van Helsing has gone to confer with Mrs. Harker and Harker, Quincey, Art, and Singleton are all out following up the clues as to the earth boxes. I shall finish my round of work and perhaps have a relaxing chat with Kate before the men meet again tonight.

Mina Harker's Journal

1 October—It is strange to me to be kept in the dark as I am today, after Jonathan's full confidence for so many years, to see him manifestly avoid certain matters, and those the most vital of all. This morning I slept late after the fatigues of yesterday, and though Jonathan was late too, he was the earlier. He spoke to me before he went out, never more sweetly or tenderly, but he never mentioned a word of what had happened in the visit to the Count's house. And yet he must have known how terribly anxious I was. Poor dear fellow! I suppose it must have distressed him even more than it did me. They all agreed that it was best that I should not be drawn further into this awful work, and I acquiesced. But to think that he keeps anything from me! And now I am crying like a silly fool, when I

know it comes from my husband's great love and from the good, good wishes of those other strong men.

That has done me good. Some day Jonathan will tell me all himself. And lest it should ever be that he should think for a moment that I kept anything from him, I still keep my journal as usual. Then if he has feared of my trust I shall show it to him, with every thought of my heart put down for his dear eyes to read. I feel strangely sad and low-spirited today. I suppose it is the reaction from the terrible excitement.

Last night I went to bed when the men had gone, simply because they told me to. I didn't feel sleepy, and I did feel full of devouring anxiety. I kept thinking over everything that has been ever since Jonathan came to see me in London, and it all seems like a horrible tragedy, with fate pressing on relentlessly to some destined end. Everything that one does seems, no matter how right it may be, to bring on the very thing which is most to be deplored. If I hadn't gone to Whitby, perhaps poor dear Lucy would be with us now. She hadn't taken to visiting the churchyard till I came, and if she hadn't come there in the day time with me she wouldn't have walked in her sleep. And if she hadn't gone there at night and asleep, that monster couldn't have destroyed her as he did. Oh, why did I ever go to Whitby? There now, crying again! I wonder what has come over me today. I must hide it from Jonathan, for if he knew that I had been crying twice in one morning . . . I, who never cried on my own account, and whom he has never caused to shed a tear, the dear fellow would fret his heart out. I shall put a bold face on, and if I do feel weepy, he shall never see it. I suppose it is just one of the lessons that we poor women have to learn.

I can't quite remember how I fell asleep last night. I remember hearing the sudden barking of the dogs and a lot of queer sounds, like praying on a very tumultuous scale, from Mr. Renfield's room, which is somewhere under this. And then there was silence over everything, silence so profound that it startled me, and I got up and looked out of the window. All was dark and silent, the black shadows thrown by the moonlight seeming full of a silent mystery of their own. Not a thing seemed to be stirring, but all to be grim and fixed as death or fate, so that a thin streak of white mist, that crept with almost imperceptible slowness across the grass towards the house, seemed to have a sentience and a vitality of its own. I think that the digression of my thoughts must have done me good, for when I got back to bed I found a lethargy creeping over me. I lay a while, but could not quite sleep, so I got out and looked out of the window again. The mist was spreading, and was now close up to the house, so that I could see it lying thick against the wall, as though it were stealing up to the windows. The poor man was more loud than ever, and though I could not distinguish a word he said, I could in some way recognize in his tones some passionate entreaty on his part. Then there was the sound of a struggle, and I knew that the attendants were dealing with him. I was so frightened that I crept into bed, and pulled the clothes over my head, putting my fingers in my ears. I was not then a bit sleepy, at least so I thought, but I must have fallen asleep, for except dreams, I do not remember anything until the morning, when Jonathan woke me. I think that it took me an effort and a little time to realize where I was, and that it was Jonathan who was bending over me. My dream was very peculiar, and was almost typical of the way that waking thoughts become merged in, or continued in, dreams.

I thought that I was asleep, and waiting for Jonathan to come back. I was very anxious about him, and I was powerless to act, my feet, and my hands, and my brain were weighted, so that nothing could proceed at the usual pace. And so I slept uneasily and thought. Then it began to dawn upon me that the air was heavy, and dank, and cold. I put back the clothes from my face, and found, to my surprise, that all was dim around. The gaslight which I had left lit for Jonathan, but turned down, came only like a tiny red spark through the fog, which had evidently grown thicker and poured into the room. Then it occurred to me that I had shut the window before I had come to bed. I would have got out to make certain on the point, but some leaden lethargy seemed to chain my limbs and even my will. I lay still and endured, that was all. I closed my eyes, but could still see through my eyelids. (It is wonderful what tricks our dreams play us, and how conveniently we can imagine.) The mist grew thicker and thicker and I could see now how it came in, for I could see it like smoke, or with the white energy of boiling water, pouring in, not through the window, but through the joinings of the door. It got thicker and thicker, till it seemed as if it became concentrated into a sort of pillar of cloud in the room, through the top of which I could see the light of the gas shining like a red eye. Things began to whirl through my brain just as the cloudy column was now whirling in the room, and through it all came the scriptural words "a pillar of cloud by day and of fire by night." Was it indeed such spiritual guidance that was coming to me in my sleep? But the pillar was composed of both the day and the night guiding, for the fire was in the red eye, which at the thought got a new fascination for me, till, as I looked, the fire divided, and seemed to shine on me through the fog like two red eyes, such as Lucy told me of in her momentary mental wandering when, on the cliff, the dying sunlight struck the windows of St. Mary's Church. Suddenly the horror burst upon me that it was thus that Jonathan had seen those awful women growing into reality through the whirling mist in the moonlight, and in my dream I must have fainted, for all became black darkness. The last conscious effort which imagination made was to show me a livid white face bending over me out of the mist.

I must be careful of such dreams, for they would unseat one's reason if there were too much of them. I would get Dr. Van Helsing or Dr. Seward to prescribe something for me which would make me sleep, only that I fear to alarm them. Such a dream at the present time would become woven into their fears for me.

Tonight I shall strive hard to sleep naturally. If I do not, I shall tomorrow night get them to give me a dose of chloral, that cannot hurt me for once, and it will give me a good night's sleep. Last night tired me more than if I had not slept at all.

2 October 10 P.M.—Last night I slept, but did not dream. I must have slept soundly, for I was not waked by Jonathan coming to bed, but the sleep has not refreshed me, for today I feel terribly weak and spiritless. I spent all yesterday trying to read, or lying down dozing. In the afternoon, Mr. Renfield asked if he might see me. Poor man, he was very gentle, and when I came away he kissed my hand and bade God bless me. Some way it affected me much. I am crying when I think of him. This is a new weakness, of which I must be careful. Jonathan would be miserable if he knew I had been crying. He and the others were out till dinner time, and they all came in tired. I did what I could to brighten them up, and I suppose that the effort did me good, for I forgot how tired I was. After dinner they sent me to bed, and all went off to smoke together, as they said, but I knew that they wanted to tell each other of what had occurred to each during the day. I could see from Jonathan's manner that he had something important to communicate. I was not so sleepy as I should have been, so before they went I asked Dr. Seward to give me a little opiate of some kind, as I had not slept well the night before. He very kindly made me up a sleeping draught, which he gave to me, telling me that it would do me no harm, as it was very mild . . . I have taken it, and am waiting for sleep, which still keeps aloof. I hope I have not done wrong, for as sleep begins to flirt with me, a new fear comes, that I may have been foolish in thus depriving myself of the power of waking. I might want it. Here comes sleep. Goodnight.

CHAPTER TWENTY-EIGHT[177]

Jonathan Harker's Journal

1 October, evening—I found Thomas Snelling in his house at Bethnal Green, but unhappily he was not in a condition to remember anything. The very prospect of beer which my expected coming had opened to him had proved too much, and he had begun too early on his expected debauch. I learned, however, from his wife, who seemed a decent, poor soul, that he was only the assistant of Smollet, who of the two mates was the responsible person. So off I drove to Walworth, and found Mr. Joseph Smollet at home and in his shirtsleeves, taking a late tea out of a saucer. He is a decent, intelligent fellow, distinctly a good, reliable type of workman, and with a headpiece of his own. He remembered all about the incident of the boxes, and from a wonderful dog-eared notebook, which he produced from some mysterious receptacle about the seat of his trousers, and which had hieroglyphical entries in thick, half-obliterated pencil, he gave me the destinations of the boxes. There were, he said, six in the cartload which he took from Carfax and left at 197 Chicksand Street, Mile End New Town, and another six which he deposited at Jamaica Lane, Bermondsey. If then the Count meant to scatter these ghastly refuges of his over London, these places were chosen as the first of delivery, so that later he might distribute more fully. The systematic manner in which this was done made me think that he could not mean to confine himself to two sides of London. He was now fixed on the far east on the northern shore, on the east of the southern shore, and on the south. The north and west were surely never meant to be left out of his diabolical scheme, let alone the City itself and the very heart of fashionable London in the south-west and west. I went back to Smollet, and asked him if he could tell us if any other boxes had been taken from Carfax.

He replied, "Well guv'nor, you've treated me very 'an'some," I had given him half a sovereign, "an' I'll tell yer all I know. I heard a man by the name of Bloxam say four nights ago in the 'Are an' 'Ounds, in Pincher's Alley, as 'ow he an' his mate 'ad 'ad a rare dusty job in a old 'ouse at Purfleet. There ain't a many such jobs as this 'ere, an' I'm thinkin' that maybe Sam Bloxam could tell ye summut."

I asked if he could tell me where to find him. I told him that if he could get me the address it would be worth another half sovereign to him. So he gulped down the rest of his tea and stood up, saying that he was going to begin the search then and there.

At the door he stopped, and said, "Look 'ere, guv'nor, there ain't no sense in me a keepin' you 'ere. I may find Sam soon, or I mayn't, but anyhow he ain't like to be in a way to tell ye much tonight. Sam is a rare one when he starts on the booze. If you can give me a envelope with a stamp on it, and put yer address on it, I'll find out where Sam is to be found and post it ye tonight. But ye'd better be up arter 'im soon in the mornin,' never mind the booze the night afore."

This was all practical, so one of the children went off with a penny to buy an envelope and a sheet of paper, and to keep the change. When she came back, I addressed the envelope and stamped it, and when Smollet had again faithfully promised to post the address when found, I took my way to home. We're on the track anyhow. I am tired tonight, and I want to sleep. Mina is fast asleep, and looks a little too pale. Her eyes look as though she had been crying. Poor dear, I've no doubt it frets her to be kept in the dark, and it may make her doubly anxious about me and the others. But it is best as it is. It is better to be disappointed and worried in such a way now than to have her nerve broken. The doctors were quite right to insist on her being kept out of this dreadful business. I must be firm, for on me this particular burden of silence must rest. I shall not ever enter on the subject with her under any circumstances. Indeed, It may not be a hard task, after all, for she herself has become reticent on the subject, and has not spoken of the Count or his doings ever since we told her of our decision.

2 October, evening—A long and trying and exciting day. By the first post I got my directed envelope with a dirty scrap of paper enclosed, on which was written with a carpenter's pencil in a sprawling hand, "Sam Bloxam, Korkrans, 4 Poters Cort, Bartel Street, Walworth. Arsk for the depite."

I got the letter in bed, and rose without waking Mina. She looked heavy and sleepy and pale, and far from well. I determined not to wake her, but that when I should return from this new search, I would arrange for her going back to Exeter. I think she would be happier in our own home, with her daily tasks to interest her, than in being here amongst us and in ignorance. I only saw Dr. Seward for a moment, and told him where I was off to, promising to come back and tell the rest so soon as I should have found out anything. I drove to Walworth and found, with some difficulty, Potter's Court. Mr. Smollet's spelling misled me, as I asked for Poter's Court instead of Potter's Court. However, when I had found the court, I had no difficulty in discovering Corcoran's lodging house.

When I asked the man who came to the door for the "depite," he shook his head, and said, "I dunno 'im. There ain't no such a person 'ere. I never 'eard of 'im in all my bloomin' days. Don't believe there ain't nobody of that kind livin' 'ere or anywheres."

I took out Smollet's letter, and as I read it seemed to me that the lesson of the spelling of the name of the court might guide me. "What are you?" I asked.

"I'm the depity," he answered.

I saw at once that I was on the right track. Phonetic spelling had again misled me. A half crown tip put the deputy's knowledge at my disposal, and I learned that Mr. Bloxam, who had slept off the remains of his beer on the previous night at Corcoran's, had left for his work at Poplar at five o'clock that morning. He could not tell me where the place of work was situated, but he had a vague idea that it was some kind of a "new-fangled ware'us," and with this slender clue I had to start for Poplar. It was twelve o'clock before I got any satisfactory hint of such a building, and this I got at a coffee shop, where some workmen were having their dinner. One of them suggested that there was being erected at Cross Angel Street a new "cold storage" building, and as this suited the condition of a "new-fangled ware'us," I at once drove to it. An interview with a surly gatekeeper and a surlier foreman, both of whom were appeased with the coin of the realm, put me on the track of Bloxam. He was sent for on my suggestion that I was willing to pay his days wages to his foreman for the privilege of asking him a few questions on a private matter. He was a smart enough fellow, though rough of speech and bearing. When I had promised to pay for his information and given him an earnest, he told me that he had made two journeys between Carfax and a house in Piccadilly, and had taken from this house to the latter nine great boxes, "main heavy ones," with a horse and cart hired by him for this purpose.

I asked him if he could tell me the number of the house in Piccadilly, to which he replied, "Well, guv'nor, I forgits the number, but it was only a few door from a big white church, or somethink of the kind, not long built. It was a dusty old 'ouse, too, though nothin' to the dustiness of the 'ouse we tooked the bloomin' boxes from." That matched with the mansion Miss Reed described as being across from her own.

"How did you get in if both houses were empty?"

"There was the old party what engaged me a waitin' in the 'ouse at Purfleet. He 'elped me to lift the boxes and put them in the dray. Curse me, but he was the strongest chap I ever struck, an' him a old feller, with a white moustache, one that thin you would think he couldn't throw a shadder."

How this phrase thrilled through me!

"Why, 'e took up 'is end o' the boxes like they was pounds of tea, and me a puffin' an' a blowin' afore I could upend mine anyhow, an' I'm no chicken, neither."

"How did you get into the house in Piccadilly?" I asked.

"There was another man there too. He looked akin to that old feller, but younger, with a dark beard. He 'elped me carry the boxes into the 'all."

"The whole nine?" I asked.

"Yus, there was five in the first load an' four in the second. It was main dry work, an' I don't so well remember 'ow I got 'ome."

I interrupted him, "Were the boxes left in the hall?"

"Yus, it was a big 'all, an' there was nothin' else in it."

I made one more attempt to further matters. "You didn't have any key?"

"Never used no key nor nothink. The old gent, he opened the door 'isself an' shut it again when I druv off. I don't remember the last time, but that was the beer."

"And you can't remember the number of the house?"

"No, sir. But ye needn't have no difficulty about that. It's a 'igh 'un with a stone front with a bow on it, an' 'igh steps up to the door. I know them steps, 'avin' 'ad to carry the boxes up with three loafers what come round to earn a copper. The old gent give them shillin's, an' they seein' they got so much, they wanted more. But 'e took one of them by the shoulder and was like to throw 'im down the steps, till the lot of them went away cussin.'"

I thought that with this description I could find the house, even if I wasn't already sure by now that is would be across from Miss Reed's own 346, so having paid my friend for his information, I started off for Piccadilly. I had gained a new painful experience. The Count could, it was evident, handle the earth boxes himself. What's more, it appeared he could grow old or young again at will, and so disguise himself . . . unless, of course, there are indeed two of them as Miss Reed fears—God help us! If so, time was precious, for now that he had achieved a certain amount of distribution, he could, by choosing his own time and his own form, complete the task unobserved. At Piccadilly Circus I discharged my cab, and walked westward. Beyond the Junior Constitutional I came across the house described and was satisfied that this was the next of the lairs arranged by Dracula. The house looked as though it had been long untenanted. The windows were encrusted with dust, and the shutters were up. All the framework was black with time, and from the iron the paint had mostly scaled away. It was evident that up to lately there had been a large notice board in front of the balcony. It had, however, been roughly torn away, the uprights which had supported it still remaining. Behind the rails of the balcony I saw there were some loose boards, whose raw edges looked white. I would have given a good deal to have been able to see the notice board intact, as it would, perhaps, have given some clue to the ownership of the house. I remembered my experience of the investigation and purchase of Carfax, and I could not but feel that if I could find the former owner there might be some means discovered of gaining access to the house.

There was at present nothing to be learned from the Piccadilly side, and nothing could be done, so I went around to the back to see if anything could be gathered from this quarter. The mews were active, the Piccadilly houses being mostly in occupation. I asked one or two of the grooms and helpers whom I saw around if they could tell me anything about the empty house. One of them said that he heard it had lately been taken, but he couldn't say from whom. He told me, however, that up to very lately there had been a notice board of "For Sale" up, and that perhaps Mitchell, Sons, & Candy the house agents could tell me something, as he thought he remembered seeing the name of that firm on the board. I did not wish to seem too eager, or to let my informant know or guess too much, so thanking him in the usual manner, I strolled away. It was now growing dusk, and the autumn night was closing in, so I did not lose any time. Having learned the address of Mitchell, Sons, & Candy from a directory at the Berkeley, I was soon at their office in Sackville Street.

The gentleman who saw me was particularly suave in manner, but uncommunicative in equal proportion. Having once told me that the Piccadilly house, which throughout our interview he called a "mansion," was sold, he considered my business as concluded. When I asked who had purchased it, he opened his eyes a thought wider, and paused a few seconds before replying, "It is sold, sir."

"Pardon me," I said, with equal politeness, "but I have a special reason for wishing to know who purchased it."

Again he paused longer, and raised his eyebrows still more. "It is sold, sir," was again his laconic reply.

"Surely," I said, "you do not mind letting me know so much."

"But I do mind," he answered. "The affairs of their clients are absolutely safe in the hands of Mitchell, Sons, & Candy."

This was manifestly a prig of the first water, and there was no use arguing with him. I thought I had best meet him on his own ground, so I said, "Your clients, sir, are happy in having so resolute a guardian of their confidence. I am myself a professional man."

Here I handed him my card. "In this instance I am not prompted by curiosity, I act on the part of Lord Godalming, who wishes to know something of the property which was, he understood, lately for sale."

These words put a different complexion on affairs. He said, "I would like to oblige you if I could, Mr. Harker, and especially would I like to oblige his lordship. We once carried out a small matter of renting some chambers for him when he was the honourable Arthur Holmwood. If you will let me have his lordship's address

I will consult the House on the subject, and will, in any case, communicate with his lordship by tonight's post. It will be a pleasure if we can so far deviate from our rules as to give the required information to his lordship."

I wanted to secure a friend, and not to make an enemy, so I thanked him, gave the address at Dr. Seward's and came away. It was now dark, and I was tired and hungry. I got a cup of tea at the Aerated Bread Company and came down to Purfleet by the next train.

I found all the others at home. Mina was looking tired and pale, but she made a gallant effort to be bright and cheerful. It wrung my heart to think that I had had to keep anything from her and so caused her inquietude. Thank God, this will be the last night of her looking on at our conferences, and feeling the sting of our not showing our confidence. It took all my courage to hold to the wise resolution of keeping her out of our grim task. She seems somehow more reconciled, or else the very subject seems to have become repugnant to her, for when any accidental allusion is made she actually shudders. I am glad we made our resolution in time, as with such a feeling as this, our growing knowledge would be torture to her.

I could not tell the others of the day's discovery till we were alone, so after dinner, followed by a little music to save appearances even amongst ourselves, I took Mina to her room and left her to go to bed. The dear girl was more affectionate with me than ever, and clung to me as though she would detain me, but there was much to be talked of and I came away. Thank God, the ceasing of telling things has made no difference between us.

When I came down again I found the others all gathered round the fire in the study. In the train I had written my diary so far, and simply read it off to them as the best means of letting them get abreast of my own information.

When I had finished Van Helsing said, "This has been a great day's work, friend Jonathan. Doubtless we are on the track of the missing boxes. If we find them all in that house, then our work is near the end. But if there be some missing, we must search until we find them. Then shall we make our final coup, and hunt the wretch to his real death."

We all sat silent awhile and all at once Mr. Morris spoke, "Say! How are we going to get into that house?"

"We got into the other," answered Lord Godalming quickly.

"But, Art, this is different. We broke house at Carfax, but we had night and a walled park to protect us. It will be a mighty different thing to commit burglary in Piccadilly, either by day or night. I confess I don't see how we are going to get in unless that agency duck can find us a key of some sort."

Lord Godalming's brows contracted, and he stood up and walked about the room. By-and-by he stopped and said, turning from one to another of us, "Quincey's head is level. This burglary business is getting serious. We got off once all right, but we have now a rare job on hand. Unless we can find the Count's key basket."

As nothing could well be done before morning, and as it would be at least advisable to wait till Lord Godalming should hear from Mitchell's, we decided not to take any active step before breakfast time. For a good while we sat and smoked, discussing the matter in its various lights and bearings. I took the opportunity of bringing this diary right up to the moment. I am very sleepy and shall go to bed . . .

Just a line. Mina sleeps soundly and her breathing is regular. Her forehead is puckered up into little wrinkles, as though she thinks even in her sleep. She is still too pale, but does not look so haggard as she did this morning. Tomorrow will, I hope, mend all this. She will be herself at home in Exeter. Oh, but I am sleepy!

Dr. Seward's Case-Book

1 October—I am puzzled afresh about Renfield. His moods change so rapidly that I find it difficult to keep touch of them, and as they always mean something more than his own well-being, they form a more than interesting study. This morning, when I went to see him after his repulse of Van Helsing, his manner was that of a man commanding destiny. He was, in fact, commanding destiny, subjectively. He did not really care for any of the things of mere earth, he was in the clouds and looked down on all the weaknesses and wants of us poor mortals.

I thought I would improve the occasion and learn something, so I asked him, "What about the flies these times?"

He smiled on me in quite a superior sort of way, such a smile as would have become the face of Malvolio, as he answered me, "The fly, my dear sir, has one striking feature. It's wings are typical of the aerial powers of the psychic faculties. The ancients did well when they typified the soul as a butterfly!"

I thought I would push his analogy to its utmost logically, so I said quickly, "Oh, it is a soul you are after now, is it?"

His madness foiled his reason, and a puzzled look spread over his face as, shaking his head with a decision which I had but seldom seen in him.

He said, "Oh, no, oh no! I want no souls. Life is all I want." Here he brightened up. "I am pretty indifferent about it at present. Life is all right. I have all I want. You must get a new patient, doctor, if you wish to study zoophagy!"

This puzzled me a little, so I drew him on. "Then you command life. You are a god, I suppose?"

He smiled with an ineffably benign superiority. "Oh no! Far be it from me to arrogate to myself the attributes of the Deity. I am not even concerned in His especially spiritual doings. If I may state my intellectual position I am, so far as concerns things purely terrestrial, somewhat in the position which Enoch occupied spiritually!"

This was a poser to me. I could not at the moment recall Enoch's appositeness, so I had to ask a simple question, though I felt that by so doing I was lowering myself in the eyes of the lunatic. "And why with Enoch?"

"Because he walked with God."

I could not see the analogy, but did not like to admit it, so I harked back to what he had denied. "So you don't care about life and you don't want souls. Why not?" I put my question quickly and somewhat sternly, on purpose to disconcert him.

The effort succeeded, for an instant he unconsciously relapsed into his old servile manner, bent low before me, and actually fawned upon me as he replied. "I don't want any souls, indeed, indeed! I don't. I couldn't use them if I had them. They would be no manner of use to me. I couldn't eat them or . . ."

He suddenly stopped and the old cunning look spread over his face, like a wind sweep on the surface of the water.

"And doctor, as to life, what is it after all? When you've got all you require, and you know that you will never want, that is all. I have friends, good friends, like you, Dr. Seward." This was said with a leer of inexpressible cunning. "I know that I shall never lack the means of life!"

I think that through the cloudiness of his insanity he saw some antagonism in me, for he at once fell back on the last refuge of such as he, a dogged silence. After a short time I saw that for the present it was useless to speak to him. He was sulky, and so I came away.

Later in the day he sent for me. Ordinarily I would not have come without special reason, but just at present I am so interested in him that I would gladly make an effort. Besides, I am glad to have anything to help pass the time. Harker is out, following up clues, and so are Lord Godalming and Quincey. Van Helsing sits in my study with Mr. Singleton, poring over the record prepared by the Harkers and debating between themselves certain esoteric points beyond my ken. Both seem to think that by accurate knowledge and correct interpretation of all details they will light up on some clue, though they apparently differ on what that interpretation may be. They do not wish to be disturbed in the work, without cause. I would have taken Van Helsing with me to see the patient, only I thought that after his last repulse he might not care to go again. There was also another reason. Renfield might not speak so freely before a third person as when he and I were alone.

I found him sitting in the middle of the floor on his stool, a pose which is generally indicative of some mental energy on his part. When I came in, he said at once, as though the question had been waiting on his lips. "What about souls?"

It was evident then that my surmise had been correct. Unconscious cerebration was doing its work, even with the lunatic. I determined to have the matter out.

"What about them yourself?" I asked.

He did not reply for a moment but looked all around him, and up and down, as though he expected to find some inspiration for an answer.

"I don't want any souls!" He said in a feeble, apologetic way. The matter seemed preying on his mind, and so I determined to use it, to "be cruel only to be kind." So I said, "You like life, and you want life?"

"Oh yes! But that is all right. You needn't worry about that!"

"But," I asked, "how are we to get the life without getting the soul also?"

This seemed to puzzle him, so I followed it up, "A nice time you'll have some time when you're flying out here, with the souls of thousands of flies and spiders and birds and cats buzzing and twittering and moaning all around you. You've got their lives, you know, and you must put up with their souls!"

Something seemed to affect his imagination, for he put his fingers to his ears and shut his eyes, screwing them up tightly just as a small boy does when his face is being soaped. There was something pathetic in it that touched me. It also gave me a lesson, for it seemed that before me was a child, only a child, though the features were worn, and the stubble on the jaws was white. It was evident that he was undergoing some process of mental disturbance, and knowing how his past moods had interpreted things seemingly foreign to himself, I thought I would enter into his mind as well as I could and go with him

The first step was to restore confidence, so I asked him, speaking pretty loud so that he would hear me through his closed ears, "Would you like some sugar to get your flies around again?"

He seemed to wake up all at once, and shook his head. With a laugh he replied, "Not much! Flies are poor things, after all!" After a pause he added, "But I don't want their souls buzzing round me, all the same."

"Or spiders?" I went on.

"Blow spiders! What's the use of spiders? There isn't anything in them to eat or . . ." He stopped suddenly as though reminded of a forbidden topic.

"So, so!" I thought to myself, "this is the second time he has suddenly stopped at the word 'drink.' What does it mean?"

Renfield seemed himself aware of having made a lapse, for he hurried on, as though to distract my attention from it, "I don't take any stock at all in such matters. 'Rats and mice and such small deer,' as Shakespeare has it, 'chicken feed of the larder' they might be called. I'm past all that sort of nonsense. You might as well ask a man to eat molecules with a pair of chopsticks, as to try to interest me about the less carnivora, when I know of what is before me."

"I see," I said. "You want big things that you can make your teeth meet in? How would you like to breakfast on an elephant?"

"What ridiculous nonsense you are talking!" He was getting too wide awake, so I thought I would press him hard.

"I wonder," I said reflectively, "what an elephant's soul is like!"

The effect I desired was obtained, for he at once fell from his high-horse and became a child again.

"I don't want an elephant's soul, or any soul at all!" he said. For a few moments he sat despondently. Suddenly he jumped to his feet, with his eyes blazing and all the signs of intense cerebral excitement. "To hell with you and your souls!" he shouted. "Why do you plague me about souls? Haven't I got enough to worry, and pain, to distract me already, without thinking of souls?"

He looked so hostile that I thought he was in for another homicidal fit, so I blew my whistle.

The instant, however, that I did so he became calm, and said apologetically, "Forgive me, Doctor. I forgot myself. You do not need any help. I am so worried in my mind that I am apt to be irritable. If you only knew the problem I have to face, and that I am working out, you would pity, and tolerate, and pardon me. Pray do not put me in a strait waistcoat. I want to think and I cannot think freely when my body is confined. I am sure you will understand!"

He had evidently self-control, so when the attendants came I told them not to mind, and they withdrew. Renfield watched them go. When the door was closed he said with considerable dignity and sweetness, "Dr. Seward, you have been very considerate towards me. Believe me that I am very, very grateful to you!"

I thought it well to leave him in this mood, and so I came away. There is certainly something to ponder over in this man's state. Several points seem to make what the American interviewer calls "a story," if one could only get them in proper order. Here they are:

- Will not mention "drinking."
- Fears the thought of being burdened with the "soul" of anything.
- Has no dread of wanting "life" in the future.
- Despises the meaner forms of life altogether, though he dreads being haunted by their souls.
- Logically all these things point one way! He has assurance of some kind that he will acquire some higher life.
- He dreads the consequence, the burden of a soul. Then it is a human life he looks to!
- And the assurance . . . ?

Merciful God! The Count has been to him, and there is some new scheme of terror afoot!

Later—I went after my round to Van Helsing and told him my suspicion. Mr. Singleton had departed for a time, so we were free to speak with greater candor. He grew very grave, and after thinking the matter over for a while asked me to take him to Renfield. I did so. As we came to the door we heard the lunatic within singing gaily, as he used to do in the time which now seems so long ago.

When we entered we saw with amazement that he had spread out his sugar as of old. The flies, lethargic with the autumn, were beginning to buzz into the room. We tried to make him talk of the subject of our previous conversation, but he would not attend. He went on with his singing, just as though we had not been present. He had got a scrap of paper and was folding it into a notebook. We had to come away as ignorant as we went in.

His is a curious case indeed. We must watch him tonight.

Letter, Mitchell, Sons & Candy to Lord Godalming[178]

1 October.

My Lord,

We have no objection whatever to give you the information concerning which you have written to us, and are only too pleased to be able to meet your Lordship's wishes. We beg, with regard to the desire of your Lordship, expressed by Mr. Harker on your behalf, to supply the following information concerning the sale and purchase of No. 347, Piccadilly. It is true that we effected the sale of 347, Piccadilly. The original vendors were the executors of the late Mr. Archibald Winter-Suffield, who placed this property with some other real estate in our hand for disposal. The other properties passed into other vendors' hands—Mr. Trollope and Mr. Pickford. With regard to the property in question, we had on the 4. September about two o'clock a call from a gentleman who said he was Count De Ville, and that he had called to make a purchase of the house in Piccadilly. As such purchases are not generally effected over the Counter, so to speak—if your Lordship will pardon the trade familiarity of the phrase our—Mr. Leitch who was attending to him suggested a reference or the name of his solicitor, while at the same time explaining (since the gentleman was evidently a stranger and, in spite of the purity of his accent, evidently a foreigner) the usual process of the purchase of he real estate. The gentleman simply asked how much was the price and on our Mr Leitch naming the sum £2,000 he took from his pocket a cheque book and said "When you have received the money from the bank please to have the deed of sale made out in my favour. I shall call for it in two days," and walked out. He has evidently been accustomed to an offhand method of business. The cheque was duly honoured by Messrs. Coutts & Co and the deed of sale was made out to him. The Christian name had to be left blank but at our request he filled it up himself when he called with he name De Ville. We handed him the keys and we have no since heard of or from him.

We are, my Lord,
Your Lordship's humble servants,
Mitchell, Sons & Candy

Dr. Seward's Case-Book

2 October—I placed a man in the corridor last night, and told him to make an accurate note of any sound he might hear from Renfield's room, and gave him instructions that if there should be anything strange he was to call me. After dinner, when we had all gathered round the fire in the study, Mrs. Harker having gone to bed, we discussed the attempts and discoveries of the day. Harker was the only one who had any result, and we are in great hopes that his clue may be an important one.

Before going to bed I went round to the patient's room and looked in through the observation trap. He was sleeping soundly, his heart rose and fell with regular respiration.

This morning the man on duty reported to me that a little after midnight he was restless and kept saying his prayers somewhat loudly. I asked him if that was all. He replied that it was all he heard. There was something about his manner, so suspicious that I asked him point blank if he had been asleep. He denied sleep, but admitted to having "dozed" for a while. It is too bad that men cannot be trusted unless they are watched.

Today Harker is out following up his clue. Art and Quincey are looking after horses. Godalming thinks that it will be well to have horses always in readiness, for when we get the information which we seek there will be no time to lose. We must sterilize all the imported earth between sunrise and sunset. We shall thus catch the Count at his weakest, and without a refuge to fly to. Van Helsing is off to the British Museum looking up some authorities on ancient medicine. The old physicians took account of things which their followers do not accept, and the Professor is searching for witch and demon cures which may be useful to us later.

I sometimes think we must be all mad and that we shall wake to sanity in strait waistcoats.

Inspector Cotford's Case Notes

2 October—I have just read through the collection of journals that Mrs. Harker had compiled for the third time. I must confess that I am now somewhat further away from understanding this case than I was before procuring this document. There is certainly much to be found within the journals, this collection of fascinating details which have the potential to shed new light upon all that has transpired over the previous weeks and months. And still, there is also so much reason to doubt the truthfulness of what each writer has recorded. To wit:

Katherine Reed and Alfred Singleton, though perhaps the most honest of the lot—relatively speaking, that is—have been until recently so far removed from the bulk of the happenings, and are so involved with their own self-interests, that their testimony is of little help.

Jonathan Harker, whose recollections were seemingly the beginning of this whole affair, was, and to some degree may still be, suffering from brain fever, and has clearly exhibited all the symptoms of anxiety and paranoia and hallucination that such a condition can bring about. Though I still maintain my assessment of him as a fine and honest man, I cannot but wonder as to how much of his tale is pure fancy born out of the fever. (*mem.*, I note in his Journal that he had Tokay wine while abroad at the castle. Being something of a connoisseur of wines, I seem to recall that Tokay is prone to going bad in the Spring, when the frozen plants are first coming back to life. Could this have been the cause of Harker's illness?)[179].

His wife, Wilhelmina Harker (*née* Murray), who first served as the historian of Lucy Westenra and now is stenographer for the party—though she is admittedly far more precise in her writing than most women—still suffers from the same naivety which plagues all her sex, for she has assumed a degree of innocence in her companions that is clearly not present.

As for Lucy Westenra, who until recently was the focus of all attention, her words can be trusted not at all. It is a near certainty that she was having illicit romantic liaisons—though whether with one or more of her suitors, or with another man entirely, it is yet difficult to say—and would naturally wish to cover up such affairs with misdirection. And later, as with Mr. Harker, she grew ill and was clearly unable to discern what was dream and what was waking reality. Alternately, I must concede that she may well have had a doppelganger, a repressed alter ego which manifested as the "sleepwalker," and it was in this state she met with her lover or lovers. In either event, she was most certainly buried alive, and then later awoke in her own tomb—perhaps confused or deranged by the harrowing experience, or perhaps with her alter ego now fully to the fore—only to be hunted and murdered outright by her own suitors. Such a thing as living burial is not unheard of: I recall hearing an account of a woman named Guasser who suffered from a kind of catalepsy twice each day, during which time her limbs grew hard like stone, had only the faintest pulse, and did not respond to pain. And of course there was Col. Townshend; three men—Dr. Cheyne, Dr. Baynard, and Mr. Skrine—observed him "die" and remain as such for a full half hour, with no pulse or breath, after which time he awoke as if from sleep[180].

The intentions of Arthur Holmwood, Quincey P. Morris, and Dr. John Seward are also deeply suspect, for how is it that three long-time companions would propose to the same girl on the same day, and then have a meeting shortly thereafter to discuss things that would "make their ears tingle," as Holmwood puts it? Was Holmwood intending to inherit the Westenra estate, as well as his father's, through murder? Was Seward poisoning Miss Westenra all along—it was always on his watch that she worsened—for the sake of Holmwood's plan or for his own revenge?

Worst of all is Professor Abraham Van Helsing. It seems clear to me that, while there once was and may yet be intelligence within his great brain, his wits are not all about him, and indeed he may be mad (a possibility that Dr. John Seward, a better judge of insanity than myself, has alluded to more than once in his clever diary). It appears his misdiagnosis and subsequent treatment of Lucy Westenra led, more so than anything, to her decline and her living entombment, followed by her murder. It appears he has stirred the others into a frenzy of superstitious and murderous hysteria with a series of contradictory speeches, and now plans to commit murder yet again, this time upon a man of foreign nobility.

There can be no more delay; I shall return to Purfleet at once with Wright to confront these men and sift the truth from lies before anyone else can be harmed.

Dr. Seward's Case-Book

2 October—We have met again. We seem at last to be on the track, and our work of tomorrow may be the beginning of the end. I wonder if Renfield's quiet has anything to do with this. His moods have so followed the doings of the Count, that the coming destruction of the monster may be carried to him in some subtle way. If we could only get some hint as to what passed in his mind, between the time of my argument with him today and his resumption of fly-catching, it might afford us a valuable clue. He is now seemingly quiet for a spell . . . Is he? That wild yell seemed to come from his room . . .

The attendant came bursting into my room and told me that Renfield had somehow met with some accident. He had heard him yell, and when he went to him found him lying on his face on the floor, all covered with blood. Too much is happening at once; there is just now someone arriving at the front door, but I can not stay to greet them, whomever they might be. I must go at once . . .

CHAPTER
TWENTY-NINE[181]

Dr. Seward's Case-Book

3 October—Let me put down with exactness all that happened, as well as I can remember, since last I made an entry. Not a detail that I can recall must be forgotten. In all calmness I must proceed.

When I came to Renfield's room I found him lying on the floor on his left side in a glittering pool of blood. When I went to move him, it became at once apparent that he had received some terrible injuries. There seemed none of the unity of purpose between the parts of the body which marks even lethargic sanity. As the face was exposed I could see that it was horribly bruised, as though it had been beaten against the floor. Indeed it was from the face wounds that the pool of blood originated.

The attendant who was kneeling beside the body said to me as we turned him over, "I think, sir, his back is broken. See, both his right arm and leg and the whole side of his face are paralysed." How such a thing could have happened puzzled the attendant beyond measure. He seemed quite bewildered, and his brows were gathered in as he said, "I can't understand the two things. He could mark his face like that by beating his own head on the floor. I saw a young woman do it once at the Eversfield Asylum before anyone could lay hands on her. And I suppose he might have broken his neck by falling out of bed, if he got in an awkward kink. But for the life of me I can't imagine how the two things occurred. If his back was broke, he couldn't beat his head, and if his face was like that before the fall out of bed, there would be marks of it."

I said to him, "Go to Dr. Van Helsing, and ask him to kindly come here at once. I want him without an instant's delay."

The man ran off, but within a few minutes returned alone. "Sir, the good doctor and the other men are at present detained with two inspectors, who have arrived to question them about certain matters."

We had tried hard to avoid an inquest, but with so many deaths and strange occurrences, it was, I suppose, inevitable that the police would ultimately become involved. I thought hard for a moment, but the patient was now breathing stertorously and it was easy to see that he had suffered some terrible injury. It was clear that time was of the essence, and what Renfield might have to tell us could mean the life or death for many. So I sent the attendant back to retrieve Van Helsing, even if it meant bringing the inspectors in as well.

In short order the Professor appeared with one of the inspectors. The detective (whose name I later learned was Cotford) was a young man clean-shaven, tall and slight, with an eagle face and bright, quick eyes that seemed to take in everything around him at a glance[182].

When the Professor saw Renfield on the ground, he looked keenly at him a moment, and then turned to me. I think he recognized my thought in my eyes, for he said very quietly, manifestly for the ears of the inspector and the attendant, "Ah, a sad accident! He will need very careful watching, and much attention. I shall stay with you myself, but I shall first dress myself. If you will remain I shall in a few minutes join you."

Van Helsing returned with extraordinary celerity, bearing with him a surgical case, and being accompanied by the rest of the men and, as I feared, both inspectors. As we went into a strict examination of the patient, the detective who was now present with Cotford, when he saw the attitude and state of the patient, and noted the horrible pool on the floor, said softly, "My God! What has happened to him? Poor, poor devil!" Yes, what indeed? The wounds of the face were superficial. The real injury was a depressed fracture of the skull, extending right up through the motor area. The Professor thought a moment and said, "We must reduce the pressure and get back to normal conditions, as far as can be. The rapidity of the suffusion shows the terrible nature of his injury. The whole motor area seems affected. The suffusion of the brain will increase quickly, so we must trephine at once or it may be too late." We all watched in patience as the Professor continued to contemplate the situation. "We shall wait," said Van Helsing, "just long enough to fix the best spot for trephining, so that we may most quickly and perfectly remove the blood clot, for it is evident that the haemorrhage is increasing."

The minutes during which we waited passed with fearful slowness. I had a horrible sinking in my heart, and from Van Helsing's face I gathered that he felt some fear or apprehension as to what was to come. I dreaded the words Renfield might speak, and I dreaded even more that the inspectors would also be present to hear them. I was positively afraid to think. But the conviction of what was coming was on me, as I have read of men who have heard the death watch. The poor man's breathing came in uncertain gasps. Each instant he seemed as though he would open his eyes and speak, but then would follow a prolonged stertorous breath, and he would relapse into a more fixed insensibility. Inured as I was to sick beds and death, this suspense grew and grew upon me. I could almost hear the beating of my own heart, and the blood surging through my temples sounded like blows from a hammer. The silence finally became agonizing. I looked at my companions, one after another, and saw from their flushed faces and damp brows that they were enduring equal torture. The inspectors, for their part, remained mercifully patient and quiet, simply observing and analyzing all that was transpiring before them. There was a nervous suspense over us all, as though overhead some dread bell would peal out powerfully when we should least expect it.

At last there came a time when it was evident that the patient was sinking fast. He might die at any moment. I looked up at the Professor and caught his eyes fixed on mine. His face was sternly set as he spoke, "There is no time to lose. His words may be worth many lives. I have been thinking so, as I stood here. It may be there is a soul at stake! We shall operate just above the ear."

Without another word he made the operation. For a few moments the breathing continued to be stertorous. Then there came a breath so prolonged that it seemed as though it would tear open his chest. Suddenly his eyes opened, and became fixed in a wild, helpless stare. This was continued for a few moments, then it was softened into a glad surprise, and from his lips came a sigh of relief. He moved convulsively, and as he did so, said, "I'll be quiet, Doctor. Tell them to take off the strait waistcoat. I have had a terrible dream, and it has left me so weak that I cannot move. What's wrong with my face? It feels all swollen, and it smarts dreadfully."

He tried to turn his head, but even with the effort his eyes seemed to grow glassy again so I gently put it back. Then Van Helsing said in a quiet grave tone, "Tell us your dream, Mr. Renfield."

As he heard the voice his face brightened, through its mutilation, and he said, "That is Dr. Van Helsing. How good it is of you to be here. Give me some water, my lips are dry, and I shall try to tell you. I dreamed . . ."

He stopped and seemed fainting. I called quietly to Quincey, "The brandy, it is in my study, quick!" He flew and returned with a glass, the decanter of brandy and a carafe of water. We moistened the parched lips, and the patient quickly revived.

It seemed, however, that his poor injured brain had been working in the interval, for when he was quite conscious, he looked at me piercingly with an agonized confusion which I shall never forget, and said, "I must not deceive myself. It was no dream, but all a grim reality." Then his eyes roved round the room. As they caught sight of the figures sitting patiently on the edge of the bed and standing around him, he went on, "If I were not sure already, I would know from them."

For an instant his eyes closed, not with pain or sleep but voluntarily, as though he were bringing all his faculties to bear. When he opened them he said, hurriedly, and with more energy than he had yet displayed, "Quick, Doctor, quick, I am dying! I feel that I have but a few minutes, and then I must go back to death, or worse! Wet my lips with brandy again. I have something that I must say before I die. Or before my poor crushed brain dies anyhow. Thank you! It was that night after you left me, when I implored you to let me go away. I couldn't speak then, for I felt my tongue was tied. But I was as sane then, except in that way, as I am now. I was in an agony of despair for a long time after you left me, it seemed hours. Then there came a sudden peace to me. My brain seemed to become cool again, and I realised where I was. I heard the dogs bark behind our house, but not where He was!"

As he spoke, Van Helsing's eyes never blinked, but his hand came out and met mine and gripped it hard. He did not, however, betray himself. He nodded slightly and said, "Go on," in a low voice.

Renfield proceeded. "He came up to the window in the mist, as I had seen him often before, but he was solid then, not a ghost, and his eyes were fierce like a man's when angry. He was laughing with his red mouth, the sharp white teeth glinted in the moonlight when he turned to look back over the belt of trees, to where the dogs were barking. I wouldn't ask him to come in at first, though I knew he wanted to, just as he had wanted all along. Then he began promising me things, not in words but by doing them."

He was interrupted by a word from the Professor, "How?"

"By making them happen. Just as he used to send in the flies when the sun was shining. Great big fat ones with steel and sapphire on their wings. And big moths, in the night, with skull and cross-bones on their backs."

Van Helsing nodded to him as he whispered to me unconsciously, "The *Acherontia Atropos* of the Sphinges, what you call the 'Death's-head Moth'?"

The patient went on without stopping, "Then he began to whisper. 'Rats, rats, rats! Hundreds, thousands, millions of them, and every one a life. And dogs to eat them, and cats too. All lives! All red blood, with years of life in it, and not merely buzzing flies!' I laughed at him, for I wanted to see what he could do. Then the dogs howled, away beyond the dark trees in His house. He beckoned me to the window. I got up and looked out, and He raised his hands, and seemed to call out without using any words. A dark mass spread over the grass, coming on like the shape of a flame of fire. And then He moved the mist to the right and left, and I could see that there were thousands of rats with their eyes blazing red, like His only smaller. He held up his hand, and they all stopped.

"I said to myself 'I must truly be mad'—I believed I had only thought it in my mind, but I must have said it aloud, for a voice that was not my own answered me, saying 'No Renfield, you are not mad, and I can prove you sane.'[183] When I asked how this could be, the voice replied 'You must put your theory of obtaining life to the test. If you are wrong, then you are surely mad, but if you are right, and you go on living for ever, then your theory will be proven correct, and your sanity redeemed![184] Come, Renfield, all these lives will I give you, ay, and many more and greater, through countless ages, if you will fall down and worship me!' And then a red cloud, like the colour of blood, seemed to close over my eyes, and before I knew what I was doing, I found myself opening the sash and saying to Him, 'Come in, Lord and Master!' The rats were all gone, but He slid into the room through the sash, though it was only open an inch wide, just as the Moon herself has often come in through the tiniest crack and has stood before me in all her size and splendour."

His voice was weaker, so I moistened his lips with the brandy again, and he continued, but it seemed as though his memory had gone on working in the interval for his story was further advanced. I was about to call him back to the point, but Van Helsing whispered to me, "Let him go on. Do not interrupt him. He cannot go back, and maybe could not proceed at all if once he lost the thread of his thought."

He proceeded, "All day I waited to hear from him, but he did not send me anything, not even a blowfly, and when the moon got up I was pretty angry with him. When he did slide in through the window, though it was shut, and did not even knock, I got mad with him. He sneered at me, and his white face looked out of the mist with his red eyes gleaming, and he went on as though he owned the whole place, and I was no one. He didn't even smell the same as he went by me. I couldn't hold him. I thought that, somehow, Mrs. Harker had come into the room."

The inspectors came closer, standing behind him so that he could not see them, but where they could hear better. They were silent, but the Professor started and quivered. His face, however, grew grimmer and sterner still. Renfield went on without noticing, "When Mrs. Harker came in to see me this afternoon she wasn't the same. It was like tea after the teapot has been watered." Here we all moved, but no one said a word.

He went on, "I didn't know that she was here till she spoke, and she didn't look the same. I don't care for the pale people. I like them with lots of blood in them, and hers all seemed to have run out. I didn't think of it at the time, but when she went away I began to think, and it made me mad to know that He had been taking the life out of her." I could feel that the rest quivered, as I did. But we remained otherwise still. "So when He came tonight I was ready for Him. I saw the mist stealing in, and I grabbed it tight. I had heard that madmen have unnatural strength. And as I knew I was a madman, at times anyhow, I resolved to use my power. Ay, and He felt it too, for He had to come out of the mist to struggle with me. I held tight, and I thought I was going to win, for I didn't mean Him to take any more of her life, till I saw His eyes. They burned into me, and my strength became like water. He slipped through it, and when I tried to cling to Him, He raised me up and flung me down. There was a red cloud before me, and a noise like thunder, and the mist seemed to steal away under the door."

His voice was becoming fainter and his breath more stertorous. Van Helsing stood up instinctively.

"We know the worst now," he said. "He is here, and we know his purpose. It may not be too late. Let us be armed, the same as we were the other night, but lose no time, there is not an instant to spare." Here he turned to the inspectors, who had thus far watched these grim proceedings in silence. "You have come here, as is your good and just duty, in search of answers to those questions, and more, which you had begun to ask of us earlier. Come with us now, and find the answers you seek."

There was no need to put our fear, nay our conviction, into words, we shared them in common. We all hurried and took from our rooms the same things that we had when we entered the Count's house. The Professor had his ready, and as we met in the corridor he pointed to them significantly as he said, "They never leave me, and they shall not till this unhappy business is over. Be wise also, my friends. It is no common enemy that we deal with. Alas! Alas! That dear Madam Mina should suffer!" He stopped, his voice was breaking, and I do not know if rage or terror predominated in my own heart.

Outside the Harkers' door we paused. Art and Quincey held back, and the latter said, "Should we disturb her?"

"We must," said Van Helsing grimly. "If the door be locked, I shall break it in."

"May it not frighten her terribly?" one of the inspectors insisted. "It is unusual to break into a lady's room!"

Van Helsing said solemnly, "You are right. But this is life and death. All chambers are alike to the doctor. And even were they not they are all as one to me tonight. Friend John, when I turn the handle, if the door does not open, do you put your shoulder down and shove. And you too, my friends. Now!"

He turned the handle as he spoke, but the door did not yield. We threw ourselves against it. With a crash it burst open, and we almost fell headlong into the room. The Professor did actually fall, and I saw across him as he gathered himself up from hands and knees. What I saw appalled me. I felt my hair rise like bristles on the back of my neck, and my heart seemed to stand still.

The moonlight was so bright that through the thick yellow blind the room was light enough to see. On the bed beside the window lay Jonathan Harker, his face flushed and breathing heavily as though in a stupor. Kneeling on the near edge of the bed facing outwards was the white-clad figure of his wife. By her side stood a tall, thin man, clad in black. His face was turned from us, but the instant we saw we all recognized the Count, in every way, even to the scar on his forehead. With his left hand he held both Mrs. Harker's hands, keeping them away with her arms at full tension. His right hand gripped her by the back of the neck, forcing her face down on his bosom. Her white nightdress was smeared with blood, and a thin stream trickled down the man's bare chest which was shown by his torn-open dress. The attitude of the two had a terrible resemblance to a child forcing a kitten's nose into a saucer of milk to compel it to drink.

As we burst into the room, the Count turned his face, and the hellish look that I had heard described seemed to leap into it. His eyes flamed red with devilish passion. The great nostrils of the white aquiline nose opened wide and quivered at the edge, and the white sharp teeth, behind the full lips of the blood dripping mouth, clamped together like those of a wild beast. With a wrench, which threw his victim back upon the bed as though hurled from a height, he turned and sprang at us. The inspectors, accustomed as they must be to unexpected dangers, instantly drew their revolvers and fired, but the bullets either missed (rather an unlikely possibility at such a range) or else passed harmlessly through him.

But by this time the Professor had gained his feet, and was holding towards him the envelope which contained the Sacred Wafer. The Count suddenly stopped, just as poor Lucy had done outside the tomb, and cowered back. Further and further back he cowered, as we, lifting our crucifixes, advanced. Even then at that awful moment with such a tragedy before my eyes, the figure of Mephistopheles in the Opera cowering before Margaret's lifted cross swam up before man and for an instant I wondered if I were mad. The moonlight suddenly failed, as a great black cloud sailed across the sky. And when the gaslight sprang up under Quincey's match, we saw nothing but a faint vapour. This, as we looked, trailed under the door, which with the recoil from its bursting open, had swung back to its old position. Van Helsing, Art, and I moved forward to Mrs. Harker, who by this time had drawn her breath and with it had given a scream so wild, so ear-piercing, so despairing that it seems to me now that it will ring in my ears till my dying day. For a few seconds she lay in her helpless attitude and disarray. Her face was ghastly, with a pallor which was accentuated by the blood which smeared her lips and cheeks and chin. From her throat trickled a thin stream of blood. Her eyes were mad with terror. Then she put before her face her poor crushed hands, which bore on their whiteness the red mark of the Count's terrible grip, and from behind them came a low desolate wail which made the terrible scream seem only the quick expression of an endless grief.

By this time Kate, having undoubtedly been awakened by the commotion, had rushed into the room and, sizing up something of the situation in the space of a long breath, stepped forward and drew the coverlet gently over Mrs Harker and sat with her, whilst Art, after looking at her face for an instant despairingly, ran out of the room.

Van Helsing whispered to me, "Jonathan is in a stupor such as we know the Vampire can produce. We can do nothing with poor Madam Mina for a few moments till she recovers herself. I must wake him!"

He dipped the end of a towel in cold water and with it began to flick him on the face, his wife all the while holding her face between her hands and sobbing in a way that was heart breaking to hear. I raised the blind, and looked out of the window. There was much moonshine, and as I looked I could see Quincey Morris run across the lawn and hide himself in the shadow of a great yew tree. It puzzled me to think why he was doing this. But at the instant I heard Harker's quick exclamation as he woke to partial consciousness, and turned to the bed. On his face, as there might well be, was a look of wild amazement. He seemed dazed for a few seconds, and then full consciousness seemed to burst upon him all at once, and he started up.

His wife was aroused by the quick movement, and turned to him with her arms stretched out, as though to embrace him. Instantly, however, she drew them in again, and putting her elbows together, held her hands before her face, and shuddered till the bed beneath her shook.

"In God's name what does this mean?" Harker cried out. "Dr. Seward, Dr. Van Helsing, what is it? What has happened? What is wrong? Mina, dear, what is it? What does that blood mean? My God, my God! Has it come to this!" And, raising himself to his knees, he beat his hands wildly together. "Good God help us! Help her! Oh, help her!"

With a quick movement he jumped from bed, and began to pull on his clothes, all the man in him awake at the need for instant exertion. "What has happened? Tell me all about it!" he cried without pausing. "Dr. Van Helsing you love Mina, I know. Oh, do something to save her. It cannot have gone too far yet. Guard her while I look for him!"

His wife, through her terror and horror and distress, saw some sure danger to him. Instantly forgetting her own grief, she seized hold of him and cried out.

"No! No! Jonathan, you must not leave me. I have suffered enough tonight, God knows, without the dread of his harming you. You must stay with me. Stay with these friends who will watch over you!" Her expression became frantic as she spoke. And, he yielding to her, she pulled him down sitting on the bedside, and clung to him fiercely.

Van Helsing and I tried to calm them both. The Professor held up his golden crucifix, and said with wonderful calmness, "Do not fear, my dear. We are here, and whilst this is close to you no foul thing can approach. You are safe for tonight, and we must be calm and take counsel together."

She shuddered and was silent, holding down her head on her husband's breast. When she raised it, his white nightrobe was stained with blood where her lips had touched, and where the thin open wound in the neck had sent forth drops. The instant she saw it she drew back, with a low wail, and whispered, amidst choking sobs.

"Unclean, unclean! I must touch him or kiss him no more. Oh, that it should be that it is I who am now his worst enemy, and whom he may have most cause to fear."

To this he spoke out resolutely, "Nonsense, Mina. It is a shame to me to hear such a word. I would not hear it of you. And I shall not hear it from you. May God judge me by my deserts, and punish me with more bitter suffering than even this hour, if by any act or will of mine anything ever come between us!"

He put out his arms and folded her to his breast. And for a while she lay there sobbing. He looked at us over her bowed head, with eyes that blinked damply above his quivering nostrils. His mouth was set as steel.

After a while her sobs became less frequent and more faint, and then he said to me, speaking with a studied calmness which I felt tried his nervous power to the utmost.

"And now, Dr. Seward, tell me all about it. Too well I know the broad fact. Tell me all that has been."

I told him exactly what had happened and he listened with seeming impassiveness, but his nostrils twitched and his eyes blazed as I told how the ruthless hands of the Count had held his wife in that terrible and horrid position, with her mouth to the open wound in his breast. It interested me, even at that moment, to see that whilst the face of white set passion worked convulsively over the bowed head, the hands tenderly and lovingly stroked the ruffled hair. Just as I had finished, Quincey and Godalming knocked at the door. They entered in obedience to our summons. Van Helsing looked at me questioningly. I understood him to mean if we were to take advantage of their coming to divert if possible the thoughts of the unhappy husband and wife from each other and from themselves. So on nodding acquiescence to him he asked them what they had seen or done. To which Lord Godalming answered.

"I could not see him anywhere in the passage, or in any of our rooms. I looked in the study but, though he had been there, he had gone. He had, however . . ." He stopped suddenly, looking first at the poor drooping figure on the bed, then to the inspectors.

Van Helsing said gravely, "Go on, friend Arthur. We want here no more concealments. Our hope now is in knowing all. Tell freely!"

So Art went on, "He had been there, and though it could only have been for a few seconds, he made rare hay of the place. All the manuscript had been burned, and the blue flames were flickering amongst the white ashes. The cylinders of your phonograph too were thrown on the fire, and the wax had helped the flames. Everything is destroyed." Here I noticed the inspectors exchange knowing glances, but Art went on. "I ran downstairs then, but could see no sign of him. I looked into Renfield's room, but there was no trace there except . . ." Again he paused.

"Go on," said Harker hoarsely. So he bowed his head and moistening his lips with his tongue, added, "except that the poor fellow is dead."

Mrs. Harker raised her head, looking from one to the other of us she said solemnly, "God's will be done!"

I could not but feel that Art was keeping back something. But, as I took it that his new silence was with a purpose—perhaps owing to the presence of the police—I said nothing.

Van Helsing turned to Morris and asked, "And you, friend Quincey, have you any to tell?"

"A little," he answered. "It may be much eventually, but at present I can't say. I thought it well to know if possible where the Count would go when he left the house. I did not see him, but I saw a bat rise from Renfield's window, and flap westward. I expected to see him in some shape go back to Carfax, but he evidently sought some other lair. He will not be back tonight, for the sky is reddening in the east, and the dawn is close. We must work tomorrow!"

He said the latter words through his shut teeth. For a space of perhaps a couple of minutes there was silence, and I could fancy that I could hear the sound of our hearts beating.

Then Van Helsing said, placing his hand tenderly on Mrs. Harker's head, "And now, Madam Mina, poor dear, dear, Madam Mina, tell us exactly what happened. God knows that I do not want that you be pained, but it is need that we know all. For now more than ever has all work to be done quick and sharp, and in deadly earnest. The day is close to us that must end all, if it may be so, and now is the chance that we may live and learn."

The poor dear lady shivered, and I could see the tension of her nerves as she clasped her husband closer to her and bent her head lower and lower still on his breast. Then she raised her head proudly, and held out one hand to Van Helsing who took it in his, and after stooping and kissing it reverently, held it fast. The other hand was locked in that of her husband, who held his other arm thrown round her protectingly. After a pause in which she was evidently ordering her thoughts, she began.

"I took the sleeping draught which you had so kindly given me, but for a long time it did not act. I seemed to become more wakeful, and myriads of horrible fancies began to crowd in upon my mind. All of them connected with death, and vampires, with blood, and pain, and trouble." Her husband involuntarily groaned as she turned to him and said lovingly, "Do not fret, dear. You must be brave and strong, and help me through the horrible task. If you only knew what an effort it is to me to tell of this fearful thing at all, you would understand how much I need your help. Well, I saw I must try to help the medicine to its work with my will, if it was to do me any good, so I resolutely set myself to sleep. Sure enough sleep must soon have come to me, for I remember no more. Jonathan coming in had not waked me, for he lay by my side when next I remember. There was in the room the same thin white mist that I had before noticed. But I forget now if you know of this. You will find it in my diary which I shall show you later. I felt the same vague terror which had come to me before and the same sense of some presence. I turned to wake Jonathan, but found that he slept so soundly that it seemed as if it was he who had taken the sleeping draught, and not I. I tried, but I could not wake him. This caused me a great fear, and I looked around terrified. Then indeed, my heart sank within me. Beside the bed, as if he had stepped out of the mist, or rather as if the mist had turned into his figure, for it had entirely disappeared, stood a tall, thin man, all in black. I knew him at once from the description of the others. The waxen face, the high aquiline nose, on which the light fell in a thin white line, the parted red lips, with the sharp white teeth showing between, and the red eyes that I had seemed to see in the sunset on the windows of St. Mary's Church at Whitby. I knew, too, the red scar on his forehead where Jonathan had struck him. For an instant my heart stood still, and I would have screamed out, only that I was paralyzed. In the pause he spoke in a sort of keen, cutting whisper, pointing as he spoke to Jonathan.

"'Silence! If you make a sound I shall take him and dash his brains out before your very eyes.' I was appalled and was too bewildered to do or say anything. With a mocking smile, he placed one hand upon my shoulder and, holding me tight, bared my throat with the other, saying as he did so, 'First, a little refreshment to reward my exertions. You may as well be quiet. It is not the first time, or the second, that your veins have appeased my thirst!' I was bewildered, and strangely enough, I did not want to hinder him. I suppose it is a part of the horrible curse that such is, when his touch is on his victim. And oh, my God, my God, pity me! He placed his reeking lips upon my throat!" Her husband groaned again. She clasped his hand harder, and looked at him pityingly, as if he were the injured one, and went on.

"I felt my strength fading away, and I was in a half swoon. How long this horrible thing lasted I know not, but it seemed that a long time must have passed before he took his foul, awful, sneering mouth away. I saw it drip with the fresh blood!" The remembrance seemed for a while to overpower her, and she drooped and would have sunk down but for her husband's sustaining arm. With a great effort she recovered herself and went on.

"Then he spoke to me mockingly, 'And so you, like the others, would play your brains against mine. You would help these men to hunt me and frustrate me in my design! You know now, and they know in part already, and will know in full before long, what it is to cross my path. They should have kept their energies for use closer to home. Whilst they played wits against me, against me who commanded nations, and intrigued for them, and fought for them, hundreds of years before they were born, I was countermining them. And you, their best beloved one, are now to me, flesh of my flesh, blood of my blood, kin of my kin, my bountiful wine-press for a while, and shall be later on my companion and my helper. You shall be avenged in turn, for not one of them but shall minister to your needs. But as yet you are to be punished for what you have done. You have aided in thwarting me. Now you shall come to my call. When my brain says "Come!" to you, you shall cross land or sea to do my bidding. And to that end this! You shall have the Vampire's baptism of blood!'

"With that he pulled open his shirt, and with his long sharp nails opened a vein in his breast. When the blood began to spurt out, he took my hands in one of his, holding them tight, and with the other seized my neck and pressed my mouth to the wound, so that I must either suffocate or swallow some to the . . . Oh, my God! My God! What have I done? What have I done to deserve such a fate, I who have tried to walk in meekness and righteousness all my days. God pity me! Look down on a poor soul in worse than mortal peril. And in mercy pity those to whom she is dear!" Then she began to rub her lips as though to cleanse them from pollution.

As she was telling her terrible story, the eastern sky began to quicken, and everything became more and more clear. Harker was still and quiet. But over his face, as the awful narrative went on, came a grey look which deepened and deepened in the morning light, till when the first red streak of the coming dawn shot up, the flesh stood darkly out against the whitening hair.

The inspectors asked several questions of us. As it quickly became clear that they somehow had acquired an impressive knowledge of ourselves and of the various happenings up until now, or rather until our meeting last night, we had little choice but to answer them in all honesty. They have since left for a time to consult among themselves.

As for our party, we have arranged that one of us is to stay within call of the unhappy pair till we can meet together and arrange about taking action.

Of this I am sure. The sun rises today on no more miserable house in all the great round of its daily course.

BOOK IV

PUNISHMENT[185]

CHAPTER THIRTY[186]

Jonathan Harker's Journal

3 October—As I must do something or go mad, I write this diary. It is now six o'clock, and we are to meet in the study in half an hour and take something to eat, for Dr. Van Helsing and Dr. Seward are agreed that if we do not eat we cannot work our best. Our best will be, God knows, required today. I must keep writing at every chance, for I dare not stop to think. All, big and little, must go down. Perhaps at the end the little things may teach us most. The teaching, big or little, could not have landed Mina or me anywhere worse than we are today. However, we must trust and hope. Poor Mina told me just now, with the tears running down her dear cheeks, that it is in trouble and trial that our faith is tested. That we must keep on trusting, and that God will aid us up to the end. The end! Oh my God! What end? . . . To work! To work!

When Dr. Van Helsing and Dr. Seward had come back from seeing poor Renfield, we went gravely into what was to be done. First, Dr. Seward told us that when he and Dr. Van Helsing had gone down to the room below they had found Renfield lying on the floor, all in a heap. His face was all bruised and crushed in, and the bones of the neck were broken.

Dr. Seward asked the attendant who was on duty in the passage if he had heard anything. He said that he had been sitting down, he confessed to half dozing, when he heard loud voices in the room, and then Renfield had called out loudly several times, "God! God! God!" After that there was a sound of falling, and when he entered the room he found him lying on the floor, face down, just as the doctors had seen him. Van Helsing asked if he had heard "voices" or "a voice," and he said he could not say. That at first it had seemed to him as if there were two, but as there was no one in the room it could have been only one. He could swear to it, if required, that the word "God" was spoken by the patient.

Dr. Seward said to us, when we were alone, that an inquest was assured at this point, as two inspectors from Scotland Yard had seen Renfield and heard his dying confession. Had the case been otherwise, it never would have done to put forward the truth, as no one would believe it, and that on the attendant's evidence he could have given a certificate of death by misadventure in falling from bed. But now there would be a formal inquest, if it was not already underway, when the inspectors returned.

When the question began to be discussed as to what should be our next step, the very first thing we decided was that Mina should be in full confidence. That nothing of any sort, no matter how painful, should be kept from her. She herself agreed as to its wisdom, and it was pitiful to see her so brave and yet so sorrowful, and in such a depth of despair.

"There must be no concealment," she said. "Alas! We have had too much already. And besides there is nothing in all the world that can give me more pain than I have already endured, than I suffer now! Whatever may happen, it must be of new hope or of new courage to me!"

Van Helsing was looking at her fixedly as she spoke, and said, suddenly but quietly, "But dear Madam Mina, are you not afraid. Not for yourself, but for others from yourself, after what has happened?"

Her face grew set in its lines, but her eyes shone with the devotion of a martyr as she answered, "Ah no! For my mind is made up!"

"To what?" he asked gently, whilst we were all very still, for each in our own way we had a sort of vague idea of what she meant.

Her answer came with direct simplicity, as though she was simply stating a fact, "Because if I find in myself, and I shall watch keenly for it, a sign of harm to any that I love, I shall die!"

"You would not kill yourself?" Mr. Singleton asked, hoarsely.

"I would. If there were no friend who loved me, who would save me such a pain, and so desperate an effort!" She looked at him meaningly as she spoke.

Van Helsing was sitting down, but now he rose and came close to her and put his hand on her head as he said solemnly. "My child, there is such an one if it were for your good. For myself I could hold it in my account with God to find such an euthanasia for you, even at this moment if it were best. Nay, were it safe! But my child . . ."

For a moment he seemed choked, and a great sob rose in his throat. He gulped it down and went on, "There are here some who would stand between you and death. You must not die. You must not die by any hand, but least of all your own. Until the other, who has fouled your sweet life, is true dead you must not die. For if he is still with the quick Undead, your death would make you even as he is. No, you must live! You must struggle and strive to live, though death would seem a boon unspeakable. You must fight Death himself, though he come to you in pain or in joy. By the day, or the night, in safety or in peril! On your living soul I charge you that you do not die. Nay, nor think of death, till this great evil be past."

The poor dear grew white as death, and shook and shivered, as I have seen a quicksand shake and shiver at the incoming of the tide. We were all silent. We could do nothing. At length she grew more calm and turning to him said sweetly, but oh so sorrowfully, as she held out her hand, "I promise you, my dear friend, that if God will let me live, I shall strive to do so. Till, if it may be in His good time, this horror may have passed away from me."

She was so good and brave that we all felt that our hearts were strengthened to work and endure for her, and we began to discuss what we were to do. I told her that she was to have all the papers in the safe, and all the papers or diaries and phonographs we might hereafter use, and was to keep the record as she had done before. She was pleased with the prospect of anything to do, if "pleased" could be used in connection with so grim an interest.

As usual Van Helsing had thought ahead of everyone else, and was prepared with an exact ordering of our work.

"It is perhaps well," he said, "that at our meeting after our visit to Carfax we decided not to do anything with the earth boxes that lay there. Had we done so, the Count must have guessed our purpose, and would doubtless have taken measures in advance to frustrate such an effort with regard to the others. But now he does not know our intentions. Nay, more, in all probability, he does not know that such a power exists to us as can sterilize his lairs, so that he cannot use them as of old.

"We are now so much further advanced in our knowledge as to their disposition that, when we have examined the house in Piccadilly, we may track the very last of them. Today then, is ours, and in it rests our hope. The sun that rose on our sorrow this morning guards us in its course. Until it sets tonight, that monster must retain whatever form he now has. He is confined within the limitations of his earthly envelope. He cannot melt into thin air nor disappear through cracks or chinks or crannies. If he go through a doorway, he must open the door like a mortal. And so we have this day to hunt out all his lairs and sterilize them. So we shall, if we have not yet catch him and destroy him, drive him to bay in some place where the catching and the destroying shall be, in time, sure."

Here I started up for I could not contain myself at the thought that the minutes and seconds so preciously laden with Mina's life and happiness were flying from us, since whilst we talked action was impossible. But Van Helsing held up his hand warningly.

"Nay, friend Jonathan," he said, "in this, the quickest way home is the longest way, so your proverb say. We shall all act and act with desperate quick, when the time has come. But think, in all probable the key of the situation is in that house in Piccadilly. The Count may have many houses which he has bought. Of them he will have deeds of purchase, keys and other things. He will have paper that he write on. He will have his book of cheques. There are many belongings that he must have somewhere. Why not in this place so central, so quiet, where he come and go by the front or the back at all hours, when in the very vast of the traffic there is none to notice. We shall go there and search that house. And when we learn what it holds, then we do what our friend Arthur call, in his phrases of hunt 'stop the earths' and so we run down our old fox, so? Is it not?"

"Then let us come at once," I cried, "we are wasting the precious, precious time!"

The Professor did not move, but simply said, "And how are we to get into that house in Piccadilly?"

"Any way!" I cried. "Mr. Morris can open the lock, as he did at Carfax. Failing that, we shall break in if need be."

"And your police? Those inspectors who were here last night? Where will they be, and what will they say?"

I was staggered, but I knew that if he wished to delay he had a good reason for it. So I said, as quietly as I could, "Don't wait more than need be. You know, I am sure, what torture I am in."

"Ah, my child, that I do. For I too have been through such torture at the hand of the Undead, when the lives of loved ones hung in the balance of time. I was not patient then, and so failed in my duty. Indeed there is no wish of me to add to your anguish. But just think, what can we do, until all the world be at movement. Then will come our time. I have thought and thought, and it seems to me that the simplest way is the best of all. Now we wish to get into the house, but we have no key. Is it not so?" I nodded.

"Now suppose that you were, in truth, the owner of that house, and could not still get in. And think there was to you no conscience of the housebreaker, what would you do?"

"I should get a respectable locksmith, and set him to work to pick the lock for me."

"And your police, they would interfere, would they not?"

"Oh no! Not if they knew the man was properly employed."

"Then," he looked at me as keenly as he spoke, "all that is in doubt is the conscience of the employer, and the belief of your policemen as to whether or not that employer has a good conscience or a bad one. Your police must indeed be zealous men and clever, oh so clever, in reading the heart, that they trouble themselves in such matter. No, no, my friend Jonathan, you go take the lock off a hundred empty houses in this your London, or of any city in the world, and if you do it as such things are rightly done, and at the time such things are rightly done, no one will interfere. I have read of a gentleman who owned a so fine house in London, and when he went for months of summer to Switzerland and lock up his house, some burglar come and broke window at back and got in. Then he went and made open the shutters in front and walk out and in through the door, before the very eyes of the police. Then he have an auction in that house, and advertise it, and put up big notice. And when the day come he sell off by a great auctioneer all the goods of that other man who own them. Then he go to a builder, and he sell him that house, making an agreement that he pull it down and take all away within a certain time. And your police and other authority help him all they can. And when that owner come back from his holiday in Switzerland he find only an empty hole where his house had been. This was all done *en regle*, and in our work we shall be *en regle* too. We shall not go so early that the policemen who have then little to think of, shall deem it strange. But we shall go after ten o'clock, when there are many about, and such things would be done were we indeed owners of the house."

I could not but see how right he was and the terrible despair of Mina's face became relaxed in thought. There was hope in such good counsel.

Van Helsing went on, "When once within that house we may find more clues. At any rate some of us can remain there whilst the rest find the other places where there be more earth boxes, at Bermondsey and Mile End."

Lord Godalming stood up. "I can be of some use here," he said. "I shall wire to my people to have horses and carriages where they will be most convenient."[187]

"Look here, old fellow," said Morris, "it is a capital idea to have all ready in case we want to go horse backing, but don't you think that one of your snappy carriages with its heraldic adornments in a byway of Walworth or Mile End would attract too much attention for our purpose? It seems to me that we ought to take cabs when we go south or east. And even leave them somewhere near the neighbourhood we are going to."

"Friend Quincey is right!" said the Professor. "His head is what you call in plane with the horizon. It is a difficult thing that we go to do, and we do not want no peoples to watch us if so it may."

"To that end, I must come with you!" said Miss Reed. The Professor began at once to object, but she would not let him. "Good sir, I have not seen my friend for many days now, or even know if he still lives, or is now dead, or worse, and cannot bear to wait a moment longer. But, to appease your conscience, please think on this, that I myself live upon that very street! The neighbours and police see me walking up and down that path most every day, though they may not have a precise idea as to where exactly I live. Would not my presence there add credence to our task?"

Though the Professor's mouth was fixed at the start, as Miss Reed was speaking his countenance grew first resigned and then even pleased.

"My dear Miss Reed," Van Helsing said, "I dare say your head, pretty though it may be, is just as much in plane as our American friend!"

Mina took a growing interest in everything and I was rejoiced to see that the exigency of affairs was helping her to forget for a time the terrible experience of the night. She was very, very pale, almost ghastly, and so thin that her lips were drawn away, showing her teeth in somewhat of prominence. I did not mention this last, lest it should give her needless pain, but it made my blood run cold in my veins to think of what had occurred with poor Lucy when the Count had sucked her blood. As yet there was no sign of the teeth growing sharper, but the time as yet was short, and there was time for fear.

When we came to the discussion of the sequence of our efforts and of the disposition of our forces, there were new sources of doubt. It was finally agreed that before starting for Piccadilly we should destroy the Count's lair close at hand. In case he should find it out too soon, we should thus be still ahead of him in our work of destruction. And his presence in his purely material shape, and at his weakest, might give us some new clue.

As to the disposal of forces, it was suggested by the Professor that, after our visit to Carfax, we should all enter the house in Piccadilly. That the Professor, Lord Godalming and I should remain there, whilst Quincey and Mr. Singleton, and the doctor and Miss Reed, each acting in pairs, found the lairs at Bermondsey and Mile End and destroyed them.

It was possible, if not likely, the Professor urged, that the Count might appear in Piccadilly during the day, and that if so we might be able to cope with him then and there. At any rate, we might be able to follow him in force. To this plan I strenuously objected, and so far as my going was concerned, for I said that I intended to stay and protect Mina. I thought that my mind was made up on the subject, but Mina would not listen to my objection. She said that there might be some law matter in which I could be useful. That amongst the Count's papers might be some clue which I could understand out of my experience in Transylvania. And that, as it was, all the strength we could muster was required to cope with the Count's extraordinary power. I had to give in, for Mina's resolution was fixed. She said that it was the last hope for her that we should all work together.

"As for me," she said, "I have no fear. Things have been as bad as they can be. And whatever may happen must have in it some element of hope or comfort. Go, my husband! God can, if He wishes it, guard me as well alone as with any one present."

So I started up crying out, "Then in God's name let us come at once, for we are losing time. The Count may come to Piccadilly earlier than we think, and the police may return to prevent us from performing our task!"

"We shall be gone from here ere the inspectors return. As for the Count's rising early this day . . . Not so!" said Van Helsing, holding up his hand.

"But why?" I asked.

"Do you forget," he said, with actually a smile, "that last night he banqueted heavily, and will sleep late?"

Did I forget! Shall I ever . . . can I ever! Can any of us ever forget that terrible scene! Mina struggled hard to keep her brave countenance, but the pain overmastered her and she put her hands before her face, and shuddered whilst she moaned. Van Helsing had not intended to recall her frightful experience. He had simply lost sight of her and her part in the affair in his intellectual effort.

When it struck him what he said, he was horrified at his thoughtlessness and tried to comfort her.

"Oh, Madam Mina," he said, "dear, dear, Madam Mina, alas! That I of all who so reverence you should have said anything so forgetful. These stupid old lips of mine and this stupid old head do not deserve so, but you will forget it, will you not?" He bent low beside her as he spoke.

She took his hand, and looking at him through her tears, said hoarsely, "No, I shall not forget, for it is well that I remember. And with it I have so much in memory of you that is sweet, that I take it all together. Now, you must all be going soon. Breakfast is ready, and we must all eat that we may be strong."

Breakfast was a strange meal to us all. We tried to be cheerful and encourage each other, and Mina was the brightest and most cheerful of us. When it was over, Van Helsing stood up and said, "Now, my dear friends, we go forth to our terrible enterprise. Are we all armed, as we were on that night when first we visited our enemy's lair. Armed against ghostly as well as carnal attack?"

We all assured him.

"Then it is well. Now, Madam Mina, you are in any case quite safe here until the sunset. And before then we shall return . . . if . . . We shall return! But before we go let me see you armed against personal attack. I have myself, since you came down, prepared your chamber by the placing of things of which we know, so that He may not enter. Now let me guard yourself. On your forehead I touch this piece of Sacred Wafer in the name of the Father, the Son, and . . ."

There was a fearful scream which almost froze our hearts to hear. As he had placed the Wafer on Mina's forehead, it had seared it . . . had burned into the flesh as though it had been a piece of white-hot metal. My poor darling's brain had told her the significance of the fact as quickly as her nerves received the pain of it, and the two so overwhelmed her that her overwrought nature had its voice in that dreadful scream.

But the words to her thought came quickly. The echo of the scream had not ceased to ring on the air when there came the reaction, and she sank on her knees on the floor in an agony of abasement. Pulling her beautiful hair over her face, as the leper of old his mantle, she wailed out.

"Unclean! Unclean! Even the Almighty shuns my polluted flesh! I must bear this mark of shame upon my forehead until the Judgement Day."

They all paused. I had thrown myself beside her in an agony of helpless grief, and putting my arms around held her tight. For a few minutes our sorrowful hearts beat together, whilst the friends around us turned away their eyes that ran tears silently. Then Van Helsing turned and said gravely, so gravely that I could not help feeling that he was in some way inspired, and was stating things outside himself.

"It may be that you may have to bear that mark till God himself see fit, as He most surely shall, on the Judgement Day, to redress all wrongs of the earth and of His children that He has placed thereon. And oh, Madam Mina, my dear, my dear, may we who love you be there to see, when that red scar, the sign of God's knowledge of what has been, shall pass away, and leave your forehead as pure as the heart we know. For so surely as we live, that scar shall pass away when God sees right to lift the burden that is hard upon us. Till then we bear our Cross, as His Son did in obedience to His Will. It may be that we are chosen instruments of His good pleasure, and that we ascend to His bidding as that other through stripes and shame. Through tears and blood. Through doubts and fear, and all that makes the difference between God and man."

There was hope in his words, and comfort. And they made for resignation. Mina and I both felt so, and simultaneously we each took one of the old man's hands and bent over and kissed it. Then without a word we all knelt down together, and all holding hands, swore to be true to each other. We pledged ourselves to raise the veil of sorrow from the head of her whom, each in his own way, we loved. And we prayed for help and guidance in the terrible task which lay before us. It was then time to start. So I said farewell to Mina, a parting which neither of us shall forget to our dying day, and we set out.

To one thing I have made up my mind. If we find out that Mina must be a vampire in the end, then she shall not go into that unknown and terrible land alone. I suppose it is thus that in old times one vampire meant many. Just as their hideous bodies could only rest in sacred earth, so the holiest love was the recruiting sergeant for their ghastly ranks.

We entered Carfax without trouble and found all things the same as on the first occasion. Of course this was Miss Reed's first venture into the abode, and though she was wide eyed and full of questions, she kept up her nerve. It was hard to believe that amongst so prosaic surroundings of neglect and dust and decay there was any ground for such fear as already we knew. Had not our minds been made up, and had there not been terrible memories to spur us on, we could hardly have proceeded with our task. We found no papers, or any sign of use in the house. And in the old chapel the great boxes looked just as we had seen them last.

Dr. Van Helsing said to us solemnly as we stood before him, "And now, my friends, we have a duty here to do. We must sterilize this earth, so sacred of holy memories, that he has brought from a far distant land for such fell use. He has chosen this earth because it has been holy. Thus we defeat him with his own weapon, for we make it more holy still. It was sanctified to such use of man, now we sanctify it to God."

As he spoke he took from his bag a screwdriver and a wrench, and very soon the top of one of the cases was thrown open. The earth smelled musty and close, but we did not somehow seem to mind, for our attention was concentrated on the Professor. Taking from his box a piece of the Sacred Wafer he laid it reverently on the earth, and then shutting down the lid began to screw it home, we aiding him as he worked.

One by one we treated in the same way each of the great boxes, and left them as we had found them to all appearance. But in each was a portion of the Host. When we closed the door behind us, the Professor said solemnly, "So much is already done. It may be that with all the others we can be so successful, then the sunset of this evening may shine on Madam Mina's forehead all white as ivory and with no stain!"

As we passed across the lawn on our way to the station to catch our train we could see the front of the asylum. I looked eagerly, and in the window of my own room saw Mina. I waved my hand to her, and nodded to tell that our work there was successfully accomplished. She nodded in reply to show that she understood. The last I saw, she was waving her hand in farewell. It was with a heavy heart that we sought the station and just caught the train, which was steaming in as we reached the platform. I have written this in the train.

Piccadilly, 12:30 o'clock—Just before we reached Fenchurch Street Lord Godalming said to me, "Miss Reed and I will find a locksmith. You had better not come with us in case there should be any difficulty. For under the circumstances it wouldn't seem so bad for us to break into an empty house. But you are a solicitor and the Incorporated Law Society might tell you that you should have known better."

I demurred as to my not sharing any danger even of odium, but he went on, "Besides, it will attract less attention if there are not too many of us. My title and Miss Reed's presence will make it all right with the locksmith, and with any policeman that may come along. You had better go with the others and stay in the Green Park. Somewhere in sight of the house, and when you see the door opened and the smith has gone away, do you all come across. We shall be on the lookout for you, and shall let you in."

"The advice is good!" said Van Helsing, so we said no more. Godalming and Miss Reed hurried off in a cab, we following in another. At the corner of Arlington Street our contingent got out and strolled into the Green Park. My heart beat as I saw the house on which so much of our hope was centred, looming up grim and silent in its deserted condition amongst its more lively and spruce-looking neighbours. We sat down on a bench within good view, and began to smoke cigars so as to attract as little attention as possible. The minutes seemed to pass with leaden feet as we waited for the coming of the others.

At length we saw a four-wheeler drive up. Out of it, in leisurely fashion, got Lord Godalming and Miss Reed. And down from the box descended a thick-set working man with his rush-woven basket of tools. Godalming paid the cabman, who touched his hat and drove away. Together the three ascended the steps, and Lord Godalming pointed out what he wanted done. The workman took off his coat leisurely and hung it on one of the spikes of the rail, saying something to a policeman who just then sauntered along. The policeman nodded acquiescence, and the man kneeling down placed his bag beside him. After searching through it, he took out a selection of tools which he proceeded to lay beside him in orderly fashion. Then he stood up, looked in the keyhole, blew into it, and turning to his employers, made some remark. Lord Godalming smiled, and the man lifted a good sized bunch of keys. Selecting one of them, he began to probe the lock, as if feeling his way with it. After fumbling about for a bit he tried a second, and then a third. All at once the door opened under a slight push from him, and he and the two others entered the hall. We sat still. My own cigar burnt furiously, but Van Helsing's went cold altogether. We waited patiently as we saw the workman come out and bring his bag. Then he held the door partly open, steadying it with his knees, whilst he fitted a key to the lock. This he finally handed to Lord Godalming, who took out his purse and gave him something. The man touched his hat, took his bag, put on his coat and departed. Not a soul took the slightest notice of the whole transaction.

When the man had fairly gone, we four crossed the street and knocked at the door. It was immediately opened by Miss Reed, beside whom stood Lord Godalming lighting a cigar.

"The place smells so vilely," said the latter as we came in. It did indeed smell vilely. Like the old chapel at Carfax. And with our previous experience it was plain to us that the Count had been using the place pretty freely. We moved to explore the house, all keeping together in case of attack, for we knew we had a strong and wily enemy to deal with, and as yet we did not know whether the Count might not be in the house.

In the dining room, which lay at the back of the hall, we found eight boxes of earth. Eight boxes only out of the nine which we sought! Our work was not over, and would never be until we should have found the missing box.

First we opened the shutters of the window which looked out across a narrow stone flagged yard at the blank face of a stable, pointed to look like the front of a miniature house. There were no windows in it, so we were not afraid of being overlooked. We did not lose any time in examining the chests. With the tools which we had brought with us we opened them, one by one, and treated them as we had treated those others in the old chapel. It was evident to us that the Count was not at present in the house, and we proceeded to search for any of his effects.

After a cursory glance at the rest of the rooms, from basement to attic, we came to the conclusion that the dining room contained any effects which might belong to the Count. And so we proceeded to minutely examine them. They lay in a sort of orderly disorder on the great dining room table.

There were a clothes brush, a brush and comb, and a jug and basin. The latter containing dirty water which was reddened as if with blood. There were also two sets of keys, which undoubtedly belonged to the other houses.

There were also papers; title deeds of the Piccadilly house in a great bundle, deeds of the purchase of the houses at Mile End and Bermondsey, which the papers indicate had been facilitated by a Mr. Pickford and a Mr. Trollope, respectively.[188] To our surprise, each house had been owned by the same man before he died, one Archibald Winter-Suffield, the same as who had owned Carfax. There were also notepaper, envelopes, and pens and ink. All of these were covered up in thin wrapping paper to keep them from the dust.

Among these papers, there were slips, indicating that the Count had obtained two servants—a man and a woman from a prison workhouse. The slip on the man had the notation of "murderer," while on the woman's was written "dumb"[189].

While examining this last find, we came across, amidst the various legal documents, a rather gushing letter addressed to "King Death," which was signed by none other than Miss Reed's own Francis Aytown. Miss Reed's face grew quite pale to read the letter, and looked as though she would faint. For a moment I regretted the Professor's having allowed her to come with us. But my doubts were without merit, for after she had read the note, and then had re-read it to make sure that it indeed said what it did, proceeded to join the rest of us in our examination of the Count's effects, as though nothing had transpired. An amazing woman, indeed. I can now understand something of what Dr. Seward sees in her.

When at last our examination was at an end, the pairs of Quincey Morris and Alfred Singleton, and Dr. Seward and Miss Reed, each took accurate notes of the various addresses of the houses in the East and the South, and took with them the keys, and set out to destroy the boxes in these places. The rest of us are, with what patience we can, waiting their return, or the coming of the Count.

CHAPTER
THIRTY-ONE[190]

Alfred Singleton's Notes

3 October—Mr. Morris and I crossed the Thames and arrived in Bermondsey with no trouble, but when we came to the house noted in the Count's papers, we could not help but wonder if we had somehow erred, for while the Carfax and the Piccadilly houses had the appearance of being long desolate, this one was quite different.

The building was old, to be sure, and most certainly in great need of repair. And yet, it did not appear entirely uninhabited; the tall hedge around the property had been recently trimmed, and the glass of the windows had been washed. Indeed, even as we were observing the scene from a distance, a woman came around the corner of the house, going about her business as if she had every right to be there.

She was rather under a woman's average height, and was far thinner than a proper diet should have allowed. Her face was smudged with soot and dirt, and her hair unkempt; she was dressed in little more than the rags of a workhouse hand, and presently busied herself with gathering up sticks and clutter from about the yard. Mr. Morris and I discussed our options briefly, but, really having little other choice in the matter, we decided to approach her directly.

"Pardon us, miss, but might we have a moment of your time?" I called out to her when we drew near, but she did not answer us, or turn her head, or give any indication she had even heard my call. "I say, miss, may we ask you a few questions?" I called again, louder this time, but with the same response—or rather, the lack there of. So we continued walking toward her, and were nearly upon her before she turned, seemingly for some other purpose, and started when she saw us, her eyes going wide in surprise, and an odd whining moan escaped her lips.

"I'm sorry, miss. We didn't mean to startle you, but we called to you twice without reply, and . . ." Here I paused, for I had noticed, as I was speaking and moving about and gesturing, that the woman was making a concerted effort to keep her eyes fixed upon my mouth. I realised, then, that she was deaf, and so was trying to watch the movements of my lips, so that she might, in her own way, "hear" what I was saying. I apologized all over again, this time being sure to keep my face toward her at all times, and use the smallest words I could think of, for the sake of our communication. She seemed at last to understand what I was saying, for she smiled and nodded in a comprehending and half-apologetic way. Here I paused again, not quite certain as to how to proceed with this unexpected situation, when Mr. Morris, in his forthright American manner, caught the woman's attention and came straight to the point.

"Pardon us, ma'am, but is the Count at home?" No sooner than his mouth formed the word "Count" than the woman's eyes grew wide with fright, and she backed away, shaking her head from side to side, voicing another peculiar moan. It appeared she could not speak any more than she could hear; this then was the "dumb" woman from the workhouse. She hurried away from us and into the house. Quickly we followed, and made it to the door before she could close it upon us, and pushed our way through to the inside. Thankfully, the tall hedge all but obscured the view of the hall door from the street, thus preventing any passerby from having a clear view of what we were doing; nor could the woman call out, seeing as she was dumb.

We found, upon entering the house, that some effort had been made to tidy up the residence, for much of the dust and grime that had covered floor and wall and furniture at the other two houses had here been removed for the most part.

As for the woman, she was still backing away from us, and continued to make more of those unintelligible mewling sounds. In truth, though, we were only half-watching her, as we turned this way and that, on the lookout for an attack from the Count. Our alertness served us well, for an attack of sorts did indeed come, though it was not from the Count. A man, dressed in the garb of a prisoner, his hair cut close to his scalp, came at us out of the shadows brandishing a shovel, a murderous gleam in his eyes.

Mr. Morris handled the situation with a degree of calmness and stoicism that was a credit to his great state. In a single graceful movement, he pulled free his revolver and brought it level to the head of the approaching man. The man, a criminal though he may have been, was apparently no fool, and, quickly sizing up the situation, checked his attack and came to an abrupt halt. At a gesture from Mr. Morris, the man dropped the shovel to the floor, a scowl marring his visage. So there the four of us stood for a long breath, before Mr. Morris spoke.

"All right, we've all had our fun, but now the jig is up," he said laconically to the man. "We're just here to settle a score with the Count. So if you'd be so kind as to fork over those six boxes, we'll wind up our business and be on our way." The man's face showed genuine surprise for an instant, but then the scowl returned, and he shook his head to indicate his refusal, though he made no sound. For a moment I took his silence as proof that he too was like the woman, but then dismissed the notion just as quickly, for he showed no signs of having any difficulty in hearing us. It merely seemed that he was unwilling—or unable—to speak. "These must be the two convicts we found papers on," Mr. Morris realised aloud. "I can keep an eye on these two, if you want to hunt after those boxes."

While the American kept the two covered with his revolver, I made a quick search of the house, but none of the rooms on the two floors turned up the Count's effects, neither the attic nor the cellar. I returned to hall, where Mr. Morris still watched over the two servants, to confess my failure. In response, he made a gesture at the man who had rushed us.

"I'd take him to be a regular curly wolf, but I'd bet the house he knows the Count's secret," Morris declared. "The trick's gonna be getting' him to fess up." I looked the silent man up and down, wondering what to do about him, and it was then that I noticed his shoes were covered in fresh mud. The shovel that he had been wielding also had mud caked on its blade.

"He may not have to," I said, a thought dawning in my mind. "Wait here." I quickly followed the trail of muddy footprints though the house and out the back, where I found six great holes, each about the size of a grave, freshly dug. Peering in, I saw that the six wooden crates were present and accounted for, one in each pit. I returned and shared the news of my find with Morris.

Though the woman, who was obviously having difficulty following the train of our conversation, not having a clear view of our mouths, had no reaction to our discussion, the man's eyes grew wide to hear I had found out the Count's hiding place for his boxes. His agitation only grew when he realised that we had some plan in mind for the Count's effects, and his eyes began to shift between the Texan's gun and the shovel on the floor, as if weighing his chances against us. There was no murderous hate in his eyes now, though, only fear—undoubtedly fear for himself, for he had failed to hide the boxes under the earth in time to prevent their discovery, and he had failed to deal with the two of us, and now was dreading the retribution of his master that was now sure to come his way.

Mr. Morris, also catching the man's shifty gaze, quickly forced the two of them through the house and into the kitchen pantry, which was minimally stocked with the most meager choices of food (undoubtedly for the two servants, as we had already concluded the Count did not eat a mortal's fare). After they were safely inside, we closed the doors to the pantry and barred them shut.

"That should serve as a calaboose for the time being," my companion mused lazily. "Enough time, at least, for us to finish with those boxes, and tip off the police to the whereabouts of these two mudsills."

And with that, we set about our task. How fortunate we were to have made our move against the Count now, for to have delayed even one day would have made discovering the boxes nearly impossible. But, as always, the hand of Providence moves His chess pieces in the proper time, and box by box we consecrated the foreign soil.

After we were satisfied with our work, we sent a note to the police, then watched from a safe distance away to see what would transpire. In time, three policemen came to the house and, finding the door ajar (as we had purposefully left it) entered the building. In short order they emerged, one holding the woman and two restraining the man. Though the two servants might think ill of us now, in truth the workhouse will be a better life for them than being the slaves—or worse—of the Count . . .

Dr. Seward's Case-Book

3 October—Kate and I traveled along the north embankment—by way of the Strand, Upper Thames Street, Fenchurch Street—and then veered away from the river along Whitechapel Road, until we came into Mile End. Here the side streets and alleyways became rather confusing, but with the notes we had taken from the Count's maps, we had no trouble at all finding the house; a left turn onto Brick Lane and a quick right again put us on Chicksand Street, where sat the quiet house at 197.

In fact, "quiet" was not the proper word to apply to it—desolation was the only term conveying any suitable idea of its isolation. It was an old rambling, heavy-built house of the Jacobean style, with heavy gables and windows, unusually small, and set higher than was customary in such houses. It was surrounded with a high brick wall massively built. Indeed, on examination, it looked more like a fortified house than an ordinary dwelling[191].

Gaining entry to the house was far easier than we had imagined, for when we reached the door, we found, to our amazement, that it had been forced open! Cautiously we entered, and, each of us taking a lamp in one hand, we went all through this quaint and beautiful an old house that had been so long neglected. The carving of the oak on the panels of the wainscot was fine, and on and round the doors and windows it was beautiful and of rare merit. There were some old pictures on the walls, but they were coated so thick with dust and dirt that we could not distinguish any detail of them, though we held our lamps as high as we could over our heads. Here and there as we went round we saw some crack or hole blocked for a moment by the face of a rat with its bright eyes glittering in the light, but in an instant it was gone, and a squeak and a scamper followed[192].

Then it was that we began to notice for the first time what a noise the rats were making. It was evident that at first the rats had been frightened at the presence of strangers, and the light of lamps; but that as the time went on they had grown bolder and were now disporting themselves as was their wont. How busy they were! and hark to the strange noises! Up and down behind the old wainscot, over the ceiling and under the floor they raced, and gnawed, and scratched!

As we passed through the living room, Kate let out a surprised gasp. I lifted the shade of my lamp and, holding it up, went and stood opposite the pictures that she was staring at with such a fixed gaze, a deadly pallor having overspread her face. I saw that her knees shook, and heavy drops of sweat came on her forehead, and she trembled like an aspen. But she was young and plucky, and before I could say anything she had pulled herself together, and after the pause of a few seconds had stepped forward again, raised her own lamp, and examined the paintings which stood out clearly from the dark and dusty walls.

The first was most certainly a personification of Death, judging by his black attire and skeletal face, who was depicted leaning sensually over a woman clad only in her dressing gown, her face half hidden amidst the ripples of her dark hair, who had swooned across a bench. The scene was eerily lit by a full moon, and a graveyard overfilled with headstones comprised much of the background. It was a masterful piece, and one quite suited to hang on the wall of the Count's house.

The second was a portrait of the Count himself, though in his younger guise. His face was strong and merciless, evil, crafty, and vindictive, with a sensual mouth and a hooked nose shaped like the beak of a bird of prey. The rest of the face was of a cadaverous colour, and, if one looked closely, seemed quite translucent, so that the bones and sinews could be seen beneath the flesh. The eyes were of peculiar brilliance and with a terribly malignant expression. He was seated in a great high-backed carved oak chair, on the right-hand side of a great stone fireplace. With a feeling of something like horror, I recognised the scene of the room as the very one in which we now stood, and gazed around in an awestruck manner as though expecting to find some strange presence behind us.[193]

"This is Francis' work!" Kate breathed. "This graveyard is the one at Whitby," she continued, staring at the rendition of Death and his victim, "and the seat where Mina and poor Lucy were wont to sit." It must have struck her then, even as it struck me, as to just exactly who and what this painting was depicting. "My God! He really and truly had seen them that night! He must have known . . . all this time he must have known . . ." Suddenly she turned and buried her face into my shoulder, sobbing. "He left a note for the Count, told that creature where he lived . . . where I lived! Oh Jack, he *told* that thing where to find us!"

I stroked her hair and said what comforting things came to mind, and found that there was a small part of myself that was pleased to have her cling to me and to hear her once again call me "Jack." For the most part, though, a great anger burned within me against her friend, who knew what had befallen poor sweet Lucy, and did nothing about it, save to ingratiate himself to the very fiend. But then I thought of Renfield, and what terrible control that evil had slowly and surely gained over him, and made him suffer in a way I would not wish upon my greatest enemy.

"We must not be his judges, Kate," I said, for her benefit as well as my own, in what I imagine must have been in a clumsy and awkward sort of way. "We do not know the how and why of his choice, or even if he made it of his own free will. Van Helsing said the Vampire can twist around a person's thoughts, and bend them to his will. Did not Mr. Singleton note the Count's power over your friend at your dinner party?" Slowly Kate began to relax, and her breathing, which before had been choking sobs, slowed to something more manageable.

Kate, now with perhaps an ember of hope for her friend's soul rekindled, recovered something of her former self-control, and we made our way back to the main hall. By now our eyes had adjusted to the gloom of the house, and the shadows thrown by our lamps, and so it was that we caught sight of foot prints. While the dust upon the floor of Carfax had been thick and untouched save for our own feet, here there were many foot prints going to and fro through the dust; and not just one set, but several different sizes and shapes. Though some led into and out of different rooms, the main bulk of them were facing in one direction or the other along a path which led from the main door further into the dark recesses of the house. Carefully we followed these back into a windowless room that was rank with that corrupt scent that so permeated the air of Carfax and the Piccadilly home, and which was filled with a number of large wooden crates.

For a brief moment I rejoiced, for there upon the floor rested not the expected six, but rather seven wooden boxes, and so it seemed we had thus located the one missing from Piccadilly. But upon closer examination we found that the seventh box was different from the others, fashioned of newer wood, more narrow than the others, like a proper coffin, and quite empty, save for a few newspaper clippings.

The articles themselves were of great interest, which detailed various murders in this vicinity, and made note of a tall man with a dark beard who dressed all in black, who spoke with a foreign accent. Even so, the find was over all a disappointment, for one of the Count's boxes was still missing. But we couldn't dwell upon that, for there was much work to be done. Kate and I quickly set about our task, and, by prying open each box and laying a piece of the Sacred Wafer onto the earth within, we thus destroyed six more resting places for that fiend. As we found nothing else of relevance, we made our way out into the fresh air . . . only to be met at the doorstep a policeman!

"See 'ere!" the man said in a stern and accusing tone, "who are ye, an' what're ye doin' up there?" For a moment my mind was completely emptied, and my tongue tied. But Kate, always the clever one, answered him in an instant.

"My name is Mrs. Reed, and this is my husband, Dr. Reed," she told the man in an outright lie. I didn't know whether to be stunned or relieved that she had answered him thus, though I did feel my ears burn to hear her having us married in such a manner.

"Well, well, we have a doctor here, do we? We've been told to keep an eye out for a doctor snoopin' around these parts. You're name wouldn't happen to be 'Jack,' would it?" Again I was stunned into silence—for how could the police know my name? Could it be that the Count somehow anticipated my arrival and stirred up some sort of trouble in my name? But again Kate came to my defense.

"Sir, we're only here to look for our good friend, a painter by the name of Francis Aytown, who we understood had taken up residence here not long ago."

"Oh, are ye now? An' what did this 'good friend' of yers look like?" demanded the policeman, but there was a certain pitch to his voice that gave me the glimmer of hope that he actually believed Kate.

"He is twenty-four years old, rather over average height, with a heavy jaw and straight hair," was her reply.

"Then ye must come with me at once," the officer insisted, but in a lighter tone of voice, "for we've found your friend!"

While en route to the nearby London Hospital at Whitechapel, the policeman explained the situation to us in greater detail. "We came arount jest this mornin' to see 'bout some strange noises comin' from that house, an' we heard 'em ourselves when we came to the door—a kind of low moanin,' it was. What with all the murders takin' place, we didn't want to leave anything to chance, so we forced the door open, and followed the moanin,' until we comes to a dark room filled with great wooden boxes like coffins. And there in one of them coffins lays your friend, Mr. Aytown, was 'is name? At first we thought him to be drunk, but then we sees he's all pale and sickly, so we brings him straightaway to the hospital. The doctor there says he has a bad case of brain fever." Kate and I exchanged sharp glances at the policeman's words, both of us remembering Mr. Harker's diagnosis after his prolonged contact with the Count.

Upon arriving at Whitechapel's hospital, we found Mr. Aytown lying in his sick bed in a half-conscious stupor, his breathing stertorous. Quickly I pulled back one corner of his mouth, and found his teeth were long and white and sharp. Kate saw this as well, and moaned in despair.

"I have driven him to this end," she muttered to herself, and then to me she said "Can you do anything for him?"

"I fear not," I replied after a moment's thought. "There are not marks on his throat, so he has not been fed from and thus is not suffering from aenemia. A transfusion of blood would do him no good, even if the hospital were to permit such a thing." Seeing Kate become crestfallen, I was quick to add "Perhaps . . .

perhaps with the lack of the aenemia to compound the problem, he may well survive long enough for us to end his curse at its source and thus free him before it's too late."

Presently, Mr. Aytown opened his eyes—dull and dark—to look at Kate.

"Francis!" Kate said, kneeling by his bed.

"Kate . . . you . . . you're here," he muttered dreamily.

"Yes, we're here."

"We?" the patient inquired.

"This is Jack," she said, gesturing toward me. "He came to see you before, in Piccadilly, remember? He's a doctor, and can help you be rid of this . . ." Kate cut her introduction short, for a sinister change had come over her friend's face, twisting it into something very malign indeed.

"Oh, it's just 'Jack' now is it? And what would you have him rid me of, Katherine?" he hissed, his eyes now seeming to smolder with a light of their own. "I am already rid of you, and am all the better for it!" Kate reeled back as if struck, but the man continued on without notice or care for her heart. "And how short of a time it's been since I turned down your proposal, if you could even call it that, and already you've found for yourself another man. You are no better that the whores who walk these very streets!"

"Sir!" I began hotly, but he now seemed to have forgotten my presence entirely, and focused his rage on Kate.

"Why did you put me in such a ridiculous position? That is the worst of you women. You're always wanting me to do something I don't want to do, or crying . . . A fellow should go away so that he wouldn't have to swear lies. Women are always wanting money, or worse, to be married! First there was you, then Polly, and that sickly Annie girl with the dark hair, and of course that fine pair a few days back . . . Confound you! Why couldn't you have let me know that you were fond of me in some decent way, without all that formal theatrical proposing? It's a deuced annoying thing in the long run the way the women get fond of me. Though it's nice enough in some ways while it lasts![194] But I am down on you, and all those like you, and I shant quit . . . quit . . ." He made as if to rise from his bed, but even as he did so a cold sweat broke out across his brow, and he sank back from the exertion, his eyes glazing over and closing in unconsciousness.

"That wasn't him speaking, Kate, you must know that," I insisted, for her eyes were already red with tears. "It was the darkness that has corrupted his soul. Come, let us go to put an end to all this, before it's too late for him and the others . . ."

And so we left Mr. Aytown in the hospital, and are presently en route to Piccadilly. Kate is very silent as she sits beside me, her gaze far off, her thoughts no doubt lost somewhere between contemplation and sorrow.

CHAPTER
THIRTY-TWO[195]

Alfred Singleton's Notes

3 October—We returned to the Piccadilly house, and found the Professor, Harker, and Lord Godalming waiting for us. Of the Count there had been no sign, but neither had there been any word from Dr. Seward and Miss Reed. We told the Professor of our encounter with the Count's servants, and our treatment of his boxes.

The time seemed terribly long whilst we were waiting for the return of the others. The Professor tried to keep our minds active by using them all the time. I could see his beneficent purpose, by the side glances which he threw from time to time at Harker. The poor fellow is overwhelmed in a misery that is appalling to see. Last night he was a frank, happy-looking man, with strong, youthful face, full of energy, and with dark brown hair. Today he is a drawn, haggard old man, whose white hair matches well with the hollow burning eyes and grief-written lines of his face. His energy is still intact. In fact, he is like a living flame. This may yet be his salvation, for if all go well, it will tide him over the despairing period. He will then, in a kind of way, wake again to the realities of life. Poor fellow!

The Professor knows this well enough, and is doing his best to keep his mind active. What he has been saying was, under the circumstances, of absorbing interest. So well as I can remember, here it is:

"I have studied, over and over again since they came into my hands, until the time they were destroyed, all the papers relating to this monster, and the more I have studied, the greater seems the necessity to utterly stamp him out. All through there are signs of his advance. Not only of his power, but of his knowledge of it. As I learned from the researches of my friend Arminius of Buda-Pesth, he was in life a most wonderful man. Soldier, statesman, and alchemist. Which latter

390

was the highest development of the science knowledge of his time. He had a mighty brain, a learning beyond compare, and a heart that knew no fear and no remorse. He dared even to attend the Scholomance, and there was no branch of knowledge of his time that he did not essay.

"Though it is not often so with the Undead, in him the brain powers survived the physical death. Though it would seem that memory was not all complete. In some faculties of mind he has been, and is, only a child. But he is growing, and some things that were childish at the first are now of man's stature. He is experimenting, and doing it well. And if it had not been that we have crossed his path he would be yet, he may be yet if we fail, the father or furtherer of a new order of beings, whose road must lead through Death, not Life."

Harker groaned and said, "And this is all arrayed against my darling! But how is he experimenting? The knowledge may help us to defeat him!"

"He has all along, since his coming, been trying his power, slowly but surely. That big child-brain of his is working. Well for us, it is as yet a child-brain. For had he dared, at the first, to attempt certain things he would long ago have been beyond our power. However, he means to succeed, and a man who has centuries before him can afford to wait and to go slow. *Festina lente* may well be his motto."

"I fail to understand," said Harker wearily. "Oh, do be more plain to me! Perhaps grief and trouble are dulling my brain."

The Professor laid his hand tenderly on his shoulder as he spoke, "Ah, my child, I will be plain. Do you not see how, of late, this monster has been creeping into knowledge experimentally. How he has been making use of the zoophagous patient to effect his entry into friend John's home. For your Vampire, though in all afterwards he can come when and how he will, must at the first make entry only when asked thereto by an inmate. But these are not his most important experiments.

"These papers here, and the testimony of our good friends, show how he acquired for himself two servants to give one of his houses the appearance of being inhabited by one of the living. And see how he chooses them with the utmost care, for neither of them did speak! Thus they would be all the harder pressed to betray his secrets.

"And do we not see how at the first all these so great boxes were moved by others. He knew not then but that must be so. But all the time that so great child-brain of his was growing, and he began to consider whether he might not himself move the box. So he began to help. And then, when he found that this be all right, he try to move them all alone. And so he progress, and he scatter these graves of him. And none but he know where they are hidden.

"He may have intend to bury them deep in the ground. So that only he use them in the night, or at such time as he can change his form, they do him equal well, and none may know these are his hiding place! But, my child, do not despair, this knowledge came to him just too late! Already all of his lairs but one be sterilize as for him. And before the sunset this shall be so. Then he have no place where he can move and hide. I delayed this morning that so we might be sure. Is there not more at stake for us than for him? Then why not be more careful than him? By my clock it is one hour and already, if all be well, friend Jack and Miss Kate are on their way to us. Today is our day, and we must go sure, if slow, and lose no chance. See! There are seven of us when those absent ones return."

Whilst we were speaking we were startled by a knock at the hall door, the double postman's knock of the telegraph boy. We all moved out to the hall with one impulse, and Van Helsing, holding up his hand to us to keep silence, stepped to the door and opened it. The boy handed in a dispatch. The Professor closed the door again, and after looking at the direction, opened it and read aloud.

> "Look out for D. He has just now, 12:45, come from Carfax hurriedly
> and hastened towards the South. He seems to be going the round and
> may want to see you—Mina."

There was a pause, broken by Jonathan Harker's voice, "Now, God be thanked, we shall soon meet!"

Van Helsing turned to him quickly and said, "God will act in His own way and time. Do not fear, and do not rejoice as yet. For what we wish for at the moment may be our own undoings."

"I care for nothing now," he answered hotly, "except to wipe out this brute from the face of creation. I would sell my soul to do it!"

"Oh, hush, hush, my child!" said Van Helsing. "God does not purchase souls in this wise, and the Devil, though he may purchase, does not keep faith. But God is merciful and just, and knows your pain and your devotion to that dear Madam Mina. Think you, how her pain would be doubled, did she but hear your wild words. Do not fear any of us, we are all devoted to this cause, and today shall see the end. The time is coming for action. Today this Vampire is limit to the powers of man, and till sunset he may not change. It will take him time to arrive here, see it is twenty minutes past one, and there are yet some times before he can hither come, be he never so quick. What we must hope for is that Jack and Miss Kate arrive first."

About half an hour after we had received Mrs. Harker's telegram, there came a quiet, resolute knock at the hall door. It was just an ordinary knock, such as is given hourly by thousands of gentlemen, but it made the Professor's heart and mine beat loudly. We looked at each other, and together moved out into the hall. We each held ready to use our various armaments, the spiritual in the left hand, the mortal in the right. Van Helsing pulled back the latch, and holding the door half open, stood back, having both hands ready for action. The gladness of our hearts must have shown upon our faces when on the step, close to the door, we saw Dr. Seward. He came quickly in and closed the door behind him as he moved along the hall.

"It is all right. We found the house. Six boxes in it, and we destroyed them all."

"Destroyed?" asked the Professor.

"For him!"

"And Miss Kate?" pressed the Professor.

"She is on her way to Purfleet, to comfort Mrs. Harker, and to be comforted by her."

"Though I am all the more pleased she will be out of harm's way, for what reason does she want for comfort?"

"We found, at the Whitechapel hospital, near the Mile End house, her friend Mr. Aytown. That was the cause for our delay. He was very pale and weak, and it seems certain that the Count's venom runs through his veins, though we found no marks on this throat. Could it be that the Vampire may infect others purely with his blood, without the need to feed at the first?"

Having no answer to this, we were silent for a minute, and then Quincey said, "There's nothing to do but to wait here. If, however, he doesn't turn up by five o'clock, we must start off. For it won't do to leave Mrs. Harker alone after sunset."

"He will be here before long now," said Van Helsing, who had been consulting his pocketbook. "*Nota bene*, in Madam's telegram he went south from Carfax. That means he went to cross the river, and he could only do so at slack of tide, which should be something before one o'clock. That he went south has a meaning for us. He is as yet only suspicious, and he went from Carfax first to the place where he would suspect interference least. You must have been at Bermondsey only a short time before him. That he is not here already shows that he went to Mile End next. This took him some time, for he would then have to be carried over the river in some way. Believe me, my friends, we shall not have long to wait now. We should have ready some plan of attack, so that we may throw away no chance. Hush, there is no time now. Have all your arms! Be ready!" He held up a warning hand as he spoke, for we all could hear a key softly inserted in the lock of the hall door . . .

Dr. Seward's Case-Book

3 October—After seeing Kate off at the station, I returned to Piccadilly. Quincey and Mr. Singleton had been successful in their task, as had we, though none had yet located that one box. It was not long after I gave them an account of our time in Mile End and the London Hospital when we heard the key turn in hall door.

I could not but admire, even at such a trying moment as we experienced at the Piccadilly house, the way in which a dominant spirit asserted itself. In all our hunting parties and adventures in different parts of the world, Quincey Morris had always been the one to arrange the plan of action, and Arthur and I had been accustomed to obey him implicitly. Now, the old habit seemed to be renewed instinctively. With a swift glance around the room, he at once laid out our plan of attack, and without speaking a word, with a gesture, placed us each in position. Van Helsing, Harker, and I were just behind the door, so that when it was opened the Professor could guard it whilst we two stepped between the incomer and the door. Godalming and Singleton behind, and Quincey in front stood just out of sight, his hand on his Bowie knife,—which I had seen him use with such effect on a jaguar in Brazil—ready to move in front of the window. We waited in a suspense that made the seconds pass with nightmare slowness. The slow, careful steps came along the hall. The Count was evidently prepared for some surprise, at least he feared it.

Suddenly with a single bound he leaped into the room. Winning a way past us before any of us could raise a hand to stay him. There was something so pantherlike in the movement, something so unhuman, that it seemed to sober us all from the shock of his coming. The first to act was Harker, who with a quick movement, threw himself before the door leading into the room in the front of the house. As the Count saw us, a horrible sort of snarl passed over his face, showing the eyeteeth long and pointed. But the evil smile as quickly passed into a cold stare of lion-like disdain. His expression again changed as, with a single impulse, we all advanced upon him. It was a pity that we had not some better organized plan of attack, for even at the moment I wondered what we were to do. I did not myself know whether our lethal weapons would avail us anything.

Harker evidently meant to try the matter, for he had ready his great Kukri knife and made a fierce and sudden cut at him. The blow was a powerful one. Only the diabolical quickness of the Count's leap back saved him. A second less and the trenchant blade had shorn through his heart. As it was, the point just cut the cloth of his coat, making a wide gap whence a bundle of bank notes and a stream of gold fell out. The expression of the Count's face was so hellish, that for a moment I feared for Harker, though I saw him throw the terrible knife aloft again for another stroke. Instinctively I moved forward with a protective impulse, holding the Crucifix and Wafer in my left hand.

I felt a mighty power fly along my arm, and it was without surprise that I saw the monster cower back before a similar movement made spontaneously by each one of us. It would be impossible to describe the expression of hate and baffled malignity, of anger and hellish rage, which came over the Count's face. His waxen hue became greenish-yellow by the contrast of his burning eyes, and the red scar on the forehead showed on the pallid skin like a palpitating wound. The next instant, with a sinuous dive he swept under Harker's arm, ere his blow could fall, and grasping a handful of the money from the floor, dashed across the room, threw himself at the window. Amid the crash and glitter of the falling glass, he tumbled into the flagged area below. Through the sound of the shivering glass I could hear the "ting" of the gold, as some of the sovereigns fell on the flagging.

We ran over and saw him spring unhurt from the ground. He, rushing up the steps, crossed the flagged yard, and pushed open the stable door. There he turned and spoke to us.

"You think to baffle me, you with your pale faces all in a row, like sheep in a butcher's. You shall be sorry yet, each one of you! You think you have left me without a place to rest, but I have more. My revenge is just begun! I spread it over centuries, and time is on my side. Your girls that you all love are mine already. And through them you and others shall yet be mine, my creatures, to do my bidding and to be my jackals when I want to feed. Bah!"

With a contemptuous sneer, he passed quickly through the door, and we heard the rusty bolt creak as he fastened it behind him. A door beyond opened and shut. Realizing the difficulty of following him through the stable, we moved toward the hall. Godalming and Singleton had rushed out into the yard and down the street to where they had cabs waiting, while Harker and Morris had lowered themselves from the window to follow the Count. Van Helsing and I made our way onto the street and climbed into the cabs that had just pulled up. We quickly rounded the corner to find Harker and Singleton waiting for us.

"He's headed north!" cried Harker as he climbed into the cab with Van Helsing and Singleton, as Quincey jumped in with Art and myself. And so we raced after him, slowly but surely closing the gap between us. Though he was diabolically fast, the Count undoubtedly realised he could not outdistance our horses. We caught sight of his thin, black-clad form disappearing into Regents Park as we drew near.

"He seeks Miss Lucy's tomb!" Van Helsing called out to us from his cab. "Follow him through the park, and we will go to Hampstead directly!" At the park our cabs parted ways, ours taking one of the paths, while the other veered to the east, and then north along Hampstead Road.

The pursuit through the park was slow going, as the Count knew it would be, and it was all we could do to keep sight of his form in the distance. By the time we were through the park, we had lost sight of the creature, but at least we knew where he was going. As we approached the Kingstead cemetery, we heard an inhuman bellow of rage and frustration that chilled us to the bone. When we pulled up to the gate, we found the other cab already there and emptied of its passengers. We rushed through the cemetery to the Westenra tomb, where we saw that the door had been forced open. Lying prone on the ground nearby was a gravedigger, blood matting his hair. As Art and Quincey rushed inside, I paused to check on the wounded man; seeing as the wound did not appear overly serious, I too made my way into the tomb, and found Van Helsing and the others standing about the sarcophagus[196].

"The Count has been here," Van Helsing said, "but he found Miss Lucy's bed closed to him, barred by the purifying grace of God, just as we had left it. But he has fled now, to where we yet know not. Still, we have learnt something . . . much! Notwithstanding his brave words, he fears us. He fears time, he fears want! For if not, why he hurry so? His very tone betray him, or my ears deceive. Why take that money? Let us return to the house, and make sure that nothing there may be of use to him, if so that he returns."

Mr. Singleton said he would meet up with us in Purfleet this evening, as there was the matter of our chase through London that many would have seen, as well as the matter of the injured man, that would have to be dealt with in some manner that would keep ourselves from being involved any more than necessary.

When we at last found ourselves back in the Piccadilly house, Godalming went to the table and put the money remaining in his pocket, and took the title deeds in the bundle as Harker had left them. Van Helsing retrieved the letter Mr. Aytown had left for the Count, and swept the remaining things into the open fireplace, where he set fire to them with a match.

It was now late in the afternoon, and sunset was not far off. We had to recognize that our game was up. With heavy hearts we agreed with the Professor when he said, "Let us go back to Madam Mina. Poor, poor dear Madam Mina. All we can do just now is done, and we can there, at least, protect her. But we need not despair. There is but one more earth box, and we must try to find it. When that is done all may yet be well."

I could see that he spoke as bravely as he could to comfort Harker. The poor fellow was quite broken down, now and again he gave a low groan which he could not suppress. He was thinking of his wife.

With sad hearts we came back to my house, where we found Kate as well as Inspector Cotford. Mrs. Harker too was waiting us, with an appearance of cheerfulness which did honour to her bravery and unselfishness. When she saw our faces, her own became as pale as death. For a second or two her eyes were closed as if she were in secret prayer.

And then she said cheerfully, "I can never thank you all enough. Oh, my poor darling!" As she spoke, she took her husband's grey head in her hands and kissed it. "Lay your poor head here and rest it. All will yet be well, dear! God will protect us if He so will it in His good intent." The poor fellow groaned. There was no place for words in his sublime misery.

Inspector Cotford, seeing that we had all been through a trying time, delayed his questions for a time, and we all had a sort of perfunctory supper together, and I think it cheered us all up somewhat. It was, perhaps, the mere animal heat of food to hungry people, for none of us had eaten anything since breakfast, or the sense of companionship may have helped us, but anyhow we were all less miserable, and saw the morrow as not altogether without hope.

True to our promise, we told Mrs. Harker everything which had passed, and in full hearing of the inspector, in the hopes that we might win him as an ally, rather than have him prevent us from our urgent duty. And although Mrs. Harker grew snowy white at times when danger had seemed to threaten her husband, and red at others when his devotion to her was manifested she listened bravely and with calmness. When we came to the part where Harker had rushed at the Count so recklessly, she clung to her husband's arm, and held it tight as though her clinging could protect him from any harm that might come. She said nothing, however, till the narration was all done, and matters had been brought up to the present time.

Then without letting go her husband's hand she stood up amongst us and spoke. Oh, that I could give any idea of the scene. Of that sweet, sweet, good, good woman in all the radiant beauty of her youth and animation, with the red scar on her forehead, of which she was conscious, and which we saw with grinding of our teeth, remembering whence and how it came. Her loving kindness against our grim hate. Her tender faith against all our fears and doubting. And we, knowing that so far as symbols went, she with all her goodness and purity and faith, was outcast from God.

"Jonathan," she said, and the word sounded like music on her lips it was so full of love and tenderness, "Jonathan dear, and you all my true, true friends, I want you to bear something in mind through all this dreadful time. I know that you must fight. That you must destroy even as you destroyed the false Lucy so that the true Lucy might live hereafter. But it is not a work of hate. That poor soul who has wrought all this misery is the saddest case of all. Just think what will be his joy when he, too, is destroyed in his worser part that his better part may have spiritual immortality. You must be pitiful to him, too, though it may not hold your hands from his destruction."

As she spoke I could see her husband's face darken and draw together, as though the passion in him were shriveling his being to its core. Instinctively the clasp on his wife's hand grew closer, till his knuckles looked white. She did not flinch from the pain which I knew she must have suffered, but looked at him with eyes that were more appealing than ever.

As she stopped speaking he leaped to his feet, almost tearing his hand from hers as he spoke.

"May God give him into my hand just for long enough to destroy that earthly life of him which we are aiming at. If beyond it I could send his soul forever and ever to burning hell I would do it!"

"Oh, hush! Oh, hush in the name of the good God. Don't say such things, Jonathan, my husband, or you will crush me with fear and horror. Just think, my dear . . . I have been thinking all this long, long day of it . . . that . . . perhaps . . .

some day . . . I, too, may need such pity, and that some other like you, and with equal cause for anger, may deny it to me! Oh, my husband! My husband, indeed I would have spared you such a thought had there been another way. But I pray that God may not have treasured your wild words, except as the heart-broken wail of a very loving and sorely stricken man. Oh, God, let these poor white hairs go in evidence of what he has suffered, who all his life has done no wrong, and on whom so many sorrows have come."

We men were all in tears now, save for Cotford, who observed the proceedings with a stoicism that was not cold hearted, but understandably necessary. As for the rest of us, there was no resisting the tears, and we wept openly. She wept, too, to see that her sweeter counsels had prevailed. Her husband flung himself on his knees beside her, and putting his arms round her, hid his face in the folds of her dress. Van Helsing beckoned to us and we stole out of the room, leaving the two loving hearts alone with their God.

About this time Mr. Singleton returned, looking very weary, yet in some small way triumphant, and carried with him a clipping from this evening's edition of the "Sporting Life" newspaper. It seems that his position as an independent correspondent allowed him to write up a brief article on the Count, warning the citizens of London to be on the look out for such a man. The Professor seemed pleased.

"Excellent, friend Alfred. This will slow his movements, for he must be cautious now."

Before they retired the Professor fixed up the room against any coming of the Vampire, and assured Mrs. Harker that she might rest in peace. She tried to school herself to the belief, and manifestly for her husband's sake, tried to seem content. It was a brave struggle, and was, I think and believe, not without its reward. Van Helsing had placed at hand a bell which either of them was to sound in case of any emergency. When they had retired, Quincey, Godalming, and I arranged that we should sit up, dividing the night between us, and watch over the safety of the poor stricken lady. The first watch falls to Quincey, so the rest of us shall be off to bed as soon as we can.

The inspector has insisted upon staying the night as well, and I have had a room prepared for him. I can only hope he will side with us in this battle, for any delay now could cost Mrs. Harker more than just her life.

Godalming has already turned in, for his is the second watch. Now that my work is done I, too, shall go to bed.

Inspector Cotford's Case Notes

3 October—This case is becoming akin to Pandora's Box, with some new quandary emerging every day. Attributing the sheer number of suspicious deaths to the possibility of poisoning was certainly straightforward enough, at least in

the beginning. Then added to that was the apparent living entombment of the Westenra girl, followed by her subsequent murder. Though not common, there are certainly documented cases of people being buried alive and then emerging from their own tombs, especially when poisons were involved.

But then this manuscript came into evidence, this compilation of journals which weave together a fanciful, if somewhat contradictory, tale of supernatural horror. "What is the significance of these journals?" I said to myself, after reading through them. "Are the journals intentional misdirection, written by these allies of Arthur Holmwood, aimed at concealing the truth behind the deaths? Or are the journals honest misinterpretations of the events their writers have witnessed?" Though the answer eluded me at the time, and to a degree still does, I found that with regard to this case it made little difference—if the journals were written as intentional misdirection to hide Holmwood's activities, then that simply meant Holmwood had allies helping him; but if the journals were written with the intention of honesty, though within the limited scope of their writers' knowledge, then, even through the grievous misinterpretations and superstitions, the guilt of murder still remained clear enough.

And yet, the possibility that the supernatural events recorded in the diaries might in any way be accurate never entered my mind until this morning, when I witnessed for myself the dying confession of the mad patient Renfield, as well as Count Dracula actually feeding his own blood to Mrs. Harker. Even those events, in and of themselves, may not have convinced me, but when the Count was fired upon at close range by Wright and myself with seemingly no effect whatsoever, and then when immediately thereafter the Count vanished into thin air when confronted by mere religious icons . . .

Later—I have spent the day with Wright, digging yet deeper into these matters. With regard to Mr. Renfield, the Inns (which have in their possession all of Renfield's records, seeing as he had no partner or clerk to take over his business) show him to have been an accomplished solicitor, who spent as much time in Munich and Buda-Pesth as he did here. His records confirmed that he had, as one of his clients, one Archibald Winter-Suffield, who had indeed been the owner of Carfax and the Piccadilly mansion mentioned in the journals. (*mem.*, that Mr. Winter-Suffield had taken his own life may now be in question, given Renfield's ties to the present situation; one must consider the possibility of murder, or perhaps of somehow being driven to suicide). Furthermore, Renfield also had Edward Holmwood as a client for a time. Curiously, it would appear that both the late Lord Godalming and Mr. Renfield had made several journeys together abroad; their last trip together was to Munich—in the same year that young Arthur was adopted—after which they apparently parted ways.

As for "Count Dracula," we could find no mention of the man in any list of foreign royalty. The closest we came was a document from Nürnberg entitled

Dracole Waida, which began with the line "In the year of Our Lord 1456 Dracole did many dreadful and curious things."[197] The document went on to detail a number of tortures and murders committed by this warlord, but proved of little help for the case at hand.

I returned to the Purfleet asylum with Wright, to find that, of the party in question, only Mrs. Harker remained. To our surprise, she now bore a bright red burn across her brow, as if she had been seared with hot metal. She explained that Professor Van Helsing was going to bless her with the use of a Host, but that its touch burned her "unclean flesh," as she put it. Though suspicious of this account, I was hardly in a position to question it at present, and did not wish to trouble her further.

Mrs. Harker was understandably weak and pale from her recent ordeals, but nevertheless put up a brave façade. When asked about the whereabouts of the others, her answer seemed perfectly candid, and was spoken with a confidence born of absolute faith: "They have gone to the Count's homes about London, to consecrate his earth boxes which he must have concealed there, so that he may have no more respite in them." When asked how they would do this thing, she replied "Through the power of God, as embodied in the Host that the Professor brought with him."

It was about this time that Miss Reed returned to the house, though she was quite alone, and had obviously been crying. When pressed for an explanation, she revealed that she had at last found her friend, Mr. Aytown, at the London Hospital in Whitechapel, and that he had been "infected," to use her word, by the Count, and that he must soon become like the Count, if nothing were done. At once I sent Wright to see about this matter, reminding him of what "signs" the Harkers' manuscript said to look for with regards to this supposed vampirism. I am now awaiting his response, while the two women console one another with their tears.

Telegram, from Johnny Wright to Inspector Cotford

3 October

Sir, confirmed Mr. Aytown at hospital. Very pale and weak. Checked teeth as requested: longer and sharper than typical. Awaiting further instructions.

—Wright

Telegram, Cotford to Wright

3 October

Remain with patient to see he is safe and cared for. Inform me immediately should his condition change.

—Cotford

Inspector Cotford's Case Notes

3 October, night—The others returned late in the afternoon, save for Mr. Singleton, who they say had an errand to perform first. After they dined (which I allowed them to do without interruption, for it was clear they were quite famished), they reported having entered four houses belonging to the Count—in Purfleet, Piccadilly, Mile End, and Bermondsey—and "consecrated" the earth held within forty-nine of the fifty boxes they had sought, though they had been unable to locate the last box. After this, they confronted the Count in Piccadilly, who fled to Hampstead, where he eluded them. They spent much time wavering between moods of hatred and sadness, all of which seemed so honest that I began to wonder if more than less of all of this business about the Count was quite true.

Shortly before we were all to retire for the evening, Mr. Singleton returned with a cutting from "Sporting Life"—an article he apparently wrote himself, which describes, to a certain degree, the most recent activities of the Count to the London readers.

Cutting from *Sporting Life*, 3 October

(inserted as evidence into Inspector Cotford's Case Notes)
Man Hurt by Foreigner[198]

The good people of London are warned this evening to keep a wary eye out for a foreign man, dressed all in black, who has proven himself to be a danger to one and all. This man, who is described as being "tall, clean-shaven, save for a white moustache, with a beaky nose and hellish eyes, with a bright red scar upon his brow," has caused much havoc in and about Piccadilly this day.

After being seen breaking a window of the Piccadilly mews, eyewitnesses say that when a band of concerned citizens attempted to detain him, he fled north through Regent Park, through Hampstead, and into Kingstead Cemetery. There the man apparently assaulted a gravedigger, knocking him to the ground and wounding him, before fleeing once more. It is possible that he was heading to the Mile End and Whitechapel area, or to Bermondsey, for such a man has been reported in those areas as well.

Be warned, this foreigner is strong and fast, more so than his apparent age would indicate. What's more, he is clever, and may attempt to disguise himself—an actor's brown stage beard to cover his face, and a hat to cover his scar, would be the most likely choices he would make. And indeed, such a man has already been seen in the vicinity of Whitechapel in connection with a number of murders that have taken place there in recent weeks.

Jonathan Harker's Journal

3-4 October, close to midnight—I thought yesterday would never end. There was over me a yearning for sleep, in some sort of blind belief that to wake would be to find things changed, and that any change must now be for the better. Before we parted, we discussed what our next step was to be, but we could arrive at no result. All we knew was that one earth box remained, and that the Count alone knew where it was. If he chooses to lie hidden, he may baffle us for years. And in the meantime, the thought is too horrible, I dare not think of it even now. This I know, that if ever there was a woman who was all perfection, that one is my poor wronged darling. I loved her a thousand times more for her sweet pity of last night, a pity that made my own hate of the monster seem despicable. Surely God will not permit the world to be the poorer by the loss of such a creature. This is hope to me. We are all drifting reefwards now, and faith is our only anchor.

Thank God! Mina is sleeping, and sleeping without dreams. I fear what her dreams might be like, with such terrible memories to ground them in. She has not been so calm, within my seeing, since the sunset. Then, for a while, there came over her face a repose which was like spring after the blasts of March. I thought at the time that it was the softness of the red sunset on her face, but somehow now I think it has a deeper meaning. I am not sleepy myself, though I am weary . . . weary to death. However, I must try to sleep. For there is tomorrow to think of, and there is no rest for me until . . .

Later—I must have fallen asleep, for I was awakened by Mina, who was sitting up in bed, with a startled look on her face. I could see easily, for we did not leave the room in darkness. She had placed a warning hand over my mouth, and now she whispered in my ear, "Hush! There is someone in the corridor!" I got up softly, and crossing the room, gently opened the door.

Just outside, stretched on a mattress, lay Mr. Morris, wide awake. He raised a warning hand for silence as he whispered to me, "Hush! Go back to bed. It is all right. One of us will be here all night. We don't mean to take any chances!"

His look and gesture forbade discussion, so I came back and told Mina. She sighed and positively a shadow of a smile stole over her poor, pale face as she put her arms round me and said softly, "Oh, thank God for good brave men!" With a sigh she sank back again to sleep. I write this now as I am not sleepy, though I must try again.

4 October, morning—Once again during the night I was wakened by Mina. This time we had all had a good sleep, for the grey of the coming dawn was making the windows into sharp oblongs, and the gas flame was like a speck rather than a disc of light.

She said to me hurriedly, "Go, call the Professor. I want to see him at once."
"Why?" I asked.

"I have an idea. I suppose it must have come in the night, and matured without my knowing it. He must hypnotize me before the dawn, and then I shall be able to speak. Go quick, dearest, the time is getting close."

I went to the door. Dr. Seward was resting on the mattress, and seeing me, he sprang to his feet.

"Is anything wrong?" he asked, in alarm.

"No," I replied. "But Mina wants to see Dr. Van Helsing at once."

"I will go," he said, and hurried into the Professor's room.

Two or three minutes later Van Helsing was in the room in his dressing gown, and Mr. Morris and Lord Godalming were with Dr. Seward at the door. Inspector Cotford made his dutiful appearance as well, asking questions. When the Professor saw Mina a smile, a positive smile ousted the anxiety of his face.

He rubbed his hands as he said, "Oh, my dear Madam Mina, this is indeed a change. See! Friend Jonathan, we have got our dear Madam Mina, as of old, back to us today!" Then turning to her, he said cheerfully, "And what am I to do for you? For at this hour you do not want me for nothing."

"I want you to hypnotize me!" she said. "Do it before the dawn, for I feel that then I can speak, and speak freely. Be quick, for the time is short!" Without a word he motioned her to sit up in bed.

Looking fixedly at her, he commenced to make passes in front of her, from over the top of her head downward, with each hand in turn. Mina gazed at him fixedly for a few minutes, during which my own heart beat like a trip hammer, for I felt that some crisis was at hand. Gradually her eyes closed, and she sat, stock still. Only by the gentle heaving of her bosom could one know that she was alive. The Professor made a few more passes and then stopped, and I could see that his forehead was covered with great beads of perspiration. Mina opened her eyes, but she did not seem the same woman. There was a far-away look in her eyes, and her voice had a sad dreaminess which was new to me. Raising his hand to impose silence, the Professor motioned to me to bring the others in. They came on tiptoe, closing the door behind them, and stood at the foot of the bed, looking on. Mina appeared not to see them. The stillness was broken by Van Helsing's voice speaking in a low level tone which would not break the current of her thoughts.

"Where are you?" The answer came in a neutral way.

"I do not know. Sleep has no place it can call its own." For several minutes there was silence. Mina sat rigid, and the Professor stood staring at her fixedly.

The rest of us hardly dared to breathe. The room was growing lighter. Without taking his eyes from Mina's face, Dr. Van Helsing motioned me to pull up the blind. I did so, and the day seemed just upon us. A red streak shot up, and a rosy light seemed to diffuse itself through the room. On the instant the Professor spoke again.

"Where are you now?"

The answer came dreamily, but with intention. It were as though she were interpreting something. I have heard her use the same tone when reading her shorthand notes.

"I do not know. It is all strange to me!"

"What do you see?"

"I can see nothing. It is all dark."

"What do you hear?" I could detect the strain in the Professor's patient voice.

"The lapping of water. It is gurgling by, and little waves leap. I can hear them on the outside."

"Then you are on a ship?'"

We all looked at each other, trying to glean something each from the other. We were afraid to think.

The answer came quick, "Oh, yes!"

"What else do you hear?"

"The sound of men stamping overhead as they run about. There is the creaking of a chain, and the loud tinkle as the check of the capstan falls into the ratchet."

"What are you doing?"

"I am still, oh so still. It is like death!" The voice faded away into a deep breath as of one sleeping, and the open eyes closed again.

By this time the sun had risen, and we were all in the full light of day. Dr. Van Helsing placed his hands on Mina's shoulders, and laid her head down softly on her pillow. She lay like a sleeping child for a few moments, and then, with a long sigh, awoke and stared in wonder to see us all around her.

"Have I been talking in my sleep?" was all she said. She seemed, however, to know the situation without telling, though she was eager to know what she had told. The Professor repeated the conversation, and she said, "Then there is not a moment to lose. It may not be yet too late!"

Mr. Morris and Lord Godalming started for the door but the Inspector's calm voice called them back.

"Where are you going?" he asked rhetorically, in a manner that bordered between being instructive and amused. "That ship, wherever it was, was weighing anchor at the moment. Which port do you seek? And which ship in that port?"

"The wisdom offered by the detective is sound," the Professor said to the rest of us, and then turned to address the inspector. "Will you then aid us in our quest to right these many wrongs?" After a long, tense pause, Inspector Cotford gave his answer, choosing his words with extreme care.

"Let us say that, for the time being, I will at the very least not hinder you, until I can understand fully all that is happening." I believe everyone in the room gave a sigh of relief. Then the Professor spoke.

"God be thanked that we have once again a clue, though whither it may lead us we know not. We have been blind somewhat. Blind after the manner of men, since when we can look back we see what we might have seen looking forward if we had been able to see what we might have seen! Alas, but that sentence is a puddle, is it not? We can know now what was in the Count's mind, when he seize that money, though Jonathan's so fierce knife put him in the danger that even he dread. He meant escape. Hear me, ESCAPE! He saw that with but one earth box left, and a pack of men following like dogs after a fox, this London was no place for him. He have take his last earth box on board a ship, and he leave the land. He think to escape, but no! We follow him. Tally Ho! As friend Arthur would say when he put on his red frock! Our old fox is wily. Oh! So wily, and we must follow with wile. I, too, am wily and I think his mind in a little while. In meantime we may rest and in peace, for there are waters between us which he do not want to pass, and which he could not if he would. Unless the ship were to touch the land, and then only at full or slack tide. See, and the sun is just rose, and all day to sunset is to us. Let us take bath, and dress, and have breakfast which we all need, and which we can eat comfortably since he be not in the same land with us."

Mina looked at him appealingly as she asked, "But why need we seek him further, when he is gone away from us?"

He took her hand and patted it as he replied, "Ask me nothing as yet. When we have breakfast, then I answer all questions." He would say no more, and we separated to dress.

After breakfast Mina repeated her question. He looked at her gravely for a minute and then said sorrowfully, "Because my dear, dear Madam Mina, now more than ever must we find him even if we have to follow him to the jaws of Hell!"

She grew paler as she asked faintly, "Why?"

"Because," he answered solemnly, "he can live for centuries, and you are but mortal woman. Time is now to be dreaded, since once he put that mark upon your throat."

I was just in time to catch her as she fell forward in a faint.

Cutting from *The East London Advertiser*, 6 October[199]

A Thirst For Blood

The two fresh murders which have been committed in Whitechapel have aroused the indignation and excited the imagination of London to a degree without parallel. Men feel that they are face to face with some awful and extraordinary freak of nature. So inexplicable and ghastly are the circumstances surrounding the crimes that people are affected by them in the same way as children are by the recital of a weird and terrible story of the supernatural. It is so impossible to account, on any ordinary hypothesis, for these revolting acts of blood that the mind turns as it were instinctively to some theory of occult force, and the myths of the Dark Ages rise before the imagination. Ghouls, vampires, bloodsuckers, and all the ghastly array of fables which have been accumulated throughout the course of centuries take form, and seize hold of the excited fancy. Yet the most morbid imagination can conceive nothing worse than this terrible reality; for what can be more appalling than the thought that there is a being in human shape stealthily moving about a great city, burning with the thirst for human blood, and endowed with such diabolical astuteness, as to enable him to gratify his fiendish lust with absolute impunity?

CHAPTER THIRTY-THREE[200]

Dr. Seward's Phonograph Diary

Spoken by Van Helsing

This to Jonathan Harker.

You are to stay with your dear Madam Mina. We shall go to make our search, if I can call it so, for it is not search but knowing, and we seek confirmation only. But do you stay and take care of her today. This is your best and most holiest office. This day nothing can find him here.

Let me tell you that so you will know what we four know already, for I have tell them. He, our enemy, have gone away. He have gone back to his Castle in Transylvania. I know it so well, as if a great hand of fire wrote it on the wall. He have prepare for this in some way, and that last earth box was ready to ship somewheres. For this he took the money. For this he hurry at the last, lest we catch him before the sun go down. It was his last hope, save that he might hide in the tomb that he think poor Miss Lucy, being as he thought like him, keep open to him. But there he found her tomb closed to him. When that fail he make straight for his last resource, his last earth-work I might say did I wish double entente. He is clever, oh so clever! He know that his game here was finish. And so he decide he go back home. He find ship going by the route he came, and he go in it.

We go off now to find what ship, and whither bound. When we have discover that, we come back and tell you all. Then we will comfort you and poor Madam Mina with new hope. For it will be hope when you think it over, that all is not lost. This very creature that we pursue, he take hundreds of years to get so far as London. And yet in one day, when we know of the disposal of him we drive him out. He is finite, though he is powerful to do much harm and suffers not as we do. But we are strong, each in our purpose, and we are all more strong together. Take heart afresh, dear husband of Madam Mina. This battle is but begun and in the end we shall win. So sure as that God sits on high to watch over His children. Therefore be of much comfort till we return.

—Van Helsing

Jonathan Harker's Journal

4 October—When I read to Mina, Van Helsing's message in the phonograph, the poor girl brightened up considerably. Already the certainty that the Count is out of the country has given her comfort. And comfort is strength to her. For my own part, now that his horrible danger is not face to face with us, it seems almost impossible to believe in it. Even my own terrible experiences in Castle Dracula seem like a long forgotten dream. Here in the crisp autumn air in the bright sunlight.

Alas! How can I disbelieve! In the midst of my thought my eye fell on the red scar on my poor darling's white forehead. Whilst that lasts, there can be no disbelief. Mina and I fear to be idle, so we have been over all the diaries again and again. Somehow, although the reality seem greater each time, the pain and the fear seem less. There is something of a guiding purpose manifest throughout, which is comforting. Mina says that perhaps we are the instruments of ultimate good. It may be! I shall try to think as she does. We have never spoken to each other yet of the future. It is better to wait till we see the Professor and the others after their investigations.

The day is running by more quickly than I ever thought a day could run for me again. It is now three o'clock.

Campaign Diary, kept my Mina Harker

5 October, 5 P.M.—Our meeting for report. Present: Professor Van Helsing, Lord Godalming, Inspector Cotford, Mr. Alfred Singleton, Mr. Quincey Morris, Dr. Seward, Miss Katherine Reed, Jonathan Harker, Mina Harker.

Dr. Van Helsing described what steps were taken during the day to discover on what boat and whither bound Count Dracula made his escape.

"As I knew that he wanted to get back to Transylvania, I felt sure that he must go by the Danube mouth, or by somewhere in the Black Sea, since by that way he come. He had been only so far north and east as Munich and this in experiment and so he know not at first quite how he get fro London to there. It was a dreary blank that was before us. *Omne Ignotum pro magnifico*. And so with heavy hearts we start to find what ships leave for the Black Sea last night. He was in sailing ship, since Madam Mina tell of sails being set. These not so important as to go in your list of the shipping in the *Times*, and so we go, by suggestion of Inspector Cotford, to your Lloyd's, where are note of all ships that sail, however so small. There we find that only one Black Sea bound ship go out with the tide. She is the *Czarina Catherine*, and she sail from Doolittle's Wharf for Varna, and thence to other ports and up the Danube. 'So!' said I, 'this is the ship whereon is the Count.' So off we go to Doolittle's Wharf, and there we find a man in an office. From him we inquire of the goings of the *Czarina Catherine*. He swear much, and he red face and loud of voice, but he good fellow all the same. And when Quincey give him something from his pocket which crackle as he roll it up, and put it in a so small bag which he have hid deep in his clothing, he still better fellow and humble servant to us. He come with us, and ask many men who are rough and hot. These be better fellows too when they have been no more thirsty. They say much of blood and bloom, and of others which I comprehend not, though I guess what they mean. But nevertheless they tell us all things which we want to know.

"They make known to us among them, how last afternoon at about five o'clock comes a man so hurry. A tall man, thin and pale, with high nose and teeth so white, and eyes that seem to be burning. That he be all in black, except that he have a hat of straw which suit not him or the time. That he scatter his money in making quick inquiry as to what ship sails for the Black Sea and for where. Some took him to the office and then to the ship, where he will not go aboard but halt at shore end of gangplank, and ask that the captain come to him. The captain come, when told that he will be pay well, and though he swear much at the first he agree to term. Then the thin man go and some one tell him where horse and cart can be hired. He go there and soon he come again, himself driving cart on which was two great boxes. These he himself lift down, though it take several to put them on truck for the ship. He give much talk to captain as to how and where his boxes are to be place. But the captain like it not and swear at him in many tongues, and tell him that if he like he can come and see where they shall be. But he say 'no,' that he come not yet, for that he have much to do. Whereupon the captain tell him that he had better be quick, with blood, for that his ship will leave the place, of blood, before the turn of the tide, with blood. Then the thin man smile and say that of course he must go when he think fit, but he will be surprise if he go quite so soon. The captain swear again, polyglot, and the thin man make him bow, and thank him, and say that he will so far intrude on his kindness as to come aboard before the sailing. Final the captain, more red than ever, and in more tongues, tell him that he doesn't want no Frenchmen, with bloom upon them and also with blood, in his ship, with blood on her also. And so, after asking where he might purchase ship forms, he departed.

"No one knew where he went 'or bloomin' well cared' as they said, for they had something else to think of, well with blood again. For it soon became apparent to all that the *Czarina Catherine* would not sail as was expected. A thin mist began to creep up from the river, and it grew, and grew. Till soon a dense fog enveloped the ship and all around her. The captain swore polyglot, very polyglot, polyglot with bloom and blood, but he could do nothing. The water rose and rose, and he began to fear that he would lose the tide altogether. He was in no friendly mood, when just at full tide, the thin man came up the gangplank again and asked to see where his boxes had been stowed. Then the captain replied that he wished that he and his boxes, old and with much bloom and blood, were in hell. But the thin man did not be offend, and went down with the mate and saw where they was place, and came up and stood awhile on deck in fog. He must have come off by himself, for none notice him. Indeed they thought not of him, for soon the fog begin to melt away, and all was clear again. My friends of the thirst and the language that was of bloom and blood laughed, as they told how the captain's swears exceeded even his usual polyglot, and was more than ever full of picturesque, when on questioning other mariners who were on movement up and down the river that hour, he found that few of them had seen any of fog at all, except where it lay round the wharf. However, the ship went out on the ebb tide, and was doubtless by morning far down the river mouth. She was then, when they told us, well out to sea.

"And so, my dear Madam Mina, it is that we have to rest for a time, for our enemy is on the sea, with the fog at his command, on his way to the Danube mouth. To sail a ship takes time, go she never so quick. And when we start to go on land more quick, and we meet him there. Our best hope is to come on him when in the box between sunrise and sunset. For then he can make no struggle, and we may deal with him as we should. There are days for us, in which we can make ready our plan. We know all about where he go. For we have seen the owner of the ship, who have shown us invoices and all papers that can be. The box we seek is to be landed in Varna, and to be given to an agent, one Ristics who will there present his credentials. And so our merchant friend will have done his part. When he ask if there be any wrong, for that so, he can telegraph and have inquiry made at Varna, we say 'no,' for what is to be done is not for their police or of the customs. It must be done by us alone and in our own way."

When Dr. Van Helsing had done speaking, I asked him if he were certain that the Count had remained on board the ship. He replied, "We have the best proof of that, your own evidence, when in the hypnotic trance this morning." I then asked him why the Count had shipped two boxes, if there was but one of the fifty that remained unaccounted for. He said "I know not. But the Vampire is old, and may have, over long time, gained many things he value and take with him."

I asked him again if it were really necessary that they should pursue the Count, for oh! I dread Jonathan leaving me, and I know that he would surely go if the others went. He answered in growing passion, at first quietly. As he went on, however, he grew more angry and more forceful, till in the end we could not but see wherein was at least some of that personal dominance which made him so long a master amongst men.

"Yes, it is necessary, necessary, necessary! For your sake in the first, and then for the sake of humanity. This monster has done much harm already, in the narrow scope where he find himself, and in the short time when as yet he was only as a body groping his so small measure in darkness and not knowing. All this have I told these others. You, my dear Madam Mina, will learn it in the phonograph of my friend John, or in that of your husband. I have told them how the measure of leaving his own barren land, barren of peoples, and coming to a new land where life of man teems till they are like the multitude of standing corn, was the work of centuries. Were another of the Undead, like him, to try to do what he has done, perhaps not all the centuries of the world that have been, or that will be, could aid him.

"But with this one, all the forces of nature that are occult and deep and strong must have worked together in some wonderous way. The very place, where he have been alive, Undead for all these centuries, is full of strangeness of the geologic and chemical world. There are deep caverns and fissures that reach none know whither. There have been volcanoes, some of whose openings still send out waters of strange properties, and gases that kill or make to vivify. Doubtless, there is something magnetic or electric in some of these combinations of occult forces which work for physical life in strange way, and in himself were from the first some great qualities. In a hard and warlike time he was celebrate that he have more iron nerve, more subtle brain, more braver heart, than any man. In him some vital principle have in strange way found their utmost. And as his body keep strong and grow and thrive, so his brain grow too. All this without that diabolic aid which is surely to him. For it have to yield to the powers that come from, and are, symbolic of good. And now this is what he is to us. He have infect you, oh forgive me, my dear, that I must say such, but it is for good of you that I speak. He infect you in such wise, that even if he do no more, you have only to live, to live in your own old, sweet way, and so in time, death, which is of man's common lot and with God's sanction, shall make you like to him. And not only you, but the friend of Miss Kate, and all those children found upon Hampstead Heath, and who knows how many more we know not of. This must not be! We have sworn together that it must not. Thus are we ministers of God's own wish. That the world, and men for whom His Son die, will not be given over to monsters, whose very existence would defame Him. He have allowed us to redeem one soul already, and we go out as the old knights of the Cross to redeem more. Like them we shall travel towards the sunrise. And like them, if we fall, we fall in good cause."

He paused and I said, "But will not the Count take his rebuff wisely? Since he has been driven from England, will he not avoid it, as a tiger does the village from which he has been hunted?"

"Aha!" he said, "your simile of the tiger good, for me, and I shall adopt him. Your maneater, as they of India call the tiger who has once tasted blood of the human, care no more for the other prey, but prowl unceasing till he get him. This that we hunt from our village is a tiger, too, a maneater, and he never cease to prowl. Nay, in himself he is not one to retire and stay afar. In his life, his living life, he go over the Turkey frontier and attack his enemy on his own ground. He be beaten back, but did he stay? No! He come again, and again, and again. Look at his persistence and endurance. With the child-brain that was to him he have long since conceive the idea of coming to a great city. What does he do? He find out the place of all the world most of promise for him. Then he deliberately set himself down to prepare for the task. He find in patience just how is his strength, and what are his powers. He study new tongues. He learn new social life, new environment of old ways, the politics, the law, the finance, the science, the habit of a new land and a new people who have come to be since he was. His glimpse that he have had, whet his appetite only and enkeen his desire. Nay, it help him to grow as to his brain. For it all prove to him how right he was at the first in his surmises. He have done this alone, all alone! From a ruin tomb in a forgotten land. What more may he not do when the greater world of thought is open to him. He that can smile at death, as we know him. Who can flourish in the midst of diseases that kill off whole peoples. Oh! If such a one was to come from God, and not the Devil, what a force for good might he not be in this old world of ours. But we are pledged to set the world free. Our toil must be in silence, and our efforts all in secret. For in this enlightened age, when men believe not even what they see, the doubting of wise men would be his greatest strength. It would be at once his sheath and his armor, and his weapons to destroy us, his enemies, who are willing to peril even our own souls for the safety of one we love. For the good of mankind, and for the honour and glory of God."

After a general discussion it was determined that for tonight nothing be definitely settled. That we should all sleep on the facts, and try to think out the proper conclusions. Tomorrow, at breakfast, we are to meet again, and after making our conclusions known to one another, we shall decide on some definite cause of action . . .

I feel a wonderful peace and rest tonight. It is as if some haunting presence were removed from me. Perhaps . . .

My surmise was not finished, could not be, for I caught sight in the mirror of the red mark upon my forehead, and I knew that I was still unclean.

Dr. Seward's Case-Book

5 October—We all arose early, and I think that sleep did much for each and all of us. When we met at early breakfast there was more general cheerfulness than any of us had ever expected to experience again.

It is really wonderful how much resilience there is in human nature. Let any obstructing cause, no matter what, be removed in any way, even by death, and we fly back to first principles of hope and enjoyment. More than once as we sat around the table, my eyes opened in wonder whether the whole of the past days had not been a dream. It was only when I caught sight of the red blotch on Mrs. Harker's forehead that I was brought back to reality. Even now, when I am gravely revolving the matter, it is almost impossible to realize that the cause of all our trouble is still existent. Even Mrs. Harker seems to lose sight of her trouble for whole spells. It is only now and again, when something recalls it to her mind, that she thinks of her terrible scar. We are to meet here in my study in half an hour and decide on our course of action. I see only one immediate difficulty, I know it by instinct rather than reason. We shall all have to speak frankly. And yet I fear that in some mysterious way poor Mrs. Harker's tongue is tied. I know that she forms conclusions of her own, and from all that has been I can guess how brilliant and how true they must be. But she will not, or cannot, give them utterance. I have mentioned this to Van Helsing, and he and I are to talk it over when we are alone. I suppose it is some of that horrid poison which has got into her veins beginning to work. The Count had his own purposes when he gave her what he called "the Vampire's baptism of blood." Well, there may be a poison that distills itself out of good things. In an age when the existence of ptomaines is a mystery we should not wonder at anything! One thing I know, that if my instinct be true regarding poor Mrs. Harker's silences, then there is a terrible difficulty, an unknown danger, in the work before us. The same power that compels her silence may compel her speech. I dare not think further, for so I should in my thoughts dishonour a noble woman!

Later—When the Professor came in, we talked over the state of things. I could see that he had something on his mind, which he wanted to say, but felt some hesitancy about broaching the subject. After beating about the bush a little, he said, "Friend John, there is something that you and I must talk of alone, just at the first at any rate. Later, we may have to take the others into our confidence."

Then he stopped, so I waited. He went on, "Madam Mina, our poor, dear Madam Mina is changing."

A cold shiver ran through me to find my worst fears thus endorsed. Van Helsing continued.

"With the sad experience of Miss Lucy, we must this time be warned before things go too far. Our task is now in reality more difficult than ever, and this new trouble makes every hour of the direst importance. I can see the characteristics of the vampire coming in her face. It is now but very, very slight. But it is to be seen if we have eyes to notice without prejudge. Her teeth are sharper, and at times her eyes are more hard. But these are not all, there is to her the silence now often, as so it was with Miss Lucy. She did not speak, even when she wrote that which she wished to be known later. Now my fear is this. If it be that she can, by our hypnotic trance, tell what the Count see and hear, is it not more true that he who have hypnotize her first, and who have drink of her very blood and make her drink of his, should if he will, compel her mind to disclose to him that which she know?"

I nodded acquiescence. He went on, "Then, what we must do is to prevent this. We must keep her ignorant of our intent, and so she cannot tell what she know not. This is a painful task! Oh, so painful that it heartbreak me to think of it, but it must be. When today we meet, I must tell her that for reason which we will not to speak she must not more be of our council, but be simply guarded by us."

He wiped his forehead, which had broken out in profuse perspiration at the thought of the pain which he might have to inflict upon the poor soul already so tortured. I knew that it would be some sort of comfort to him if I told him that I also had come to the same conclusion. For at any rate it would take away the pain of doubt. I told him, and the effect was as I expected.

It is now close to the time of our general gathering. Van Helsing has gone away to prepare for the meeting, and his painful part of it. I really believe his purpose is to be able to pray alone.

Later—At the very outset of our meeting a great personal relief was experienced by both Van Helsing and myself. Mrs. Harker had sent a message by her husband to say that she would not join us at present, as she thought it better that we should be free to discuss our movements without her presence to embarrass us. The Professor and I looked at each other for an instant, and somehow we both seemed relieved. For my own part, I thought that if Mrs. Harker realised the danger herself, it was much pain as well as much danger averted. Under the circumstances we agreed, by a questioning look and answer, with finger on lip, to preserve silence in our suspicions, until we should have been able to confer alone again. We went at once into our Plan of Campaign.

Van Helsing roughly put the facts before us first, "The *Czarina Catherine* left the Thames yesterday morning. It will take her at the quickest speed she has ever made at least three weeks to reach Varna. But we can travel overland to the same place in three days. Now, if we allow for two days less for the ship's voyage, owing to such weather influences as we know that the Count can bring to bear, and if we allow a whole day and night for any delays which may occur to us, then we have a margin of nearly two weeks.

"Thus, in order to be quite safe, we must leave here on 17th at latest. Then we shall at any rate be in Varna a day before the ship arrives, and able to make such preparations as may be necessary. Of course we shall all go armed, armed against evil things, spiritual as well as physical."

Here Quincey Morris added, "I understand that the Count comes from a wolf country, and it may be that he shall get there before us. I propose that we add Winchesters to our armament. I have a kind of belief in a Winchester when there is any trouble of that sort around. Do you remember, Art, when we had the pack after us at Tobolsk? What wouldn't we have given then for a repeater apiece!"

"Good!" said Van Helsing, "Winchesters it shall be. Quincey's head is level at times, but most so when there is to hunt, metaphor be more dishonour to science than wolves be of danger to man. In the meantime we can do nothing here. And as I think that Varna is not familiar to any of us, why not go there more soon? It is as long to wait here as there. Tonight and tomorrow we can get ready, and then if all be well, we six can set out on our journey."

"We six?" said Kate interrogatively, looking from one to another of us.

"Of course!" answered the Professor quickly. "You must remain here to take care of your good friend in the hospital, and Harker must remain to take care of his so sweet wife!"

Kate's face flushed, but she held her peace for the moment. Harker, too, was silent for awhile and then said in a hollow voice, "Let us talk of that part of it in the morning. I want to consult with Mina."

I thought that now was the time for Van Helsing to warn him not to disclose our plan to her, but he took no notice. I looked at him significantly and coughed. For answer he put his finger to his lips and turned away.

Jonathan Harker's Journal

5 October, afternoon—For some time after our meeting this morning I could not think. The new phases of things leave my mind in a state of wonder which allows no room for active thought. Mina's determination not to take any part in the discussion set me thinking. And as I could not argue the matter with her, I could only guess. I am as far as ever from a solution now. The way the others received it, too, puzzled me. The last time we talked of the subject we agreed that there was to be no more concealment of anything amongst us. Mina is sleeping now, calmly and sweetly like a little child. Her lips are curved and her face beams with happiness. Thank God, there are such moments still for her.

Later—How strange it all is. I sat watching Mina's happy sleep, and I came as near to being happy myself as I suppose I shall ever be. As the evening drew on, and the earth took its shadows from the sun sinking lower, the silence of the room grew more and more solemn to me.

All at once Mina opened her eyes, and looking at me tenderly said, "Jonathan, I want you to promise me something on your word of honour. A promise made to me, but made holily in God's hearing, and not to be broken though I should go down on my knees and implore you with bitter tears. Quick, you must make it to me at once."

"Mina," I said, "a promise like that, I cannot make at once. I may have no right to make it."

"But, dear one," she said, with such spiritual intensity that her eyes were like pole stars, "it is I who wish it. And it is not for myself. You can ask Dr. Van Helsing if I am not right. If he disagrees you may do as you will. Nay, more if you all agree, later you are absolved from the promise."

"I promise!" I said, and for a moment she looked supremely happy. Though to me all happiness for her was denied by the red scar on her forehead.

She said, "Promise me that you will not tell me anything of the plans formed for the campaign against the Count. Not by word, or inference, or implication, not at any time whilst this remains to me!" And she solemnly pointed to the scar. I saw that she was in earnest, and said solemnly, "I promise!" and as I said it I felt that from that instant a door had been shut between us.

Later, midnight—Mina has been bright and cheerful all the evening. So much so that all the rest seemed to take courage, as if infected somewhat with her gaiety. As a result even I myself felt as if the pall of gloom which weighs us down were somewhat lifted. We all retired early. Mina is now sleeping like a little child. It is wonderful thing that her faculty of sleep remains to her in the midst of her terrible trouble. Thank God for it, for then at least she can forget her care. Perhaps her example may affect me as her gaiety did tonight. I shall try it. Oh! For a dreamless sleep.

6 October, morning—Another surprise. Mina woke me early, about the same time as yesterday, and asked me to bring Dr. Van Helsing. I thought that it was another occasion for hypnotism, and without question went for the Professor. He had evidently expected some such call, for I found him dressed in his room. His door was ajar, so that he could hear the opening of the door of our room. He came at once. As he passed into the room, he asked Mina if the others might come, too.

"No," she said quite simply, "it will not be necessary. You can tell them just as well. I must go with you on your journey."

Dr. Van Helsing was as startled as I was. After a moment's pause he asked, "But why?"

"You must take me with you. I am safer with you, and you shall be safer, too."

"But why, dear Madam Mina? You know that your safety is our solemnest duty. We go into danger, to which you are, or may be, more liable than any of us from . . . from circumstances . . . things that have been." He paused embarrassed.

As she replied, she raised her finger and pointed to her forehead. "I know. That is why I must go. I can tell you now, whilst the sun is coming up. I may not be able again. I know that when the Count wills me I must go. I know that if he tells me to come in secret, I must by wile. By any device to hoodwink, even Jonathan." God saw the look that she turned on me as she spoke, and if there be indeed a Recording Angel that look is noted to her ever-lasting honour. I could only clasp her hand. I could not speak. My emotion was too great for even the relief of tears.

She went on. "You men are brave and strong. You are strong in your numbers, for you can defy that which would break down the human endurance of one who had to guard alone. Besides, I may be of service, since you can hypnotize me and so learn that which even I myself do not know."

Dr. Van Helsing said gravely, "Madam Mina, you are, as always, most wise. You shall with us come. And together we shall do that which we go forth to achieve."

When he had spoken, Mina's long spell of silence made me look at her. She had fallen back on her pillow asleep. She did not even wake when I had pulled up the blind and let in the sunlight which flooded the room. Van Helsing motioned to me to come with him quietly. We went to his room, and within a minute Lord Godalming, Dr. Seward, and Mr. Morris were with us also, as were Mr. Singleton and Inspector Cotford.

He told them what Mina had said, and went on. "In the morning we shall leave for Varna. We have now to deal with a new factor, Madam Mina. Oh, but her soul is true. It is to her an agony to tell us so much as she has done. But it is most right, and we are warned in time. There must be no chance lost, and in Varna we must be ready to act the instant when that ship arrives."

"Then I must come with you as well," a voice said from behind us. All of us to a one started a bit, and turned to find Miss Reed, who had silently approached. "I can do nothing for Francis while I am here, but if I come with you, then at least I may be of some service. And in any event," she added quickly, to forestall any objections, "it would not seem proper to have so many men traveling with but a single lady. Such may be of no importance now, but later there may be unnecessary scandal from it." Seeing as there would be no arguing with her, Van Helsing consented.

"What shall we do exactly?" asked Mr. Morris laconically.

The Professor paused before replying, "We shall at the first board that ship. Then, when we have identified the box, we shall place a branch of the wild rose on it. This we shall fasten, for when it is there none can emerge, so that at least says the superstition. And to superstition must we trust at the first. It was man's faith in the early, and it have its root in faith still. Then, when we get the opportunity that we seek, when none are near to see, we shall open the box, and . . . and all will be well."

"Meaning no disrespect, Professor," said Morris, "but you said yesterday that it would take three weeks for his ship to reach dry land. I'm not so certain I can hold still for that long. So I've been thinking, why don't I just mosey over into the wolf country when you head out for Varna, to scout out the territory, as it were. It couldn't hurt, and it may save us from bein' dry-gulched by some trap the Count has layin' in wait for us[201]. I can catch up with you in Varna, and if somehow you are delayed and the ship makes it there before you, I shall not wait for any opportunity. When I see the box I shall open it and destroy the monster, though there were a thousand men looking on, and if I am to be wiped out for it the next moment!" I grasped his hand instinctively and found it as firm as a piece of steel. I think he understood my look. I hope he did.

"Good boy," said Dr. Van Helsing. "Brave boy. Quincey is all man. God bless him for it. My child, believe me none of us shall lag behind or pause from any fear. I do but say what we may do . . . what we must do. But, indeed, indeed we cannot say what we may do. There are so many things which may happen, and their ways and their ends are so various that until the moment we may not say. We shall all be armed, in all ways. And when the time for the end has come, our effort shall not be lack. Now let us today put all our affairs in order. Let all things which touch on others dear to us, and who on us depend, be complete. For none of us can tell what, or when, or how, the end may be. As for me, my own affairs are regulate, and as I have nothing else to do, I shall go make arrangements for the travel. I shall have all tickets and so forth for our journey."

There was nothing further to be said, and we parted. I shall now settle up all my affairs of earth, and be ready for whatever may come.

Later—It is done. My will is made, given to Cotford for safe keeping, and all complete. Mina if she survive is my sole heir. If it should not be so, then the others who have been so good to us shall have remainder.

It is now drawing towards the sunset. Mina's uneasiness calls my attention to it. I am sure that there is something on her mind which the time of exact sunset will reveal. These occasions are becoming harrowing times for us all. For each sunrise and sunset opens up some new danger, some new pain, which however, may in God's will be means to a good end. I write all these things in the diary since my darling must not hear them now. But if it may be that she can see them again, they shall be ready. She is calling to me.

Letter, Kate to Mr. and Mrs. Reed

11 October

Dearest Mamma and Papa,

Please forgive me for not having written for so long, but so much has happened since our last correspondence. Francis has been found, but he is very sick, and near death—or worse—having been poisoned, or perhaps infected would be a more correct word?, by the very Count I have written you of.

Since my last letter to you, I have, thanks to your kind prayers, become acquainted with a band of good people, who themselves have suffered much at the hands of this Count. Tomorrow, we shall leave on an expedition, in the hopes of tracking down this fiend, and give to him the justice he so deserves . . . and, perhaps, the redemption he so needs.

Francis is at the Whitechapel hospital; please do see to his care while I am away. And if, God forbid, I should not return to you, please know that I have always loved you.

Your loving daughter,
Kate

Dr. Seward's Case-Book

11 October, Evening—Jonathan Harker has asked me to note this, as he says he is hardly equal to the task, and he wants an exact record kept.

I think that none of us were surprised when we were asked to see Mrs. Harker a little before the time of sunset. We have of late come to understand that sunrise and sunset are to her times of peculiar freedom. When her old self can be manifest without any controlling force subduing or restraining her, or inciting her to action. This mood or condition begins some half hour or more before actual sunrise or sunset, and lasts till either the sun is high, or whilst the clouds are still aglow with the rays streaming above the horizon. At first there is a sort of negative condition, as if some tie were loosened, and then the absolute freedom quickly follows. When, however, the freedom ceases the change back or relapse comes quickly, preceded only by a spell of warning silence.

Tonight, when we met, she was somewhat constrained, and bore all the signs of an internal struggle. I put it down myself to her making a violent effort at the earliest instant she could do so.

A very few minutes, however, gave her complete control of herself. Then, motioning her husband to sit beside her on the sofa where she was half reclining, she made the rest of us bring chairs up close.

Taking her husband's hand in hers, she began, "We are all here together in freedom, for perhaps the last time! I know that you will always be with me to the end." This was to her husband whose hand had, as we could see, tightened upon her. "In the morning we go out upon our task, and God alone knows what may be in store for any of us. You are going to be so good to me to take me with you. I know that all that brave earnest men can do for a poor weak woman, whose soul perhaps is lost, no, no, not yet, but is at any rate at stake, you will do. But you must remember that I am not as you are. There is a poison in my blood, in my soul, which may destroy me, which must destroy me, unless some relief comes to us. Oh, my friends, you know as well as I do, that my soul is at stake. And though I know there is one way out for me, you must not and I must not take it!" She looked appealingly to us all in turn, beginning and ending with her husband.

"What is that way?" asked Van Helsing in a hoarse voice. "What is that way, which we must not, may not, take?"

"That I may die now, either by my own hand or that of another, before the greater evil is entirely wrought. I know, and you know, that were I once dead you could and would set free my immortal spirit, even as you did my poor Lucy's. Were death, or the fear of death, the only thing that stood in the way I would not shrink to die here now, amidst the friends who love me. But death is not all. I cannot believe that to die in such a case, when there is hope before us and a bitter task to be done, is God's will. Therefore, I on my part, give up here the certainty of eternal rest, and go out into the dark where may be the blackest things that the world or the nether world holds!"

We were all silent, for we knew instinctively that this was only a prelude. The faces of the others were set, and Harker's grew ashen grey. Perhaps, he guessed better than any of us what was coming.

She continued, "This is what I can give into the hotch-pot." I could not but note the quaint legal phrase which she used in such a place, and with all seriousness. "What will each of you give? Your lives I know," she went on quickly, "that is easy for brave men. Your lives are God's, and you can give them back to Him, but what will you give to me?" She looked again questioningly, but this time avoided her husband's face. Quincey seemed to understand, he nodded, and her face lit up. "Then I shall tell you plainly what I want, for there must be no doubtful matter in this connection between us now. You must promise me, one and all, even you, my beloved husband, that should the time come, you will kill me."

"What is that time?" The voice was Quincey's, but it was low and strained.

"When you shall be convinced that I am so changed that it is better that I die that I may live. When I am thus dead in the flesh, then you will, without a moment's delay, drive a stake through me and cut off my head, or do whatever else may be wanting to give me rest!"

Quincey was the first to rise after the pause. He knelt down before her and taking her hand in his said solemnly, "I'm only a rough fellow, who hasn't, perhaps, lived as a man should to win such a distinction, but I swear to you by all that I hold sacred and dear that, should the time ever come, I shall not flinch from the duty that you have set us. And I promise you, too, that I shall make all certain, for if I am only doubtful I shall take it that the time has come!"

"My true friend!" was all she could say amid her fast-falling tears, as bending over, she kissed his hand.

"I swear the same, my dear Madam Mina!" said Van Helsing. "And I!" said Lord Godalming, each of them in turn kneeling to her to take the oath. I followed, myself.

Then her husband turned to her wan-eyed and with a greenish pallor which subdued the snowy whiteness of his hair, and asked, "And must I, too, make such a promise, oh, my wife?"

"You too, my dearest," she said, with infinite yearning of pity in her voice and eyes. "You must not shrink. You are nearest and dearest and all the world to me. Our souls are knit into one, for all life and all time. Think, dear, that there have been times when brave men have killed their wives and their womenkind, to keep them from falling into the hands of the enemy. Their hands did not falter any the more because those that they loved implored them to slay them. It is men's duty towards those whom they love, in such times of sore trial! And oh, my dear, if it is to be that I must meet death at any hand, let it be at the hand of him that loves me best. Dr. Van Helsing, I have not forgotten your mercy in poor Lucy's case to him who loved." She stopped with a flying blush, and changed her phrase, "to him who had best right to give her peace. If that time shall come again, I look to you to make it a happy memory of my husband's life that it was his loving hand which set me free from the awful thrall upon me."

"Again I swear!" came the Professor's resonant voice.

Mrs. Harker smiled, positively smiled, as with a sigh of relief she leaned back and said, "And now one word of warning, a warning which you must never forget. This time, if it ever come, may come quickly and unexpectedly, and in such case you must lose no time in using your opportunity. At such a time I myself might be . . . nay! If the time ever come, shall be, leagued with your enemy against you.

"One more request," she became very solemn as she said this, "it is not vital and necessary like the other, but I want you to do one thing for me, if you will."

We all acquiesced, but no one spoke. There was no need to speak.

"I want you to read the Burial Service." She was interrupted by a deep groan from her husband. Taking his hand in hers, she held it over her heart, and continued. "You must read it over me some day. Whatever may be the issue of all this fearful state of things, it will be a sweet thought to all or some of us. You, my dearest, will I hope read it, for then it will be in your voice in my memory forever, come what may!"

"But oh, my dear one," he pleaded, "death is afar off from you."

"Nay," she said, holding up a warning hand. "I am deeper in death at this moment than if the weight of an earthly grave lay heavy upon me!"

"Oh, my wife, must I read it?" he said, before he began.

"It would comfort me, my husband!" was all she said, and he began to read when she had got the book ready.

How can I, how could anyone, tell of that strange scene, its solemnity, its gloom, its sadness, its horror, and withal, its sweetness. Even a sceptic, who can see nothing but a travesty of bitter truth in anything holy or emotional, would have been melted to the heart had he seen that little group of loving and devoted friends kneeling round that stricken and sorrowing lady. Or heard the tender passion of her husband's voice, as in tones so broken and emotional that often he had to pause, he read the simple and beautiful service from the Burial of the Dead. I cannot go on . . . words . . . and v-voices . . . f-fail m-me!

She was right in her instinct. Strange as it was, bizarre as it may hereafter seem even to us who felt its potent influence at the time, it comforted us much. And the silence, which showed Mrs. Harker's coming relapse from her freedom of soul, did not seem so full of despair to any of us as we had dreaded.

CHAPTER
THIRTY-FOUR[202]

Report of Quincey Morris[203]

14 October, night—I'm not one to write letters or keep diaries, and quite frankly I don't have the knack for it. But the good Professor was very keen on accurate records being kept of everything I can learn about the Count and his old stomping grounds, so I reckon I'll just have to try my hand at it.

The morning after we all swore our terrible pledge to that dear little girl, and read the prayer of the dead over her, we made our way from Jack's house to the Charing Cross, not so very far from the Count's own house in Piccadilly (which now belongs to Art, as do all of the lairs, since he, God bless'm, pinched the deeds right from the Count's own table!). After a long day of travel, we made it to Paris just in the nick of time to board the Orient Express. It was a queer night on the train, like being in a hotel and saloon on wheels, but the Harkers quite enjoyed it, for they do love their trains, and I think it took their mind off darker matters for a spell. The following day we reached Buda-Pesth, where we saw each other off with a fond farewell. I'd grown mighty fond of these good folks, and hated to leave them to wait it out in Varna without me, but seeing as we had to get the bulge on the Count, I knew this was the best way to go about it. So we all did our best to keep from taking on, and said our good byes.

Once the train was out of sight, I set out for the big university in Pesth, on the banks of the wide river Danube. To hear tell, the university was at its first a sort of doxology works, but then it was moved here some four or five score years past, first into Buda and then across the river into Pesth, where it was made into a proper school. The University was a powerful big building, like nothing we have back in America—not even in the Old States, and seemed to almost be a castle in its own right. As I passed through the great door, I noticed I was walking under a fancy coat of arms, with two angels to each side of the big shield, I couldn't help but thinking of them as being a good omen for us.

Of course, I didn't speak a word of German or Magyar, but seeing as this was an ace-high school, it didn't take me long to find someone who could understand me. After I told the man who I was and who I was here to see, and handed him the letter of introduction the Professor wrote for me, he excused himself to look into the matter, but in no time at all he came back, saying that Arminius Vambery[204] was expecting me and could see me right away. Van Helsing must be an even bigger bug than I ever imagined, that a word from him would have this here Vambery fellow, as important as he must be in this burg, drop what he's doing to make time for me.

When I was shown into the professor's office, I found Vambery to be a noble looking Jew, with fifty or so years under his belt, not so much hair on his crown, but with a good deal of it under his chin. He was wearing his best bib and tucker (though I imagine that's how all these fancy professor types dress around here), and held himself with a fierce amount of pride. When he came over to meet me, I saw he leaned heavy on a cane, but for him that only added to his character, for it was clear that he'd been through the mill but stood the gaff all the same.

"Quincey Morris, is it not?" he asked in near perfect English, "The American inventor and friend to Van Helsing?"

"And you must be Professor Vambery," I replied with a nod.

"Call me Arminius," he insisted, and we shook hands like old friends . . . for any friend of Van Helsing's would ever be a friend of mine, and it was clear he thought the same.

Though I wanted to get a wiggle on why I was here, he would hear none of it until we had a good meal and drink. He had brought to us something he called Fugas, some fish from a Barlaton Lake, some Spatchcock with that red Paprika pepper Harker mentioned, some cabbage filled with rice and meat and spices (which Arminius named as something I couldn't begin to pronounce), and watermelon. Between us we drank a bottle of Neszmelys, which was something between Hock and Chablis[205].

Afterward he had himself a good smoke. Of course I couldn't have a cigar myself, seeing as the doc back home warned that I was well on my way to being a lunger, and smoking would only worsen the consumption, so I cut a good plug for myself. He wanted to hear all about the States, especially Texas, and my particular trade of locksmithing. In turn, he spun a few good yarns of his own . . .

He had been to Central Asia, following after centuries the track of Marco Polo and was full of experiences fascinating to hear. I asked him if when in Thibet he never felt any fear. He answered:

"Fear of death—no; but I am afraid of torture. I protected myself against that, however!"

"However did you manage that?"

"I had always a poison pill fastened here, where the lappet of my coat now is. This I could always reach with my mouth in case my hands were tied. I knew they could not torture me, and then I did not care!"

He is a wonderful linguist, writes twelve languages, speaks freely sixteen, and knows over twenty. He told me once that when the Empress Eugenie remarked to him that it was odd that he who was lame should have walked so much, he replied:

"Ah, Madam, in Central Asia we travel not on the feet but on the tongue."[206]

He was an odd stick, to be sure, but his insistence that we just dicker stories back and forth got me to relax for an hour or so, and have a word and a thought that did not have to do with the Count. I reckon I didn't quite realize just how wound up I had been until that point. Arminius must have seen the change in me, for directly he said:

"Ah, good! When you came in, your American blood was pumping so hard that you wouldn't have been able to hear my answers over the drumming of your heart! But now your hot blood has cooled a bit, yes? and you can ask your questions, and I will give you my answers."

"Professor," I began, "is it so that you sent the good Doctor Van Helsing some information on Count Dracula?"

"Yes and no," he answered me at once. "I did provide that good friend of both mine and yours with some of the history of the Draculas, but none of his line was ever a Count. The first of them was Voivode, a sort of warlord prince, you might say, who the bulk of my papers to Van Helsing dealt with. Though some who came after held that title as well, most were simply boyar—those of wealth and power."

"That first Dracula, the Voivode fellow . . . let's say, just for the sake of argument, that he all of a sudden came back to life. Where might such a man look to hole up for the day, if the world was against him and he were coppering his bets?" Arminius didn't seem to think the question bosh, and mulled over in all seriousness for a moment before he answered.

"There are six places that might suite his fancy—the Transylvanian town of Sighisoara, the Wallachian city of Targoviste, the Castle Arges, the Monastery of Snagov, the Borgo Pass, and the Scholomance."

When I asked him to elaborate a bit on these, he was more than happy to do so, and began thus:

"Dracula, or simply 'Vlad,' as was his name, was born in Transylvania, in the town of Sighisoara. His father was called 'Dracul'—the Dragon—for in 1431, the same year his son was born, he was invested into the secretive Order of the Dragon. Because of his father, in time the young Vlad came to be known as 'Dracula'—Son of the Dragon.

"Though born in Transylvania, Dracula ruled as Voivode in the province to the south, called Wallachia, from the city stronghold of Targoviste. He was a harsh ruler, but the people there loved him dearly, and even to this day hail him as a hero and saint, for he overthrew the corrupt boyars, did away with all crime through fear of horrible tortures, and saved their land again and again from the Turk. There he became famous for impaling his enemies on long shafts of sharpened wood, thus earning him the dubious title of 'Tepes'—the Impaler. It is even said he at one time had erected a veritable forest of the impaled, where he dined on bread dipped in the blood of the dying.

"West of Targoviste, at the source of the river Arges, Dracula forced many boyar (whom he blamed, and perhaps rightly so, for the murder of his father) to rebuild the old Dacian fortress, once called the Castle Arges, stone by stone, so that he might have a place of respite. Many boyar died in the building of it, and their blood and bones became a part of that fortress. Dracula's first wife threw herself into the river there, drowning herself after vengeful Turks shot an arrow through her window with a note bearing false news of her husband's death.

"Eventually, the Voivode was killed in battle against the armies of his brother Radu, who had from early on sided with the Turks. By then Dracula had been declared anathema—excommunicated, you would say—by the Eastern Church, for his various crimes, thus condemning his body to remain incorrupt, his soul cursed to wander the earth, until the Day of Judgement. So his body was collected in secret, and buried in the monastery of Snagov, which had many close ties to the Dracula family.

"But when he was yet alive, he fathered a number of children, some of whom managed to survive the dangers of battle and assassination, and lived to father children of their own. In time, the last of his race, descendants of the Voivode's second wife, settled near the Borgo Pass, where they have since faded into obscurity."

"And what about that Scholomance?" I pressed. "I heard Van Helsing make mention of that name as well."

"Ah, now there is a fascinating tale, to be sure. Some two millennia ago, there lived in Transylvania a people called the Dacians. They worshiped a god of sorts named Zalmoxis, who was mentioned by name in the writings of Plato and Herodotus as a god of the underworld. He was said to have taught the Dacians a great many things, how to forge iron that did not rust, how to build great towers of stone without the need for mortar, how to fashion burnt clay pipes to carry water. More than that, his followers believed he could control the weather, and could teach his people to become as wolves, and even bestow immortality. His disciples offered sacrifices to him regularly by throwing living men upon rows of spikes, impaling them unto death.

"So impressive were the disciples of Zalmoxis, these 'Dacian Wolves' as they were called, that even their enemies respected them. Their greatest enemy, the

Romans, even went so far as to erect the Trajan Column in Rome to commemorate their battles, where it remains to this day.

"In the Carpathians above what is now Hermanstadt, Zalmoxis hollowed out for himself a great underground cave near a lake, where he would disappear for long periods of time, sometimes alone, sometimes with a number of his disciples. As the centuries passed, this cave became known as the Scholomance. The legend of it grew, as legends often will, and it is now said that the Devil himself teaches sorcery and alchemy to ten students there once every generation, but in the end only releases nine of them back into the world, for the tenth is kept at the Scholomance to serve the Devil and tend to the great dragon which dwells in the lake."

"Do you believe any of that Scholomance yarn to be true?" I asked.

"While the Accuser may be real enough, I daresay that the 'Devil' of the Scholomance is but a man who, when his time there has come to an end, selects his successor from his ten students, who then takes his place as the new 'Devil.' And so the cycle continues from generation to generation, from the days of Zalmoxis until now, with the headmaster being raised up from a student, who then, in his time, raises up the next student, and so on.

"And as for the dragon, who's to say? According to legend, there are such monsters of vast size and power, such as legend attributes to vast fens or quags where there was illimitable room for expansion. A glance at a geological map will show that whatever truth there may have been of the actuality of such monsters in the early geologic periods, at least there was plenty of possibility. In Transylvania there were places where the plentiful supply of water could gather. The streams were deep and slow, and there were holes of abysmal depth, where any kind and size of antediluvian monster could find a habitat. In places were mud-holes a hundred or more feet deep. Who can tell us when the age of the monsters which flourished in slime came to an end? There must have been places and conditions which made for greater longevity, greater size, greater strength than was usual. Such over-lappings may have come down even to our earlier centuries. Nay, are there not now creatures of a vastness of bulk regarded by the generality of men as impossible? Even in our own day there are seen the traces of animals, if not the animals themselves, of stupendous size—veritable survivals from earlier ages, preserved by some special qualities in their habitats. I remember meeting a distinguished man in India, who had the reputation of being a great shikaree, who told me that the greatest temptation he had ever had in his life was to shoot a giant snake which he had come across in the Terai of Upper India. He was on a tiger-shooting expedition, and as his elephant was crossing a nullah, it squealed. He looked down from his howdah and saw that the elephant had stepped across the body of a snake which was dragging itself through the jungle. 'So far as I could see,' he said, 'it must have been eighty or one hundred feet in length. Fully forty or fifty feet was on each side of the track, and though the weight which it dragged had thinned it, it was as thick round as a man's body. I suppose you know that when you are after tiger, it is a point of honour not to shoot at anything else, as life may depend on it. I could easily have spined this monster, but I felt that I must not—so, with regret, I had to let it go.'"[207]

By this time the hour was growing late, and I felt the need to pony up. Arminius kindly gave me maps of Transylvania and Wallachia, so I would be able to find my way without having to ask for directions (which would be a problem, seeing as I don't speak in the same tongue as these folks). I thanked the man profusely, and he bid me a fond farewell.

I've packed up all the supplies I might need—I have the maps the good Arminius gave me, and all the food and water I can carry. I'm heeled with my revolver and rifle, and I have my trusty Bowie knife, of course. I also have the cross and wafer the Professor gave me. And, just for good measure, I've brought along the new portable "Maxim" gun[208] I have been working on perfecting, as well as a few sticks of dynamite as well. Seeing as there's no need to investigate the Borgo Pass, for we already know that to be one of the Count's lairs, I believe I'll scout out Sighisoara first, as it's the closest one to the Pass.

15 October, evening—I found Sighisoara to be a quaint little medieval burg, with narrow cobblestone lanes and old German houses, and fortified all around with great walls and towers. The folk here are simple, and look and dress just as Harker wrote about them on his first trip through these lands. Though it's a pretty sight, sure enough, I'll not dawdle here. Sighisoara is quite far from Varna, with no direct route of travel. What's more, it's a small burg, as cities go, and in small burgs people are tight knit with one another, and know who's a neighbor and who's not, and keep a sharp eye on the comings an goings of strangers, and would notice right away if a fellow like the Count were to make an appearance. Seeing as how our vampire's probably wanting to lay low, I think it's safe to say he wouldn't want to be coming here.

16 October—In Wallachia now. Here the folk are a bit different than up north. The men dress in tartar fur caps with jackets of sheepskin with the fur worn outwards, and shirts with their tails outside white trousers, with either Russian boots or sandals bound over rough garters, into which the trousers are tucked. The women all have white kerchiefs on their heads, and loose chemises fastened at the neck and waist with strings, which reach the ankles and are otherwise open down to the waist, with baggy sleeves tucked up at their elbows. The ladies also wear a sort of belt or girdle with fringes of black and scarlet reaching down to the ankles[209].

17 October—To my surprise, I found that Snagov was an island, and sits in the middle of a lake near Bucharest. Surely the Count wouldn't come here, for even

if he made it to the island, he could be easily trapped there by the water which he dare not cross. I reckon that was why he was buried there in the first place; if they knew he was cursed to rise again, they'd want to keep him trapped by the sacred relics of the monastery, and by the ring of water. I wonder how he managed to escape?

19 October—Targoviste's also a wash. This was the Count's old stomping ground, to be sure, and he's still well remembered here. There are statues of him, and paintings, and carvings, and the like all over the place. If the Count wanted to hide out in a city where he'd be known on sight, he would have settled down here instead of making the trek all the way over to London. I'm figuring he doesn't want to be recognized at all, not even by people who still think of him as a hero.

20 October—The Castle Arges, as Arminius called it, turned out to be no castle at all, but just a pile of stones that were half fallen down the cliff to the river below. Now, that's not to say that back in the Count's living days this wasn't something to see. It was a powerful hard trek getting up here, and the pile's up on a cliff that'd be easy to defend. But there's been no one here for a long, long time, and everything's come a cropper. There wouldn't even be a place to hide his box out from under the sun, even if he did decide to pay his old house a visit.

22 October—The Scholomance was right where Arminius said it would be, though it was not quite what I was expecting, at least from the outside, and I almost overlooked it. After passing through Hermanstadt—which, I must say, looked much like the pictures of Nuremburg I've seen now and again—I traveled through the Carpathians along the Red Tower Pass. Though I knew I was quite a hike from the Borgo Pass, I couldn't help but remember how Mr. Harker described his journey through the mountains; and a fine man he was for not turning tail, for seein' with my own eyes those jagged peaks rising up so high as if they'd topple down on my head at the drop of a hat was enough to want to make me shin out too.

The road seemed to wind on an on, until at last I found a stream spillin' down into the pass. I turned my horse and followed the water up and up and up until I came to its source—a wide lake sitting in a clearing amongst the mountain peaks. I reined in my horse for a drink, but he wouldn't go near the water, and shied away from it and whinnied and cowered all the while. Now, I'm a mighty fine judge of horses, if I do say so myself, so I knew I hadn't saddled any crowbait, but I couldn't for the life of me see what had'm spooked (though there was a time or two I fancied I saw out of the corner of my eye something sleek and long break the surface of the water, but when I looked again it was gone and only a few slight ripples remained).

As I was hunting around, I caught sight of a small rust-red tower, mostly grown over with moss and vines, way over on the other side. So I tied up my horse out of sight back in the trees, and made my way around the lake on foot.

The tower was a queer sight, all squat on the bottom and narrower at the top, and made out of large red stones that were cut just right so they'd fit together without mortar, and looked to be very old. The doors to the tower were massive, made of iron, and were fastened with a lock nearly a foot square, of a kind I had never seen before. It took me longer than my pride would like to have me admit to get that lock open, but open it I did, and went inside.

I saw, as I entered the tower, that it was very strong, almost as strong and as heavy as if it had been intended as a fortress. I made my way down a steep set of stairs, worn smooth by long use, and then followed a cave that looked more like the borrow of a snake than anything carved by man, back, back until I came to a blood red room of considerable size[210], hollowed right out of the mountain stone. From this vast chamber many tunnels, akin to what I had just come through, led away in all directions, with no end in sight to any of them. The red room itself was filled all around with books and scrolls, and clay jars of powders, and archaic devices of all sorts. In the middle of the room was a wide wheel or round table of sorts carved from a single piece of stone. Around the table sat eleven chairs, each also from a single stone, with one being quite larger than the others. I found, upon touching the table, that it turned with surprising ease.[211] In the middle of the great wheel, which was dark in places, as if stained again and again with old blood, there opened up a wide sunk well, which looked to go deep underground. There was no windlass nor any trace of there ever having been any—no rope—nothing.

Now, I had heard tell that the Romans had wells of immense depth, from which the water was lifted by the 'old rag rope'; that at Woodhull used to be nearly a thousand feet. Here, then, I reckoned we had simply an enormously deep well-hole. And yet, there was a sort of green light—very clouded, very dim—which came up from the well. Not a fixed light, but intermittent and irregular—quite unlike anything I had ever seen. And from the well came a nauseating smell, like that of a bilge or rank swamp, akin to the stench we came across back at Carfax.

I figured that if the Count were going to hole up anywhere around here, this tower would be the place he'd choose, and I aimed to do something about it. After rummaging through the room, I found many of the powders to be right nasty—sulfur and black powder and the like, which I easily recognized from my own work back home—so I dumped the whole kit and caboodle down the hole. Then, having climbed the stairs to the door, I lit all the dynamite and tossed'm down the shaft of the tower into the well-hole . . . and then skedaddled!

As I ran, from behind me there rose from the tower a powerful crashin' sound, mixed up with an inhuman scream so appalling that I, as stout of heart as any Texan ever was, felt my blood turn into ice. The shrieks continued, though less sharp in sound, as if they'd been muffled. In the midst of all that screaming was a terrific explosion, seemingly from deep down in the earth. When I felt I was a safe enough distance away, I climbed up a tall rock and took a gander at my handywork.

Though it was now getting on toward dusk, the flames that rose up from the tower made all around almost as light as day, and my eyes were able to make out a good bit of detail. The heat of the burning tower caused the iron doors to warp and collapse. I watched as they fell open and exposed the interior. I could now see clear through to the room beyond, where the well-hole yawned. From this the agonised shrieks were rising, growing ever more terrible with each second that passed.

And what I saw in that room was enough to fill me up with enough evil dreams to last me the rest of my life. The whole place looked as if a sea of blood had been crashing against it. Each of the explosions from below had thrown out from the well-hole, as if it were the mouth of some great cannon, a mass of fine mountain sand mixed with fresh blood, and great red pieces of torn-up meat. As the explosions kept on, more and more of this gore was shot up, though most of the lot fell back in again into the hole. Many of the awful fragments were of something which had lately been alive, by the look of 'em, and they quivered and shook as though they were still in torment. Some of those pieces of raw meat were partially covered with scaled skin, like some great lizard or rattler, and there were what looked to have been the entrails of a monster torn into shreds. All in all, I reckon all the blood and gore was from that Scholomance dragon which Arminius had chatted about.

Then I got a right nasty surprise, as the underground fires evidently reached the main stash of pots I had tossed into the hole. All of a sudden the ground heaved and opened up in long deep chasms, whose edges shook and fell in, throwing up clouds of sand which fell back and hissed as it landed atop the churning lake water. The tower, though heavy and strong, shook to its foundations. Some of the great hard stones, squared and grooved, were thrown up as if from a volcano. I watched as they broke and split in mid air as though dashed by some infernal power. Even the trees near the tower were torn up by the roots and hurled into the air.

And as for me, I found myself thrown through the air by that concussive force, and felt a stabbin' pain shoot through my side, and then silence brooded over all—silence so complete that it seemed in itself a sentient thing—silence which seemed like incarnate darkness . . . [212]

CHAPTER
THIRTY-FIVE[213]

Jonathan Harker's Journal

15 October, Varna—We left Charing Cross on the morning of the 12th, got to Paris the same night, and took the places secured for us in the Orient Express. At Buda-Pesth, Morris disembarked to begin his "scouting out the territory," as he put it. The parting was a sad one, for we all had come to draw strength from his own.

From Buda-Pesth we traveled night and day, arriving here at about five o'clock. Lord Godalming went to the Consulate to see if any telegram had arrived for him, whilst the rest of us came on to this hotel, "the Odessus." The journey may have had incidents. I was, however, too eager to get on, to care for them. Until the *Czarina Catherine* comes into port there will be no interest for me in anything in the wide world. Thank God! Mina is well, and looks to be getting stronger. Her colour is coming back. She sleeps a great deal. Throughout the journey she slept nearly all the time. Before sunrise and sunset, however, she is very wakeful and alert. And it has become a habit for Van Helsing to hypnotize her at such times. At first, some effort was needed, and he had to make many passes. But now, she seems to yield at once, as if by habit, and scarcely any action is needed. He seems to have power at these particular moments to simply will, and her thoughts obey him. He always asks her what she can see and hear.

She answers to the first, "Nothing, all is dark."

And to the second, "I can hear the waves lapping against the ship, and the water rushing by. Canvas and cordage strain and masts and yards creak. The wind is high . . . I can hear it in the shrouds, and the bow throws back the foam."

It is evident that the *Czarina Catherine* is still at sea, hastening on her way to Varna. Lord Godalming has just returned. He had four telegrams, one each day since we started, and all to the same effect. That the *Czarina Catherine* had not been reported to Lloyd's from anywhere. He had arranged before leaving London that his agent should send him every day a telegram saying if the ship had been reported. He was to have a message even if she were not reported, so that he might be sure that there was a watch being kept at the other end of the wire.

There was also a telegram waiting from Mr. Morris, dated 14 October from Buda-Pesth, which read "Met with Professor Vambery. Will scout out the Count's old stomping grounds, and send reports." Even as we were reading it, another one arrived fresh from today: "Strolled through Sighisoara, where the Count was born. A bit too close-knit for his tastes, I'd think. Will look elsewhere."

We had dinner and went to bed early. Tomorrow we are to see the Vice Consul, and to arrange, if we can, about getting on board the ship as soon as she arrives. Van Helsing says that our chance will be to get on the boat between sunrise and sunset. The Count, even if he takes the form of a bat, cannot cross the running water of his own volition, and so cannot leave the ship. As he dare not change to man's form without suspicion, which he evidently wishes to avoid, he must remain in the box as a corpse. If, then, we can come on board after sunrise, he is at our mercy, for we can open the box and make sure of him, as we did of poor Lucy, before he wakes. What mercy he shall get from us all will not count for much. We think that we shall not have much trouble with officials or the seamen. Thank God! This is the country where bribery can do anything, and we are well supplied with money. We have only to make sure that the ship cannot come into port between sunset and sunrise without our being warned, and we shall be safe. Judge Moneybag will settle this case, I think!

16 October—Mina's report still the same. Lapping waves and rushing water, darkness and favouring winds. We are evidently in good time, and when we hear of the *Czarina Catherine* we shall be ready. As she must pass the Dardanelles we are sure to have some report.

17 October—Everything is pretty well fixed now, I think, to welcome the Count on his return from his tour. Godalming told the ship owner Mr. Hopgood that he fancied that one or both of the boxes sent aboard might contain something stolen from him, and got a half consent that he might open it at his own risk. The owner gave him a paper telling the Captain to give him every facility in doing whatever he chose on board the ship, and also a similar authorization to his agent at Varna. We have seen the agent, who was much impressed with Godalming's kindly manner to him, and we are all satisfied that whatever he can do to aid our wishes will be done.

We have already arranged what to do in case we get the box open. If the Count is there, Van Helsing and Seward will cut off his head at once and drive a stake through his heart, with Cotford presiding over the affair to insure, for the sake of the law, that the body therein, which we intend to mutilate, is not that of a living man. Singleton and Godalming and I shall prevent interference, even if we have to use the arms which we shall have ready. The Professor says that if we can so treat the Count's body, it will soon after fall into dust, given that it would revert to its proper age of centuries. In such case there would be no evidence against us, in case any suspicion of murder were aroused. But even if it were not, we should stand or fall by our act, and perhaps some day this very script may be evidence to come between some of us and a rope. Inspector Cotford would, no doubt, see to that, for as kind and honourable of a man as he seems to be, he is still a man of the law, and must do his sworn duty to that law. For myself, I should take the chance only too thankfully if it were to come. We mean to leave no stone unturned to carry out our intent. We have arranged with certain officials that the instant the *Czarina Catherine* is seen, we are to be informed by a special messenger.

17 October, evening—Telegram from Morris, sent from Bucharest: "Nothing here for the Count; his old tomb is closed in on all sides by water."

22 October—Still no news from Morris. We are all growing anxious over his safety, and pray for him often.

24 October—A whole week of waiting. Daily telegrams to Godalming, but only the same story. "Not yet reported." Mina's morning and evening hypnotic answer is unvaried. Lapping waves, rushing water, and creaking masts.

One bright ray in this darkness, though, is that Mr. Morris has returned to us, safe and sound. He looked worn and weary from his travels, and had a great gash in his side which still oozed blood, but was as pleased to see us as we were him. After Dr. Seward tended to his wounds, we all sat around to listen to him "spin yarns," as he called it, about his exploration of the Count's old haunts, and his perilous adventure at the Scholomance, from which he barely escaped with his life. When asked about what happened when he regained consciousness from the explosion, he finished the tale he had not had time or energy to finish recording before his return to us:

"I must have been out cold for the whole of the night, for I awoke to the warmth of the sun upon my face. The morning was bright and cheerful, as a morning sometimes is after a devastating storm. All nature was bright and joyous, and it was a queer thing to see in the middle of all that the wrecked tower, all burnt-out and ruined as it was.

"The only sign that the Scholomance had ever been there at all was a shapeless huddle of shattered stones, which I could just barely make out as the breeze pushed aside some of the smoke that still poured from its ruins. The trees of the clearing were still there—or at least some of them—standing tall in the haze of smoke. Their mighty trunks looked to be as solid as ever, but the larger branches were broken and twisted and cracked, with bark stripped and chipped, and the smaller twigs were broken or missing outright.

"The absolute destruction of the place and everything in it, being seen as it was in the broad daylight, was something I had trouble wrapping my mind around. Something had changed there since the time I had been knocked out. It almost seemed as if Nature herself had tried to obliterate the evil signs of what had once been here. Now that the sun was up, I was able to get a good gander at the tower ruins. The broken stonework looked worse than before; the upheaved foundations, the chunks of masonry, the fissures in the torn earth like little canyons—all looked right awful. I could still see the well-hole, a round pit seemingly leading down into the very bowels of Hell itself. But all that blood and slime, the torn and evil-smelling flesh, and the sickening remnants of the dragon's violent death, were gone. I reckon the later explosions had thrown up from the deep some lake water which, though nasty in itself, had still some cleansing power left, or else the writhing mass which stirred from far below had helped to drag down and obliterate the items of horror. A red dust, partly of fine sand, partly of the waste of the falling ruin, covered everything, and, though ghastly itself, helped to mask something still worse.

"And yet, after a few minutes of watching, it became clear that even now the turmoil below hadn't let up quite yet. Every now and then some hell-broth in the hole seemed to boil up. It rose and fell again and turned over, showing me even more nauseous details than I had seen before. The worst parts were the great masses of the flesh of the monstrous dragon, in all its red and sickening aspect. Such fragments had been bad enough before, but now they were infinitely worse. I guess corruption may come mighty fast upon those creatures whose existence was an insult to nature, for the whole mass seemed to have become rotten overnight! The whole surface of the fragments, alive only a day before, was now covered with insects, worms, and vermin of all kinds. The sight was horrible enough, but, with the awful smell added, was simply unbearable. The hole appeared to breathe forth death in its most repulsive forms.[214]

"I could stand no more, so I found my horse—which by some miracle was spared from both the explosion and from the wolves which most roam these parts—and left as fast as his four hooves would carry me. I've been through many things in my day, but bein' caught in a blast like that damn near did me in. I dare say that I would not make it through another one."

Though his adventures were most fascinating and entertaining to hear tell of, and assured us that the Vampire had fewer refuges to flee to than we first thought, we were now more than ever anxious for the Count's ship to arrive and be done with the matter once and for all.

Telegram, 24 October

Rufus Smith, Lloyd's, London, to Lord Godalming,
care of H.B.M. Vice Consul, Varna

Czarina Catherine reported this morning from Dardanelles.

Dr. Seward's Case-Book

25 October—How I miss my phonograph! To write a diary with a pen is irksome
to me! But Van Helsing says I must. We were all wild with excitement yesterday
when Godalming got his telegram from Lloyd's. I know now what men feel in
battle when the call to action is heard. Even Kate seemed eager to bring about
an end to this matter, even knowing what that end must entail. Mrs. Harker,
alone of our party, did not show any signs of emotion. After all, it is not strange
that she did not, for we took special care not to let her know anything about
it, and we all tried not to show any excitement when we were in her presence.
In old days she would, I am sure, have noticed, no matter how we might have
tried to conceal it. But in this way she is greatly changed during the past three
weeks. The lethargy grows upon her, and though she seems strong and well,
and is getting back some of her colour, Van Helsing, Singleton, and I are not
satisfied. We talk of her often. We have not, however, said a word to the others.
It would break poor Harker's heart, certainly his nerve, if he knew that we had
even a suspicion on the subject. Van Helsing examines, he tells me, her teeth
very carefully, whilst she is in the hypnotic condition, for he says that so long
as they do not begin to sharpen there is no active danger of a change in her. If
this change should come, it would be necessary to take steps! We both know
what those steps would have to be, though we do not mention our thoughts to
each other. We should neither of us shrink from the task, awful though it be to
contemplate. "Euthanasia" is an excellent and a comforting word! I am grateful
to whoever invented it.

It is only about 24 hours' sail from the Dardanelles to here, at the rate
the *Czarina Catherine* has come from London. She should therefore arrive
some time in the morning, but as she cannot possibly get in before noon,
we are all about to retire early. We shall get up at one o'clock, so as to be
ready.

25 October, Noon—No news yet of the ship's arrival. Mrs. Harker's hypnotic
report this morning was the same as usual, so it is possible that we may get news
at any moment. We men are all in a fever of excitement, except Harker, who is
calm. His hands are cold as ice, and an hour ago I found him whetting the edge
of the great Ghoorka knife which he now always carries with him. It will be a

bad lookout for the Count if the edge of that "Kukri" ever touches his throat, driven by that stern, ice-cold hand!

Van Helsing and I were a little alarmed about Mrs. Harker today. About noon she got into a sort of lethargy which we did not like. Although we kept silence to the others, we were neither of us happy about it. She had been restless all the morning, so that we were at first glad to know that she was sleeping. When, however, her husband mentioned casually that she was sleeping so soundly that he could not wake her, we went to her room to see for ourselves. She was breathing naturally and looked so well and peaceful that we agreed that the sleep was better for her than anything else. Poor girl, she has so much to forget that it is no wonder that sleep, if it brings oblivion to her, does her good.

Later—Our opinion was justified, for when after a refreshing sleep of some hours she woke up, she seemed brighter and better than she had been for days. At sunset she made the usual hypnotic report. Wherever he may be in the Black Sea, the Count is hurrying to his destination. To his doom, I trust!

26 October—Another day and no tidings of the *Czarina Catherine*. She ought to be here by now. That she is still journeying somewhere is apparent, for Mrs. Harker's hypnotic report at sunrise was still the same. It is possible that the vessel may be lying by, at times, for fog. Some of the steamers which came in last evening reported patches of fog both to north and south of the port. We must continue our watching, as the ship may now be signalled any moment.

27 October, Noon—Most strange. No news yet of the ship we wait for. Mrs. Harker reported last night and this morning as usual. "Lapping waves and rushing water," though she added that "the waves were very faint." The telegrams from London have been the same, "no further report." Van Helsing is terribly anxious, and told me just now that he fears the Count is escaping us.

He added significantly, "I did not like that lethargy of Madam Mina's. Souls and memories can do strange things during trance." I was about to ask him more, but Harker just then came in, and he held up a warning hand. We must try tonight at sunset to make her speak more fully when in her hypnotic state.

Telegram, 28 October

Rufus Smith, London, to Lord Godalming,
care of H.B.M. Vice Consul, Varna

Czarina Catherine reported entering Galatz at one o'clock today.

Dr. Seward's Case-Book

28 October—When the telegram came announcing the arrival in Galatz I do not think it was such a shock to any of us as might have been expected. True, we did not know whence, or how, or when, the bolt would come. But I think we all expected that something strange would happen. The day of arrival at Varna made us individually satisfied that things would not be just as we had expected. We only waited to learn where the change would occur. None the less, however, it was a surprise. I suppose that nature works on such a hopeful basis that we believe against ourselves that things will be as they ought to be, not as we should know that they will be. Transcendentalism is a beacon to the angels, even if it be a will-o'-the-wisp to man. Van Helsing raised his hand over his head for a moment, as though in remonstrance with the Almighty. But he said not a word, and in a few seconds stood up with his face sternly set.

Lord Godalming grew very pale, and sat breathing heavily. I was myself half stunned and looked in wonder at one after another. Quincey Morris tightened his belt with that quick movement which I knew so well. In our old wandering days it meant "action." Cotford and Singleton were quiet and contemplative, their analytical minds undoubtedly hard at work on the matter. Mrs. Harker grew ghastly white, so that the scar on her forehead seemed to burn, but she folded her hands meekly and looked up in prayer as Kate drew close to her in comfort. Harker smiled, actually smiled, the dark, bitter smile of one who is without hope, but at the same time his action belied his words, for his hands instinctively sought the hilt of the great Kukri knife and rested there.

"When does the next train start for Galatz?" said Van Helsing to us generally.

"At 6:30 tomorrow morning!" We all started, for the answer came from Mrs. Harker.

"How on earth do you know?" said Art.

"You forget, or perhaps you do not know, though Jonathan does and so does Dr. Van Helsing, that I am the train fiend. At home in Exeter I always used to make up the time tables, so as to be helpful to my husband. I found it so useful sometimes, that I always make a study of the time tables now. I knew that if anything were to take us to Castle Dracula we should go by Galatz, or at any rate through Bucharest, so I learned the times very carefully. Unhappily there are not many to learn, as the only train tomorrow leaves as I say."

"Wonderful woman!" murmured the Professor.

"Can't we get a special?" asked Lord Godalming.

Van Helsing shook his head, "I fear not. This land is very different from yours or mine. Even if we did have a special, it would probably not arrive as soon as our regular train. Moreover, we have something to prepare. We must think. Now let us organize. You, friend Arthur, go to the train and get the tickets and arrange that all be ready for us to go in the morning. You, friend Jonathan, go to the agent of the ship and get from him letters to the agent in Galatz, with authority to make a search of the ship just as it was here. If you would, Inspector, please do go with him, as you presence may ensure his success. Quincey Morris, you and friend Alfred see the Vice Consul, and get his aid with his fellow in Galatz and all he can do to make our way smooth, so that no times be lost when over the Danube. Miss Kate will stay with Madam Mina, while John and I consult. For so if time be long you may be delayed. And it will not matter when the sun set, since I am here with Madam to make report."

"And I," said Mrs. Harker brightly, and more like her old self than she had been for many a long day, "shall try to be of use in all ways, and shall think and write for you as I used to do. Something is shifting from me in some strange way, and I feel freer than I have been of late!"

The others—save for perhaps Singleton, who is quite knowledgeable in the occult, if not in medicine—looked happier at the moment as they seemed to realize the significance of her words. But Van Helsing and I, turning to each other, met each a grave and troubled glance. We said nothing at the time, however.

When the men had gone out to their tasks, and Kate was conversing with Mrs. Harker, and the door was shut, he said to me, "We mean the same! Speak out!"

"Here is some change. It is a hope that makes me sick, for it may deceive us."

"Quite so. In the moment when Madam Mina said those words that arrest both our understanding, an inspiration came to me. In the trance of three days ago the Count sent her his spirit to read her mind. Or more like he took her to see him in his earth box in the ship with water rushing, just as it go free at rise and set of sun. He learn then that we are here, for she have more to tell in her open life with eyes to see and ears to hear than he, shut as he is, in his coffin box. Now he make his most effort to escape us. At present he want her not.

"He is sure with his so great knowledge that she will come at his call. But he cut her off, take her, as he can do, out of his own power, that so she come not to him. Ah! There I have hope that our man brains that have been of man so long and that have not lost the grace of God, will come higher than his child-brain that lie in his tomb for centuries, that grow not yet to our stature, and that do only work selfish and therefore small.

"Here comes Madam Mina. Not a word to her of her trance! She knows it not, and it would overwhelm her and make despair just when we want all her hope, all her courage, when most we want all her great brain which is trained like man's brain, but is of sweet woman and have a special power which the Count give her, and which he may not take away altogether, though he think not so. Hush! Let me speak, and you shall learn. Oh, John, my friend, we are in awful straits. I fear, as I never feared before. We can only trust the good God. Silence! Here she comes!"

I thought that the Professor was going to break down and have hysterics, just as he had when Lucy died, but with a great effort he controlled himself and was at perfect nervous poise when Mrs. Harker tripped into the room, bright and happy looking, and seemingly forgetful of her misery.

As she came in, Van Helsing said to her, "Madam Mina, though our manuscript is lost to us, burned in that fire the Count did set to confound us, your mind is young and nimble, and may recall many things which our minds, being somewhat more aged, may not. Could you, pray tell, recite for us your recollection of your husband's diary, where he records the Count's history of invading Turkey?"

Mina closed her eyes and thought for a time, then, with her eyes still closed, began to speak, as if reading. "That other of his race who, in a later age, again and again, brought his forces over The Great River into Turkey Land, who when he was beaten back, came again, and again, and again, though he had to come alone from the bloody field where his troops were being slaughtered, since he knew that he alone could ultimately triumph."

"How wonderful you are, Madam! Friend John, to you with so much experience already, and you too, dear Madam Mina, that are young, here is a lesson. Do not fear ever to think. A half thought has been buzzing often in my brain, but I fear to let him loose his wings. Here now, with more knowledge, I go back to where that half thought come from and I find that he be no half thought at all. That be a whole thought, though so young that he is not yet strong to use his little wings. Nay, like the 'Ugly Duck' of my friend Hans Andersen, he be no duck thought at all, but a big swan thought that sail nobly on big wings, when the time come for him to try them. So we have heard here what Jonathan have once written. What does this tell us? Not much? No! The Count's child thought see nothing, therefore he speak so free. Your man thought see nothing. My man thought see nothing, till just now. No! But there comes another word from some one who speak without thought because she, too, know not what it mean, what it might mean. Just as there are elements which rest, yet when in nature's course they move on their way and they touch, then pouf! And there comes a flash of light, heaven wide, that blind and kill and destroy some. But that show up all earth below for leagues and leagues. Is it not so? Well, I shall explain. To begin, have you ever study the philosophy of crime? 'Yes' and 'No.' You, John, yes, for it is a study of insanity. You, no, Madam Mina, for crime touch you not, not but once. Still, your mind works true, and argues not *a particulari ad universale*. There is this peculiarity in criminals. It is so constant, in all countries and at all times, that even police, who know not much from philosophy, come to know it empirically, that it is. That is to be empiric. The criminal always work at one crime, that is the true criminal who seems predestinate to crime, and who will of none other. This criminal has not full man brain. He is clever and cunning and resourceful, but he be not of man stature as to brain. He be of child brain in much. Now this criminal of ours is predestinate to crime also. He, too, have child brain, and it is of the child to do what he have done. The little bird, the little fish, the little animal learn not by principle, but empirically. And when he learn to do, then there is to him the ground to start from to do more. 'Dos pou sto,' said Archimedes. 'Give me a fulcrum, and I shall move the world!' To do once, is the fulcrum whereby child brain become man brain. And until he have the purpose to do more, he continue to do the same again every time, just as he have done before! Oh, my dear, I see that your eyes are opened, and that to you the lightning flash show all the leagues," for Mrs. Harker began to clap her hands and her eyes sparkled.

He went on, "Now you shall speak. Tell us two dry men of science what you see with those so bright eyes." He took her hand and held it whilst he spoke. His finger and thumb closed on her pulse, as I thought instinctively and unconsciously, as she spoke.

"The Count is a criminal and of criminal type. Nordau and Lombroso would so classify him, and qua criminal he is of an imperfectly formed mind. Thus, in a difficulty he has to seek resource in habit. His past is a clue, and the one page of it that we know, and that from his own lips, tells that once before, when in what Mr. Morris would call a 'tight place,' he went back to his own country from the land he had tried to invade, and thence, without losing purpose, prepared himself for a new effort. He came again better equipped for his work, and won. So he came to London to invade a new land. He was beaten, and when all hope of success was lost, and his existence in danger, he fled back over the sea to his home. Just as formerly he had fled back over the Danube from Turkey Land."

"Good, good! Oh, you so clever lady!" said Van Helsing, enthusiastically, as he stooped and kissed her hand. A moment later he said to me, as calmly as though we had been having a sick room consultation, "A pulse of seventy-two only, and in all this excitement. I have hope."

Turning to her again, he said with keen expectation, "But go on. Go on! There is more to tell if you will. Be not afraid. John and I know. I do in any case, and shall tell you if you are right. Speak, without fear!"

"I will try to. But you will forgive me if I seem too egotistical."

"Nay! Fear not, you must be egotist, for it is of you that we think."

"Then, as he is criminal he is selfish. And as his intellect is small and his action is based on selfishness, he confines himself to one purpose. That purpose is remorseless. As he fled back over the Danube, leaving his forces to be cut to pieces, so now he is intent on being safe, careless of all. So his own selfishness frees my soul somewhat from the terrible power which he acquired over me on that dreadful night. I felt it! Oh, I felt it! Thank God, for His great mercy! My soul is freer than it has been since that awful hour. And all that haunts me is a fear lest in some trance or dream he may have used my knowledge for his ends."

The Professor stood up, "He has so used your mind, and by it he has left us here in Varna, whilst the ship that carried him rushed through enveloping fog up to Galatz, where, doubtless, he had made preparation for escaping from us. But his child mind only saw so far. And it may be that as ever is in God's Providence, the very thing that the evil doer most reckoned on for his selfish good, turns out to be his chiefest harm. The hunter is taken in his own snare, as the great Psalmist says. For now that he think he is free from every trace of us all, and that he has escaped us with so many hours to him, then his selfish child brain will whisper him to sleep. He think, too, that as he cut himself off from knowing your mind, there can be no knowledge of him to you. There is where he fail! That terrible baptism of blood which he give you makes you free to go to him in spirit, as you have as yet done in your times of freedom, when the sun rise and set. At such times you go by my volition and not by his. And this power to good of you and others, you have won from your suffering at his hands. This is now all more precious that he know it not, and to guard himself have even cut himself off from his knowledge of our where. We, however, are not selfish, and we believe that God is with us through all this blackness, and these many dark hours. We shall follow him, and we shall not flinch. Even if we peril ourselves that we become like him. Friend John, this has been a great hour, and it have done much to advance us on our way. You must be scribe and write him all down, so that when the others return from their work you can give it to them, then they shall know as we do."

And so I have written it whilst we wait their return, and Mrs. Harker has written with the typewriter all since that day when the older diaries were burned and we had to start anew.

CHAPTER
THIRTY-SIX[215]

Dr. Seward's Case-Book, Continued

29 October—This is written in the train from Varna to Galatz. Last night we all assembled a little before the time of sunset. Each of us had done his work as well as he could, so far as thought, and endeavour, and opportunity go, we are prepared for the whole of our journey, and for our work when we get to Galatz. When the usual time came round Mrs. Harker prepared herself for her hypnotic effort, and after a longer and more serious effort on the part of Van Helsing than has been usually necessary, she sank into the trance. Usually she speaks on a hint, but this time the Professor had to ask her questions, and to ask them pretty resolutely, before we could learn anything. At last her answer came.

"I can see nothing. We are still. There are no waves lapping, but only a steady swirl of water softly running against the hawser. I can hear men's voices calling, near and far, and the roll and creak of oars in the rowlocks. A gun is fired somewhere, the echo of it seems far away. There is tramping of feet overhead, and ropes and chains are dragged along. What is this? There is a gleam of light. I can feel the air blowing upon me."

Here she stopped. She had risen, as if impulsively, from where she lay on the sofa, and raised both her hands, palms upwards, as if lifting a weight. Van Helsing and I looked at each other with understanding. Quincey raised his eyebrows slightly and looked at her intently, whilst Harker's hand instinctively closed round the hilt of his Kukri. There was a long pause. We all knew that the time when she could speak was passing, but we felt that it was useless to say anything.

Suddenly she sat up, and as she opened her eyes said sweetly, "Would none of you like a cup of tea? You must all be so tired!"

We could only make her happy, and so acqueisced. She bustled off to get tea. When she had gone Van Helsing said, "You see, my friends. He is close to land. He has left his earth chest. But he has yet to get on shore. In the night he may lie hidden somewhere, but if he be not carried on shore, or if the ship do not touch it, he cannot achieve the land. In such case he can, if it be in the night, change his form and jump or fly on shore, then, unless he be carried he cannot escape. And if he be carried, then the customs men may discover what the box contain. Thus, in fine, if he escape not on shore tonight, or before dawn, there will be the whole day lost to him. We may then arrive in time. For if he escape not at night we shall come on him in daytime, boxed up and at our mercy. For he dare not be his true self, awake and visible, lest he be discovered."

There was no more to be said, so we waited in patience until the dawn, at which time we might learn more from Mrs. Harker.

Early this morning we listened, with breathless anxiety, for her response in her trance. The hypnotic stage was even longer in coming than before, and when it came the time remaining until full sunrise was so short that we began to despair. Van Helsing seemed to throw his whole soul into the effort. At last, in obedience to his will she made reply.

"All is dark. I hear lapping water, level with me, and some creaking as of wood on wood." She paused, and the red sun shot up. We must wait till tonight.

And so it is that we are travelling towards Galatz in an agony of expectation. We are due to arrive between two and three in the morning. But already, at Bucharest, we are three hours late, so we cannot possibly get in till well after sunup. Thus we shall have two more hypnotic messages from Mrs. Harker! Either or both may possibly throw more light on what is happening.

Later—Sunset has come and gone. Fortunately it came at a time when there was no distraction. For had it occurred whilst we were at a station, we might not have secured the necessary calm and isolation. Mrs. Harker yielded to the hypnotic influence even less readily than this morning. I am in fear that her power of reading the Count's sensations may die away, just when we want it most. It seems to me that her imagination is beginning to work. Whilst she has been in the trance hitherto she has confined herself to the simplest of facts. If this goes on it may ultimately mislead us. If I thought that the Count's power over her would die away equally with her power of knowledge it would be a happy thought. But I am afraid that it may not be so.

When she did speak, her words were enigmatical, "Something is going out. I can feel it pass me like a cold wind. I can hear, far off, confused sounds, as of men talking in strange tongues, fierce falling water, and the howling of wolves." She stopped and a shudder ran through her, increasing in intensity for a few seconds, till at the end, she shook as though in a palsy. She said no more, even in answer to the Professor's imperative questioning. When she woke from the trance, she was cold, and exhausted, and languid, but her mind was all alert. She could not remember anything, but asked what she had said. When she was told, she pondered over it deeply for a long time and in silence.

30 October, 7 A.M.—We are near Galatz now, and I may not have time to write later. Sunrise this morning was anxiously looked for by us all. Knowing of the increasing difficulty of procuring the hypnotic trance, Van Helsing began his passes earlier than usual. They produced no effect, however, until the regular time, when she yielded with a still greater difficulty, only a minute before the sun rose. The Professor lost no time in his questioning.

Her answer came with equal quickness, "All is dark. I hear water swirling by, level with my ears, and the creaking of wood on wood. Cattle low far off. There is another sound, a queer one like . . ." She stopped and grew white, and whiter still.

"Go on, go on! Speak, I command you!" said Van Helsing in an agonized voice. At the same time there was despair in his eyes, for the risen sun was reddening even Mrs. Harker's pale face. She opened her eyes, and we all started as she said, sweetly and seemingly with the utmost unconcern.

"Oh, Professor, why ask me to do what you know I can't? I don't remember anything." Then, seeing the look of amazement on our faces, she said, turning from one to the other with a troubled look, "What have I said? What have I done? I know nothing, only that I was lying here, half asleep, and heard you say 'go on! speak, I command you!' It seemed so funny to hear you order me about, as if I were a bad child!"

"Oh, Madam Mina," he said, sadly, "it is proof, if proof be needed, of how I love and honour you, when a word for your good, spoken more earnest than ever, can seem so strange because it is to order her whom I am proud to obey!"

The whistles are sounding. We are nearing Galatz. We are on fire with anxiety and eagerness.

Mina Harker's Journal

30 October—Mr. Morris took me to the hotel where our rooms had been ordered by telegraph, he being the one who could best be spared, since he does not speak any foreign language. The forces were distributed much as they had been at Varna, except that Lord Godalming went to the Vice Consul, as his rank might serve as an immediate guarantee of some sort to the official, we being in extreme hurry. Jonathan and the two doctors went to the shipping agent to learn particulars of the arrival of the *Czarina Catherine*.

Later—Lord Godalming has returned. The Consul is away, and the Vice Consul sick. So the routine work has been attended to by a clerk. He was very obliging, and offered to do anything in his power.

Jonathan Harker's Journal

30 October—At nine o'clock Dr. Van Helsing, Dr. Seward, and I called on Messrs. Mackenzie & Steinkoff, the agents of the London firm of Hapgood. They had received a wire from London, in answer to Lord Godalming's telegraphed request, asking them to show us any civility in their power. They were more than kind and courteous, and took us at once on board the *Czarina Catherine*, which lay at anchor out in the river harbor. There we saw the Captain, Donelson by name, who told us of his voyage. He said that in all his life he had never had so favourable a run.

"Man!" he said, "but it made us afeard, for we expect it that we should have to pay for it wi' some rare piece o' ill luck, so as to keep up the average. It's no canny to run frae London to the Black Sea wi' a wind ahint ye, as though the Deil himself were blawin' on yer sail for his ain purpose. An' a' the time we could no speer a thing. Gin we were nigh a ship, or a port, or a headland, a fog fell on us and travelled wi' us, till when after it had lifted and we looked out, the deil a thing could we see. We ran by Gibraltar wi' oot bein' able to signal. An' til we came to the Dardanelles and had to wait to get our permit to pass, we never were within hail o' aught. At first I inclined to slack off sail and beat about till the fog was lifted. But whiles, I thocht that if the Deil was minded to get us into the Black Sea quick, he was like to do it whether we would or no. If we had a quick voyage it would be no to our miscredit wi'the owners, or no hurt to our traffic, an' the Old Mon who had served his ain purpose wad be decently grateful to us for no hinderin' him."

This mixture of simplicity and cunning, of superstition and commercial reasoning, aroused Van Helsing, who said, "Mine friend, that Devil is more clever than he is thought by some, and he know when he meet his match!"

The skipper was not displeased with the compliment, and went on, "When we got past the Bosphorus the men began to grumble. Some o' them, the Roumanians, came and asked me to heave overboard two big boxes which had been put on board by a queer lookin' old man just before we had started frae London. I had seen them speer at the fellow, and put out their twa fingers when they saw him, to guard them against the evil eye. Man! but the supersteetion of foreigners is pairfectly rideeculous! I sent them aboot their business pretty quick, but as just after a fog closed in on us I felt a wee bit as they did anent something, though I wouldn't say it was again the big boxes. Well, on we went, and as the fog didn't let up for five days I joost let the wind carry us, for if the Deil wanted to get somewheres, well, he would fetch it up a'reet. An' if he didn't, well, we'd keep a sharp lookout anyhow. Sure eneuch, we had a fair way and deep water all the time. And two days ago, when the mornin' sun came through the fog, we found ourselves just in the river opposite Galatz. The Roumanians were wild, and wanted me right or wrong to take out the boxes and fling 'm in the river. I had to argy wi' them aboot it wi' a handspike. An' when the last o' them rose off the deck wi' his head in his hand, I had convinced them that, evil eye or no evil eye, the property and the trust of my owners were better in my hands than in the river Danube. They had, mind ye, taken the boxes on the deck ready to fling in, and as it was marked Galatz via Varna, I thocht I'd let 'm lie till we discharged in the port an' get rid o'm althegither. We didn't do much clearin' that day, an' had to remain the nicht at anchor. But in the mornin,' braw an' airly, an hour before sunup, a man came aboard wi' an order, written to him from England, to receive two boxes marked for one Count Dracula. Sure eneuch the matter was one ready to his hand. He had his papers a' reet, an' glad I was to be rid o' the dam' thing, for I was beginnin' masel' to feel uneasy at it. If the Deil did have any luggage aboord the ship, I'm thinkin' it was nane ither than that same!"

"What was the name of the man who took them?" asked Dr. Van Helsing with restrained eagerness.

"I'll be tellin' ye quick!" he answered, and stepping down to his cabin, produced a receipt signed "Immanuel Hildesheim." Burgen-strasse 16 was the address. We found out that this was all the Captain knew, so with thanks we came away.

We found Hildesheim in his office, a Hebrew of rather the Adelphi Theatre type, with a nose like a sheep, and a fez. His arguments were pointed with specie, we doing the punctuation, and with a little bargaining he told us what he knew. This turned out to be simple but important. He had received a letter from Mr. DeVille[216] of London, telling him to receive, if possible before sunrise so as to avoid customs, two boxes which would arrive at Galatz in the *Czarina Catherine*. These he was to give in charge to a certain Petrof Skinsky, who dealt with the Slovaks who traded down the river to the port. He had been paid for his work by an English bank note, which had been duly cashed for gold at the Danube International Bank. When Skinsky had come to him, he had taken him to the ship and handed over the boxes, so as to save porterage. That was all he knew.

We then sought for Skinsky, but were unable to find him. One of his neighbors, who did not seem to bear him any affection, said that he had gone away two days before, no one knew whither. This was corroborated by his landlord, who had received by messenger the key of the house together with the rent due, in English money. This had been between ten and eleven o'clock last night. We were at a standstill again.

Whilst we were talking one came running and breathlessly gasped out that the body of Skinsky had been found inside the wall of the churchyard of St. Peter, and that the throat had been torn open as if by some wild animal. Those we had been speaking with ran off to see the horror, the women crying out. "This is the work of a Slovak!" We hurried away lest we should have been in some way drawn into the affair, and so detained.

As we came home we could arrive at no definite conclusion. We were all convinced that the boxes were on their way, by water, to somewhere, but where that might be we would have to discover. With heavy hearts we came home to the hotel to Mina.

When we met together, the first thing was to consult as to taking Mina again into our confidence. Things are getting desperate, and it is at least a chance, though a hazardous one. As a preliminary step, I was released from my promise to her.

Mina Harker's Journal

30 October, evening—They were so tired and worn out and dispirited that there was nothing to be done till they had some rest, so I asked them all to lie down for half an hour whilst I should enter everything up to the moment. I feel so grateful to the man who invented the "Traveller's" typewriter, and to Mr. Morris for getting this one for me. I should have felt quite astray doing the work if I had to write with a pen . . .

It is all done. Poor dear, dear Jonathan, what he must have suffered, what he must be suffering now. He lies on the sofa hardly seeming to breathe, and his whole body appears in collapse. His brows are knit. His face is drawn with pain. Poor fellow, maybe he is thinking, and I can see his face all wrinkled up with the concentration of his thoughts. Oh! if I could only help at all. I shall do what I can.

I have asked Dr. Van Helsing, and he has got me all the papers that I have not yet seen. Whilst they are resting, I shall go over all carefully, and perhaps I may arrive at some conclusion. I shall try to follow the Professor's example, and think without prejudice on the facts before me . . .

I do believe that under God's providence I have made a discovery. I shall get the maps and look over them.

I am more than ever sure that I am right. My new conclusion is ready, so I shall get our party together and read it. They can judge it. It is well to be accurate, and every minute is precious.

Mina Harker's Memorandum

(entered in her journal)

Ground of inquiry—Count Dracula's problem is to get back to his own place.

(a) He must be brought back by some one. This is evident. For had he power to move himself as he wished he could go either as man, or wolf, or bat, or in some other way. He evidently fears discovery or interference, in the state of helplessness in which he must be, confined as he is between dawn and sunset in his wooden box.

(b) How is he to be taken?—Here a process of exclusions may help us. By road, by rail, by water?

1. By Road—There are endless difficulties, especially in leaving the city.

   (x) There are people. And people are curious, and investigate. A hint, a surmise, a doubt as to what might be in his own box, would destroy him.

   (y) There are, or there may be, customs and octroi officers to pass.

   (z) His pursuers might follow. This is his highest fear. And in order to prevent his being betrayed he has repelled, so far as he can, even his victim, me!

2. By Rail—There is no one in charge of the boxes. He would have to take his chance of being delayed, and delay would be fatal, with enemies on the track. True, he might escape at night. But what would he be, if left in a strange place with no refuge that he could fly to? This is not what he intends, and he does not mean to risk it.

3. By Water—Here is the safest way, in one respect, but with most danger in another. On the water he is powerless except at night. Even then he can only summon fog and storm and snow and his wolves. But were he wrecked, the living water would engulf him, helpless, and he would indeed be lost. He could have the vessel drive to land, but if it were unfriendly land, wherein he was not free to move, his position would still be desperate.

We know from the record that he was on the water, so what we have to do is to ascertain what water. The first thing is to realize exactly what he has done as yet. We may, then, get a light on what his task is to be.

Firstly we must differentiate between what he did in London as part of his general plan of action, when he was pressed for moments and had to arrange as best he could.

Secondly we must see, as well as we can surmise it from the facts we know of, what he has done here.

As to the first, he evidently intended to arrive at Galatz, and sent invoice to Varna to deceive us lest we should ascertain his means of exit from England. His immediate and sole purpose then was to escape. The proof of this, is the letter of instructions sent to Immanuel Hildesheim to clear and take away the boxes before sunrise. There is also the instruction to Petrof Skinsky. These we must only guess at, but there must have been some letter or message, since Skinsky came to Hildesheim.

That, so far, his plans were successful we know. The *Czarina Catherine* made a phenomenally quick journey. So much so that Captain Donelson's suspicions were aroused. But his superstition united with his canniness played the Count's game for him, and he ran with his favouring wind through fogs and all till he brought up blindfold at Galatz. That the Count's arrangements were well made, has been proved. Hildesheim cleared the boxes, took them off, and gave them to Skinsky. Skinsky took them, and here we lose the trail. We only know that the box is somewhere on the water, moving along. The customs and the octroi, if there be any, have been avoided.

Now we come to what the Count must have done after his arrival, on land, at Galatz. The boxes were given to Skinsky before sunrise. At sunrise the Count could appear in his own form. Here, we ask why Skinsky was chosen at all to aid in the work? In my husband's diary, Skinsky is mentioned as dealing with the Slovaks who trade down the river to the port. And the man's remark, that the murder was the work of a Slovak, showed the general feeling against his class. The Count wanted isolation.

My surmise is this, that in London the Count decided to get back to his castle by water, as the most safe and secret way. He was brought from the castle by Szgany, and probably they delivered their cargo to Slovaks who took the boxes to Varna, for there they were shipped to London. Thus the Count had knowledge of the persons who could arrange this service. When the boxes were on land, before sunrise or after sunset, he came out from his own box, met Skinsky and instructed him what to do as to arranging the carriage of the boxes up some river. When this was done, and he knew that all was in train, he blotted out his traces, as he thought, by murdering his agent.

I have examined the map and find that the river most suitable for the Slovaks to have ascended is either the Pruth or the Sereth. I read in the typescript that in my trance I heard cows low and water swirling level with my ears and the creaking of wood. The Count in his box, then, was on a river in an open boat, propelled probably either by oars or poles, for the banks are near and it is working against stream. There would be no such if floating down stream.

Of course it may not be either the Sereth or the Pruth, but we may possibly investigate further. Now of these two, the Pruth is the more easily navigated, but the Sereth is, at Fundu, joined by the Bistritza which runs up round the Borgo Pass. The loop it makes is manifestly as close to Dracula's castle as can be got by water.

Mina Harker's Journal, Continued

When I had done reading, Jonathan took me in his arms and kissed me. The others kept shaking me by both hands, and Dr. Van Helsing said, "Our dear Madam Mina is once more our teacher. Her eyes have been where we were blinded. Now we are on the track once again, and this time we may succeed. Our enemy is at his most helpless. And if we can come on him by day, on the water, our task will be over. He has a start, but he is powerless to hasten, as he may not leave his box lest those who carry him may suspect. For them to suspect would be to prompt them to throw him in the stream where he perish. This he knows, and will not. Now men, to our Council of War, for here and now, we must plan what each and all shall do."

"I shall get a steam launch and follow him," said Lord Godalming.

"And I, horses to follow on the bank lest by chance he land," said Mr. Morris.

"Good!" said the Professor, "both good. But neither must go alone. There must be force to overcome force if need be. The Slovak is strong and rough, and he carries rude arms. Parties of three each would be most wise." All the men smiled, for amongst them they carried a small arsenal.

Said Mr. Morris, "I have brought some Winchesters. They are pretty handy in a crowd, and there may be wolves. The Count, if you remember, took some other precautions. He made some requisitions on others that Mrs. Harker could not quite hear or understand. We must be ready at all points."

Dr. Seward said, "I think I had better go with Quincey. We have been accustomed to hunt together, and we, well armed, will be a match for whatever may come along."

"I'll come with you too," offered Mr. Singleton. "I'm not a such bad shot, myself, and may be of assistance."

"Good," Seward nodded, then turned to Lord Godalming. "You must not be alone either, Art. It may be necessary to fight the Slovaks, and a chance thrust, for I don't suppose these fellows carry guns, would undo all our plans. There must be no chances, this time. We shall not rest until the Count's head and body have been separated, and we are sure that he cannot reincarnate."

"I believe I shall accompany Lord Godalming," Inspector Cotford stated simply, in a tone that brooked no room for argument.

"That makes to for that party. Who shall be the third?" asked Dr. Seward. He looked at Jonathan as he spoke, and Jonathan looked at me. I could see that the poor dear was torn about in his mind. Of course he wanted to be with me. But then the boat service would, most likely, be the one which would destroy the . . . the . . . Vampire. (Why did I hesitate to write the word?)

He was silent awhile, and during his silence Dr. Van Helsing spoke, "Friend Jonathan, this is to you for twice reasons. First, because you are young and brave and can fight, and all energies may be needed at the last. And again that it is your right to destroy him. That, which has wrought such woe to you and yours. Be not afraid for Madam Mina. Miss Kate will be with her, and they both will be my care, if I may. I am old. My legs are not so quick to run as once. And I am not used to ride so long or to pursue as need be, or to fight with lethal weapons. But I can be of other service. I can fight in other way. And I can die, if need be, as well as younger men. Now let me say that what I would is this. While you, my Lord Godalming and friend Jonathan go in your so swift little steamboat up the river, and whilst John and Quincey guard the bank where perchance he might be landed, Miss Kate and I will take Madam Mina right into the heart of the enemy's country. Whilst the old fox is tied in his box, floating on the running stream whence he cannot escape to land, where he dares not raise the lid of his coffin box lest his Slovak carriers should in fear leave him to perish, we shall go in the track where Jonathan went, from Bistritz over the Borgo, and find our way to the Castle of Dracula. Here, Madam Mina's hypnotic power will surely help, and we shall find our way, all dark and unknown otherwise, after the first sunrise when we are near that fateful place. There is much to be done, and other places to be made sanctify, so that that nest of vipers be obliterated."

Here Jonathan interrupted him hotly, "Do you mean to say, Professor Van Helsing, that you would bring Mina, in her sad case and tainted as she is with that devil's illness, right into the jaws of his deathtrap? Not for the world! Not for Heaven or Hell!"

He became almost speechless for a minute, and then went on, "Do you know what the place is? Have you seen that awful den of hellish infamy, with the very moonlight alive with grisly shapes, and every speck of dust that whirls in the wind a devouring monster in embryo? Have you felt the Vampire's lips upon your throat?"

Here he turned to me, and as his eyes lit on my forehead he threw up his arms with a cry, "Oh, my God, what have we done to have this terror upon us?" and he sank down on the sofa in a collapse of misery.

The Professor's voice, as he spoke in clear, sweet tones, which seemed to vibrate in the air, calmed us all.

"Oh, my friend, it is because I would save Madam Mina from that awful place that I would go. God forbid that I should take her into that place. There is work, wild work, to be done before that place can be purify. Remember that we are in terrible straits. If the Count escape us this time, and he is strong and subtle and cunning, he may choose to sleep him for a century, and then in time our dear one," he took my hand, "would come to him to keep him company, and would be as those others that you, Jonathan, saw. You have told us of their gloating lips.

You heard their ribald laugh as they clutched the nursing boy that the Count threw to them. You shudder, and well may it be. Forgive me that I make you so much pain, but it is necessary. My friend, is it not a dire need for that which I am giving, possibly my life? If it were that any one went into that place to stay, it is I who would have to go to keep them company."

"Do as you will," said Jonathan, with a sob that shook him all over, "we are in the hands of God!"

Later—Oh, it did me good to see the way that these brave men worked. How can women help loving men when they are so earnest, and so true, and so brave! And, too, it made me think of the wonderful power of money! What can it not do when basely used. I felt so thankful that Lord Godalming is rich, and both he and Mr. Morris, who also has plenty of money, are willing to spend it so freely. For if they did not, our little expedition could not start, either so promptly or so well equipped, as it will within another hour. It is not three hours since it was arranged what part each of us was to do. And now Lord Godalming, Inspector Cotford, and Jonathan have a lovely steam launch, with steam up ready to start at a moment's notice. Dr. Seward, Mr. Singleton, and Mr. Morris have half a dozen good horses, well appointed. We have all the maps and appliances of various kinds that can be had. Professor Van Helsing, Kate, and I are to leave by the 11:40 train tonight for Veresti, where we are to get a carriage to drive to the Borgo Pass. We are bringing a good deal of ready money, as we are to buy a carriage and horses. We shall drive ourselves, for we have no one whom we can trust in the matter. The Professor knows something of a great many languages, so we shall get on all right. We have all got arms, even Kate, who is skilled with a rifle. As for me, I have a large bore revolver. Jonathan would not be happy unless I was armed like the rest. Alas! I cannot carry one arm that the rest do, the scar on my forehead forbids that. Dear Dr. Van Helsing comforts me by telling me that I am fully armed as there may be wolves. The weather is getting colder every hour, and there are snow flurries which come and go as warnings.

Later—It took all my courage to say goodbye to my darling. We may never meet again. Courage, Mina! The Professor is looking at you keenly. His look is a warning. There must be no tears now, unless it may be that God will let them fall in gladness.

Jonathan Harker's Journal

30 October, night—I am writing this in the light from the furnace door of the steam launch. Lord Godalming is firing up. He is an experienced hand at the work, as he has had for years a launch of his own on the Thames, and another on

the Norfolk Broads. Regarding our plans, we finally decided that Mina's guess was correct, and that if any waterway was chosen for the Count's escape back to his Castle, the Sereth and then the Bistritza at its junction, would be the one. We took it, that somewhere about the 47th degree, north latitude, would be the place chosen for crossing the country between the river and the Carpathians. We have no fear in running at good speed up the river at night. There is plenty of water, and the banks are wide enough apart to make steaming, even in the dark, easy enough. Lord Godalming tells me to sleep for a while, as it is enough for the present for one to be on watch. But I cannot sleep, how can I with the terrible danger hanging over my darling, and her going out into that awful place . . .

My only comfort is that we are in the hands of God. Only for that faith it would be easier to die than to live, and so be quit of all the trouble. Mr. Singleton, Mr. Morris, and Dr. Seward were off on their long ride before we started. They are to keep up the right bank, far enough off to get on higher lands where they can see a good stretch of river and avoid the following of its curves. They have, for the first stages, three men to ride and lead their spare horses, six in all, so as not to excite curiosity. When they dismiss the men, which shall be shortly, they shall themselves look after the horses. It may be necessary for us to join forces. If so they can mount our whole party. One of the saddles has a moveable horn, and can be easily adapted for Mina, if required.

It is a wild adventure we are on. Here, as we are rushing along through the darkness, with the cold from the river seeming to rise up and strike us, with all the mysterious voices of the night around us, it all comes home. We seem to be drifting into unknown places and unknown ways. Into a whole world of dark and dreadful things. Godalming is shutting the furnace door . . .

31 October—Still hurrying along. The day has come, and Godalming is sleeping. Cotford is on watch, though I notice how his eyes are half on Godalming. I don't think he trusts the man, though as to why I cannot say. As for me, I cannot sleep, so I write . . .

The morning is bitterly cold, the furnace heat is grateful, though we have heavy fur coats. As yet we have passed only a few open boats, but none of them had on board any box or package of anything like the size of the ones we seek. The men were scared every time we turned our electric lamp on them, and fell on their knees and prayed.

1 November, evening—No news all day. We have found nothing of the kind we seek. We have now passed into the Bistritza, and if we are wrong in our surmise our chance is gone. We have overhauled every boat, big and little. Early this morning, one crew took us for a Government boat, and treated us accordingly. We saw in this a way of smoothing matters, so at Fundu, where the Bistritza runs into the Sereth, we got a

Roumanian flag which we now fly conspicuously. With every boat which we have overhauled since then this trick has succeeded. We have had every deference shown to us, and not once any objection to whatever we chose to ask or do. Some of the Slovaks tell us that a big boat passed them, going at more than usual speed as she had a double crew on board. This was before they came to Fundu, so they could not tell us whether the boat turned into the Bistritza or continued on up the Sereth. At Fundu we could not hear of any such boat, so she must have passed there in the night.

I am feeling very sleepy. The cold is perhaps beginning to tell upon me, and nature must have rest some time. Godalming insists that he shall keep the first watch. God bless him for all his goodness to poor dear Mina and me.

2 November, morning—It is broad daylight. That good fellow would not wake me or Cotford. He says it would have been a sin to, for I slept peacefully and was forgetting my trouble. It seems brutally selfish to me to have slept so long, and let him watch all night, but he was quite right. I am a new man this morning. And, as I sit here and watch him sleeping, I can do all that is necessary both as to minding the engine, steering, and keeping watch. I can feel that my strength and energy are coming back to me. I wonder where Mina is now. She should have got to Veresti about noon on Wednesday, with Van Helsing and Miss Reed. It would take them some time to get the carriage and horses. So if they had started and travelled hard, they would be about now at the Borgo Pass. God guide and help them! I am afraid to think what may happen. If we could only go faster. But we cannot. The engines are throbbing and doing their utmost. I wonder how Seward, Singleton, and Morris are getting on. There seem to be endless streams running down the mountains into this river, but as none of them are very large, at present, at all events, though they are doubtless terrible in winter and when the snow melts, the horsemen may not have met much obstruction. I hope that before we get to Strasba we may see them. For if by that time we have not overtaken the Count, it may be necessary to take counsel together what to do next.

Dr. Seward's Case-Book

2 November—Three days on the road. No news, and no time to write it if there had been, for every moment is precious. We have had only the rest needful for the horses. But we are both bearing it wonderfully. Those adventurous days of ours are turning up useful. We must push on. We shall never feel happy till we get the launch in sight again.

3 November—We heard at Fundu that the launch had gone up the Bistritza. I wish it wasn't so cold. There are signs of snow coming. And if it falls heavy it will stop us. In such case we must get a sledge and go on, Russian fashion.

4 November—Today we heard of the launch having been detained by an accident when trying to force a way up the rapids. The Slovak boats get up all right, by aid of a rope and steering with knowledge. Some went up only a few hours before. Godalming is an amateur fitter himself, and evidently it was he who put the launch in trim again.

Finally, they got up the rapids all right, with local help, and are off on the chase afresh. I fear that the boat is not any better for the accident, the peasantry tell us that after she got upon smooth water again, she kept stopping every now and again so long as she was in sight. We must push on harder than ever. Our help may be wanted soon.

Mina Harker's Journal

31 October—Arrived at Veresti at noon. The Professor tells me that this morning at dawn he could hardly hypnotize me at all, and that all I could say was, "dark and quiet." He is off now buying a carriage and horses. He says that he will later on try to buy additional horses, so that we may be able to change them on the way. We have something more than 70 miles before us. The country is lovely, and most interesting. If only we were under different conditions, how delightful it would be to see it all. If Jonathan and I were driving through it alone what a pleasure it would be. To stop and see people, and learn something of their life, and to fill our minds and memories with all the colour and picturesqueness of the whole wild, beautiful country and the quaint people! But, alas!

Later—Dr. Van Helsing has returned. He has got the carriage and horses; we are to have some dinner, and to start in an hour. The landlady is putting us up a huge basket of provisions; it seems enough for a company of soldiers. The Professor encourages her, and whispers to me that it may be a week before we can get any good food again. He has been shopping too, and has sent home such a wonderful lot of fur coats ad wraps, and all sorts of warm things. There will not be any chance of our being cold.

We shall soon be off. I am afraid to think what may happen to us. We are truly in the hands of God. He alone knows what may be, and I pray Him, with all the strength of my sad and humble soul, that He will watch over my beloved husband; that whatever may happen, Jonathan may know that I loved him and honoured him more than I can say, and that my latest and truest thought will be always for him.

CHAPTER THIRTY-SEVEN[217]

Mina Harker's Journal

1 November—All day long we have travelled, and at a good speed. The horses seem to know that they are being kindly treated, for they go willingly their full stage at best speed. We have now had so many changes and find the same thing so constantly that we are encouraged to think that the journey will be an easy one. Dr. Van Helsing is laconic, he tells the farmers that he is hurrying to Bistritz, and pays them well to make the exchange of horses. We get hot soup, or coffee, or tea, and off we go. It is a lovely country. Full of beauties of all imaginable kinds, and the people are brave, and strong, and simple, and seem full of nice qualities. They are very, very superstitious. In the first house where we stopped, when the woman who served us saw the scar on my forehead, she crossed herself and put out two fingers towards me, to keep off the evil eye. I believe they went to the trouble of putting an extra amount of garlic into our food, and I can't abide garlic. Ever since then I have taken care not to take off my hat or veil, and so have escaped their suspicions. We are travelling fast, and as we have no driver with us to carry tales, we go ahead of scandal. But I daresay that fear of the evil eye will follow hard behind us all the way. The Professor and Kate seem tireless. All day they took turns driving, and made me sleep for a long spell.

At sunset time Van Helsing hypnotized me, and he says I answered as usual, "darkness, lapping water and creaking wood." So our enemy is still on the river. I am afraid to think of Jonathan, but somehow I have now no fear for him, or for myself. I write this whilst we wait in a farmhouse for the horses to be ready. Dr. Van Helsing is sleeping. Kate says he looks very tired and old and grey, but I pointed out to her how his mouth is set as firmly as a conqueror's. Even in his sleep he is intense with resolution. When we have well started I must make him and Kate rest whilst I drive. I shall tell them that we have days before us, and they cannot do all the work between only the two of them. Kate may have the vigor of youth, but Van Helsing does not, and he must not break down when most of all his strength will be needed . . .

All is ready. We are off shortly.

2 November, morning—I was successful, and we took turns driving all night. Now the day is on us, bright though cold. There is a strange heaviness in the air. I say heaviness for want of a better word. I mean that it oppresses us all. It is very cold, and only our warm furs keep us comfortable. At dawn Van Helsing hypnotized me. He says I answered "darkness, creaking wood and roaring water," so the river is changing as they ascend. I do hope that my darling will not run any chance of danger, more than need be, but we are in God's hands.

2 November, night—All day long driving. The country gets wilder as we go, and the great spurs of the Carpathians, which at Veresti seemed so far from us and so low on the horizon, now seem to gather round us and tower in front. We three seem in good spirits, though the oppressiveness of the air at times concerns us.[218] I think we make an effort each to cheer the other, in the doing so we cheer ourselves. Dr. Van Helsing says that by morning we shall reach the Borgo Pass. The houses are very few here now, and the Professor says that the last horse we got will have to go on with us, as we may not be able to change. He got one in addition to the three we changed, so that now we have a rude four-in-hand. The dear horses are patient and good, and they give us no trouble. We are not worried with other travellers, and so Kate and I can drive. We shall get to the Pass in daylight. We do not want to arrive before. So we take it easy, and have each a long rest in turn. Oh, what will tomorrow bring to us? We go to seek the place where my poor darling suffered so much. God grant that we may be guided aright, and that He will deign to watch over my husband and those dear to us, and who are in such deadly peril. As for me, I am not worthy in His sight. Alas! I am unclean to His eyes, and shall be until He may deign to let me stand forth in His sight as one of those who have not incurred His wrath.

Memorandum by Abraham Van Helsing

4 November—This to my old and true friend John Seward, M.D., of Purfleet, London, in case I may not see him. It may explain. It is morning, and I write by a fire which all the night I have kept alive, Miss Kate and Madam Mina aiding me. There are atmospheric disturbances which I know not and which much concern me. It is cold, cold. So cold that the grey heavy sky is full of snow, which when

it falls will settle for all winter as the ground is hardening to receive it, and yet the thermometer go up and up and up. I would that my old friend Palmieri of Naples were here and with him his wonderful seismograph for he could give me some clue to what is happening—or about to happen. Whatever it is, it seems to have affected Madam Mina. She has been so heavy of head all day that she was not like herself. She sleeps, and sleeps, and sleeps! She who is usual so alert, have done literally nothing all the day. She even have lost her appetite. She make no entry into her little diary, she who write so faithful at every pause. Something whisper to me that all is not well. However, tonight she is more *vif.* Her long sleep all day have refresh and restore her, for now she is all sweet and bright as ever. At sunset I try to hypnotize her, but alas! with no effect. The power has grown less and less with each day, and tonight it fail me altogether. Well, God's will be done, whatever it may be, and whithersoever it may lead!

Now to the historical, for as Madam Mina write not in her stenography, and Miss Kate keep no diary at all, I must, in my cumbrous old fashion, that so each day of us may not go unrecorded.

We got to the Borgo Pass just after sunrise yesterday morning. When I saw the signs of the dawn I got ready for the hypnotism. We stopped our carriage, and got down so that there might be no disturbance. Miss Kate made a couch with furs, and Madam Mina, lying down, yield herself as usual, but more slow and more short time than ever, to the hypnotic sleep. As before, came the answer, "darkness and the swirling of water." Then she woke, bright and radiant and we go on our way and soon reach the Pass. At this time and place, she become all on fire with zeal. Some new guiding power be in her manifested, for she point to a road and say, "This is the way."

"How know you it?" I ask.

"Of course I know it," she answer, and with a pause, add, "Have not my Jonathan travelled it and wrote of his travel?"

At first I think somewhat strange, but soon I see that there be only one such byroad. It is used but little, and very different from the coach road from the Bukovina to Bistritz, which is more wide and hard, and more of use.

So we came down this road. When we meet other ways, not always were we sure that they were roads at all, for they be neglect and light snow have fallen, the horses know and they only. I give rein to them, and they go on so patient. By and by we find all the things which Jonathan have note in that wonderful diary of him. Then we go on for long, long hours and hours. At the first, I tell Madam Mina to sleep. She try, and she succeed. She sleep all the time, till at the last, I feel myself to suspicious grow, and have Miss Kate attempt to wake her. But she sleep on, and her friend may not wake her though she try. I do not wish to try too hard lest we harm her. For I know that she have suffer much, and sleep at times be all-in-all to her. I think I drowse myself, for all of sudden I feel guilt, as though I have done something. I find myself bolt up, and find the reins in Miss Kate's hand, and the good horses go along jog, jog, just as ever. I look down and find Madam Mina still asleep. It is now not far off sunset time, and over the snow the light of the sun flow in big yellow flood, so that we throw great long shadow on where the mountain rise so steep. For we are going up, and up, and all is oh, so wild and rocky, as though it were the end of the world.

Then, as Miss Kate drive, I arouse Madam Mina. This time she wake with not much trouble, and then I try to put her to hypnotic sleep. But she sleep not, being as though I were not. Still I try and try, till all at once I find we three in dark, so I look round, and find that the sun have gone down. Madam Mina laugh, and I turn and look at her. She is now quite awake, and look so well as I never saw her since that night at Carfax when we first enter the Count's house. I am amaze, and not at ease then. But she is so bright and tender and thoughtful for me that I forget all fear. I light a fire, for we have brought supply of wood with us, and she prepare food while Miss Kate and I undo the horses and set them, tethered in shelter, to feed. Then when we return to the fire she have our supper ready. I go to help her, but she smile, and tell me that she have eat already. That she was so hungry that she would not wait. I like it not, and I have grave doubts. I see from her look that Miss Kate too have doubts. But we fear to affright her, and so are both silent of it. So Miss Kate and I eat, and then we wrap in fur and lie beside the fire, and I tell them to sleep while I watch. But presently I forget all of watching. And when I sudden remember that I watch, I find Miss Kate asleep, but Madam Mina lying quiet, but awake, and looking at me with so bright eyes. Once, twice more the same occur, and I get much sleep till before morning. When I wake I try to hypnotize her, but alas! Though she shut her eyes obedient, she may not sleep. The sun rise up, and up, and up, and then sleep come to her too late, but so heavy that she will not wake. We have to lift her up, and place her sleeping in the carriage when we have harnessed the horses and made all ready. Madam still sleep, and she look in her sleep more healthy and more redder than before. And I like it not. The air is still more upsetting and I wish more and more that Palmieri were here to tell me what is going to happen. And I am afraid, afraid, afraid! I am afraid of all things, even to think but I must go on my way. The stake we play for is life and death, or more than these, and we must not flinch.

5 November, morning—Let me be accurate in everything, for though you and I have seen some strange things together, you may at the first think that I, Van Helsing, am mad. That the many horrors and the so long strain on nerves has at the last turn my brain.

All yesterday we travel, always getting closer to the mountains, and moving into a more and more wild and desert land. There are great, frowning precipices and much falling water, and Nature seem to have held sometime her carnival. Madam Mina still sleep and sleep. And though we did have hunger and appeased it, we could not waken her, even for food. I began to fear that the fatal spell of the place was upon her, tainted as she is with that Vampire baptism. "Well," said I to Miss Kate, "if it be that she sleep all the day, it shall also be that I do not sleep at night." As we travel on the rough road, for a road of an ancient and imperfect kind there was, I held down my head and slept as Kate held the reigns.

Again I waked with a sense of guilt and of time passed, and found Madam Mina still sleeping, and the sun low down. But all was indeed changed. The frowning mountains seemed further away, and we were near the top of a steep rising hill, on summit of which was such a castle as Jonathan tell of in his diary. At once I exulted and feared. For now, for good or ill, the end was near.

I woke Madam Mina, and again tried to hypnotize her, but alas! unavailing till too late. Then, ere the great dark came upon us, for even after down sun the heavens reflected the gone sun on the snow, and all was for a time in a great twilight. Miss Kate and I took out the horses and fed them in what shelter we could. Then we make a fire, and near it I make Madam Mina, now awake and more charming than ever, sit comfortable amid her rugs. We got ready food, but she would not eat, simply saying that she had not hunger. I did not press her, knowing her unavailingness. But I myself eat, as did Miss Kate, for we two must needs now be strong for all. Then, with the fear on me of what might be, I drew a ring so big for her comfort, round where Madam Mina sat. And over the ring I passed some of the wafer, and I broke it fine so that all was well guarded. She sat still all the time, so still as one dead. And she grew whiter and even whiter till the snow was not more pale, and no word she said. But when Miss Kate drew near, she clung to her, and I could see that the poor soul shook her from head to feet with a tremor that was pain to see.

I said to her presently, when she had grown more quiet, "Will you not come over to the fire?" for I wished to make a test of what she could. She rose obedient from her friend, but when she have made a step she stopped, and stood as one stricken.

"Why not go on?" I asked. She shook her head, and coming back, sat down in her place. Then, looking at me with open eyes, as of one waked from sleep, she said simply, "I cannot!" and remained silent. I rejoiced, for I knew that what she could not, none of those that we dreaded could. Though there might be danger to her body, yet her soul was safe!

Presently the horses began to scream, and tore at their tethers till I came to them and quieted them. When they did feel my hands on them, they whinnied low as in joy, and licked at my hands and were quiet for a time. Many times through the night did I or Miss Kate come to them, till it arrive to the cold hour when all nature is at lowest, and every time our coming was with quiet of them.

In the cold hour the fire began to die, and I was about stepping forth to replenish it, for now the snow came in flying sweeps and with it a chill mist. Even in the dark there was a light of some kind, as there ever is over snow, and it seemed as though the snow flurries and the wreaths of mist took shape as of women with trailing garments. All was in dead, grim silence only that the horses whinnied and cowered, as if in terror of the worst. I began to fear, horrible fears. But then came to me the sense of safety in that ring wherein we stood. I began too, to think that my imaginings were of the night, and the gloom, and the unrest that I have gone through, and all the terrible anxiety. It was as though my memories of all Jonathan's horrid experience were befooling me. For the snow flakes and the mist began to wheel and circle round, till I could get as though a shadowy glimpse of those women that would have kissed him. And then the horses cowered lower and lower, and moaned in terror as men do in pain. Even the madness of fright was not to them, so that they could break away. I feared for my dear Madam Mina when these weird figures drew near and circled round. I looked at her, but she sat calm, and smiled at me. When I would have stepped to the fire to replenish it, she caught me and held me back, and whispered, like a voice that one hears in a dream, so low it was.

"No! No! Do not go without. Here you are safe!"

I turned to her, and looking in her eyes said, "But you? It is for you that I fear!"

Whereat she laughed, a laugh low and unreal, and said, "Fear for me! Why fear for me? None safer in all the world from them than I am," and as I wondered at the meaning of her words, a puff of wind made the flame leap up, and I see the red scar on her forehead. Then, alas! I knew. Did I not, I would soon have learned, for the wheeling figures of mist and snow came closer, but keeping ever without the Holy circle. Then they began to materialize till, if God have not taken away my reason, for I saw it through my eyes. There were before us in actual flesh the same three women that Jonathan saw in the room, when they would have kissed his throat. I knew the swaying round forms, the bright hard eyes, the white teeth, the ruddy colour, the voluptuous lips. They smiled ever at poor dear Madam Mina. And as their laugh came through the silence of the night, they twined their arms and pointed to her, and said in those so sweet tingling tones that Jonathan said were of the intolerable sweetness of the water glasses, "Come, sister. Come to us. Come!"

In fear I turned to my poor Madam Mina, and my heart with gladness leapt like flame. For oh! the terror in her sweet eyes, the repulsion, the horror, told a story to my heart that was all of hope. God be thanked she was not, yet, of them. As Miss Kate sought to comfort Madam, I seized some of the firewood which was by me, and holding out some of the Wafer, advanced on them towards the fire. They drew back before me, and laughed their low horrid laugh. I fed the fire, and feared them not. For I knew that we were safe within the ring, which she could not leave no more than they could enter. The horses had ceased to moan, and lay still on the ground. The snow fell on them softly, and they grew whiter. I knew that there was for the poor beasts no more of terror.

And so we remained till the red of the dawn began to fall through the snow gloom. I was desolate and afraid, and full of woe and terror. But when that beautiful sun began to climb the horizon life was to me again. At the first coming of the dawn the horrid figures melted in the whirling mist and snow. The wreaths of transparent gloom moved away towards the castle, and were lost. I saw them one more, wild whirling figures of women on the tower,[219] seething with rage at my defiance of them, but then in a flash they were gone.

Instinctively, with the dawn coming, I turned to Madam Mina, intending to hypnotize her. But she lay in a deep and sudden sleep, her head in her friend's lap, from which I could not wake her. I tried to hypnotize through her sleep, but she made no response, none at all, and the day broke. I fear yet to stir. I have made our fire and have seen the horses, they are all dead. Today I have much to do here, and I keep waiting till the sun is up high. For there may be places where I must go, where that sunlight, though snow and mist obscure it, will be to me a safety. The oppression in the air grows more, and more I know not what is to happen.

I will strengthen me with breakfast, and then I will do my terrible work. Madam Mina still sleeps under Miss Kate's watchful eye, and God be thanked! She is calm in her sleep . . .

Jonathan Harker's Journal

4 November, evening—The accident to the launch has been a terrible thing for us. Only for it we should have overtaken the boat long ago, and by now my dear Mina would have been free. I fear to think of her, off on the wolds near that horrid place. We have got horses, and we follow on the track. I note this whilst Godalming and Cotford are getting ready. I think Cotford somehow blames Godalming for our delay, though he has not said as much. We have our arms. The Szgany must look out if they mean to fight. Oh, if only the others were with us. We must only hope! If I write no more, Goodbye Mina! God bless and keep you.

Singleton's Notes

5 November—With the dawn we saw the body of Szgany before us dashing away from the river with their leiter wagon. They surrounded it in a cluster, and hurried along as though beset. The snow is falling lightly and there is a strange excitement in the air. It may be our own feelings, but the depression is strange. Far off I hear the howling of wolves. The snow brings them down from the mountains, and there are dangers to all of us, and from all sides. The horses are nearly ready, and

we are soon off. We ride to death of some one. God alone knows who, or where, or what, or when, or how it may be . . .

Dr. Van Helsing's Memorandum

5 November, afternoon—I am at least sane. Thank God for that mercy at all events, though the proving it has been dreadful. When I left Madam Mina sleeping, watched over by her friend, within the Holy circle, I took my way to the castle. The blacksmith hammer which I took in the carriage from Veresti was useful, though the doors were all open I broke them off the rusty hinges, lest some ill intent or ill chance should close them, so that being entered I might not get out. Jonathan's bitter experience served me here. By memory of his diary I found my way to the old chapel, for I knew that here my work lay. The air was oppressive. It seemed as if there was some sulphurous fume, which at times made me dizzy. Either there was a roaring in my ears or I heard afar off the howl of wolves. Then I bethought me of my dear Madam Mina and Miss Kate, and I was in terrible plight. The dilemma had me between his horns.

They, I had not dare to take into this place, but left safe from the Vampire in that Holy circle. And yet even there would be the wolf! Though Madam slept, Miss Kate remained awake with her rifle, so I resolve me that my work lay here, and that as to the wolves we must submit, if it were God's will. At any rate it was only death and freedom beyond. So did I choose for them. Had it but been for myself the choice had been easy, the maw of the wolf were better to rest in than the grave of the Vampire! So I make my choice to go on with my work.

I knew that there were at least three graves to find, graves that are inhabit. So I search, and search, and I find one of them. She lay in her Vampire sleep, so full of life and voluptuous beauty that I shudder as though I have come to do murder. Ah, I doubt not that in the old time, when such things were, many a man who set forth to do such a task as mine, found at the last his heart fail him, and then his nerve. So he delay, and delay, and delay, till the mere beauty and the fascination of the wanton Undead have hypnotize him. And he remain on and on, till sunset come, and the Vampire sleep be over. Then the beautiful eyes of the fair woman open and look love, and the voluptuous mouth present to a kiss, and the man is weak. And there remain one more victim in the Vampire fold. One more to swell the grim and grisly ranks of the Undead! . . .

There is some fascination, surely, when I am moved by the mere presence of such an one, even lying as she lay in a tomb fretted with age and heavy with the dust of centuries, though there be that horrid odour such as the lairs of the Count have had. Yes, I was moved. I, Van Helsing, with all my purpose and with my motive for hate. I was moved to a yearning for delay which seemed to paralyze my faculties and to clog my very soul. It may have been that the need of

natural sleep, and the strange oppression of the air were beginning to overcome
me. Certain it was that I was lapsing into sleep, the open eyed sleep of one who
yields to a sweet fascination, when there came through the snow stilled air a long,
low wail, so full of woe and pity that it woke me like the sound of a clarion. For
it was the voice of my dear Madam Mina that I heard.

Then I braced myself again to my horrid task, and found by wrenching away
tomb tops one other of the sisters, the other dark one. I dared not pause to look
on her as I had on her sister, lest once more I should begin to be enthrall. But I go
on searching until, presently, I find in a high great tomb as if made to one much
beloved that other fair sister which, like Jonathan I had seen to gather herself
out of the atoms of the mist. She was so fair to look on, so radiantly beautiful,
so exquisitely voluptuous, that the very instinct of man in me, which calls some
of my sex to love and to protect one of hers, made my head whirl with new
emotion. But God be thanked, that soul wail of my dear Madam Mina had not
died out of my ears. And, before the spell could be wrought further upon me, I
had nerved myself to my wild work. By this time I had searched all the tombs
in the chapel, so far as I could tell. And as there had been only three of these
Undead phantoms around us in the night, I took it that there were no more of
active Undead existent. There was one great tomb more lordly than all the rest.
Huge it was, and nobly proportioned. On it was but one word.

DRACULA

This then was the Undead home of the King Vampire, to whom so many
more were due. Its emptiness spoke eloquent to make certain what I knew. Before
I began to restore these women to their dead selves through my awful work, I
laid in Dracula's tomb some of the Wafer, and so banished him from it, Undead,
for ever.

Then began my terrible task, and I dreaded it. Had it been but one, it had
been easy, comparative. But three! To begin twice more after I had been through
a deed of horror. For it was terrible with the sweet Miss Lucy, what would it not
be with these strange ones who had survived through centuries, and who had
been strengthened by the passing of the years. Who would, if they could, have
fought for their foul lives . . .

Oh, my friend John, but it was butcher work. Had I not been nerved by
thoughts of other dead, and of the living over whom hung such a pall of fear, I
could not have gone on. I tremble and tremble even yet, though till all was over,
God be thanked, my nerve did stand. Had I not seen the repose in the first place,
and the gladness that stole over it just ere the final dissolution came, as realization
that the soul had been won, I could not have gone further with my butchery. I could
not have endured the horrid screeching as the stake drove home, the plunging of

writhing form, and lips of bloody foam. I should have fled in terror and left my work undone. But it is over! And the poor souls, I can pity them now and weep, as I think of them placid each in her full sleep of death for a short moment ere fading. For, friend John, hardly had my knife severed the head of each, before the whole body began to melt away and crumble into its native dust, as though the death that should have come centuries ago had at last assert himself and say at once and loud, "I am here!"

Before I left the castle I so fixed its entrances that never more can the Count enter there Undead.

When I stepped into the circle where Madam Mina slept, she woke from her sleep and, seeing me, cried out in pain that I had endured too much.

"Come!" she said, "come away from this awful place! Let us go to meet my husband who is, I know, coming towards us." She was looking thin and pale and weak. But her eyes were pure and glowed with fervour. I was glad to see her paleness and her illness, for my mind was full of the fresh horror of that ruddy vampire sleep.

And so with trust and hope, and yet full of fear, we go eastward to meet our friends, and him, whom Madam Mina tell me that she know are coming to meet us.

CHAPTER THIRTY-EIGHT[220]

Mina Harker's Journal

6 November—It was late in the afternoon when the Professor, Kate, and I took our way towards the east whence I knew Jonathan was coming. We did not go fast, though the way was steeply downhill, for we had to take heavy rugs and wraps with us. We dared not face the possibility of being left without warmth in the cold and the snow. We had to take some of our provisions too, for we were in a perfect desolation, and so far as we could see through the snowfall, there was not even the sign of habitation. When we had gone about a mile, I was tired with the heavy walking and sat down to rest. Then we looked back and saw where the clear line of Dracula's castle cut the sky. For we were so deep under the hill whereon it was set that the angle of perspective of the Carpathian mountains was far below it. We saw it in all its grandeur, perched a thousand feet on the summit of a sheer precipice, and with seemingly a great gap between it and the steep of the adjacent mountain on any side. There was something wild and uncanny about the place. We could hear the distant howling of wolves. They were far off, but the sound, even though coming muffled through the deadening snowfall, was full of terror. I knew from the way Dr. Van Helsing was searching about that he was trying to seek some strategic point, where we would be less exposed in case of attack. The rough roadway still led downwards. We could trace it through the drifted snow.

In a little while the Professor signalled to us, so we got up and joined him. He had found a wonderful spot, a sort of natural hollow in a rock, with an entrance like a doorway between two boulders. He took me by the hand and drew me in.

"See!" he said, "here you will be in shelter. And if the wolves do come I can meet them one by one. And should I fall, Miss Kate will next stand between you and they with her rifle."

He brought in our furs, and made a snug nest for me, and got out some provisions and forced them upon me. But I could not eat, to even try to do so was repulsive to me, and much as I would have liked to please him, I could not bring myself to the attempt. He looked very sad, but did not reproach me. Taking his field glasses from the case, he stood on the top of the rock, and began to search the horizon.

Suddenly he called out, "Look! Look!"

I sprang up and stood beside him on the rock. He handed me his glasses and pointed. The snow was now falling more heavily, and swirled about fiercely, for a high wind was beginning to blow. However, there were times when there were pauses between the snow flurries and I could see a long way round. From the height where we were it was possible to see a great distance. And far off, beyond the white waste of snow, I could see the river lying like a black ribbon in kinks and curls as it wound its way. Straight in front of us and not far off, in fact so near that I wondered we had not noticed before, came a group of mounted men hurrying along. In the midst of them was a cart, a long leiter wagon which swept from side to side, like a dog's tail wagging, with each stern inequality of the road. Outlined against the snow as they were, I could see from the men's clothes that they were peasants or gypsies of some kind.

On the cart were two great square chests, one atop the other. My heart leaped as I saw it, for I felt that the end was coming. The evening was now drawing close, and well I knew that at sunset the Thing, which was till then imprisoned there, would take new freedom and could in any of many forms elude pursuit. In fear I turned to the Professor. To my consternation, however, he was not there, though Kate remained and had brought her rifle to bare. An instant later, I saw the Professor below me. Round the rock he had drawn a circle, such as we had found shelter in last night.

When he had completed it he stood beside me again saying, "At least you shall be safe here from him!" He took the glasses from Kate, who had been watching their approach, and at the next lull of the snow swept the whole space below us. "See," he said, "they come quickly. They are flogging the horses, and galloping as hard as they can."

He paused and went on in a hollow voice, "They are racing for the sunset. We may be too late. God's will be done!" Down came another blinding rush of driving snow, and the whole landscape was blotted out. It soon passed, however, and once more his glasses were fixed on the plain.

Then came a sudden cry, "Look! Look! Look! See, three horsemen follow fast, coming up from the south. It must be Quincey and Alfred and John. Take the glass. Look before the snow blots it all out!" I took it and looked. The three men might be Dr. Seward and Mr. Singleton and Mr. Morris. I knew at all events that none of them was Jonathan. At the same time I knew that Jonathan was not far off. Looking around I saw on the north side of the coming party three other men, riding at breakneck speed. One of them I knew was Jonathan, and the others I took, of course, to be Inspector Cotford and Lord Godalming. They too, were pursuing the party with the cart. When I told the Professor he shouted in glee like a schoolboy, and after looking intently till a snow fall made sight impossible, he laid his Winchester rifle ready for use against the boulder at the opening of our shelter.

"They are all converging," he said. "When the time comes we shall have gypsies on all sides." I got out my revolver ready to hand, for whilst we were speaking the howling of wolves came louder and closer. Kate was already prepared with her own rifle, with a steeled nerve that surpassed what was common for our sex. When the snow storm abated a moment we looked again. It was strange to see the snow falling in such heavy flakes close to us, and beyond, the sun shining more and more brightly as it sank down towards the far mountain tops. Sweeping the glass all around us I could see here and there dots moving singly and in twos and threes and larger numbers. The wolves were gathering for their prey.

Every instant seemed an age whilst we waited. The wind came now in fierce bursts, and the snow was driven with fury as it swept upon us in circling eddies. At times we could not see an arm's length before us. But at others, as the hollow sounding wind swept by us, it seemed to clear the air space around us so that we could see afar off. We had of late been so accustomed to watch for sunrise and sunset, that we knew with fair accuracy when it would be. And we knew that before long the sun would set. It was hard to believe that by our watches it was less than an hour that we waited in that rocky shelter before the various bodies began to converge close upon us. The wind came now with fiercer and more bitter sweeps, and more steadily from the north. It seemingly had driven the snow clouds from us, for with only occasional bursts, the snow fell. We could distinguish clearly the individuals of each party, the pursued and the pursuers. Strangely enough those pursued did not seem to realize, or at least to care, that they were pursued. They seemed, however, to hasten with redoubled speed as the sun dropped lower and lower on the mountain tops.

Closer and closer they drew. We crouched down behind our rock, and held our weapons ready. I could see that the Professor was determined that they should not pass. One and all were quite unaware of our presence.

All at once two voices shouted out to "Halt!" One was my Jonathan's, raised in a high key of passion. The other Mr. Morris' strong resolute tone of quiet command. The gypsies may not have known the language, but there was no mistaking the tone, in whatever tongue the words were spoken. Instinctively they reined in, and at the instant Jonathan, with Lord Godalming and Inspector Cotford, dashed up at one side and Dr. Seward and Mr. Singleton and Mr. Morris on the other. The leader of the gypsies, a splendid looking fellow who sat his horse like a centaur, waved them back, and in a fierce voice gave to his companions some word to proceed. They lashed the horses which sprang forward. But the six men raised their Winchester rifles, and in an unmistakable way commanded them to stop. At the same moment we rose behind the rock and pointed our weapons at them. Seeing that they were surrounded the men tightened their reins and drew up. The leader turned to them and gave a word at which every man of the gypsy party drew what weapon he carried, knife or pistol, and held himself in readiness to attack. Issue was joined in an instant.

The leader, with a quick movement of his rein, threw his horse out in front, and pointed first to the sun, now close down on the hill tops, and then to the castle, said something which I did not understand. For answer, all six men of our party threw themselves from their horses and dashed towards the cart. I should have felt terrible fear at seeing Jonathan in such danger, but that the ardor of battle must have been upon me as well as the rest of them. I felt no fear, but only a wild, surging desire to do something. Seeing the quick movement of our parties, the leader of the gypsies gave a command. His men instantly formed round the cart in a sort of undisciplined endeavour, each one shouldering and pushing the other in his eagerness to carry out the order.

In the midst of this I could see that Jonathan on one side of the ring of men, and Quincey on the other, were forcing a way to the cart. It was evident that they were bent on finishing their task before the sun should set. Nothing seemed to stop or even to hinder them. Neither the levelled weapons nor the flashing knives of the gypsies in front, nor the howling of the wolves behind, appeared to even attract their attention. Jonathan's impetuosity, and the manifest singleness of his purpose, seemed to overawe those in front of him. Instinctively they cowered aside and let him pass. In an instant he had jumped upon the cart, and with a strength which seemed incredible, raised the first of the two great boxes, and flung it over the wheel to the ground. In the meantime, Mr. Morris had had to use force to pass through his side of the ring of Szgany. All the time I had been breathlessly watching Jonathan I had, with the tail of my eye, seen him pressing desperately forward, and had seen the knives of the gypsies flash as he won a way through them, and they cut at him. He had parried with his great bowie knife, and at first I thought that he too had come through in safety. But as he sprang beside Jonathan, who had by now jumped from the cart, I could see that with his left hand he was clutching at his side, and that the blood was spurting through his fingers from the wound which must have re-opened during his struggles. He did not delay notwithstanding this, for as Jonathan, with desperate energy, attacked one end of the chest, attempting to prize off the lid with his great Kukri knife,

he attacked the other frantically with his bowie. Under the efforts of both men
the lid began to yield. I could only pray that it was this box, and not the other,
that held the body of the Count. The nails drew with a screeching sound, and
the top of the box was thrown back.

By this time the gypsies, seeing themselves covered by the Winchesters, and
at our mercy, had given in and made no further resistance. The sun was almost
down on the mountain tops, and the shadows of the whole group fell upon the
snow. I saw the Count lying within the box upon the earth, some of which the
rude falling from the cart had scattered over him. He was deathly pale, just like
a waxen image, and the red eyes glared with the horrible vindictive look which
I knew so well.

As I looked, the eyes saw the sinking sun, and the look of hate in them
turned to triumph.

But, on the instant, came the sweep and flash of Jonathan's great knife. I
shrieked as I saw it shear through the throat. Whilst at the same moment Mr.
Morris's bowie knife plunged into the heart.

It was like a miracle, but before our very eyes, and almost in the drawing of
a breath, the whole body crumbled into dust and passed from our sight.

I shall be glad as long as I live that even in that moment of final dissolution,
there was in the face a look of peace, such as I never could have imagined might
have rested there.

At that moment, the lid of the second box[221] was thrown open from within.
From its confines arose none other than Renfield, his skin as pale and his eyes
as red as ever the Count's were. All the signs of his violent death had vanished,
leaving him with an appearance of strength and youth that belied his sixty odd
years. Afterward, upon reflection, all the warnings were present that Renfield had
been infected with the Count's poison—his intuitive knowledge of the Count's
comings and goings, his desire to consume life, his comments of having been
assured eternal life—but none of us took heed to them then. And now, because
of our remissness, he stood before us as one of the UnDead, and at his full power
now that the sun had set.

In a flash, Renfield sprang upon the closest man of our party, which was Mr.
Morris. Morris was quick to meet the attack with his bowie knife, but it availed
him not at all, for now that the hour of sunset was upon us, the same blade which
had served to destroy the Count only moments ago now seemed to pass through
the madman as if through fog. Morris was thrown to the ground; the wound in
his side opened all the wider, and his blood flowed freely from it upon the snow.
Kate and I, who were at present free from having to keep the gypsies at bay, fired
our weapons, but our bullets, as with the knife, proved useless.

"Fools!" the madman laughed at us as he stood over the prone form of our
poor American friend, "Fools, all of you to a one! Did I not warn you to send me

away? But you heeded me not. You thought I was mad, but I was sane! All along I was sane, and the Master has proven it so, for I was right—the blood *is* the life, and now it shall be mine! All of it mine! Look around you, you pathetic sheep, you lambs to the slaughter; there are more gypsies here than you have bullets, should they all come at you at once. And they will come at you, even at the cost of their own lives, with but a word from me. And lo, if they fail, what will you do against these?" And even as he spoke, he raised his arms, as if beckoning, and we saw the circle of wolves draw closer in around us. "The Master is a part of me, and all that was His is mine to command!"

But in that instant Lord Godalming had rushed forward, holding up the Host that the Professor had given him. And Renfield, for all his boasting, cowered back before him, spitting and snarling like a cat.

"Renfield!" Godalming bellowed. "Did you think I had not recognized you, even after all these years? I was only a child when you gave me to the Holmwoods, but I am a child no longer! I know you Renfield; I know all that you've done. It was you, in your madness and weakness, who betrayed Lucy's secret; we should have been together for all eternity, but because of you was I forced to see her destroyed by my own hand. And now, even now, have you stolen what was to be mine. For all of this and more, I will see you suffer!"

Godalming advanced upon him, and Renfield, unable to stand before the presence of the Host, turned and fled toward the castle. As we looked on, his form seemed to blur and shift, and within the space of a breath, a great wolf could be seen running where a man's form had just been. Notwithstanding, Lord Godalming was quick to follow, and his rage was sufficient to keep him from falling too very far behind the bounding wolf. The Professor called for him to stop, but he paid him no heed. As they approached the great door of the castle, the ground began to shake beneath us all[222].

The castle of Dracula now stood out against the red sky and every stone of its broken battlements was articulated against the light. As we looked there came a terrible convulsion of the earth so that we seemed to rock to and fro and fell to our knees. At the same moment with a roar which seemed to shake the very heavens, the whole castle and the rock and even the hill on which it stood seemed to rise into the air and scatter in fragments while a mighty cloud of black and yellow smoke, volume on volume in rolling grandeur, was shot upwards with inconceivable rapidity. Then there was a stillness in nature as the echoes of that thunderous report seemed to come as with the hollow boom of a thunder clap—the long, reverberating roll which seems as though the floors of heaven shook. Then down in a mighty rain falling whence they rose came the fragments that had been tossed skywards in the cataclysm. From where we stood it seemed as though the one fierce volcano burst had satisfied the need of nature and that the castle and the structure of the hill had sunk again into the void. We were so appalled with the suddenness and the grandeur that we forgot to think of ourselves.[223]

As we looked on, we saw Godalming and the wolf that had been Renfield hurled from the precipice by the force of the blast, their bodies disappearing into the river a thousand feet below.[224] Despite the dangers around us, Van Helsing dropped his rifle and broke down upon the very spot, and wept openly and bitterly, as if he had lost his own son.

The gypsies, taking us as in some way the cause of the earthquakes as well as the extraordinary disappearance of the dead man, turned, without a word, and rode away as if for their lives. Those who were unmounted jumped upon the leiter wagon and shouted to the horsemen not to desert them. The wolves, which had withdrawn to a safe distance, followed in their wake, leaving us alone.

Mr. Morris, who had not risen from the ground like the rest of us, leaned on his elbow, holding his hand pressed to his side. The blood still gushed through his fingers. I flew to him, for the Holy circle did not now keep me back. Jonathan knelt behind him and the wounded man laid back his head on his shoulder. With a sigh he took, with a feeble effort, my hand in that of his own which was unstained.

He must have seen the anguish of my heart in my face, for he smiled at me and said, "I am only too happy to have been of service! Oh, God!" he cried suddenly, struggling to a sitting posture and pointing to me. "It was worth for this to die! Look! Look!"

The last red gleams of the sunset sky came through the thin smoke of the earthquake and fell upon my face, so that it was bathed in rosy light. With one impulse the men sank on their knees and a deep and earnest "Amen" broke from all as their eyes followed the pointing of his finger.

The dying man spoke, "Now God be thanked that all has not been in vain! See! The snow is not more stainless than her forehead! The curse has passed away!"

And, to our bitter grief, with a smile and in silence, he died, a gallant gentleman.

Note, Inspector Cotford to Mr. and Mrs. Harker left with package containing manuscript

9 November

Dear Sir and Madam,

I'm glad this case is over; and over it is, so far as I am concerned. I received word on our return journey that Mr. Aytown has vanished to God knows where. And of course, the only other people who might have shed further light on the case—the Count, the Holmwoods, and perhaps the mad solicitor Renfield—are no more. We'll be told officially, I suppose, that it was all a series of unrelated accidents, or sleep-walking, or superstitious hysteria, or something of the kind, to satisfy the conscience of our Record Department; and that will be the end. As for me, I tell you frankly that it will be the saving of me. I verily believe I was beginning to get dotty over it all. There were too many mysteries, that aren't in my line, for me to be really satisfied as to either facts or the causes of them. Now I'll be able to wash my hands of it, and get back to clean, wholesome, criminal work[225].

I have included with this letter a package, containing one of the manuscript copies you thought destroyed in the fire. I have included with them copies of my own case notes, if for no other purpose than to be an apology of sorts for having taken it in the first place . . . though as you will see in my notes, it appeared quite justified at the time. I feel free to return this to you, now that Lord Godalming is no more, for despite all that transpired with the Count, I am certain that Holmwood had, for reasons of his own, burned what he thought were the only copies of the diaries. After all, how could the Count have been the one to burn them, if he was already being pursued outside by Mr. Morris even as Holmwood was leaving the room? I am certain he destroyed it to eradicate—or so he thought—any evidence connecting his family to the Count, for that there was a connection is evident. And yet, if that were so, why did Holmwood . . .

But there! I keep thinking of it still. I must look out and keep a check on myself, or I shall think of it when I have to keep my mind on other things. I wish you both the very best.

In all sincerity,
Inspector Cotford

Letter, Kate to Mr. and Mrs. Reed

9 November

Dearest Mamma and Papa,

God be praised! We were successful in our hunt, though that success did not come without a price. The Count, who proved himself to be a vampire, led us on a long chase through the wilds of Transylvania, which ended at his castle high in the Carpathians. It was there, amid the freezing snow and fierce gypsies and savage wolves, that Jonathan (who is the husband of friend Mina) severed the head of the fiend that had visited so many horrors upon us, and we all watched as he crumbled into a cloud of dust which in an instant blew away on the winds. But even so, I was not so certain of the Count's destruction. How could I be? The vampire had already proven himself capable of dissolving into dust and mist upon the setting of the sun, and where was the blood and writhing and screeching that I have read marked the death of friend Lucy's death and the three vampire women we encountered at the castle? But so impressive was the destruction of the castle—which seemed to have been previously held together by only the will or some spell of the Count—fell apart only moments after the creature vanished, and so dramatic was the change that came over Mina, that my momentary doubts were appeased.

I returned to London with the others (save for the noble Quincey Morris, and Lord Godalming whose motives I have come to question of late[226], both of whom perished in Transylvania), all the while filled with hope that Francis would now be free of the Count's influence. I wasted no time in making my way to the hospital in Whitechapel, only to find that Francis had vanished on the very night of our battle in the Carpathians. Jack saw me to my house, where we found all of Francis' belongings to be missing. It would appear that he has indeed chosen to remove himself from my life. Though I am saddened by the loss of one friendship, I am happy to say that another has been rekindled.

I must say that I am not the same woman who had pushed Jack away last year, nor is he the same man. We are both changed, and having been passed through God's fires, we are both the better for it. In time, perhaps, that friendship will grow into something more.

Until then, I trust that I am now quite done with all matters of blood and death and the occult . . .

Your Loving Daughter,
Kate

Cutting from *The London Times*, 10 November[227]

Another Whitechapel Murder

During the early hours of yesterday morning another murder of a most revolting and fiendish character took place in Spitalfields. This is the seventh which has occurred in this immediate neighbourhood, and the character of the mutilations leaves very little doubt that the murderer in this instance is the same person who has committed the previous ones, with which the public are fully acquainted.

A Final Note

Seven years[228] ago we all went through the flames. And the happiness of some of us since then is, we think, well worth the pain we endured. It is an added joy to Mina and to me that our boy's birthday is the same day as that on which Quincey Morris died. His mother holds, I know, the secret belief that some of our brave friend's spirit has passed into him. His bundle of names links all our little band of men together. But we call him Quincey.

In the summer of this year we made a journey to Transylvania, and went over the old ground which was, and is, to us so full of vivid and terrible memories. It was almost impossible to believe that the things which we had seen with our own eyes and heard with our own ears were living truths. Every trace of all that had been was blotted out—the site of the castle was a desert waste where as yet no seed could flourish and whence came no bird or insect or even a crawling thing. In its cold sulphurous silent loneliness it was the very abomination of desolation.[229] Even so, the legacy of our battle endures, for while in Transylvania we were regaled with the account of that fateful day, as a gypsy tale told to entertain travelers. How queer it was, to hear our own struggle recounted as a tourist's tale[230].

When we got home we were talking of the old time, which we could all look back on without despair, for Seward and Kate are now happily married. Their joy had taken its own time in arriving, however, for upon our return seven years ago we found that Mr. Aytown had mysteriously disappeared from the Whitechapel hospital, and on the very same day the Count met his end. Where he may have gone, and in what form—living or undead, we know not. But in that same year there was a series of heinous crimes in the vicinity of Whitechapel, committed by a murderer who made himself out to be—deliberately, one might think—someone much like our own good doctor Jack. Some of the newspapers seemed to think as much, though for myself, I thought the murderer seemed more akin to a demented artist than to a doctor. But whoever the killer may have been—Mr. Aytown, or a second vampire count as Kate feared all along, or someone else entirely—the crimes came to an end in fairly short order. And if any of our little band had a hand in that end, they have not said, and I have not inquired[231].

Today I took the papers from the safe where they had been ever since our return so long ago. We were struck with the fact, that in all the mass of material of which the record is composed, there is hardly one authentic document. Nothing but a mass of typewriting, except the Inspector's notes, the later notebooks of Mina and Seward and myself, and Van Helsing's memorandum.

Singleton had once attempted to have our story told by the *Journal of the Occult*, but it proved too fanciful, even for a publication such as that, to accept. But our friend from the Lyceum, whom Mina and the Sewards have since introduced me to, has offered to serve as our editor, so that our story may at last be told. Still, we could hardly ask any one, even did we wish to, to accept these as proofs of so wild a story. Van Helsing summed it all up as he said, with our boy on his knee.

"We want no proofs. We ask none to believe us! This boy will some day know what a brave and gallant woman his mother is. Already he knows her sweetness and loving care. Later on he will understand how some men so loved her, that they did dare much for her sake."

—Jonathan Harker

ENDNOTES

[1] Bram Stoker's writing notes make it clear on page 31b verso ("verso" means the back-side of the page) that he originally intended the novel to be called *The Un-Dead*. In fact, it was still titled as such when he submitted it for publication. Only a last-minute change made it *Dracula*. Indeed, the original manuscript of *Dracula*, which changed hands a few years ago through Christie's auction house, still has the hand-written words *The Un-Dead* on its title page. The lettering of the title you see at the start of this book was faithfully recreated from Stoker's own handwriting from that manuscript.

[2] At the Rosenbach Museum and Library in Philadelphia, Pennsylvania, there are housed Bram Stoker's personal writing notes—which from here on will simply be called "The Notes" (an efficient trick borrowed from Elizabeth Miller)—which record his thoughts and research for the seven years leading up to the first publication of *Dracula*. In these Notes are found various characters and events that never made it into the final 1897 publication.

[3] Hommy-Beg is a nickname for Thomas, literally meaning "Little Tommy." Though the identity of this mysterious Thomas has been debated over the years, most scholars now believe him to have been Stoker's friend Thomas Hall Caine, who dedicated a work of his own—*Cap'n Davy's Honeymoon*—to Stoker.

[4] Only this first paragraph comprised the introduction that appeared in the original 1897 publication. What follows after is a very-slightly modified introduction that first appeared in the 1901 Icelandic edition of the novel, which was later translated back into English and reprinted in various publications on *Dracula* and Stoker, such as *A Bram Stoker Omnibus*, *Dracula Unearthed* and *Dracula: A Documentary Volume*. Readers are encouraged to visit Elizabeth Miller's website (www.blooferland.com) to read the original text.

[5] Stoker did indeed change several of the characters' names from what they were originally (according to pages 1, 5, 31b verso, 35a, and 35a verso), as we will see in later notations. . .

6   Amazing! Here, in the rarely-seen version of the introduction, Bram Stoker is working into *Dracula* the infamous Jack the Ripper murders of 1888.

7   Stoker here sets up a member of the London aristocracy to disappear without a trace during the course of the novel.

8   The Notes (on page 2) reveal that the novel was intended to be divided into four sections, or "books." The first was originally entitled "Styria to London" (back when Stoker had intended to set the novel in Styria, a literary nod to Le Fanu's *Carmilla*), and then was changed to "Transylvania to London." In this work, I have shortened it to be simply called "Transylvania," to match with the other one-word titles of the subsequent books ("Tragedy," "Discovery," and "Punishment").

9   This is a new chapter, not found in Stoker's 1897 publication. In The Notes (on pages 5, 26a, 26b, and 35a verso) there were to be a series of correspondences which would set the stage for Jonathan Harker's eventual journey to Transylvania. These correspondences were to consist of several letters between the Count, Sir John Paxton, Peter Hawkins, and Jonathan Harker. There was also to be an exchange of letters between Lucy Westenra and Kate Reed (a character who never made it into the final publication), as well as a note regarding the use of a kind of fortune-telling called *sortes virgiliane*.

10   Pinning down the exact year the events of *Dracula* occurred has always been a challenge. If the reader is to suspend disbelief and accept the content of *Dracula* as a factual account, as Stoker insists it is in his introduction, then the events recorded in the text logically occurred before its publication in 1897. . . but how long before? Certain cultural details within the novel—such as a possible reference to the death of the famous neurologist Jean-Martin Charcot, and the common-place use of the term "New Woman"—would seem to place the year of *Dracula* in or around 1893. What's more, the calendar dates listed in The Notes match up with those of 1893. Thus, there can be little doubt as to Stoker's having used 1893 as his "model" year when writing his book. However, Harker's final note at the end of the book places the bulk of the events at least seven years *before* it was published, thus requiring the story to have occurred before 1890, despite the previously-mentioned support for 1893. Now, thanks to the rarely-seen Icelandic version of the introduction, we have Stoker specifically linking the timeframe of *Dracula* to the infamous Jack the Ripper murders. This would then place the events of the novel in 1888, when Jack the Ripper committed his crimes. Though 1888 may not have been Stoker's original intent, it appears he eventually settled on that timeframe.

11   The basic contents of this letter are described in The Notes (pages 5, 26a, and 35a verso). Page 5 reads "Sir Robert Parton *[that is, Sir John Paxton]*, President I.L.S., to Peter Hawkins, Cathedral Place, Exeter, stating letter received from Count Wampyr *[that is, Count Dracula]*." Page 35a verso reads "Letter from ditto *[that is, the "President Incorporated Law Society" mentioned in a previous notation on page 35a verso]* to Abraham Aaronson, solicitor *[that is, Peter Hawkins]*, enclosing copy of references." Page 26a gives the date of Parton's letter, "March 21, Tuesday—Sir Robert Parton's letter to Hawkins."

[12] A last minute change must have made this law society president's name into John Paxton, but all throughout The Notes it is consistently "Robert Parton" (as on pages 5, 31b verso). Oddly enough, the name John Paxton also appears later in the novel as a name on a Whitby tombstone, as well as in The Notes (on page 77) where it reads "John Paxton drowned off Cape Farewell 4th April 1778."

[13] In The Notes, Hawkins was originally named either "Abraham Aaronson" (as on page 35a, where it reads "Lawyer—Aaronson" and on 35a verso, where it reads "Abraham Aaronson, solicitor") or "Arthur Abbott" (as on page 1, where "Lawyer Arthur Abbott" was actually crossed off and replaced with "John Hawkins," which in turn was replaced with "Peter Hawkins").

[14] The basic contents of this letter are described in The Notes (pages 5, 26a, 35a verso). Page 5 reads "Count Wampyr *[later crossed out and replaced with "Dracula"]*, Transylvania, to Peter Hawkins asking him to purchase estate." Page 35a verso simply reads "Letter to President Incorporated Law Society." Page 26a gives the date of the Count's letter, "March 16 Wednesday—Dracula's letter to Hawkins (dated 4 March Old Style)"

[15] This is March 16 by Western reckoning. During the Victorian Era, Eastern Europe still recorded dates by the older Julian calendar (which is about two weeks "behind" the modern Gregorian), and would continue to do so up until the end of the First World War. The Notes make it clear (on page 26a) that Dracula dates his letters in the "Old Style."

[16] Early on in his conceptualizing, it appears Stoker had no intention of having his vampire be Dracula, calling him instead "Count Wampyr" in his Notes (as on page 5). Only later, when he learned the sordid history of Voivode Dracula—who we now know to be Vlad Dracula the Impaler—did he finalize the identity of the vampire. It is important to note here that Stoker did not necessarily *base* his vampire on Vlad; it is likely he already had his vampire's concept and appearance worked out before he learned of and "tacked on" the historical identity of Voivode Dracula.

[17] The basic contents of this letter are described in The Notes (pages 5 and 26a). Page 5 reads "Peter Hawkins to Count Wampyr, replying & stating has gout but will send Harker, asking some kind of idea of place required." Page 26a gives the date of Hawkins' letter "March 23—Hawkins letter to Dracula."

[18] The basic contents of this letter are described in The Notes (pages 5, 26a, 35a verso). Page 5 reads "Count Wampyr *[later crossed out and replaced with "Dracula"]*, to Peter Hawkins giving information." Page 35a verso reads at the bottom of the page (a confusing place, to be sure, as the letters were mainly described at the top) "requirements consecrated church in grounds, near river."

[19] This is March 30 by Western reckoning.

[20] Dracula's requirement of having a "consecrated church in the grounds" (page 35a verso) is certainly a peculiar one, given the Count's susceptibility to holy icons, and yet, according to Stoker's mythology of vampirism, it makes sense. Later in the book, Van Helsing will say "There have been from the loins of this very one great men

and good women, and their graves make sacred the earth where alone this foulness can dwell. For it is not the least of its terrors that this evil thing is rooted deep in all good, in soil barren of holy memories it cannot rest."

21   The Notes make mention (on page 38b) of Dracula's "attitude with regard to religion—only moved by relics older than own real date." Dracula—who Stoker ultimately decided was Vlad Dracula (or "that Voivode Dracula who won his name against the Turk," according to the speech later given by Van Helsing)—lived during the fifteenth century, his tomb/bed must also be at least that old. Thus, ironically, Dracula tells the truth in this letter, and again later when he talks with Harker at his castle, when he says that to live in a new home would kill him.

22   Dracula's requirement of having his home "near river" (page 35a verso), is not explained. It is possible that Dracula is still functioning with a warlord's mindset, and desires a fresh water supply for his soldiers and servants. . . or perhaps simply for any imprisoned "blood donors" he may choose to keep at his house.

23   Such an attribute should be obvious, but Dracula specifically requests trustworthiness (page 35a verso, which reads "send trustworthy lawyer"), probably with regard to being able to be discreet with the details of the Count, as later in the novel, Peter Hawkins will make the point of telling the Count that Harker is "discreet and silent."

24   Dracula's requirement of having a lawyer "who does not speak German" (page 35a verso) is not explained. It is tempting to think that Dracula resents the Austrian occupation of his homeland, and that he does not want to deal with anyone who may have pro-Austrian sentiments. Indeed, Stoker makes a point of recording (on page 61 of his Notes) that since the Battle of Mohacs "No Szekely or Saxon elected to office of prince, which was reserved for Hungarian nobility." As the Count later identifies himself as a Szekely, this theory may be so. . .

Or perhaps the Count wants to make sure Harker will have to use English with him, so he can practice without an accent (and later in the novel, the Count will in fact say to Harker "But alas! As yet I only know your tongue through books. To you, my friend, I look that I know it to speak"). Or, quite possibly, he simply wants Harker to have as little opportunity as possible in understanding the peasants' warnings about him. Harker, as it turns out, does know a "smattering of German," as he puts it, but certainly not enough to be considered fluent in the language.

25   The date and basic contents of this letter is described in The Notes, on page 26b which reads "April 12 Wednesday—Harker goes to Purfleet / April 13 Thursday—continues search } letter 12 & 13 Harker to Hawkins."

26   The date and basic contents of this letter is described in The Notes, on page 26b which reads "April 12 Wednesday—Harker goes to Purfleet / April 13 Thursday—continues search / letter 12 & 13 Harker to Hawkins."

27   Page 26b reads "April 15 Saturday—Harker's letter to Hawkins."

28   The basic contents of this letter are described in The Notes (pages 5 and 26b). Page 5 reads "Kate Reed to Lucy Westenra, telling of Harker's visit to the school to see

Mina Murray & of Mina's confidence & her story, with postscript telling how she thought after writing it would be well to ask Mina's permission before telling her story." Page 26b gives the date of Harker's visit, "April 16 Sunday—Harker visits Mina at school," and of Kate's letter, "April 17 Monday—Kate's letter to Lucy."

[29] Kate Reed is a character mentioned on page 1 of The Notes ("Friend & schoolfellow of above *[that is, of "Wilhelmina Murray" who was mentioned earlier on that page]*—Kate Reed"), but she never made it into the 1897 publication... except, perhaps, for a brief mention by Lucy to Mina that "someone has evidently been telling tales" about her romance with Arthur, and Mina's comments about the "New Woman." Though not many specifics are given about her in the Notes (except that she is fairly straightforward and a bit of a gossip, given the contents of her letter listed in a previous endnote), I have made her out to be a "New Woman"—that is, a Victorian era woman who considered herself equal to a man in every way, especially in terms of social and legal rights. In this way Kate makes a good third female character to complement and contrast Mina and Lucy. It is clear that Mina is Stoker's view of the ideal woman, "one of God's own women" as Van Helsing calls her. She is competent and self-sufficient, and yet is a helper and partner to her husband, like the woman of Proverbs 31. Then there is Lucy, who is flighty, subservient, and mainly decorative—a traditional and stereotypical Victorian Era woman. So, on the other end of the spectrum from Lucy, we now have Kate. Like Mina, Kate is quite competent, but she has also completely rebelled against the traditional role of women that Lucy has fallen prey to, thus forsaking both the Biblical merits of that role along with the unfortunate flaws her society had added to it. Please note that our version of Kate is in NO WAY meant to have anything to do with the Kate Reed character from Kim Newman's excellent ***Anno Dracula*** series, other than that both Kate Reeds were named as such because of The Notes.

[30] The very independent heroine from Stoker's ***The Man***, inserted here as a contemporary of Kate, and one that she, as a New Woman, would identify with.

[31] These last words are from the simple proposal found in Stoker's ***The Lady of the Shroud***, a later novel also written in journal form, and dealing with vampiric themes.

[32] Though this may come as a surprise to many readers, Mina's being Scottish and an orphan is nothing new, but is straight out of ***Dracula***. Mina writes to Lucy of Peter Hawkins' death, and says "I never knew either father or mother, so that the dear old man's death is a real blow to me." As for being Scottish, while the evidence for her nationality is more circumstantial, we know that her last name of Murray is certainly of Scottish origin, and she records that in her leading Lucy home from her first sleepwalking encounter with the Count that she "hid in a door till he had disappeared up an opening such as there are here, steep little closes, or 'wynds,' as they call them in Scotland," thus implying a first-hand familiarity with Scotland (probably as a child, for how else would a poor orphan have made her way to Scotland?).

33 This short passage about Mina leaving teaching after marriage was adapted from Stoker's theatre script for *Dracula: or The Un-Dead*.

34 The basic contents of this letter are described in The Notes on page 5, which reads "she knows it all dear long ago & that she goes & stays with her on summer holiday at Whitby."

35 In The Notes, Quincey was named either "Brutus M. Marix" (on page 1, which reads "a Texan—Brutus M. Marix") or "Quincey P. Adams" (page 31b verso)

36 The Notes (on page 1) lists an "American inventor from Texas." Rather than adding yet another Texan to the group, I have simply made Quincey an inventor by trade. In the original 1897 publication of **Dracula**, Stoker took the time to give everyone's profession, except for Quincey's, so I've filled in that missing bit of information in this manner.

37 Francis Aytown is a character mentioned on page 1 of The Notes ("A painter—Francis Aytown"), but he never made it into the 1897 publication. . . except, perhaps, for a brief mention by Mina of "The experience was not lost on the painters, and doubtless some of the sketches of the 'Prelude to the Great Storm' will grace the R.A and R.I. walls in May next." That originally having a painter in the story was clear, as Stoker lists one of the vampire's traits (on page 38b) as "Painters cannot paint him—their likenesses always like some one else." It is very possible that Stoker had the poet Oscar Wilde in mind when formulating this character. Wilde was a contemporary of Stoker, and was involved in the Aesthetic and Decadent movements of his day. He is perhaps most famous for three things: The first is his novel **The Picture of Dorian Gray**—a tale of the beautiful, morally corrupt, and *immortal* Dorian Gray, and of the painter Basil Hallward who becomes infatuated with him and paints a portrait of him, a portrait which in time grows hideous and distorted. The second is his being literally convicted of "committing acts of gross indecency with other male persons," which probably amounted to having homosexual affairs. And the third is his courting Florence Balcombe, only to have her marry Bram Stoker instead. So I have made Francis somewhat bohemian and effeminate—a perception that those of the Victorian era had of Oscar Wilde, and of artists and poets in general—and thus have paired him with Kate, who is more masculine.

38 Page 26b reads "April 18 Tuesday—Harker's letter to Hawkins."

39 Both the old silent German film **Nosferatu** and the original 1931 Hollywood film **Dracula**, as well as later films, have Renfield being a solicitor (that is, a lawyer) involved to varying degrees in the purchase of the Count's new home.

40 The basic contents of this letter are described in The Notes (pages 5 and 26b). Page 5 reads "Peter Hawkins to Count Wampyr *[later crossed out and replaced with "Dracula"]*, place secured in official, enclosing copies (2) of letters from Harker regarding estate of Purfleet." Page 26b gives the date of Hawkins' letter, "April 19 Wednesday—Hawkins letter to Dracula."

41 The basic contents of this telegram are described in The Notes (pages 5 and 26b). Page 5 reads "Telegram, Dracula to Hawkins to get Harker start for Munich."

Page 26b gives the date of Dracula's telegram, "April 24 Monday—Telegram from Dracula." It seems somehow out of place for Dracula, an anachronistic warlord from a bygone era, to be making use of something as modern as a telegraph! Yet Stoker is clear in his Notes that this is indeed the method of communication he uses for his last correspondence with Hawkins.

[42] The practice of fortune-telling, of seeking some insight into the future with regard to a particular situation, by opening a copy of Virgil's *Aeneid* to a random page and line, and reading what that line of poetry says, and then applying that line to the situation at hand. Such a practice is mentioned in The Notes, on pages 2, 35a, 35a verso, and 35b verso. While the other pages are merely references to the name "sortes virgilianae," page 35a reads, in reference to Aaronson, who we know to be Peter Hawkins, "ditto—(sortes virgilianae) conveyance of body."

[43] This is most likely the line of the *Aeneid* that The Notes reference as the "conveyance of body" on page 35a.

[44] On page 66 of The Notes, on a page entitled "The Theory of Dreams," there is a paragraph which reads "Simonides buried a body and was advised by it in a dream not to start the next day—He took the advice and all those who sailed were lost. Told by the Stoics."

[45] This is a new chapter, not found in Stoker's 1897 publication. In The Notes (on pages 6, 26b, 27a, and 38a) we find more omitted events which were to have taken place in and around Munich prior to Jonathan Harker's May 3rd journal entry which began Stoker's final version of the story.

Page 6 reads "Journal in shorthand of Jonathan Harker on his first journey abroad. Directions in letter of Count to go to Munich, stop at Quatre Saisons & await instructions. Start on same day & arrive direct service. Visit to Pinnacothek Museum & to Dead House, telling how brought about. Sees old man on bier, describe—then to babies, then hears talk &listens—man went to bier corpse—where taken—returned on inquiry & find corpse gone. Harker has seen the corpse but does not ask to take part in discussion."

Page 26b into 27a reads "April 25 Tuesday—Leave London 8:50 P.M. / April 26 Wednesday—Arrive Paris 5:50 A.M., Leave Paris 8:25 A.M., Arrive Munich 8:35 P.M. / April 27 Thursday—Snow storm and wolf *[an event that was moved to a later date, for reasons that will be explained in a later footnote]* / April 29 Saturday—Home all day / April 30 Sunday—Flying Dutchman / May 1 Monday—Walpurgis Nacht, Dead House *[an event that was moved back to take the place of the "snow storm and wolf" event, for reasons that will be explained in a later footnote]*."

Page 38a reads "At Munich Dead House see face among flowers—think corpse, but is alive."

[46] Page 6 of The Notes mentions that Harker will "Start on same day & arrive direct service."

[47] On page 26b of The Notes, on the "April 13 Thursday" line, there is a note jotted down that says "Dracula writes to the maître d'hôtel Quatre Saisons."

[48]   In actuality, the Marienbad and the Auracher Hof were the hotels Stoker was originally considering for Harker's stay in Germany, but on page 6 of The Notes we see that these alternatives have been crossed out.

[49]   While the "snow storm and wolf" events of the *Dracula's Guest* short story ultimately take place on Walpurgis Night—a night of supernatural evil between 30 April and 1 May, in The Notes (as we saw in the earlier endnote regarding 26b and 27a), they were supposed to take place on 27 April, with the "Dead House" instead being on Walpurgis Night. But since *Dracula's Guest* is now the "official canon," as it were, I have simply switched the two dates; so the events of *Dracula's Guest* remain on Walpurgis Night (as seen in the upcoming Chapter Three), while events of the museum, opera and Dead House begin with the date of 27 April.

[50]   On page 6 of The Notes, he misspells this museum as "Pinnacothek."

[51]   This is an authentic painting by an unknown 15th century Austrian painter, depicting the presence of Vlad Dracula the Impaler at the martyrdom of St. Andrew. Its image can be found in the book *In Search of Dracula* by McNally and Florescu.

[52]   The description of the opera's theatre stage is a modified exerpt from Stoker's short story *The Coming of Abel Behenna*, in which he records a most vivid description of a harbor.

[53]   The description of the undying Captain was adapted from Stoker's *Personal Reminiscences of Henry Irving.*

[54]   From Stoker's own critique of Irving's performance, found in *Personal Reminiscences of Henry Irving.*

[55]   This description of the Count's eyes can be found in The Notes (page 35a verso), where he has "dead dark eyes."

[56]   This whole peculiar visit to the Dead House is described on page 6 of The Notes, where it reads "Sees old man on bier, describe—then to babies, then hears talk &listens—man went to bier corpse—where taken—returned on inquiry & find corpse gone. Harker has seen the corpse but does not ask to take part in discussion."

[57]   This is a new chapter, not found in Stoker's 1897 publication, and is essentially *Dracula's Guest*, with only a few changes here and there. The Notes mention an event involving a snowstorm and a wolf—page 26b reads "snow storm and wolf," 35c verso reads "Harker's diary Munich wolf." What's more, in 1914 Florence (Bram Stoker's widow) had published a short story entitled *Dracula's Guest*, which she says was an "unpublished episode from *Dracula*. It was originally excised owing to the length of the book, and may prove of interest to the many readers of what is considered my husband's most remarkable work." The Notes about the snowstorm and wolf certainly support the planned existence of such a chapter, and there are a number of pages missing from the beginning of Stoker's original *Un-Dead* manuscript, denoting a large section had been removed prior to being given to the publisher.

[58]   This is an obvious literary nod to Le Fanu's *Carmilla*, which was set in Styria and makes mention of a "ruined village" that had been "troubled by revenants." In Le

Fanu's work, there is also "a gentleman, dressed in black, who looked particularly elegant and distinguished, with this drawback, that his face was the most deadly pale I ever saw, except in death." It is important to note that the vampiress that Harker sees within the tomb is not necessarily the Countess Dolingen whose tomb this is; as we will see later in the novel, the grave of a suicide (which the Countess was, given that she "sought and found death") is a safe haven for any vampire.

59 The events of this chapter correspond to those of the first chapter of Stoker's 1897 publication, though the text has been modified slightly.

60 This reference to the Munich Dead House is taken directly from the original manuscript, indicating that Stoker had very nearly included that scene in his final publication.

61 This reference to the storm and wolf is taken directly from the original manuscript, indicating that the tale of "Dracula's Guest"—the "deleted chapter" status of which has been hotly debated over the years—was indeed originally a scene in Stoker's work and indeed nearly made it through to final publication.

62 The events of this chapter correspond to those of the second chapter of Stoker's 1897 publication, though the text has been modified slightly.

63 This addition of recounting the Munich adventures comes from two unused and incomplete sentences in the Manuscript (which I have combined here into a single thought), further proving that **Dracula's Guest** was indeed a part of the novel until just before publication.

64 A remark from the Manuscript about the wound left by the wolf—not a bite, mind you, but a red and raw mark from its tongue—again confirming the legitimacy of **Dracula's Guest** as part of the Dracula story.

65 Stoker makes a point, on page 43a verso, of noting "green taper with blue flame in Count's house."

66 A reference to "sortes virgilianae" is mentioned on page 35a verso in The Notes, among other things Harker finds at the castle, "books and books, English law directory, sortes virgilianae." Odd, that both the Count and Peter Hawkins would use the same methods of scrying. . .

67 In the Manuscript, Harker did not ask this question, but rather the Count brings it up himself. Harker writes "but then it struck me as an odd thing that he should know of the episode for I was sure I had not told him of it."

68 Despite Harker's flawed translation, Carfax actually means "crossroads," and it is well known that a crossroads is where suicides are buried and where the undead are said to dwell (Stoker even says as much in the "Dracula's Guest" chapter). It is inconceivable that Stoker named the estate Carfax without knowing its true meaning; perhaps he intended to have the name be brought up again later, or he assumed that the reader of his era would have caught the play on words and thus be amused at Harker's ignorance. In any event, this line was added for the benefit of the modern reader and to help rekindle this lost plot thread.

69 On page 35a verso of The Notes, he says that the "central name marked with point of knife."

70 The events of this chapter correspond to those of the third chapter of Stoker's 1897 publication, though the text has been modified slightly.

71 Later in the text, according to the Manuscript, when Van Helsing is listing items that vampires have no power against, he also mentions "the rye which Jonathan experience." In folklore, werewolves—which is Stoker's day were still equated with vampires—are allergic to the rye plant. On page 43 verso b of the Notes, in which Stoker records his research from Baring-Gould's *The Book of Were-Wolves*, states "Ww. [that is, werewolves]—no power in rye field."

72 Yet another reference to *Dracula's Guest* taken from the Manuscript. The vampiress' displeasure calls into question just who or what the Munich wolf was. Was it one of Dracula's pets, or was it Dracula himself in wolf form? If the fair vampiress was the woman in the tomb (as will be discussed shortly), the wolf could have certainly been her . . . though there is no reason for her to now show disgust at her own handiwork. Perhaps it was even another vampire altogether (hence Dracula's earlier excitement at Harker's recounting of the incident) . . .

73 Here, perhaps, is the most telling connection to *Dracula's Guest* found in the original Manuscript, that "she was the woman—or her image—that I had seen on Walpurgis night." This is not simply a reference to Munich or snow or a wolf, but a reference to a scene from *Dracula's Guest* with a direct link to the vampiress Harker is now facing.

74 The events of this chapter correspond to those of the fourth chapter of Stoker's 1897 publication, though the text has been modified slightly.

75 The addition of this Shakespeare reference is from the Manuscript.

76 There was a small but curious change in text between the original 1897 British edition of Dracula and the 1899 American edition. The British edition reads "Tomorrow, tomorrow night is yours!," whereas the American edition reads "Tonight is mine! Tomorrow night is yours?" In this version, both are used.

77 Thus begins the second book of Stoker's original concept for a four book arrangement for his novel (on page 2 of The Notes, which reads "Book II Tragedy")

78 The events of this chapter correspond to those of the fifth chapter of Stoker's 1897 publication, though the text has been somewhat modified.

79 Starting with this addition regarding her mother and social situations, Lucy's letters to Mina are longer than in the original text, expanded in several places with sections from the Manuscript that reveal more of Lucy's thoughts and personality.

80 On page 11 of The Notes, the text reads "Developments of study—Lucy visits asylum—her effect on mad patient with flies—curiosity concerning closed estate—peeks over wall— Seward promises to get leave to show it to her. The notice board down—mystery."

81 Though Lucy, drawn to Seward as she is, turns him down here, early in The Notes she had accepted his proposal (page 1 reads "Doctor of Mad House—Seward / Girl engaged to him—Lucy Westenra").

82   Throughout The Notes, this pivotal character is referred to only as "Mad Patient"
      (page 1) or "Flyman" (page 35b verso) or "Fly Patient" (page 2). . . but never by the
      name Renfield. In fact, in reviewing Stoker's original "cut-and-paste" manuscript,
      one can see that "Renfield" was hand-written into the already typed text, making it
      a last minute choice for Stoker.

83   The events of this chapter correspond to those of the sixth chapter of Stoker's 1897
      publication, though the text has been significantly modified.

84   This man, who we come to know as "Mr. Swales," may have simply been called the
      "Crank" in The Notes (page 1). Stoker mentions the "Crank" early on in his notes,
      but does not mention him again. Perhaps this was an early character concept that
      was dropped, only to be rekindled later on after his visit to Whitby?

85   Stoker's Notes (on pages 41a, 41b, 41a verso, and 41b verso) show that he painstakingly
      researched the Yorkshire dialect of Whitby. The translation of Mr. Swales' speech
      reads, more or less, as "I wouldn't worry myself about them, miss. Such things don't
      exist. Keep in mind that I'm not saying that they never existed, but I am saying
      that they never existed in my time. Such things are good for entertaining tourists
      and the like, but not for a nice young lady like you. Those tourists from York and
      Leeds—the ones who are always eating cured herring and drinking tea and looking
      for opportunities to buy cheap black jet-stone—they would believe such things.
      Though I've wondered myself who would bother to tell them such lies, if even the
      newspapers would, which is otherwise so full of foolishness."

86   The translation of this speech of Mr. Swales' reads, more or less, as "I must on my
      way home now, miss. My grand-daughter doesn't like to be kept waiting when the
      tea is ready, and it takes me a long time to hobble along through the tombstones,
      for there are a lot of them, and anyway, miss, it's time for me to eat."

87   In Stoker's original 1897 publication, Mr. Swales had a grand-daughter who remained
      nameless. I have merged that character with Kate, to provide a reason for her to be
      in Whitby.

88   These two epitaphs are actual Whitby tombstone inscriptions, which are specifically
      mentioned—along with several others—in The Notes (all listed on pages 75 through
      84). Page 76 reads "Ann Swales. 6th Feb. 1795. aet 100." Page 81 reads "James Reed
      drowned Liverpool 7/1/59 aet 23."

89   The translation of this speech of Mr. Swales' reads, more or less, as "It's all foolish-talk,
      every bit of it, that's what it is and nothing else. These ghosts and such are nothing
      but ways to make children and silly women scream. They're nothing but air bubbles.
      Such things, as well as dark tales and omens and warnings, are all invented by church
      pastors and evil men and cheap advertisers to scare and disturb children, and to get
      people to do something that they wouldn't otherwise want to. It makes me angry
      to think of those people. Why, it's those same people that—not being content with
      printing their lies on paper and preaching them out of pulpits—also want to carve
      them on the tombstones. Look here all around you, in whatever direction you want.

All of those stones, holding up their heads as well as they can out of their pride, are leaning over and falling down from the weight of the lies wrote on them. 'Here lies the body' or 'Sacred to the memory' are the words written on all of them, and yet in about half of the graves there are not even any bodies present at all, and their memories are cared for less than a pinch of snuff is, much less being held as 'sacred.' Lies all of them, nothing but lies of one kind or another! My God, but it'll be a strange confusion on the Day of Judgment, when they rise up in their death-clothes, all bogged down together and trying to drag their tombstones with them to prove how good they were, some of them shaking and slow, with their hands so wrinkled and slippery from lying in the sea that they can't even keep their grip on them."

[90] The translation of this speech of Mr. Swales' reads, more or less, as "Nonsense! There may be a very few of them correct, except where they make out the people to be overly good, for there be people who would call a bowl of water the ocean when describing their own goodness. The whole thing is only lies. For example, you have come here a stranger, and you have seen this graveyard?" I nodded, for I thought it better to assent, though I did not quite understand his dialect. I knew it had something to do with the church. He went on, "And you believe that all these stones are above the people that are supposed to be buried here, all snug and tidy?" I assented again. "And that is just where the lie begins. Why, there be dozens of these graves that are as empty as old Dun's tobacco box on a Friday night!" He nudged one of his companions, and they all laughed. "And, my God! How could they be otherwise? Look at that one, the farthest one from past the bank, read it!"

[91] The translation of this speech of Mr. Swales' reads, more or less, as "Who brought him home, I wonder, to bury him here? Murdered off the coast of Andres! And you believe his body rests here! Why, I could tell you a dozen names whose bones still lie in the Greenland seas to the north," he pointed northwards, "or to wherever the currants may have taken them. There are their stones all around you. You can, with your young eyes, read the small print of the lies from here. There's Braithwaite Lowery (I knew his father), who was lost in the Lively off Greenland in '20, or Andrew Woodhouse, who drowned in those same seas in 1777, or John Paxton, who drowned off Cape Farewell a year later, or old John Rawlings, whose grandfather sailed with me, drowned in the Gulf of Finland in '50. Do ye think that all these men will have to make a rush to Whitby when the trumpet sounds? I have my doubts about it! I tell you that if they get here they'd be pushing and shoving one another so much that it would be like a fight up north on the ice, like in the old days, when we'd be fighting one another from daylight to dark, and then trying to bandage our cuts by the northern lights!"

[92] The translation of this speech of Mr. Swales' reads, more or less, as "You don't see anything funny! Ha-ha! But that's because you don't know that the mourning mother was a hell-cat that hated him because he was a cripple—quite lame, he was—and he hated her so much that he committed suicide in order that she might not get the

insurance money she had put on his life. He blew most of the top of his own head off with an old musket that they used for scaring crows. It wasn't to scare crows then, for it brought the crows and the flies to him! And that's the way he fell off the rocks. And, as to hopes of a glorious resurrection, I've often heard him say myself that he hoped he'd go to hell, for his mother was so pious that she'd be sure to go to heaven, and he didn't want to be where she was. Now isn't that stone, in any event," he hammered it with his stick as he spoke, "a pack of lies? And won't it make Gabriel laugh when Geordie comes panting up the grass with the tombstone balanced on his back, and asks for it to be taken as evidence!"

93   The translation of this speech of Mr. Swales' reads, more or less, as "That won't harm you, my pretty one, and it may make poor Geordie happy to have so trim a girl as you sitting on his lap. That won't hurt you. Why, I've sat here off and on for about the last twenty years, and it hasn't done me any harm. Don't you worry about those that lie under you, or that don't lie there at all, as the case may be! The time for you to be getting scared is when you see the tombstones vanish, and the place becomes as bare as a stubble-field. There's the clock, and I must be going now. My service to you, ladies!"

94   Stoker notes (on page 43a verso) that werewolves are "told not to bite thumb nail of left hand." So why does Renfield have a long thumb nail? Hmm. . .

95   The translation of this speech of Mr. Swales' reads, more or less, as "I'm afraid, my dear, that I must have shocked you by all the wicked things I've been saying about the dead, and the like, for the past few weeks, but I didn't mean them, and I want you to remember that when I'm gone. We old folks are stupid, and have one foot above the grave, don't really like to think about it, and we don't want to feel scared of it, and that's why I've started making jokes about it, so that I'd cheer up my own heart a bit. But, Lord love you, miss, I'm not afraid of dying, not a bit, only I don't want to die if I can help it. My time must be close at hand now, for I am old, and to live a hundred years is too much for any man to expect. And I'm so close to death that the Old Man is already whetting his scythe. You see, I can't get out of the habit of complaining about it all at once. These jaws of mine still wag just like they be used to. Some day soon the Angel of Death will sound his trumpet for me. But don't you cry and grieve, my dear!"—for he saw that I was crying—"if he should come this very night I'd not refuse to answer his call. For life is, after all, only a time to wait for something other than what we're doing here, and death is all that we can truly depend on. But I'm content, for it's coming to me, my dear, and coming quick. It may be coming while we're looking and wondering. Maybe it's in that wind out over the sea that's bringing with it loss and wreck, and sore distress, and sad hearts. Look! Look!" he cried suddenly. "There's something in that wind and in what's beyond that sounds, and looks, and tastes, and smells like death. It's in the air. I feel it coming. Lord, make me answer cheerful, when my call comes."

96   The events of this chapter correspond to those of the seventh chapter of Stoker's 1897 publication, though the text has been somewhat modified, and the section of

journal entries which were to appear after the newspaper clipping have been relocated to the next chapter for editing purposes.

[97] The original point of arrival in England for Dracula was to be Dover (per page 38a in The Notes, which reads "Doctor at Dover customs house sees him a corpse"), though it was changed to Whitby after Stoker enjoyed a holiday there.

[98] From The Notes (pages 1 and 2 both have "The Auctioneer"... though both are also crossed out)

[99] From reading The Notes, it seems clear that the idea of having Dracula as a great dog (i.e. a wolf) leaping from the ship as it came ashore was added much later; earlier in his planning, Stoker had Dracula being in one of the crates still aboard the ship. Page 13 in his Notes reads "ship full of clay—coffin found aboard."

[100] The presence of a doctor to inspect the coffined body of Dracula upon its arrival in England can be found in The Notes (page 38a), where it reads "Doctor at Dover customs house sees him a corpse."

[101] The Notes (on page 13) do originally have the bodies of the crew wash up on shore after the ship. However, as Stoker eventually decided on having the crew disappear several days prior, and much further out to sea, there was no way to reasonably insert this minor detail. But Stoker did use the concept elsewhere in his writings, as in this line from *The Coming of Abel Behenna*: "In the morning the storm was over and all was smiling again, except that the sea was still boisterous with its unspent fury. Great pieces of wreck drifted into the port, and the sea around the island rock was strewn with others. Two bodies also drifted into the harbour—one the master of the wrecked ketch, the other a strange seaman whom no one knew."

[102] Pages 40 and 40 verso of The Notes are filled with research on a ship called the *Demetry*, how it wrecked at Whitby in 1885, and even what the weather conditions were during that storm. Interestingly, in the original Manuscript, the ship's name was the *Demetrius Pupoff*.

[103] The Notes about finding the Count's body at the custom's house describe how one wrong coffin was brought over to England; page 38a reads "coffins selected to be taken over—one wrong one brought."

[104] This interesting addition about photographing the dead dog's eyes is from the Manuscript. It is in reference to the notion that the last thing a person or animal sees is somehow imprinted on the eyes' retinas.

[105] On page 47b of The Notes, it reads "local dog found ripped open & graves torn up."

[106] This chapter is a composite of modified journal entries transplanted from the end of the last chapter, as well as a significant amount of new material not found in Stoker's 1897 publication.

[107] There is a fascinating account in The Notes which describes Lucy finding a brooch on the shore after the storm. Page 14 reads "Whitby. Lucy finds strange brooch on shore & puts it on—she becomes fond of dreaming & walks in sleep (renewing old habit)."

108   This is a description of the jewel found in a hat that the historical Vlad Dracula is often seen wearing in paintings and portraits.

109   This section on Lucy's sleepwalking is actually pieced together from Mina's account in the previous chapter (excised from her 26 July and 3 August entries) and a section earlier in this chapter (excised from her 8 August entry). The reasoning for this is that The Notes (as we've already seen, on page 14) make it clear that Lucy's sleepwalking started up *after* the brooch was found, thus making a definite connection between the two.

110   The events of this chapter correspond to those of the eighth chapter of Stoker's 1897 publication, though the text has been significantly modified.

111   The Notes on page 14 read "Finds Mina *[should read "Lucy"]* asleep on bench. Wound in throat & brooch covered with blood."

112   This reference to Dracula sinking into the ground after feeding is mentioned in Stoker's stage play *Dracula or The Un-Dead*.

113   This is a modified version of the letter that Bram Stoker actually wrote to his idol Walt Whitman in 1872, which it then took him four years to build the courage to send. A copy of it can be found in the Whitman Archives, or in Haining and Tremayne's book **The Un-Dead: The Legend of Bram Stoker and Dracula**.

114   This early witnessing of Dracula by Seward was added to support a later reference by Van Helsing—reinserted from the Manuscript—which states "Friend John saw that when he meet you on this road here. Alas! That you did not know of him then!"

115   This is a brief exerpt (modified, of course) from a reply letter that Walt Whitman sent to Bram Stoker after reading what Stoker had finally mailed to him.

116   This is a new chapter, not found in Stoker's 1897 publication.

117   Oddly, Mina and Lucy's hair color is not described in detail, either in the original publication or in The Notes. Lucy's hair color is mentioned only twice in the 1897 publication, once as having "sunny ripples" (which was in later editions changed to "shiny ripples" to avoid confusion; this version uses "shiny" as well) and once as being "dark." Thus, we can conclude Lucy has dark, shiny hair. Mina's hair is not described at all, but given the Scottish surname Murray, she has been made a red head, to help differentiate her from Lucy.

118   The painter's difficulty in capturing a vampire's face correctly, and having that face look different, even skeletal, is mentioned in The Notes (on page 38b), which reads "Painters cannot paint him—their likenesses always like someone else" and again "Could not Kodak him—come out black or like skeleton corpse."

119   On the first page of The Notes, there is the mention of "Lawyer—Wm. Young," though it is heavily crossed out. Just below that, there are the words (also crossed out) "His sister."

120   As Stoker already had a self-assured law student make his way aboard the Demeter, I have simply made him into Mr. Young, for the sake of "fleshing out" characters Stoker already had in place.

[121] The Notes, on page 35a, again makes mention of this lawyer and his sister, and describes the man as "shrewd and skeptical"

[122] The account of the doctor being asked to see the man in the coffin, in lieu of the sick regional surgeon, who then restores the man to life, can be found in The Notes, on page 38c, which reads "The divisional surgeon being sick, the doctor is asked to see man in coffin, restores him to life." Of course, the "doctor" mentioned here was meant to be Dr. Seward, but as making that happen would have required altering too much of Stoker's final work, I opted to have Dr. Caffyn be this doctor instead (which makes sense, seeing as Stoker already has him board the ship at Whitby to examine the captain).

[123] This line is in honor of an anecdote supposedly told by Stoker's son Noel, in which the author first conceived of the idea for *Dracula* after having a nightmare that he blamed on his eating of dressed crab that day.

[124] This dinner party game was specifically mentioned in The Notes, on page 38c, which reads "The dinner party at the mad doctor's. Thirteen—each has a number, each asked to tell something strange—order of numbers make the story complete—at the end the Count comes in." Again, Dr. Caffyn was substituted here for Dr. Seward, the "mad doctor."

[125] The tale which the guests compose is actually a minimally modified portion of an obscure short story written by Stoker, called *Under the Sunset*.

[126] In Stoker's original 1897 publication, Dracula on more than one occasion used the name Count DeVille for himself while in England.

[127] This is a new chapter, not found in Stoker's 1897 publication. The last chapter covered the storytelling game mentioned on page 38c, so this chapter will deal with the arrival of the Count, which was to occur at the end of the game. The concept that Dracula would attend a dinner with his victims actually made it into one of the movie adaptations—the 1979 version of *Dracula*, staring Frank Langella, upon which the structure and dialogue of this chapter has been loosely based. The Notes indicate this scenario was intended to be at Dr. Seward's, but as he later changed his storyline to make it a surprise to Seward that Dracula's house was across from his, it would no longer make sense to have the dinner in Purfleet. So for the sake of continuity, this dinner party was moved to be across from the Count's London address, with a different group of protagonists.

[128] The Notes (on page 38b) list one of the traits of a vampire as an "absolute despisal of death & the dead."

[129] The Notes (on page 38b) list one of the traits of a vampire as an "insensibility to music"

[130] As seen earlier in the endnotes, Stoker originally intended Dracula to arrive by way of Dover (as seen in his Notes, on page 38a, where it reads ""Doctor at Dover customs house sees him a corpse").

[131] The events of this chapter correspond to those of the ninth chapter of Stoker's 1897 publication, though the text has been significantly modified.

132 Stoker originally intended for Lucy to be a witness to their marriage; page 15 of his Notes reads "Jonathan & Mina are married—Lucy at wedding."

133 Emily Gerard's *Transylvanian Superstitions* is one book Stoker definitely used in his research for writing *Dracula*, as it appears referenced in his Notes.

134 This is an exerpt from a real 1888 newspaper covering the Jack the Ripper murders.

135 The Notes (on page 15) show that it was originally Mina, not Arthur, who first alerts Dr. Seward to Lucy's ailments, as the text reads "Lucy grows worse. Mina goes about her to Dr. Seward." But, as Stoker decided to have Mina and Seward's meeting much later, Arthur remains the informer.

136 In The Notes, on page 1, Van Helsing was originally named "A German Professor—Max Windshoeffel"

137 This is an excerpt from a real 1888 newspaper covering the Jack the Ripper murders.

138 This events of this chapter correspond to those of the tenth chapter of Stoker's 1897 publication.

139 Though a relatively small addition from the original Manuscript, this "no sugar in mine thank you" phrase warrants an explanation. Though being light-hearted here, Lucy is essentially refusing to have the garlic in her room. This is what provokes Van Helsing's harsh response, which seemed quite out of place in the original *Dracula* publication.

140 The events of this chapter correspond to those of the eleventh chapter of Stoker's 1897 publication, though the text has been significantly modified.

141 This whole account is taken from page 16 in The Notes, where he writes "Lucy's Diary. A Night of Terror. Mem., attempts of Count Dracula to get into Lucy's room in various ways—bird & beast & dark mass—scratching out window pane—threatening—finally covers glass with mass of blood, this seems to throw it out of bounds—she is guarded by some spell (?) placed accidentally (describe beforehand) Dracula's rage—insensibility—recovery."

142 The Notes (on page 38b) note that while the Count is at the Zoological Gardens, there is the "rage of eagle & lion."

143 This is a new chapter, not found in Stoker's 1897 publication. This chapter has been adapted from an exerpt from Stoker's novel *The Man*.

144 The events of this chapter correspond to those of the twelfth chapter of Stoker's 1897 publication, though the text has been significantly modified.

145 Stokers Notes (on page 38b) states "Could not Kodak him—come out black or like skeleton corpse."

146 These events of this chapter correspond to those of the thirteenth chapter of Stoker's 1897 publication, though the text has been significantly modified.

147 The Notes mention a "A Detectivc—Cotford" on page 1, and later, on page 35a, an unnamed "detective inspector."

148 Thus begins the third book of Stoker's original concept for a four book arrangement for his novel (on page 2 of The Notes, which reads "Book III Discovery")

149   The events of this chapter correspond to those of the fourteenth chapter of Stoker's 1897 publication, though the text has been significantly modified.

150   According to The Notes (on pages 21 and 25), the account of Jonathan seeing the Count in London for the first time, followed by Mina opening his journal, was to take place in Book III. Thus, this journal entry was removed from the last chapter (which ended Book II) and was placed here, where it seems a more natural fit anyway.

151   A reference to Harker's earlier adventures in Munich (which never made it into the final publication), found in the Manuscript.

152   Page 25 of The Notes reads "Harker sees the Count—met him in the Munich Dead House."

153   Yet another reference in the Manuscript to Harker's adventures in Munich.

154   A title of nobility used in England since 1440; according to The Notes (on page 31b verso, which reads "Viscount Godalming"), it is the actual title for Lord Godalming, though the "Viscount" was not used in the 1897 publication, perhaps to avoid confusion with the "Count."

155   Page 38a of The Notes reads "Money always old gold—traced to Salzburg banking house." Hmm. . . what are the Holmwoods doing with it?

156   The events of this chapter correspond to those of the fifteenth chapter of Stoker's 1897 publication, though the text has been significantly modified.

157   The events of this chapter correspond to those of the sixteenth chapter of Stoker's 1897 publication, though the first section of Dr. Seward's journal was transplanted from the end of the last chapter, and the text has been modified slightly.

158   In the Manuscript, it appears Van Helsing is using both the holy wafer *and* the sacramental wine.

159   This is a new chapter, not found in Stoker's 1897 publication.

160   The concept of the Count gaining control of a maid of his victim's house first made it's way into the **Dracula** story through Hamilton Deane's 1924 stage production, followed by the Deane-Balterston's 1927 version.

161   The engagement of the undertaker's man to a maid is mentioned briefly in The Notes, on page 35a, where it reads "undertaker's man" and "maid engaged undertaker's man."

162   This is an excerpt from a real 1888 newspaper covering the Jack the Ripper murders.

163   The name of an assistant investigator from Stoker's *The Jewel of Seven Stars*.

164   The events of this chapter correspond to those of the seventeenth chapter of Stoker's 1897 publication, though the text has been significantly modified.

165   This mention of papers from Arthur is found only in the original Manuscript. No such papers find there way into Mina's final collection of documents, neither in the Manuscript nor in the published version . . . which may indicate that they were purposefully withheld or destroyed.

166   The events of this chapter correspond to those of the eighteenth chapter of Stoker's 1897 publication, though the text has been significantly modified.

167   Stoker makes a point of recording (on page 49 of his Notes) that "Magyars are the
      4th branch of Finnish stock viz. the Ugric" and a few lines later "wehrwolf legend
      through Fins."

168   From The Notes (page 38b), which reads "power of creating evil thoughts or banishing
      good ones in others."

169   On page 4 of The Notes, amidst a list of vampiric traits, there is a particularly
      mysterious line that reads simply "Immortaliable—Gladstone," with no further
      explanation. "Immortaliable," by its etymology, of course implies the potential to live
      forever and/or to grant such potential to others. Furthermore, in a letter that Stoker
      sent to William Gladstone (available at the British Library, or Elizabeth Miller's
      website www.blooferland.com), he writes of his novel that "It has I think pretty well
      all the vampire legend as to limitations and these may in some way interest you who
      have made as bold a guess at 'immortaliability.'" William Gladstone was, in his day,
      a rather vocal advocate of Conditional Immortality, a doctrine which states that (1)
      the human soul is not inherently immortal, but (2) that a human may attain or be
      granted a certain limited form of immortality though the physical transformation
      or resurrection of the body from the dead.

170   An idea jotted down amongst more scholarly research in The Notes (page 56), which
      reads "horses to be disturbed at approach of Count Dracula and smell blood."

171   Another jotted down idea amidst Stoker's research (page 50), which reads "leeches—
      attracted to Count Dracula, and then repelled."

172   Page 39b of The Notes reads "Vampire cause drought—to get rain seek & destroy
      vampire." Though a seemingly an odd trait for the Count to have, the reader of the
      original *Dracula* will note that, once the Count is on shore in England—a land
      where the stereotype is that everyone carries umbrellas—there is not one drop of
      rain mentioned throughout the original text.

173   The events of this chapter correspond to those of the nineteenth chapter of Stoker's
      1897 publication, though the text has been significantly modified.

174   A reference to Stoker's employer, the actor Sir Henry Irving, found in the Manuscript.
      Quincey is saying here that either Renfield is perfectly sane, or he's as good of an
      actor as Irving.

175   The act of picking the lock originally fell to Dr. Seward, but seemed more appropriate
      for Quincey, given his new role as inventor.

176   The act of summoning the dogs originally fell to Arthur, but seemed more appropriate
      for Singleton, given his established interest in dogs as enemies of supernatural evil.

177   The events of this chapter correspond to those of the twentieth chapter of Stoker's
      1897 publication, though the text has been significantly modified.

178   What follows is a combination of the letter found in the traditional publication of
      Dracula and the longer version found in the Manuscript. Of note is that fact that in the
      Manuscript version mentions other property owned by Winter-Suffield. Note that the
      mention of Trollope and Pickford appear in neither *Dracula* nor the Manuscript.

[179] Page 58 of The Notes reads "Sometimes Tokay (wine) gets sick in Spring—the time when the sap rises in living plants (mem. Guess cause)."

[180] Stoker records these cases in his Notes. Page 67 reads ". . . a woman named Guasser who got kind of catalepsy twice a day, limbs grew hard like stone, little pulse but respiration as in sleep, had no feeling though flesh scarified. . ." and page 68 reads "See 'Cheyne's English Malady' where Col. Townshend who had nephritic complaint had power of dying and coming to life at pleasure. Dr. Cheyne, Dr. Baynard and Mr. Skrine saw that at Bath when for half an hour he died. No motion of heart. Mirror held over mouth not even soiled, etc."

[181] The events of this chapter correspond to those of the twenty-first chapter of Stoker's 1897 publication, though the text has been significantly modified.

[182] The description of Sergeant Daw, one of the main characters of Stoker's *The Jewel of Seven Stars*.

[183] In The Notes (on page 24), it reads "Count offers to prove in his way if patient sane—proves it."

[184] On page 1 of The Notes, it describes Renfield as "Mad Patient { Theory of getting life—instinctively goes for Count & follows up idea with mad cunning."

[185] Thus begins the fourth book of Stoker's original concept for a four book arrangement for his novel (on page 2 of The Notes, which reads "Book IV Punishment")

[186] The events of this chapter correspond to those of the twenty-second chapter in Stoker's original 1897 publication, though the text has been significantly modified.

[187] The Manuscript shows that Stoker had continued with idea—writing "So it was arranged that Lord Godalming was to have three horses ready at Piccadilly close to the Junior Constitutional Club where they would not attract attention. He also arranged for a groom to . . ." before Stoker ultimately decided to have Quincey and Van Helsing veto the idea.

[188] On page 29a of the writing Notes, Stoker has the Count contacting someone named Pickford and another someone named Trollope, who make no further appearances.

[189] Pages 1 of The Notes reads "A Deaf Mute Woman / A Silent Man } English Servants of the Count." Page 35a mentions them again, where it reads "Silent man & dumb woman—Count's London servants, in power of Count, some terrible fear, man knows secret." In addition, there is a penciled-in comment in The Notes (page 58) indicates that "Count Dracula in prison picks out murderer." I have combined these two thoughts together, so that the Count has leased a couple of servants from a prison workhouse.

[190] This is a new chapter, not found in Stoker's original 1897 publication.

[191] The description of this house is taken from Stoker's short story *The Judge's House*.

[192] Save for a few modifications, this description of the interior of the house is taken from Stoker's *The Judge's House*. Note the presence of rats. Rats are a recurring theme in Stoker's works; not only are they in *Dracula*, but in other works such as *The Judge's House* and *The Burial of Rats*.

193   Though heavily modified, this description of finding the painting is also taken from Stoker's *The Judge's House*. The figure in the painting has, of course, been altered somewhat to be the Count's. . . but note how similar Stoker's evil Judge is to the Count in the original short story: "His face was strong and merciless, evil, crafty, and vindictive, with a sensual mouth, hooked nose of ruddy colour, and shaped like the beak of a bird of prey. The rest of the face was of a cadaverous colour. The eyes were of peculiar brilliance and with a terribly malignant expression." This image—the hooked nose, the sensual mouth, the glowing eyes—must have struck a particular chord of horror within Stoker.

194   Francis' rant is a modified exerpt from Stoker's *The Man*.

195   The events of this chapter correspond to those of the twenty-third chapter in Stoker's original 1897 publication, though the text has been significantly modified.

196   In Stoker's original 1897 publication, the protagonists do not pursue the Count. However, in The Notes (on page 34) he details the chase he intended to have happen here. Page 34 reads "Art, Morris & Seward follow, Van Helsing & Jonathan go to the place direct, Dracula goes through park, we follow, others on two sides up Hampstead, they follow him through cemetery." Elsewhere in the Notes (on page 33a) it records "October 3—Off on search, see Count at Piccadilly, to churchyard, baffled at tomb. . ."

197   A real document of anti-Dracula propaganda, published in 1488.

198   From page 34 in The Notes, in which, in the aftermath of pursuing the Count, there is a mention of a "cutting from Sporting Life—man hurt."

199   This is an excerpt from a real 1888 newspaper covering the Jack the Ripper murders.

200   The events of this chapter correspond to those of the twenty-fourth chapter in Stoker's original 1897 publication, as well as the first part of the twenty-fifth chapter (moved to the end of this chapter for editing purposes), though the text has been significantly modified.

201   Page 21 of The Notes states that the "Texan offers to go to Transylvania."

202   This is a new chapter, not found in Stoker's original 1897 publication.

203   In The Notes (pages 2 and 35b verso), we find that the "Texan" actually makes a trip to Transylvania to gain more information on their enemy. Page 2 reads "On the track, Texan in Transylvania." Page 35b verso reads "Texan's diary—Transylvania." The context of the Notes would indicate that he goes to Transylvania and returns prior to Van Helsing's big lecture on vampires. However, as Stoker ultimately settled on having Book III take place over a very short period of time, Quincey could not have made a reasonable round trip to Transylvania, much less have any adventures while there, and make it back before Van Helsing's lecture. So, I have given him his adventure now, during the otherwise long and uneventful wait for the Count's ship to arrive in Varna. . . a long waiting game that the brash American adventurer would probably not sit still for anyway.

[204]   Arminius Vambery, who earlier Van Helsing says provided him with information about the Dracula family, was a very famous professor at the Budapest University.

[205]   Stoker mentions this meal on page 65 of his Notes: "Dinner at Pesth. Fugas (pronounced 'Fogush'), fish of Barlaton Lake, Spatchcock with red pepper ('Paprika'), Töltött Kaposzta (cabbage filled with rice, meat and spice) delicious but dyspeptic. Watermelon—green outside... red inside. Bottle of Neszmelyi—between Hock and Chablis."

[206]   Starting with the line "He had been to Central Asia" and until this endnote number, this section is taken directly from Stoker's *Personal Reminiscences of Henry Irving*.

[207]   This paragraph on dragons was adapted from Stoker's *The Lair of the White Worm*.

[208]   Page 34 verso of the Notes makes mention of "Quincey to rescue with maxim gun." A maxim gun was a primitive sort of machine gun that was invented in the 1880's.

[209]   Though Jonathan never made it into Wallachia (the province south of Transylvania), Stoker makes a record of that region anyway; on pages 60 through 61 his Notes read "Wallachia. Men in Tartar fur caps, sheepskin jackets—fur outwards, shirts with tails outside white trousers, and Russian boots or trousers tucked into garters made of rough cloth over which sandals are bound—Women with white kerchief on head, loose chemise with baggy sleeves tucked up at elbow—reaching to ankle, open down to waist: has strings to fasten at neck and waist—and belt or girdle from which is suspended the Obreska—with fringe of black and scarlet reaching to ankle."

[210]   The mention of a "blood red room" can be found in various places throughout The Notes (such as pages 1, 2, and 35b verso), though where exactly this room was to be located was never mentioned. The Scholomance is supposed to be in the Carpathian mountains that tower above the Transylvanian city of Hermanstadt, and there just happens to be a mountain pass near Hermanstadt called the "Red Tower Pass." Combining the legendary Scholomance, the real Red Tower Pass, and the Red Room from The Notes seemed the logical way to go.

[211]   An excerpt from Silvia Chitimia's *Les Traces de l'Occulte dans le Folklore Roumain*, which was kindly translated for me by Elizabeth Miller, reads, "The second kind of round table (made of stone) transmitted down through Romanian folklore is, in fact, a spinning stone . . . strange sorcerers were called Solomonari. The Solomonari passed three to seven years in a mysterious school in order to learn to master both dragons and the weather . . . The initiation ritual of the Solomonari in the school of the Dragon made use of a type of round table or rock disk. The students were seated on the round stone, which turned with great speed. It is said that, under these circumstances, one of them was always overwhelmed by a demon. This suggests the archaic sacrifice offered to the demon of the wheel."

[212]   The description of the Scholomance, and its destruction, was adapted from Stoker's *The Lair of the White Worm.*

[213]   The events of this chapter correspond to those of the twenty-fifth chapter in Stoker's original 1897 publication, though the first section was removed and relocated to a previous chapter for editing purposes, and the remaining text has been significantly modified.

[214] The aftermath Morris describes was adapted from Stoker's *The Lair of the White Worm*.

[215] The events of this chapter correspond to those of the twenty-sixth chapter in Stoker's original 1897 publication, though the text has been significantly modified.

[216] According to the Manuscript, the original alias Dracula chose to use here and elsewhere was "D. Mandevill."

[217] The events of this chapter correspond to those of the first half of the twenty-seventh chapter in Stoker's original 1897 publication, though the text has been significantly modified.

[218] This is the first of several concerns about the quality of the air mentioned in the Manuscript.

[219] This scene was added in honor of page 34 verso of the Notes, which reads "Wild whirling figures of women on tower—obliterated by lightening." Originally, the vampiresses were to have survived Dracula's destruction, only to be destroyed along with the castle in a great storm. Here, at least, some of that lost scene is preserved.

[220] The events of this chapter correspond to those of the second half of the twenty-seventh chapter in Stoker's original 1897 publication, though the text has been significantly modified.

[221] Up until now, the original text has been modified to show that Dracula is transporting two boxes, not just one, and for this very reason of Renfield's presence. But having two secret boxes instead of one is not a new idea, for there is a section in the original Manuscript, during the scene where the protagonists are tracking down Dracula's coffin boxes in London, and they say "there were still two missing to which we had as yet no clue of any kind."

[222] In The Notes, he called his ending a "Tourists Tale." Page 35b verso reads "A Tourists Tale—Flyman & Texan & ____." Thus, he notes this ending involves the Flyman (his early name for Renfield), the Texan (who is, of course, Quincey), and "___" (an underlined blank space left for a third person). Stoker never filled in that blank, so I chose Arthur as the candidate. On page 2 of the Notes, Stoker has a couple of addendums to his "Tourists Tale"—the first stating "bring in the Texan" and the second stating that "one killed by wolf(wehr?)." Thus, again, the Texan is involved, as is a werewolf (which, in the mythology of Stoker's day, was synonymous with "vampire"). Thus, the conclusion is that Quincey was to be killed by Renfield, who is now a vampire (which is, of course, the only way Renfield *could* be involved in the ending anyway, seeing as he "died" back in Purfleet many chapters earlier). As for Arthur, he too dies in this rendition, to fulfill Stoker's foreshadowing in his Icelandic preface in which he says "the aristocracy here in London; and some will remember that one of them disappeared suddenly without apparent reason, leaving no trace." This missing aristocrat, then, is none other than Arthur.

[223] This is the famous "deleted ending" to Dracula, which was found in Stoker's manuscript, that has at long last been re-inserted into its proper place.

[224] On page 33b of The Notes, it reads "Look down at end of Castle & see figures vanish in river."

225 This is a somewhat modified excerpt from a speech that Sergeant Daw gives in
     Stoker's *The Jewel of Seven Stars*.

226 One addition to the plot, and a rather major one at that, arose neither from Stoker's
     notes nor from any other source, but rather came from the text of **Dracula** itself.
     This change was in essence the deliberate increase of suspicion surrounding Arthur
     Holmwood. So why was poor Arthur made to be the unwanted center of such
     attention? Because, in his novel, Stoker set up far too many suspicious occurrences
     surrounding Arthur to go unnoticed. From the original 1897 text, these are:

     [1] Arthur Holmwood and his two very close friends—Quincey Morris and
     John Seward—all propose to Lucy on the same day. Afterward, they all get together
     to discuss things which, as Arthur says in his telegram, will "make their ears tingle."
     [2] Arthur always seems to be mysteriously absent during those times when Lucy's
     health gets worse. [3] Arthur's fiancé Lucy, Lucy's mother, and Arthur's father all die
     within a day or two of each other. (Jonathan's employer Hawkins dies at this same
     time as well, though he appeared to have no direct connection to the Holmwoods
     in the original **Dracula**). [4] In addition to his own inheritance, Arthur also receives
     the estates of both Lucy and her mother, through a legal arrangement so peculiar
     that even the lawyers of Lucy's mother tried to talk her out of it. [5] Dr. Seward
     notes Arthur was withholding information when he returned to report the diaries
     were burned. [6] Renfield is well acquainted with the Holmwoods, and reveals to
     the party that he knew Arthur's father from the Windham. [7] In his hysterics after
     Lucy's death, Van Helsing reveals that his wife was mad and their son lost, yet he
     says he loves Arthur as a father loves a son because Arthur looks exactly like his son
     would have looked, had he grown up!

227 This is an excerpt from a real 1888 newspaper covering the Jack the Ripper murders.

228 The Manuscript has this number as "Eleven years."

229 This description of a wasteland comes right out of the Manuscript.

230 The Notes (pages 2 and 35b verso) have the story end with a "tourist's tale."

231 A final tie-in to Stoker's deliberate mention of Jack the Ripper in his Icelandic version
     of the introduction, thus closing the loop and giving the reader the opportunity to
     draw his or her own conclusion about any ties that Francis or the Count may have
     had with the Ripper.

CPSIA information can be obtained at www.ICGtesting.com
Printed in the USA
LVOW12s0707150215

427085LV00002B/105/P